9 Short Novels

9 SHORT NOVELS

SECOND EDITION

Edited by

RICHARD M. LUDWIG
Princeton University

and

MARVIN B. PERRY, JR.
The University of Virginia

D. C. HEATH AND COMPANY
Lexington, Massachusetts

Printed in the United States of America

Library of Congress Number: 61-15583

To our parents

Preface

The title of this volume is intended to be descriptive, not definitive. In selecting these nine stories, we hope to offer not only representatives of a specific genre, the short novel or novella, but also examples of relatively short fiction which combine mastery of technique with maturity of theme. There is no need to define at length the so-called short novel or to trace its historical development, from Boccaccio's *novella* through the German *novelle* and Henry James' "blest *nouvelle.*" The term used in the title is an arbitrary one. In length these selections fall between fifteen and fifty thousand words. With the unity and immediacy of impact of the short story, they combine something of the intricacy and extended development of character and theme proper to the full-length novel. Whether as long short stories, as *nouvelles,* or as embryo novels, they furnish rich material for a mature and careful study of the methods of fiction.

At the end of this volume each author is identified briefly. We have tried to avoid superfluous biographical details here, but when the facts of an author's life are germane to his story, as for example, in Mann's *Tonio Kröger* or Kafka's *Metamorphosis,* we have supplied them. Dogmatic critical estimates and categorical assertions we have avoided as far as possible. Stimulation of independent critical judgment by a close reading of the text, not dissemination of professorial opinions, is the chief aim of this collection.

R. M. L.
M. B. P., Jr.

Contents

9 Short Novels

STEPHEN CRANE

The Red Badge of Courage

The cold passed reluctantly from the earth, and the retiring fogs revealed an army stretched out on the hills, resting. As the landscape changed from brown to green, the army awakened, and began to tremble with eagerness at the noise of rumors. It cast its eyes upon the roads, which were growing from long troughs of liquid mud to proper thoroughfares. A river, amber-tinted in the shadow of its banks, purled at the army's feet; and at night, when the stream had become of a sorrowful blackness, one could see across it the red, eyelike gleam of hostile camp fires set in the low brows of distant hills.

Once a certain tall soldier developed virtues and went resolutely to wash a shirt. He came flying back from a brook waving his garment bannerlike. He was swelled with a tale he had heard from a reliable friend, who had heard it from a truthful cavalryman, who had heard it from his trustworthy brother, one of the orderlies at division headquarters. He adopted the important air of a herald in red and gold.

"We're goin' t' move t' morrah—sure," he said pompously to a group in the company street. "We're goin' 'way up the river, cut across, an' come around in behint 'em."

To his attentive audience he drew a loud and elaborate plan of a very brilliant campaign. When he had finished, the blue-clothed men scattered into small arguing groups between the rows of squat brown huts. A negro teamster who had been dancing upon a cracker box with the hilarious encouragement of two-score soldiers was deserted. He sat mournfully down. Smoke drifted lazily from a multitude of quaint chimneys.

"It's a lie! that's all it is—a thunderin' lie!" said another private loudly. His smooth face was flushed, and his hands were thrust sulkily into his trousers' pockets. He took the matter as an affront to him. "I don't believe the derned old army's ever going to move. We're set. I've got ready to move eight times in the last two weeks, and we ain't moved yet."

The tall soldier felt called upon to defend the truth of a rumor he himself had introduced. He and the loud one came near to fighting over it.

A corporal began to swear before the assemblage. He had just put a costly board floor in his house, he said. During the early spring he had refrained from adding extensively to the comfort of his environment because he had felt that the army might start on the march at any moment. Of late, however, he had been impressed that they were in a sort of eternal camp.

Many of the men engaged in a spirited debate. One outlined in a peculiarly lucid manner all the plans of the commanding general. He was opposed by men who advocated that there were other plans of campaign. They clamored at each other, numbers making futile bids for the popular attention. Meanwhile, the soldier who had fetched the rumor bustled about with much importance. He was continually assailed by questions.

"What's up, Jim?"

"Th' army's goin' t' move."

"Ah, what yeh talkin' about? How yeh know it is?"

"Well, yeh kin b'lieve me er not, jest as yeh like. I don't care a hang."

There was much food for thought in the manner in which he replied. He came near to convincing them by disdaining to produce proofs. They grew much excited over it.

There was a youthful private who listened with eager ears to the words of the tall soldier and to the varied comments of his comrades. After receiving a fill of discussions concerning marches and attacks, he went to his hut and crawled through an intricate hole that served it as a door. He wished to be alone with some new thoughts that had lately come to him.

He lay down on a wide bunk that stretched across the end of the room. In the other end, cracker boxes were made to serve as furniture. They were grouped about the fireplace. A picture from an illustrated weekly was upon the log walls, and three rifles were paralleled on pegs. Equipments hung on handy projections, and some tin dishes lay upon a small pile of firewood. A folded tent was serving as a roof. The sunlight, without, beating upon it, made it glow a light yellow shade. A small window shot an oblique square of whiter light upon the cluttered floor. The smoke from the fire at times neglected the clay chimney and wreathed into the room, and this flimsy chimney of clay and sticks made endless threats to set ablaze the whole establishment.

The youth was in a little trance of astonishment. So they were at last going to fight. On the morrow, perhaps, there would be a battle, and he would be in it. For a time he was obliged to labor to make himself believe. He could not accept with assurance an omen that he was about to mingle in one of those great affairs of the earth.

He had, of course, dreamed of battles all his life—of vague and bloody conflicts that had thrilled him with their sweep and fire. In visions he had seen himself in many struggles. He had imagined peoples secure in the shadow of his eagle-eyed prowess. But awake he had regarded battles as crimson blotches on the pages of the past. He had put them as things of the bygone with his thought-images of heavy crowns and high castles. There was a portion of the world's history which he had regarded as the time of wars, but it, he thought, had been long gone over the horizon and had disappeared forever.

From his home his youthful eyes had looked upon the war in his own country with distrust. It must be some sort of a play affair. He had long despaired of witnessing a Greeklike struggle. Such would be no more, he had said. Men were better, or more timid. Secular and religious education had effaced the throat-grappling instinct, or else firm finance held in check the passions.

He had burned several times to enlist. Tales of great movements shook the land. They might not be distinctly Homeric, but there seemed to be much glory in them. He had read of marches, sieges, conflicts, and he had longed to see it all. His busy mind had drawn for him large pictures extravagant in color, lurid with breathless deeds.

But his mother had discouraged him. She had affected to look with some contempt upon the quality of his war ardor and patriotism. She could calmly seat herself and with no apparent difficulty give him many hundreds of reasons why he was of vastly more importance on the farm than on the field of battle. She had had certain ways of expression that told him that her statements on the subject came from a deep conviction. Moreover, on her side, was his belief that her ethical motive in the argument was impregnable.

At last, however, he had made firm rebellion against this yellow light thrown upon the color of his ambitions. The newspapers, the gossip of the village, his own picturings, had aroused him to an uncheckable degree. They were in truth fighting finely down there. Almost every day the newspapers printed accounts of a decisive victory.

One night, as he lay in bed, the winds had carried to him the clangoring of the church bell as some enthusiast jerked the rope frantically to tell the twisted news of a great battle. This voice of the people rejoicing in the night had made him shiver in a prolonged ecstasy of excitement. Later, he had gone down to his mother's room and had spoken thus: "Ma, I'm going to enlist."

"Henry, don't you be a fool," his mother had replied. She had then covered her face with the quilt. There was an end to the matter for that night.

Nevertheless, the next morning he had gone to a town that was near his mother's farm and had enlisted in a company that was forming there. When he had returned home his mother was milking the brindle cow. Four others stood waiting. "Ma, I've enlisted," he had said to her diffidently. There was a short silence. "The Lord's will be done, Henry," she had finally replied, and had then continued to milk the brindle cow.

When he had stood in the doorway with his soldier's clothes on his back, and with the light of excitement and expectancy in his eyes almost defeating the glow of regret for the home bonds, he had seen two tears leaving their trails on his mother's scarred cheeks.

Still, she had disappointed him by saying nothing whatever about returning with his shield or on it. He had privately primed himself for a beautiful scene. He had prepared certain sentences which he thought could be used with touching effect. But her words destroyed his plans. She had doggedly peeled potatoes and addressed him as follows: "You watch out, Henry, an' take good care of yerself in this here fighting business—you watch out, an' take good care of yerself. Don't go a-thinkin' you can lick the hull rebel army at the start, because yeh can't. Yer jest one little feller amongst a hull lot of others, and yeh've got to keep quiet an' do what they tell yeh. I know how you are, Henry.

"I've knet yeh eight pair of socks, Henry, and I've put in all yer best shirts, because I want my boy to be jest as warm and comf'able as anybody in the army. Whenever they get holes in 'em, I want yeh to send 'em rightaway back to me, so's I kin dern 'em.

"An' allus be careful an' choose yer comp'ny. There's lots of bad men in the army, Henry. The army makes 'em wild, and they like nothing better than the job of leading off a young feller like you, as ain't never been away from home much and has allus had a mother, an' a-learning 'em to drink and swear. Keep clear of them folks, Henry. I don't want yeh to ever do anything, Henry, that yeh would be 'shamed to let me know about. Jest think as if I was a-watchin' yeh. If yer keep that in yer mind allus, I guess yeh'll come out about right.

"Yeh must allus remember yer father, too, child, an' remember he never drunk a drop of licker in his life, and seldom swore a cross oath.

"I don't know what else to tell yeh, Henry, excepting that yeh must never do no shirking, child, on my account. If so be a time comes when yeh have to be kilt or do a mean thing, why, Henry, don't think of anything 'cept what's right, because there's many a woman has to bear up 'ginst sech things these times, and the Lord 'll take keer of us all.

"Don't forgit about the socks and the shirts, child; and I've put a cup of blackberry jam with yer bundle, because I know yeh like it above all things. Good-by, Henry. Watch out, and be a good boy."

He had, of course, been impatient under the ordeal of this speech. It had not been quite what he expected, and he had borne it with an air of irritation. He departed feeling vague relief.

Still, when he had looked back from the gate, he had seen his mother kneeling among the potato parings. Her brown face, upraised, was stained with tears, and her spare form was quivering. He bowed his head and went on, feeling suddenly ashamed of his purposes.

From his home he had gone to the seminary to bid adieu to many schoolmates. They had thronged about him with wonder and admiration. He had felt the gulf now between them and had swelled with calm pride. He and some of his fellows who had donned blue were quite overwhelmed with privileges for all of one afternoon, and it had been a very delicious thing. They had strutted.

A certain light-haired girl had made vivacious fun at his martial spirit, but there was another and darker girl whom he had gazed at steadfastly, and he thought she grew demure and sad at sight of his blue and brass. As he had walked down the path between the rows of oaks, he had turned his head and detected her at a window watching his departure. As he perceived her, she had immediately begun to stare up through the high tree branches at the sky. He had seen a good deal of flurry and haste in her movement as she changed her attitude. He often thought of it.

On the way to Washington his spirit had soared. The regiment was fed and caressed at station after station until the youth had believed that he must be a hero. There was a lavish expenditure of bread and cold meats, coffee, and pickles and cheese. As he basked in the smiles of the girls and was patted and complimented by the old men, he had felt growing within him the strength to do mighty deeds of arms.

After complicated journeyings with many pauses, there had come months of monotonous life in a camp. He had had the belief that real war was a series of death struggles with small time in between for sleep and meals; but since his regiment had come to the field the army had done little but sit still and try to keep warm.

He was brought then gradually back to his old ideas. Greeklike struggles would be no more. Men were better, or more timid. Secular and religious education had effaced the throat-grappling instinct, or else firm finance held in check the passions.

He had grown to regard himself merely as a part of a vast blue demonstration. His province was to look out, as far as he could, for his personal comfort. For recreation he could twiddle his thumbs and speculate on the thoughts which must agitate the minds of the generals. Also, he was drilled and drilled and reviewed, and drilled and drilled and reviewed.

The only foes he had seen were some pickets along the river bank. They were a sun-tanned philosophical lot, who sometimes shot reflectively at the blue pickets. When reproached for this afterward, they usually expressed sorrow, and swore by their gods that the guns had exploded without their permission. The youth, on guard during one night, conversed across the stream with one of them. He was a slightly ragged man, who spat skillfully between his shoes and possessed a great fund of bland and infantile assurance. The youth liked him personally.

"Yank," the other had informed him, "yer a right dum good feller." This sentiment, floating to him upon the still air, had made him temporarily regret war.

Various veterans had told him tales. Some talked of gray, bewhiskered hordes who were advancing with relentless curses and chewing tobacco with unspeakable valor; tremendous bodies of fierce soldiery who were sweeping along like the Huns. Others spoke of tattered and eternally hungry men who fired despondent powders. "They'll charge through hell's fire an' brimstone t' git a holt on a haversack, an' sech stomachs ain't a-lastin' long," he was told. From the stories, the youth imagined the red, live bones sticking out through slits in the faded uniforms.

Still, he could not put a whole faith in veterans' tales, for recruits were their prey. They talked much of smoke, fire, and blood, but he could not tell how much might be lies. They persistently yelled "Fresh fish!" at him, and were in no wise to be trusted.

However, he perceived now that it did not greatly matter what kind of soldiers he was going to fight, so long as they fought, which fact no one disputed. There was a more serious problem. He lay in his bunk pondering upon it. He tried to mathematically prove to himself that he would not run from a battle.

Previously he had never felt obliged to wrestle too seriously with this question. In his life he had taken certain things for granted, never challenging his belief in ultimate success, and bothering little about means and roads. But here he was confronted with a thing of moment. It had suddenly appeared to him that perhaps in a battle he might run. He was forced to admit that as far as war was concerned he knew nothing of himself.

A sufficient time before he would have allowed the problem to kick its heels at the outer portals of his mind, but now he felt compelled to give serious attention to it.

A little panic-fear grew in his mind. As his imagination went forward to a fight, he saw hideous possibilities. He contemplated the lurking menaces of the future, and failed in an effort to see himself standing stoutly in the midst of them. He recalled his visions of broken-bladed glory, but in the shadow of the impending tumult he suspected them to be impossible pictures.

He sprang from the bunk and began to pace nervously to and fro. "Good Lord, what's th' matter with me?" he said aloud.

He felt that in this crisis his laws of life were useless. Whatever he had learned of himself was here of no avail. He was an unknown quantity. He saw that he would again be obliged to experiment as he had in early youth. He must accumulate information of himself, and meanwhile he resolved to remain close upon his guard lest those qualities of which he knew nothing should everlastingly disgrace him. "Good Lord!" he repeated in dismay.

After a time the tall soldier slid dexterously through the hole. The loud private followed. They were wrangling.

"That's all right," said the tall soldier as he entered. He waved his hand expressively. "You can believe me or not, jest as you like. All you got to do is to sit down and wait as quiet as you can. Then pretty soon you'll find out I was right."

His comrade grunted stubbornly. For a moment he seemed to be searching for a formidable reply. Finally he said: "Well, you don't know everything in the world, do you?"

"Didn't say I knew everything in the world," retorted the other sharply. He began to stow various articles snugly into his knapsack.

The youth, pausing in his nervous walk, looked down at the busy figure. "Going to be a battle, sure, is there, Jim?" he asked.

"Of course there is," replied the tall soldier. "Of course there is. You jest wait 'til tomorrow, and you'll see one of the biggest battles ever was. You jest wait."

"Thunder!" said the youth.

"Oh, you'll see fighting this time, my boy, what'll be regular out-and-out fighting," added the tall soldier, with the air of a man who is about to exhibit a battle for the benefit of his friends.

"Huh!" said the loud one from a corner.

"Well," remarked the youth, "like as not this story 'll turn out jest like them others did."

"Not much it won't," replied the tall soldier, exasperated. "Not much it won't. Didn't the cavalry all start this morning?" He glared about him. No one denied his statement. "The cavalry started this morning," he continued. "They say there ain't hardly any cavalry left in camp. They're going to Richmond, or some place, while we fight all the Johnnies. It's some dodge like that. The regiment's got orders, too. A feller what seen 'em go to headquarters told me a little while ago. And they're raising blazes all over camp—anybody can see that."

"Shucks!" said the loud one.

The youth remained silent for a time. At last he spoke to the tall soldier. "Jim!"

"What?"

"How do you think the reg'ment 'll do?"

"Oh, they'll fight all right, I guess, after they once get into it," said the other with cold judgment. He made a fine use of the third person. "There's been heaps of fun poked at 'em because they're new, of course, and all that; but they'll fight all right, I guess."

"Think any of the boys 'll run?" persisted the youth.

"Oh, there may be a few of 'em run, but there's them kind in every regiment, 'specially when they first goes under fire," said the other in a tolerant way. "Of course it might happen that the hull kit-and-boodle might start and run, if some big fighting came first-off, and then again they might stay and fight like fun. But you can't bet on nothing. Of course they ain't never been under fire yet, and it ain't likely they'll lick the hull rebel army all-to-oncet the first time; but I think they'll fight better than some, if worse than others. That's the way I figger. They call the reg'ment 'Fresh fish' and everything; but the boys come of good stock, and most of 'em 'll fight like sin after they oncet git shootin'," he added, with a mighty emphasis on the last four words.

"Oh, you think you know—" began the loud soldier with scorn.

The other turned savagely upon him. They had a rapid altercation, in which they fastened upon each other various strange epithets.

The youth at last interrupted them. "Did you ever think you might run yourself, Jim?" he asked. On concluding the sentence he laughed as if he had meant to aim a joke. The loud soldier also giggled.

The tall private waved his hand. "Well," said he profoundly, "I've thought it might get too hot for Jim Conklin in some of them scrimmages, and if a whole lot of boys started and run, why, I s'pose I'd start and run. And if I once started to run, I'd run like the devil, and no mistake. But if everybody was a-standing and a-fighting, why, I'd stand and fight. Be jiminey, I would. I'll bet on it."

"Huh!" said the loud one.

The youth of this tale felt gratitude for these words of his comrade. He had feared that all of the untried men possessed a great and correct confidence. He now was in a measure reassured.

2

The next morning the youth discovered that his tall comrade had been the fast-flying messenger of a mistake. There was much scoffing at the latter by those who had yesterday been firm adherents of his views, and there was even a little sneering by men who had never believed the rumor. The tall one fought with a man from Chatfield Corners and beat him severely.

The youth felt, however, that his problem was in no wise lifted from him. There was, on the contrary, an irritating prolongation. The tale had created in him a great concern for himself. Now, with the newborn question in his mind, he was compelled to sink back into his old place as part of a blue demonstration.

For days he made ceaseless calculations, but they were all wondrously unsatisfactory. He found that he could establish nothing. He finally concluded that the only way to prove himself was to go into the blaze, and then figuratively to watch his legs to discover their merits and faults. He reluctantly admitted that he could not sit still and with a mental slate and pencil derive an answer. To gain it, he must have blaze, blood, and danger, even as a chemist requires this, that, and the other. So he fretted for an opportunity.

Meanwhile he continually tried to measure himself by his comrades. The tall soldier, for one, gave him some assurance. This man's serene unconcern dealt him a measure of confidence, for he had known him since childhood, and from his intimate knowledge he did not see how he could be capable of anything that was beyond him, the youth. Still, he thought that his comrade might be mistaken about himself. Or, on the other hand, he might be a man heretofore doomed to peace and obscurity, but, in reality, made to shine in war.

The youth would have liked to have discovered another who suspected himself. A sympathetic comparison of mental notes would have been a joy to him.

He occasionally tried to fathom a comrade with seductive sentences. He looked about to find men in the proper mood. All attempts failed to bring forth any statement which looked in any way like a confession to those doubts which he privately acknowledged in himself. He was afraid to make an open declaration of his concern, because he dreaded to place some unscrupulous confidant upon the high plane of the unconfessed from which elevation he could be derided.

In regard to his companions his mind wavered between two opinions, according to his mood. Sometimes he inclined to believing them all heroes. In fact, he usually admitted in secret the superior development of the higher qualities in others. He could conceive of men going very insignificantly about the world bearing a load of courage unseen, and, although he had known many of his comrades through boyhood, he began to fear that his judgment of them had been blind. Then, in other moments, he flouted these theories, and assured himself that his fellows were all privately wondering and quaking.

His emotions made him feel strange in the presence of men who talked excitedly of a prospective battle as of a drama they were about to witness, with nothing but eagerness and curiosity apparent in their faces. It was often that he suspected them to be liars.

He did not pass such thoughts without severe condemnation of himself. He dinned reproaches at times. He was convicted by himself of many shameful crimes against the gods of traditions.

In his great anxiety his heart was continually clamoring at what he considered the intolerable slowness of the generals. They seemed content to perch tranquilly on the river bank, and leave him bowed down by the weight of a great problem. He wanted it settled forthwith. He could not long bear such a load, he said. Sometimes his anger at the commanders reached an acute stage, and he grumbled about the camp like a veteran.

One morning, however, he found himself in the ranks of his prepared regiment. The men were whispering speculations and recounting the old rumors. In the gloom before the break of the day their uniforms glowed a deep purple hue. From across the river the red eyes were still peering. In the eastern sky there was a yellow patch like a rug laid for the feet of the coming sun; and against it, black and patternlike, loomed the gigantic figure of the colonel on a gigantic horse.

From off in the darkness came the trampling of feet. The youth could occasionally see dark shadows that moved like monsters. The regiment stood at rest for what seemed a long time. The youth grew impatient. It was unendurable the way these affairs were managed. He wondered how long they were to be kept waiting.

As he looked all about him and pondered upon the mystic gloom, he began to believe that at any moment the ominous distance might be aflare, and the rolling crashes of an engagement come to his ears. Staring once at the red eyes across the river, he conceived them to be growing larger, as the orbs of a row of dragons advancing. He turned toward the colonel and saw him lift his gigantic arm and calmly stroke his mustache.

At last he heard from along the road at the foot of the hill the clatter of a horse's galloping hoofs. It must be the coming of orders. He bent forward, scarce breathing. The exciting clickety-click, as it grew louder and louder, seemed to be beating upon his soul. Presently a horseman with jangling equipment drew rein before the colonel of the regiment. The two held a short, sharp-worded conversation. The men in the foremost ranks craned their necks.

As the horseman wheeled his animal and galloped away he turned to shout over his shoulder, "Don't forget that box of cigars!" The colonel mumbled in reply. The youth wondered what a box of cigars had to do with war.

A moment later the regiment went swinging off into the darkness. It was now like one of those moving monsters wending with many feet. The air was heavy, and cold with dew. A mass of wet grass, marched upon, rustled like silk.

There was an occasional flash and glimmer of steel from the backs of all these huge crawling reptiles. From the road came creakings and grumblings as some surly guns were dragged away.

The men stumbled along still muttering speculations. There was a subdued debate. Once a man fell down, and as he reached for his rifle a comrade, unseeing, trod upon his hand. He of the injured fingers swore bitterly and aloud. A low, tittering laugh went among his fellows.

Presently they passed into a roadway and marched forward with easy strides. A dark regiment moved before them, and from behind also came the tinkle of equipments on the bodies of marching men.

The rushing yellow of the developing day went on behind their backs. When the sunrays at last struck full and mellowingly upon the earth, the youth saw that the landscape was streaked with two long, thin, black columns which disappeared on the brow of a hill in front and rearward vanished in a wood. They were like two serpents crawling along the cavern of the night.

The river was not in view. The tall soldier burst into praises of what he thought to be his powers of perception.

Some of the tall one's companions cried with emphasis that they, too, had evolved the same thing, and they congratulated themselves upon it. But there were others who said that the tall one's plan was not the true one at all. They persisted with other theories. There was a vigorous discussion.

The youth took no part in them. As he walked along in careless line he was engaged with his own eternal debate. He could not hinder himself from dwelling upon it. He was despondent and sullen, and threw shifting glances about him. He looked ahead, often expecting to hear from the advance the rattle of firing.

But the long serpents crawled slowly from hill to hill without bluster of smoke. A dun-colored cloud of dust floated away to the right. The sky overhead was of a fairy blue.

The youth studied the faces of his companions, ever on the watch to detect kindred emotions. He suffered disappointment. Some ardor of the air which was causing the veteran commands to move with glee—almost with song—had infected the new regiment. The men began to speak of victory as of a thing they knew. Also, the tall soldier received his vindication. They were certainly going to come around in behind the enemy. They expressed commiseration for that part of the army which had been left upon the river bank, felicitating themselves upon being a part of a blasting host.

The youth, considering himself as separated from the others, was saddened by the blithe and merry speeches that went from rank to rank. The company wags all made their best endeavors. The regiment tramped to the tune of laughter.

The blatant soldier often convulsed whole files by his biting sarcasms aimed at the tall one.

And it was not long before all the men seemed to forget their mission. Whole brigades grinned in unison, and regiments laughed.

A rather fat soldier attempted to pilfer a horse from a dooryard. He planned to load his knapsack upon it. He was escaping with his prize when a young girl rushed from the house and grabbed the animal's mane. There followed a wrangle. The young girl, with pink cheeks and shining eyes, stood like a dauntless statue.

The observant regiment, standing at rest in the roadway, whooped at once, and entered whole-souled upon the side of the maiden. The men became so engrossed in this affair that they entirely ceased to remember their own large war. They jeered the piratical private, and called attention to various defects in his personal appearance; and they were wildly enthusiastic in support of the young girl.

To her, from some distance, came bold advice. "Hit him with a stick."

There were crows and catcalls showered upon him when he retreated without the horse. The regiment rejoiced at his downfall. Loud and vociferous congratulations were showered upon the maiden, who stood panting and regarding the troops with defiance.

At nightfall the column broke into regimental pieces, and the fragments went into the fields to camp. Tents sprang up like strange plants. Camp fires, like red, peculiar blossoms, dotted the night.

The youth kept from intercourse with his companions as much as circumstances would allow him. In the evening he wandered a few paces into the gloom. From this little distance the many fires, with the black forms of men passing to and fro before the crimson rays, made weird and satanic effects.

He lay down in the grass. The blades pressed tenderly against his cheek. The moon had been lighted and was hung in a treetop. The liquid stillness of the night enveloping him made him feel vast pity for himself. There was a caress in the soft winds; and the whole mood of the darkness, he thought, was one of sympathy for himself in his distress.

He wished, without reserve, that he was at home again making the endless rounds from the house to the barn, from the barn to the fields, from the fields to the barn, from the barn to the house. He remembered he had often cursed the brindle cow and her mates, and had sometimes flung milking stools. But, from his present point of view, there was a halo of happiness about each of their heads, and he would have sacrificed all the brass buttons on the continent to have been enabled to return to them. He told himself that he was not formed for a soldier. And he mused seriously upon the radical differences between himself and those men who were dodging implike around the fires.

As he mused thus he heard the rustle of grass, and, upon turning his head, discovered the loud soldier. He called out, "Oh, Wilson!"

The latter approached and looked down. "Why, hello, Henry; is it you? What you doing here?"

"Oh, thinking," said the youth.

The other sat down and carefully lighted his pipe. "You're getting blue, my boy. You're looking thundering peeked. What the dickens is wrong with you?"

"Oh, nothing," said the youth.

The loud soldier launched then into the subject of the anticipated fight. "Oh, we've got 'em now!" As he spoke his boyish face was wreathed in a gleeful smile, and his voice had an exultant ring. "We've got 'em now. At last, by the eternal thunders, we'll lick 'em good!"

"If the truth was known," he added, more soberly, "*they've* licked *us* about every clip up to now; but this time—this time—we'll lick 'em good!"

"I thought you was objecting to this march a little while ago," said the youth coldly.

"Oh, it wasn't that," explained the other. "I don't mind marching, if there's going to be fighting at the end of it. What I hate is this getting moved here and moved there, with no good coming of it, as far as I can see, excepting sore feet and damned short rations."

"Well, Jim Conklin says we'll get a plenty of fighting this time."

"He's right for once, I guess, though I can't see how it come. This time we're in for a big battle, and we've got the best end of it, certain sure. Gee rod! how we will thump 'em!"

He arose and began to pace to and fro excitedly. The thrill of his enthusiasm made him walk with an elastic step. He was sprightly, vigorous, fiery in his belief in success. He looked into the future with clear, proud eye, and he swore with the air of an old soldier.

The youth watched him for a moment in silence. When he finally spoke his voice was as bitter as dregs. "Oh, you're going to do great things, I s'pose!"

The loud soldier blew a thoughtful cloud of smoke from his pipe. "Oh, I don't know," he remarked with dignity; "I don't know. I s'pose I'll do as well as the rest. I'm going to try like thunder." He evidently complimented himself upon the modesty of this statement.

"How do you know you won't run when the time comes?" asked the youth.

"Run?" said the loud one; "run?—of course not!" He laughed.

"Well," continued the youth, "lots of good-a-'nough men have thought they was going to do great things before the fight, but when the time come they skedaddled."

"Oh, that's all true, I s'pose," replied the other; "but I'm not going to skedaddle. The man that bets on my running will lose his money, that's all." He nodded confidently.

"Oh, shucks!" said the youth. "You ain't the bravest man in the world, are you?"

"No, I ain't," exclaimed the loud soldier indignantly; "and I didn't say I was the bravest man in the world, neither. I said I was going to do my share of fighting—that's what I said. And I am, too. Who are you, anyhow? You talk as if you thought you was Napoleon Bonaparte." He glared at the youth for a moment, and then strode away.

The youth called in a savage voice after his comrade: "Well, you needn't git mad about it!" But the other continued on his way and made no reply.

He felt alone in space when his injured comrade had disappeared. His failure to discover any mite of resemblance in their viewpoints made him more miserable than before. No one seemed to be wrestling with such a terrific personal problem. He was a mental outcast.

He went slowly to his tent and stretched himself on a blanket by the side of the snoring tall soldier. In the darkness he saw visions of a thousand-tongued fear that would babble at his back and cause him to flee, while others were going coolly about their country's business. He admitted that he would not be able to cope with this monster. He felt that every nerve in his body would be an ear to hear the voices, while other men would remain stolid and deaf.

And as he sweated with the pain of these thoughts, he could hear low, serene sentences. "I'll bid five." "Make it six." "Seven." "Seven goes."

He stared at the red, shivering reflection of a fire on the white wall of his tent until, exhausted and ill from the monotony of his suffering, he fell asleep.

3

When another night came the columns, changed to purple streaks, filed across two pontoon bridges. A glaring fire wine-tinted the waters of the river. Its rays, shining upon the moving masses of troops, brought forth here and there sudden gleams of silver or gold. Upon the other shore a dark and mysterious range of hills was curved against the sky. The insect voices of the night sang solemnly.

After this crossing the youth assured himself that at any moment they might be suddenly and fearfully assaulted from the caves of the lowering woods. He kept his eyes watchfully upon the darkness.

But his regiment went unmolested to a camping place, and its soldiers slept the brave sleep of wearied men. In the morning they were routed out with early energy, and hustled along a narrow road that led deep into the forest.

It was during this rapid march that the regiment lost many of the marks of a new command.

The men had begun to count the miles upon their fingers, and they grew tired. "Sore feet an' damned short rations, that's all," said the loud soldier. There were perspiration and grumblings. After a time they began to shed their knapsacks. Some tossed them unconcernedly down; others hid them carefully, asserting their plans to return for them at some convenient time. Men extricated themselves from thick shirts. Presently few carried anything but their necessary clothing, blankets, haversacks, canteens, and arms and ammunition. "You can now eat and shoot," said the tall soldier to the youth. "That's all you want to do."

There was sudden change from the ponderous infantry of theory to the light and speedy infantry of practice. The regiment, relieved of a burden, received a new impetus. But there was much loss of valuable knapsacks, and, on the whole, very good shirts.

But the regiment was not yet veteranlike in appearance. Veteran regiments in the army were likely to be very small aggregations of men. Once, when the command had first come to the field, some perambulating veterans, noting the length of their column, had accosted them thus: "Hey, fellers, what brigade is that?" And when the men had replied that they formed a regiment and not a brigade, the older soldiers had laughed, and said, "O Gawd!"

Also, there was too great a similarity in the hats. The hats of a regiment should properly represent the history of headgear for a period of years. And, moreover, there were no letters of faded gold speaking from the colors. They were new and beautiful, and the color bearer habitually oiled the pole.

Presently the army again sat down to think. The odor of the peaceful pines was in the men's nostrils. The sound of monotonous axe blows rang through the forest, and the insects, nodding upon their perches, crooned like old women. The youth returned to his theory of a blue demonstration.

One gray dawn, however, he was kicked in the leg by the tall soldier, and then, before he was entirely awake, he found himself running down a wood road in the midst of men who were panting from the first effects of speed. His canteen banged rhythmically upon his thigh, and his haversack bobbed softly. His musket bounced a trifle from his shoulder at each stride and made his cap feel uncertain upon his head.

He could hear the men whisper jerky sentences: "Say—what's all this—about?" "What th' thunder—we—skedaddlin' this way fer?" "Billie—keep off m' feet. Yeh run—like a cow." And the loud soldier's shrill voice could be heard: "What th' devil they in sich a hurry for?"

The youth thought the damp fog of early morning moved from the rush of a great body of troops. From the distance came a sudden spatter of firing.

He was bewildered. As he ran with his comrades he strenuously tried to think, but all he knew was that if he fell down those coming behind would tread upon him. All his faculties seemed to be needed to guide him over and past obstructions. He felt carried along by a mob.

The sun spread disclosing rays, and, one by one, regiments burst into view like armed men just born of the earth. The youth perceived that the time had come. He was about to be measured. For a moment he felt in the face of his great trial like a babe, and the flesh over his heart seemed very thin. He seized time to look about him calculatingly.

But he instantly saw that it would be impossible for him to escape from the regiment. It inclosed him. And there were iron laws of tradition and law on four sides. He was in a moving box.

As he perceived this fact it occurred to him that he had never wished to come to the war. He had not enlisted of his free will. He had been dragged by the merciless government. And now they were taking him out to be slaughtered.

The regiment slid down a bank and wallowed across a little stream. The mournful current moved slowly on, and from the water, shaded black, some white bubble eyes looked at the men.

As they climbed the hill on the farther side artillery began to boom. Here the youth forgot many things as he felt a sudden impulse of curiosity. He scrambled up the bank with a speed that could not be exceeded by a bloodthirsty man.

He expected a battle scene.

There were some little fields girted and squeezed by a forest. Spread over the grass and in among the tree trunks, he could see knots and waving lines of skirmishers who were running hither and thither and firing at the landscape. A dark battle line lay upon a sunstruck clearing that gleamed orange color. A flag fluttered.

Other regiments floundered up the bank. The brigade was formed in line of battle, and after a pause started slowly through the woods in the rear of the receding skirmishers, who were continually melting into the scene to appear again farther on. They were always busy as bees, deeply absorbed in their little combats.

The youth tried to observe everything. He did not use care to avoid trees and branches, and his forgotten feet were constantly knocking against stones or getting entangled in briers. He was aware that these battalions with their commotions were woven red and startling into the gentle fabric of softened greens and browns. It looked to be a wrong place for a battle field.

The skirmishers in advance fascinated him. Their shots into thickets and at distant and prominent trees spoke to him of tragedies—hidden, mysterious, solemn.

Once the line encountered the body of a dead soldier. He lay upon his back staring at the sky. He was dressed in an awkward suit of yellowish brown. The youth could see that the soles of his shoes had been worn to the thinness of writing paper, and from a great rent in one the dead foot projected piteously. And it was as if fate had betrayed the soldier. In death it exposed to his enemies that poverty which in life he had perhaps concealed from his friends.

The ranks opened covertly to avoid the corpse. The invulnerable dead man forced a way for himself. The youth looked keenly at the ashen face. The wind raised the tawny beard. It moved as if a hand were stroking it. He vaguely desired to walk around and around the body and stare; the impulse of the living to try to read in dead eyes the answer to the Question.

During the march the ardor which the youth had acquired when out of view of the field rapidly faded to nothing. His curiosity was quite easily satisfied. If an intense scene had caught him with its wild swing as he came to the top of the bank, he might have gone roaring on. This advance upon Nature was too calm. He had opportunity to reflect. He had time in which to wonder about himself and to attempt to probe his sensations.

Absurd ideas took hold upon him. He thought that he did not relish the landscape. It threatened him. A coldness swept over his back, and it is true that his trousers felt to him that they were no fit for his legs at all.

A house standing placidly in distant fields had to him an ominous look. The shadows of the woods were formidable. He was certain that in this vista there lurked fierce-eyed hosts. The swift thought came to him that the generals did not know what they were about. It was all a trap. Suddenly those close forests would bristle with rifle barrels. Ironlike brigades would appear in the rear. They were all going to be sacrificed. The generals were stupids. The enemy would presently swallow the whole command. He glared about him, expecting to see the stealthy approach of his death.

He thought that he must break from the ranks and harangue his comrades. They must not all be killed like pigs; and he was sure it would come to pass unless they were informed of these dangers. The generals were idiots to send them marching into a regular pen. There was but one pair of eyes in the corps. He would step forth and make a speech. Shrill and passionate words came to his lips.

The line, broken into moving fragments by the ground, went calmly on through fields and woods. The youth looked at the men nearest him, and saw, for the most part, expressions of deep interest, as if they were investigating something that had fascinated them. One or two stepped with overvaliant airs as if they were already plunged into war. Others walked as upon thin ice. The greater part of the untested men appeared quiet and absorbed. They were going to look at war, the red animal—war, the blood-swollen god. And they were deeply engrossed in this march.

As he looked the youth gripped his outcry at his throat. He saw that even if the men were tottering with fear they would laugh at his warning. They would jeer him, and, if practicable, pelt him with missiles. Admitting that he might be wrong, a frenzied declamation of the kind would turn him into a worm.

He assumed, then, the demeanor of one who knows that he is doomed alone to unwritten responsibilities. He lagged, with tragic glances at the sky.

He was surprised presently by the young lieutenant of his company, who began heartily to beat him with a sword, calling out in a loud and insolent voice: "Come, young man, get up into ranks there. No skulking 'll do here." He mended his pace with suitable haste. And he hated the lieutenant, who had no appreciation of fine minds. He was a mere brute.

After a time the brigade was halted in the cathedral light of a forest. The busy skirmishers were still popping. Through the aisles of the wood could be seen the floating smoke from their rifles. Sometimes it went up in little balls, white and compact.

During this halt many men in the regiment began erecting tiny hills in front of them. They used stones, sticks, earth, and anything they thought might turn a bullet. Some built comparatively large ones, while others seemed content with little ones.

This procedure caused a discussion among the men. Some wished to fight like duelists, believing it to be correct to stand erect and be, from their feet to their foreheads, a mark. They said they scorned the devices of the cautious. But the others scoffed in reply, and pointed to the veterans on the flanks who were digging at the ground like terriers. In a short time there was quite a barricade along the regimental fronts. Directly, however, they were ordered to withdraw from that place.

This astounded the youth. He forgot his stewing over the advance movement. "Well, then, what did they march us out here for?" he demanded of the tall soldier. The latter with calm faith began a heavy explanation, although he had been compelled to leave a little protection of stones and dirt to which he had devoted much care and skill.

When the regiment was aligned in another position each man's regard for his safety caused another line of small intrenchments. They ate their noon meal behind a third one. They were moved from this one also. They were marched from place to place with apparent aimlessness.

The youth had been taught that a man became another thing in a battle. He saw his salvation in such a change. Hence this waiting was an ordeal to him. He was in a fever of impatience. He considered that there was denoted a lack of purpose on the part of the generals. He began to complain to the tall soldier. "I can't stand this much longer," he cried. "I don't see what good it does to make us wear out our legs for nothin'." He wished to return to camp, knowing that this affair was a blue demonstration; or else to go into a battle and discover that he had been a fool in his doubts, and was, in truth, a man of traditional courage. The strain of present circumstances he felt to be intolerable.

The philosophical tall soldier measured a sandwich of cracker and pork and swallowed it in a nonchalant manner. "Oh, I suppose we must go reconnoitering around the country jest to keep 'em from getting too close, or to develop 'em, or something."

"Huh!" said the loud soldier.

"Well," cried the youth, still fidgeting, "I'd rather do anything 'most than go tramping 'round the country all day doing no good to nobody and jest tiring ourselves out."

"So would I," said the loud soldier. "It ain't right. I tell you if anybody with any sense was a-runnin' this army it—"

"Oh, shut up!" roared the tall private. "You little fool. You little damn' cuss. You ain't had that there coat and them pants on for six months, and yet you talk as if—"

"Well, I wanta do some fighting anyway," interrupted the other. "I didn't come here to walk. I could 'ave walked to home—'round an 'round the barn, if I jest wanted to walk."

The tall one, red-faced, swallowed another sandwich as if taking poison in despair.

But gradually, as he chewed, his face became again quiet and contented. He could not rage in fierce argument in the presence of such sandwiches. During his meals he always wore an air of blissful contemplation of the food he had swallowed. His spirit seemed then to be communing with the viands.

He accepted new environment and circumstance with great coolness, eating from his haversack at every opportunity. On the march he went along with the stride of a hunter, objecting to neither gait nor distance. And he had not raised his voice when he had been ordered away from three little protective piles of earth and stone, each of which had been an engineering feat worthy of being made sacred to the name of his grandmother.

In the afternoon the regiment went out over the same ground it had taken in the morning. The landscape then ceased to threaten the youth. He had been close to it and become familiar with it.

When, however, they began to pass into a new region, his old fears of stupidity and incompetence reassailed him, but this time he doggedly let them babble. He was occupied with his problem, and in his desperation he concluded that the stupidity did not greatly matter.

Once he thought he had concluded that it would be better to get killed directly and end his troubles. Regarding death thus out of the corner of his eye, he conceived it to be nothing but rest, and he was filled with a momentary astonishment that he should have made an extraordinary commotion over the mere matter of getting killed. He would die; he would go to some place where he would be understood. It was useless to expect appreciation of his profound and fine senses from such men as the lieutenant. He must look to the grave for comprehension.

The skirmish fire increased to a long clattering sound. With it was mingled far-away cheering. A battery spoke.

Directly the youth would see the skirmishers running. They were pursued by the sound of musketry fire. After a time the hot, dangerous flashes of the rifles were visible. Smoke clouds went slowly and insolently across the fields like observant phantoms. The din became crescendo, like the roar of an oncoming train.

A brigade ahead of them and on the right went into action with a rending roar. It was as if it had exploded. And thereafter it lay stretched in the distance behind a long gray wall, that one was obliged to look twice at to make sure that it was smoke.

The youth, forgetting his neat plan of getting killed, gazed spellbound. His eyes grew wide and busy with the action of the scene. His mouth was a little ways open.

Of a sudden he felt a heavy and sad hand laid upon his shoulder. Awakening from his trance of observation he turned and beheld the loud soldier.

"It's my first and last battle, old boy," said the latter, with intense gloom. He was quite pale and his girlish lip was trembling.

"Eh?" murmured the youth in great astonishment.

"It's my first and last battle, old boy," continued the loud soldier. "Something tells me—"

"What?"

"I'm a gone coon this first time and—and I w-want you to take these here things—to—my—folks." He ended in a quavering sob of pity for himself. He handed the youth a little packet done up in a yellow envelope.

"Why, what the devil—" began the youth again.

But the other gave him a glance as from the depths of a tomb, and raised his limp hand in a prophetic manner and turned away.

4

The brigade was halted in the fringe of a grove. The men crouched among the trees and pointed their restless guns out at the fields. They tried to look beyond the smoke.

Out of this haze they could see running men. Some shouted information and gestured as they hurried.

The men of the new regiment watched and listened eagerly, while their tongues ran on in gossip of the battle. They mouthed rumors that had flown like birds out of the unknown.

"They say Perry has been driven in with big loss."

"Yes, Carrott went t' th' hospital. He said he was sick. That smart lieutenant is commanding 'G' Company. Th' boys say they won't be under Carrott no more if they all have t' desert. They allus knew he was a—"

"Hannises' batt'ry is took."

"It ain't either. I saw Hannises' batt'ry off on th' left not more'n fifteen minutes ago."

"Well—"

"Th' general, he ses he is goin' t' take th' hull command of th' 304th when we go inteh action, an' then he ses we'll do sech fightin' as never another one reg'ment done."

"They say we're catchin' it over on th' left. They say th' enemy driv' our line inteh a devil of a swamp an' took Hannises' batt'ry."

"No sech thing. Hannises' batt'ry was 'long here 'bout a minute ago."

"That young Hasbrouck, he makes a good off'cer. He ain't afraid 'a nothin'."

"I met one of th' 148th Maine boys an' he ses his brigade fit th' hull rebel army fer four hours over on th' turnpike road an' killed about five thousand of 'em. He ses one more sech fight as that an' th' war'll be over."

"Bill wasn't scared either. No, sir! It wasn't that. Bill ain't a-gittin' scared easy. He was jest mad, that's what he was. When that feller trod on his hand, he up an' sed that he was willin' t' give his hand t' his country, but he be dumbed if he was goin' t' have every dumb bushwacker in th' kentry walkin' 'round on it. So he went t' th' hospital disregardless of th' fight. Three fingers was crunched. Th' dern doctor wanted t' amputate 'm, an' Bill, he raised a heluva row, I hear. He's a funny feller."

The din in front swelled to a tremendous chorus. The youth and his fellows were frozen to silence. They could see a flag that tossed in the smoke angrily. Near it were the blurred and agitated forms of troops. There came a turbulent stream of men across the fields. A battery changing position at a frantic gallop scattered the stragglers right and left.

A shell screaming like a storm banshee went over the huddled heads of the reserves. It landed in the grove, and exploding redly flung the brown earth. There was a little shower of pine needles.

Bullets began to whistle among the branches and nip at the trees. Twigs and leaves came sailing down. It was as if a thousand axes, wee and invisible, were being wielded. Many of the men were constantly dodging and ducking their heads.

The lieutenant of the youth's company was shot in the hand. He began to swear so wondrously that a nervous laugh went along the regimental line. The officer's profanity sounded conventional. It relieved the tightened senses of the new men. It was as if he had hit his fingers with a tack hammer at home.

He held the wounded member carefully away from his side so that the blood would not drip upon his trousers.

The captain of the company, tucking his sword under his arm, produced a handkerchief and began to bind with it the lieutenant's wound. And they disputed as to how the binding should be done.

The battle flag in the distance jerked about madly. It seemed to be struggling to free itself from an agony. The billowing smoke was filled with horizontal flashes.

Men running swiftly emerged from it. They grew in numbers until it was seen that the whole command was fleeing. The flag suddenly sank down as if dying. Its motion as it fell was a gesture of despair.

Wild yells came from behind the walls of smoke. A sketch in gray and red dissolved into a moblike body of men who galloped like wild horses.

The veteran regiments on the right and left of the 304th immediately began to jeer. With the passionate song of the bullets and the banshee shrieks of shells were mingled loud catcalls and bits of facetious advice concerning places of safety.

But the new regiment was breathless with horror. "Gawd! Saunders's got crushed!" whispered the man at the youth's elbow. They shrank back and crouched as if compelled to await a flood.

The youth shot a swift glance along the blue ranks of the regiment. The profiles were motionless, carven; and afterward he remembered that the color sergeant was standing with his legs apart, as if he expected to be pushed to the ground.

The following throng went whirling around the flank. Here and there were officers carried along on the stream like exasperated chips. They were striking about them with their swords and with their left fists, punching every head they could reach. They cursed like highwaymen.

A mounted officer displayed the furious anger of a spoiled child. He raged with his head, his arms, and his legs.

Another, the commander of the brigade, was galloping about bawling. His hat was gone and his clothes were awry. He resembled a man who has come from bed to go to a fire. The hoofs of his horse often threatened the heads of the running men, but they scampered with singular fortune. In this rush they were apparently all deaf and blind. They heeded not the largest and longest of the oaths that were thrown at them from all directions.

Frequently over this tumult could be heard the grim jokes of the critical veterans; but the retreating men apparently were not even conscious of the presence of an audience.

The battle reflection that shone for an instant in the faces on the mad current made the youth feel that forceful hands from heaven would not have been able to have held him in place if he could have got intelligent control of his legs.

There was an appalling imprint upon these faces. The struggle in the smoke had pictured an exaggeration of itself on the bleached cheeks and in the eyes wild with one desire.

The sight of this stampede exerted a floodlike force that seemed able to drag sticks and stones and men from the ground. They of the reserves had to hold on. They grew pale and firm, and red and quaking.

The youth achieved one little thought in the midst of this chaos. The composite monster which had caused the other troops to flee had not then appeared. He resolved to get a view of it, and then, he thought he might very likely run better than the best of them

5

There were moments of waiting. The youth thought of the village street at home before the arrival of the circus parade on a day in the spring. He remembered how he had stood, a small, thrillful boy, prepared to follow the dingy lady upon the white horse, or the band in its faded chariot. He saw the yellow road, the lines of expectant people, and the sober houses. He particularly remembered an old fellow who used to sit upon a cracker box in front of the store and feign to despise such exhibitions. A thousand details of color and form surged in his mind. The old fellow upon the cracker box appeared in middle prominence.

Some one cried, "Here they come!"

There was rustling and muttering among the men. They displayed a feverish desire to have every possible cartridge ready to their hands. The boxes were pulled around into various positions, and adjusted with great care. It was as if seven hundred new bonnets were being tried on.

The tall soldier, having prepared his rifle, produced a red handkerchief of some kind. He was engaged in knitting it about his throat with exquisite attention to its position, when the cry was repeated up and down the line in a muffled roar of sound.

"Here they come! Here they come!" Gun locks clicked.

Across the smoke-infested fields came a brown swarm of running men who were giving shrill yells. They came on, stooping and swinging their rifles at all angles. A flag, tilted forward, sped near the front.

As he caught sight of them the youth was momentarily startled by a thought that perhaps his gun was not loaded. He stood trying to rally his faltering intellect so that he might recollect the moment when he had loaded, but he could not.

A hatless general pulled his dripping horse to a stand near the colonel of the 304th. He shook his fist in the other's face. "You've got to hold 'em back!" he shouted, savagely; "you've got to hold 'em back!"

In his agitation the colonel began to stammer. "A-all r-right, General, all right, by Gawd! We-we'll do our—we-we'll d-d-do—do our best, General." The general made a passionate gesture and galloped away. The colonel, perchance to relieve his feelings, began to scold like a wet parrot. The youth, turning swiftly to make sure that the rear was unmolested, saw the commander regarding his men in a highly resentful manner, as if he regretted above everything his association with them.

The man at the youth's elbow was mumbling, as if to himself: "Oh, we're in for it now! oh, we're in for it now!"

The captain of the company had been pacing excitedly to and fro in the rear. He coaxed in schoolmistress fashion, as to a congregation of boys with primers. His talk was an endless repetition. "Reserve your fire, boys—don't shoot till I tell you—save your fire—wait till they get close up—don't be damned fools—"

Perspiration streamed down the youth's face, which was soiled like that of a weeping urchin. He frequently, with a nervous movement, wiped his eyes with his coat sleeve. His mouth was still a little way open

He got the one glance at the foe-swarming field in front of him, and instantly ceased to debate the question of his piece being loaded. Before he was ready to begin—before he had announced to himself that he was about to fight—he threw the obedient, well-balanced rifle into position and fired a first wild shot. Directly he was working at his weapon like an automatic affair.

He suddenly lost concern for himself, and forgot to look at a menacing fate. He became not a man but a member. He felt that something of which he was a part—a regiment, an army, a cause, or a country—was in a crisis. He was welded into a common personality which was dominated by a single desire. For some moments he could not flee, no more than a little finger can commit a revolution from a hand.

If he had thought the regiment was about to be annihilated perhaps he could have amputated himself from it. But its noise gave him assurance. The regiment was like a firework that, once ignited, proceeds superior to circumstances until its blazing vitality fades. It wheezed and banged with a mighty power. He pictured the ground before it as strewn with the discomfited.

There was a consciousness always of the presence of his comrades about him. He felt the subtle battle brotherhood more potent even than the cause for which they were fighting. It was a mysterious fraternity born of the smoke and danger of death.

He was at a task. He was like a carpenter who has made many boxes, making still another box, only there was furious haste in his movements. He, in his thought, was careering off in other places, even as the carpenter who as he works whistles and thinks of his friend or his enemy, his home or a saloon. And these jolted dreams were never perfect to him afterward, but remained a mass of blurred shapes.

Presently he began to feel the effects of the war atmosphere—a blistering sweat, a sensation that his eyeballs were about to crack like hot stones. A burning roar filled his ears.

Following this came a red rage. He developed the acute exasperation of a pestered animal, a well-meaning cow worried by dogs. He had a mad feeling against his rifle, which could only be used against one life at a time. He wished to rush forward and strangle with his fingers. He craved a power that would enable him to make a world-sweeping gesture and brush all back. His impotency appeared to him, and made his rage into that of a driven beast.

Buried in the smoke of many rifles his anger was directed not so much against men whom he knew were rushing toward him as against the swirling battle phantoms which were choking him, stuffing their smoke robes down his parched throat. He fought frantically for respite for his senses, for air, as a babe being smothered attacks the deadly blankets.

There was a blare of heated rage mingled with a certain expression of intentness on all faces. Many of the men were making low-toned noises with their mouths, and these subdued cheers, snarls, imprecations, prayers, made a wild, barbaric song that went as an undercurrent of sound, strange and chantlike with the resounding chords of the war march. The man at the youth's elbow was babbling. In it there was something soft and tender like the monologue of a babe. The tall soldier was swearing in a loud voice. From his lips came a black procession of curious oaths. Of a sudden another broke out in a querulous way like a man who has mislaid his hat. "Well, why don't they support us? Why don't they send supports? Do they think–"

The youth in his battle sleep heard this as one who dozes hears.

There was a singular absence of heroic poses. The men bending and surging in their haste and rage were in every impossible attitude. The steel ramrods clanked and clanged with incessant din as the men pounded them furiously into the hot rifle barrels. The flaps of the cartridge boxes were all unfastened, and bobbed idiotically with each movement. The rifles, once loaded, were jerked to the shoulder and fired without apparent aim into the smoke or at one of the blurred and shifting forms which upon the field before the regiment had been growing larger and larger like puppets under a magician's hand.

The officers, at their intervals, rearward, neglected to stand in picturesque attitudes. They were bobbing to and fro roaring directions and encouragements. The dimensions of their howls were extraordinary. They expended their lungs with prodigal wills. And often they nearly stood upon their heads in their anxiety to observe the enemy on the other side of the tumbling smoke.

The lieutenant of the youth's company had encountered a soldier who had fled screaming at the first volley of his comrades. Behind the lines these two were acting a little isolated scene. The man was blubbering and staring with sheeplike eyes at the lieutenant, who had seized him by the collar and was pommeling him. He drove him back into the ranks with many blows. The soldier went mechanically, dully, with his animal-like eyes upon the officer. Perhaps there was to him a divinity expressed in the voice of the other–stern, hard, with no reflection of fear in it. He tried to reload his gun, but his shaking hands prevented. The lieutenant was obliged to assist him.

The men dropped here and there like bundles. The captain of the youth's company had been killed in an early part of the action. His body lay stretched out in the position of a tired man resting, but upon his face there was an astonished and sorrowful look, as if he thought some friend had done him an ill turn. The babbling man was grazed by a shot that made the blood stream widely down his face. He clapped both hands to his head. "Oh!" he said, and ran. Another grunted suddenly as if he had been struck by a club in the stomach. He sat down and gazed ruefully. In his eyes there was mute, indefinite reproach. Farther up the line a man, standing behind a tree, had had his knee joint splintered by a ball. Immediately he had dropped his rifle and gripped the tree with both arms. And there he remained, clinging desperately and crying for assistance that he might withdraw his hold upon the tree.

At last an exultant yell went along the quivering line. The fire dwindled from an uproar to a last vindictive popping. As the smoke slowly eddied away, the youth saw that the charge had been repulsed. The enemy were scattered into reluctant groups. He saw a man climb to the top of the fence, straddle the rail, and fire a parting shot. The waves had receded, leaving bits of dark *débris* upon the ground.

Some in the regiment began to whoop frenziedly. Many were silent. Apparently they were trying to contemplate themselves.

After the fever had left his veins, the youth thought that at last he was going to suffocate. He became aware of the foul atmosphere in which he had been struggling. He was grimy and dripping like a laborer in a foundry. He grasped his canteen and took a long swallow of the warmed water.

A sentence with variations went up and down the line. "Well, we've helt 'em back. We've helt 'em back; derned if we haven't." The men said it blissfully, leering at each other with dirty smiles.

The youth turned to look behind him and off to the right and off to the left. He experienced the joy of a man who at last finds leisure in which to look about him.

Under foot there were a few ghastly forms motionless. They lay twisted in fantastic contortions. Arms were bent and heads were turned in incredible ways. It seemed that the dead men must have fallen from some great height to get into such positions. They looked to be dumped out upon the ground from the sky.

From a position in the rear of the grove a battery was throwing shells over it. The flash of the guns startled the youth at first. He thought they were aimed directly at him. Through the trees he watched the black figures of the gunners as they worked swiftly and intently. Their labor seemed a complicated thing. He wondered how they could remember its formula in the midst of confusion.

The guns squatted in a row like savage chiefs. They argued with abrupt violence. It was a grim pow-wow Their busy servants ran hither and thither.

A small procession of wounded men were going drearily toward the rear. It was a flow of blood from the torn body of the brigade.

To the right and to the left were the dark lines of other troops. Far in front he thought he could see lighter masses protruding in points from the forest. They were suggestive of unnumbered thousands.

Once he saw a tiny battery go dashing along the line of the horizon. The tiny riders were beating the tiny horses.

From a sloping hill came the sound of cheerings and clashes. Smoke welled slowly through the leaves.

Batteries were speaking with thunderous oratorical effort. Here and there were flags, the red in the stripes dominating. They splashed bits of warm color upon the dark lines of troops.

The youth felt the old thrill at the sight of the emblem. They were like beautiful birds strangely undaunted in a storm.

As he listened to the din from the hillside, to a deep pulsating thunder that came from afar to the left, and to the lesser clamors which came from many directions, it occurred to him that they were fighting, too, over there, and over there, and over there. Heretofore he had supposed that all the battle was directly under his nose.

As he gazed around him the youth felt a flash of astonishment at the blue, pure sky and the sun gleaming on the trees and fields. It was surprising that Nature had gone tranquilly on with her golden process in the midst of so much devilment.

6

The youth awakened slowly. He came gradually back to a position from which he could regard himself. For moments he had been scrutinizing his person in a dazed way as if he had never before seen himself. Then he picked up his cap from the ground. He wriggled in his jacket to make a more comfortable fit, and kneeling relaced his shoe. He thoughtfully mopped his reeking features.

So it was all over at last! The supreme trial had been passed. The red, formidable difficulties of war had been vanquished.

He went into an ecstasy of self-satisfaction. He had the most delightful sensations of his life. Standing as if apart from himself, he viewed that last scene. He perceived that the man who had fought thus was magnificent.

He felt that he was a fine fellow. He saw himself even with those ideals which he had considered as far beyond him. He smiled in deep gratification.

Upon his fellows he beamed tenderness and good will. "Gee! ain't it hot, hey?" he said affably to a man who was polishing his streaming face with his coat sleeves

"You bet!" said the other, grinning sociably. "I never seen sech dumb hotness." He sprawled out luxuriously on the ground. "Gee, yes! An' I hope we don't have no more fightin' till a week from Monday."

There were some handshakings and deep speeches with men whose features were familiar, but with whom the youth now felt the bonds of tied hearts. He helped a cursing comrade to bind up a wound of the shin.

But, of a sudden, cries of amazement broke out along the ranks of the new regiment. "Here they come ag'in! Here they come ag'in!" The man who had sprawled upon the ground started up and said, "Gosh!"

The youth turned quick eyes upon the field. He discerned forms begin to swell in masses out of a distant wood. He again saw the tilted flag speeding forward.

The shells, which had ceased to trouble the regiment for a time, came swirling again, and exploded in the grass or among the leaves of the trees. They looked to be strange war flowers bursting into fierce bloom.

The men groaned. The luster faded from their eyes. Their smudged countenances now expressed a profound dejection. They moved their stiffened bodies slowly, and watched in sullen mood the frantic approach of the enemy. The slaves toiling in the temple of this god began to feel rebellion at his harsh tasks.

They fretted and complained each to each. "Oh, say, this is too much of a good thing! Why can't somebody send us supports?"

"We ain't never goin' to stand this second banging. I didn't come here to fight the hull damn' rebel army."

There was one who raised a doleful cry. "I wish Bill Smithers had trod on my hand, insteader me treddin' on his'n." The sore joints of the regiment creaked as it painfully floundered into position to repulse.

The youth stared. Surely, he thought, this impossible thing was not about to happen. He waited as if he expected the enemy to suddenly stop, apologize, and retire bowing. It was all a mistake.

But the firing began somewhere on the regimental line and ripped along in both directions. The level sheets of flame developed great clouds of smoke that tumbled and tossed in the mild wind near the ground for a moment, and then rolled through the ranks as through a gate. The clouds were tinged an earthlike yellow in the sunrays and in the shadow were a sorry blue. The flag was sometimes eaten and lost in this mass of vapor, but more often it projected, sun-touched, resplendent.

Into the youth's eyes there came a look that one can see in the orbs of a jaded horse. His neck was quivering with nervous weakness and the muscles of his arms felt numb and bloodless. His hands, too, seemed large and awkward as if he was wearing invisible mittens. And there was a great uncertainty about his knee joints.

The words that comrades had uttered previous to the firing began to recur to him. "Oh, say, this is too much of a good thing! What do they take us for—why don't they send supports? I didn't come here to fight the hull damned rebel army."

He began to exaggerate the endurance, the skill, and the valor of those who were coming. Himself reeling from exhaustion, he was astonished beyond measure at such persistency. They must be machines of steel. It was very gloomy struggling against such affairs, wound up perhaps to fight until sundown.

He slowly lifted his rifle and catching a glimpse of the thickspread field he blazed at a cantering cluster. He stopped then and began to peer as best he could through the smoke. He caught changing views of the ground covered with men who were all running like pursued imps, and yelling.

To the youth it was an onslaught of redoubtable dragons. He became like the man who lost his legs at the approach of the red and green monster. He waited in a sort of a horrified, listening attitude. He seemed to shut his eyes and wait to be gobbled.

A man near him who up to this time had been working feverishly at his rifle suddenly stopped and ran with howls. A lad whose face had borne an expression of exalted courage, the majesty of he who dares give his life, was, at an instant, smitten abject. He blanched like one who has come to the edge of a cliff at midnight and is suddenly made aware. There was a revelation. He, too, threw down his gun and fled. There was no shame in his face. He ran like a rabbit.

Others began to scamper away through the smoke. The youth turned his head, shaken from his trance by this movement as if the regiment was leaving him behind. He saw the few fleeting forms.

He yelled then with fright and swung about. For a moment, in the great clamor, he was like a proverbial chicken. He lost the direction of safety. Destruction threatened him from all points.

Directly he began to speed toward the rear in great leaps. His rifle and cap were gone. His unbuttoned coat bulged in the wind. The flap of his cartridge box bobbed wildly, and his canteen, by its slender cord, swung out behind. On his face was all the horror of those things which he imagined.

The lieutenant sprang forward bawling. The youth saw his features wrathfully red, and saw him make a dab with his sword. His one thought of the incident was that the lieutenant was a peculiar creature to feel interested in such matters upon this occasion.

He ran like a blind man. Two or three times he fell down. Once he knocked his shoulder so heavily against a tree that he went headlong.

Since he had turned his back upon the fight his fears had been wondrously magnified. Death about to thrust him between the shoulder blades was far more dreadful than death about to smite him between the eyes. When he thought of it later, he conceived the impression that it is better to view the appalling than to be merely within hearing. The noises of the battle were like stones; he believed himself liable to be crushed.

As he ran on he mingled with others. He dimly saw men on his right and on his left, and he heard footsteps behind him. He thought that all the regiment was fleeing, pursued by these ominous crashes.

In his flight the sound of these following footsteps gave him his one meager relief. He felt vaguely that death must make a first choice of the men who were nearest; the initial morsels for the dragons would be then those who were following him. So he displayed the zeal of an insane sprinter in his purpose to keep them in the rear. There was a race.

As he, leading, went across a little field, he found himself in a region of shells. They hurtled over his head with long wild screams. As he listened he imagined them to have rows of cruel teeth that grinned at him. Once one lit before him and the livid lightning of the explosion effectually barred the way in his chosen direction. He groveled on the ground and then springing up went careering off through some bushes.

He experienced a thrill of amazement when he came within view of a battery in action. The men there seemed to be in conventional moods, altogether unaware of the impending annihilation. The battery was disputing with a distant antagonist and the gunners were wrapped in admiration of their shooting. They were continually bending in coaxing postures over the guns. They seemed to be patting them on the back and encouraging them with words. The guns, stolid and undaunted, spoke with dogged valor.

The precise gunners were coolly enthusiastic. They lifted their eyes every chance to the smoke-wreathed hillock from whence the hostile battery addressed them. The youth pitied them as he ran. Methodical idiots! Machinelike fools! The refined joy of planting shells in the midst of the other battery's formation would appear a little thing when the infantry came swooping out of the woods.

The face of a youthful rider, who was jerking his frantic horse with an abandon of temper he might display in a placid barnyard, was impressed deeply upon his mind. He knew that he looked upon a man who would presently be dead.

Too, he felt a pity for the guns, standing, six good comrades, in a bold row.

He saw a brigade going to the relief of its pestered fellows. He scrambled upon a wee hill and watched it sweeping finely, keeping formation in difficult places. The blue of the line was crusted with steel color, and the brilliant flags projected. Officers were shouting.

This sight also filled him with wonder. The brigade was hurrying briskly to be gulped into the infernal mouths of the war god. What manner of men were they, anyhow? Ah, it was some wondrous breed! Or else they didn't comprehend—the fools.

A furious order caused commotion in the artillery. An officer on a bounding horse made maniacal motions with his arms. The teams went swinging up from the rear, the guns were whirled about, and the battery scampered away. The cannon with their noses poked slantingly at the ground grunted and grumbled like stout men, brave but with objections to hurry.

The youth went on, moderating his pace since he had left the place of noises.

Later he came upon a general of division seated upon a horse that pricked its ears in an interested way at the battle. There was a great gleaming of yellow and patent leather about the saddle and bridle. The quiet man astride looked mouse-colored upon such a splendid charger.

A jingling staff was galloping hither and thither. Sometimes the general was surrounded by horsemen and at other times he was quite alone. He looked to be much harassed. He had the appearance of a business man whose market is swinging up and down.

The youth went slinking around this spot. He went as near as he dared trying to overhear words. Perhaps the general, unable to comprehend chaos, might call upon him for information. And he could tell him. He knew all concerning it. Of a surety the force was in a fix, and any fool could see that if they did not retreat while they had opportunity—why—

He felt that he would like to thrash the general, or at least approach and tell him in plain words exactly what he thought him to be. It was criminal to stay calmly in one spot and make no effort to stay destruction. He loitered in a fever of eagerness for the division commander to apply to him.

As he warily moved about, he heard the general call out irritably: "Tompkins, go over an' see Taylor, an' tell him not t' be in such an all-fired hurry; tell him t' halt his brigade in th' edge of th' woods; tell him t' detach a reg'ment—say I think th' center 'll break if we don't help it out some; tell him t' hurry up."

A slim youth on a fine chestnut horse caught these swift words from the mouth of his superior. He made his horse bound into a gallop almost from a walk in his haste to go upon his mission. There was a cloud of dust.

A moment later the youth saw the general bounce excitedly in his saddle.

"Yes, by heavens, they have!" The officer leaned forward. His face was aflame with excitement. "Yes, by heavens, they've held 'im! They've held 'im!"

He began to blithely roar at his staff: "We'll wallop 'im now. We'll wallop 'im now. We've got 'em sure." He turned suddenly upon an aid: "Here—you—Jones—quick—ride after Tompkins—see Taylor—tell him t' go in—everlastingly—like blazes—anything."

As another officer sped his horse after the first messenger, the general beamed upon the earth like a sun. In his eyes was a desire to chant a paean. He kept repeating, "They've held 'em, by heavens!"

His excitement made his horse plunge, and he merrily kicked and swore at it. He held a little carnival of joy on horseback.

7

The youth cringed as if discovered in a crime. By heavens, they had won after all! The imbecile line had remained and become victors. He could hear cheering.

He lifted himself upon his toes and looked in the direction of the fight. A yellow fog lay wallowing on the treetops. From beneath it came the clatter of musketry. Hoarse cries told of an advance.

He turned away amazed and angry. He felt that he had been wronged.

He had fled, he told himself, because annihilation approached. He had done a good part in saving himself, who was a little piece of the army. He had considered the time, he said, to be one in which it was the duty of every little piece to rescue itself if possible. Later the officers could fit the little pieces together again, and make a battle front. If none of the little pieces were wise enough to save themselves from the flurry of death at such a time, why, then, where would be the army? It was all plain that he had proceeded according to very correct and commendable rules. His actions had been sagacious things. They had been full of strategy. They were the work of a master's legs.

Thoughts of his comrades came to him. The brittle blue line had withstood the blows and won. He grew bitter over it. It seemed that the blind ignorance and stupidity of those little pieces had betrayed him. He had been overturned and crushed by their lack of sense in holding the position, when intelligent deliberation would have convinced them that it was impossible. He, the enlightened man who looks afar in the dark, had fled because of his superior perceptions and knowledge. He felt a great anger against his comrades. He knew it could be proved that they had been fools.

He wondered what they would remark when later he appeared in camp. His mind heard howls of derision. Their destiny would not enable them to understand his sharper point of view.

He began to pity himself acutely. He was ill used. He was trodden beneath the feet of an iron injustice. He had proceeded with wisdom and from the most righteous motives under heaven's blue only to be frustrated by hateful circumstances.

A dull, animal-like rebellion against his fellows, war in the abstract, and fate grew within him. He shambled along with bowed head, his brain in a tumult of agony and despair. When he looked loweringly up, quivering at each sound, his eyes had the expression of those of a criminal who thinks his guilt and his punishment great, and knows that he can find no words.

He went from the fields into a thick woods, as if resolved to bury himself. He wished to get out of hearing of the cracking shots which were to him like voices.

The ground was cluttered with vines and bushes, and the trees grew close and spread out like bouquets. He was obliged to force his way with much noise. The creepers, catching against his legs, cried out harshly as their sprays were torn from the barks of trees. The swishing saplings tried to make known his presence to the world. He could not conciliate the forest. As he made his way, it was always calling out protestations. When he separated embraces of trees and vines the disturbed foliages waved their arms and turned their face leaves toward him. He dreaded lest these noisy motions and cries should bring men to look at him. So he went far, seeking dark and intricate places.

After a time the sound of musketry grew faint and the cannon boomed in the distance. The sun, suddenly apparent, blazed among the trees. The insects were making rhythmical noises. They seemed to be grinding their teeth in unison. A woodpecker stuck his impudent head around the side of a tree. A bird flew on lighthearted wing.

Off was the rumble of death. It seemed now that Nature had no ears.

This landscape gave him assurance. A fair field holding life. It was the religion of peace. It would die if its timid eyes were compelled to see blood. He conceived Nature to be a woman with a deep aversion to tragedy.

He threw a pine cone at a jovial squirrel, and he ran with chattering fear. High in a treetop he stopped, and, poking his head cautiously from behind a branch, looked down with an air of trepidation.

The youth felt triumphant at this exhibition. There was the law, he said. Nature had given him a sign. The squirrel, immediately upon recognizing danger, had taken to his legs without ado. He did not stand stolidly baring his furry belly to the missile, and die with an upward glance at the sympathetic heavens. On the contrary, he had fled as fast as his legs could carry him; and he was but an ordinary squirrel, too—doubtless no philosopher of his race. The youth wended, feeling that Nature was of his mind. She re-enforced his argument with proofs that lived where the sun shone.

Once he found himself almost into a swamp. He was obliged to walk upon bog tufts and watch his feet to keep from the oily mire. Pausing at one time to look about him he saw, out at some black water, a small animal pounce in and emerge directly with a gleaming fish.

The youth went again into the deep thickets. The brushed branches made a noise that drowned the sounds of cannon. He walked on, going from obscurity into promises of a greater obscurity.

At length he reached a place where the high, arching boughs made a chapel. He softly pushed the green doors aside and entered. Pine needles were a gentle brown carpet. There was a religious half light.

Near the threshold he stopped, horror-stricken at the sight of a thing.

He was being looked at by a dead man who was seated with his back against a columnlike tree. The corpse was dressed in a uniform that once had been blue, but was now faded to a melancholy shade of green. The eyes, staring at the youth, had changed to the dull hue to be seen on the side of a dead fish. The mouth was open. Its red had changed to an appalling yellow. Over the gray skin of the face ran little ants. One was trundling some sort of a bundle along the upper lip.

The youth gave a shriek as he confronted the thing. He was for moments turned to stone before it. He remained staring into the liquid-looking eyes. The dead man and the living man exchanged a long look. Then the youth cautiously put one hand behind him and brought it against a tree. Leaning upon this he retreated, step by step, with his face still toward the thing. He feared that if he turned his back the body might spring up and stealthily pursue him.

The branches, pushing against him, threatened to throw him over upon it. His unguided feet, too, caught aggravatingly in brambles; and with it all he received a subtle suggestion to touch the corpse. As he thought of his hand upon it he shuddered profoundly.

At last he burst the bonds which had fastened him to the spot and fled, unheeding the underbrush. He was pursued by a sight of the black ants swarming greedily upon the gray face and venturing horribly near to the eyes.

After a time he paused, and, breathless and panting, listened. He imagined some strange voice would come from the dead throat and squawk after him in horrible menaces.

The trees about the portals of the chapel moved soughingly in a soft wind. A sad silence was upon the little guarding edifice.

8

The trees began softly to sing a hymn of twilight. The sun sank until slanted bronze rays struck the forest. There was a lull in the noises of insects as if they had bowed their beaks and were making a devotional pause. There was silence save for the chanted chorus of the trees.

Then, upon this stillness, there suddenly broke a tremendous clangor of sounds. A crimson roar came from the distance.

The youth stopped. He was transfixed by this terrific medley of all noises. It was as if worlds were being rended. There was the ripping sound of musketry and the breaking crash of the artillery.

His mind flew in all directions. He conceived the two armies to be at each other panther fashion. He listened for a time. Then he began to run in the direction of the battle. He saw that it was an ironical thing for him to be running thus toward that which he had been at such pains to avoid. But he said, in substance, to himself that if the earth and the moon were about to clash, many persons would doubtless plan to get upon the roofs to witness the collision.

As he ran, he became aware that the forest had stopped its music, as if at last becoming capable of hearing the foreign sounds. The trees hushed and stood motionless. Everything seemed to be listening to the crackle and clatter and ear-shaking thunder. The chorus pealed over the still earth.

It suddenly occurred to the youth that the fight in which he had been was, after all, but perfunctory popping. In the hearing of this present din he was doubtful if he had seen real battle scenes. This uproar explained a celestial battle; it was tumbling hordes a-struggle in the air.

Reflecting, he saw a sort of humor in the point of view of himself and his fellows during the late encounter. They had taken themselves and the enemy very seriously and had imagined that they were deciding the war. Individuals must have supposed that they were cutting the letters of their names deep into everlasting tablets of brass, or enshrining their reputations forever in the hearts of their countrymen, while, as to fact, the affair would appear in printed reports under a meek and immaterial title. But he saw that it was good, else, he said, in battle every one would surely run save forlorn hopes and their ilk.

He went rapidly on. He wished to come to the edge of the forest that he might peer out.

As he hastened, there passed through his mind pictures of stupendous conflicts. His accumulated thought upon such subjects was used to form scenes. The noise was as the voice of an eloquent being, describing.

Sometimes the brambles formed chains and tried to hold him back. Trees, confronting him, stretched out their arms and forbade him to pass. After its previous hostility this new resistance of the forest filled him with a fine bitterness. It seemed that Nature could not be quite ready to kill him.

But he obstinately took roundabout ways, and presently he was where he could see long gray walls of vapor where lay battle lines. The voices of cannon shook him. The musketry sounded in long irregular surges that played havoc with his ears. He stood regardant for a moment. His eyes had an awestruck expression. He gawked in the direction of the fight.

Presently he proceeded again on his forward way. The battle was like the grinding of an immense and terrible machine to him. Its complexities and powers, its grim processes, fascinated him. He must go close and see it produce corpses.

He came to a fence and clambered over it. On the far side, the ground was littered with clothes and guns. A newspaper, folded up, lay in the dirt. A dead soldier was stretched with his face hidden in his arm. Farther off there was a group of four or five corpses keeping mournful company. A hot sun had blazed upon the spot.

In this place the youth felt that he was an invader. This forgotten part of the battle ground was owned by the dead men, and he hurried, in the vague apprehension that one of the swollen forms would rise and tell him to begone.

He came finally to a road from which he could see in the distance dark and agitated bodies of troops, smoke-fringed. In the lane was a blood-stained crowd streaming to the rear. The wounded men were cursing, groaning, and wailing. In the air, always, was a mighty swell of sound that it seemed could sway the earth. With the courageous words of the artillery and the spiteful sentences of the musketry mingled red cheers. And from this region of noises came the steady current of the maimed.

One of the wounded men had a shoeful of blood. He hopped like a schoolboy in a game. He was laughing hysterically.

One was swearing that he had been shot in the arm through the commanding general's mismanagement of the army. One was marching with an air imitative of some sublime drum major. Upon his features was an unholy mixture of merriment and agony. As he marched he sang a bit of doggerel in a high and quavering voice:

"Sing a song 'a vic'try,
A pocketful 'a bullets,
Five an' twenty dead men
Baked in a—pie."

Parts of the procession limped and staggered to this tune.

Another had the gray seal of death already upon his face. His lips were curled in hard lines and his teeth were clinched. His hands were bloody from where he had pressed them upon his wound. He seemed to be awaiting the moment when he should pitch headlong. He stalked like the specter of a soldier, his eyes burning with the power of a stare into the unknown.

There were some who proceeded sullenly, full of anger at their wounds, and ready to turn upon anything as an obscure cause.

An officer was carried along by two privates. He was peevish. "Don't joggle so, Johnson, yeh fool," he cried. "Think m' leg is made of iron? If yeh can't carry me decent, put me down an' let some one else do it."

He bellowed at the tottering crowd who blocked the quick march of his bearers. "Say, make way there, can't yeh? Make way, dickens take it all."

They sulkily parted and went to the roadsides. As he was carried past they made pert remarks to him. When he raged in reply and threatened them, they told him to be damned.

The shoulder of one of the tramping bearers knocked heavily against the spectral soldier who was staring into the unknown.

The youth joined this crowd and marched along with it. The torn bodies expressed the awful machinery in which the men had been entangled.

Orderlies and couriers occasionally broke through the throng in the roadway, scattering wounded men right and left, galloping on, followed by howls. The melancholy march was continually disturbed by the messengers, and sometimes by bustling batteries that came swinging and thumping down upon them, the officers shouting orders to clear the way.

There was a tattered man, fouled with dust, blood and powder stain from hair to shoes, who trudged quietly at the youth's side. He was listening with eagerness and much humility to the lurid descriptions of a bearded sergeant. His lean features wore an expression of awe and admiration. He was like a listener in a country store to wondrous tales told among the sugar barrels. He eyed the story-teller with unspeakable wonder. His mouth was agape in yokel fashion.

The sergeant, taking note of this, gave pause to his elaborate history while he administered a sardonic comment. "Be keerful, honey, you'll be a-ketchin' flies," he said.

The tattered man shrank back abashed.

After a time he began to sidle near to the youth, and in a different way try to make him a friend. His voice was gentle as a girl's voice and his eyes were pleading. The youth saw with surprise that the soldier had two wounds, one in the head, bound with a blood-soaked rag, and the other in the arm, making that member dangle like a broken bough.

After they had walked together for some time the tattered man mustered sufficient courage to speak. "Was pretty good fight, wasn't it?" he timidly said. The youth, deep in thought, glanced up at the bloody and grim figure with its lamblike eyes. "What?"

"Was pretty good fight, wa'n't it?"

"Yes," said the youth shortly. He quickened his pace.

But the other hobbled industriously after him. There was an air of apology in his manner, but he evidently thought that he needed only to talk for a time, and the youth would perceive that he was a good fellow.

"Was pretty good fight, wa'n't it?" he began in a small voice, and then he achieved the fortitude to continue. "Dern me if I ever see fellers fight so. Laws, how they did fight! I knowed th' boys 'd like when they onct got square at it. Th' boys ain't had no fair chanct up t' now, but this time they showed what they was. I knowed it 'd turn out this way. Yeh can't lick them boys. No, sir! They're fighters, they be."

He breathed a deep breath of humble admiration. He had looked at the youth for encouragement several times. He received none, but gradually he seemed to get absorbed in his subject.

"I was talkin' 'cross pickets with a boy from Georgie, onct, an' that boy, he ses, 'Your fellers 'll all run like hell when they onct hearn a gun,' he ses. 'Mebbe they will,' I ses, 'but I don't b'lieve none of it,' I ses; 'an' b'jiminey,' I ses back t' 'um, 'mebbe your fellers 'll all run like hell when they onct hearn a gun,' I ses. He larfed. Well, they didn't run t'-day, did they, hey? No, sir! They fit, an' fit, an' fit."

His homely face was suffused with a light of love for the army which was to him all things beautiful and powerful.

After a time he turned to the youth, "Where yeh hit, ol' boy?" he asked in a brotherly tone.

The youth felt instant panic at this question, although at first its full import was not borne in upon him

"What?" he asked.

"Where yeh hit?" repeated the tattered man.

"Why," began the youth, "I—I—that is—why—I—"

He turned away suddenly and slid through the crowd. His brow was heavily flushed, and his fingers were picking nervously at one of his buttons. He bent his head and fastened his eyes studiously upon the button as if it were a little problem.

The tattered man looked after him in astonishment.

9

The youth fell back in the procession until the tattered soldier was not in sight. Then he started to walk on with the others.

But he was amid wounds. The mob of men was bleeding. Because of the tattered soldier's question he now felt that his shame could be viewed. He was continually casting sidelong glances to see if the men were contemplating the letters of guilt he felt burned into his brow.

At times he regarded the wounded soldiers in an envious way. He conceived persons with torn bodies to be peculiarly happy. He wished that he, too, had a wound, a red badge of courage.

The spectral soldier was at his side like a stalking reproach. The man's eyes were still fixed in a stare into the unknown. His gray, appalling face had attracted attention in the crowd, and men, slowing to his dreary pace, were walking with him. They were discussing his plight, questioning him and giving him advice. In a dogged way he repelled them, signing to them to go on and leave him alone. The shadows of his face were deepening and his tight lips seemed holding in check the moan of great despair. There could be seen a certain stiffness in the movements of his body, as if he were taking infinite care not to arouse the passion of his wounds. As he went on, he seemed always looking for a place, like one who goes to choose a grave.

Something in the gesture of the man as he waved the bloody and pitying soldiers away made the youth start as if bitten. He yelled in horror. Tottering forward he laid a quivering hand upon the man's arm. As the latter slowly turned his waxlike features toward him, the youth screamed:

"Gawd! Jim Conklin!"

The tall soldier made a little commonplace smile. "Hello, Henry," he said.

The youth swayed on his legs and glared strangely. He stuttered and stammered. "Oh, Jim—oh, Jim—oh, Jim—"

The tall soldier held out his gory hand. There was a curious red and black combination of new blood and old blood upon it. "Where yeh been, Henry?" he asked. He continued in a monotonous voice, "I thought mebbe yeh got keeled over. There's been thunder t' pay t'-day. I was worryin' about it a good deal."

The youth still lamented. "Oh, Jim—oh, Jim—oh, Jim—"

"Yeh know," said the tall soldier, "I was out there." He made a careful gesture. "An', Lord, what a circus! An', b'jiminey, I got shot—I got shot. Yes, b'jiminey, I got shot." He reiterated this fact in a bewildered way, as if he did not know how it came about.

The youth put forth anxious arms to assist him, but the tall soldier went firmly on as if propelled. Since the youth's arrival as a guardian for his friend, the other wounded men had ceased to display much interest. They occupied themselves again in dragging their own tragedies toward the rear.

Suddenly, as the two friends marched on, the tall soldier seemed to be overcome by a terror. His face turned to a semblance of gray paste. He clutched the youth's arm and looked all about him, as if dreading to be overheard. Then he began to speak in a shaking whisper:

"I tell yeh what I'm 'fraid of, Henry—I'll tell yeh what I'm 'fraid of. I'm 'fraid I'll fall down—an' then yeh know—them damned artillery wagons—they like as not 'll run over me. That's what I'm 'fraid of—"

The youth cried out to him hysterically: "I'll take care of yeh, Jim! I'll take care of yeh! I swear t' Gawd I will!"

"Sure—will yeh, Henry?" the tall soldier beseeched.

"Yes—yes—I tell yeh—I'll take care of yeh, Jim!" protested the youth. He could not speak accurately because of the gulpings in his throat.

But the tall soldier continued to beg in a lowly way. He now hung babelike to the youth's arm. His eyes rolled in the wildness of his terror. "I was allus a good friend t' yeh, wa'n't I, Henry? I've allus been a pretty good feller, ain't I? An' it ain't much t' ask, is it? Jest t' pull me along outer th' road? I'd do it fer you, wouldn't I, Henry?"

He paused in piteous anxiety to await his friend's reply.

The youth had reached an anguish where the sobs scorched him. He strove to express his loyalty, but he could only make fantastic gestures.

However, the tall soldier seemed suddenly to forget all those fears. He became again the grim, stalking specter of a soldier. He went stonily forward. The youth wished his friend to lean upon him, but the other always shook his head and strangely protested. "No—no—no—leave me be—leave me be—"

His look was fixed again upon the unknown. He moved with mysterious purpose, and all of the youth's offers he brushed aside. "No—no—leave me be—leave me be—"

The youth had to follow.

Presently the latter heard a voice talking softly near his shoulders. Turning he saw that it belonged to the tattered soldier. "Ye'd better take 'im outa th' road, pardner. There's a batt'ry comin' helitywhoop down th' road an' he'll git runned over. He's a goner anyhow in about five minutes —yeh kin see that. Ye'd better take 'im outa th' road. Where th' blazes does he git his stren'th from?"

"Lord knows!" cried the youth. He was shaking his hands helplessly.

He ran forward presently and grasped the tall soldier by the arm. "Jim! Jim!" he coaxed, "come with me."

The tall soldier weakly tried to wrench himself free. "Huh," he said vacantly. He stared at the youth for a moment. At last he spoke as if dimly comprehending. "Oh! Inteh th' fields? Oh!"

He started blindly through the grass.

The youth turned once to look at the lashing riders and jouncing guns of the battery. He was startled from this view by a shrill outcry from the tattered man.

"Gawd! He's runnin'!"

Turning his head swiftly, the youth saw his friend running in a staggering and stumbling way toward a little clump of bushes. His heart seemed to wrench itself almost free from his body at this sight. He made a noise of pain. He and the tattered man began a pursuit. There was a singular race.

When he overtook the tall soldier he began to plead with all the words he could find. "Jim—Jim—what are you doing—what makes you do this way—you'll hurt yerself."

The same purpose was in the tall soldier's face. He protested in a dulled way, keeping his eyes fastened on the mystic place of his intentions. "No—no—don't tech me—leave me be—leave me be—"

The youth, aghast and filled with wonder at the tall soldier, began quaveringly to question him. "Where yeh goin', Jim? What you thinking about? Where you going? Tell me, won't you, Jim?"

The tall soldier faced about as upon relentless pursuers. In his eyes there was a great appeal. "Leave me be, can't yeh? Leave me be fer a minnit."

The youth recoiled. "Why, Jim," he said, in a dazed way, "what's the matter with you?"

The tall soldier turned and, lurching dangerously, went on. The youth and the tattered soldier followed, sneaking as if whipped, feeling unable to face the stricken man if he should again confront them. They began to have thoughts of a solemn ceremony. There was something ritelike in these movements of the doomed soldier. And there was a resemblance in him to a devotee of a mad religion, blood-sucking, muscle-wrenching, bone-crushing. They were awed and afraid. They hung back lest he have at command a dreadful weapon.

At last, they saw him stop and stand motionless. Hastening up, they perceived that his face wore an expression telling that he had at last found the place for which he had struggled. His spare figure was erect; his bloody hands were quietly at his side. He was waiting with patience for something that he had come to meet. He was at the rendezvous. They paused and stood, expectant.

There was a silence.

Finally, the chest of the doomed soldier began to heave with a strained motion. It increased in violence until it was as if an animal was within and was kicking and tumbling furiously to be free.

This spectacle of gradual strangulation made the youth writhe, and once as his friend rolled his eyes, he saw something in them that made him sink wailing to the ground. He raised his voice in a last supreme call.

"Jim—Jim—Jim—"

The tall soldier opened his lips and spoke. He made a gesture. "Leave me be—don't tech me—leave me be—"

There was another silence while he waited.

Suddenly, his form stiffened and straightened. Then it was shaken by a prolonged ague. He stared into space. To the two watchers there was a curious and profound dignity in the firm lines of his awful face.

He was invaded by a creeping strangeness that slowly enveloped him. For a moment the tremor of his legs caused him to dance a sort of hideous hornpipe. His arms beat wildly about his head in expression of implike enthusiasm.

His tall figure stretched itself to its full height. There was a slight rending sound. Then it began to swing forward, slow and straight, in the manner of a falling tree. A swift muscular contortion made the left shoulder strike the ground first.

The body seemed to bounce a little way from the earth. "God!" said the tattered soldier.

The youth had watched, spellbound, this ceremony at the place of meeting. His face had been twisted into an expression of every agony he had imagined for his friend.

He now sprang to his feet and, going closer, gazed upon the pastelike face. The mouth was opened and the teeth showed in a laugh.

As the flap of the blue jacket fell away from the body, he could see that the side looked as if it had been chewed by wolves.

The youth turned, with sudden, livid rage, toward the battlefield. He shook his fist. He seemed about to deliver a philippic.

"Hell—"

The red sun was pasted in the sky like a wafer.

10

The tattered man stood musing.

"Well, he was reg'lar jim-dandy fer nerve, wa'n't he," said he finally in a little awestruck voice. "A reg'lar jim-dandy." He thoughtfully poked one of the docile hands with his foot. "I wonner where he got 'is stren'th from? I never seen a man do like that before. It was a funny thing. Well, he was a reg'lar jim-dandy."

The youth desired to screech out his grief. He was stabbed, but his tongue lay dead in the tomb of his mouth. He threw himself again upon the ground and began to brood.

The tattered man stood musing.

"Look-a-here, pardner," he said, after a time. He regarded the corpse as he spoke. "He's up an' gone, ain't 'e, an' we might as well begin t' look out fer ol' number one. This here thing is all over. He's up an' gone, ain't 'e? An' he's all right here. Nobody won't bother 'im. An' I must say I ain't enjoying any great health m'self these days."

The youth, awakened by the tattered soldier's tone, looked quickly up. He saw that he was swinging uncertainly on his legs and that his face had turned to a shade of blue.

"Good Lord!" he cried, "you ain't goin' t'—not you, too."

The tattered man waved his hand. "Nary die," he said. "All I want is some pea soup an' a good bed. Some pea soup," he repeated dreamfully.

The youth arose from the ground. "I wonder where he came from. I left him over there." He pointed. "And now I find 'im here. And he was coming from over there, too." He indicated a new direction. They both turned toward the body as if to ask of it a question.

"Well," at length spoke the tattered man, "there ain't no use in our stayin' here an' tryin' t' ask him anything."

The youth nodded an assent wearily. They both turned to gaze for a moment at the corpse.

The youth murmured something.

"Well, he was a jim-dandy, wa'n't 'e?" said the tattered man as if in response.

They turned their backs upon it and started away. For a time they stole softly, treading with their toes. It remained laughing there in the grass.

"I'm commencin' t' feel pretty bad," said the tattered man, suddenly breaking one of his little silences. "I'm commencin' t' feel pretty damn' bad."

The youth groaned. "O Lord!" He wondered if he was to be the tortured witness of another grim encounter.

But his companion waved his hand reassuringly. "Oh, I'm not goin' t' die yit! There's too much dependin' on me fer me t' die yit. No, sir! Nary die; I *can't!* Ye'd oughta see th' swad a' chil'ren I've got, an' all like that."

The youth glancing at his companion could see by the shadow of a smile that he was making some kind of fun.

As they plodded on the tattered soldier continued to talk. "Besides, if I died, I wouldn't die th' way that feller did. That was th' funniest thing. I'd jest flop down, I would. I never seen a feller die th' way that feller did.

"Yeh know Tom Jamison, he lives next door t' me up home. He's a nice feller, he is, an' we was allus good friends. Smart, too. Smart as a steel trap. Well, when we was a-fightin' this atternoon, all-of-a-sudden he begin t' rip up an' cuss an' beller at me. 'Yer shot, yeh blamed infernal!'—he swear horrible—he ses t' me. I put up m' hand t' m' head an' when I looked at m' fingers, I seen, sure 'nough, I was shot. I give a holler an' begin t' run, but b'fore I could git away another one hit me in th' arm an' whirl' me clean 'round. I got skeared when they was all a-shootin' b'hind me an' I run t' beat all, but I cotch it pretty bad. I've an idee I'd a' been fightin' yit, if t'wasn't fer Tom Jamison."

Then he made a calm announcement: "There's two of 'em—little ones—but they're beginnin' t' have fun with me now. I don't b'lieve I kin walk much furder."

They went slowly on in silence. "Yeh look pretty peek-ed yerself," said the tattered man at last. "I bet yeh 've got a worser one than yeh think. Ye'd better take keer of yer hurt. It don't do t' let sech things go. It might be inside mostly, an' them plays thunder. Where is it located?" But he continued his harangue without waiting for a reply. "I see' a feller git hit plum in th' head when my reg'ment was a-standin' at ease onct. An' everybody yelled out to 'im: Hurt, John? Are yeh hurt much? 'No,' ses he. He looked kinder surprised, an' he went on tellin' 'em how he felt. He sed he didn't feel nothin'. But, by dad, th' first thing that feller knowed he was dead. Yes, he was dead—stone dead. So, yeh wanta watch out. Yeh might have some queer kind 'a hurt yerself. Yeh can't never tell. Where is your'n located?"

The youth had been wriggling since the introduction of this topic. He now gave a cry of exasperation and made a furious motion with his hand. "Oh, don't bother me!" he said. He was enraged against the tattered man, and could have strangled him. His companions seemed ever to play intolerable parts. They were ever upraising the ghost of shame on the stick of their curiosity. He turned toward the tattered man as one at bay. "Now, don't bother me," he repeated with desperate menace.

"Well, Lord knows I don't wanta bother anybody," said the other. There was a little accent of despair in his voice as he replied, "Lord knows I've gota 'nough m' own t' tend to."

The youth, who had been holding a bitter debate with himself and casting glances of hatred and contempt at the tattered man, here spoke in a hard voice. "Good-by," he said.

The tattered man looked at him in gaping amazement. "Why—why, pardner, where yeh goin'?" he asked unsteadily. The youth looked at him, could see that he, too, like that other one, was beginning to act dumb and animal-like. His thoughts seemed to be floundering about in his head. "Now—now—look—a—here, you Tom Jamison—now—I won't have this—this here won't do. Where—where yeh goin'?"

The youth pointed vaguely. "Over there," he replied.

"Well, now look—a—here—now," said the tattered man, rambling on in idiot fashion. His head was hanging forward and his words were slurred. "This thing won't do, now, Tom Jamison. It won't do. I know yeh, yeh pigheaded devil. Yeh wanta go trompin' off with a bad hurt. It ain't right—now—Tom Jamison—it ain't. Yeh wanta leave me take keer of yeh, Tom Jamison. It ain't—right—it ain't—fer yeh t' go—trompin' off—with a bad hurt—it ain't—ain't—ain't right—it ain't."

In reply the youth climbed a fence and started away. He could hear the tattered man bleating plaintively.

Once he faced about angrily. "What?"

"Look—a—here, now, Tom Jamison—now—it ain't—"

The youth went on. Turning at a distance he saw the tattered man wandering about helplessly in the field.

He now thought that he wished he was dead. He believed that he envied those men whose bodies lay strewn over the grass of the fields and on the fallen leaves of the forest.

The simple questions of the tattered man had been knife thrusts to him. They asserted a society that probes pitilessly at secrets until all is apparent. His late companion's chance persistency made him feel that he could not keep his crime concealed in his bosom. It was sure to be brought plain by one of those arrows which cloud the air and are constantly pricking, discovering, proclaiming those things which are willed to be forever hidden. He admitted that he could not defend himself against this agency. It was not within the power of vigilance.

11

He became aware that the furnace roar of the battle was growing louder. Great brown clouds had floated to the still heights of air before him. The noise, too, was approaching. The woods filtered men and the fields became dotted.

As he rounded a hillock, he perceived that the roadway was now a crying mass of wagons, teams, and men. From the heaving tangle issued exhortations, commands, imprecations. Fear was sweeping it all along. The cracking whips bit and horses plunged and tugged. The white-topped wagons strained and stumbled in their exertions like fat sheep.

The youth felt comforted in a measure by this sight. They were all retreating. Perhaps, then, he was not so bad after all. He seated himself and watched the terror-stricken wagons. They fled like soft, ungainly animals. All the roarers and lashers served to help him to magnify the dangers and horrors of the engagement that he might try to prove to himself that the thing with which men could charge him was in truth a symmetrical act. There was an amount of pleasure to him in watching the wild march of this vindication.

Presently the calm head of a forward-going column of infantry appeared in the road. It came swiftly on. Avoiding the obstructions gave it the sinuous movement of a serpent. The men at the head butted mules with their musket stocks. They prodded teamsters indifferent to all howls. The men forced their way through parts of the dense mass by strength. The blunt head of the column pushed. The raving teamsters swore many strange oaths.

The commands to make way had the ring of a great importance in them. The men were going forward to the heart of the din. They were to confront the eager rush of the enemy. They felt the pride of their onward movement when the remainder of the army seemed trying to dribble down this road. They tumbled teams about with a fine feeling that it was no matter so long as their column got to the front in time. This importance made their faces grave and stern. And the backs of the officers were very rigid.

As the youth looked at them the black weight of his woe returned to him. He felt that he was regarding a procession of chosen beings. The separation was as great to him as if they had marched with weapons of flame and banners of sunlight. He could never be like them. He could have wept in his longings.

He searched about in his mind for an adequate malediction for the indefinite cause, the thing upon which men turn the words of final blame. It—whatever it was—was responsible for him, he said. There lay the fault.

The haste of the column to reach the battle seemed to the forlorn young man to be something much finer than stout fighting. Heroes, he thought, could find excuses in that long seething lane. They could retire with perfect self-respect and make excuses to the stars.

He wondered what those men had eaten that they could be in such haste to force their way to grim chances of death. As he watched his envy grew until he thought that he wished to change lives with one of them. He would have liked to have used a tremendous force, he said, throw off himself and become a better. Swift pictures of himself, apart, yet in himself, came to him—a blue desperate figure leading lurid charges with one knee forward and a broken blade high—a blue, determined figure standing before a crimson and steel assault, getting calmly killed on a high place before the eyes of all. He thought of the magnificent pathos of his dead body.

These thoughts uplifted him. He felt the quiver of war desire. In his ears, he heard the ring of victory. He knew the frenzy of a rapid successful charge. The music of the trampling feet, the sharp voices, the clanking arms of the column near him made him soar on the red wings of war. For a few moments he was sublime.

He thought that he was about to start for the front. Indeed, he saw a picture of himself, dust-stained, haggard, panting, flying to the front at the proper moment to seize and throttle the dark, leering witch of calamity.

Then the difficulties of the thing began to drag at him. He hesitated, balancing awkwardly on one foot.

He had no rifle; he could not fight with his hands, said he resentfully to his plan. Well, rifles could be had for the picking. They were extraordinarily profuse.

Also, he continued, it would be a miracle if he found his regiment. Well, he could fight with any regiment.

He started forward slowly. He stepped as if he expected to tread upon some explosive thing. Doubts and he were struggling.

He would truly be a worm if any of his comrades should see him returning thus, the marks of his flight upon him. There was a reply that the intent fighters did not care for what happened rearward saving that no hostile bayonets appeared there. In the battle-blur his face would in a way be hidden, like the face of a cowled man.

But then he said that his tireless fate would bring forth, when the strife lulled for a moment, a man to ask of him an explanation. In imagination he felt the scrutiny of his companions as he painfully labored through some lies.

Eventually, his courage expended itself upon these objections. The debates drained him of his fire.

He was not cast down by this defeat of his plan, for, upon studying the affair carefully, he could not but admit that the objections were very formidable.

Furthermore, various ailments had begun to cry out. In their presence he could not persist in flying high with the wings of war; they rendered it almost impossible for him to see himself in a heroic light. He tumbled headlong.

He discovered that he had a scorching thirst. His face was so dry and grimy that he thought he could feel his skin crackle. Each bone of his body had an ache in it, and seemingly threatened to break with each movement. His feet were like two sores. Also, his body was calling for food. It was more powerful than a direct hunger. There was a dull, weight-like feeling in his stomach, and, when he tried to walk, his head swayed and he tottered. He could not see with distinctness. Small patches of green mist floated before his vision.

While he had been tossed by many emotions, he had not been aware of ailments. Now they beset him and made clamor. As he was at last compelled to pay attention to them, his capacity for self-hate was multiplied. In despair, he declared that he was not like those others. He now conceded it to be impossible that he should ever become a hero. He was a craven loon. Those pictures of glory were piteous things. He groaned from his heart and went staggering off.

A certain mothlike quality within him kept him in the vicinity of the battle. He had a great desire to see, and to get news. He wished to know who was winning.

He told himself that, despite his unprecedented suffering, he had never lost his greed for a victory, yet, he said, in a half-apologetic manner to his conscience, he could not but know that a defeat for the army this time might mean many favorable things for him. The blows of the enemy would splinter regiments into fragments. Thus, many men of courage, he considered, would be obliged to desert the colors and scurry like chickens. He would appear as one of them. They would be sullen brothers in distress, and he could then easily believe he had not run any farther or faster than they. And if he himself could believe in his virtuous perfection, he conceived that there would be small trouble in convincing all others.

He said, as if in excuse for this hope, that previously the army had encountered great defeats and in a few months had shaken off all blood and tradition of them, emerging as bright and valiant as a new one; thrusting out of sight the memory of disaster, and appearing with the valor and confidence of unconquered legions. The shrilling voices of the people at home would pipe dismally for a time, but various generals were usually compelled to listen to these ditties. He of course felt no compunctions for proposing a general as a sacrifice. He could not tell who the chosen for the barbs might be, so he could center no direct sympathy upon him. The people were afar and he did not conceive public opinion to be accurate at long range. It was quite probable they would hit the wrong man who, after he had recovered from his amazement would perhaps spend the rest of his days in writing replies to the songs of his alleged failure. It would be very unfortunate, no doubt, but in this case a general was of no consequence to the youth.

In a defeat there would be a roundabout vindication of himself. He thought it would prove, in a manner, that he had fled early because of his superior powers of perception. A serious prophet upon predicting a flood should be the first man to climb a tree. This would demonstrate that he was indeed a seer.

A moral vindication was regarded by the youth as a very important thing. Without salve, he could not, he thought, wear the sore badge of his dishonor through life. With his heart continually assuring him that he was despicable, he could not exist without making it, through his actions, apparent to all men.

If the army had gone gloriously on he would be lost. If the din meant that now his army's flags were tilted forward he was a condemned wretch. He would be compelled to doom himself to isolation. If the men were advancing, their indifferent feet were trampling upon his chances for a successful life.

As these thoughts went rapidly through his mind, he turned upon them and tried to thrust them away. He denounced himself as a villain. He said that he was the most unutterably selfish man in existence. His mind pictured the soldiers who would place their defiant bodies before the spear of the yelling battle fiend, and as he saw their dripping corpses on an imagined field, he said that he was their murderer.

Again he thought that he wished he was dead. He believed that he envied a corpse. Thinking of the slain, he achieved a great contempt for some of them, as if they were guilty for thus becoming lifeless. They might have been killed by lucky chances, he said, before they had had opportunities to flee or before they had been really tested. Yet they would receive laurels from tradition. He cried out bitterly that their crowns were stolen and their robes of glorious memories were shams. However, he still said that it was a great pity he was not as they.

A defeat of the army had suggested itself to him as a means of escape from the consequences of his fall. He considered, now, however, that it was useless to think of such a possibility. His education had been that success for that mighty blue machine was certain; that it would make victories as a contrivance turns out buttons. He presently discarded all his speculations in the other direction. He returned to the creed of soldiers.

When he perceived again that it was not possible for the army to be defeated, he tried to bethink him of a fine tale which he could take back to his regiment, and with it turn the expected shafts of derision.

But, as he mortally feared these shafts, it became impossible for him to invent a tale he felt he could trust. He experimented with many schemes, but threw them aside one by one as flimsy. He was quick to see vulnerable places in them all.

Furthermore, he was much afraid that some arrow of scorn might lay him mentally low before he could raise his protecting tale.

He imagined the whole regiment saying: "Where's Henry Fleming? He run, didn't 'e? Oh, my!" He recalled various persons who would be quite sure to leave him no peace about it. They would doubtless question him with sneers, and laugh at his stammering hesitation. In the next engagement they would try to keep watch of him to discover when he would run.

Wherever he went in camp, he would encounter insolent and lingeringly cruel stares. As he imagined himself passing near a crowd of comrades, he could hear some one say, "There he goes!"

Then, as if the heads were moved by one muscle, all the faces were turned toward him with wide, derisive grins. He seemed to hear some one make a humorous remark in a low tone. At it the others all crowed and cackled. He was a slang phrase

12

The column that had butted stoutly at the obstacles in the roadway was barely out of the youth's sight before he saw dark waves of men come sweeping out of the woods and down through the fields. He knew at once that the steel fibers had been washed from their hearts. They were bursting from their coats and their equipments as from entanglements. They charged down upon him like terrified buffaloes.

Behind them blue smoke curled and clouded above the treetops, and through the thickets he could sometimes see a distant pink glare. The voices of the cannon were clamoring in interminable chorus.

The youth was horrorstricken. He stared in agony and amazement. He forgot that he was engaged in combating the universe. He threw aside his mental pamphlets on the philosophy of the retreated and rules for the guidance of the damned.

The fight was lost. The dragons were coming with invincible strides. The army, helpless in the matted thickets and blinded by the overhanging night, was going to be swallowed. War, the red animal, war, the blood-swollen god, would have bloated fill.

Within him something bade to cry out. He had the impulse to make a rallying speech, to sing a battle hymn, but he could only get his tongue to call into the air: "Why—why—what—what's th' matter?"

Soon he was in the midst of them. They were leaping and scampering all about him. Their blanched faces shone in the dusk. They seemed, for the most part, to be very burly men. The youth turned from one to another of them as they galloped along. His incoherent questions were lost. They were heedless of his appeals. They did not seem to see him.

They sometimes gabbled insanely. One huge man was asking of the sky: "Say, where de plank road? Where de plank road?" It was as if he had lost a child. He wept in his pain and dismay.

Presently, men were running hither and thither in all ways. The artillery booming, forward, rearward, and on the flanks made jumble of ideas of direction. Landmarks had vanished into the gathered gloom. The youth began to imagine that he had got into the center of the tremendous quarrel, and he could perceive no way out of it. From the mouths of the fleeing men came a thousand wild questions, but no one made answers.

The youth, after rushing about and throwing interrogations at the heedless bands of retreating infantry, finally clutched a man by the arm. They swung around face to face.

"Why—why—" stammered the youth struggling with his balking tongue.

The man screamed: "Let go me! Let go me!" His face was livid and his eyes were rolling uncontrolled. He was heaving and panting. He still grasped his rifle, perhaps having forgotten to release his hold upon it. He tugged frantically, and the youth being compelled to lean forward was dragged several paces.

"Let go me! Let go me!"

"Why—why—" stuttered the youth.

"Well, then!" bawled the man in a lurid rage. He adroitly and fiercely swung his rifle. It crushed upon the youth's head. The man ran on.

The youth's fingers had turned to paste upon the other's arm. The energy was smitten from his muscles. He saw the flaming wings of lightning flash before his vision. There was a deafening rumble of thunder within his head.

Suddenly his legs seemed to die. He sank writhing to the ground. He tried to arise. In his efforts against the numbing pain he was like a man wrestling with a creature of the air.

There was a sinister struggle.

Sometimes he would achieve a position half erect, battle with the air for a moment, and then fall again, grabbing at the grass. His face was of a clammy pallor. Deep groans were wrenched from him.

At last, with a twisting movement, he got upon his hands and knees, and from thence, like a babe trying to walk, to his feet. Pressing his hands to his temples he went lurching over the grass.

He fought an intense battle with his body. His dulled senses wished him to swoon and he opposed them stubbornly, his mind portraying unknown dangers and mutilations if he should fall upon the field. He went tall soldier fashion. He imagined secluded spots where he could fall and be unmolested. To search for one he strove against the tide of his pain.

Once he put his hand to the top of his head and timidly touched the wound. The scratching pain of the contact made him draw a long breath through his clinched teeth. His fingers were dabbled with blood. He regarded them with a fixed stare.

Around him he could hear the grumble of jolted cannon as the scurrying horses were lashed toward the front. Once, a young officer on a besplashed charger nearly ran him down. He turned and watched the mass of guns, men, and horses sweeping in a wide curve toward a gap in a fence. The officer was making excited motions with a gauntleted hand. The guns followed the teams with an air of unwillingness, of being dragged by the heels.

Some officers of the scattered infantry were cursing and railing like fishwives. Their scolding voices could be heard above the din. Into the unspeakable jumble in the roadway rode a squadron of cavalry. The faded yellow of their facings shone bravely. There was a mighty altercation.

The artillery were assembling as if for a conference.

The blue haze of evening was upon the field. The lines of forest were long purple shadows. One cloud lay along the western sky partly smothering the red.

As the youth left the scene behind him, he heard the guns suddenly roar out. He imagined them shaking in black rage. They belched and howled like brass devils guarding a gate. The soft air was filled with the tremendous remonstrance. With it came the shattering peal of opposing infantry. Turning to look behind him, he could see sheets of orange light illumine the shadowy distance. There were subtle and sudden lightnings in the far air. At times he thought he could see heaving masses of men.

He hurried on in the dusk. The day had faded until he could barely distinguish place for his feet. The purple darkness was filled with men who lectured and jabbered. Sometimes he could see them gesticulating against the blue and somber sky. There seemed to be a great ruck of men and munitions spread about in the forest and in the fields.

The little narrow roadway now lay lifeless. There were overturned wagons like sun-dried bowlders. The bed of the former torrent was choked with the bodies of horses and splintered parts of war machines.

It had come to pass that his wound pained him but little. He was afraid to move rapidly, however, for a dread of disturbing it. He held his head very still and took many precautions against stumbling. He was filled with anxiety, and his face was pinched and drawn in anticipation of the pain of any sudden mistake of his feet in the gloom.

His thoughts, as he walked, fixed intently upon his hurt. There was a cool, liquid feeling about it and he imagined blood moving slowly down under his hair. His head seemed swollen to a size that made him think his neck to be inadequate.

The new silence of his wound made much worriment. The little blistering voices of pain that had called out from his scalp were, he thought, definite in their expression of danger. By them he believed that he could measure his plight. But when they remained ominously silent he became frightened and imagined terrible fingers that clutched into his brain.

Amid it he began to reflect upon various incidents and conditions of the past. He bethought him of certain meals his mother had cooked at home, in which those dishes of which he was particularly fond had occupied prominent positions. He saw the spread table. The pine walls of the kitchen were glowing in the warm light from the stove. Too, he remembered how he and his companions used to go from the schoolhouse to the bank of a shaded pool. He saw his clothes in disorderly array upon the grass of the bank. He felt the swash of the fragrant water upon his body. The leaves of the overhanging maple rustled with melody in the wind of youthful summer.

He was overcome presently by a dragging weariness. His head hung forward and his shoulders were stooped as if he were bearing a great bundle. His feet shuffled along the ground.

He held continuous arguments as to whether he should lie down and sleep at some near spot, or force himself on until he reached a certain haven. He often tried to dismiss the question, but his body persisted in rebellion and his senses nagged at him like pampered babies.

At last he heard a cheery voice near his shoulder: "Yeh seem t' be in a pretty bad way, boy?"

The youth did not look up, but he assented with thick tongue. "Uh!"

The owner of the cheery voice took him firmly by the arm. "Well," he said, with a round laugh, "I'm goin' your way. Th' hull gang is goin' your way. An' I guess I kin give yeh a lift." They began to walk like a drunken man and his friend.

As they went along, the man questioned the youth and assisted him with the replies like one manipulating the mind of a child. Sometimes he interjected anecdotes. "What reg'ment do yeh b'long teh? Eh? What's that? Th' 304th N' York? Why, what corps is that in? Oh, it is? Why, I thought they wasn't engaged t'-day—they're 'way over in th' center. Oh, they was, eh? Well, pretty nearly everybody got their share 'a fightin' t'-day. By dad, I give myself up fer dead any number 'a times. There was shootin' here an' shootin' there, an' hollerin' here an hollerin' there, in th' damn' darkness, until I couldn't tell t' save m' soul which side I was on. Sometimes I thought I was sure 'nough from Ohier, an' other times I could a' swore I was from th' bitter end of Florida. It was th' most mixed up dern thing I ever see. An' these here hull woods is a reg'lar mess. It'll be a miracle if we find our reg'ments t'-night. Pretty soon, though, we'll meet a-plenty of guards an' provost-guards, an' one thing an' another. Ho! there they go with an off'cer, I guess. Look at his hand a-draggin'. He's got all th' war he wants, I bet. He won't be talkin' so big about his reputation an' all when they go t' sawin' off his leg. Poor feller! My brother's got whiskers jest like that. How did yeh git 'way over here, anyhow? Your reg'ment is a long way from here, ain't it? Well, I guess we can find it. Yeh know there was a boy killed in my comp'ny t'-day that I thought th' world an' all of. Jack was a nice feller. By ginger, it hurt like thunder t' see ol' Jack jest git knocked flat. We was a-standin' purty peaceable fer a spell, 'though there was men runnin' ev'ry way all 'round us, an' while we was a-standin' like that, 'long come a big fat feller. He began t' peck at Jack's elbow, an' he ses: 'Say, where 's th' road t' th' river?' An' Jack, he never paid no attention, an' th' feller kept on a-peckin' at his elbow an' sayin': 'Say, where's th' road t' th' river?' Jack was a-lookin' ahead all th' time tryin' t' see th' Johnnies comin' through th' woods, an' he never paid no attention t' this big fat feller fer a long time, but at last he turned 'round an' he ses: 'Ah, go t' hell an' find th' road t' th' river!' An' jest then a shot slapped him bang on th' side th' head. He was a sergeant, too Them was his last words. Thunder, I wish we was sure 'a findin' our reg'ments t'-night. It's goin' t' be long huntin'. But I guess we kin do it."

In the search which followed, the man of the cheery voice seemed to the youth to possess a wand of a magic kind. He threaded the mazes of the tangled forest with a strange fortune. In encounters with guards and patrols he displayed the keenness of a detective and the valor of a gamin. Obstacles fell before him and became of assistance. The youth, with his chin still on his breast, stood woodenly by while his companion beat ways and means out of sullen things.

The forest seemed a vast hive of men buzzing about in frantic circles, but the cheery man conducted the youth without mistakes, until at last he began to chuckle with glee and self-satisfaction. "Ah, there yeh are! See that fire?"

The youth nodded stupidly.

"Well, there's where your reg'ment is. An' now, good-by, ol' boy, good luck t' yeh."

A warm and strong hand clasped the youth's languid fingers for an instant, and then he heard a cheerful and audacious whistling as the man strode away. As he who had so befriended him was thus passing out of his life, it suddenly occurred to the youth that he had not once seen his face.

13

The youth went slowly toward the fire indicated by his departed friend. As he reeled, he bethought him of the welcome his comrades would give him. He had a conviction that he would soon feel in his sore heart the barbed missiles of ridicule. He had no strength to invent a tale; he would be a soft target

He made vague plans to go off into the deeper darkness and hide, but they were all destroyed by the voices of exhaustion and pain from his body. His ailments, clamoring, forced him to seek the place of food and rest, at whatever cost.

He swung unsteadily toward the fire. He could see the forms of men throwing black shadows in the red light, and as he went nearer it became known to him in some way that the ground was strewn with sleeping men.

Of a sudden he confronted a black and monstrous figure. A rifle barrel caught some glinting beams. "Halt! halt!" He was dismayed for a moment, but he presently thought that he recognized the nervous voice. As he stood tottering before the rifle barrel, he called out: "Why, hello, Wilson, you—you here?"

The rifle was lowered to a position of caution and the loud soldier came slowly forward. He peered into the youth's face. "That you, Henry?"

"Yes it's—it's me."

"Well, well, ol' boy," said the other, "by ginger, I'm glad t' see yeh! I give yeh up fer a goner. I thought yeh was dead sure enough." There was husky emotion in his voice.

The youth found that now he could barely stand upon his feet. There was a sudden sinking of his forces. He thought he must hasten to produce his tale to protect him from the missiles already at the lips of his redoubtable comrades. So, staggering before the loud soldier, he began. "Yes, yes. I've—I've had an awful time. I've been all over. Way over on th' right. Ter'ble fightin' over there. I had an awful time. I got separated from th' reg'ment. Over on th' right, I got shot. In th' head. I never see sech fightin'. Awful time. I don't see how I could a' got separated from th' reg'ment. I got shot, too."

His friend had stepped forward quickly. "What? Got shot? Why didn't yeh say so first? Poor ol' boy, we must—hol' on a minnit; what am I doin'? I'll call Simpson."

Another figure at that moment loomed in the gloom. They could see that it was the corporal. "Who yeh talkin' to, Wilson?" he demanded. His voice was anger-toned. "Who yeh talkin' to? Yeh th' derndest sentinel—why—hello, Henry, you here? Why, I thought you was dead four hours ago! Great Jerusalem, they keep turnin' up every ten minutes or so! We thought we'd lost forty-two men by straight count, but if they keep on a-comin' this way, we'll git th' comp'ny all back by mornin' yit. Where was yeh?"

"Over on th' right. I got separated"—began the youth with considerable glibness.

But his friend had interrupted hastily. "Yes, an' he got shot in th' head an' he's in a fix, an' we must see t' him right away." He rested his rifle in the hollow of his left arm and his right around the youth's shoulder.

"Gee, it must hurt like thunder!" he said.

The youth leaned heavily upon his friend. "Yes, it hurts—hurts a good deal," he replied. There was a faltering in his voice.

"Oh," said the corporal. He linked his arm in the youth's and drew him forward. "Come on, Henry. I'll take keer 'a yeh."

As they went on together the loud private called out after them: "Put 'im t' sleep in my blanket, Simpson. An'—hol' on a minnit—here's my canteen. It's full 'a coffee. Look at his head by th' fire an' see how it looks. Maybe it's a pretty bad un. When I git relieved in a couple 'a minnits, I'll be over an' see t' him."

The youth's senses were so deadened that his friend's voice sounded from afar and he could scarcely feel the pressure of the corporal's arm. He submitted passively to the latter's directing strength. His head was in the old manner hanging forward upon his breast. His knees wobbled.

The corporal led him into the glare of the fire. "Now, Henry," he said, "let's have look at yer ol' head."

The youth sat down obediently and the corporal, laying aside his rifle, began to fumble in the bushy hair of his comrade. He was obliged to turn the other's head so that the full flush of the fire light would beam upon it. He puckered his mouth with a critical air. He drew back his lips and whistled through his teeth when his fingers came in contact with the splashed blood and the rare wound.

"Ah, here we are!" he said. He awkwardly made further investigations. "Jest as I thought," he added, presently. "Yeh've been grazed by a ball. It's raised a queer lump jest as if some feller had lammed yeh on th' head with a club. It stopped a-bleedin' long time ago. Th' most about it is that in th' mornin' yeh'll feel that a number ten hat wouldn't fit yeh. An' your head 'll be all het up an' feel as dry as burnt pork. An' yeh may git a lot 'a other sicknesses, too, by mornin'. Yeh can't never tell. Still, I don't much think so. It's jest a damn' good belt on th' head, an' nothin' more. Now, you jest sit here an' don't move, while I go rout out th' relief. Then I'll send Wilson t' take keer 'a yeh."

The corporal went away. The youth remained on the ground like a parcel. He stared with a vacant look into the fire.

After a time he aroused, for some part, and the things about him began to take form. He saw that the ground in the deep shadows was cluttered with men, sprawling in every conceivable posture. Glancing narrowly into the more distant darkness, he caught occasional glimpses of visages that loomed pallid and ghostly, lit with a phosphorescent glow. These faces expressed in their lines the deep stupor of the tired soldiers. They made them appear like men drunk with wine. This bit of forest might have appeared to an ethereal wanderer as a scene of the result of some frightful debauch.

On the other side of the fire the youth observed an officer asleep, seated bolt upright, with his back against a tree. There was something perilous in his position. Badgered by dreams, perhaps, he swayed with little bounces and starts, like an old, toddy-stricken grandfather in a chimney corner. Dust and stains were upon his face. His lower jaw hung down as if lacking strength to assume its normal position. He was the picture of an exhausted soldier after a feast of war.

He had evidently gone to sleep with his sword in his arms. These two had slumbered in an embrace, but the weapon had been allowed in time to fall unheeded to the ground. The brass-mounted hilt lay in contact with some parts of the fire.

Within the gleam of rose and orange light from the burning sticks were other soldiers, snoring and heaving, or lying deathlike in slumber. A few pairs of legs were stuck forth, rigid and straight. The shoes displayed the mud or dust of marches and bits of rounded trousers, protruding from the blankets, showed rents and tears from hurried pitchings through the dense brambles.

The fire crackled musically. From it swelled light smoke. Overhead the foliage moved softly. The leaves, with their faces turned toward the blaze, were colored shifting hues of silver, often edged with red. Far off to the right, through a window in the forest, could be seen a handful of stars lying, like glittering pebbles, on the black level of the night.

Occasionally, in this low-arched hall, a soldier would arouse and turn his body to a new position, the experience of his sleep having taught him of uneven and objectionable places upon the ground under him. Or, perhaps, he would lift himself to a sitting posture, blink at the fire for an unintelligent moment, throw a swift glance at his prostrate companion, and then cuddle down again with a grunt of sleepy content.

The youth sat in a forlorn heap until his friend, the loud young soldier, came swinging two canteens by their light strings. "Well, now, Henry, ol' boy," said the latter, "we'll have yeh fixed up in jest about a minnit."

He had the bustling ways of an amateur nurse. He fussed around the fire and stirred the sticks to brilliant exertions. He made his patient drink largely from the canteen that contained the coffee. It was to the youth a delicious draught. He tilted his head afar back and held the canteen long to his lips. The cool mixture went caressingly down his blistered throat. Having finished, he sighed with comfortable delight.

The loud young soldier watched his comrade with an air of satisfaction. He later produced an extensive handkerchief from his pocket. He folded it into a manner of bandage and soused water from the other canteen upon the middle of it. This crude arrangement he bound over the youth's head, tying the ends in a queer knot at the back of the neck.

"There," he said, moving off and surveying his deed, "yeh look like th' devil, but I bet yeh feel better."

The youth contemplated his friend with grateful eyes. Upon his aching and swelling head the cold cloth was like a tender woman's hand.

"Yeh don't holler ner say nothin'," remarked his friend approvingly. "I know I'm a blacksmith at takin' keer 'a sick folks, an' yeh never squeaked.

Yer a good un, Henry. Most 'a men would a' been in th' hospital long ago. A shot in th' head ain't foolin' business."

The youth made no reply, but began to fumble with the buttons of his jacket.

"Well, come, now," continued his friend, "come on. I must put yeh t' bed an' see that yeh git a good night's rest."

The other got carefully erect, and the loud young soldier led him among the sleeping forms lying in groups and rows. Presently he stooped and picked up his blankets. He spread the rubber one upon the ground and placed the woolen one about the youth's shoulders.

"There now," he said, "lie down an' git some sleep."

The youth, with his manner of doglike obedience, got carefully down like a crone stooping. He stretched out with a murmur of relief and comfort. The ground felt like the softest couch.

But of a sudden he ejaculated: "Hol' on a minnit! Where you goin' t' sleep?"

His friend waved his hand impatiently. "Right down there by yeh."

"Well, but hol' on a minnit," continued the youth. "What yeh goin' t' sleep in? I've got your—"

The loud young soldier snarled: "Shet up an' go on t' sleep. Don't be makin' a damn' fool 'a yerself," he said severely.

After the reproof the youth said no more. An exquisite drowsiness had spread through him. The warm comfort of the blanket enveloped him and made a gentle languor. His head fell forward on his crooked arm and his weighted lids went slowly down over his eyes. Hearing a splatter of musketry from the distance, he wondered indifferently if those men sometimes slept. He gave a long sigh, snuggled down into his blanket, and in a moment was like his comrades.

14

When the youth awoke it seemed to him that he had been asleep for a thousand years, and he felt sure that he opened his eyes upon an unexpected world. Gray mists were slowly shifting before the first efforts of the sunrays. An impending splendor could be seen in the eastern sky. An icy dew had chilled his face, and immediately upon arousing he curled farther down into his blankets. He stared for a while at the leaves overhead, moving in a heraldic wind of the day.

The distance was splintering and blaring with the noise of fighting. There was in the sound an expression of a deadly persistency, as if it had not begun and was not to cease.

About him were the rows and groups of men that he had dimly seen the previous night. They were getting a last draught of sleep before the awakening. The gaunt, careworn features and dusty figures were made plain by this quaint light at the dawning, but it dressed the skin of the men in corpselike hues and made the tangled limbs appear pulseless and dead. The youth started up with a little cry when his eyes first swept over this motionless mass of men, thick-spread upon the ground, pallid, and in strange postures. His disordered mind interpreted the hall of the forest as a charnel place. He believed for an instant that he was in the house of the dead, and he did not dare to move lest these corpses start up, squalling and squawking. In a second, however, he achieved his proper mind. He swore a complicated oath at himself. He saw that this somber picture was not a fact of the present, but a mere prophecy.

He heard then the noise of a fire crackling briskly in the cold air, and, turning his head, he saw his friend pottering busily about a small blaze. A few other figures moved in the fog, and he heard the hard cracking of axe blows.

Suddenly there was a hollow rumble of drums. A distant bugle sang faintly. Similar sounds, varying in strength, came from near and far over the forest. The bugles called to each other like brazen gamecocks. The near thunder of the regimental drums rolled.

The body of men in the woods rustled. There was a general uplifting of heads. A murmuring of voices broke upon the air. In it there was much bass of grumbling oaths. Strange gods were addressed in condemnation of the early hours necessary to correct war. An officer's peremptory tenor rang out and quickened the stiffened movement of the men. The tangled limbs unraveled. The corpse-hued faces were hidden behind fists that twisted slowly in the eye sockets.

The youth sat up and gave vent to an enormous yawn. "Thunder!" he remarked petulantly. He rubbed his eyes, and then putting up his hand felt carefully of the bandage over his wound. His friend, perceiving him to be awake, came from the fire. "Well, Henry, ol' man, how do yeh feel this mornin'?" he demanded.

The youth yawned again. Then he puckered his mouth to a little pucker. His head, in truth, felt precisely like a melon, and there was an unpleasant sensation at his stomach.

"Oh, Lord, I feel pretty bad," he said.

"Thunder!" exclaimed the other. "I hoped ye'd feel all right this mornin'. Let's see th' bandage—I guess it's slipped." He began to tinker at the wound in rather a clumsy way until the youth exploded.

"Gosh-dern it!" he said in sharp irritation; "you're the hangdest man I ever saw! You wear muffs on your hands. Why in good thunderation can't you be more easy? I'd rather you'd stand off an' throw guns at it. Now, go slow, an' don't act as if you was nailing down carpet."

He glared with insolent command at his friend, but the latter answered soothingly. "Well, well, come now, an' git some grub," he said. "Then, maybe, yeh'll feel better."

At the fireside the loud young soldier watched over his comrade's wants with tenderness and care. He was very busy marshaling the little black vagabonds of tin cups and pouring into them the steaming, iron colored mixture from a small and sooty tin pail. He had some fresh meat, which he roasted hurriedly upon a stick. He sat down then and contemplated the youth's appetite with glee.

The youth took note of a remarkable change in his comrade since those days of camp life upon the river bank. He seemed no more to be continually regarding the proportions of his personal prowess. He was not furious at small words that pricked his conceits. He was no more a loud young soldier. There was about him now a fine reliance. He showed a quiet belief in his purposes and his abilities. And this inward confidence evidently enabled him to be indifferent to little words of other men aimed at him.

The youth reflected. He had been used to regarding his comrade as a blatant child with an audacity grown from his inexperience, thoughtless, headstrong, jealous, and filled with a tinsel courage. A swaggering babe accustomed to strut in his own dooryard. The youth wondered where had been born these new eyes; when his comrade had made the great discovery that there were many men who would refuse to be subjected by him. Apparently, the other had now climbed a peak of wisdom from which he could perceive himself as a very wee thing. And the youth saw that ever after it would be easier to live in his friend's neighborhood.

His comrade balanced his ebony coffee cup on his knee. "Well, Henry," he said, "what d'yeh think th' chances are? D'yeh think we'll wallop 'em?"

The youth considered for a moment. "Day-b'fore-yestirday," he finally replied, with boldness, "you would 'a' bet you'd lick the hull kit-an'-boodle all by yourself."

His friend looked a trifle amazed. "Would I?" he asked. He pondered. "Well, perhaps I would," he decided at last. He stared humbly at the fire.

The youth was quite disconcerted at this surprising reception of his remarks. "Oh, no, you wouldn't either," he said, hastily trying to retrace.

But the other made a deprecating gesture. "Oh, yeh needn't mind, Henry," he said. "I believe I was a pretty big fool in those days." He spoke as after a lapse of years.

There was a little pause.

"All th' officers say we've got th' rebs in a pretty tight box," said the friend, clearing his throat in a commonplace way. "They all seem t' think we've got 'em jest where we want 'em."

"I don't know about that," the youth replied. "What I seen over on th' right makes me think it was th' other way about. From where I was, it looked as if we was gettin' a good poundin' yestirday."

"D'yeh think so?" inquired the friend. "I thought we handled 'em pretty rough yestirday."

"Not a bit," said the youth. "Why, Lord, man, you didn't see nothing of the fight. Why!" Then a sudden thought came to him. "Oh! Jim Conklin's dead."

His friend started. "What? Is he? Jim Conklin?"

The youth spoke slowly. "Yes. He's dead. Shot in th' side."

"Yeh don't say so. Jim Conklin . . . poor cuss!"

All about them were other small fires surrounded by men with their little black utensils. From one of these near came sudden sharp voices in a row. It appeared that two light-footed soldiers had been teasing a huge, bearded man, causing him to spill coffee upon his blue knees. The man had gone into a rage and had sworn comprehensively. Stung by his language, his tormentors had immediately bristled at him with a great show of resenting unjust oaths. Possibly there was going to be a fight.

The friend arose and went over to them, making pacific motions with his arms. "Oh, here, now, boys, what's th' use?" he said. "We'll be at th' rebs in less'n an hour. What's th' good fightin' 'mong ourselves?"

One of the light-footed soldiers turned upon him red-faced and violent. "Yeh needn't come around here with yer preachin'. I s'pose yeh don't approve 'a fightin' since Charley Morgan licked yeh; but I don't see what business this here is 'a yours or anybody else."

"Well, it ain't," said the friend mildly. "Still I hate t' see—"

That was a tangled argument.

"Well, he—," said the two, indicating their opponent with accusative forefingers.

The huge soldier was quite purple with rage. He pointed at the two soldiers with his great hand, extended clawlike. "Well, they—"

But during this argumentative time the desire to deal blows seemed to pass, although they said much to each other. Finally the friend returned to his old seat. In a short while the three antagonists could be seen together in an amiable bunch.

"Jimmie Rogers ses I'll have t' fight him after th' battle t'-day," announced the friend as he again seated himself. "He ses he don't allow no interferin' in his business. I hate t' see th' boys fightin' 'mong themselves."

The youth laughed. "Yer changed a good bit. Yeh ain't at all like yeh was. I remember when you an' that Irish feller—" He stopped and laughed again.

"No, I didn't use t' be that way," said his friend thoughtfully. "That's true 'nough."

"Well, I didn't mean—" began the youth.

The friend made another deprecatory gesture. "Oh, yeh needn't mind, Henry."

There was another little pause.

"Th' reg'ment lost over half th' men yestirday," remarked the friend eventually. "I thought a course they was all dead, but, laws, they kep' a-comin' back last night until it seems, after all, we didn't lose but a few. They'd been scattered all over, wanderin' around in th' woods, fightin' with other reg'ments, an' everything. Jest like you done."

"So?" said the youth.

15

The regiment was standing at order arms at the side of a lane, waiting for the command to march, when suddenly the youth remembered the little packet enwrapped in a faded yellow envelope which the loud young soldier with lugubrious words had intrusted to him. It made him start. He uttered an exclamation and turned toward his comrade.

"Wilson!"

"What?"

His friend, at his side in the ranks, was thoughtfully staring down the road. From some cause his expression was at that moment very meek. The youth, regarding him with sidelong glances, felt impelled to change his purpose. "Oh, nothing," he said.

His friend turned his head in some surprise, "Why, what was yeh goin' t' say?"

"Oh, nothin'," repeated the youth.

He resolved not to deal the little blow. It was sufficient that the fact made him glad. It was not necessary to knock his friend on the head with the misguided packet.

He had been possessed of much fear of his friend, for he saw how easily questionings could make holes in his feelings. Lately, he had assured himself that the altered comrade would not tantalize him with a persistent curiosity, but he felt certain that during the first period of leisure his friend would ask him to relate his adventures of the previous day.

He now rejoiced in the possession of a small weapon with which he could prostrate his comrade at the first signs of a cross-examination. He was master. It would now be he who could laugh and shoot the shafts of derision.

The friend had, in a weak hour, spoken with sobs of his own death. He had delivered a melancholy oration previous to his funeral, and had doubtless in the packet of letters, presented various keepsakes to relatives. But he had not died, and thus he had delivered himself into the hands of the youth.

The latter felt immensely superior to his friend, but he inclined to condescension. He adopted toward him an air of patronizing good humor.

His self-pride was now entirely restored. In the shade of its flourishing growth he stood with braced and self-confident legs, and since nothing could now be discovered he did not shrink from an encounter with the eyes of judges, and allowed no thoughts of his own to keep him from an attitude of manfulness. He had performed his mistakes in the dark, so he was still a man.

Indeed, when he remembered his fortunes of yesterday, and looked at them from a distance he began to see something fine there. He had license to be pompous and veteranlike.

His panting agonies of the past he put out of his sight.

In the present, he declared to himself that it was only the doomed and the damned who roared with sincerity at circumstance. Few but they ever did it. A man with a full stomach and the respect of his fellows had no business to scold about anything that he might think to be wrong in the ways of the universe, or even with the ways of society. Let the unfortunates rail; the others may play marbles.

He did not give a great deal of thought to these battles that lay directly before him. It was not essential that he should plan his ways in regard to them. He had been taught that many obligations of a life were easily avoided. The lessons of yesterday had been that retribution was a laggard and blind. With these facts before him he did not deem it necessary that he should become feverish over the possibilities of the ensuing twenty-four hours. He could leave much to chance. Besides, a faith in himself had secretly blossomed. There was a little flower of confidence growing within him. He was now a man of experience. He had been out among the dragons, he said, and he assured himself that they were not so hideous as he had imagined them. Also, they were inaccurate; they did not sting with precision. A stout heart often defied, and defying, escaped.

And, furthermore, how could they kill him who was the chosen of gods and doomed to greatness?

He remembered how some of the men had run from the battle. As he recalled their terror-struck faces he felt a scorn for them. They had surely been more fleet and more wild than was absolutely necessary. They were weak mortals. As for himself, he had fled with discretion and dignity.

He was aroused from this reverie by his friend, who, having hitched about nervously and blinked at the trees for a time, suddenly coughed in an introductory way, and spoke.

"Fleming!"

"What?"

The friend put his hand up to his mouth and coughed again. He fidgeted in his jacket.

"Well," he gulped, at last, "I guess yeh might as well give me back them letters." Dark, prickling blood had flushed into his cheeks and brow.

"All right, Wilson," said the youth. He loosened two buttons of his coat, thrust in his hand, and brought forth the packet. As he extended it to his friend the latter's face was turned from him.

He had been slow in the act of producing the packet because during it he had been trying to invent a remarkable comment upon the affair. He could conjure nothing of sufficient point. He was compelled to allow his friend to escape unmolested with his packet. And for this he took unto himself considerable credit. It was a generous thing.

His friend at his side seemed suffering great shame. As he contemplated him, the youth felt his heart grow more strong and stout. He had never been compelled to blush in such manner for his acts; he was an individual of extraordinary virtues.

He reflected, with condescending pity: "Too bad! Too bad! The poor devil, it makes him feel tough!"

After this incident, and as he reviewed the battle pictures he had seen, he felt quite competent to return home and make the hearts of the people glow with stories of war. He could see himself in a room of warm tints telling tales to listeners. He could exhibit laurels. They were insignificant; still, in a district where laurels were infrequent, they might shine.

He saw his gaping audience picturing him as the central figure in blazing scenes. And he imagined the consternation and the ejaculations of his mother and the young lady at the seminary as they drank his recitals. Their vague feminine formula for beloved ones doing brave deeds on the field of battle without risk of life would be destroyed.

16

A sputtering of musketry was always to be heard. Later, the cannon had entered the dispute. In the fog-filled air their voices made a thudding sound. The reverberations were continued. This part of the world led a strange, battleful existence.

The youth's regiment was marched to relieve a command that had lain long in some damp trenches. The men took positions behind a curving line of rifle pits that had been turned up, like a large furrow, along the line of woods. Before them was a level stretch, peopled with short, deformed stumps. From the woods beyond came the dull popping of the skirmishers and pickets, firing in the fog. From the right came the noise of a terrific fracas.

The men cuddled behind the small embankment and sat in easy attitudes awaiting their turn. Many had their backs to the firing. The youth's friend lay down, buried his face in his arms, and almost instantly, it seemed, he was in a deep sleep.

The youth leaned his breast against the brown dirt and peered over at the woods and up and down the line. Curtains of trees interfered with his ways of vision. He could see the low line of trenches but for a short distance. A few idle flags were perched on the dirt hills. Behind them were rows of dark bodies with a few heads sticking curiously over the top.

Always the noise of skirmishers came from the woods on the front and left, and the din on the right had grown to frightful proportions. The guns were roaring without an instant's pause for breath. It seemed that the cannon had come from all parts and were engaged in a stupendous wrangle. It became impossible to make a sentence heard.

The youth wished to launch a joke—a quotation from newspapers. He desired to say, "All quiet on the Rappahannock," but the guns refused to permit even a comment upon their uproar. He never successfully concluded the sentence. But at last the guns stopped, and among the men in the rifle pits rumors again flew, like birds, but they were now for the most part black creatures who flapped their wings drearily near to the ground and refused to rise on any wings of hope. The men's faces grew doleful from the interpreting of omens. Tales of hesitation and uncertainty on the part of those high in place and responsibility came to their ears. Stories of disaster were borne into their minds with many proofs. This din of musketry on the right, growing like a released genie of sound, expressed and emphasized the army's plight.

The men were disheartened and began to mutter. They made gestures expressive of the sentence: "Ah, what more can we do?" And it could always be seen that they were bewildered by the alleged news and could not fully comprehend a defeat.

Before the gray mists had been totally obliterated by the sunrays, the regiment was marching in a spread column that was retiring carefully through the woods. The disordered, hurrying lines of the enemy could sometimes be seen down through the groves and little fields. They were yelling, shrill and exultant.

At this sight the youth forgot many personal matters and became greatly enraged. He exploded in loud sentences. "B'jiminey, we're generaled by a lot 'a lunkheads."

"More than one feller has said that t'-day," observed a man.

His friend, recently aroused, was still very drowsy. He looked behind him until his mind took in the meaning of the movement. Then he sighed. "Oh, well, I s'pose we got licked," he remarked sadly.

The youth had a thought that it would not be handsome for him to freely condemn other men. He made an attempt to restrain himself, but the words upon his tongue were too bitter. He presently began a long and intricate denunciation of the commander of the forces.

"Mebbe, it wa'n't all his fault—not all together. He did th' best he knowed. It's our luck t' git licked often," said his friend in a weary tone. He was trudging along with stooped shoulders and shifting eyes like a man who has been caned and kicked.

"Well, don't we fight like the devil? Don't we do all that men can?" demanded the youth loudly.

He was secretly dumbfounded at this sentiment when it came from his lips. For a moment his face lost its valor and he looked guiltily about him. But no one questioned his right to deal in such words, and presently he recovered his air of courage. He went on to repeat a statement he had heard going from group to group at the camp that morning. "The brigadier said he never saw a new reg'ment fight the way we fought yestirday, didn't he? And we didn't do better than many another reg'ment, did we? Well, then, you can't say it's th' army's fault, can you?"

In his reply, the friend's voice was stern. " 'A course not," he said. "No man dare say we don't fight like th' devil. No man will ever dare say it. Th' boys fight like hell-roosters. But still—still, we don't have no luck."

"Well, then, if we fight like the devil an' don't ever whip, it must be the general's fault," said the youth grandly and decisively. "And I don't see any sense in fighting and fighting and fighting, yet always losing through some derned old lunkhead of a general."

A sarcastic man who was tramping at the youth's side, then spoke lazily. "Mebbe yeh think yeh fit th' hull battle yestirday, Fleming," he remarked.

The speech pierced the youth. Inwardly he was reduced to an abject pulp by these chance words. His legs quaked privately. He cast a frightened glance at the sarcastic man.

"Why, no," he hastened to say in a conciliating voice, "I don't think I fought the whole battle yesterday."

But the other seemed innocent of any deeper meaning. Apparently, he had no information. It was merely his habit. "Oh!" he replied in the same tone of calm derision.

The youth, nevertheless, felt a threat. His mind shrank from going near to the danger, and thereafter he was silent. The significance of the sarcastic man's words took from him all loud moods that would make him appear prominent. He became suddenly a modest person.

There was low-toned talk among the troops. The officers were impatient and snappy, their countenances clouded with the tales of misfortune. The troops, sifting through the forest, were sullen. In the youth's company once a man's laugh rang out. A dozen soldiers turned their faces quickly toward him and frowned with vague displeasure.

The noise of firing dogged their footsteps. Sometimes, it seemed to be driven a little way, but it always returned again with increased insolence. The men muttered and cursed, throwing black looks in its direction.

In a clear space the troops were at last halted. Regiments and brigades, broken and detached through their encounters with thickets, grew together again and lines were faced toward the pursuing bark of the enemy's infantry.

This noise, following like the yellings of eager, metallic hounds, increased to a loud and joyous burst, and then, as the sun went serenely up the sky, throwing illuminating rays into the gloomy thickets, it broke forth into prolonged peelings. The woods began to crackle as if afire.

"Whoop-a-dadee," said a man, "here we are! Everybody fightin'. Blood an' destruction."

"I was willin' t' bet they'd attack as soon as th' sun got fairly up," savagely asserted the lieutenant who commanded the youth's company. He jerked without mercy at his little mustache. He strode to and fro with dark dignity in the rear of his men, who were lying down behind whatever protection they had collected.

A battery had trundled into position in the rear and was thoughtfully shelling the distance. The regiment, unmolested as yet, awaited the moment when the gray shadows of the woods before them should be slashed by the lines of flame. There was much growling and swearing.

"Good Gawd," the youth grumbled, "we're always being chased around like rats! It makes me sick. Nobody seems to know where we go or why we go. We just get fired around from pillar to post and get licked here and get licked there, and nobody knows what it's done for. It makes a man feel like a damn' kitten in a bag. Now, I'd like to know what the eternal thunders we was marched into these woods for anyhow, unless it was to give the rebs a regular pot shot at us. We came in here and got our legs all tangled up in these cussed briers, and then we begin to fight and the rebs had an easy time of it. Don't tell me it's just luck! I know better. It's this derned old—"

The friend seemed jaded, but he interrupted his comrade with a voice of calm confidence. "It'll turn out all right in th' end," he said.

"Oh, the devil it will! You always talk like a dog-hanged parson. Don't tell me! I know—"

At this time there was an interposition by the savage-minded lieutenant, who was obliged to vent some of his inward dissatisfaction upon his men. "You boys shut right up! There no need 'a your wastin' your breath in long-winded arguments about this an' that an' th' other. You've been jawin' like a lot 'a old hens. All you've got t' do is to fight, an' you'll get plenty 'a that t' do in about ten minutes. Less talkin' an' more fightin' is what's best for you boys. I never saw sech gabbling jackasses."

He paused, ready to pounce upon any man who might have the temerity to reply. No words being said, he resumed his dignified pacing.

"There's too much chin music an' too little fightin' in this war, anyhow," he said to them, turning his head for a final remark.

The day had grown more white, until the sun shed his full radiance upon the thronged forest. A sort of a gust of battle came sweeping toward that part of the line where lay the youth's regiment. The front shifted a trifle to meet it squarely. There was a wait. In this part of the field there passed slowly the intense moments that precede the tempest.

A single rifle flashed in a thicket before the regiment. In an instant it was joined by many others. There was a mighty song of clashes and crashes that went sweeping through the woods. The guns in the rear, aroused and enraged by shells that had been thrown burrlike at them, suddenly involved themselves in a hideous altercation with another band of guns. The battle roar settled to a rolling thunder, which was a single, long explosion.

In the regiment there was a peculiar kind of hesitation denoted in the attitudes of the men. They were worn, exhausted, having slept but little and labored much. They rolled their eyes toward the advancing battle as they stood awaiting the shock. Some shrank and flinched. They stood as men tied to stakes.

17

This advance of the enemy had seemed to the youth like a ruthless hunting. He began to fume with rage and exasperation. He beat his foot upon the ground, and scowled with hate at the swirling smoke that was approaching like a phantom flood. There was a maddening quality in this seeming resolution of the foe to give him no rest, to give him no time to sit down and think. Yesterday he had fought and had fled rapidly. There had been many adventures. For to-day he felt that he had earned opportunities for contemplative repose. He could have enjoyed portraying to uninitiated listeners various scenes at which he had been a witness or ably discussing the processes of war with other proved men. Too it was important that he should have time for physical recuperation. He was sore and stiff from his experiences. He had received his fill of all exertions, and he wished to rest.

But those other men seemed never to grow weary; they were fighting with their old speed. He had a wild hate for the relentless foe. Yesterday, when he had imagined the universe to be against him, he had hated it, little gods and big gods; to-day he hated the army of the foe with the same great hatred. He was not going to be badgered of his life, like a kitten chased by boys, he said. It was not well to drive men into final corners; at those moments they could all develop teeth and claws.

He leaned and spoke into his friend's ear. He menaced the woods with a gesture. "If they keep on chasing us, by Gawd, they'd better watch out. Can't stand *too* much."

The friend twisted his head and made a calm reply. "If they keep on a-chasin' us they'll drive us all inteh th' river."

The youth cried out savagely at this statement. He crouched behind a little tree, with his eyes burning hatefully and his teeth set in a curlike snarl. The awkward bandage was still about his head, and upon it, over his wound, there was a spot of dry blood. His hair was wondrously tousled, and some straggling, moving locks hung over the cloth of the bandage down toward his forehead. His jacket and shirt were open at the throat, and exposed his young bronzed neck. There could be seen spasmodic gulpings at his throat.

His fingers twined nervously about his rifle. He wished that it was an engine of annihilating power. He felt that he and his companions were being taunted and derided from sincere convictions that they were poor and puny. His knowledge of his inability to take vengeance for it made his rage into a dark and stormy specter, that possessed him and made him dream of abominable cruelties. The tormentors were flies sucking insolently at his blood, and he thought that he would have given his life for a revenge of seeing their faces in pitiful plights.

The winds of battle had swept all about the regiment, until the one rifle, instantly followed by others, flashed in its front. A moment later the regiment roared forth its sudden and valiant retort. A dense wall of smoke settled slowly down. It was furiously slit and slashed by the knifelike fire from the rifles.

To the youth the fighters resembled animals tossed for a death struggle into a dark pit. There was a sensation that he and his fellows, at bay, were pushing back, always pushing fierce onslaughts of creatures who were slippery. Their beams of crimson seemed to get no purchase upon the bodies of their foes; the latter seemed to evade them with ease, and come through, between, around, and about with unopposed skill.

When, in a dream, it occurred to the youth that his rifle was an impotent stick, he lost sense of everything but his hate, his desire to smash into pulp the glittering smile of victory which he could feel upon the faces of his enemies.

The blue smoke-swallowed line curled and writhed like a snake stepped upon. It swung its ends to and fro in an agony of fear and rage.

The youth was not conscious that he was erect upon his feet. He did not know the direction of the ground. Indeed, once he even lost the habit of balance and fell heavily. He was up again immediately. One thought went through the chaos of his brain at the time. He wondered if he had fallen because he had been shot. But the suspicion flew away at once. He did not think more of it.

He had taken up a first position behind the little tree, with a direct determination to hold it against the world. He had not deemed it possible that his army could that day succeed, and from this he felt the ability to fight harder. But the throng had surged in all ways, until he lost directions and locations, save that he knew where lay the enemy.

The flames bit him, and the hot smoke broiled his skin. His rifle barrel grew so hot that ordinarily he could not have borne it upon his palms; but he kept on stuffing cartridges into it, and pounding them with his clanking, bending ramrod. If he aimed at some changing form through the smoke, he pulled his trigger with a fierce grunt, as if he were dealing a blow of the fist with all his strength.

When the enemy seemed falling back before him and his fellows, he went instantly forward, like a dog who, seeing his foes lagging, turns and insists upon being pursued. And when he was compelled to retire again, he did it slowly, sullenly, taking steps of wrathful despair.

Once he, in his intent hate, was almost alone, and was firing, when all those near him had ceased. He was so engrossed in his occupation that he was not aware of a lull.

He was recalled by a hoarse laugh and a sentence that came to his ears in a voice of contempt and amazement. "Yeh infernal fool, don't yeh know enough t' quit when there ain't anything t' shoot at? Good Gawd!"

He turned then and, pausing with his rifle thrown half into position, looked at the blue line of his comrades. During this moment of leisure they seemed all to be engaged in staring with astonishment at him. They had become spectators. Turning to the front again he saw, under the lifted smoke, a deserted ground.

He looked bewildered for a moment. Then there appeared upon the glazed vacancy of his eyes a diamond point of intelligence. "Oh," he said, comprehending.

He returned to his comrades and threw himself upon the ground. He sprawled like a man who had been thrashed. His flesh seemed strangely on fire, and the sounds of the battle continued in his ears. He groped blindly for his canteen.

The lieutenant was crowing. He seemed drunk with fighting. He called out to the youth: "By heavens, if I had ten thousand wild cats like you I could tear th' stomach outa this war in less'n a week!" He puffed out his chest with large dignity as he said it.

Some of the men muttered and looked at the youth in awe-struck ways. It was plain that as he had gone on loading and firing and cursing without the proper intermission, they had found time to regard him. And they now looked upon him as a war devil.

The friend came staggering to him. There was some fright and dismay in his voice. "Are yeh all right, Fleming? Do yeh feel all right? There ain't nothin' th' matter with yeh, Henry, is there?"

"No," said the youth with difficulty. His throat seemed full of knobs and burrs.

These incidents made the youth ponder. It was revealed to him that he had been a barbarian, a beast. He had fought like a pagan who defends his religion. Regarding it, he saw that it was fine, wild, and, in some ways, easy. He had been a tremendous figure, no doubt. By this struggle he had overcome obstacles which he had admitted to be mountains. They had fallen like paper peaks, and he was now what he called a hero. And he had not been aware of the process. He had slept and, awakening, found himself a knight.

He lay and basked in the occasional stares of his comrades. Their faces were varied in degrees of blackness from the burned powder. Some were utterly smudged. They were reeking with perspiration, and their breaths came hard and wheezing. And from these soiled expanses they peered at him.

"Hot work! Hot work!" cried the lieutenant deliriously. He walked up and down, restless and eager. Sometimes his voice could be heard in a wild, incomprehensible laugh.

When he had a particularly profound thought upon the science of war he always unconsciously addressed himself to the youth.

There was some grim rejoicing by the men. "By thunder, I bet this army'll never see another new reg'ment like us!"

"You bet!

'A dog, a woman, an' a walnut tree,
Th' more yeh beat 'em, th' better they be!'

That's like us."

"Lost a piler men, they did. If an' ol' woman swep' up th' woods she'd git a dustpanful."

"Yes, an' if she'll come around ag'in in 'bout an' hour she'll git a pile more."

The forest still bore its burden of clamor. From off under the trees came the rolling clatter of the musketry. Each distant thicket seemed a strange porcupine with quills of flame. A cloud of dark smoke, as from smoldering ruins, went up toward the sun now bright and gay in the blue, enameled sky.

18

The ragged line had respite for some minutes, but during its pause the struggle in the forest became magnified until the trees seemed to quiver from the firing and the ground to shake from the rushing of the men. The voices of the cannon were mingled in a long and interminable row. It seemed difficult to live in such an atmosphere. The chests of the men strained for a bit of freshness, and their throats craved water.

There was one shot through the body, who raised a cry of bitter lamentation when came this lull. Perhaps he had been calling out during the fighting also, but at that time no one had heard him. But now the men turned at the woeful complaints of him upon the ground.

"Who is it? Who is it?"

"It's Jimmie Rogers. Jimmie Rogers."

When their eyes first encountered him there was a sudden halt, as if they feared to go near. He was thrashing about in the grass, twisting his shuddering body into many strange postures. He was screaming loudly. This instant's hesitation seemed to fill him with a tremendous, fantastic contempt, and he damned them in shrieked sentences.

The youth's friend had a geographical illusion concerning a stream, and he obtained permission to go for some water. Immediately canteens were showered upon him. "Fill mine, will yeh?" "Bring me some, too." "And me, too." He departed, laden. The youth went with his friend, feeling a desire to throw his heated body into the stream and, soaking there, drink quarts.

They made a hurried search for the supposed stream, but did not find it. "No water here," said the youth. They turned without delay and began to retrace their steps.

From their position as they again faced toward the place of the fighting, they could of course comprehend a greater amount of the battle than when their visions had been blurred by the hurling smoke of the line. They could see dark stretches winding along the land, and on one cleared space there was a row of guns making gray clouds, which were filled with large flashes of orange-colored flame. Over some foliage they could see the roof of a house. One window, glowing a deep murder red, shone squarely through the leaves. From the edifice a tall leaning tower of smoke went far into the sky.

Looking over their own troops, they saw mixed masses slowly getting into regular form. The sunlight made twinkling points of the bright steel. To the rear there was a glimpse of a distant roadway as it curved over a slope. It was crowded with retreating infantry. From all the interwoven forest arose the smoke and bluster of the battle. The air was always occupied by a blaring.

Near where they stood shells were flip-flapping and hooting. Occasional bullets buzzed in the air and spanged into tree trunks. Wounded men and other stragglers were slinking through the woods.

Looking down an aisle of the grove, the youth and his companion saw a jangling general and his staff almost ride upon a wounded man who was crawling on his hands and knees. The general reined strongly at his charger's opened and foamy mouth and guided it with dexterous horsemanship past the man. The latter scrambled in wild and torturing haste. His strength evidently failed him as he reached a place of safety. One of his arms suddenly weakened, and he fell, sliding over upon his back. He lay stretched out, breathing gently.

A moment later the small, creaking cavalcade was directly in front of the two soldiers. Another officer, riding with the skillful abandon of a cowboy, galloped his horse to a position directly before the general. The two unnoticed foot soldiers made a little show of going on, but they lingered near in the desire to overhear the conversation. Perhaps, they thought, some great inner historical things would be said.

The general, whom the boys knew as the commander of their division, looked at the other officer and spoke coolly, as if he were criticising his clothes. "Th' enemy's formin' over there for another charge," he said. "It'll be directed against Whiterside, an' I fear they'll break through there unless we work like thunder t' stop them."

The other swore at his restive horse, and then cleared his throat. He made a gesture toward his cap. "It'll be hell t' pay stoppin' them," he said shortly.

"I presume so," remarked the general. Then he began to talk rapidly and in a lower tone. He frequently illustrated his words with a pointing finger. The two infantrymen could hear nothing until finally he asked: "What troops can you spare?"

The officer who rode like a cowboy reflected for an instant. "Well," he said, "I had to order in th' 12th to help th' 76th, an' I haven't really got any. But there's th' 304th. They fight like a lot 'a mule drivers. I can spare them best of any."

The youth and his friend exchanged glances of astonishment.

The general spoke sharply. "Get 'em ready, then. I'll watch developments from here, an' send you word when t' start them. It'll happen in five minutes."

As the other officer tossed his fingers toward his cap and wheeling his horse, started away, the general called out to him in a sober voice: "I don't believe many of your mule drivers will get back."

The other shouted something in reply. He smiled.

With scared faces, the youth and his companion hurried back to the line.

These happenings had occupied an incredibly short time, yet the youth felt that in them he had been made aged. New eyes were given to him. And the most startling thing was to learn suddenly that he was very insignificant. The officer spoke of the regiment as if he referred to a broom. Some part of the woods needed sweeping, perhaps, and he merely indicated a broom in a tone properly indifferent to its fate. It was war, no doubt, but it appeared strange.

As the two boys approached the line, the lieutenant perceived them and swelled with wrath. "Fleming—Wilson—how long does it take yeh to git water, anyhow—where yeh been to."

But his oration ceased as he saw their eyes, which were large with great tales. "We're goin' t' charge—we're goin' t' charge!" cried the youth's friend, hastening with his news.

"Charge?" said the lieutenant. "Charge? Well, b'Gawd! Now; this is real fightin'." Over his soiled countenance there went a boastful smile. "Charge? Well, b'Gawd!"

A little group of soldiers surrounded the two youths. "Are we, sure 'nough? Well, I'll be derned! Charge? What fer? What at? Wilson, you're lyin'."

"I hope to die," said the youth, pitching his tones to the key of angry remonstrance. "Sure as shooting, I tell you."

And his friend spoke in re-enforcement. "Not by a blame sight, he ain't lyin'. We heard 'em talkin'."

They caught sight of two mounted figures a short distance from them. One was the colonel of the regiment and the other was the officer who had received orders from the commander of the division. They were gesticulating at each other. The soldier, pointing at them, interpreted the scene.

One man had a final objection: "How could yeh hear 'em talkin'?" But the men, for a large part, nodded, admitting that previously the two friends had spoken truth.

They settled back into reposeful attitudes with airs of having accepted the matter. And they mused upon it, with a hundred varieties of expression. It was an engrossing thing to think about. Many tightened their belts carefully and hitched at their trousers.

A moment later the officers began to bustle among the men, pushing them into a more compact mass and into a better alignment. They chased those that straggled and fumed at a few men who seemed to show by their attitudes that they had decided to remain at that spot. They were like critical shepherds struggling with sheep.

Presently, the regiment seemed to draw itself up and heave a deep breath. None of the men's faces were mirrors of large thoughts. The soldiers were bended and stooped like sprinters before a signal. Many pairs of glinting eyes peered from the grimy faces toward the curtains of the deeper woods. They seemed to be engaged in deep calculations of time and distance.

They were surrounded by the noises of the monstrous altercation between the two armies. The world was fully interested in other matters. Apparently, the regiment had its small affair to itself.

The youth, turning, shot a quick, inquiring glance at his friend. The latter returned to him the same manner of look. They were the only ones who possessed an inner knowledge. "Mule drivers—hell t' pay—don't believe many will get back." It was an ironical secret. Still, they saw no hesitation in each other's faces, and they nodded a mute and unprotesting assent when a shaggy man near them said in a meek voice: "We'll git swallowed."

19

The youth stared at the land in front of him. Its foliage now seemed to veil powers and horrors. He was unaware of the machinery of orders that started the charge, although from the corners of his eyes he saw an officer, who looked like a boy a-horseback, come galloping, waving his hat. Suddenly he felt a straining and heaving among the men. The line fell slowly forward like a toppling wall, and, with a convulsive gasp that was intended for a cheer, the regiment began its journey. The youth was pushed and jostled for a moment before he understood the movement at all, but directly he lunged ahead and began to run.

He fixed his eye upon a distant and prominent clump of trees where he had concluded the enemy were to be met, and he ran toward it as toward a goal. He had believed throughout that it was a mere question of getting over an unpleasant matter as quickly as possible, and he ran desperately, as if pursued for a murder. His face was drawn hard and tight with the stress of his endeavor. His eyes were fixed in a lurid glare. And with his soiled and disordered dress, his red and inflamed features surmounted by the dingy rag with its spot of blood, his wildly swinging rifle and banging accouterments, he looked to be an insane soldier.

As the regiment swung from its position out into a cleared space the woods and thickets before it awakened. Yellow flames leaped toward it from many directions. The forest made a tremendous objection.

The line lurched straight for a moment. Then the right wing sprung forward; it in turn was surpassed by the left. Afterward the center careered to the front until the regiment was a wedge-shaped mass, but an instant later the opposition of the bushes, trees, and uneven places on the ground split the command and scattered it into detached clusters.

The youth, light-footed, was unconsciously in advance. His eyes still kept note of the clump of trees. From all places near it the clannish yell of the enemy could be heard. The little flames of rifles leaped from it. The song of the bullets was in the air and shells snarled among the treetops. One tumbled directly into the middle of a hurrying group and exploded in crimson fury. There was an instant's spectacle of a man, almost over it, throwing up his hands to shield his eyes.

Other men, punched by bullets, fell in grotesque agonies. The regiment left a coherent trail of bodies.

They had passed into a clearer atmosphere. There was an effect like a revelation in the new appearance of the landscape. Some men working madly at a battery were plain to them, and the opposing infantry's lines were defined by the gray walls and fringes of smoke.

It seemed to the youth that he saw everything. Each blade of the green grass was bold and clear. He thought that he was aware of every change in the thin, transparent vapor that floated idly in sheets. The brown or gray trunks of the trees showed each roughness of their surfaces. And the men of the regiment, with their starting eyes and sweating faces, running madly, or falling, as if thrown headlong, to queer, heaped-up corpses —all were comprehended. His mind took a mechanical but firm impression, so that afterward everything was pictured and explained to him, save why he himself was there.

But there was a frenzy made from this furious rush. The men, pitching forward insanely, had burst into cheerings, moblike and barbaric, but tuned in strange keys that can arouse the dullard and the stoic. It made a mad enthusiasm that, it seemed, would be incapable of checking itself before granite and brass. There was the delirium that encounters despair and death, and is heedless and blind to the odds. It is a temporary but sublime absence of selfishness. And because it was of this order was the reason, perhaps, why the youth wondered, afterward, what reasons he could have had for being there.

Presently the straining pace ate up the energies of the men. As if by agreement, the leaders began to slacken their speed. The volleys directed against them had had a seeming windlike effect. The regiment snorted and blew. Among some stolid trees it began to falter and hesitate. The men, staring intently, began to wait for some of the distant walls of smoke to move and disclose to them the scene. Since much of their strength and their breath had vanished, they returned to caution. They were become men again.

The youth had a vague belief that he had run miles, and he thought, in a way, that he was now in some new and unknown land.

The moment the regiment ceased its advance the protesting splutter of musketry became a steadied roar. Long and accurate fringes of smoke spread out. From the top of a small hill came level belchings of yellow flame that caused an inhuman whistling in the air.

The men, halted, had opportunity to see some of their comrades dropping with moans and shrieks. A few lay under foot, still or wailing. And now for an instant the men stood, their rifles slack in their hands, and watched the regiment dwindle. They appeared dazed and stupid. This spectacle seemed to paralyze them, overcome them with a fatal fascination. They stared woodenly at the sights, and, lowering their eyes, looked from face to face. It was a strange pause, and a strange silence.

Then, above the sounds of the outside commotion, arose the roar of the lieutenant. He strode suddenly forth, his infantile features black with rage.

"Come on, yeh fools!" he bellowed. "Come on! Yeh can't stay here. Yeh must come on." He said more, but much of it could not be understood.

He started rapidly forward, with his head turned toward the men. "Come on," he was shouting. The men stared with blank and yokel-like eyes at him. He was obliged to halt and retrace his steps. He stood then with his back to the enemy and delivered gigantic curses into the faces of the men. His body vibrated from the weight and force of his imprecations. And he could string oaths with the facility of a maiden who strings beads.

The friend of the youth aroused. Lurching suddenly forward and dropping to his knees, he fired an angry shot at the persistent woods. This action awakened the men. They huddled no more like sheep. They seemed suddenly to bethink them of their weapons, and at once commenced firing. Belabored by their officers, they began to move forward. The regiment, involved like a cart involved in mud and muddle, started unevenly with many jolts and jerks. The men stopped now every few paces to fire and load, and in this manner moved slowly on from trees to trees.

The flaming opposition in their front grew with their advance until it seemed that all forward ways were barred by the thin leaping tongues, and off to the right an ominous demonstration could sometimes be dimly discerned. The smoke lately generated was in confusing clouds that made it difficult for the regiment to proceed with intelligence. As he passed through each curling mass the youth wondered what would confront him on the farther side.

The command went painfully forward until an open space interposed between them and the lurid lines. Here, crouching and cowering behind some trees, the men clung with desperation, as if threatened by a wave. They looked wild-eyed, and as if amazed at this furious disturbance they had stirred. In the storm there was an ironical expression of their importance. The faces of the men, too, showed a lack of a certain feeling of responsibility for being there. It was as if they had been driven. It was the dominant animal failing to remember in the supreme moments the forceful causes of various superficial qualities. The whole affair seemed incomprehensible to many of them.

As they halted thus the lieutenant again began to bellow profanely. Regardless of the vindictive threats of the bullets, he went about coaxing, berating, and bedamning. His lips, that were habitually in a soft and childlike curve, were now writhed into unholy contortions. He swore by all possible deities.

Once he grabbed the youth by the arm. "Come on, yeh lunkhead!" he roared. "Come on! We'll all git killed if we stay here. We've on'y got t' go across that lot. An' then"—the remainder of his idea disappeared in a blue haze of curses.

The youth stretched forth his arm. "Cross there?" His mouth was puckered in doubt and awe.

"Certainly. Jest 'cross th' lot! We can't stay here," screamed the lieutenant. He poked his face close to the youth and waved his bandaged hand.

"Come on!" Presently he grappled with him as if for a wrestling bout. It was as if he planned to drag the youth by the ear on to the assault.

The private felt a sudden unspeakable indignation against his officer. He wrenched fiercely and shook him off.

"Come on yerself, then," he yelled. There was a bitter challenge in his voice.

They galloped together down the regimental front. The friend scrambled after them. In front of the colors the three men began to bawl: "Come on! come on!" They danced and gyrated like tortured savages.

The flag, obedient to these appeals, bended its glittering form and swept toward them. The men wavered in indecision for a moment, and then with a long, wailful cry the dilapidated regiment surged forward and began its new journey.

Over the field went the scurrying mass. It was a handful of men splattered into the faces of the enemy. Toward it instantly sprang the yellow tongues. A vast quantity of blue smoke hung before them. A mighty banging made ears valueless.

The youth ran like a madman to reach the woods before a bullet could discover him. He ducked his head low, like a football player. In his haste his eyes almost closed, and the scene was a wild blur. Pulsating saliva stood at the corners of his mouth.

Within him, as he hurled himself forward, was born a love, a despairing fondness for this flag which was near him. It was a creation of beauty and invulnerability. It was a goddess, radiant, that bended its form with an imperious gesture to him. It was a woman, red and white, hating and loving, that called him with the voice of his hopes. Because no harm could come to it he endowed it with power. He kept near, as if it could be a saver of lives, and an imploring cry went from his mind.

In the mad scramble he was aware that the color sergeant flinched suddenly, as if struck by a bludgeon. He faltered, and then became motionless, save for his quivering knees.

He made a spring and a clutch at the pole. At the same instant his friend grabbed it from the other side. They jerked at it, stout and furious, but the color sergeant was dead, and the corpse would not relinquish its trust. For a moment there was a grim encounter. The dead man, swinging with bended back, seemed to be obstinately tugging, in ludicrous and awful ways, for the possession of the flag.

It was past in an instant of time. They wrenched the flag furiously from the dead man, and, as they turned again, the corpse swayed forward with bowed head. One arm swung high, and the curved hand fell with heavy protest on the friend's unheeding shoulder

20

When the two youths turned with the flag they saw that much of the regiment had crumbled away, and the dejected remnant was coming back. The men, having hurled themselves in projectile fashion, had presently expended their forces. They slowly retreated, with their faces still toward the spluttering woods, and their hot rifles still replying to the din. Several officers were giving orders, their voices keyed to screams.

"Where in hell yeh goin'?" the lieutenant was asking in a sarcastic howl. And a red-bearded officer, whose voice of triple brass could plainly be heard, was commanding: "Shoot into 'em! Shoot into 'em, Gawd damn their souls!" There was a *mêlée* of screeches, in which the men were ordered to do conflicting and impossible things.

The youth and his friend had a small scuffle over the flag. "Give it t' me!" "No, let me keep it!" Each felt satisfied with the other's possession of it, but each felt bound to declare, by an offer to carry the emblem, his willingness to further risk himself. The youth roughly pushed his friend away.

The regiment fell back to the stolid trees. There it halted for a moment to blaze at some dark forms that had begun to steal upon its track. Presently it resumed its march again, curving among the tree trunks. By the time the depleted regiment had again reached the first open space they were receiving a fast and merciless fire. There seemed to be mobs all about them.

The greater part of the men, discouraged, their spirits worn by the turmoil, acted as if stunned. They accepted the pelting of the bullets with bowed and weary heads. It was of no purpose to strive against walls. It was of no use to batter themselves against granite. And from this consciousness that they had attempted to conquer an unconquerable thing there seemed to arise a feeling that they had been betrayed. They glowered with bent brows, but dangerously, upon some of the officers, more particularly upon the red-bearded one with the voice of triple brass.

However, the rear of the regiment was fringed with men, who continued to shoot irritably at the advancing foes. They seemed resolved to make every trouble. The youthful lieutenant was perhaps the last man in the disordered mass. His forgotten back was toward the enemy. He had been shot in the arm. It hung straight and rigid. Occasionally he would cease to remember it, and be about to emphasize an oath with a sweeping gesture. The multiplied pain caused him to swear with incredible power.

The youth went along with slipping, uncertain feet. He kept watchful eyes rearward. A scowl of mortification and rage was upon his face. He had thought of a fine revenge upon the officer who had referred to him and his fellows as mule drivers. But he saw that it could not come to pass. His dreams had collapsed when the mule drivers, dwindling rapidly, had wavered and hesitated on the little clearing, and then had recoiled. And now the retreat of the mule drivers was a march of shame to him.

A dagger-pointed gaze from without his blackened face was held toward the enemy, but his greater hatred was riveted upon the man, who, not knowing him, had called him a mule driver.

When he knew that he and his comrades had failed to do anything in successful ways that might bring the little pangs of a kind of remorse upon the officer, the youth allowed the rage of the baffled to possess him. This cold officer upon a monument, who dropped epithets unconcernedly down, would be finer as a dead man, he thought. So grievous did he think it that he could never possess the secret right to taunt truly in answer.

He had pictured red letters of curious revenge. "We *are* mule drivers, are we?" And now he was compelled to throw them away.

He presently wrapped his heart in the cloak of his pride and kept the flag erect. He harangued his fellows, pushing against their chests with his free hand. To those he knew well he made frantic appeals, beseeching them by name. Between him and the lieutenant, scolding and near to losing his mind with rage, there was felt a subtle fellowship and equality. They supported each other in all manner of hoarse, howling protests.

But the regiment was a machine run down. The two men babbled at a forceless thing. The soldiers who had heart to go slowly were continually shaken in their resolves by a knowledge that comrades were slipping with speed back to the lines. It was difficult to think of reputation when others were thinking of skins. Wounded men were left crying on this black journey.

The smoke fringes and flames blustered always. The youth, peering once through a sudden rift in a cloud, saw a brown mass of troops, interwoven and magnified until they appeared to be thousands. A fierce-hued flag flashed before his vision.

Immediately, as if the uplifting of the smoke had been prearranged, the discovered troops burst into a rasping yell, and a hundred flames jetted toward the retreating band. A rolling gray cloud again interposed as the regiment doggedly replied. The youth had to depend again upon his misused ears, which were trembling and buzzing from the *mêlée* of musketry and yells.

The way seemed eternal. In the clouded haze men became panic-stricken with the thought that the regiment had lost its path, and was proceeding in a perilous direction. Once the men who headed the wild procession turned and came pushing back against their comrades, screaming that they were being fired upon from points which they had considered to be toward their own lines. At this cry a hysterical fear and dismay beset the troops. A soldier, who heretofore had been ambitious to make the regiment into a wise little band that would proceed calmly amid the huge-appearing difficulties, suddenly sank down and buried his face in his arms with an air of bowing to a doom. From another a shrill lamentation rang out filled with profane allusions to a general. Men ran hither and thither, seeking with their eyes roads of escape. With serene regularity, as if controlled by a schedule, bullets buffed into men.

The youth walked stolidly into the midst of the mob, and with his flag in his hands took a stand as if he expected an attempt to push him to the ground. He unconsciously assumed the attitude of the color bearer in the fight of the preceding day. He passed over his brow a hand that trembled. His breath did not come freely. He was choking during this small wait for the crisis.

His friend came to him. "Well, Henry, I guess this is good-by—John."

"Oh, shut up, you damned fool!" replied the youth, and he would not look at the other.

The officers labored like politicians to beat the mass into a proper circle to face the menaces. The ground was uneven and torn. The men curled into depressions and fitted themselves snugly behind whatever would frustrate a bullet.

The youth noted with vague surprise that the lieutenant was standing mutely with his legs far apart and his sword held in the manner of a cane. The youth wondered what had happened to his vocal organs that he no more cursed.

There was something curious in this little intent pause of the lieutenant. He was like a babe which, having wept its fill, raises its eyes and fixes upon a distant toy. He was engrossed in this contemplation, and the soft under lip quivered from self-whispered words.

Some lazy and ignorant smoke curled slowly. The men, hiding from the bullets, waited anxiously for it to lift and disclose the plight of the regiment.

The silent ranks were suddenly thrilled by the eager voice of the youthful lieutenant bawling out: "Here they come! Right on to us, b'Gawd!" His further words were lost in a roar of wicked thunder from the men's rifles.

The youth's eyes had instantly turned in the direction indicated by the awakened and agitated lieutenant, and he had seen the haze of treachery disclosing a body of soldiers of the enemy. They were so near that he could see their features. There was a recognition as he looked at the types of faces. Also he perceived with dim amazement that their uniforms were rather gay in effect, being light gray, accented with a brilliant-hued facing. Too, the clothes seemed new.

These troops had apparently been going forward with caution, their rifles held in readiness, when the youthful lieutenant had discovered them and their movement had been interrupted by the volley from the blue regiment. From the moment's glimpse, it was derived that they had been unaware of the proximity of their dark-suited foes or had mistaken the direction. Almost instantly they were shut utterly from the youth's sight by the smoke from the energetic rifles of his companions. He strained his vision to learn the accomplishment of the volley, but the smoke hung before him

The two bodies of troops exchanged blows in the manner of a pair of boxers. The fast angry firings went back and forth. The men in blue were intent with the despair of their circumstances and they seized upon the revenge to be had at close range. Their thunder swelled loud and valiant. Their curving front bristled with flashes and the place resounded with the clangor of their ramrods. The youth ducked and dodged for a time and achieved a few unsatisfactory views of the enemy. There appeared to be many of them and they were replying swiftly. They seemed moving toward the blue regiment, step by step. He seated himself gloomily on the ground with his flag between his knees.

As he noted the vicious, wolflike temper of his comrades he had a sweet thought that if the enemy was about to swallow the regimental broom as a large prisoner, it could at least have the consolation of going down with bristles forward.

But the blows of the antagonist began to grow more weak. Fewer bullets ripped the air, and finally, when the men slackened to learn of the fight, they could see only dark, floating smoke. The regiment lay still and gazed. Presently some chance whim came to the pestering blur, and it began to coil heavily away. The men saw a ground vacant of fighters. It would have been an empty stage if it were not for a few corpses that lay thrown and twisted into fantastic shapes upon the sward.

At sight of this tableau, many of the men in blue sprang from behind their covers and made an ungainly dance of joy. Their eyes burned and a hoarse cheer of elation broke from their dry lips.

It had begun to seem to them that events were trying to prove that they were impotent. These little battles had evidently endeavored to demonstrate that the men could not fight well. When on the verge of submission to these opinions, the small duel had showed them that the proportions were not impossible, and by it they had revenged themselves upon their misgivings and upon the foe.

The impetus of enthusiasm was theirs again. They gazed about them with looks of uplifted pride, feeling new trust in the grim, always confident weapons in their hands. And they were men

21

Presently they knew that no fighting threatened them. All ways seemed once more opened to them. The dusty blue lines of their friends were disclosed a short distance away. In the distance there were many colossal noises, but in all this part of the field there was a sudden stillness.

They perceived that they were free. The depleted band drew a long breath of relief and gathered itself into a bunch to complete its trip.

In this last length of journey the men began to show strange emotions. They hurried with nervous fear. Some who had been dark and unfaltering in the grimmest moments now could not conceal an anxiety that made them frantic. It was perhaps that they dreaded to be killed in insignificant ways after the times for proper military deaths had passed. Or, perhaps, they thought it would be too ironical to get killed at the portals of safety. With backward looks of perturbation, they hastened.

As they approached their own lines there was some sarcasm exhibited on the part of a gaunt and bronzed regiment that lay resting in the shade of trees. Questions were wafted to them.

"Where th' hell yeh been?"

"What yeh comin' back fer?"

"Why didn't yeh stay there?"

"Was it warm out there, sonny?"

"Goin' home now, boys?"

One shouted in taunting mimicry: "Oh, mother, come quick an' look at th' sojers!"

There was no reply from the bruised and battered regiment, save that one man made broadcast challenges to fist fights and the red-bearded officer walked rather near and glared in great swashbuckler style at a tall captain in the other regiment. But the lieutenant suppressed the man who wished to fist fight, and the tall captain, flushing at the little fanfare of the red-bearded one, was obliged to look intently at some trees.

The youth's tender flesh was deeply stung by these remarks. From under his creased brows he glowered with hate at the mockers. He meditated upon a few revenges. Still, many in the regiment hung their heads in criminal fashion, so that it came to pass that the men trudged with sudden heaviness, as if they bore upon their bended shoulders the coffin of their honor. And the youthful lieutenant, recollecting himself, began to mutter softly in black curses.

They turned when they arrived at their old position to regard the ground over which they had charged.

The youth in this contemplation was smitten with a large astonishment.

He discovered that the distances, as compared with the brilliant measurings of his mind, were trivial and ridiculous. The stolid trees, where much had taken place, seemed incredibly near. The time, too, now that he reflected, he saw to have been short. He wondered at the number of emotions and events that had been crowded into such little spaces. Elfin thoughts must have exaggerated and enlarged everything, he said.

It seemed, then, that there was bitter justice in the speeches of the gaunt and bronzed veterans. He veiled a glance of disdain at his fellows who strewed the ground, choking with dust, red from perspiration, misty-eyed, disheveled.

They were gulping at their canteens, fierce to wring every mite of water from them, and they polished at their swollen and watery features with coat sleeves and bunches of grass.

However, to the youth there was a considerable joy in musing upon his performances during the charge. He had had very little time previously in which to appreciate himself, so that there was now much satisfaction in quietly thinking of his actions. He recalled bits of color that in the flurry had stamped themselves unawares upon his engaged senses.

As the regiment lay heaving from its hot exertions the officer who had named them as mule drivers came galloping along the line. He had lost his cap. His tousled hair streamed wildly, and his face was dark with vexation and wrath. His temper was displayed with more clearness by the way in which he managed his horse. He jerked and wrenched savagely at his bridle, stopping the hard-breathing animal with a furious pull near the colonel of the regiment. He immediately exploded in reproaches which came unbidden to the ears of the men. They were suddenly alert, being always curious about black words between officers.

"Oh, thunder, MacChesnay, what an awful bull you made of this thing!" began the officer. He attempted low tones, but his indignation caused certain of the men to learn the sense of his words. "What an awful mess you made! Good Lord, man, you stopped about a hundred feet this side of a very pretty success! If your men had gone a hundred feet farther you would have made a great charge, but as it is—what a lot of mud diggers you've got anyway!"

The men, listening with bated breath, now turned their curious eyes upon the colonel. They had a ragamuffin interest in this affair.

The colonel was seen to straighten his form and put one hand forth in oratorical fashion. He wore an injured air; it was as if a deacon had been accused of stealing. The men were wiggling in an ecstasy of excitement.

But of a sudden the colonel's manner changed from that of a deacon to that of a Frenchman. He shrugged his shoulders. "Oh, well, general, we went as far as we could," he said calmly.

"As far as you could? Did you, b'Gawd?" snorted the other. "Well, that wasn't very far, was it?" he added, with a glance of cold contempt into the other's eyes. "Not very far, I think. You were intended to make a diversion in favor of Whiterside. How well you succeeded your own ears can now tell you." He wheeled his horse and rode stiffly away.

The colonel, bidden to hear the jarring noises of an engagement in the woods to the left, broke out in vague damnations.

The lieutenant, who had listened with an air of impotent rage to the interview, spoke suddenly in firm and undaunted tones. "I don't care what a man is—whether he is a general or what—if he says th' boys didn't put up a good fight out there he's a damned fool."

"Lieutenant," began the colonel, severely, "this is my own affair, and I'll trouble you—"

The lieutenant made an obedient gesture. "All right, colonel, all right," he said. He sat down with an air of being content with himself.

The news that the regiment had been reproached went along the line. For a time the men were bewildered by it. "Good thunder!" they ejaculated, staring at the vanishing form of the general. They conceived it to be a huge mistake.

Presently, however, they began to believe that in truth their efforts had been called light. The youth could see this conviction weigh upon the entire regiment until the men were like cuffed and cursed animals, but withal rebellious.

The friend, with a grievance in his eye, went to the youth. "I wonder what he does want," he said. "He must think we went out there an' played marbles! I never see sech a man!"

The youth developed a tranquil philosophy for these moments of irritation. "Oh, well," he rejoined, "he probably didn't see nothing of it at all and got mad as blazes, and concluded we were a lot of sheep, just because we didn't do what he wanted done. It's a pity old Grandpa Henderson got killed yestirday—he'd have known that we did our best and fought good. It's just our awful luck, that's what."

"I should say so," replied the friend. He seemed to be deeply wounded at an injustice. "I should say we did have awful luck! There's no fun in fightin' fer people when everything yeh do—no matter what—ain't done right. I have a notion t' stay behind next time an' let 'em take their ol' charge an' go t' th' devil with it."

The youth spoke soothingly to his comrade. "Well, we both did good. I'd like to see the fool what'd say we both didn't do as good as we could!"

"Of course we did," declared the friend stoutly. "An' I'd break th' feller's neck if he was as big as a church. But we're all right, anyhow, for I heard one feller say that we two fit th' best in th' reg'ment, an' they had a great argument 'bout it. Another feller, 'a course, he had t' up an' say it was a lie—he seen all what was goin' on' an' he never seen us from th' beginnin' t' th' end. An' a lot more struck in an' ses it wasn't a lie—we did fight like thunder, an' they give us quite a send-off. But this is what I can't stand—these everlastin' ol' soldiers, titterin' an' laughin', an' then that general, he's crazy."

The youth exclaimed with sudden exasperation: "He's a lunkhead! He makes me mad. I wish he'd come along next time. We'd show 'im what—"

He ceased because several men had come hurrying up. Their faces expressed a bringing of great news.

"O Flem, yeh jest oughta heard!" cried one, eagerly.

"Heard what?" said the youth.

"Yeh jest oughta heard!" repeated the other, and he arranged himself to tell his tidings. The others made an excited circle. "Well, sir, th' colonel met your lieutenant right by us—it was damnedest thing I ever heard—an' he ses: 'Ahem! ahem!' he ses. 'Mr. Hasbrouck!' he ses, 'by th' way, who was that lad what carried th' flag?' he ses. There, Flemin', what d' yeh think 'a that? 'Who was th' lad what carried th' flag?' he ses, an' th' lieutenant, he speaks up right away: 'That's Flemin', an' he's a jimhickey,' he ses, right away. What? I say he did. 'A jimhickey,' he ses—those 'r his words. He did, too. I say he did. If you kin tell this story better than I kin, go ahead an' tell it. Well, then, keep yer mouth shet. Th' lieutenant, he ses: 'He's a jimhickey,' an' th' colonel, he ses: 'Ahem! ahem! he is, indeed, a very good man t' have, ahem! He kep' th' flag 'way t' th' front. I saw 'im. He's a good un,' ses th' colonel. 'You bet,' ses th' lieutenant, 'he an' a feller named Wilson was at th' head 'a th' charge, an' howlin' like Indians all th' time,' he ses. 'Head a' th' charge all th' time,' he ses. 'A feller named Wilson,' he ses. There, Wilson, m'boy, put that in a letter an' send it hum t' yer mother, hay? 'A feller named Wilson,' he ses. An' th' colonel, he ses: 'Were they, indeed? Ahem! ahem! My sakes!' he ses. 'At th' head a' th' reg'ment?' he ses. 'They were,' ses th' lieutenant. 'My sakes!' ses th' colonel. He ses: 'Well, well, well,' he ses, 'those two babies?' 'They were,' ses th' lieutenant. 'Well, well,' ses th' colonel, 'they deserve t' be major-generals,' he ses. 'They deserve t' be major-generals.' "

The youth and his friend had said: "Huh!" "Yer lyin', Thompson." "Oh, go t' blazes!" "He never sed it." "Oh, what a lie!" "Huh!" But despite these youthful scoffings and embarrassments, they knew that their faces were deeply flushing from thrills of pleasure. They exchanged a secret glance of joy and congratulation.

They speedily forgot many things. The past held no pictures of error and disappointment. They were very happy, and their hearts swelled with grateful affection for the colonel and the youthful lieutenant.

22

When the woods again began to pour forth the dark-hued masses of the enemy the youth felt serene self-confidence. He smiled briefly when he saw men dodge and duck at the long screechings of shells that were thrown in giant handfuls over them. He stood, erect and tranquil, watching the attack begin against a part of the line that made a blue curve along the side of an adjacent hill. His vision being unmolested by smoke from the rifles of his companions, he had opportunities to see parts of the hard fight. It was a relief to perceive at last from whence came some of these noises which had been roared into his ears.

Off a short way he saw two regiments fighting a little separate battle with two other regiments. It was in a cleared space, wearing a set-apart look. They were blazing as if upon a wager, giving and taking tremendous blows. The firings were incredibly fierce and rapid. These intent regiments apparently were oblivious of all larger purposes of war, and were slugging each other as if at a matched game.

In another direction he saw a magnificent brigade going with the evident intention of driving the enemy from a wood. They passed in out of sight and presently there was a most awe-inspiring racket in the wood. The noise was unspeakable. Having stirred this prodigious uproar, and, apparently, finding it too prodigious, the brigade, after a little time, came marching airily out again with its fine formation in nowise disturbed. There were no traces of speed in its movements. The brigade was jaunty and seemed to point a proud thumb at the yelling wood.

On a slope to the left there was a long row of guns, gruff and maddened, denouncing the enemy, who, down through the woods, were forming for another attack in the pitiless monotony of conflicts. The round red discharges from the guns made a crimson flare and a high, thick smoke. Occasional glimpses could be caught of groups of the toiling artillerymen. In the rear of this row of guns stood a house, calm and white, amid bursting shells. A congregation of horses, tied to a long railing, were tugging frenziedly at their bridles. Men were running hither and thither.

The detached battle between the four regiments lasted for some time. There chanced to be no interference, and they settled their dispute by themselves. They struck savagely and powerfully at each other for a period of minutes, and then the lighter-hued regiments faltered and drew back, leaving the dark-blue lines shouting. The youth could see the two flags shaking with laughter amid the smoke remnants.

Presently there was a stillness, pregnant with meaning. The blue lines shifted and changed a trifle and stared expectantly at the silent woods and fields before them. The hush was solemn and churchlike, save for a distant battery that, evidently unable to remain quiet, sent a faint rolling thunder over the ground. It irritated, like the noises of unimpressed boys. The men imagined that it would prevent their perched ears from hearing the first words of the new battle.

Of a sudden the guns on the slope roared out a message of warning. A spluttering sound had begun in the woods. It swelled with amazing speed to a profound clamor that involved the earth in noises. The splitting crashes swept along the lines until an interminable roar was developed. To those in the midst of it it became a din fitted to the universe. It was the whirring and thumping of gigantic machinery, complications among the smaller stars. The youth's ears were filled up. They were incapable of hearing more.

On an incline over which a road wound he saw wild and desperate rushes of men perpetually backward and forward in riotous surges. These parts of the opposing armies were two long waves that pitched upon each other madly at dictated points. To and fro they swelled. Sometimes, one side by its yells and cheers would proclaim decisive blows, but a moment later the other side would be all yells and cheers. Once the youth saw a spray of light forms go in houndlike leaps toward the waving blue lines. There was much howling, and presently it went away with a vast mouthful of prisoners. Again, he saw a blue wave dash with such thunderous force against a gray obstruction that it seemed to clear the earth of it and leave nothing but trampled sod. And always in their swift and deadly rushes to and fro the men screamed and yelled like maniacs.

Particular pieces of fence or secure positions behind collections of trees were wrangled over, as gold thrones or pearl bedsteads. There were desperate lunges at these chosen spots seemingly every instant, and most of them were bandied like light toys between the contending forces. The youth could not tell from the battle flags flying like crimson foam in many directions which color of cloth was winning.

His emaciated regiment bustled forth with undiminished fierceness when its time came. When assaulted again by bullets, the men burst out in a barbaric cry of rage and pain. They bent their heads in aims of intent hatred behind the projected hammers of their guns. Their ramrods clanged loud with fury as their eager arms pounded the cartridges into the rifle barrels. The front of the regiment was a smoke-wall penetrated by the flashing points of yellow and red.

Wallowing in the fight, they were in an astonishingly short time resmudged. They surpassed in stain and dirt all their previous appearances. Moving to and fro with strained exertion, jabbering the while, they were, with their swaying bodies, black faces, and glowing eyes, like strange and ugly fiends jigging heavily in the smoke.

The lieutenant, returning from a tour after a bandage, produced from a hidden receptacle of his mind new and portentous oaths suited to the emergency. Strings of expletives he swung lashlike over the backs of his men, and it was evident that his previous efforts had in nowise impaired his resources.

The youth, still the bearer of the colors, did not feel his idleness. He was deeply absorbed as a spectator. The crash and swing of the great drama made him lean forward, intent-eyed, his face working in small contortions. Sometimes he prattled, words coming unconsciously from him in grotesque exclamations. He did not know that he breathed, that the flag hung silently over him, so absorbed was he.

A formidable line of the enemy came within dangerous range. They could be seen plainly—tall, gaunt men with excited faces running with long strides toward a wandering fence.

At sight of this danger the men suddenly ceased their cursing monotone. There was an instant of strained silence before they threw up their rifles and fired a plumping volley at the foes. There had been no order given; the men, upon recognizing the menace, had immediately let drive their flock of bullets without waiting for word of command.

But the enemy were quick to gain the protection of the wandering line of fence. They slid down behind it with remarkable celerity, and from this position they began briskly to slice up the blue men.

These latter braced their energies for a great struggle. Often, white clinched teeth shone from the dusky faces. Many heads surged to and fro, floating upon a pale sea of smoke. Those behind the fence frequently shouted and yelped in taunts and gibelike cries, but the regiment maintained a stressed silence. Perhaps, at this new assault the men recalled the fact that they had been named mud diggers, and it made their situation thrice bitter. They were breathlessly intent upon keeping the ground and thrusting away the rejoicing body of the enemy. They fought swiftly and with a despairing savageness denoted in their expressions

The youth had resolved not to budge whatever should happen. Some arrows of scorn that had buried themselves in his heart had generated strange and unspeakable hatred. It was clear to him that his final and absolute revenge was to be achieved by his dead body lying, torn and gluttering, upon the field. This was to be a poignant retaliation upon the officer who had said "mule drivers," and later "mud diggers," for in all the wild graspings of his mind for a unit responsible for his sufferings and commotions he always seized upon the man who had dubbed him wrongly. And it was his idea, vaguely formulated, that his corpse would be for those eyes a great and salt reproach.

The regiment bled extravagantly. Grunting bundles of blue began to drop. The orderly sergeant of the youth's company was shot through the cheeks. Its supports being injured, his jaw hung afar down, disclosing in the wide cavern of his mouth a pulsing mass of blood and teeth. And with all he made attempts to cry out In his endeavor there was a dreadful earnestness, as if he conceived that one great shriek would make him well.

The youth saw him presently go rearward. His strength seemed in nowise impaired. He ran swiftly, casting wild glances for succor.

Others fell down about the feet of their companions. Some of the wounded crawled out and away, but many lay still, their bodies twisted into impossible shapes.

The youth looked once for his friend. He saw a vehement young man, powder-smeared and frowzled, whom he knew to be him. The lieutenant, also, was unscathed in his position at the rear. He had continued to curse, but it was now with the air of a man who was using his last box of oaths.

For the fire of the regiment had begun to wane and drip. The robust voice, that had come strangely from the thin ranks, was growing rapidly weak.

23

The colonel came running along back of the line. There were other officers following him. "We must charge'm!" they shouted. "We must charge'm!" they cried with resentful voices, as if anticipating a rebellion against this plan by the men.

The youth, upon hearing the shouts, began to study the distance between him and the enemy. He made vague calculations. He saw that to be firm soldiers they must go forward. It would be death to stay in the present place, and with all the circumstances to go backward would exalt too many others. Their hope was to push the galling foes away from the fence.

He expected that his companions, weary and stiffened, would have to be driven to this assault, but as he turned toward them he perceived with a certain surprise that they were giving quick and unqualified expressions of assent. There was an ominous, clanging overture to the charge when the shafts of the bayonets rattled upon the rifle barrels. At the yelled words of command the soldiers sprang forward in eager leaps. There was new and unexpected force in the movement of the regiment. A knowledge of its faded and jaded condition made the charge appear like a paroxysm, a display of the strength that comes before a final feebleness. The men scampered in insane fever of haste, racing as if to achieve a sudden success before an exhilarating fluid should leave them. It was a blind and despairing rush by the collection of men in dusty and tattered blue, over a green sward and under a sapphire sky, toward a fence, dimly outlined in smoke, from behind which spluttered the fierce rifles of enemies.

The youth kept the bright colors to the front. He was waving his free arm in furious circles, the while shrieking mad calls and appeals, urging on those that did not need to be urged, for it seemed that the mob of blue men hurling themselves on the dangerous group of rifles were again grown suddenly wild with an enthusiasm of unselfishness. From the many firings starting toward them, it looked as if they would merely succeed in making a great sprinkling of corpses on the grass between their former position and the fence. But they were in a state of frenzy, perhaps because of forgotten vanities, and it made an exhibition of sublime recklessness. There was no obvious questioning, nor figurings, nor diagrams. There were, apparently, no considered loopholes. It appeared that the swift wings of their desires would have shattered against the iron gates of the impossible.

He himself felt the daring spirit of a savage religion mad. He was capable of profound sacrifices, a tremendous death. He had no time for dissections, but he knew that he thought of the bullets only as things that could prevent him from reaching the place of his endeavor. There were subtle flashings of joy within him that thus should be his mind.

He strained all his strength. His eyesight was shaken and dazzled by the tension of thought and muscle. He did not see anything excepting the mist of smoke gashed by the little knives of fire, but he knew that in it lay the aged fence of a vanished farmer protecting the snuggled bodies of the gray men.

As he ran a thought of the shock of contact gleamed in his mind. He expected a great concussion when the two bodies of troops crashed together. This became a part of his wild battle madness. He could feel the onward swing of the regiment about him and he conceived of a thunderous, crushing blow that would prostrate the resistance and spread consternation and amazement for miles. The flying regiment was going to have a catapultian effect. This dream made him run faster among his comrades, who were giving vent to hoarse and frantic cheers.

But presently he could see that many of the men in gray did not intend to abide the blow. The smoke, rolling, disclosed men who ran, their faces still turned. These grew to a crowd, who retired stubbornly. Individuals wheeled frequently to send a bullet at the blue wave.

But at one part of the line there was a grim and obdurate group that made no movement. They were settled firmly down behind posts and rails. A flag, ruffled and fierce, waved over them and their rifles dinned fiercely.

The blue whirl of men got very near, until it seemed that in truth there would be a close and frightful scuffle. There was an expressed disdain in the opposition of the little group, that changed the meaning of the cheers of the men in blue. They became yells of wrath, directed, personal. The cries of the two parties were now in sound an interchange of scathing insults.

They in blue showed their teeth; their eyes shone all white. They launched themselves as at the throats of those who stood resisting. The space between dwindled to an insignificant distance.

The youth had centered the gaze of his soul upon that other flag. Its possession would be high pride. It would express bloody minglings, near blows. He had a gigantic hatred for those who made great difficulties and complications. They caused it to be as a craved treasure of mythology, hung amid tasks and contrivances of danger.

He plunged like a mad horse at it. He was resolved it should not escape if wild blows and darings of blows could seize it. His own emblem, quivering and aflare, was winging toward the other. It seemed there would shortly be an encounter of strange beaks and claws, as of eagles.

The swirling body of blue men came to a sudden halt at close and disastrous range and roared a swift volley. The group in gray was split and broken by this fire, but its riddled body still fought. The men in blue yelled again and rushed in upon it.

The youth, in his leapings, saw, as through a mist, a picture of four or five men stretched upon the ground or writhing upon their knees with bowed heads as if they had been stricken by bolts from the sky. Tottering among them was the rival color bearer, whom the youth saw had been bitten vitally by the bullets of the last formidable volley. He perceived this man fighting a last struggle, the struggle of one whose legs are grasped by demons. It was a ghastly battle. Over his face was the bleach of death, but set upon it were the dark and hard lines of desperate purpose. With this terrible grin of resolution he hugged his precious flag to him and was stumbling and staggering in his design to go the way that led to safety for it.

But his wounds always made it seem that his feet were retarded, held, and he fought a grim fight, as with invisible ghouls fastened greedily upon his limbs. Those in advance of the scampering blue men, howling cheers, leaped at the fence. The despair of the lost was in his eyes as he glanced back at them.

The youth's friend went over the obstruction in a tumbling heap and sprang at the flag as a panther at prey. He pulled at it and, wrenching it free, swung up its red brilliancy with a mad cry of exultation even as the color bearer, gasping, lurched over in a final throe and, stiffening convulsively, turned his dead face to the ground. There was much blood upon the grass blades.

At the place of success there began more wild clamorings of cheers. The men gesticulated and bellowed in an ecstasy. When they spoke it was as if they considered their listener to be a mile away. What hats and caps were left to them they often slung high in the air.

At one part of the line four men had been swooped upon, and they now sat as prisoners. Some blue men were about them in an eager and curious circle. The soldiers had trapped strange birds, and there was an examination. A flurry of fast questions was in the air.

One of the prisoners was nursing a superficial wound in the foot. He cuddled it, baby-wise, but he looked up from it often to curse with an astonishing utter abandon straight at the noses of his captors. He consigned them to red regions; he called upon the pestilential wrath of strange gods. And with it all he was singularly free from recognition of the finer points of the conduct of prisoners of war. It was as if a clumsy clod had trod upon his toe and he conceived it to be his privilege, his duty, to use deep, resentful oaths.

Another, who was a boy in years, took his plight with great calmness and apparent good nature. He conversed with the men in blue, studying their faces with his bright and keen eyes. They spoke of battles and conditions. There was an acute interest in all their faces during this exchange of viewpoints. It seemed a great satisfaction to hear voices from where all had been darkness and speculation.

The third captive sat with a morose countenance. He preserved a stoical and cold attitude. To all advances he made one reply without variation, "Ah, go t' hell!"

The last of the four was always silent and, for the most part, kept his face turned in unmolested directions. From the views the youth received he seemed to be in a state of absolute dejection. Shame was upon him, and with it profound regret that he was, perhaps, no more to be counted in the ranks of his fellows. The youth could detect no expression that would allow him to believe that the other was giving a thought to his narrowed future, the pictured dungeons, perhaps, and starvations and brutalities, liable to the imagination. All to be seen was shame for captivity and regret for the right to antagonize.

After the men had celebrated sufficiently they settled down behind the old rail fence, on the opposite side to the one from which their foes had been driven. A few shot perfunctorily at distant marks.

There was some long grass. The youth nestled in it and rested, making a convenient rail support the flag. His friend, jubilant and glorified, holding his treasure with vanity, came to him there. They sat side by side and congratulated each other.

24

The roarings that had stretched in a long line of sound across the face of the forest began to grow intermittent and weaker. The stentorian speeches of the artillery continued in some distant encounter, but the crashes of the musketry had almost ceased. The youth and his friend of a sudden looked up, feeling a deadened form of distress at the waning of these noises, which had become a part of life. They could see changes going on among the troops. There were marchings this way and that way. A battery wheeled leisurely. On the crest of a small hill was the thick gleam of many departing muskets.

The youth arose. "Well, what now, I wonder?" he said. By his tone he seemed to be preparing to resent some new monstrosity in the way of dins and smashes. He shaded his eyes with his grimy hand and gazed over the field.

His friend also arose and stared. "I bet we're goin' t' git along out of this an' back over th' river," said he.

"Well, I swan!" said the youth.

They waited, watching. Within a little while the regiment received orders to retrace its way. The men got up grunting from the grass, regretting the soft repose. They jerked their stiffened legs, and stretched their arms over their heads. One man swore as he rubbed his eyes. They all groaned "O Lord!" They had as many objections to this change as they would have had to a proposal for a new battle.

They trampled slowly back over the field across which they had run in a mad scamper.

The regiment marched until it had joined its fellows. The reformed brigade, in column, aimed through a wood at the road. Directly they were in a mass of dust-covered troops, and were trudging along in a way parallel to the enemy's lines as these had been defined by the previous turmoil.

They passed within view of a stolid white house, and saw in front of it groups of their comrades lying in wait behind a neat breastwork. A row of guns were booming at a distant enemy. Shells thrown in reply were raising clouds of dust and splinters. Horsemen dashed along the line of intrenchments.

At this point of its march the division curved away from the field and went winding off in the direction of the river. When the significance of this movement had impressed itself upon the youth he turned his head and looked over his shoulder toward the trampled and *débris*-strewed ground. He breathed a breath of new satisfaction. He finally nudged his friend. "Well, it's all over," he said to him.

His friend gazed backward. "B'Gawd, it is," he assented. They mused.

For a time the youth was obliged to reflect in a puzzled and uncertain way. His mind was undergoing a subtle change. It took moments for it to cast off its battleful ways and resume its accustomed course of thought. Gradually his brain emerged from the clogged clouds, and at last he was enabled to more closely comprehend himself and circumstance.

He understood then that the existence of shot and counter-shot was in the past. He had dwelt in a land of strange, squalling upheavals and had come forth. He had been where there was red of blood and black of passion, and he was escaped. His first thoughts were given to rejoicings at this fact.

Later he began to study his deeds, his failures, and his achievements. Thus, fresh from scenes where many of his usual machines of reflection had been idle, from where he had proceeded sheeplike, he struggled to marshal all his acts.

At last they marched before him clearly. From this present view point he was enabled to look upon them in spectator fashion and to criticize them with some correctness, for his new condition had already defeated certain sympathies.

Regarding his procession of memory he felt gleeful and unregretting, for in it his public deeds were paraded in great and shining prominence. Those performances which had been witnessed by his fellows marched now in wide purple and gold, having various deflections. They went gayly with music. It was pleasure to watch these things. He spent delightful minutes viewing the gilded images of memory.

He saw that he was good. He recalled with a thrill of joy the respectful comments of his fellows upon his conduct.

Nevertheless, the ghost of his flight from the first engagement appeared to him and danced. There were small shoutings in his brain about these matters. For a moment he blushed, and the light of his soul flickered with shame.

A specter of reproach came to him. There loomed the dogging memory of the tattered soldier—he who, gored by bullets and faint for blood, had fretted concerning an imagined wound in another; he who had loaned his last of strength and intellect for the tall soldier; he who, blind with weariness and pain, had been deserted in the field.

For an instant a wretched chill of sweat was upon him at the thought that he might be detected in the thing. As he stood persistently before his vision, he gave vent to a cry of sharp irritation and agony.

His friend turned. "What's the matter, Henry?" he demanded. The youth's reply was an outburst of crimson oaths.

As he marched along the little branch-hung roadway among his prattling companions this vision of cruelty brooded over him. It clung near him always and darkened his view of these deeds in purple and gold. Whichever way his thoughts turned they were followed by the somber phantom of the desertion in the fields. He looked stealthily at his companions, feeling sure that they must discern in his face evidences of this pursuit. But they were plodding in ragged array, discussing with quick tongues the accomplishments of the late battle.

"Oh, if a man should come up an' ask me, I'd say we got a dum good lickin'."

"Lickin'—in yer eye! We ain't licked, sonny. We're going down here aways, swing aroun', an' come in behint 'em."

"Oh, hush with your comin' in behint 'em. I've seen all 'a that I wanta. Don't tell me about comin' in behint—"

"Bill Smithers, he ses he'd rather been in ten hundred battles than been in that heluva hospital. He ses they got shootin' in th' night-time, an' shells dropped plum among 'em in th' hospital. He ses sech hollerin' he never see."

"Hasbrouck? He's th' best off'cer in this here reg'ment. He's a whale."

"Didn't I tell yeh we'd come aroun' in behint 'em? Didn't I tell yeh so? We—"

"Oh, shet yer mouth!"

For a time this pursuing recollection of the tattered man took all elation from the youth's veins. He saw his vivid error, and he was afraid that it would stand before him all his life. He took no share in the chatter of his comrades, nor did he look at them or know them, save when he felt sudden suspicion that they were seeing his thoughts and scrutinizing each detail of the scene with the tattered soldier.

Yet gradually he mustered force to put the sin at a distance. And at last his eyes seemed to open to some new ways. He found that he could look back upon the brass and bombast of his earlier gospels and see them truly. He was gleeful when he discovered that he now despised them.

With the conviction came a store of assurance. He felt a quiet manhood, nonassertive but of sturdy and strong blood. He knew that he would no more quail before his guides wherever they should point. He had been to touch the great death, and found that, after all, it was but the great death. He was a man.

So it came to pass that as he trudged from the place of blood and wrath his soul changed. He came from hot plowshares to prospects of clover tranquilly, and it was as if hot plowshares were not. Scars faded as flowers.

It rained. The procession of weary soldiers became a bedraggled train, despondent and muttering, marching with churning effort in a trough of liquid brown mud under a low, wretched sky. Yet the youth smiled, for he saw that the world was a world for him, though many discovered it to be made of oaths and walking sticks. He had rid himself of the red sickness of battle. The sultry nightmare was in the past. He had been an animal blistered and sweating in the heat and pain of war. He turned now with a lover's thirst to images of tranquil skies, fresh meadows, cool brooks—an existence of soft and eternal peace.

Over the river a golden ray of sun came through the hosts of leaden rain clouds.

KAY BOYLE

The Crazy Hunter

The woman and the girl began undressing in the bushes near the water, modestly taking their garments off at a little distance from each other and with their backs turned so as not to surprise each other's abashed flesh. The sun came thin but warm through the just opening buds and the tight flickering leaves of the branches, dappling the two lowered faces and the bared arms and legs with shadow. The girl had ripped her jersey over her head and flung it aside and kicked her sandals off; the tweed skirt lay discarded behind her on the earth beneath the burgeoning spring-like twigs. When she had pulled the tight blue woolen swimming suit up over her belly and breasts, she straightened up and came out onto the bank, buttoning one strap over the shoulder still, and stood there looking: the white naked legs drawn close together, slender and the flesh delicate as southern dogwood flowers, the head held straight upon the round slender neck, the temples hollow and bare with the black hair drawn back above the ears and falling almost to the shoulders. The hair and the skin's untroubled purity, and the wide, uptilted, the seemingly drugged or glazed transparent eyes gave her a look un-English as the Orient. And now the woman in her bathing-dress came stooping out, picking her own clothes up carefully and folding them over and laying them in order on the meadow grass above the wall of sedges that grew from the running water.

"Fold your things up, Nan," the woman said. "Pick your clothes up and put them somewhere all together so you'll know where they are when you get out," saying it not so much from will or habit as from the need to stop quickly this or any gap of silence between them. The arms, like the body in the black skirted bathing-dress, were full, powder-white, unblemished: these (with the forebone long and prominent in them, despite their unstained beauty, and the flesh gone slack), and the thickening, sloping shoulders and the neck's yoke signs of the consummation between flesh and time. From now on was the decline, the deterioration towards age, to come. Only the hands, reaching for the plaid blouse to smooth it out and fold it, and the face and the narrow feet in the black tennis shoes, were part still of a thinner, shyer woman's corporeity: perhaps one who had never entered into marriage willingly or given birth but who remained still tentative, still virgin, still unformed. "Nan, pick up your clothes before you go in," she said, the slow, still-innocent eyes searching the ground itself for flaw, saying it hopelessly into youth's deafness and imperviousness.

But the cold was on the girl's feet already, the water rising slowly on the pure legs as she slid down the bank's edge to the stream: the blurred face lowered, part in ecstasy, part fear, to watch the thin silver line of cold pass the ankles and mount the flesh to the knees and pass them, rising, until it had clasped her waist, her breasts, her throat, and for an instant twisted her shocked face in consternation. Then her arms began moving and she was swimming against the pouring current, the teeth shaking in her head with cold. So the last time I did this I was fifteen, two years back, she began thinking quickly against the rushing slabs of water. I hadn't been away yet and I wasn't afraid. I didn't know what it was yet. Now I can feel everything stopping, the heart, the blood, the muscles hardening as if I were working my way through ice and becoming ice and the land and sky congealing tight around me. But the mother standing on her big bare legs on the grass saw the sun falling on the soft short hair that mounted black against the current, and the girl's slim arms falling and rising, the shoulders and the bent arms as they fell chalk-white in motion through the dark water, thrusting it down behind her with small quick strokes like someone quickly mounting a steep ladder or jerking up a greased pole at a country fair.

"How is it, Nan?" she called out. "Cold?" And now her own body slumped over and broke through the sedge and the reed-sweet into the stream's fast deep bed. For a moment she swam strongly, without gasping and her chin high, and then she turned lazily onto her back and rode there, the blue rubber cap edging the longish, pale face, the big arms thrashing backwards. "Warm," she called peacefully across the water's rapid murmuring. "Just the first plunge that takes your breath off. . . ."

The way home takes it from you and doesn't return it, the girl was saying, because every year of youth is still there in the furniture and the rugs and the marks on the glass. There is a school of children everywhere with me here, all of them that one child I was once running along the house's east ivy-covered wall and down through the stables and pastures; home putting short skirts on me and picture-books on the shelves in my room. The child who scratched that drawing with a nursery pin on the inside of the banisters above the sixth bar on the first flight is still your bone, your skin, your muscle of the eye, your nail and tooth, the same physically projected child that dies now in the water's ice. She let the current turn and draw her down-stream towards the blue rubber cap, past the water-beaded floating head with its face turned upward in repose to the sun's light hanging palely on the meadows and trees.

"I'm not so good as I used to be," Nan said. "I'm going to get out, mother. I've forgotten how to swim in cold water after swimming over there."

"Climbing mountains ought to give you wind enough," the woman said, floating quietly with the stream. She lay vast, wide, bloated-seeming, her arms and legs dangling swollen under water.

"Sometimes when you learn one thing you forget another," Nan said, her teeth knocking in her mouth again. She reached up for the willow's roots and pulled herself, straining, out of the water. "I spoke German until I learned French, and in Italy I forgot everything I knew in French." On her hands and knees she sought under the bushes for the towel, tossed the tweed skirt and the jersey aside on the fresh, glinting earth, saying: "One year I know algebra and another year geometry. I never know them both the same winter." In a moment she turned on her knees and came back to the bank and sat there hunched in the towel, shaking, her toenails showing bluish at the edge. "Or when I get halfway good in charcoal drawing I forget how to work with oils, and the year I took architectural design I couldn't do life-class afterwards." She started drying her hair at the back with her hand inside the towel, shaking the soft dark locks loose. "And it's the same thing if I admire things," she said, stopping to pick a blade of pressed grass from her knee inside the towel's shade. "When I was so keen on the Renaissance I couldn't—"

"You're tucked up, that's what it is," said the woman smartly from the water, churning backwards with her arms. "You're still growing, you know, and you've been wearing yourself out with all this studying. Yesterday I saw one thing," she said, drifting wide and peaceful. "You haven't forgot how to ride a horse."

Nor have I forgotten to breathe or speak my native tongue, only how to walk into the house and through its rooms as if I belonged there any longer, or swim in water that knew me young, or sit under this tree that knew my legs climbing up it once, or how to look at her and talk to her because she is still talking Then and I am ahead in what there will be for me or in Now. I am home now, this is home, and there is no place for me because every place is taken by that child who will not die.

"I don't think I'm still growing," she said. "Anyway, my feet aren't growing. I've worn the same size shoes for two years now. I got my navy suède brogues to wear on my fifteenth birthday to go to Pellton to Mary's lunch party, and I can still wear them without them hurting."

"Look at your riding-breeches!" said the mother, floating near the sedges. "You've shot up four inches at least since September. That's why

I don't want to get you a top-price twill. You'll be out of it in six months. It isn't worth it."

"Yes," she said, "yes," almost in pain, and then as if that was the end of it she sat without speaking, rubbing the damp hair off her neck with her hand inside the towel. Mother, I know my bones, I live in this flesh, I know I have stopped growing. Look at me, I am another woman sitting up here on the grass, only not established, not recognized yet, but I am a woman sitting here watching you refuse the stream its current by your will. Just let me say this and say without looking at you that I've been three days, no, three nights and two days back and I can't stay. It's June, but it's just spring here because things are late this year. That's why the water is cold and the buds hardly open and the sedges the way rushes are in May usually, everything a month or more than that behind the season. But in other countries, in southern countries, things would be different now: the roses out strong and hot and sweet in the gardens, and the students, poets, painters coming back to their rooms along the river not looking like other people, their eyes different, and their voices not like other people's, and their shoes older, and their heads bare the way mine was bare all winter through the galleries and in the art museums and even in the churches, for even in Italy they don't seem to care if you put a handkerchief over your hair in respect any more. You walk in at noon out of the hot streets and the sun and your blood is consecrated, it becomes cool and pious with the devout pace of your feet across the stones, and you kneel down under the rising pillars in the granite dark, believing, believing. It is not religion, or Catholicism, or the belief of the Church of England, but it is your spirit on its knees at last just learning the words for its articulation. Students, she did not say aloud but sat silent rubbing her cold breasts dry beneath the towel, their faces looking different from other faces because they are still on the adventure, looking for a thing nobody here wants or has heard of wanting: knowledge or the way to knowledge or else simply the way, because of what families or convention want, of keeping curious and keeping free. All last winter I wore my clothes the way they did, as if I were a student instead of just making the pretense at it, and walked like that, and now she watched her mother emerge from the water, draw herself out by the feminine thinnish hand which seized the damp rope of the tree's uncovered root. The stuff of the wet bathing-skirt shaped the firm muscles in the thighs that gripped toward land, and in some hopeless and unreclaimed contrition, the girl stretched her own bare arm out from the towel and saw the goose-flesh powdering her skin whitely to the wrist as her arm stiffened to aid the other woman up the bank. When their fingers met and clasped, the girl's face flashed suddenly up, fervent, humble, eager, but now the mother burst out laughing, slipping and scrambling there on her broad knees in the mud; either knowing what was to come or else not knowing quite and fearful of what the words might be, she pulled herself finally up laughing onto the grass and ripped the blue rubber casing from her head and shook out her short graying curled hair and glanced quickly across the sky.

"Well, the sun's thinning out all right, Nan. Your hand's as cold as charity," she said, the voice light, inconsequential, speaking merely for the sake of sound. "You're foolish not to have taken your suit right off as soon as you were out. It chills you sitting in it like that." She was moving off, rump-high, groping on wet hands and knees to the pile of folded clothing. "Come along. We'll get our things on and run up to the paddocks," she said.

It was she who led the way along the foot-worn, cattle- and man-marked path that ran between the wild hedge and the rushes in the water, and the daughter followed, listening to the talk which led up to money now and stopped short there. The price of the seventh broodmare, and the stud fees; on went the mother's voice ahead, talking of buying wider pasture while the big arm and the bathing-bag swung at the foxtails as she passed. Nan came over the pressed grass of the walk behind her, her feet in sandals, the vague, dream-drugged, rapt eyes watching the weeds and the branches move in the sun while the water slid off through the fields and the woman's voice went on before her:

"There's no worse business than this kind of thing we have to do, growing horses on the same ground year after year. I keep racking my brains for some way out of it and how to get hold of another set of paddocks to make use of alternate years like a rich man's stud where money is no object. There's the saying that a sheep's foot is golden and that's what has saved the ground from going horse-proud." The voice went quickly, ceaselessly on, faintly contentious, acrimonious, in the drifting light of afternoon. The back of her neck stood broad and thickening beneath her sailor hat and the cropped hairs lay, wet from swimming, flat against the dust-white skin. "Putting cattle on and off the paddocks, in and out while the stud is going on, it's a heartbreaking business. Salting the rough grasses so the cattle will eat them off or mowing the grasses off and getting the sheep in, there's no end to it." She hit out at the foxtails with her bag. "I know what I want," she said savagely, coming closer to the bitter statement of it. "If I had enough money for it. Grassland kept in good heart by resting, d' y' see, Nan? Acres of fresh rested cock's foot and rye grass and fiorin. Ah, I can see it all right in my mind's eye, but what can I do about it? Anyone knowing anything about horses would see it like this, but the one man who has anything to do with it goes using the money up in other ways—"

This was not the beginning of it or anywhere near the beginning: it was merely the high-spot of the story re-stated so that she could begin to tell it all over again. It had started in those letters written to the young ladies' boarding-school in Florence, crossed land and water to another country and begun abruptly in the big wide Italian room with the girls' three beds in it: "Nan, I had put money aside towards buying new pasture and what did your father do but up and buy this stag-faced gelding without any rhyme or reason for doing it, except he'd had too much to drink."

He hasn't any preferences or any real will of his own, it went on in the letters or else in the voice carrying it along the cattle and dairy path ahead. He does it out of, what's the word I want, Nan, I don't mean out of spite but something almost like it only queerer, because I'm the one who has the money, born with it, kept it, doubled it after your grandfather died, and your father has to show he's somebody with something, even if it's only the say-so. He wants to prove to me and everybody else what a man he is by going out and buying an animal I haven't had a finger or an eye on, and drawing the check out to fool them into thinking any of it's his, doing it after a few drinks to show them what it's like, a man's signature and a man's bank account. And he knows I'll stand by him; it's what he trades on, that I won't let him down. Seven, eight years back he spent that fortune on cattle when he knew, sober anyway he knew, that polled cattle were the only kind we could use with horses on the farm. He had the breed names in his notebook when he went off to the fair: Galloways, Red Polls or Aberdeen Angus I'd put down for him, thinking to give him the satisfaction of the responsibility. But after whatever he had at the Ship he must have said to himself, I'll show her. If she's British and the money's hers, I'm Canadian and I'll have the choice and the say. I cried a week over it after but that didn't do any good, and the cattle once re-sold fetched half the price of what he'd paid at the public sales, and I had to swallow that too. And next was the unproved sire he brought home instead of a high-class stallion, without running out its pedigree even. Try always if you can to nick with the *sire's* dam's blood and leave the *sire's* sire's blood as your outcross whenever it's possible to do it, I'd told him since the beginning. I'd written it down for him, but nothing scientific ever mattered to him. If he likes the look of a thing, or if he's had enough of someone knowing better than he does, or after a drink or two, he'll have his head for once whatever the price, so home he comes with this horse and there we were with it, a practical dead-loss on our hands. But even with it down in print before him you can't teach a Canadian anything about a horse's predominate blood. Ah, it's been a heart-breaking business with your father, Nan; if he kept his hands on paints or chess sets it would be one thing, but after he's started drinking at the sales and has the bee in his bonnet that he knows, it would break your heart wide open. But I've never put my foot down about the joint account and that's what I should have done from the beginning. I've always let him go on drawing on the money for the sake of his manliness, or like giving him the tail-end of a career or an occupation because he never had one of his own. And why do I keep on doing it like a fool?—only because he comes back crying over what he's done once he's seen the folly of it, crying and sorry and swearing never to do it again and ready to die for it and willing to pay back every penny out of tobacco money, and swearing to paint a picture worth more than everything he's lost. . . .

"He's only spent the money wrong like that about twice, mother," the girl said. Hatless, stockingless, she walked behind, the dream-rapt eyes watching the weeds and branches stir and quiver in the sun.

"Three times!" the woman ahead cried out. "There were the horned cattle and the worthless sire, and now this time it's this crazy hunter! He brings in this stag-faced hack at the price you'd lay out for a thoroughbred beast, and never thinking after what he'd had to drink, of having him up to pass the vet. Jolly as can be he comes in without a certificate either way, and the man who'd sold it to him out of the country so it happened. And why did your father do it? Just to show me he can get the money out of my hands when he wants! We're stocking a stud-farm, I told him, not a riding-school. But the money was already gone and the price of new paddocks shot again—"

"Was it much? Could it have been as much as that?" the girl said, the black hair back from the hollow temples, the eyes wild-violet soft and tender, the bare blue-veined feet in the sandals wandering dreamily, soundlessly on by the stream.

"Ah, no, not so much as the price of new land, no," said the mother, striking at the tall fox-grasses with her bag. "Nothing like what has been paid for horses, nothing compared to what Sir Mallaby Deeley paid for 'Solario,' for instance," she said with bitter irony. "Never forty-odd thousand pounds, of course, but still for me it was something. It was enough to put off looking at land or even thinking of new paddocks for another year or more until something has had the time to collect and stop the hole up—"

The girl started talking quietly behind her.

"Candy says he bought Brigand for me," she was saying. "He says he wants me to have Brigand to ride and do with as I please. I told Candy I didn't want to hunt any more and he said I could have him anyway for mine—if I wanted him—I mean, if I stay—"

"He's leggy," the mother said quickly, almost quick enough to stop the sound of the last words short before she would have to hear them said, and she went on talking loud and fast. "There's bad blood in him somewhere, sire or dam; he's queer. Your father picked him for his shoulders, but anyone who knows will tell you that's a luxury item. A bad horse can trick a novice time and again with pretty shoulders."

Home three days, the mother began thinking now a little wildly, and already that face as if they'd put her in prison for life, and already the words beginning to be dropped and the hints. She went along the stream's side, irritated now, hitting impatiently at the heads of the weeds, thinking of the girl following a little way behind her and thinking It's her good-looks that have done it. None of us thought she'd turn out like that, and now summer's good enough to be wasted at home but later she'll have to be off where the remarks men on the street or men she's met pass about her will be nourishment enough. Ah, I know very well what it is you want, she thought slyly, and at the same time with an impatient recognition of the slyness, and I'm your mother and I'll keep you from it as long as I can. It's all very fine for you but it isn't fine enough, Nan; you're seventeen, you can very well wait till you're twenty to know what you want and to hear the things they'll always have to say about your face and figure.

"Your father—" she began, but suddenly, as if wakened from the walking dream and crying out in sleep, the girl called:

"Mother, look at that bird up there!"

Once they had been walking along here to the paddocks, perhaps two years back it was, anyway before the boarding-school in Florence, and it was something else that stopped them short like this on the path, and the mother now, as then, turned with her bathing-bag in her hand and the identical sailor hat (which perhaps was not the same one from summer to summer but which might have been) shaded her face from what was not sun or even light so much as merely the absence of rain. I can't look, if I can't look down there again I can't. I can't bear looking at it, I can't look again, said Nan's voice over the two years of almost having forgotten what its shape was and how it lay against the bottom in the mud.

"What are you talking about, Nan?" said the mother with no alteration in the tone or face, neither more impatient or less, saying it now exactly as she had said it then.

"Mother, look, there's a bird caught up there in the trees," the girl said, thinking: Two years ago the thing was lying in the water and I couldn't look down at it again. I stood staring at her face until she finally turned her face down to see, the hat brim lowering so that I couldn't see her eyes any more, only the nostrils whitening along the edges and her mouth opening as if to make a sound but not making it, and then she threw her bag down on the path. We'll have to get him out quick, she said. Nan, I'll go down and get him and if you can get hold of his arms from the bank while I push him from below we ought to make it. He's got his cap on still, the mother said. Mother, I can't, I can't do anything, said Nan's voice, dying. I can't. I'm too afraid.

So slowly, the act witnessed only by herself because the girl crouched on the path had covered her face with her hands, the mother turned the body over in the water, kneeling in her clothes in the stream while the water ran cold across her doubled-up legs and to her hips. It's Sykes, she said without looking up. What I thought. It's Sykes. He's dead. And slowly, breathing hard with the effort, she got him out over the rushes and up the bank alone, thought Nan, while I sat here shaking and crying and trying not to see. But still I saw, because I remember seeing his head fall backwards on his neck and hit the grass and concrete by the paddock's post and his adam's apple jerk up higher in his throat and stop there and not come down again the way a living man's would. I remember her saying He must have drowned last Saturday night (and this was Monday afternoon), dead drunk, perhaps drinking with your father. She stood up and stood looking down at him, and then she leaned over and pulled the beak of the black-and-white checkered cap he was wearing down across his face. He wasn't a good groom anyway, the mother said wiping her hands in her handkerchief. I've been thinking for two days he'd gone off dishonestly but this was honest enough, the old souse, she said.

Holding her bathing-bag now and looking off in the direction of the trees clumped at a little distance in the meadow, she said:

"Where? A bird caught? I can't see it, Nan. Where?" Because she must turn around to look for it, her back was put now to where the paddocks lay beyond the stream's next bend, masked by the drooping willows, and this was more than she had the patience left for, for she'd already got the smell of horses down the wind. "Where in the world can you possibly see a bird caught?" she said almost in irritation.

"There," the girl said, and the lifted hand was narrow and angular as a boy's hand set strangely at the white arm's extremity. "It's holding onto something in the tree there, or else it's caught by something," she said, the hand lifted, pointing, square at the fingertips and the resolute square nails cut short on a doer's not a dreamer's hand.

The trees they looked at were various and of variable green, standing high and lovely now against the misting heavens, their pale and dark, strong and fanciful greens shaking and beckoning in a breeze that did not touch the woman's or the girl's lifted face. Now that the mother saw the bird hanging too, they set off through the field, walking side by side through the half-grown unbroken weeds the short way there was to go. Ahead stood the trees: it might have been that a fistful of seed, no two alike, had been flung down, years back, upon that place—oak, ash, beech, juniper, elder and their underbrush—and this almost circular island of uneven, incongruous mast and foliage had sprung up there in the open sea of grass. The mother and the girl did not speak as they walked but watched those forward branches of the oak where the bird hung, rising and falling.

"There's a sling on his neck," said the woman, standing under him now and letting the bag drop behind her into the grass.

"They've tried to hang him!" the girl cried out in anger. "Boys, of course! They've strung him up there simply for the fun of it!"

"Rubbish," said the woman. They stood with their heads thrown back, the mother taller, stronger, their faces lifted to the flapping captive bird.

"He's got his head tangled in it somehow. He's a thrush—a silly, thieving thrush, out after something for his nest and this is the trouble he's got himself into."

As they stood under him watching, he fluttered wildly upward and lit in panic on the branch above. There he paused, his beak gaping weakly, his eye, bright, wounded, desperate, on them. Below him the string that held him tethered loop down, swinging loose as a hammock on the delicate air.

"So now I suppose you see what you've got yourself into?" the woman called up to him from the ground. "Now you see what it means to go snooping and nosing around instead of staying in the woods where you belong!" The bird sat high above them, unmoving on the branch, his beak as if pried open, his motionless body throbbing under the leaves like a feathered, stricken heart. "I've a good mind to leave you right where you are like that," she said, and she added: "He's too high to reach from here."

"I can climb to him," the girl said. "I can easily get up to him."

She leaned and undid her sandals, and then the boy hands reached up and closed on the oak's lowest bough and her feet swung off the ground. The bare feet ran quickly up the trunk's hide and she stood upright in the first fork with one arm around the tree's girth. Seeing her there, taller and closer in menace, the bird fell threshing again from the branch and hung, the eye on her small, bright, alert, jerking at the string's extremity. It will be like having a moth fly in the room at night, the girl said climbing higher; I'll feel the flesh moving up my back and swear not to shudder and all the time I'll be crawling cold with terror. When I get my hands around him to lift him down, I'll have to keep my eyes shut, and even then I won't be able to bear the feel of his feathers beating and fluttering on my skin.

"Move out along the branch towards him from where you are," the mother called up. Her face was lifted and the sailor-hat brim hung limp across her brow and ears.

"Yes," said the girl, not moving. "That's what I'm going to do."

Or the feel of his feet, I won't be able to stand it. They'll be cold, naked, unbearable, like a sick thing's or a dying baby's fingers. If I touch him I'll have to choke him in terror, I'll have to break his legs in two, I'll have to do it. She crouched waiting at the tree's second fork before beginning the journey out, her fingers and bare feet holding to the tree's heavy hide. And now, ahead, she could see how the string lay coiled around the branch and the fiber of it, like good fishing-line. Exactly like fishing-gut, she thought, her eyes shifting quickly, steadily from the bird's hanging body beating among the leaves to the way out along the slowly yielding curve of the wood.

"A yard more and you've got him," said the mother, carefully, step by step, keeping pace with her on the ground below; and now the branch sagged gently with the girl's weight, dipped whispering and creaking lower while the mother said cautiously: "Go a little further and then I can reach up and get him."

"But don't pull him!" the girl said. Pausing there, crouched animal-like, wide-eyed on the branch, she saw suddenly what it was. "It is fishing-line!" she said. "Look! He's swallowed the worm and hook, that's what he's done—"

She began unwinding the broken gut string from the bough, squatting on her bare legs and feet and reaching out, and now the terrible, wild, tugging life freed of the branch pulled on the string her hands held, tore through the leaves in frantic terror like a fish leaping underwater with the hook caught in him. In a minute he'll rip his tongue out and I'll go crazy, she thought, feeding the line down to her mother, and below her the woman lifted her arms high and raised her empty hands.

"Can you get him? Have you got him?" the girl said, and she closed her eyes so as to see it no longer and crouched blind, dazed in the tree with the nightmare of frail desperate life tearing, beak, claw, and wing, at the string's vein through her fingers.

"Yes, let the string go," said the mother's hushed voice. "Let it go. I have him," and the movement ceased suddenly, halted with an abruptness closer to extinction than release as the woman took him in her lifted hands.

The girl swung herself from the second branch down to the first, and hung from the first for a moment before dropping to the ground. The woman held him fast, the beak wide open in her fingers while with the right hand she manipulated the hook forked deep within his throat. The breath came audibly through her nostrils as she worked and her face hung over him, and it was at the face the girl looked, not at the bird, as she stood beside her. She looked at the long pale cheek and the lips set and she said, Mother, not speaking aloud, you can touch these things, you can touch death and wipe it off in your handkerchief afterwards and touch pain without shrinking from it but you cannot take me in your arms any more and when I am with you I am afraid. Mother, she said in silence not looking at the bird, come out of your stone flesh and touch me too and see how tall I am, my eye almost up to your eye, and how big my feet and hands are, like a woman's. But the cheek did not alter and did not color, and the girl made herself look down now at the bird. For a while there was no sign of blood, only the stretched gagging throat and tongue, and then suddenly it came, fine as thread and dark across the seemingly unliving substance of the beak and across the cushion of the woman's finger prying it wide.

"There," she said, and she flung the freed hook and the length of the fishing-line from her and lifted the bird closer in her fist to see deeper into the hopelessly defended and betrayed secrets of its throat and sight. And now, eye to eye with her, he closed his beak violently on her finger, the flat tiny poll bristling with outrage, the beak striking and closing and striking again out of the small held feathered body in a paroxysm of hate.

"Now what will he do? Will he be able to eat?" the girl asked in a whisper, watching, and while she said it the woman opened the hand that held him and he struggled queerly forward, his feathers damp from the pressure of the palm and fingers and their human moisture and the thread of black blood streaking across his bill and breast. He did not fly at once: first he soiled the woman's hand and then he wheeled falteringly off under the trees.

"He can't fly straight yet," the mother said, and she stooped and wiped her hand off on the grasses. "Perhaps hanging all night there—"

And now as if the exact hour to speak had struck, as if it were this surprised and perhaps unpermanent moment of tenderness or frailty or default they had been waiting for, the girl put her hand up to the dark hair above her brow, shielding her eyes a little from the absolute committance of sight and began saying:

"Mother, I want to know now, I want to know it so much now so I'll be certain . . . I've been trying to say it to you since I've been back . . . I want to know if you and Candy will let me . . . I want to know it so I can plan about it and talk and write letters . . . I mean, if you will let me go again in September . . . it's June now, I mean in about three months could I . . . I mean, to study somewhere, of course, not just to have a good time but to really learn . . ."

The mother had turned away and stooped, and with her head down picked up the bathing-bag where she had dropped it in the grass.

"Where? Where do you want to go?" she said, her hands dragging the bag's strings tighter, the face turned off under the old hat's brim and the dry lips trembling a little, not speaking loud.

"I thought perhaps back to Florence only not . . . I mean, I don't want to go to Miss Easter's again . . . I thought . . . You see, I want to paint. I thought live with a family in Paris or Florence or somewhere like that and go to classes . . . I thought . . . I mean . . ." She stopped saying it when the mother turned, her chin lifted.

"Nan, don't talk drivel," she said. "Think what you're saying. A girl of your age turned loose in a city. You'd soon enough see the folly of it—"

She was facing the stream again, the path, the willows concealing at the water's bend what lay so richly, ripely, fragrantly beyond. She had begun to move towards it, her back to the girl, the bag swinging, escaping towards the wind's smell, the myriad sound and stamp, the eager substance and heart of horses in their paddocks. Behind her the girl stood waiting, trembling, silent a moment before she too began walking.

"Not loose," she said after her. "Mother, not loose," but the tears rising in her throat stopped the sound of it with pain.

2

After she had opened the stable door and let the sun run in she stood watching him an instant: his head was high but quiet, his ears alive, his mahogany flank gleamed richly in the light from the part-opened door. Out of the shallow dimness of the boxes she could hear the groom's voice, continuous in the soothing swageing words of horse-talk as she crossed the floor, hearing it steady as water murmuring while she crossed the separately rounded and hoof-scarred timbers to where the hunter stood beyond his gate. His loins and quarters shone bright and firm and he stood on all four feet, without a hoof cocked, even though at ease. "You Brigand, you troublemaker," she said half-aloud and he turned his head on his shoulder to watch her come inside and close the latch behind her, and then he shifted to one side. At his head she raised her bare arm and laid her hand, gloved to the wrist, beneath his mane.

Now the delusion of darkness was clearing, ebbing fast, as her eyes altered, towards light: she could see the knots in the boards of the stall and the mare's head and neck beyond and her full ripe dappled shoulder over the partitions that stood between, and the strings of white hair, like a witch's, hanging on the brood-mare's neck. "I like this horse, Apby," the girl said, with her hand laid under the hunter's mane. She stood looking beyond into the clearing obscurity at the mare's head and the unseen crouching groom, saying it to his goodafternoon and the voice's low ceaseless cajoling. The windows were open the stable's length and the air was clean with avenues of myriad sparkling light running with sun to the forage of oaten straw and striking there and igniting it like flame. "Apby, I like him. I like the way he went yesterday. He's a good horse," she said. She was wearing breeches, old ones, too tight and darned across the knees, and a sport shirt undone at the neck. The gloves with the buttons missing and the brown leather wearing through white at the fingers' ends were turned inside out at her bare wrists and flapped back loose across her hands.

"Yes, Miss," said the groom, not lifting his voice to say it but letting the sound go murmuring on. "Bees swarming all the morning kept them nervy. They was all over the windows and wood." So hush now, so be still now, it went on gently, gently to the brood-mare as he squatted beside her using the paring-knife on her unshod foot. "Out yonder the wall was black with them, thick," he said in the same low, tempered, wooing tone. "They didn't like them, did you, lady? Oh, not at all, they didn't like them. I got them away with sulphur, burning it here and there in dishes outside and in."

"Apby, what do you think of him as a horse?" the girl said. "What do you think of this animal? He's turned out to be mine." She stood looking into the horse's dark clear eye with the lash, thick, black, fernlike, brushing on the lid, and the blood turned warm, the marrow melted softly in her from the power of the delicate, quick body breathing near. "What do you think of this upstart, this Brigand with his bony face?" she said. The smell of his coat was sweet and the neck's arch sprang firm and meaty underneath her hand.

"I will say he's got a good rein," the groom's voice began saying warily from the brood-mare's side. "He's got quite a bit in front of him, and that gives a horse an air. But I wouldn't—"

"He's got a foolish head, my fine horse has," said the girl with love, and she pulled the near ear gently down and drew the pointed fur tip of it across her face. And now, as if just recognizing the words the groom's voice had shaped or just receiving now their sense on some vague undulation of retarded hearing, she stopped short and stared across the stalls' partitions at the mare's head and shoulder and the unseen groom. "But you wouldn't what?" she said. "You wouldn't what?"

"It might be that I would never have thought of picking him out for a buy," the groom's voice went on. "But if he's stag-faced, as Mrs. Lombe has it, it don't hurt him none for riding. No one's going to ask nothing else of him, the way I understand it." He did not look up, the head, the soiled brown cap lowered over the bent foot as he worked at the mare's side, the same gentle assuaging murmur of contemporation crooning: "If he runs to hollowness towards the nose, there's no foal going to bear it on. Whatever his faults are or his points either, it stops with him there and no harm come to, at least the way I look at it."

She stood with her hand stopped under the black hairs of the mane still, her obsessed rapt gaze moving from the ear's soft flick and the passive brow down the nasal bones to the nostril, her own dream-stupored, half-slumbering eye level with the horse's proud soft brilliant eye. So this is how they think of you, my horse, she said in silence to him. She lifted her other hand and touched the wide hard cheek-bone's blade. Not my first horse or my second or even the third, but this time my horse in protest, my hunter in defiance; not with race and nervousness flickering down your crest and loins, but my bony-legged monster to gentle, to murmur alone to in fortification of my father's errors; the substance of identity and revolt and love to hold to, until I can see you like the oriflamme of what is nothing more violent than Candy and me walking down a street arm in arm together in another country, she said, the gloved hand moving on his neck under the mane's coarse glossy hair. With one finger she lifted the velvet of his lip and looked at the upper teeth laid bare in his mouth, breathing the warm hay-sweetened breath while the physical stab of love thrust in her. He drew his head up from her hand, but tractably, the nostril opening dry as silk and rosy and the hairs quivering on his vulnerable unmottled lip.

"Apby, what age would you give him?" she said, watching in grave passionate pride how his teeth met evenly, touching one on the other almost vertically.

"I'd give him off five," the groom said from the other box, and the girl looked up in sudden sharpness and Brigand's ears flicked on his lifted head.

"Off five!" she said. "What rubbish, Apby! Have you taken the trouble to look at him instead of just making up your mind about him without— Look here, his side front teeth are hardly cut. I'd say he's just off three."

"Come first July I'd give him rising six," the groom said, the peaceful, persistently assuaging voice unaltered. "He's cutting his tush and that's what's maybe thrown you off," but when he heard her jerk the bridle down off the peg he stood up in the mare's box. "I'll have him ready for you straight away, Miss, if you're taking him out," he said.

"No, I'll do it," she said shortly. "I don't see how in the world you handle him at all, feeling about him the way you do." Her hand in its glove lifted the hunter's hair and drew the forelock free of the browband onto his face and buckled the cheek-pieces tighter, working in quick stubborn rebuke. "You'd let them tell you anything and believe it, true or not," she said. She did not look for an instant over the box's panel to where the groom stood, the dwarfed arms hanging from the waistcoat's cramp and the blunt soiled fingers turning the paring-knife in harried, slow humility. He saw the sun coming through the open window onto her hair and head as she loosened the throat-lash on the horse's neck: the dark soft longish hair with the strong light on it and the pale face and throat and the mouth's color warm but pallid and he began saying in expiation:

"They're up to all kinds of tricks you'd never suspect if you wasn't onto them. Copers'll file off the seven-year notch and nobody the wiser if they get hold of a buyer what wouldn't know. You got to keep your eyes open, I tell you, you can't trust anybody, you just got to look sharp." He stood watching her from the other box and turning the paring-knife in his fingers, as if just to keep on talking no matter what the words were would be enough to set it right at last. "Bishoping's another coper's trick," he said. "They'll level the teeth off short and gouge the centers out and blacken them with caustic if they think it'll sell a ten-year old for a six," he said, and then he said abruptly and painfully: "I didn't mean no offense about his age, Miss," standing with the brown cloth cap turned back to front and lending him the look now of a tough stunted gladiator halted in the arena, unchârioted, bewildered, and unarmed. When he said this to her over the box's panel, she raised her lids and looked with the heavy, seemingly drugged wide-spaced eyes across the crib-bitten wood at him, the eyes' substance transparent as glass in the sunlight and clear bright icy blue.

"All right," she said, lifting the saddle over the gate. She stooped to girth it, and now the groom returned to his work again and his voice to cajoling, saying to the mare or the girl or to their quiet This is the way I came to say it or how I came to think it or Here's the explanation of it if you want it and this is the truth, s'help me, soothing them, lulling them, rocking them to sleep with the low half-querulous murmur of his self-palliation as he raised the mare's forefoot onto his lowered knee.

Saddled and bridled the horse waited while she unlatched the gate, and then turned in his box to follow her out. He carried his head down and the reins loose on his neck, but the ears were pointing in expectancy, his hoofs thudding loud and full on the timber as he came. His sloping shoulders flowed under the loose burnished skin and on the left side of his neck his mane hung dark and glossy. At the stable door the girl turned and took the double reins and ran them over her arm; when she lifted the door's handle and pushed the half of it out, the daylight fell like a wedge through the stable's dark.

"Apby," she said, looking back, and the groom stood up and answered, "Yes, Miss," touching his cap as he stood helpless, hopeless in the box by the mare. "Brigand's my show now," she said. "I'll be in to do him every morning," and the groom answered bleakly, "Yes, Miss" again, and touched his cap again with his fingers, and then he suddenly began saying: "Sometimes even old hands at the game'll make a slip, like a breeder I knew of once was thrown off by the corner teeth. You'll see them coming through around four years and rising five, nine times out of ten you will, but like this time I was speaking about, there was the exception proving the rule, as they say, and knowing the horse I knew when he was foaled, a bay colt nice as anything you've seen—"

"All right," the girl said from the doorway, the voice cold, implacable still.

"That Brigand there, he has the kind of look like he might break a rule," the groom said, speaking louder as if the mere sound of his impetration must set it right no matter what the words were. "When Mr. Lombe brought him in a month or something back, I said right off to Mrs. Lombe, I said if ever I saw a horse that looked like he'd—"

"All right," she said, stepping clear of the beam. "All right." She watched the horse pick his way over after her and she said: "All right, Apby, I'll see to him myself when I bring him in. Don't wait around for him," and she closed the door.

Candy Lombe had put his dark green felt on looking at himself, the roundish, soft, bright face, the swollen aggrieved eyes, looking straight into the vestibule's long glass and bringing the brim down right; the small hand with the signet dark red ring drawing tighter the cravat on which the beagles ran against his throat, the head held back to get the light while he slipped his fingers along the short mustaches' bristles on his upper lip and smelled the bay rum and the shaving-soap that lingered. He had gone off from the house in the afternoon feeling the curse lying heavy on him: the bane and the wrong that there was no shape to his life and none in the past since youth (and youth shaped by what, after all, but the imminence of hope), and now youth gone and the curse of nothing else to come. The forty-three or forty-four years (he couldn't or didn't want to remember which) must for a long time now have been these fragments, discarded over some vague period of space or time: vestiges of a thing as irreplaceable as life that had been given him entire and that he had let fall, the separate pieces lost in separate countries, before knowing there was any value to the thing or even that he carried anything at all.

Ah, trouble, trouble, there are the two different kinds of it, he thought, going bitterly alone up through the green June fields; there's the one you give and the other you take. I gave, I gave freely, he said to the curse, the bane, the wrong of his life. It is more blessèd to give than to receive, so I gave. I gave trouble at home until I was twenty for the ordeal of art alone; not for the fact or the accomplishment of art but the organized slaughter of what the idle said was not Art, the Glorified, the Exalted; I gave trouble year after year for the willful murder of what They (family) recognized as comfort like a mouse its hole by Me (individual) who must (for what reason time has never made clear) be saved from mediocrity for the crowning and the final wide and loud acclaim. I wore a smock and a beret on the streets of Montreal, did Candy Lombe, by God, and what is he now but a squire in his English squire's jacket strolling up the country with a good felt hat on telling himself he'll get a thumb-nail sketch, a bird's eye view instead of a kick in the seat for his forty-odd years of caring, not making the pretense any more of carrying a water-color box or a palette and tubes and boards but out with his golf hose fitting his ankles right and his heart gone rotten in him.

Because nobody ever made me understand that it was up to me and nobody ever helped me with it or told me what to do, said the petulance, the querulousness which even rising anger could not dignify with heat; me, colonial in England, pauper, painter, each imposing their segregation from country, status, convention. Everyone with their hands lifted hard and high against what I have to be: the intruder on somebody else's soil when I should have stayed home and gone on with what my father was (the visionary, the preacher), and the intruder on some woman's money even if I did give her my name in exchange, and the last tentative intrusion made and abandoned on some other kind of man's career. Me, the painter, tradition of Goya, Velasquez, me, charcoal sketching in night-schools, water-painting landscapes up to thirty like a school-boy, hanging up little canvases in fancy rooms with decorated peasant china and hand-embroidered table linen, all for sale, even the pretty pastel-colored canvases, all at a price for the ladies who come in to tea. Me, an artist, never able to memorize right the lines I wasn't intended to speak or recognizing the cues when I heard them, but somehow trying to take part in the performance, making my exits and entrances blushing, stammering, always backwards and on the wrong side of the stage.

The lane he had come into now had wild hedge growing thick on either side of it and ruts cutting deep and dry into its bed. Long pale grasses sprang up in the crescents marked by draught-horses' feet on the center rise of ground between the stone-hard troughs their cart wheels had hollowed. In a while he knew he would come out onto the dairy farm, not suddenly but piece by piece upon it: first the wall with the moss along it beginning to wind in low, unbroken meandering beyond the orchard trunks, the stones washed light as lime but slightly golden, and after the flash of a white cat with a striped auburn tail past the milk-tins tilted up to sweeten in the sun; step by step coming to it, the familiarly rain-drenched or else the shimmering completely silent, rural scene. It might have been something printed on a postcard, or still more a faintly tinted photograph joined by a silk cord with tassels to a wall calendar for the year. C. Lombe, Esq., he said walking measuredly in silence towards it, taking his forty-three or forty-four years of protest against, dreams of, demands for whispered or spoken or cried aloud at night, to this stage laid for still unaccumulated action, to this hushed homely amphitheater where the classic drama of neurosis might play itself out to destruction; Candy Lombe taking the not even colossal failure of these expended years out for a stroll this afternoon as I did yesterday afternoon and as I will take it out into the air tomorrow, exactly as you'd take a horse out, two hours of gentle exercise a day, to tire him for his body's peace and wear him down to time's passivity for his soul's. Lure the days one after another like this, as the years have been inveigled to a lonely spot where their cries cannot be heard and cut their throats for them and fling them, virgin still, upon the manure-heaps, the stable-rakings, the horse offal of this part of England. They can't stink more than stud-farms do of sex and monstrous matings and foalings brutaler than murders.

Through his shoes he could feel the scars the horses' irons had left in the lane-bed's clay, the shape of them set hard into his shoe leather like in his memory: the calkins, the feather-edge, the plain, the

Rodway shoe. Nowhere in this countryside could you get away from the mark of horses on the soil, the smell of horses, of horses' droppings, the rose-headed and counter-sunk shoe-nails found on the roads and lanes and scattered through the pastures. Horses pulled carts when I was young, he thought, walking; they were nothing to me, neither to be liked or not. They never entered into life's substance; their place was allotted, not mine. They were not the established order and I the outcast lost to society and human intercourse for want of a proper name. And now, to elude their wild extravagant possession, Candy Lombe instead of signing canvases walks through a county fetid with horse, rank with horse, pock-marked and stampeded by them; here he is, paddocked at middle-age, hobbled without a choice of pasture or forage, buckled and strapped and gelded and going thick in the wind.

"I feel so sorry for Candy, although he looks such a dandy," he began, making it up, half aloud. "His squire's jacket is black and white, and his something something fits him tight—right—I feel so sorry for Candy," he started over again, "although his color's so—though his color's fresh and dandy. His hair and his mustache are neat, but he's sick of the sight of horses' feet. I feel so VERY sorry for him—tum-te-tum, te-tum-te-tum. He used to be young and his paunch was thin, but rigs and fillies have done him in. I feel so sorry for—"

Now the first sight of the dairy began through the apple trees and he stopped making his verses up and watched for the wings and the dreamy faintly blowing back-drop and the familiar properties set to the right and left. There was the stage, the rural lovely scene, and no players on the boards yet, as yet no sign of horse-dirt fouling the prepared ground here where the lane widened slowly towards the farm's court and halted. Oh, Candy Lombe, he used to paint, he said to himself, the idle English gentleman wandering towards the picturesque little dairy farm on the June afternoon. But all the praise he got was faint. He thought: if I stop saying this I'm lost, if I stop saying Oh, Candy Lombe, he used to think in the days before he took to—if I stop saying it I'll see the curse hanging there before me, weighted and choked with death and incongruous in the sun as a corpse hanging in his old clothes behind the house there by his neck and swinging gently, or a railway tramp lying iron-dead in a freight-car of red apples. Oh, Nancy, Nancy, give me ear, he went on, like whistling in the dark; oh, hasten to your father, dear! Oh, Candy Lombe stepped out from home, he began rapidly again, and then he saw the first movement of life, furtive and quick as something stirring in the twilight of early morning or evening: the white cat flashing past the up-turned milk-tins as it had done yesterday afternoon, only a little earlier, just as he had been a few yards back crossing the orchard grass. Now, it seemed, had the overture to action been executed at last, and immediately the ducks, neat and immaculate as linen, reeled slowly around the corner of the dairy farmhouse and started for the water-trough.

After a time, still standing there in his gray knickerbockers and his trimly gartered wool hose and watching the ducks beguile themselves gravely across the water's surface, their bills dipping and fumbling below the brink, he began to hear the sound of the horse's hoofs coming. For a while he did not turn his head to see or even begin conjecturing, but stood with his hands in his jacket pockets, the narrow, cleanly manicured thumbs showing, the hatbrim smartly down, seeming to watch the ducks in the water but perhaps seeing nothing beyond the lost, corrupted vision of his youth or hearing nothing but the sound of its despair. But when the horse had come close behind him and the rider drew rein, he started and turned in guilt, his right arm involuntarily raised partly in some gesture of greeting and partly as if to ward off the violence of actual sight or being seen by whoever had come on him undefended and unaware.

"Hello, Candy," said Nan from the horse's back, and here were their eyes meeting down the slant of the mahogany shoulder, the same marvelously glazed, indolently cast eyes obliquely and rather shyly spanning the distance's acclivity from mount to ground, and their mouths smiling.

"Why, hello there, Nancy," the father said with an American and disproportionate heartiness that only from uneasiness and hesitation sought to cloak, conceal, secrete nothing but the soul's timidity.

"I was looking for you," the girl said. "I rode him up here because I thought you came this way."

"I've got the habit of walking up here in the afternoons," he said in a bright sociable tone, almost but not quite as if seeking to keep from her some reason for his having come. He laid one hand, palm down, on the horse's shoulder and looked up at her from under the smartly dipping fine felt brim. "Gets me away from the stud," he said, his small mouth and his chin beginning to laugh under his mustache. "I think it's more like country up here and not so much like business. Nobody's doing anything, not even the ducks." He was smiling up at her with this little defense, this eager little reserve between them as if she were a lady he had just met at tea. "I can flâner les boulevards, as it were," he said. When he put out his hand to hold the rein while she dismounted, she stopped and said:

"Don't hold him. Please, don't hold him. He won't stir."

"You've only ridden him two days," said Candy, but he stayed his hand uncertainly and watched her slide to the ground.

"He's been very nicely trained, your horse has," she said. "When I mount he stands without moving a muscle while I fix my reins or gloves or belt or fiddle with the stirrups." She brought the reins forward over the horse's head and ran them up her arm. "We did exercises at the trot this afternoon: the figure of eight on one track and hock turns and the turn about. We're getting on very well together." They walked along side by side, past the dairy farmhouse, the girl with the horse coming docilely behind her and the man with his hands in his jacket pockets, side by side out onto the country road. "Only voices worry him a little. He likes them soft and low, like you do." Their eyes slid sideways again at each other's faces, and the father laughed. "He shied twice—once at a fence and at a tree back there a minute before the dairy. I told him I wouldn't have it."

"Now, listen," said Candy. "I don't want him to get you into trouble." Here it was, the threat, the menace of horses again, the monstrous promise in their bone and hide of the mutilation, the even fatal evil they could wreak on peace sounding alarm from nerve to nerve and marking it in trepidation on his face. "Look here, Nancy, I want you to be careful with him."

"It's just a game he likes to play," she said. "He pretended he couldn't get the look of the fence right and so he shied off at the jump. He must have seen other horses' demonstrations, you know, and thinks it's smart to imitate them—you know, the way schoolgirls, I mean some do, you know, the way they imitate or pretend to talk like picture actresses they've seen—"

"The silly, adolescent creatures," Candy said severely.

"Ah, don't laugh," his daughter said, and the horse came gently, meekly on behind. "He's looking for a personality, you know, the way you have to when you're young. You can't always decide so quickly what you're going to be like. Sometimes he plays at being willful and he goes on the way he must have seen race horses do. But it doesn't mean anything, it's really rather silly of him. Coming up the hill he stopped walking and stared at a clump of buttercups as if he'd never seen anything like them before, or perhaps as if he couldn't *really* see them, and then he just walked on and I couldn't get a word out of him. But he's really, I mean underneath everything else, he's really awfully afraid of displeasing. You can see by looking at him he's very vain," she said.

"Oh, can you?" said Candy, looking back under the brim of his hat at the horse coming on behind. "Now, with all due respect, Nancy, where—"

"Ah, don't make fun of him!" she said in sudden pain. "Everyone ridiculing him and jeering at him as if he were the stable freak simply because he isn't to sire or foal or isn't a colt, or isn't to train, or hasn't a single action he's expected to perform! Simply to look the fool and hack around, but I didn't think you'd feel that about him—"

Walking in silence beside her, he put his arm in the black-and-white patterned sleeve through her bare arm's bend and drew her against him until he felt the ribs and the breast under the sport shirt moving against his squire's cloth, walking in step with her and in silence, the sharp small daughterly hip moving against his thickening hip.

"Nancy, I'm sorry. I'm sorry I said that," he said. "I didn't mean it." A freak and a fool and a hack like me, he thought in bitter, retributive guilt. In this way they walked on for a while through the scallops of shade and sun, shade cast by the thickly arching trees and sun shining palely in the open spaces on the ground; each thinking of the horse, not as it came along behind them at the end of its loose rein, but transformed to symbol for the separateness of two interpretations and two isolate despairs. "I was thinking this afternoon," the father said, "about horses. You were brought up on the brutes but I wasn't. I never had a horse anywhere near me, except pulling a milk-wagon or a tramcar, when I was young. Perhaps I keep on thinking about horses without knowing that I think of them like that, the way someone who has all the equipment bought and ready and has promised to go big-game hunting feels when he starts thinking about the game, you know, the elephants and the lions and all that. Of course, I mean somebody who doesn't like big-game hunting or big game or who doesn't even like shooting. I mean, somebody who just simply doesn't like to think about lions and elephants and other big savage animals and who would rather think about something else. Well, there it is," he said, beginning to smile uneasily under his mustache. "So I have to get out of it by being funny about horses. If I wasn't funny about them I'd have to get up and ride one and I never liked getting anywhere near them. I've climbed up on them for almost twenty years, and I respect them, they stand very high in my opinion, and I think they've got all the qualities the horse authorities claim they have. But I just don't like having much to do with them. I like to watch a good point-to-point race or a steeplechase and have some money on it, but I don't like getting into mix-ups with them. Maybe it's because I'm not really interested in showing them, you know, or anybody I'm the master. I don't like to bully anything into obeying me so that's why I don't like to have to go into their stalls or have too much to do with them. I don't mind this chap coming along behind us here because he's not as arrogant as most, but I wouldn't go out of my way–"

"I met a man last winter," the girl said, his arm through hers as she walked, her eyes watching the ground. "He'd been brought up with them, like me." They went on, arm in arm, silent for a little further and the horse came following on his rein. "At Mrs. Paddington's Wednesday teas in Florence, I met him there," she said after a minute. "He was an Irishman–about twenty or something like that. His people kept hunters and his mother had one of the best seats in Ireland, she was one of the grand women to hounds–you know, he didn't say it to brag but like a joke," she said, looking quickly at the side of her father's face. "As a matter of fact, he couldn't stick hunting. It made him sick. And I knew

I felt that way too, after he'd said it, only I'd never been able to explain it before. He'd gone off from home after a row, I think, or something, but anyway he couldn't stick the kind of hunting county people he'd been born with. He was writing a book about them. He was one of the first writers I ever met," she said.

Arm in arm, step by step they went on together, and the father's eyes slipping sideways saw the tender flesh of her neck, and the ear's lobe pale as coral, and the vulnerable temple with life beating visibly, exquisitely there. He made his tone carefully, casually bright so as not to scare her words off.

"Sounds like an interesting sort of chap," he said, clearing his throat and watching the ground below.

"Candy," said the girl in a quick, soft, eager voice, but she did not turn her head. "I want to go back in September. I don't mean back to Miss Easter's but back to Paris or somewhere else. I want to do something. I have to do something. I can't stay here. I mean, I want to go on studying painting or art or maybe how to be a sculptor and I thought after a while I might be able to make my living and then I wouldn't have to stay all the year here. It's not," she said, not looking up from the road but watching it go steadily beneath their walking feet, "I mean, it hasn't anything to do with not—with not loving you or not loving anyone, but in cities and in other places, you know, there're people all over the world, I mean like that Irishman, saying different things all the time and here nobody hears them saying them and—"

"Nancy," said the father in a tight, small, but brightly casual voice. "I suppose—that is, if it's true I thought you just might like to say it—I suppose it's possible you liked him rather well?"

"Oh, no," she said quickly. "I didn't mean that. I only saw him two or three times after that. He wasn't staying long in Florence. He was on his way to Spain." Arm in arm they walked, watching the ground move back beneath their feet, the road slipping back and away in the shade and the light and the shade from the trees as they walked small and human-voiced and human-limbed under the high fresh springing boughs. "He was going to get over there and fight against Franco, only he couldn't let the Italians hear him say it. Here you wouldn't know about anybody doing anything like that, would you, Candy? Or if you read it in the paper you'd forget about it because you wouldn't have the sound of the person's voice when they said it or how their face looked."

"No," said Candy, holding her arm tight in his. "No. I know."

"So I thought if I could do something, do some kind of work, I mean first learn to do something, like painting, the way you did," she went on, watching the ground go; and Like me, he thought, learn to sit waiting in a room alone, face a blank canvas and a notebook with a sketch or two sketches in it, the brushes clean, the paints ready, the light right, the easel set, and sit there making no mark, and fearing to make any, and sit fearing thought as impotently as act. Learn to sit still in terror before nothing, learning, the way a convict learns by heart the words of his sentence, the emptiness of one's own indecision and the elusiveness of the idiom, the pronunciation, the sound even of one's own purposeless intention. "So I thought if I could go back over there, I mean to Paris or Rome or somewhere in September," she was saying, and he went on in silence: Learn it without ever crying out in protest or bringing down in vengeance, and slowly, weakly, gradually meander to the first drink of consolation and the second, until Drink itself becomes the thing to wait for in the room's and soul's void, not the visitation youth promised of the pure and perfect substance of Art. "I thought if it could be decided now so that I'd know," she was saying, "then I could stick it out here this summer without—"

The road moved slowly, unevenly off behind them through light and shade, shade and shimmering afternoon light, poured slowly back over rut and scarcely covered stone as they walked with their heads down, the same shapely, well-turned flesh and bone, the same drugged dreamy eyes watching it run slowly, endlessly back beneath their feet.

"Yes, that's the way I must have felt," said the father. "Just about your age—almost thirty years ago, maybe about twenty-seven or -eight years back—"

"I could get a room with a family or something or live in a club," the girl said. "Then you wouldn't worry about that part of what was happening to me. You could come over with me, Candy, and find the right courses for me to take, and meet the teachers and find the place for me to live in." She was talking faster now, her breath coming quick, as if the name of the street, the size of the room, the utensils of the art itself would be designated in a minute if she could catch up with where they were. "Candy, you could even find out for me what it is I ought to do," she said, and her mouth trembled.

"Yes," said her father, holding her bare arm tight in the up-bend of his arm, his fingers lying on her wrist. "You'll have to find somebody very good; you mustn't have somebody vague to teach you the things you'll have to learn. You know, bone's there, structure's there," he said brightly, his fingers modeling at her wrist where the pulse beat light and quick in the veins. "The old skeleton's there under the rest; under all the fanciness and vagueness you've got to find out in the end that he's there and how he goes together and how he moves. That's what I never paid enough attention to, Nancy. Perhaps that's why I never made a go of things." He glanced quickly, uneasily at the side of her face, and then away, thinking Perhaps it's too late already, perhaps there is nothing more to conceal from her by now. Ever since she could think for herself, maybe, she's laid in her bed at night knowing what I am better than I've ever known it, seeing me clearer, thinking about the one water-color hanging up in the top-hall and the one in the guest room behind the door, and knowing exactly without anyone saying it to her. Out loud he said in bold shy uneasiness: "You've got to dig right down into things from the start if you want to get anywhere. I tried out too many things, got interested in one phase of a thing—you know, experimented with one thing after another, and sometimes that leads you nowhere. I might have done a lot of things if I'd got hold of something certain at the outset. I might have done some good paintings—"

"Candy, you are a great painter," the girl said gravely.

"Oh, no," he said, looking down at the road and the little twitching smile beginning on his lips. "Oh, no."

For a time they had forgotten the horse, hearing without knowing they heard the slow light clopping of his hoofs behind them, but now the rein tightened on her arm and she stopped and looked back to where the horse stood halted on the road. His head was raised and turned a little to one side, away, and when she said his name he shook it gently, then savagely, in bewilderment. He stood fixed at his rein's length, like a beast who has come to water and will not cross, the forefeet planted in advance of the full glossy breast, the shocked hoofs gripping forward for balance to the earth. He had not started to retreat yet and did not venture to come on, but stood, his legs thrusting wider and wider apart, the neck curved back burnished, voluptuous as a swan's, and the raised head tossing, gently, gently, as if seeking to cast the mask of unfamiliar and desperate confusion off.

"Brigand," said the girl softly, drawing in the rein. "Brigand, you foolish thing, be quiet now, be still."

She had turned to him and now began walking to him, but once the rein had slackened on his mouth he reeled slowly, sickeningly backwards on his heels, the last link with human ascendancy and human corporality withdrawn, leaving him staggering masterless, lost, riderless in the obscure and incommunicable reaches of his pain.

"Look out for him!" the father suddenly cried out. "Get away from him, Nancy!" She saw him make the jump forward, the color ebbed from his face and mouth, and jerk the rein from her hand, and saw the horse whirl in panic and totter towards the ditch and trees and falter, as if sensing not seeing danger there, and stop quivering on the brink. "Get away from behind him! He may start kicking, Nancy!" Candy called out. "He's had a stroke! Look out for him! He's going to fall!"

"Hush," she said savagely. "Hush, oh, hush," to man and beast and to the terror that palsied their bones. She was at the horse's head again, taking the man's clutched trembling fingers from the leather and drawing the rein's length from his hand. "Hush, now stop, now listen to me," she said, and at the sound of her voice the horse's head veered awkwardly, but meek, despairing, towards her, the ears quivering antennae-vulnerable, the raised face defeated, directionless, blind, mute. "Hush now," she said, "hush now," standing bare-armed, bare-headed between the man's and the horse's terror of each other and the terror of what mystery, violent, powerful, unstayed, had struck like paralysis with a hand numb as stone and might lift again and strike before them. "Hush now," she said, and she brought the horse's head slowly down and, talking, slipped her gloved fingers under the browband and the forelock's length of straight black hair. The gloved leather came away wet, darkened as if from the touch of blood, and the girl stood looking at it. "Sweat," she said, half-aloud, staring at her hand. "He hasn't been running and still sweating like that. . . ."

"Nancy," said the father, running his tongue along his lip. "Nancy, for God's sake, let him go."

"He's got himself into a fever, so he has, my lamb, my lamb," she said, holding his soft mouth and his head firm in the reins caught underneath his chin. "He's been worrying and worrying himself about worms or thinking about his family tree," she said, stroking the bony, prow-like nasal peak, thinking In a moment Candy may start shouting again or the thing that has struck once strike harder like a crop splitting skull and fiber across the frontal bone. "He's been eating too much, my horse has, and given himself the mad and sleepy staggers, so he has. He's got himself into a fit and he'd like a drink of water, that's what he'd like," she went on saying, thinking I must go on talking so that there's no time for anything else and no place for any other sound, I must go on in this voice because this is the voice that says to him, "So now we'll just go quietly along home because nothing has happened to my big foolish man, we'll just give him some salt and a bucket of warm water to soothe him and we'll rub his belly for him and rub him down with a straw wisp—"

"Nancy," said the father, saying it quietly now, not in a voice from which fear had gone but into which more awe than fear had come. "Look at him closely, Nancy," he said, half whispering it. He was fumbling in his pocket for something and the girl looked away from him, wondering, and up at the horse's head again. Holding him under the quivering soft lip, she looked at the bony brow with the moist forelock on it and the searching, flicking ears; looked at the hollows, throbbing and pit-like, above the eyes, and lingered on the fixed brown brilliant eyes themselves before descending the face's sharp decline to the concave nostrils, dilated, convulsed now with pain. "Look at his eyes, Nancy," Candy said, having found the matchbox and holding it in his hand, his fingers shaking still as he drew the frail match-stem along the box's side and cupped the flame against the air's movement underneath the trees. When he lifted his arm the horse gave no sign, but as the match rose higher in her father's hand, the girl began talking again in precaution, murmuring to him in the ceaseless, gentle, assuaging voice that said:

"So his mother must just take him back to his stable and cool him off and put straw under his rug for him and rub him clean and dry and give him . . ."

"Watch him," said Candy softly, and now the match's flame, made puny by the sun's light through the leaves but steadily burning, came level with the horse's eye and halted and he made no sign. "He can't see it," the father said, awe-stricken, scarcely breathing. "He doesn't even know it's there."

3

"I know we had quite a time of it," the mother was saying, sitting with her knees spread wide so that the rain would dry from her tweed skirt; talking to them while she smoked the cigarette, but half-musingly, only part given to this communication with other beings and part to her own high scrupulous contriving as she looked into the fire on the hearth. "We had one surprise after another from the moment we set foot on shore. In the first place, nobody'd given us any idea we were going to be sewed up in our clothes—"

"Ha, ha," sounded the vet's uneasy laughter, and perhaps because he caught sight of his boots below him on the rug thick with stable and road muck although he had cleaned them off on the mat outside the door, he shifted in cramped, miserable unease on the edge of the ancient shabbily upholstered chair. "Well, I should think that would have been a bit of a shock," he said, and the pale light-lashed eyes sought rather desperately for comfort around the room.

"I must say, I shan't forget it as long as I live," said Mrs. Lombe. She looked up from her contemplation of this other, this unspoken thing, and went on talking lightly of their trip, some or all of which the vet must have heard at other times, in box or paddock, or seated like this in this room. "They packed our feet and legs up in straw the very first thing," she said, "and then this garment arrangement we each of us had to put on was pulled up over the three layers of wool around our bodies and arms—" She went on making the gestures, the mouth open in speech, the words coming quickly, almost merrily; only when she looked up at her husband's and her daughter's faces did it whet to irritation in the strained, impatient eyes. This is the way to meet it, the limbs at ease in the wool skirt and the casual, ordinary cigarette and the conversational manner might have been saying: if you have to face the truth for once in your lives, accept it like this with the chin up and all flags flying from the mast; don't sit there making a tragedy of it. But the eyes ringed deep with a yearning implacable as intolerance knew and had for a long time bitterly and irritably known the uselessness of asking this or anything in reason of them. There they sat on the sofa, a little back, father and daughter facing across the rug's and the table's interval straight at the fire without seeming to see it or seeming to hear what was said. "And then they sewed us right up inside of all this," she went on saying to the vet, the blond raw-skinned young man who sat with his arms placed on his knees and his head extended over his big-wristed, uneasily clasped hands. "Stitched us up for three weeks," she said with a snort of amusement at their own audacity. "Three weeks of it! I tell you, it was an experience to have had."

"Good heavens, three weeks!" the vet echoed in a voice gone high and unbecoming in this attempt at social grace. He glanced in hope towards Mr. and Miss Lombe to see if they were joining in at last, but having seen their faces again he quickly looked away. He drew one hand slowly over the light stubble on his clefted buckling chin and swallowed, thinking now as he had been thinking without interruption that it wasn't to hear stories about where the family had been one spring that he'd come, but to see the hunter and that he'd seen it and he'd told them and the act to be performed was still there undone. But here they sat with the rain falling down outside, talking of Finland or sitting in silence, and coming no nearer to it.

"Of course, we'd taken all sorts of jackets and warm things up there but we were told to leave them where they were. They told us there wasn't any sense in us taking them out of our boxes, but just to leave them there at the hotel the way they were until we got back." She repeated the word "hotel" in sudden derision, jerking her head up from the fire again and giving the lot of them the same queer, anxious, admonishing look. "Hotel, if you please," she said. "It was a lamentable place, as you can imagine, and even for that part of the world it was just about as bad as anything could be. But that's what they called it, for the sake of appearances, I suppose, and that's where we left all our belongings, and I must say I wondered. Mr. Lombe and I had quite a laugh over it," she said and she dropped her cigarette into the fire and struck the ashes from her skirt. "We had no idea if we'd ever see any of our things again, but apparently that was the way it had to be done. Fortunately for us, there were some other English people in the party and they said they'd heard from friends who'd been out to Finland that it was always done like that. And then in the morning there was another shock in store for me," she went on. "They produced the reindeer and I really had no idea, judging from pictures and photographs where one pays more or less attention, you know, I simply hadn't imagined for a moment that a reindeer would be just about the size of a good-sized dane. I'd always thought of them as quite imposing-looking animals, something rather in the cattle line, of course, not so big as a horse," she said, and then she stopped, leaving the word suddenly there, unexpectedly bleak and alone. For an instant she could not look at any one of them but reached out for the poker's handle and took it and thrust it toward the steadily burning wood. Sitting with her knees spread in her skirt and her face turned from them, she struck the log smartly apart and the vet at least saw from his chair the sparks shower across the deep dead ash in the hearth and the chips of charred wood fall forward, smoking, on the stone. Now at the far end of the room the wind and rain drove hard against the windows, and refusing to think That horse, that crazy hunter is standing out there in the stable, stone-blind, incurable, bat-blind, Mrs. Lombe took up from where it had lapsed her own strained, almost merry locution of the other story. "Then they told us, once we'd got over that shock, that we were to lie flat down on the sleds, each one on his own individual sled, you understand, right behind the reindeer's heels." She hung the poker upright in its place again and with the side of one brogue pushed a charred bit of wood back where it belonged. "We each of us had our own separate sleds and reindeers, you see, and when they got us stretched out like that, more like Egyptian mummies than humans by that time as a matter of fact, they started to tuck us in! I kept looking at Mr. Lombe and wondering how he was going to like it!" Having achieved a certain jocularity again, she could look up at the vet and look at Candy Lombe (perhaps at him because in his fear of the heels and hoofs and the power of beasts she had one on him), but not quite yet at the girl's grave, pale, set face. "I told him I'd heard in Russia you landed the other way 'round, that is with your head to the front, guiding the thing with some kind of contraption with your hands, and your face practically under the reindeer's back heels, but that didn't seem to reassure Mr. Lombe, and I must say there were moments when I wondered how it was all going to turn out. As long as we trotted along on the flat it was clear enough sailing, but when we'd start off down those slopes at the pace they kept up, the sleds would begin going faster than the reindeer did, and that had its drawbacks! But the reindeer were beautifully trained and I must say they managed very cleverly. As soon as they felt you outstripping them from behind, they'd jump to one side of the track, skip into the snow at the side to keep you from running right under their heels. It was quite a lark, I thought," she said. "We were four days and nights on the way, sleeping right out in the snow, and we were told that some years at the roundup the wild deer stampeded. They assured us that nobody, that is, no foreigners had ever come to any harm, but the more I thought about it during that drive, the more relieved I was I hadn't taken my daughter with me." And now, having spoken the word daughter, having avowed in some distorted mimicry of declaration I care, I care! she could raise her head and look over the piece of rug and across the gate-legged table on which the Dresden dancers, the woman in a milk-white petticoat, several layers of china thick and edged with lace, on which hung flowered paniers, and the man in blue silk tails danced in formal motionless precision; looked past the vet's clasped raw uneasy hands, his arms and elbows planted on his breeches' knees, his lowered pale-haired head, to where the girl sat in her dark skirt and jersey on the sofa. There the mother's halted look pressed urgently, compellingly, and finally faded to grievousness on her. "She was about fourteen then, and those nights out in the cold, quite an experience for her of course but not quite, you know, just a bit on the rigorous side for a growing and not very robust girl. In fact, I'm not so sure any of the women liked it as much as they said they did. I loved it, but there were two Frenchwomen among us and I'm sure they must have found it very different from what they were accustomed to, their hairdressing shops and café life and everything like that."

The two others, the father and daughter, sat on the sofa motionless still; still sitting a little apart from each other, seeming to hear nothing, see nothing, like people waiting in a hospital's or prison's halls without hope but in numb unrecalcitrant endurance for the verdict to be given. When I got him into the stable last evening, the girl was repeating to herself, saying it slowly and carefully over and over as if this precision had been exacted by a judge and jury or by the gravity of life or death, I thought I must start right off doing everything for him exactly the way it's always been done so he won't think the thing that's happened to him is going to make him any different. I thought, even if he's lost the power to see, and now the word constricted like a knot jerked tighter in her: blind, gone blind, stone-blind. (Stick to the story, please, said the cold hard silent core of listening in rebuke. Tell us what actually took place, don't tell us what you thought.) I got him into his box, she went on looking straight before her across the room, and I began grooming him right away. I didn't want him to suspect yet there was anything the matter, I mean, I thought if I led him home like that, talking to him, and not riding him, he'd see it wasn't the world and the world's paraphernalia that had been wiped out or had been altered even but something as temporary and personal as a toothache that had occurred. (Very well, said the Court, bringing its mallet impatiently down. Get on with it without any dramatization, please.) I started to brush and comb him hard, the girl went on, and then when I saw the brush was annoying him because the prickles were worn down, I asked Apby for another and he handed me a new one over the gate. Apby was standing there watching me all the time I was doing Brigand down, and I did it thoroughly, it took me an hour to do it. There's a sign hanging up in the stable, my mother had it printed and put up there, and it says, "No one can groom a horse without perspiring over it," and by half an hour I was hot and I stopped and took my handkerchief out and wiped my face dry. I knew when you come into the stable in the morning after the grooming's been done you pass your hand through the coat the reverse way to see if it's been properly done, and if you see the gray line there near the hairs' roots you make the groom start his work over again, and I know Brigand was as clean as anything when I was through. After that I thought I'd never let anyone else ever, as long as I was alive and he was alive, I'd never let anyone put a hand on him again. (Please keep to the facts, said the judge or the jury's silence in jobation to her. The Court cannot admit as evidence the passage of thought, however sentimental its trend, through your mind or that of any witness.) So then I told Apby to bring me the warm water, she said, looking straight ahead. I knew I had to sponge Brigand's eyes out because if I avoided doing that, that would be the worst thing. Maybe he'd just been waiting to see if I would do it and if I would touch his eyes, and so I did it and while I did it I spoke to him in a natural tone of voice and I could see the film that was coming over his eyes now, a sort of milkiness blurring them all over, but I went right on sponging out his nostrils and then I did his dock and washed his feet. While I was drying the heel of one forefoot, he reeled a little as if he had lost his balance and he trod back on me, catching my shoe underneath his hoof. I didn't make a sound, I swear I didn't, because I thought it would be the end of him if he thought that having lost the power to see had done this other thing to him too, I mean, had crippled and disabled his legs under him or taken his sense of gravitation from him. I didn't want him to—(Unless you are willing to testify in the manner which the Court has specified, said the controlled cold accents of authority, the evidence you have given will be struck from the records as irrelevant.) Then I brushed the mane and tail, the girl repeated slowly and carefully, and took the burrs out, separating as nearly as I could each hair in his mane and bidding him keep his head low which he did. After laying the mane with water, I brushed the tail out lock by lock from the roots, talking to him about it. I decided to wash his tail at the seven o'clock grooming in the morning, that is this morning, and pick his feet out outside the stable in the sun. But this morning it began raining early, so I did not do this. Last evening then, about half-past six it was, I put his feed down myself for him. I gave him three pounds of corn and a bit over a pound of chop, and because of what had happened to him I gave him a linseed mash. I put his food on the ground for him, just the way he always had it. Apby said it would be better maybe to put his rations up in a manger or hayrack where he could find them easier, and he said he'd bring the portable rack in, but I wouldn't have it. Our horses have always eaten from the ground the way they would if they were turned out to grass and I said I was going to feed him from the ground so he'd go on thinking it couldn't be as bad as he'd thought at first or else everything wouldn't be going on exactly the same. My father had put the call in to Pellton for the veterinary-surgeon to come and I waited in the stable to see if Brigand was going to eat, and he snuffed around for a bit and after I'd talked to him he put his head down to where the food was because he knew it had always been there although now he was blind, do you understand, he was stone-blind, he couldn't see it– (Very well, said the unmoved, the untouched silence, that will be all, Miss Lombe, that will do.) But I have to tell you this! the girl cried out, and she jumped up quickly from the sofa with one hand stretched out as if in the act of arresting the irrevocable closing of a door. Wait! she cried out. Wait! You have to listen!

"I'm not going to let them destroy him. I'm not going to let anybody destroy him," she said out loud, and she stood looking around the room, bewildered now that she was on her feet and speaking: looking in fumbling surprise at her mother sitting by the fire with her face raised in offense, and at the vet jerking on the chair's edge, his head lowered as he watched the filth caking dry on the carpet under his shoes. She did not turn to look at Candy sitting behind her on the sofa now, but only at the forces mustered there against them, these two other faces and two bodies, and haltingly, separately, at the different pieces of furniture, the logs burning in the fire, the Dresden figures dancing, as if seeing for the first time what they were. "I don't believe it's something incurable," she said, the heavy, subtly glazed eyes moving off from the faces to object after object, and groping, object by object, as if through darkness, back to the faces again. "Nobody can make me believe you can't cure it if you take the care and trouble."

"There's nothing to stop us from having an opinion down from London," the vet began saying without raising his head. He sat there, bowed forward over his soiled pin-striped riding-breeches, with his arms resting on the cloth drawn tight across his legs. While he talked he wove his blunt big fingers in and out, the knuckles rubbing one against the other, and looked down as if in shame at the mud-splattered calves of his tan leather gaiters. "I'd be the first one to say hold off until we get another opinion. I say it's a clear and simple retinitis, come on maybe after influenza although I'd never have judged him convalescent when Mr. Lombe brought him in two months ago. It's the retina worked loose and the sight goes like that, sudden, and if you don't know to the contrary the history of eye-weakness may go right back through his blood. But I say have another opinion in and that would ease it up all 'round for us. Destroying a horse like that isn't anybody's Bank Holiday," he said.

"Ah," said Mrs. Lombe patiently, evenly, "there it is." She did not look at the vet but into the fire's depths for resolution, watching with calm, man-like resignation the uncertainly flickering flame; but still it was to the vet, the only other of sanity's disciples in the room, she spoke. "In-breeding may very well come to be the tragedy of the country before we know it," she said. "Look at our best dogs now, flying off the mouth with hysteria because of being in-bred generation after generation. They say you're safe if you put a mother to her son or a father to his daughter, but to keep off in-breeding from own brothers and sisters or even first cousins. But where do general rules ever get you? Here's this hunter out there with a history of eye-weakness, a double history if you look at his in-breeding, and nobody," she said but she did not look at her husband, "would have touched him with a yardstick if they'd taken the trouble to run his pedigree out and had him up to pass the vet. I'm not advocating the general importation of foreign dogs or foreign sires, but a great deal of good might be done by bringing in fresh blood pretty freely from the Dominions." Sit down, Nan, you look a fool standing up there, she did not say out loud, but the girl looked in sudden numb bewilderment from side to side a moment and then sat hesitatingly down. At once and for the first time turning and looking at her face, the father reached out and took his daughter's hand. "I think there should decidedly be a feeling of patriotism brought into it," the mother said, and now the sight of them sitting so hand in hand, drawn closer to each other on the sofa but sitting as invulnerable and grave as statues or wax figures roused her to hot, inexplicable fury. She felt the heat flaming in her face and she pushed back in irritation from the fire, thinking that words like patriotism, and thoroughbred, and blood—a horse's good quick blood—should flay them if there were any natural feeling in them. "This country is the home of the thoroughbred, my father used to say," she said, looking towards the vet's stooped horseman's shoulders and his warped strong horseman's legs in the puttees. "You probably know of him by reputation, you may have heard of Major Husen around Chelton," she said, "although he was before your time. I've often wondered if a man not English born and bred can have any gift or sense for horses." She did not look towards her husband but at the vet still who raised his head uncertainly and looked at her and parted his lips and did not speak but swallowed, the skin of his throat permanently and brightly flushed and covered with stubble as white as a sow's. "Major Husen—your grandfather, Nan," she added in stern arrogative rebuke, "he fought year after year against the exporting of our good classic blood, fought it tooth and nail, in season and out, until he was seventy-odd. He'd go up regularly to the sales and try to keep our classic winners on this side of the water by any means he could, and a dozen or more times he did it. On winter nights at home, he spent his time going through the Stud-book until he as good as knew the whole thing by heart. He knew them as well as if they were horses out of his own stables, those leading sires and the sound mares who shouldn't, for the country's sake, be lost to foreign studs." She shifted around completely from the fire, her knees spread still, and looked at them, the father and the daughter, with proud, bold, but hopelessly defeated eyes. "He kept Navan Flyer from going to the Argentine one year, and the next he kept Phronella from being lost to Germany. He wasn't afraid to stand up there and tell them what he thought!" she said, the proudly and pathetically lifted head and the tongue in her mouth scoring them unsparingly for what was weakness and womanliness far worse than sentiment that kept them sitting silent on the sofa, holding hands. "He brought Peacemaker home himself for his own stud, and the speech he made at the sales was printed everywhere. 'Tempting offers, especially from foreigners,' " she quoted him with the exact testy and gallant flavor of disvaluation for the foreigner's name, " 'must naturally seem difficult to refuse, but thank God there is one Englishman at least of patriotic sentiment among you, and thank God one Englishman's determination is enough to keep a good horse on its native sod!' "

(One summer, maybe it was the time Candy came home drunk after buying the horned cattle when he was supposed to have bought the Galloways or the Red Polls, I was upstairs in bed, maybe I was ten or eleven then, and Candy went out from down below and laid down on the lawn in the dark. That was the first time I climbed out the window and crossed the veranda roof and slid down the drainpipe, and the stars were out but it was dark and I couldn't see well, but I knew he was lying there near the hedge, perhaps because other times, earlier, months back or years back, I knew he'd laid out there even if I'd never seen him; perhaps in my sleep I'd heard him year after year when he was drunk open the downstairs door and go out and then remembered afterwards, like in a dream, the times he'd done it. I had no slippers or anything but my nightgown on and I kept out of the window's lights lying yellow on the lawn and ran over the gravel and the grass to where he was stretched on his back near the hedge, rolling a little from side to side with his hands over his face and moaning. Mother was sitting inside the house, I know she was sitting inside and knitting although I didn't see her, and the wireless was playing, and perhaps Candy didn't see me there but anyway he knew someone was sitting near him on the grass and he began saying in a low crying voice: "I want my wife. I want my real wife. I want my young little wife to come out and take care of me and save me from what I am. I want her now, my poor thin dying little wife, to start walking up the mountains with me the way she did and not be able to get any further and have to sit down and have to lie down on the pine-needles with me. I want her, I want her," the voice maybe she herself had never heard crying and moaning into his hands. "Out there dying young and living in a house with balconies built in the sun for the dying," he said not to me but to anybody who was sitting there on the cold grass in the dark beside him. "They'd built a café-bar across the road where the dying could get to it easy; before you were dead, you could get down the hall and cross over the road if nobody saw you and get up on a stool if you had enough strength left to do it, and get a drink down or a couple of drinks so later that night you wouldn't meet death too sober." He began shaking with crying now, his shoulders and his raised arms and his body shaking, and his face covered over tight with his hands as he rolled around on the grass. "I used to sit waiting for her there," he said in a moment, "watching the bed on the balcony on the other side of the road for her to be lying on it, and watching the café door for her to come in, and watching the snow on the mountains all summer, waiting and watching like a crazy man for her, my poor little girl, my poor dead dying young wife."

This was the story I had never heard before and I sat shaking with cold in my nightdress and listening to it, holding my teeth tight in my mouth and shaking because now I knew I wasn't anything to him; there'd been this woman once, this girl, this other wife and none of us knew about her, and now he was drunk he was taking the skeleton out of her bed and out of her grave and hanging these rags of memory on her. I wasn't his child any more because I hadn't been hers, I was nobody, sharing nothing with them, I was just anybody sitting there not far off in the dark for him to say it over and over to. When I thought of her, I set my teeth in the side of my hand to stop their shaking, crying half for her and the other half for what I'd once thought I was to him before I knew about her. "What are you crying for?" he said in a minute, and he had taken his hands away from his face now and was looking towards me although he couldn't have seen me in the dark, only the blurred white nightdress and my knees drawn up and my arms held tight around them. "You haven't anything to cry for. You haven't lost anything," he said, and I said, yes, I've lost something, holding my teeth clenched and not making any sound, I lost something I thought I had. He said the story over and over until I could have repeated it without changing a word or written it down exactly in a copy book, even then that first night I heard it knowing how he must have looked coming up the mountain road that August with his sketch box, and how she looked, the thin young woman standing on the balcony of the sanatorium built there for the ill seeing him for the first time and letting a small bright green feather from a boa or a feather-duster blow down because she wanted him to look up and smile. I sat in my nightgown crying, setting my teeth in the side of my hand and crying in the darkness for her beauty and her affliction and her death.

Now he lay without moving, saying the rest of it to me, and for a long time I couldn't understand. "I lost her," he said. "You never knew her young and ill. You knew somebody who came a long time after that." There were the five or six years in between after he'd married her and after he'd stopped painting the pictures and instead took her from one high place to another and into sanatoriums and out; until I began seeing she hadn't died, she couldn't have died because they cured her: the money she had, a lot of money from her father who'd bred horses, or else marrying for love, or else giving birth to the child who sat listening in the dark curing her for life so that she could take it up where her father had left off and go on breeding horses on the land. And Candy turned over on his face again and lay with the side of it against the grass. "Once in a while," he went on saying, his speech thick from the drink still, "just once in a while when she wakes up in the morning or sometimes when she's reading alone in a room, there's something left, something about her neck or her wrist or the way her hair grows, but otherwise she might just as well have died. Can you understand what I'm saying?" he said, his voice drifting off to sleep or stupor in the darkness. "Can you understand what I'm trying to say? If she hadn't wanted to come back here and live in this country there might never have been the two of them, I mean the one I knew first and the one you didn't, and the other one sitting inside the house now. Sometimes when I come home and see her, when I've had something to drink or the light's not good I see my dead young wife sitting there in the room and I walk quietly so I won't frighten her off and I put my arms around her before she has time to turn around and start talking to me, and before I have to learn it again," he said, the words coming slowly across the grass as the drunken, the flagging, drugged lament drifted hypnotically now towards sleep. "I've learned it over and over and I don't want to have to learn it any more, that there isn't any youth and age, there's only life and death," he said.)

Now he looked up from the sofa at them, looked brightly and pleasantly at his wife beyond the Dresden figures on the table, and at the vet whose lowered face watched in blank bewitchment the slow foul havoc wreaked on the carpet by his shoes. Candy Lombe might have been just the bright, fresh-skinned and well-dressed little man sitting holding to his daughter's hand still, his nose short, pretty and narrow at the nostrils, the mouth soft under the just beginning to lighten trim mustache: except for the eyes shaped long to the temples and uncannily weighted with the nameless and unarticulated dream.

"Well, now the thing is we must all try to be as reasonable as we can about this," he said, looking brightly, almost socially at his wife. It might be he had met her at tea just that day and was putting his best foot forward. "Naturally little Nancy here wants to have everything possible done before we come to a definite decision about Brigand. I think Penson's suggestion about—"

"But a blind horse, a horse incurably blind," the mother began, but now as if instead of looking across the Dresden china dancers at her Candy had spoken her name, or spoken a particular name which they had used a long time ago and in another country and in its deepest signification, she ceased speaking.

"How would you like it!" the girl suddenly cried out. "What would you feel like if sometime when you were ill they'd wanted to—" She sat on the sofa, not looking at anyone but savagely down at the dark stuff of her skirt, her face white, her teeth biting the wild shuddering sound of crying in. "What if just because you couldn't see any more, or couldn't eat any more, or—or—if you hadn't the strength any more to swim—or climb a mountain without—without losing your breath and having—having to stop and sit down—what if—"

"Hush, Nancy," said Candy softly. "Hush, Nancy," holding to the stiff relentless hand.

"What if you were ill once and nobody—nobody happened to come along and take care of you," the strained gulping voice went on, "just said 'put a bullet through where the brains are,' how would you like dying, how would anybody like dying when they're young and not ready for it yet! When you were ill and young sometime, maybe you wouldn't have been ready," she said, with the tears beginning to come down her face but still not looking at anyone, "just because older people said you were incurable and it was better to shoot you, you wouldn't have wanted it just because people who didn't care any more said it was the kindest—"

"Hush, Nancy, hush," said Candy, stroking her hand.

The vet stood up now and cleared his throat and took his watch from his waistcoat pocket and looked at its face, then slipped it back again. "If you decide on wanting me to ring up London," he said, buttoning his jacket over with his big, blunt, fumbling fingers, and Mrs. Lombe said:

"You've been extraordinarily patient with us, Mr. Penson. We'll let you know what decision we—" She was standing now, tall and soft, the eyes a little haggard on him. "I don't suppose you'd know what the fee of a London vet might be for running down?" she asked him.

4

At the end of the week the two things came: the vet called down from London and from London as well the letter from the Irishman. After all these months the letter came saying he was back from Spain, ten days back with a wound in his arm, and he would like to see her but he didn't know if the address would do still or if she had said Nancy Lombe or Nellie that afternoon. "You said at Mrs. Paddington's in Florence you might be back this summer, so I'm taking the chance that you'll remember me," he wrote, and Miss N. Lombe across the envelope outside in a shy quick nervous hand. The letter was folded in her jersey pocket, doubled over and the corners held tight and sharp in her fingers when they followed the London vet out and down the drive, the gravel fresh, wet underfoot where the rain had been that morning, holding onto it as if the mere fact of its paper inflexibility would be enough to hold to no matter what was said. The mother and the London vet walked slightly in advance and Candy was in the house still, having called through the bathroom door: "Nancy, your old pater's still at his ablutions," his voice amplified by the depth of water in the tub and the echoing tiles sounding wondrously strong and clear. "I'll be along when I'm done," he said, and the sound of water gushed into space. He did not say aloud or articulate it even to his own soft naked body bending into the bath: I will not walk down that road and into the stable and hear it, but will evade it here muffled in shaving lather as fragrant as the springtime. He did not say: I am afraid to go.

The London vet was no longer the country thing but had become a prosperous, aging man like the accepted figure of capitalism in a political cartoon: there were the well-packed jowls and the paunch and the backs of the hairy, dimpled hands. He went at once into the hunter's stall, the breath ticking in congestion through his nose, and there he forced the lids up from the eyes, first one lusterless blank pearl bulging an instant between his thumbs and then the other while the horse's head lifted sightlessly and warily away. The yellow fall of sunny misty heat poured through the box's window onto the vet's graying hair and onto his spectacles' glass while he said, not to the horse's concepts or perceptions but still in his intuitive hearing: "The poor chap will have to be put down." He looked into the hunter's set milky eye and said the local man could do the trick as he himself had not come prepared to do it. And the mother standing on the oaten bedding said they had promised to give the owner time to decide, they had promised to wait a little. "My daughter," she said of the girl standing out of sight behind him and behind the horse holding to the letter in her pocket and hearing the man's breath clogging in his nose, the thing continuing as they had read of it in textbooks: if there was any doubt in the marksman's mind or if it was to be done by a novice, a line should be drawn in chalk on the horse's forehead from the right ear to the center and from the left ear to the center and a crossline drawn down where they conjoined. "I don't see why it has to be done, I don't see why," the girl said, her voice coming suddenly hoarse and tragic and young out of the stable's shadow.

The vet did not quite turn around to see her when he said the place to aim for and hit was the exact intersection of the chalk lines, the unmistakable center of the frontal bone between the eyes. "No," the girl said, this time only half aloud. "No." She thought This is the illusion and the real time is night, and the condition not waking protest because I am lying in bed asleep with this letter held under the pillow in my hand. The vet is not breathing like that through his nose, but it is my own breathing. I am lying in bed asleep and these are the monsters of childhood: the reptile disguised as authority in dark blue wool with dandruff on his shoulders, the shape my mother has taken now the monument erected to all childhood fear. I am saying "no, no, no" in my sleep and they cannot hear me. The smell of hay and horse is memory and the light is cool and blurred like just-remembered light while the tide of breathing rises and ebbs, rises and ebbs with the strange deep machinations of the heart in sleep. If you cannot give sight to a horse, not only to this horse but any horse, to the finest grandest pedigreed champion of them all, you hand it death like a third eye through the forelock, you give it its peep at paradise through one small black-lipped hole. You do this for the horse, not for the owner nor for the world, but for the bony, mysteriously limbed and soft-mouthed beast who is stumbling in silent panic from darkness to darkness. You shatter his brow at one stroke for him the way a strong man's fist shatters the frail panels of a door to let in the light, and the constant dream of nothing in his inconstant world of rippling skin, twitching shoulder, flicking ear splinters like glass splintering loud at night. You are awake, Brigand, toss your mane. The dream of blindness has ceased, darling. You are no longer sightless, you are dead. "No!" she cried out, putting her knuckles to her teeth. "No! They won't do it! I won't let them do it!"

She ran panting, gasping, not crying yet, out the stable door and up the drying, softly steaming gravel to the house. Behind her the talk went on, armed now with a capable relentless pity: get grooms, the local vet, the huntsman to tell her their experiences with horses gone blind or crippled horses, get her a book on it that will give her the proper viewpoint. If it's her horse, then let the matter go a day or two until she's understood the thing in and out: the mercy first and then the necessity of it. Tell her you can't teach a horse to accept blindness because his world is sight, and in a while she'll come around all right, she'll see the humaneness in doing it as soon as it can be done. Ah, that she'll have to do for all our sakes; we're not a hospital here for the maimed and we need the place for the work I'm trying to get on with against odds. Against God, almost, but anyway against man who was still locked behind the bathroom door and whistling.

"Just coming!" he called out when the girl struck the door with her hand. "Just coming, Nancy!"

She leaned in despair on it in the instant before he opened it to her: first hearing the whistling cease, and then the key turn, and then she saw him there, his lips puckered up to begin the tune again but his eyes through the bathroom's haze recoiling from disaster into their own queer dream-drugged blue. His hands were lifted to smooth the bay rum onto his hair, the sleeves of toweling slipping back on his full womanish arms to the dimpled elbows, and she flung herself wild and crying against him.

"They'll do it if you don't stop them! They're going to do it if you don't stop them!"

The tears stopped suddenly at the sound of her own voice saying what was true. But it was only for a little while she believed strength could be given or taken, given by Candy or any man, or taken from the Irishman's letter. She began seeing how it was now as a savage might have seen it and made a picture of it with berry stains, or some coloring as primitive, or stitched it toughly in beads or thread on cloth: the small helpless lone island of the self out of voice's call or swimmer's reach lying among the scattered inaccessible islands of those other selves. In the three nights that came after with the horse still living and the Irishman written to, she saw that unpeopled landscape and the vast waters washing forever unspanned between the separate islands, and she touched the bones in bed with her, the bones of the shoulder, the arm, the hand, and the thigh's bones lying tenacious in her flesh, and the skull's inexorability underneath the hair. If there is any strength it is in these, it is here, not in running fast to Candy for help or in writing Dear Mr. Sheehan: It was jolly nice to have a letter from you and I hope you're wound is getting on well. I'm feeling very bad because the London vet we called down here says they'll have to destroy my horse. My father said to suggest for you to come down here one afternoon and he would be glad to meet you at the station. I know you said you knew horses, so maybe . . . lying awake at night in bed and saying over again these words that had been written down on paper and would be read on paper, she thought of the horse's unwritten, unrecorded, uncommitted world of sight and hearing, touch and smell, the horse's moving world of myriad credulous sensation, and lying so night after night the line came clearer through sleeplessness and through the room's dark until its clarity became the impulse to get up and walk with bare feet to the open window and repeat it aloud: "The horse is frightened by the bush because the bush unexpectedly turns and waves a branch."

She put her jersey on but she could not find her slippers at once in the darkness so she climbed over the windowledge without them and crossed the veranda roof and slid down the drainpipe with the cotton nightdress drawn tight between her legs. It was warm, for once here in England Italian-warm, even the grass warm under her feet as she crossed the corner of the lawn. Because of the bite of the gravel she kept to the grass and beds, going quickly towards the stable, and at the drive's curve she left the soft clipped border and ran painfully and rapidly across. No man, no woman, no girl, no Irishman, no doctor, vet, science, no kind of human knowledge can save him or give his sight back to him, she thought shouldering the door aside; he'll stand there shaking with palsy and funk in that state of incurable blindness and incurable terror until they put him down. She walked barefoot across the stable floor to where he was, and opened the door of his stall in the dark and spoke his name to him. "Brigand," she said out loud, and without seeing it she felt the shudder of fear and anguish that washed down him but he did not shift, perhaps not knowing whether to shift to right or left to let her by. There was no light, only the smell of horse and the taste of sweet clean-kept horse in the air, and she heard his stablemate rousing and moving in her stall beyond. So you'll stand there day after night, night after day, not knowing one from the other until your time's up, she said. She could feel him strong as stone but living as she shoved past him in the stall. You'll stand here, what's in you rearing for death and shaking with fright unless you listen to me. She drew his head down in the curve of her arm, firmly, almost without tenderness. Let the bush unexpectedly turn and touch your flank so you'll get the slap of its leaves like that without sight when the bush turns, she tried saying, and then she began it again: Your eyes, my friend, have clotted in your head. However, the road still flows away under the feet, the fence still bucks under you when you gather up your legs to rise, the house still pivots in the garden showing first one angle and then the other to you, the hedges have not ceased to pour by like water, the trees have never stopped waltzing, the clouds careening. It is you, my steed, who must comprehend motion without sight's limitations as long as we have dispensed with sight. Let the bush slap you full in the face and you will acknowledge its presence the same way as you did when you saw it unexpectedly turn and wave a branch.

The first night she took him out onto the drive only, leading him slowly by the head-rope through the dark. There were no stars, no wind, and the evergreens were a little wet still from the day's rain as they passed under, and the leaves of the wayfaring tree and the laurel brushed light and wet across their faces. It was after one o'clock, perhaps just on two but no bells in the village below, as there would have been in Italy, to say it, and the girl walked near him, her shoulder moving against the hunter's shoulder as they walked. She said Next time I'll wear slippers, damn it, stepping in pain on the gravel, and now with the great unseeing and unseen beast moving diffidently beside her she began the scheming: "She said they'd let me have two weeks. Because of Candy, she gave me the two weeks. I'll listen to Penson explaining it over again, and I'll hear the grooms out, and I'll read the book. But she's given me two weeks to prepare for death. That's always that. In a fortnight anything can happen."

The third night she put the bit between his teeth and the bridle on him, and on the fourth she took him down past the lower edge of the paddocks and along the path by the stream. Here the way was narrow and they went single file, the girl ahead and the horse coming after on his rein, and where the bank lowered she led him towards the water, saying aloud: "If I know this place in the dark without being able to see it any more than you can, you can believe in it too, you can reconstruct the picture out of chaos and memory's ruins," but the horse stood back, the strong, the monstrously night-magnified body halted and the head raised in bewildered innocence. "Come," she said, "come," and now the sudden jerk as she kicked her slippers off did not startle him as it had the night before when they came to grass. "Come, my man, come," she said, and she gathered the reins up beneath the quivering pendent lip. She stooped, holding him still, and in one hand raised a palmful of water to his nostrils and wet his mouth. "Smell it," she said, "smell water," and now the forefoot advanced with her, and now the other, until the stream washed across his hoofs. She paused with him in the running water, feet on the slippery submerged stones, and he stretched his neck out and then brought his head down, as the rein slackened, to the smell and murmur and the touch of water, and she heard him begin to drink. She put her hand under his cheek and felt the windpipe pull and tauten, and felt in his throat the strong passage of the water, irresistibly and powerfully channeled like the passage of electric current through his neck and jaws. In a moment she said "come" to him again, and they crossed through the stream together, the cold washing to their knees, and reached the sedges and waded through them and clambered up to land. "So you see," she said aloud, and she led him on under the beeches to where the trees grew the thickest and took him in through the underbrush, her bare feet shrinking sideways with pain, but still taking him fiercely through it. First the road that first night, she thought, and after that the grass and the water, and now the trees and what's tripping him up underfoot to say Nothing has gone, blind horse, nothing has altered. When they were through it she stopped again at the edge and drew the mayblossom branches down over his face, gently drawing them down and gently letting them brush upward like veils of some inexplicable substitute for sight. That night she took him back by the marsh where by day the yellow iris could be seen growing, and he did not falter but sought his way with her through the invisible fragrant lilies in the dark.

All day he would stand in the loose box with the mare or a filly for company two stalls away, curried and groomed and the place done out from under him, and the cat coming in through the window and rubbing along his leg. By day he was this thing, the prisoner, the condemned man in the death cell on the final stretch of living, not of a species to play cards and smoke the last cigarettes with the guards while he waited, but silently, motionlessly, completely waiting. But at night the stable door moved back and the latch of the stall gate was lifted and he moved out in blindness and wonder with her into the slowly reconstituted, slowly redeemed and infinite world; until the night came when she did not pick up the reins and bring them forward across his head to turn him in the stall and guide him across the stable out into the insect-murmurous dark. It was the sixth or seventh night and once he was bridled she pushed past him and opened the stall gate and standing alone on the stable floor she said, "Come on, handsome," the voice casual enough, but as she waited there in the stable's complete obscurity her heart began to tremble. She held her hands down fast by her sides, her eyes were closed tight as fists in her face, and she stood scarcely daring to hear the confused stamp of the hoofs seeking position as he turned, not hearing actual sound any more but seeming to hear what might come if he fumbled and missed the narrow way out. It might have been hours—

it was less than a minute—before he was clear of the stall and his nostrils came seeking the air for her, the hoofs' sound having altered from their stroke on straw-muffled brick to their thud on timber, and then he lipped her shoulder. "It's as black as your hat," she said as she took him across the threshold's beam. "I can't see any more than you can." She was shaking hard, as if in the teeth of cold.

The Irishman wrote back at once, gravely beginning it "Dear Miss Lombe," and she showed the letter to Candy. "He can't come down on account of his arm, on account of the dressings," she said. Candy had been by the morning bus to Pellton and bought two detective stories in paper covers at Woolworth's shop in Fore Street, and he sat on the veranda in the fan-backed Indian armchair reading *Wanton Killing* in mild, soft-shaven, immaculately accoutred peace (because this would kill the hours of the afternoon and a portion of the evening, this story that did not for an instant deal with people but with the familiarly stamped counterfeits of detective, family, doctor, corpse). On the corner of the ping-pong table lay the other, *Murder in Hand,* still clean and marvelously unread (instrument lying in readiness to slug tomorrow afternoon and evening in their turn into timeless insensibility). "He says he'd like to meet you, Candy, but he can't come down," the girl said, "but look, turn the page," and she turned it for him. "Look what he says about horses." The climbing roses, their leaves and new buds even mildewed by the weather, grew meagerly about them, reaching unblooming up the rusted trelliswork. The afternoon was gray and still, a warm, heavy, iron-dull day with the hawthorn and maples on the lawn standing motionless against it. The single bees that sailed loudly to the laboriously-opening black clots of rose were as incongruous as humming birds boring for succulence in granite flowers. Candy put his detective story face down and open on the end of the ping-pong table and looked at the letter he held in his hand.

" 'I've often seen and ridden horses with "wall" eyes, cataracts (very common), horses blind in one eye, and I've known one or two cases where hunters have been totally blinded by accident. They were not destroyed, though, but put onto farm work, where—' " He stopped reading it aloud, thinking If he did come down I'd meet him at the station, either at Monkton Junction or Eastleigh, and if he came by the late train the pub would be open and over a drink we might get somewhere and for that half hour, in the process of getting somewhere, we'd talk like men. Just for that half hour before we got back here to the house we would be two men talking together, until he saw me for what I am, the one flaw, the single mistake, mistaken as the futile, idle, the evasive must be mistaken in a décor of rearing, stamping, accoupling activity; and as the penniless out of their place and in disguise once unmasked are the mistaken. If he comes down, for a little while my clothes (so much like other men's) will see me through and my receptive manner, for the first half hour over the first drink they'll do; and then he'll see the murder book and the shiftless hours in which no one comes to me, no subordinate or equal, for authority or permission, and at last he'll see the empty glass under the chair.

"Go on," the girl said. "Read the rest of it," and Candy, thinking of murder book and empty glass as weapon and insignia, went on reading aloud:

" 'They were not destroyed, though, but put onto farm work, where they did very well. I don't know anything about retinitis.' " The mother came out through the dining-room door onto the veranda's stone, the basket with the trowel and fork in it on her forearm, and her old gardening gloves pulled on her hands. She paused as if the roses and not the words had stopped her, and touched the blighted leaves with the gardening scissors' beak. " 'I imagine it's not a very common affliction,' " Candy's voice went on. " 'All I know is that the retina's that part at the back of the eye which aches when we come suddenly from darkness into light.' "

"Who's this?" said the mother in a light, inconsequential tone. She stood like a stranger near them under the stricken rose vines, her eyes the perceptive, conjecturing eyes of the human meeting, or only seeking vainly to meet, the cold, unearthly vision of their wide, glazed eyes. The father looked up and cleared his throat and smiled with a sudden little show of daring under his small neat mustache.

"Oh, that's Mr. Sheehan," he said brightly. "Mr. Sheehan calling all stations."

"Who's Mr. Sheehan?" the mother said and she smiled rather bitterly at the dark riddled leaves.

"He's Irish," said Candy, turning the page of the letter as if the actual stamp of his nationality might be set there for the eye to see. "A broth of a boy—"

"I met him in Florence," the girl said. She stood quite still by the ping-pong table, her eyes stopped motionless, her lips ceased moving, her hands and the bare white slender forearms hanging absolutely quiet from the gray jersey's elbow sleeves. I know nothing about her now, nothing, the mother thought bitterly. She looked across, seeking to find and focus the gaze of her daughter's eyes, thinking Ah, yes, here I am as you see me, the old woman who can't think back that far any more, the commander of the ship that would have floundered if I hadn't stepped into the male boots and buckled on the male regalia, an old woman going to fat now in the permanently borrowed paraphernalia that a man, not a woman, should wear.

"That's quite interesting, but you don't have to be sulky about it," she said aloud.

"I'm not sulky," the girl said, and in spite of herself she began to tremble, not only the bones and the flesh but the very marrow shaking and crumbling in her. There was no gooseflesh on her bare hanging arms, but she felt her heart, her substance quaking in her and her teeth chattering in her head. "He knows a lot about horses. He says blind horses don't have to be put down."

"Yes, you are sulking," said the mother, and her hand with the gardening shears in it trembled too. "You've been up to something; now you know you've been up to something you don't want me to know about, Nan."

"He says blind horses can be put onto farm work, so if a blind horse can be put onto work, then I can ride mine, I can teach him," the girl said. She stood looking motionlessly, quietly beyond, beyond her mother and past the lawn, beyond the day even to that irresistible goal perhaps weeks or months ahead, almost visually perceiving the plane of victory on which the horse would pound homeward sightless, outstripping the clear-eyed thoroughbreds, taking the obstacles higher, the ditches wider. "I know I could teach mine," she said, trembling before the still imperfect vision of the truth. "I could take him out a little bit every day, a little bit more all the time—"

The mother reached over and took the Irishman's letter out of Candy's hand and she said:

"I won't have you riding a blind horse and killing yourself and the poor beast. Thank God, there's a more humane way of putting it down—"

"Brigand's a He," said the girl. "He's a man. You might speak of him like that."

"It's a gelding," said the mother. "There's no need to flatter it with a sex." She turned the three pages of Mr. Sheehan's letter and she said: "He's found time to write you a lot of nonsense, this young gentleman of yours," and in that oddly patient and at the same time oddly grieving voice, her thumb in the split leather, mud-whitened and caked glove holding the sheet, she read the sentences on the last page out. " 'It is easier to change an animal's receptivity of the world abruptly because in his two-dimensional existence everything enters from the outside. For animals a new sun rises every morning and a new morning comes with every dawning day. It is only human reasoning which insists that it is the same sun rising or the same moon waning. That is where Rostand did not understand the psychology of "Chantecler." The cock could not think that he woke up the sun by his crowing. To him the sun does not go to sleep, it goes into the past.' He is quite an intellectual, your Mr. Sheehan," said the mother, speaking without rancor as if she knew and accepted the end of the story now. " 'So you can quite naturally and I should think with comparative ease give your horse a new world of action by giving him a new discernment for the motions which go on around him. I think this is what you meant, or rather what—' " Suddenly the mother broke off her reading and flicked the letter back to Candy where he sat in the fan-backed chair. "This sort of business isn't going to get us anywhere," she said.

"Come now," said Candy, and he smiled at them both with the same little jerk of summoned courage as before. "From the point of view of that horse costing us anything, if I started in giving up my good tobacco, you know, and my cigars, and stuck to that kind of pipe fodder that makes my head go round, it ought to pay for that chap's food and drink for some months to come." His round neat little chin was lifted clear of his shirt's soft collar and the pale blue knitted tie and his hands held fast to the wicker arms of the chair. "I don't want Nancy to ride him, no, that I don't want," he said. "I don't want to have Nancy stumbling around on a blind horse, but I say let her have him for this summer anyway. She can take him walking up and down the drive if she wants him as badly as all that, Nan. This Irish chap here, this boy Sheehan, he seems to know—"

"Ah, your incurable softness, yours and Nan's incurable false softness," said the mother in a low bitter voice. She looked at his short, helpless hands hanging from the sleeves of the squire's jacket, the nails rounded clean and white on the childlike fingers that held to the chair's arms, and the empty glass put aside carefully beneath the chair. "Keep that animal rotting in blindness out there all the summer? What sort of sentimentality is it? For his health's sake, any horse must have his work-out, but you'd keep him closed out there with a step or two up the drive every day, and you'd break his heart and spirit for him! If you go on, you two," she said, holding onto the anger, "I'll put that crazy horse down myself, with my own hand I'll do it because I'm the only one here who'd have the compassion to do it—"

By the tenth day it was hot, a complete heat had descended on the country and the moon rose clearly at night. At supper Mrs. Lombe said they were leaving the yearlings out all night in the upland pastures, and thinking or dreaming of this the girl awoke as she always awoke now soon after midnight, quickly and without interruption rousing night after summer night as if someone entered the room at the specified hour and touched her arm and said it was time to come. She thought at once of the yearlings out in the grass, and she got up and put on her slippers and her jersey and crossed to the open window on the veranda roof. If they're out he has the right to go up there and graze near them and talk to them across the rails, or even go so far as . . . Or even go loose a while with them, the yet unthought, unspoken thing was shaping; not with the colts, she came near to establishing it as intention as she crossed the grass and the flower-beds to the stable. The colts play as wild as cats together, but the fillies are gentle, she thought, not quite coming to it as she shouldered back the stable door.

They went out the drive, and this time turned up the road towards the stud-farm, the horse waiting while she opened the pale painted gate and then following when she spoke his name. The main buildings stood on the rise ahead, bright white under the moon: the brood-mares' boxes looking south down the pasture-land, the granaries and the men's sleeping quarters to the north, and the stud-groom's cottage nearer, white under its thatch, standing to the right of the road. She thought I used to think jockeys and grooms never married, as if they weren't like men or anyway not whole men, just pieces of men cut down like that to fit a horse, but there's the stud-groom married and sleeping with his wife now behind those windows. I used to think of them all as something less than men because something more, like immortals, jockeys and grooms and huntsmen and vets, but whatever they say now I know better. I'm going to ride my horse, perhaps not tonight or tomorrow night but in the end I'm going to ride him. They came up out of the shadow of the firs and beeches, coming out of the trees' exactly defined darkness and walking into the open moon-whitened country like walking into the light of day. The home buildings and the cottage were white as bone, the fields, the moon-dappled pasture, the blackthorn hedges wrapped in stillness as they came past them, the girl and the horse keeping to the grass for quiet and their footfalls muffled as they passed the closed windows and moved out again into the open country, the two survivors moving through a bleached plague-stricken land.

Close to the buildings lay the small enclosures where the mares were turned out at once after foaling, and near by them the brood-mares' paddocks, longer, ampler, but likewise with the house standing between them and the north. Stretching farther afield (even in childhood she had felt in the sweep of the opening land the conditions of youth and its frenzy) were the yearlings' paddocks, acre on acre reaching out of sight to the orchards' drop. Far below, unseen, unheard, almost out of the moon's reach, the stream ran on. The paddocks set close to the home buildings stood empty under the wide night's light, for the mares and their foals were closed in until the dew would be off the grass in the morning: within the walls they were one still, mare and foal, mare and foal in their boxes, still sharing the same fodder-fragrant and straw-fragrant air. For a little while longer foal and dam pressed body to body, moved out in the early morning limb to limb, the mother sleeping now with her head lowered and the child with his legs bent under him, folded close, and his nose resting vulnerably on the trampled hay. Weaning time had not come yet and the child still flaunted his willful, wayward lip and eye, his glossy belly propped on stilts, for a little while longer drew milk from her, drank from the same wood bucket, licked the same salt stone. It would come, wax to its peak of sorrow, then wane like the wooing-season: they would be taken from each other, foal from dam, and dam from foal, and for two days they would not eat but run the length of the paddock rails seeking each other and calling out, while the pain numbed slowly and at last died wholly in their flesh. For two more days they would stand with their eyes set on nothing but the memory of each other until the lineaments of that too faded, but when the foal turned down his head to lip the grasses again a part of that fearless, fiery arrogance was gone, already and forever.

The girl and the horse passed by the bright white-painted gates and the posts and rails that marked out the paddocks, following up the road that lay between. And as they walked the colts began coming to the bars and whinnying out to them, first to the sound of footsteps and then to the sight of them passing in the moonlight, and the hunter lifted his head on the rein and turned it towards their high chiming voices. Not here, the girl said and she drew him on; these are the colts and they'd play too hard for you and bruise you, but still the clear foolish voices called out to him to come. It was better than half a mile to the last big paddock where the fillies were turned free on nights like this, and the length of the way the colts ran to the bars and called out after them, running lightly in couples through the moonlit grass. It was only in distances that the moon's power seemed to fail, blotted out in the far maze of firs, myrtles, and the scrub pines grown down the west side against the wind.

At first there were none of the fillies to be seen, lost somewhere in the rich clover down at the meadow's end, or standing asleep in the paddock's eight-acre stretch with their necks curved over one another's. The girl climbed to the top bar of their gate and sat there in the warm, foreign-seeming night, the slippers hanging loose on her bare feet, the short-sleeved jersey undone. "Come," she said, and for an instant he faltered as she drew him forward on the rein, without sight knowing (perhaps because my voice is coming now from above instead of beside him) that the barrier was there. "Come," she said, and now he came carefully forward until the full deep breast came to a pause against the bars. The face hung long and utterly quiet, utterly patient beside her, the long flexible lip seemingly ready to smile if only the gift of humor or whimsy were given, the damp forelock ready to curl in the dew-moist blank soft air. In another while the fillies began coming up the paddock in the moonlight, first one and then another, and now in couples, and now in threes, picking their way like deer with their heads high and their delicate ears tipped forward, until at last the nine of them had come tentatively to the railing, their noses lifted without shyness to lip the smell and substance of horse and human flesh.

None of the men asleep in the home buildings, nor the stud-groom in his cottage heard it, but Apby started suddenly out of sleep remembering the sound of a horse going past on the grass, not running but simply walking quietly by, perhaps in the grass by the roadside. He (who had sought to be a jockey and who had never raced except in country fairs) was dreaming of the colored caps, the striped satin shirts, the narrow pennants flying on the grandstand, and on the fast track of dreams and even through the sound of cheering, he heard the muffled passing of the horse's feet beneath the window. There was no horse in sight by the time he was out of bed and opened the shutters, but still he pulled his trousers on and went down the ladder into the center mixing-room, and unlocked the door and went out onto the road. For a while he stood there waiting to get the sound again, and he heard it, moving farther and farther, fainter and fainter, like two hands clapping slower and farther and fainter, until the sound had ceased completely, and he said There's a horse got loose up by the last paddocks, and he started walking that way.

5

But at least he kept the secret, he didn't tell either the other grooms or the masters because by keeping quiet about it the trouble over the hunter's age between him and the girl was finished. She was sitting on the top rail of the gate when he came up the road, and the fillies were galloping wild in the paddock, the group of them wheeling together, first one in the lead and then another; and she started talking to him without turning her head, as if she had expected him to come or just anybody she could say it to to come and stand there below her, a little to one side of her, looking over the top bar at the horses going crazy underneath the moon. She said: "That's my horse in there with them." She had her hands closed into fists and she kept beating her left fist up and down on her knee as she watched them reeling into one corner and out of it and sweeping wildly down the land. "My horse is in there running with them, look, he's with the last three, my blind horse running. . . ."

The fillies came snorting past the rails, their necks and shoulders leaning to the curve, their manes blowing, and galloped down the slope towards where the water passed and out of sight, then up the opposite side of the field they came like the rush of the wind coming, and the hunter with them, the tall, stern, bony body stretching and limbering with them as they swung across the grass. She said: "I took his bridle off and opened the gate for him," her hand clenched tight and beating on her knee as she watched them go. "I gave him a crack and he went straight in to them. I've won," she said, not turning her head to him. "I won against them all, even against you, Apby. I won."

He stood bandy-legged and seemingly dwarfed below her, leaning stubbornly on the painted gate, his arms raised and crossed on the top bar and his chin laid on them, almost classless now as he leaned insolently on the bar below her in this place where, at this hour, they had no right to be.

"No, you didn't win, you didn't win nothing at all," he said, leaning casually and boldly there below her. In a while he might take a cigarette out of his breeches' pocket and strike a match to it and stand there smoking without a saving-your-presence or a grant-your-grace and let it hang dry on his lip while he went on saying in the moonlight: "You didn't win because that's nothing you're giving a horse, that's no life for a grown horse, grazing and romping with yearlings, running like that like maybe a hundred blind horses would run with their kind. That don't get 'im anywheres," he said, and she looked quickly down at him, seeing him like a stranger now that for once the brown-and-white checked soiled cap was absent and the hair showed pressed flat from sleep against the skull; seeing the small elfin-profiled face of the doer for horses, the delicate-boned face of the administrator to their flesh, the inevitable steward to their intimacies. She thought Perhaps no one ever with big bones is good with horses, only these half men, while he said: "What have you won if you haven't found his use for 'im? This kind of thing is all right and all that, but it isn't finding his use for 'im."

"But there's no need to destroy him now," she said. "No one on earth'd put a horse down that can run like that. No one alive—"

"What kind of a deal are you giving him at that?" the groom said, his chin resting on his arms on the bar as he watched the galloping horses take the rise. "You're not offering him much by just turning him out to grass for the time he's got to go. I've known a few horses and I say as he'd rather be dead than in the stable and out year in and year out the way he'd be." The horses came head-on towards the gate, then bent their course and swerved like a flock of birds, and bending still chopped short the corner, and the girl's hair lifted in her neck with the wind of their passing and slowly sank again when they were by. "Grass ain't always the 'appy 'ome of rest," Apby said. "You've got the month of June and that's the best here, and after June the flies start driving the horses off their heads, and when it's late September and on the grass has no more taste than paper."

"Because you want him dead," she said, looking straight ahead down the paddock. "You all want it." And now the groom took his arms from the top bar and fished in his breeches' pocket for the cigarette and brought it out and straightened it in his fingers before he put it in his mouth and struck the match and held it, the fire-bright spark of what might have been life itself cupped in his hand's bones an instant while the lowered head, the tilted mouth leaned to it, and the small jaws sucked quickly at the air. "It's all system with you and all the rest of them," the girl was saying, looking at him now and watching him shake the match's flame out and let it drop into the grass. "So many boxes, so much room, so many hands for the work, so—"

"You get him his own work to do and I'll be the first to groom him," he said, folding his arms on the rail again and the cigarette hanging on his arrogant lip. "Make a horse out of him as long as you can't never now make a sire," he said, the humor turned coarse and free as if it were another groom, not girl and not employer, sitting on the gate above him. "You cut out his work for him and I'd be the first to do for him morning, noon, and night," he said, and the girl said quickly·

"I wouldn't let you touch him."

"Saddle 'im, I'd say, saddle 'im," the groom went on saying. He drew sparingly at the cigarette, letting the ash grow, sparingly letting the smoke rise. "He's queer enough for anything I'd ever seen so he'd likely let you do it. Saddle 'im up and give 'im his paces. Put 'im on a Ward Union double-bridle and just try 'im out."

And now the fillies, as if at a given signal, suddenly broke apart near the fence and quietly scattered; gentle as mares and with the same matured wisdom, they shook their manes on their necks and dropped their heads to graze. Only the throbbing flanks and bellies remained as remnant of their senseless wild abandon, and slowly, step by long-drawn lingering step, they moved off eating at the grass. For a moment the hunter was left there in isolation as they went in their separate, lingering directions, his head raised and searching, perhaps seeking sight now that the comprehensible motion of flight had ceased; and then abruptly he sought it no longer. Whether it was the sound of their still hot unsubsided breathing or the pull of their teeth at the grass that came to his ears now and calmed his heart's equivocal panic, the girl watching him from the top of the gate saw him drop his strong long head and begin to crop the herbage as did the others, and move, as did the others, step after prolonged half-arrested step, grazing at peace in the mysteriously shining night.

Two days after that, when she wrote to Mr. Sheehan again, she wrote:

"At first it didn't go very well because as long as I was on his back my horse got panicky and he wasn't sure about stepping on the road. If I got off and led he went all right, or he'd follow me all right, but when I mounted him again it was the same thing. He'd feel out the ground all the time with his forefoot before he'd go, or he'd stop short, maybe thinking there was a hole he couldn't see in front of him. But I managed to get him around the long way by the stream and into the paddock where there weren't any horses out. It's one of the colts' paddocks and it's more than eight acres square. When he remembered he couldn't see he stopped like a shot and that might be bad if you were going fast but maybe he'll get over that too. I'm trying the half-passage with him because I've seen quite a few horses and I don't see any good in just turning him out to grass," came the predication of youthful authority and youthful plagiarism. "I've noticed that turning them out like that isn't always their happy home of rest. There's only the month of June here and after that the flies begin pestering them, and everybody knows autumn grass tastes like paper to them. But a horse is no good to himself or to anybody if he hasn't got a use or any work to do, and training him to obey can give him a use so even if he's blind he can begin living his life again."

So the battle had another aspect to it now, the ranks were a little altered. On the side of death, the marvelously equipped cohorts of extinction, were the mother, the vets, the stud-groom, precedent; and on the other the Irishman nursing his arm up in London and writing to her, and Apby come to heel. Between the two federations Candy erred as a victim of amnesia might have wandered, the meaning of the issue lost in confusion, the name forgotten, only the sense of urgency, perplexed and sketchily defined but present. He stood at the dining-room window in the evening tapping out the verses with his fingertips on the anciently rain-stained glass: Oh, Nancy, Nancy, your doting parent, is afraid circumstances will warrant. Or If ever you took it into your head, to ride a horse that ought to be— Or If you ever rode that crazy hunter—punter, munter, bunter, runter. His fingertips drummed across the glass with the rhythm of what he was making up, seeking a way, if way there was, to establish a truce between will and will without he himself having to make any declaration or come to any choice. Because there must be an end to it he was almost persuaded now that the alternative lay between two deaths: either the hunter's provoked death or the girl's death if she rode him, and the menace of horse seemed imminent, the threat of equine inhuman power seemed ready to cast the dauntless and the daring down and stamp their life out underfoot. He stood tapping his fingers on the pane and watching the evening coming, the mild June evening in which thundered the defiance of the big-necked, the monstrous-thighed and bony-headed beasts who reeled towards growing timber in their madness (he had read of men willfully killed by horses who took trees as the last resort, low boughs or the trunks themselves, to strike their masters from their backs); he could see the vision of them cracking their legs on fences they'd jumped short and crashing gigantically, massive as floundering whales on the defenseless frail bodies of the mounted young; saw them in steeplechase and point-to-point and hunt, the cripplers, the murderers, striking out left and right and beneath them in their folly, the hard-hoofed, hysterical killers breaking their own backs as they fell, a mass of twisted, writhing tonnage, snapping their own necks as they collapsed across the bars on the still incredulous, still fearless young, the dying monsters killing as they died.

"Tum-te-te-tum, tum-te-te-tum, ta-ta," he hummed aloud now as something like actual physical fear began to shake his soul. He thrummed his fingertips on the window and he thought, The best horse story I ever heard was the one about the cavalry regiment galloping hard, four a-breast, up the village street, young sparks in their uniforms making their mounts take it fast to show the population, in particular the female, how they sat the saddle. Ah, but the street was narrow, lads, and ah, but vanity, that fluctuating current that deflects the blood stream in our hearts, was lashing the horses past all endurance: it seemed the eyes must boil from their heads, and their tongues spume from their jaws, and their lungs burst wide and hang in shreds upon their chests' scaffolding, when what happened but a cob and buggy turned out from a cross street and peacefully came towards them, slowly because it was summer and the driver with his feet propped on the dashboard, half asleep. The horses, remember, left six inches free on either side as they came up the village street, their necks at the extremity, their legs stretched reaching for the weapon with which to do the killing; ah, murderers, lusters, gangsters all, see the horse coming slowly and flickeringly, like in one of the first moving pictures, his feet seeming to wave from side to side like slowly waved handkerchiefs as he drew the buggy or else the buggy pushed him down the street, see the blinders on the sides of his face, if you can remember that far back, and the reins hanging slack because the driver had forgotten, just before meeting death, about the briefness of man's allotted span, and see the last touch, the comic feet propped on the dashboard. Towards this familiar (if you were alive in the horse and buggy age) and insignificant (if you did not admit time's aggregation) and helplessly advancing vehicle came the cavalry, unarmed except for haste and heat and savagery, while the buggy's shafts, like spears carried low and wary by African warriors on the trail, took aim in measured preparation.

Damn horses, in the name of youth, God damn them, Candy said, and he turned away from the window to the sight of his wife through the double-doorway, knitting by the silent radio. There were six horses less after that debacle, he told himself with pleasure: one man less, the driver dying with his legs stuck up on the dashboard still like a dead bird's legs sticking straight up in the air, because he didn't wake up in time to choose, or if he had chosen what could he have done with only a couple of yards between him and the galloping horde? But six horses less, two of them run through by the buggy's shafts and their hearts split on the skewers, and four of them with broken shoulders and broken necks trampled to death in headlong panic, six of them less to bolt and rear and stampede, and the officers only badly hurt, only disfigured. She was knitting with pink, and a towel spread over her skirt to keep the delicate wool from soiling, and he thought "badly hurt," how magical, how truly rich and sweet it is, "disfigured" or "badly hurt," the unhoped-for reprieves from death. He sauntered over the worn little islands of the rugs towards his wife, his hands in the pockets of his coat and his neat, well-manicured thumbs out, knitting what? he thought, half-jocularly asking, For God's sake, knitting what? Part of it was humorous and part tender, and part the complete if dimly credited perception that not time itself but the belief that there were lapses in it was the illusion: she might be sitting nearly twenty years back knitting something for Nancy not born yet, the same evening, the same supper, the same twilight outside the windows on which the rain had a long time dried. And at that same time, me beginning what was to be my artistic career, fatherhood the accessory not the keystone to life, envisaging clearly then the now dimmed, wasted features of what was to have been honor and accomplishment year after simultaneous year.

"Nan," he said, coming to the last island on which she sat marooned, "perhaps you ought to be making a confession to me," and he made a gesture with his thumb towards the pale wool and the needles in her hands. She heard the part-jocular, part-tender voice and she looked quickly up at him, at the rather gallant little figure in the squire's coat with the small mouth smiling under the tricky neat mustache, and for once she did not answer as she might have done. Instead she looked down again at her work and for the first time she said to him:

"I would have liked to have had a son."

To be what I'm not and never have been, he thought at once; to do the hard, thrashing, male things I've never done to land or woman or beast; not a son to carry on my blood but hers and Major Husen's, resenting now even her own father's blood in her; the stud, the wooings and the matings, to bear that on, the foalings, the deaths, the cycle turning and returning to the accouplements. He put out his hand and laid it on her shoulder without thinking of the words to use to begin saying it, but simply beginning:

"It's the people we surround ourselves with or get surrounded with, maybe, that seem to make us into something we never would have been. If you'd had a son you wouldn't have had to have been so—so—fearless. That's not quite the word but I mean—"

"I'm not fearless," she said, her head down, her hands working quickly at her knitting.

"Yes, because I'm a coward you had to be fearless," he said. "You found out you had to be fearless a long time ago, too long, and now you don't know how to be afraid any more. But I'm going to be different about things, you've heard me say that before, but this time I'm going to be different. I'm going to try to get into things more, be more active, and make things easier for you. I'd like you to be afraid and come to me afraid, not every day but some days."

"I am afraid," she said, her head down, her eyes on the knitting. For the second that he did not look at her he believed with the same complete perception as before that time did not lapse, in spite of man-conceived divisions neither receded nor advanced, and he heard her voice as his young love's and his young wife's saying:

"I am afraid. I'm afraid for Nan."

The girl worked two hours every night, sometimes longer, with the horse, worked fast with him now that the second week was closing: the half-passage for the first quarter of an hour in the paddock where the cropped grass was resting, and then the turn on the center as the simplest of the three equine turns. "The half-passage," said the textbook she lay reading in the hammock, "consists in making the horse, while keeping his whole body, from nose to croup, parallel with the sides of the enclosure, move sideways, crossing both fore feet and hind feet. The exercise should be performed only when the horse is walking well into his bridle. By asserting a strong pressure of one leg slightly drawn back the horse should move off in the required direction. Both legs on one side should cross the other two (in front, not behind) and he should gain ground all the time. His progression should therefore be at an angle of 45° to the sides of the road or the enclosure."

The second quarter of the hour was the turn on the center, the one turn the horse makes naturally, without instruction: the rider's inner knee the fulcrum, the horse's forehand turning inward, his quarters outward. Not till the last day of the week did she try the circle on two tracks, on the forehand and on the hock, and then "A strong pressure of the inward leg, which should be slightly drawn back, and the hand rein strongly applied," the textbook said. "The horse should make a complete circle, with his head facing the center and the hind legs passing along the circumference." Or for the hock circle, she read in the warm dim drowsy afternoon, with the hammock just moving, not swinging but stirring slightly and nothing more; for this "a strong pressure of the outward leg, in front of the girth, and the outward rein, with the hand on the neck pushing the horse over as it were," and now Candy came across the lawn, walking quickly, silently on rubber soles, dressed in white as if just ready for tennis although he had never so much as thought of tennis in years, but had dressed again, coolly and freshly, to kill an hour of the afternoon. He sat down without a sound, without a word, in the canvas chair by the tin table where the half-empty glass of lemonade was standing and she looked up from her book at him in the moment before he spoke and saw the small shocked face above the polo-shirt's open neck, the color gone from the mouth even. Although he had been well shaven at lunch, or must have been, the skin showed ailing as scalp now through darkish and unexpected bristles.

"Penson," he said, swallowing, and he did not look at her. His bare elbows were braced on the chair's wooden arms and his fingers interlocked before him. She put the book down, closed, and sat up in the hammock, the shape of the net's sag altering as she moved until it took and held her buttocks' shape. "Something's happened to Penson," he said, and his eyes ran from one side to the other, trapped in their sockets like marbles in a pocket. "A horse almost did him in last night. I met his wife in Pellton, ran into her on the street coming from the hospital." His eyes were running fast from the vision of it, and the girl sat before him in the scarcely moving hammock, her bare legs hanging slender and white-skinned out of her skirt and her bare feet, blue-veined and narrow in the unfastened sandals, swinging slightly just above the circle of earth worn under the hammock and the trees where feet had always swung. "Around Buxton, I think she said. He was called in to look at a horse," he went on saying, his eyes running fast, "and the damned farmers didn't hold the animal properly. It was a big draught-horse, heavily shod, and, by God, he got poor Penson square in the face. One point of the heel right in the eye, she said, and the other point hooked the roof of his mouth, and as soon as the brute had him down she says the farm hands ran a mile. They left Penson lying there in the stall calling for help until one or two of them collected their wits and came back and got him out—"

"Bright lads," said the girl, swinging.

"But by that time the horse had trampled his right arm half off, and she says it was Penson who told them what to do. 'Get me to the nearest doctor so he can stop the bleeding,' he told them," and Candy's eyes fled wildly from the sight of it, "but the doctor they got him to took one look and said he wouldn't touch that skull with a yardstick for fear of doing Penson in. 'All right,' said Penson, 'then get me to Pellton Royal Hospital quick as you can,' and she says the doctor drove him the twenty miles in half an hour." Candy's breath was shaking in his mouth but he went on saying: "Penson told the surgeon to give him a local anaesthetic but not to put him out completely because it was an operation he'd always wanted to see done. Trepanning I think they call it, only this time she said the difference was they didn't have to saw out a part of the skull because it had been kicked out already, so all the surgeon had to do was pick out the pieces from the front, and Penson had them put a mirror up where he could see, and there was Penson, Penson, by God, making suggestions!" His tongue came out to run along his lip but it brought no moisture with it, and looking at him from the hammock she thought It's not for Penson he's in a funk like this but for something that might happen to somebody else, perhaps to me or perhaps to himself, something more personal than just fear of theoretic violence but because it's a sample given, not only an instance of what happened to somebody else but of what might happen to him or me sometime, or perhaps just to me. "Three hours on the table," Candy said, "and Penson told the surgeon or the surgeon told Penson, I don't remember which way it was, that the complication could be meningitis. He told him that last night and at four o'clock this morning they recognized the symptoms. He's in for it now," Candy said, the eyes still running from it. "Mrs. Penson says they don't give her any hope. If he comes through, that'll be one more miracle like him having the courage to lie conscious on the operating table telling the surgeon what to do."

"What about the horse?" the girl said. She reached out for the glass of unfinished lemonade and took a swallow of it, but because it was too warm and sour now, she made a face after the first taste, and put it down.

"The horse?" said Candy, for the first time the eyes fixed steadily on her.

"What was wrong with the horse?" she said. "What was Penson called in to look at him for?" She sat swinging slightly in the hammock, the loose, hanging sandals just brushing above the circle worn bare in the grass. "I suppose because of all that stupidity the horse'll go on getting worse; because they'll be afraid to have another vet in to look at him. It wasn't the horse's fault. He was badly managed."

So now the thing is, Candy did not say, his fingers locked together desperately, the thing is we are afraid for you, your mother and I are afraid, we were afraid for you before and now we know exactly: you mustn't go into that blind horse's box any more and groom and feed him. He did not speak but he sat white and shocked before her, his eyes trapped in his face. You'll get Apby or someone else to do it for you, but you can't go in there, you mustn't do it, I forbid you to do it any more. You can't go in there three times a day like that and do all the things you've been doing for him. It's got to stop. Let a man be killed, let a vet die of brain fever, let the entire race of horses stamp out the race of men; but you, my delicate-wristed, my rapt-eyed daughter, you shall stay clear of death by murder, by calculating evil violence, by willful and ruthless vice; you shall remain unstained as the lilies remain pure growing by the water, fragrant as fruit-blossoms, unbruised, unplucked, unsullied. He did not speak but sat before her in his open polo-shirt and his white duck tennis trousers, looking out of his blanched face at her and listening to her.

"She said I could have a fortnight to think it over and now I've thought it over," she was saying, swinging just slightly in the hammock. "Today makes the two weeks and I haven't changed my mind about it, I mean I feel exactly the way I did and I won't let them put Brigand down. I mean, it's not just being stubborn about a thing, but the thing itself isn't the same any more, do you see what I'm trying to say, Candy? In a little while I'll be able to show you, but now it's too soon. I have to have more time before I can show you. That's what I want to talk to you about. I want you to tell mother I've got to have more time before I can prove it to her, maybe another fortnight would do. You're on my side, Candy, and you've got to tell mother to give me a little more time."

"More time for what?" he said, the eyes coming helplessly to a halt on her face.

"So I can prove they don't have to destroy him," she said. The hammock swung slightly, rhythmically, imperceptibly as breathing. "If I have more time I can show them what's happened and then they'll see there's no need to destroy him. I can't show you now, I want it to be perfect before I show you." The hammock moved her gently towards him and as gently drew her away. "I'm not glad Penson got hurt," she said, the strange, dream-stupored eyes profoundly and motionlessly drifting. "I'm not glad he got hurt, but if he's in hospital then he couldn't put Brigand down. So I want you to ask her to give me more time, just to allow me ten days longer, just enough—"

"He's got an assistant, Penson," Candy said. "He'll have someone replacing him. You needn't count on that," but he knew exactly what he would do: after a while he would get up from the canvas chair and cross the lawn and begin saying it to his wife, standing beside her wherever she was, his hands in his pockets, offering her half in apology and half in challenge the smile that placated nothing. Whether or not the very words in which he would petition the horse's reprieve were asking as well for an extension of the risks of human death, still he would go to where she fought the recalcitrant roses or whatever other insurgent manifestations of life were being chastised by her hand, and he would ask it, smiling, but still in shame and servility of her. "But, look here, Nancy," he said, staving it off a little longer. "What if you go off again in September? What about that blind horse? What would be the point in keeping him hanging on like that if you weren't here?"

"He'll have his own use by that time, he'll have his own life then," she said, swinging. "You'll see."

He thought suddenly I need a drink, that's what I need, a drink, and he stood up and looked at the watch on his warm arm. Bound to her, he thought, by that, "You're on my side," bound and committed to her, to lie for her, plead, connive. He stood looking down at her bare legs and her bare ankles and the sandals open on the blue-veined insteps' bone, and he thought, What if he kicks you to death out there in the box, what if he does, and he said out loud:

"But I want one thing, Nancy," looking rather wistfully and shyly at her as if on the point of asking some favor for himself instead of merely seeking to spare her from death. "I want you to say you won't go out and groom and feed that horse, Nancy. If I ask your mother to allow him to stay on there another fortnight, you can stay away from his heels, Nancy. You can get Apby to do him down and exercise him up the driveway." He stood in uncertainty and almost in humility before her, wanting the drink and at the same time wanting her obedience to be quickly and submissively given. Just not to be the one to wound her, to thwart her, not ever to evoke the balefulness and the defiance (that's for you, Nan, all for you, he thought of his wife; you can have every drop of her resistance, I don't want any of it for me), not now or ever to see the wide floating eyes focus in exprobration on him. "I'm just saying, Nancy, that I don't want to see your face changed, I don't want you dying in a hospital," he said. "I want you to keep on being and looking the way you are. That Irishman," he said, and he accomplished the little smile, "he mightn't like you either any other way."

She sat below him swinging in the hammock for a while, the face meditative, the foot hanging, and then she said, pronouncing the words slowly so there would be no mistake:

"All right, Candy. That's fair enough. I won't groom Brigand and I won't feed him. From now on I'll let Apby do it. I'll let Apby do him down and feed him and walk him up the drive every day. When I go way my horse'll have to get used to someone else, so he might as well start getting used to it now. I'll let Apby groom him and feed him because you ask me to," she said.

6

First Mr. Sheehan wrote about his sister marrying and and then his aunt wrote: the Hon. Lady Mary Disalt wrote asking if Nancy Lombe would come up to London as house-guest.

"There you are," said Candy. He looked brightly and saucily over the breakfast table. "They want a double wedding."

"Don't put ideas into her head," said the mother. The tone was light enough but she looked up at the girl with a measuring, a quietly conjecturing eye. "What in the world will you wear? What have you got?" she said to the sport-shirt and the fraying jersey and the too-tight riding breeches. "We'll have to go over to Pellton and get you something decent."

"Why doesn't she wear her spotted leopard with the cream lace insert?" said Candy, and the girl began laughing. She lifted her cup of tea to her mouth as if to hide its wide foolish laughing, but once on her tongue the tea spurted in explosions across the dishes. "Try on her old-gold sheath gown with the dimity bodice," Candy said, and the tea splattered onto the marmalade and the silver cover of the warming dish. "Or her emerald-green smock edged with yellow tulle," he went on saying, and the girl cried out:

"Oh, stop, Candy, stop it! You're so silly!"

"Or her pistache velvet with the raccoon slip?" he said. "As we used to say at school, 'was it Daniel Boone or the raccoon that gave the knave the name of Boone.'"

"Possum," the girl cried out, her face bright red with laughing. "I'm sure his hat was possum!"

The mother sat reading the Hon. Lady Mary's letter again, breakfast not done yet, and she did not speak, sitting now in that far and elegantly appointed study in which the words had been penned, perhaps on a russet leather-clasped blotting pad and certainly on Chippendale, with the murmur of London penetrating the bottle-bottomed studded panes and the partially drawn velvet hangings, reading: "So we should like to have her come up on Friday night, the seventh of July. Naturally, she will be met at Waterloo and chaperoned to the house." So that gives us ten days, the mother thought, but not the time for anything to be made; and the time is short like that for the very good reason that this highfaluting Mr. James Sheehan couldn't make up his mind until the last moment, not knowing whether he wanted Nancy Lombe to come or whether he didn't until probably yesterday morning. A wedding as presentable as this one is planned and the house party arranged for and invited six weeks ahead, at least six weeks, but it's plain as day that his royal highness decided just in the nick that Nancy was good enough, that Nancy Lombe, the little girl he'd met in Florence at Mrs. Patterson's one afternoon last winter, would make the grade, and would dear Aunt Mary Disalt write to those squirey people down Pellton-way who had this pretty daughter, and it took a bit of persuading because the guest list had been drawn up months ago, but in the end she did. And at least she had the grace to add: "Please excuse the unavoidable tardiness of this, but my nephew's delayed return from the continent made any planning with him virtually impossible."

"They've given us such short notice, the proper thing would be to turn them down," the mother said, and she put the point of toast crowned richly with Danish butter and bramble-jam into her mouth; but they all knew that the girl was to go. The mother knew it best perhaps, because knowing that friends, just other people found and called by that miraculously transforming name, were enough to change a girl's heart and alter her life for her; knowing this change might be the overture to final propitiation, the way to muffle at last the sound of horse's hoofs, not any horse's or all horses' hoofs, but the hoofs of the crazy hunter on his fruitless hunt galloping unflaggingly towards death through their speech and their silence and their struck bargain's commutation. She began talking of the clothes, shop-bought they'd have to be, and the sound of the galloping horse went on, and the mother thought, In London she'll meet people and she'll see things in their true proportions, but she'll have to have a suit to travel in, and at least two dresses, she's outgrown everything, and the horse's hoofs went galloping endlessly and hopelessly towards the unseen goal. Without pronouncing the name to herself even, the mother decided, It has to be done one day and it can be done without a scene, tears, arguments, if she's out of the house, and then when she comes home she'll have the fact to face, the absolutely done and finished thing. "Three dresses, you'll have to have three," she said to her daughter's bright red convulsed face. Candy was swaying in the arms of the dance, his checked coat humped up across his neck and shoulders as he waltzed between the breakfast table and the sideboard, his eyes half-closed, his head back, singing:

"'Don't tell my mother I breakfast on gin, Don't let the old folks know. Don't tell my father I'm living in sin, He'd never survive the blo-ow-ow-ow!'"

"For heaven's sake, stop singing that vile song before the servants hear you," the mother said, conjecturing the dresses, three complete outfits it would have to be, a new suit for traveling and two dresses to wear in the city. Candy started jigging, his hands on his hips, across the varnished dining-room floor.

"'I'm one of the ruins Cromwell knocked abaht a bit,'" he sang. "'Just *one* of the ruins Cromwell knocked abaht a bit,'" his feet nimbly, quickly, pattering time. "'Blimey, there reely isn't a doubt of it, All the 'istory books they shout of it–'"

"Is it you who's going up to London to the house party or is it Nancy?" the mother said, and looking at him she began to laugh. But the girl had ceased laughing now. She held her hands down in her lap, watching languidly, drowsily something outside the window perhaps, or perhaps only hearing the same quick, clapping passage of the hunter's feet on road or cobbles or muffled and throbbing across turf. She said:

"I'll go up for the day only. I'll go just for the wedding. I won't stay three days away."

So the argument that never found conclusion began groping anew past the minutiae of this issue as past the others and beyond it to the declaration of probity itself: the mother's voice strained thin with bitterness and hopelessness and, at last, with fury, across the breakfast table and later across the lunch table, before it turned back from the stubborn, outlandish but insoluble pledge the girl had made to some equivocal young honor, to some unperjured but infuriating loyalty. So there it was left, none of the spirit solved nor the will yet broken to will, but in abeyance: the girl would go up on the Friday afternoon and spend the night there, only one night away, and be down on the afternoon train that brought her in just before tea time Saturday. After the first moment of wondering, she knew there was nothing to fear; and now that the mother's voice returned to hopelessness, planning the suit and the one dress instead of the two, the girl lying in the hammock counted the granted days that had not yet elapsed, thinking I can go because I have until Monday and because Apby can feed and water him and perhaps exercise him, perhaps even that. She would go too because of this: because she could see Mr. Sheehan clearly only in profile, sitting beside her on the sofa at Mrs. Patterson's in Florence and leaning forward to lift up the plate of sandwiches and pass it, but the rest of his face had perished; the remembered hairless young hand out of the brown tweed jacket's sleeve, the locks of crinkly, rather difficult hair worn too long for convention, and the lobeless, narrow ear with the hair waving thick above it, light brown, or perhaps only touched with light in places, or perhaps burned light by the Italian sun, had not expired but she could not meet his eyes. Below the concave temple's level were the deep tiny lines (just under the eyebrow's dark delicate extremity), worn there by too much dry chortling at wit (his own or anybody else's) or else from squinting hard against the weather, radiating finely from the eye's tip. But whenever he turned in memory to pass the plate of sandwiches, the vision failed: the mouth, the nose, the eyes went out and only the brow remained with the long wrinkles across it like the marks of tide left on a beach, and the widow's peak giving a heart's shape to the face. Now that he had written her, and the aunt had written, he did not cease leaning in profile, only in profile, over the textbook's page, the hairless, youthful hand following the line as she read it:

"The 'approach' is the three strides the horse makes immediately before taking off. The problem is to get the horse to jump off his hocks, at a suitable distance away from the fence, and to jump completely under the rider's control. The rider must decide in good time upon the last three strides, counting 'one-two-three-up,' and regulate his horse's pace accordingly." She who had ridden and jumped since before she was five now making a study of it and reading: "Keep the horse at a controlled canter up to thirty feet from the fence. The length of a stride in a controlled canter is about six feet. At thirty feet from the fence increase this stride to seven feet, then to eight, and finally to nine. At this point you are six feet from the jump and should then give the horse the office for the leap–" and Mr. Sheehan leaned across the page in profile, the side of his mouth laughing, his eye squeezed up with laughing and the thick dark lashes thrusting forward, and the girl stretched in the librating, the almost imperceptibly moving hammock thought, I don't know whether I like him or not, I don't know if I really like him.

And now the rains returned again, starting in one afternoon as she lay reading the book and swinging slightly, the bare sandaled foot hanging near the ground. First the clouds gathered up behind the house and then the sun went, half the visible world lying in yellow murk for a space and half in blue rich foreboding, and then the first single shafts of rain came down, slanting long and silvery past the foliage, falling at intervals beyond her haven like deliberately lanced spears. Then came the true hard rain, driving down the lawn all afternoon and streaming along the window panes at supper; after the first quick stabs of lightning and the thunder had passed, the rain continued swiftly and relentlessly falling across the country, setting its quiet, dreary pace in the evening and then buckling down to it for the night. When the girl awoke at one in the morning, it was still raining quietly outside. She had brought her mackintosh up in the evening from below and laid it over the chair with her riding breeches, and now she put it on and tied the rubber handkerchief over her hair before going out the window. She thought I might have remembered my Wellingtons, sliding in her breeches and plaid wool bedroom slippers down the spouting drainpipe, but she had forgotten them the night before and forgot them now by the time she reached the stable. She was thinking, I just want him to be there, waiting inside, that's all I ask. I don't care if I'm soaked to the skin if he'll just understand and be there. And once inside the stable she saw him leaning beyond the shaded lantern he had set by the stall: Apby with his own black mackintosh shining with rain as he saddled the hunter.

"So you did come!" she said, and he looked up and touched his cap's beak, saying: "You said to be here, Miss," and leaned to the girth-straps again.

"I thought maybe when you saw it was raining," she said, and as she pushed in sideways past the horse's tail and croup and past the leaning groom, the blind horse turned his head on his shoulder towards the sound of her voice and her approach. She stood by his head, running her wet hand under his forelock, and she said: "I'm going up to London tomorrow. That's why I wanted to see you tonight. I wanted to ask you to carry on without me for the night and day I'm up in the city. I mean, I want you to put Brigand through his work-out the way I've been doing. One to half-past two, say, tomorrow night, and then when I come back I'm going to show them."

"Yes, Miss," said the groom, still leaning, not lifting his head.

"You can keep him on the figure eight with change and the half-passage at the canter," she said. She drew her hand down the short rough hair on the nasal bone. "You can try him out tonight with me on the half-passage and change, and if you can keep him going while I'm away, that'll be saving—" She thought of saying "my life" and then, because this brought it so near to "his life," she suddenly crossed her fingers against bad luck and stopped speaking. As Apby straightened up her eyes slid towards him a little cautiously, in slow, tentative induction. "Look," she said. "Another reason I wanted to see you tonight. I want to make him jump." She watched the groom sideways down the stall, her hand moving under the horse's forelock. "I want to take him over a fence tonight," she said.

The groom stood in his brightly gleaming coat, part in the lantern's light and part in the stable's dark, his cap on and its shadow cast grotesquely to the ceiling's beams, his hands on his hips, his dwarfed legs bowed, facsimile in miniature of tough and indomitable and muscular man.

"You can't do it, Miss," he said. "You can't make a blind horse jump. You can't do more than what nature allows for. You're just fixing him for a broken shoulder or broken neck—"

"I set up a knife-rest in the paddock three nights ago," she said, not paying any heed but standing there half-smiling, bringing her hand slowly down the pan of the hunter's cheek. "He took it. He took it back and forth a dozen times. When I come back I'll stretch him out on broader jumps."

"You can't do it," said Apby. He stood there on the straw bedding, his hands knuckled on his hips and the light shining through the arch and bow of his legs in their leather gaiters. He had shoved the beak of his cloth cap up and now it stood erect from the lining's edge above his creased short brow. "You've done up to now with a crock as what I've never heard of no one else doing, but you nor nobody can't give him the sight the time he needs it quick like that for gauging width and height. You can't do it," he said, and he said it again as he extinguished the lantern and then followed her and the horse out over the beam and into the steadily raining night. "You can't do it," he said, closing the stable door and buttoning his mackintosh's collar up to his chin while she mounted quickly from the ground. "You can't say to any horse, living or dead, this is so high this time and the next time it's so high so get ready for it, not unless he's got the power to see. Not unless you had just one jump fixed for him, say knee-high, and took him over it twenty times running, and even then. Even then," he said, "you couldn't do it."

"What I said to you first about why I wanted you to come out here tonight," she said, turning back to him on the saddle, "that wasn't the whole thing. I could have said that to you tomorrow morning or yesterday afternoon just as well. What I really wanted was for you to be here for the jump. I want you to stand at the thirty-foot mark in the paddock and call out one, two, three at the moment I cross it so I'll know how far it is to the fence."

"You can't do it," Apby said, following the horse's footfalls in the rain, not going up the stud-farm road tonight but the long way around by the running water to the paddocks. "You can't have a horse's eyes go and not pay for it, some way you got to pay for it. There wouldn't be no justice anywheres if a blind horse could do it as good as a horse without a flaw or a failing. You can't do what's impossible, because if you could there wouldn't be no end—" and not hearing the uneasy and exasperated words but only the sound of his complaint, the girl turned in the saddle and went on talking over her shoulder to him in the steadily falling rain.

"That'll tell me and tell him, that'll tell us both when we've got to the approach," she said, "and then I'll know when to give him the rise and take him over. You'll stand at the thirty-foot mark where I laid it out this morning, no, yesterday morning by this time, and you'll call out one, two, three. . . ."

"And to think," the groom's voice went on as he came booted and clopping behind, "it was me that begun this, started you off that night in the paddocks when you had him out with me— If I was to do the right thing by everybody, you and the horse included, what I'd do now is tell

Mrs. Lombe what's going on, get 'er up out-a-wer bed no matter if it's middle of the night or tomorrow morning, and she'd put 'er foot down and seen it was put a stop to. If I was to do what I ought to be doing now instead of—" He took one hand out of his mackintosh pocket and wiped the rain down his cheeks the way a comedian pretends to wipe the smile from his face, and then he started running clumsily forward through the mud and rain, stumbling ahead until he got to the horse's evenly and rhythmically riding croup and passed it, and then kept abreast the stirrup with the girl's plaid wool bedroom slipper thrust soaking in it while he said: "If I was to go to the house now and tell Mrs. Lombe, she wouldn't stand for it. She'd put a stop to it all right before anything worse came to happen, jumping on a stone-blind horse the way you say on a night that even frogs would stay home in. If I was to go back to the house now and get—"

"Only you wouldn't," the girl said, riding straight ahead. "You wouldn't do it because I need you to stand at the thirty-foot mark. If you didn't stand there, then something might happen because I couldn't judge close enough when to give him the rise. I worked it out from the book that maybe he'll jump this way if he won't jump any other. I wouldn't ask it for any other horse but just give him his rein and let him take off when he liked, maybe not elegant, according to the book, but that's the way I've always done it. The book says—"

"Oh, the book!" said Apby. Either she halted the horse or he halted of himself, but her voice and his movement ceased at the same instant and the groom looked up and, understanding what it was now, went ahead to open the paddock gate. She heard the hinges cry out and, waiting, heard Apby beginning the same arguments over in the same vexed, grieved tone.

"You can't do it no more than anybody could do it, a trainer couldn't do it and no book can tell you how to take a blind, dumb, unwitting, unwilling beast—" and she leaned forward and patted the horse's shoulder on which the rain poured like sweat.

"So you wouldn't let me down," she said as she rode in past Apby. "You'll stand at the thirty-foot mark where I made it this morning. I'll show it to you."

"Anyways," Apby said, letting the gate swing back, "if he breaks his back at it that'll be all right. They'll have to put him down tomorrow then, Mr. Penson or no Mr. Penson."

"Stand here, Apby," she said, bringing the horse to a halt in the grass. "Stand here. You can feel the bricks making a cross. That's it."

"You can't do it," Apby said again, and out of the little distance she had ridden away already, she said:

"I have done it. I did it alone with him over the knife-rest when there was moonlight, ten, fifteen times back and forth. The only difference is neither of us can see tonight. You stay where you are." The rain came quickly, quietly down, not in voluble articulation as on a house's roof or windows, but striking the face, the naked hands in silence, dropping steadily, as if forever, on the head and shoulders, the bent legs, beating softly as a moth's wings in the trees, until it was rain no longer after a while but the accumulated presence of water, more salient than the dark's or any human presence, like the presence of a vast and swiftly flowing, unseen river passing within arm's reach through the night. Apby stood with water trickling from his cap's stuff down across his face, water dripping unceasingly from the now lowered beak, one drop following another in rivulation to the corners of his mouth, into his ears until, like a bather, he put his forefingers into the ears' orifices and wrung them. "Damn the rain," was the last thing he heard her say before he heard the horse coming, and then a little later, either in imagination or in reality, saw coming towards him the dim cantering shape.

"She might have picked any other night to do it," he said half aloud, as if speaking to someone standing there with him for comfort's sake or else to split the blame with. He ran the back of his hand along his upper lip, under his water-beaded nose, and shook the drops off, and now the splatter of the horse's feet, the wind and thrash of his coming was almost ready to pass. He felt the movement of the air, the breath, the throb, heard even the saddle's creaking leather and the tossed bit's jangle, as if someone had opened a window or pushed open a door near him to let in these sounds he had not heard before in a vast darkened and silenced hall; and as the thing rushed past he leapt back and called the words out. "One, two, three!" he called out like a man crying desperately out from shore into the hopeless dark and wind to the floundered and drowning lost in a storm-pounded sea.

Mr. Sheehan, she thought for an instant, said that time in Florence that nobody should start riding too young, children being either too bold or too timid or both at the same time, and then the bold ones crack up going fast and they've no nerve left to go on the rest of their lives with, and the timid ones go on being shy with horses, or danger, or other people, or with themselves; their spirits, not their bodies, crippled. Mr. Sheehan said, England, the horse-growing country and the country as well of all the misfits, the hugger-muggers, the reticent, the mum, the evaders, because why, because what? because what except stuck up on a horse's back since generations and licked from the get-away, the lip set, both upper and lower, the eyes taught not to quail, and the heart broken in two by funk or daring at the age of five or younger. Take away the horses and you would have a fine upstanding race of men, the Britons, said Mr. Sheehan, the side of his face in profile squinted up either against laughing or against the drifting Irish weather, and for an instant she remembered the first time being thrown: the hack had cantered her up the lane to the top of the hill and there he had reared for no reason except "frightened by the bush because the bush unexpectedly turned and waved a branch," without warning dropping her the long way down. I remember being sick, terrifically sick, she thought, perhaps passing Apby at the thirty-foot mark now, and mother made me mount quickly again as soon as I was finished being sick. "If you don't mount right away," mother said, "you'll start crying and then you won't want to get up on a horse again," and now Apby's voice called out, "One, two, three," and she put her teeth together and thought in sudden wild jubilation, Tomorrow I'll be able to tell Mr. Sheehan that at thirty feet from the fence I increased the stride to seven feet, then to eight, and finally to nine, at this point being, as near as I could judge in the dark, six feet from the jump and I gave my horse the office for the leap.

"Bat," she said quickly. "I can't see any more than you can but we're going to take it." She let the head free then and the loins free, and her weight moved swiftly into the knees as they clasped the saddle-flaps. The balls of the feet were riding lightly in the stirrup irons now and she held him firmly to the fence with her legs. At once she felt him rising strongly but sweetly under her, the mouth limber, the neck pliant even though stretched to go, no sense of heat or excitement confusing him but the blood as temperate as if he still cantered easily across the paddock. Just as they cleared what, from conjecture, must have been the rail though lost and undelineated in the night's and the falling water's obscurity, she thought of the other side and the wet grass where he might bog or slip at the landing, and she said again: "Damn it, oh, damn the rain."

She leaned with him, the body that had followed through the rise and the soaring now bending with him through the descent, and as his forefeet struck the ground her knees and ankles caught the shock and broke it but her hands did not move on the reins. She let him stride on for twenty yards or more before she pulled him up and turned him on his hocks, and halted there in the rain and darkness and listening to the coming and going of his breath, she called out to the groom:

"Apby, I say, Apby, come and open the gate for us," her own voice sounding ringing and clear. "Apby!" she called, like someone tipsy with triumph, drunk and reeling with it. "Apby, hurry up! I want to take him over again."

7

On Friday afternoon, just after lunch time, the girl went up to London in her new suit, carrying her little overnight bag in her hand, and nothing happened in the country until the Saturday morning. It was then, standing by the sitting-room window and looking into the flowered and damp emptiness of still another day, that Candy saw them emerge from somewhere, perhaps from the main road outside where a two-seated car might now be standing halted close to the bank: the back of a man he had not seen before in khaki riding-breeches and a sport-shirt, and his wife in dark blue spotted all over its broad skirt and blouse with white, and her summer hat on, the sailor hat which came out of some undivulged hiding place each end of May or in the early days of June, depending on the weather. He watched them descend the drive, making the gestures of talk, and pass the rock garden where the purple foxgloves stood nobly if a little shabbily flowering in the moist sunlight, and pass the wayfaring-tree at the curve and go from sight. For a moment, standing at the window, he wondered and then without any feeling of surprise, he knew. He knew it exactly, as if the words had been said to him and knew now, moreover, that it was for this the quiet and lull of the day before and the night had been preparing. Through some irremediable error the sun had come out that morning, but otherwise the unmistakable stage was set.

When they had gone from sight he walked into the dining room and although it was only just gone ten he took the decanter of whiskey out. The ordinary glasses were kept in the pantry, and sadly, quietly he thought, I cannot go out and get one any more than I can go out there and go into the stable and stop them doing it. He opened the sideboard door, stooping to it, and selected one of the small embossed porter glasses and set it on the table, and then he filled it three-quarters full with whiskey and set the decanter down, fitting the glass stopper to it, and he drank the whiskey off at once. He thought, They'll do it humanely, they're bound to do it humanely, and he looked almost peacefully at the bottom of the empty glass. If I had any arguments or any reasons to give them I could go out there, or if I could walk into the stable like a man with a wallet fat in his pocket and slap the sides of it and say, This happens to be, just happens to be my horse, not yours, my lady. He was bought by me, paid for by me, purchased under the rules of warranty (only I never got the certificate because I had two drinks instead), as sound in wind and eyes, quiet to ride, has been hunted and capable of being hunted, so pack up your chalk and your pistol and your vet, whoever he is, in your old kit bag and go back to gardening. They'll do it humanely, he thought, and the feeling of peace spread marvelously through him, something better than mere respite or truce but the final, absolute conciliation through performed and indisputable act. The responsibility is being taken off my shoulders, he thought gently, forbearingly, the issue is being removed from my hands. I have no authority, no jurisdiction, even if I moved now towards the door and out it I could not save that horse, and the sense of actionless, speechless bliss rose richly in him; I am powerless, helpless because they know their business and I have none yet, I never found it; my wife will see that the target is properly indicated and the man in breeches will make use of the humane killer to the conclusion of this drama, this minor but grotesquely aggrandized tragedy which will fade slowly but unerringly into the past. It is not disaster but the one logical solution, he thought, and the voice drifted from some far dim plane of memory to hearing now, repeating as it had years back repeated all day at fifteen-minute intervals across the air, "The King's life is drawing peacefully to a close."

After the second porter-glassful was drunk, Candy put his hand to his back pocket and took his silver and leather hip-flask out. He unscrewed the cap and drew the cork out with his teeth, tipping his head on the side to do it, and then he filled it up from the decanter. He did not spill any, but because a little spread wet at the top, he ran his tongue around the screw-cap's thread, then corked the flask and twisted the top back on and slipped it under his jacket again. Or stamp down there, he thought, and take no nonsense from them, the artist out of pocket, out of luck, but painting alone, accomplishing alone experiments in style, subject, and treatment, working alone and making a name that people listen for in city exhibitions and museums, look for in catalogues and magazines, so that even a wife or even a vet's assistant would listen. He looked at the decanter in dispassionate meditation a moment and then he filled the porter glass again. Penson drawing his last breaths, it may be, while I stand here drinking, kicked towards kingdom come and landing on the threshold, and yet I'd face my Maker saying they haven't a damned bit of evidence against that blind staggerer out there in the stable, not a shred of anything except that he can't see the day ahead to face the firing squad. You've got to die, he said suddenly, putting the glass down. Horse, it's your turn to die. This time it's not Penson or me but you, horse not man, you blank-eyed espial spying upon the secrets of eternity, you milky-eyed deserter. You're no good to anyone, he said, but he was looking at his own face in the sideboard mirror. Because this was the affair culminated at last between himself and the very fiber and substance of his going on, he did not begin thinking of Nancy until after the fifth glass of whiskey; and when he thought of her he put the glass stopper for the last time into the decanter and went at once, walking carefully but without any semblance of drunkenness, upstairs to his own bedroom and pulled open the bottom drawer of the dresser. From under the neatly folded cardigans, he took out the revolver and made sure that it was loaded, and then he put it into his jacket pocket. There were two more glasses of liquid left in the decanter and he drank them fast.

"That makes everything neat and tidy," he said, but when he stooped to retrieve the glass stopper which had dropped to the ground, his head spun slowly, so he helped himself erect again by holding to the table with one hand. Then he started walking, careful and trim in his squire's jacket, his silk kerchief folded on his neck, down the faintly steaming drive.

The sliding door was standing open beyond the wayfaring-tree and Mrs. Lombe and the young man in breeches were in the stable. They were not in the hunter's stall but talking together as they stood on the timber floor, and beyond the box's gate the hunter's quarters shone in the light. At the first sound of Candy's step on the wood, his wife turned her head with her sailor hat on it and said:

"This is Mr. Lombe, Mr. Harrison. I've had Mr. Harrison over this morning while Nan's up in London to do what has to be done."

Candy stood against the daylight in the door, a rather jaunty figure with his hands in his jacket pockets, the back of the wrist and the left thumb showing, but this time the right thumb was out of sight. He nodded his head either in greeting or dismissal and teetered upwards, his legs planted wide apart, on his clean crepe soles.

"Where's Apby?" he said. "Does Apby know what's going on?"

"I sent him off early." She smiled a quick, tolerant, although impatient-seeming smile. "He's having the day off in Pellton. I told him I'd see the hunter got his midday meal. I haven't said anything to anybody. I just want to get it done as quickly and quietly as possible. It's not a pleasant job of work for anyone concerned. I had Richards take the mare to the village to have her shod."

"So there wouldn't be any witnesses, not so much as a mare looking on, what?" said Candy, and now her eye on him altered as she began to suspect it. "Where do you intend to do it?" Candy said. Since that first step over the threshold he had not moved and his eyes had not shifted from her face, so if he had been asked then he could not have said whether the man called Harrison was short or tall, or what the color of his hair or what his age was, only that he remembered the khaki breeches and the gaiters walking down the drive. "Where is justice to be meted out?" he said loudly, sardonically.

"Mr. Harrison is the huntsman from the local hunt," Mrs. Lombe said, saying the words pleasantly and exactly to him, as if it were a child's small, stubborn figure, not a man's and not her husband's, who stood teetering against the light. "He's been kind enough to offer to do it for us. He's an expert at it. I've arranged for the haulers to come at eleven and take the body away."

"Which body?" said Candy, and now as good as if his breath had been wafted to her over the smell of clean horse and fresh bedding and clean mixture in the stable, she knew the bitter and unacceptable truth: that he was drunk, drunk at ten in the morning, that it was not curiosity that held him standing there haranguing but drunken opposition; not only drunk but drunk before lunch for a change and drunk before a stranger.

"Don't be an idiot, Candy," she said, laughing quickly, nervously, and glancing at Mr. Harrison in invitation to him to do the only possible thing and laugh. "You'd better go back to the house so Mr. Harrison can get on with it."

But Candy began crossing the stable now, walking blank-eyed, blank-faced, deliberately towards them, not swaying or deviating from the invisible line his intention had drawn, but walking carefully and deliberately at them as if they were no longer there now that he had started walking directly to where he wanted to go. They did not obstruct his way, but as he came they drew apart, each of them drawing to one side as a crowd might have drawn apart to allow the passage of a vehicle that ran on tracks and could not alter its course, and Candy passed between the two people who stared, the man in curiosity and the woman in wonder at him, and walked to the stall where the horse stood, its head hanging peacefully now across the gate. Candy took his left hand from his pocket and put it on the latch, and the horse threw his head up and Candy hesitated an instant, and then turned his head too and looked back at the two people standing, in their turn outlined and faceless, against the sunlight in the open stable-door.

"I just wanted to know," he said, almost imperceptibly swaying. "I just wanted to ask you before I go in there how Mr. Penson is, Mr. Har— I'd like to know."

The young man took a step or two towards him—young, thought Candy, seeing him for the first time now as he stood in relief against the yellowish brightness of the day outside, young only because the legs tapered in the breeches and the shoulders were broad and unsloping, for he could not see the features of the face or the color of the hair.

"I was just telling Mrs. Lombe," the man said in a strangely gentle, girl-like voice. "I was just telling her he died. He died last night."

"So an eye for an eye, a horse for a man, that's the way you look at it," said Candy, sardonically, but the whiskey was swinging hard and sickening in his head now and he held to the gate's wood for support. "A life for a life is what you think—" He saw Mrs. Lombe with the old sailor hat on coming towards him and he remembered I mustn't take my right hand out of my pocket until I'm ready. I can get the gate open with my left hand, like this, and now he had come through it and he stood on the oaten straw bedding by the horse now, and the gate was closed between him and his wife and the man she called Mr. Harrison. "He's so expert," he said, holding to the wood and pressing away from the horse's shoulder in the stall, "that he could probably do it without drawing the chalkline or do it with his eyes closed only he's not going to. The minute he takes out his revolver, I take out mine."

"Candy, come out," said Mrs. Lombe, but the conviction had lapsed from her voice. Candy was standing as far from the horse as he could get, the bordeaux-red silk kerchief around his throat because he hadn't shaved yet, the small of his back against the rough wood of the stall.

"Please be reasonable, please come out," she said, but the power had gone from her. She stood with the straw hat pushed up off her forehead, seeking to say it with dignity.

"I'll come out when Nancy gets back," he said. "My little girl will come out here and she'll understand what I'm trying to do. She'll take shifts here with me, all summer if it has to be, hunger-strike, sleep-strike, drink-strike," he said, and at the last words the feeling of tears welled in him; and oh, heavens, heavens, thought the woman standing on the other side of the gate, what have I done that I should have to stand here before a stranger and hear him turning maudlin? What have I done that it should have to happen like this? Oh, spare me, spare me. "And if you try to stop Nancy's marriage it'll be the same thing. I won't have you interfering with her and stopping her whatever she wants to do, lift a finger, go to a dance, have a horse of her own like–" And ah, unjust, unjust, thought the mother bitterly. Who was it picked out the clothes for her to go up to London, who was it had found the school for her in Florence last year? But there had been so many years of it now that it was for nothing else but the stranger's presence that she cared. "I'll wait here for my little girl," Candy went on saying in the same low-pitched and vagrant and scarcely defiant voice, "and you can't do anything to me because this time I've got the upper hand, for once I've got it. You've got the money but this time I tricked you, I fooled you, you can't field marshal me out of here, you can't major-domo me, you can't even bribe me–" Oh, sordid, sordid, thought the mother in grief as she looked at the small contorted flushed face, ageless and queer as a dwarf's, turning from one side to the other in fear of death and fear of life on the other side of the gate. In a moment she looked towards Mr. Harrison and whether the actual word was said or merely indicated, they both moved in simultaneous dignity and forbearance towards the door, crossing the timber to the threshold, and there the young man stood deferentially to one side to let her pass before him out into the light. "You can go, but it won't make any difference to me," Candy called out, but then as the blind horse shifted a little nervously on the straw, he lowered his voice. "That's all right," he said, but when he looked at the massive shoulder and the strong hanging head his blood swooned in him. He stood leaning against the side of the stall, his hands in his pockets, seeking not to see the great, living, breathing beast with its eyes clogged blue and milky beneath the long, luxuriant lash, and then he took his left hand from the jacket's pocket and felt out the flask, and braced it against his ribs with his palm, the left hand's fingers fumbling off the cap. He did not stir his right hand but drew the cork out with his teeth and drank, and while he drank the horse brought his lowered head across the straw, the wide, soft nostrils seeking quiveringly for cognizance until the nose reached the shoes' tips and lipped across them, the monstrous, vacuous, ingesting suction of a snail mounting the ankles and the trousers to the jacket, and when the man brought his arm carefully down and his hand with the flask in it he dared move no longer but stood flattened against the stall's wood, waiting, the flask extended in his stricken hand. The horse's head lifted slowly, searchingly, the ears back, the hairs in the nostrils trembling in the blasts of breath, and now that the lips came blindly fumbling across his shoulder to his face, the cry of terror ripped from Candy's throat. "For Christ's sake!" he screamed, and the horse flung his head away in fright, swinging in the box until his quarters stood trembling now before the man, the long black tail twitching across his buttocks and the points of his hocks. "I can't, I can't," Candy said under his breath and he began whimpering as he leaned against the boards. "I'm afraid, I have a right to be afraid," he said, but now that the horse had ceased to move he managed to cork the flask, his left hand shaking, and slip it into his back pocket. Then he stood quiet there better than a quarter of an hour, his hands out of sight in his pockets, the dream of dauntlessness and sedulity vaguely augmenting and as vaguely waning, and at the last instant of fading reversing to a stronger, clearer, dizzier amplification. At the end of that little while, Mrs. Lombe and the huntsman came through the door and crossed the stable again.

"Mr. Harrison and I have been talking things over," she began in the measured, pleasant voice that must bring concurrence to logic in its wake. "Mr. Harrison thinks it might be very dangerous for you to stay in there with that horse. I explained to him the horse was not accustomed to being handled by you and he says that's where the great danger lies. It's strangers that worry them when there's anything wrong." He stood with the small of his back held against the boards, his eyes fixed sightless on the horse's rump and the long black tail that swept at intervals across it, and he did not speak. "If you're making this absurd scene for Nancy's sake," she went on, "I assure you she'd rather come home to find her ailing horse dead than to find her father in hospital—"

"Mr. Lombe," said the huntsman in his girl-like wounded voice, "it's scarcely taking the long view of things to—"

It was not Candy's passive opposition now that stopped them both, but without any warning he began to sing, lifting his head so that the back of it rested against the stall's boards, and his throat came free of the silk kerchief as he sang loudlessly, tunelessly what words he remembered of what remnants of song he salvaged from the cahotage of terror and drink and despair.

" 'I saw England's king from the top of a bus, He was riding in state so he didn't see us,' " he sang, bawling it out, and the horse flicked his ears. " 'And though—oh, tra, tra, tra, te-de dum—oh, by the Saxons we once were oppressed, I cheered, God forgive me, oh, God, oh, God, forgive me, I cheered with the rest, I—' "

Mrs. Lombe stepped a little nearer and spoke his name, and he glanced quickly at her and began at once:

'I'm one of the ruins Cromwell knocked abaht a bit, I'm *one* of the ruins Cromwell knocked abaht a bit, oh, tra, la, la, la! Outside the Cromwell Arms last Saturday night I was one of the—' "

When the haulers came a little after eleven, Mrs. Lombe went to the door with dignity and sent them off, offering to pay them extra if they would be kind enough to come back in the afternoon. Candy had been singing. " 'You remember young Peter O'Loughlin, of course? Well, here he is now at the head of the force! I met him one day while crossing the Strand—oh, God, oh, God bless him, he held up the street with one wave of his hand,' " but when he heard the men speaking outside and saw her go, proudly and discreetly as a lady might, to give them their directions, he turned his head towards the open door and shouted: " 'Don't tell my mother I'm living in sin, Don't let the old folks—' " and they closed the door and left him to it. All through lunch time he stood motionless in the stall with the small of his back against the boards, and at two he had finished the whiskey. The horse had dropped his head and began eating his bedding for they had not watered or fed him since the morning meal. It was almost three o'clock when the haulers came back: he heard their horses and their voices outside in the sunlight, and then Mr. Harrison opened the stable door and he and Mrs. Lombe crossed the timber briskly together. At a little distance from the box they came to a stop.

"You must be very hungry," she said, standing there slightly in advance of the huntsman. "I had them put out some roastbeef sandwiches and beer on the veranda for you, so if you'll just come along—"

"No," said Candy, looking at the horse. "No, it's all right. You can't trick me." He was talking thick now, leaning against the side of the stall. "I'm waiting here for my little girl, I'm waiting, I'm on the side of civilization. This horse, he isn't a horse any moren any of us are horses, he's the forces of good against the forces of destruction, he's me, just as much me as artist, foreigner, just as much an outcast, he's freak and he's love, he's got something to do with love as it works out against—against this, this empire building and this susspression of the native, what you said the other night about Gandhi being so ugly himself, thin and his teeth out and his gums like that the way you would talk about a horse, you said he was such a freak you didn't care what his beliefs were and didn't think he could have any looking like—well, this horse is against that sort of thing. He's for love. All right," he said, "now we've got it straight. This horse, he's all wrong and wherebyfore he's against everything that is your right and the world's right and Mr. Har— He's me by this time, and he's Nancy I think, or he's me and Nancy getting off to another country where everybody who speaks English is a foreigner, not only me. He's my horse, if he's a horse any more, and I bought him with your money, yes, all right, all rr-r-r-right, your money, but I bought something else at the same time, making the same purchase, my dear, something you haven't seen yet but it's there keeping me in the stable and in the stall until you get out of it and there doesn't have to be any explanation for him," mumbling it, half-crying it as he stood with his hands in his pockets staring at the horse's rump.

Mrs. Lombe made the imperceptible sign to the huntsman or spoke the unheard word, and immediately he stepped forward.

"Mr. Lombe," he said in his winning, girl-like voice, "won't you come out with us now and let events take their course?"

Candy turned his head and looked at them, perhaps assuring himself that he had heard it right, and then he began to laugh. With the small of his back pressed in against the stall's boards he began shaking with silent grotesque laughter.

"Let events *what?*" he wheezed through his laughing. "Let them do what?" He leaned his shoulders back now, his mouth half open, growing sick with laughter. "Let events–"

Mrs. Lombe again made the immediately understood sign to the young man, and again he began speaking.

"Mr. Lombe," he said, "we don't want to do it at all but if you don't come out we shall have to ask the hauler's men outside to help us. This horse has been condemned by two leading veterinary-surgeons, one of them dead now, killed in the act of discharging his duty–" and Candy's fit of strangling laughter cut off the sound of the huntsman's voice and the color came up his girlish throat and spread across his jaws. "Killed," he went on after a moment, with his eyes dropped now, "because he stood behind a horse the way you're standing now, Mr. Lombe, in the stall of an ailing, unpredictable animal," and Candy lay weak with laughing against the boards. "I said he was killed in the discharge of his duty," said the huntsman, his high voice trembling as he raised it to be heard. "While you, Mr. Lombe, are obstructing mine and wasting my Saturday for me–" and Candy's hilarious gasps rose now to cries of laughter and then stopped short in incredulous amazement.

"*Your* Satur– Mr. Har–? Your–?" he began, and the laughter convulsed him again. "Oh, please, pull-ease, stop being funny! Oh, pll-ease, pll-ease, Mr. Har–" He threw back his smooth neat little head again and the laughter squeezed out of his eyes and out of the strange contortion of his mouth. "For Christ's sake, pll-ease!" he said, and Mrs. Lombe turned and walked to the stable door and opened it. When she came back the hauler's men were with her, three good, stout countrymen who came through the door after her and stood waiting, ill-at-ease, beside her.

"Will you be so kind," she said quietly to them, but her spirit was bowed in grief and humility in her: so it has come to this, it has come to this. "Will you be good enough to assist the gentleman outside so that he will be out of danger," she said.

The three men stood awkwardly there a moment, their arms bare in their short-sleeved collarless shirts, their shoes good and almost stylish-looking as the shoes of Devonshire workmen are likely to be. They looked uncertainly at one another, and at Mrs. Lombe in her sailor hat, awkwardly seeking, and in too much of a dilemma to feign any other emotion, the unmistakable side of respectability. And then the huntsman made the gesture before them: standing with his face and his right arm averted from Candy's sight in case Candy had turned his head to see, he lifted his hand as if it held a glass in it, raised it to drink, once, twice, and then a third time. His mouth shaped the one word but he did not say it to them: drunk. Here was the shared joke now, the inaudibly communicated truth, and once in on it with the gentry the three hauler's men smiled, neither broadly nor sheepishly but simply in recognition, and after looking once more at one another for confirmation, they took the thing on. First Mrs. Lombe stepped forward, the huntsman walking to one side of her and a little back, perhaps out of native and habitual precaution, and close behind them followed the hauler's men. For an instant Candy did not see them as the march across the boards began but stood leaning back against the wood, his eyes fixed on the horse's motionless rump as if subduing and mastering it by sight alone. He leaned against the stall's side, his hands clenched in his pockets, having entered now another and more violent plane of fear. If I take my eyes off these quarters, this catapult of death, I'm done for, he thought, I'm finished, I'll die with the sight of Penson lying with his skull oozing its sense and memory out on horse's bedding. The dream-stupored and desperate eyes saw on the hunter's cool burnished croup the mark, raw as if only just branded on the flesh, of the horse's iron, the identical stamp they had found on Penson's face, with the hook of one heel jerked through the eyeball and the other heel caught in the palate's vertebrates. But when he felt their purpose advancing on him, he took his right hand out of his pocket for the first time and they saw the pistol in it.

"Don't touch the gate," he said, watching the horse's croup. "Don't touch it."

He did not shoot until Mrs. Lombe put her hand out to the latch, seeing or perhaps only divining the raising of her hand towards the box's gate, and then, without taking his eyes off the horse, he shot wildly out across them, the detonation splitting loud through the stable. The hauler's men and the huntsman ducked, but Mrs. Lombe did not stir but watched with clear stark eyes the blind horse as he whirled in his stall, spinning with forefeet slightly lifted, the tail arched and thrashing in panic across Candy's face and passing, and then the strong brutal head swinging across Candy's skull in its demented quest for sight.

"Come out, Candy," she whispered, but no one heard her. The hauler's men were out the door already and the huntsman was smoothing back his hair. "Come out, Candy," she said. "Come out."

He stood braced against the stall's side, the smoking pistol hanging in his fallen hand, his head pressed back against the board, the face small and fresh-looking, the eyes closed in an attitude of resigned and terrible waiting. He felt himself so, his body like something growing now to the wood and waiting, not for release any more in the gate's opening or Nancy's coming from the rapidly gyrating and seemingly illluminated wheels of fear, but release, as he swooned and drowned in terror, in the actual splinter of the complete and unalterably ordained end. But when he heard the huntsman's voice speaking again beyond the tide in which his body sank and perished, saying, "Let me by, Mrs. Lombe, let me by. This has got to be dealt with. This can't go on. Let me by"—he lifted the revolver again and again, but this time with his eyes closed fast against the vision of his own violent death, he fired out across the stable. And this time the horse shot upward, upright on its hocks, swung madly over him, and, whirling, smashed its heels savagely against the wooden gate. Mrs. Lombe's hand fell suddenly on Mr. Harrison's arm and her fingers clutched in anguish on his flesh, and they stood watching the horse spin, watched it fling itself from side to side in wild despair, while the little man lay pressed against the stall's side, his hands down, his head lifted, so far untouched and perhaps immuned by this passive, abeyant, this almost ludicrous posture of martyrdom.

They stood a while watching Candy pressed back against the planks, his eyes closed, his right hand hanging with the pistol in it, and watched the horse quieting again and beginning to pace restlessly back and forth, its head swinging, pacing quickly, nervously back and forth across the straw with its head lifted and swinging and its nostrils quivering as they lipped the air for warning. Then Mrs. Lombe and the huntsman, as if the inaudible word had again been said, took up their positions at the open stable door. They did not speak much, only now and again a word about the weather, and at twenty past four Mrs. Lombe said in a low voice:

"There's Nancy. There's my daughter coming," and she went forward to meet her, neither the thoughts or the words ready yet, nor the emotion nameable that shook her heart.

KATHERINE ANNE PORTER

Noon Wine

TIME: 1896–1905
PLACE: Small South Texas Farm

The two grubby small boys with tow-colored hair who were digging among the ragweed in the front yard sat back on their heels and said, "Hello," when the tall bony man with straw-colored hair turned in at their gate. He did not pause at the gate; it had swung back, conveniently half open, long ago, and was now sunk so firmly on its broken hinges no one thought of trying to close it. He did not even glance at the small boys, much less give them good-day. He just clumped down his big square dusty shoes one after the other steadily, like a man following a plow, as if he knew the place well and knew where he was going and what he would find there. Rounding the right-hand corner of the house under the row of chinaberry trees, he walked up to the side porch where Mr. Thompson was pushing a big swing churn back and forth.

Mr. Thompson was a tough weather-beaten man with stiff black hair and a week's growth of black whiskers. He was a noisy proud man who held his neck so straight his whole face stood level with his Adam's apple, and the whiskers continued down his neck and disappeared into a black thatch under his open collar. The churn rumbled and swished like the belly of a trotting horse, and Mr. Thompson seemed somehow to be driving a horse with one hand, reining it in and urging it forward; and every now and then he turned halfway around and squirted a tremendous spit of tobacco juice out over the steps. The door stones were brown and gleaming with fresh tobacco juice. Mr. Thompson had been churning quite a while and he was tired of it. He was just fetching a mouthful of juice to squirt again when the stranger came around the corner and stopped. Mr. Thompson saw a narrow-chested man with blue eyes so pale they were almost white, looking and not looking at him from a long gaunt face, under white eyebrows. Mr. Thompson judged him to be another of these Irishmen, by his long upper lip.

"Howdy do, sir," said Mr. Thompson politely, swinging his churn.

"I need work," said the man, clearly enough but with some kind of foreign accent Mr. Thompson couldn't place. It wasn't Cajun and it wasn't Nigger and it wasn't Dutch, so it had him stumped. "You need a man here?"

Mr. Thompson gave the churn a great shove and it swung back and forth several times on its own momentum. He sat on the steps, shot his quid into the grass, and said, "Set down. Maybe we can make a deal. I been kinda lookin' round for somebody. I had two niggers but they got into a cutting scrape up the creek last week, one of 'em dead now and the other in the hoosegow at Cold Springs. Neither one of 'em worth killing, come right down to it. So it looks like I'd better get somebody. Where'd you work last?"

"North Dakota," said the man, folding himself down on the other end of the steps, but not as if he were tired. He folded up and settled down as if it would be a long time before he got up again. He never had looked at Mr. Thompson, but there wasn't anything sneaking in his eye, either. He didn't seem to be looking anywhere else. His eyes sat in his head and let things pass by them. They didn't seem to be expecting to see anything worth looking at. Mr. Thompson waited a long time for the man to say something more, but he had gone into a brown study.

"North Dakota," said Mr. Thompson, trying to remember where that was. "That's a right smart distance off, seems to me."

"I can do everything on farm," said the man; "cheap. I need work."

Mr. Thompson settled himself to get down to business. "My name's Thompson, Mr. Royal Earle Thompson," he said.

"I'm Mr. Helton," said the man, "Mr. Olaf Helton." He did not move.

"Well, now," said Mr. Thompson in his most carrying voice, "I guess we'd better talk turkey."

When Mr. Thompson expected to drive a bargain he always grew very hearty and jovial. There was nothing wrong with him except that he hated like the devil to pay wages. He said so himself. "You furnish grub and a shack," he said, "and then you got to pay 'em besides. It ain't right. Besides the wear and tear on your implements," he said, "they just let everything go to rack and ruin." So he began to laugh and shout his way through the deal.

"Now, what I want to know is, how much you fixing to gouge outa me?" he brayed, slapping his knee. After he had kept it up as long as he could, he quieted down, feeling a little sheepish, and cut himself a chew. Mr. Helton was staring out somewhere between the barn and the orchard, and seemed to be sleeping with his eyes open.

"I'm good worker," said Mr. Helton as from the tomb. "I get dollar a day."

Mr. Thompson was so shocked he forgot to start laughing again at the top of his voice until it was nearly too late to do any good. "Haw, haw," he bawled. "Why, for a dollar a day I'd hire out myself. What kinda work is it where they pay you a dollar a day?"

"Wheatfields, North Dakota," said Mr. Helton, not even smiling.

Mr. Thompson stopped laughing. "Well, this ain't any wheatfield by a long shot. This is more of a dairy farm," he said, feeling apologetic. "My wife, she was set on a dairy, she seemed to like working around with cows and calves, so I humored her. But it was a mistake," he said. "I got nearly everything to do, anyhow. My wife ain't very strong. She's sick today, that's a fact. She's been porely for the last few days. We plant a little feed, and a corn patch, and there's the orchard, and a few pigs and chickens, but our main hold is the cows. Now just speakin' as one man to another, there ain't any money in it. Now I can't give you no dollar a day because ackshally I don't make that much out of it. No, sir, we get along on a lot less than a dollar a day, I'd say, if we figger up everything in the long run. Now, I paid seven dollars a month to the two niggers, three-fifty each, and grub, but what I say is, one middlin'-good white man ekals a whole passel of niggers any day in the week, so I'll give you seven dollars and you eat at the table with us, and you'll be treated like a white man, as the feller says—"

"That's all right," said Mr. Helton. "I take it."

"Well, now I guess we'll call it a deal, hey?" Mr. Thompson jumped up as if he had remembered important business. "Now, you just take hold of that churn and give it a few swings, will you, while I ride to town on a coupla little errands. I ain't been able to leave the place all week. I guess you know what to do with butter after you get it, don't you?"

"I know," said Mr. Helton without turning his head. "I know butter business." He had a strange drawling voice, and even when he spoke only two words his voice waved slowly up and down and the emphasis was in the wrong place. Mr. Thompson wondered what kind of foreigner Mr. Helton could be.

"Now just where did you say you worked last?" he asked, as if he expected Mr. Helton to contradict himself.

"North Dakota," said Mr. Helton.

"Well, one place is good as another once you get used to it," said Mr. Thompson, amply. "You're a forriner, ain't you?"

"I'm a Swede," said Mr. Helton, beginning to swing the churn.

Mr. Thompson let forth a booming laugh, as if this was the best joke on somebody he'd ever heard. "Well, I'll be damned," he said at the top of his voice. "A Swede: well, now, I'm afraid you'll get pretty lonesome around here. I never seen any Swedes in this neck of the woods."

"That's all right," said Mr. Helton. He went on swinging the churn as if he had been working on the place for years.

"In fact, I might as well tell you, you're practically the first Swede I ever laid eyes on."

"That's all right," said Mr. Helton.

Mr. Thompson went into the front room where Mrs. Thompson was lying down, with the green shades drawn. She had a bowl of water by her on the table and a wet cloth over her eyes. She took the cloth off at the sound of Mr. Thompson's boots and said, "What's all the noise out there? Who is it?"

"Got a feller out there says he's a Swede, Ellie," said Mr. Thompson; "says he knows how to make butter."

"I hope it turns out to be the truth," said Mrs. Thompson. "Looks like my head never will get any better."

"Don't you worry," said Mr. Thompson. "You fret too much. Now I'm gointa ride into town and get a little order of groceries."

"Don't you linger, now, Mr. Thompson," said Mrs. Thompson. "Don't go to the hotel." She meant the saloon; the proprietor also had rooms for rent upstairs.

"Just a coupla little toddies," said Mr. Thompson, laughing loudly, "never hurt anybody."

"I never took a dram in my life," said Mrs. Thompson, "and what's more I never will."

"I wasn't talking about the womenfolks," said Mr. Thompson.

The sound of the swinging churn rocked Mrs. Thompson first into a gentle doze, then a deep drowse from which she waked suddenly knowing that the swinging had stopped a good while ago. She sat up shading her weak eyes from the flat strips of late summer sunlight between the sill and the lowered shades. There she was, thank God, still alive, with supper to cook but no churning on hand, and her head still bewildered, but easy. Slowly she realized she had been hearing a new sound even in her sleep. Somebody was playing a tune on the harmonica, not merely shrilling up and down making a sickening noise, but really playing a pretty tune, merry and sad.

She went out through the kitchen, stepped off the porch, and stood facing the east, shading her eyes. When her vision cleared and settled, she saw a long, pale-haired man in blue jeans sitting in the doorway of the hired man's shack, tilted back in a kitchen chair, blowing away at the harmonica with his eyes shut. Mrs. Thompson's heart fluttered and sank. Heavens, he looked lazy and worthless, he did, now. First a lot of no-count fiddling darkies and then a no-count white man. It was just like Mr. Thompson to take on that kind. She did wish he would be more considerate, and take a little trouble with his business. She wanted to believe in her husband, and there were too many times when she couldn't. She wanted to believe that tomorrow, or at least the day after, life, such a battle at best, was going to be better.

She walked past the shack without glancing aside, stepping carefully, bent at the waist because of the nagging pain in her side, and went to the springhouse, trying to harden her mind to speak very plainly to that new hired man if he had not done his work.

The milk house was only another shack of weather-beaten boards nailed together hastily years before because they needed a milk house; it was meant to be temporary, and it was; already shapeless, leaning this way and that over a perpetual cool trickle of water that fell from a little grot, almost choked with pallid ferns. No one else in the whole countryside had such a spring on his land. Mr. and Mrs. Thompson felt they had a fortune in that spring, if ever they got around to doing anything with it.

Rickety wooden shelves clung at hazard in the square around the small pool where the larger pails of milk and butter stood, fresh and sweet in the cold water. One hand supporting her flat, pained side, the other shading her eyes, Mrs. Thompson leaned over and peered into the pails. The cream had been skimmed and set aside, there was a rich roll of butter, the wooden molds and shallow pans had been scrubbed and scalded for the first time in who knows when, the barrel was full of buttermilk ready for the pigs and the weanling calves, the hard packed-dirt floor had been swept smooth. Mrs. Thompson straightened up again, smiling tenderly. She had been ready to scold him, a poor man who needed a job, who had just come there and who might not have been expected to do things properly at first. There was nothing she could do to make up for the injustice she had done him in her thoughts but to tell him how she appreciated his good clean work, finished already, in no time at all. She ventured near the door of the shack with her careful steps; Mr. Helton opened his eyes, stopped playing, and brought his chair down straight, but did not look at her, or get up. She was a little frail woman with long thick brown hair in a braid, a suffering patient mouth and diseased eyes which cried easily. She wove her fingers into an eyeshade, thumbs on temples, and, winking her tearful lids, said with a polite little manner, "Howdy do, sir. I'm Miz Thompson, and I wanted to tell you I think you did real well in the milk house. It's always been a hard place to keep."

He said, "That's all right," in a slow voice, without moving.

Mrs. Thompson waited a moment. "That's a pretty tune you're playing. Most folks don't seem to get much music out of a harmonica."

Mr. Helton sat humped over, long legs sprawling, his spine in a bow, running his thumb over the square mouth-stops; except for his moving hand he might have been asleep. The harmonica was a big shiny new one, and Mrs. Thompson, her gaze wandering about, counted five others, all good and expensive, standing in a row on the shelf beside his cot. "He must carry them around in his jumper pocket," she thought, and noted there was not a sign of any other possession lying about. "I see you're mighty fond of music," she said. "We used to have an old accordion, and Mr. Thompson could play it right smart, but the little boys broke it up."

Mr. Helton stood up rather suddenly, the chair clattered under him, his knees straightened though his shoulders did not, and he looked at the floor as if he were listening carefully. "You know how little boys are," said Mrs. Thompson. "You'd better set them harmonicas on a high shelf or they'll be after them. They're great hands for getting into things. I try to learn 'em, but it don't do much good."

Mr. Helton, in one wide gesture of his long arms, swept his harmonicas up against his chest, and from there transferred them in a row to the ledge where the roof joined to the wall. He pushed them back almost out of sight.

"That'll do, maybe," said Mrs. Thompson. "Now I wonder," she said, turning and closing her eyes helplessly against the stronger western light, "I wonder what became of them little tads. I can't keep up with them." She had a way of speaking about her children as if they were rather troublesome nephews on a prolonged visit.

"Down by the creek," said Mr. Helton, in his hollow voice. Mrs. Thompson, pausing confusedly, decided he had answered her question. He stood in silent patience, not exactly waiting for her to go, perhaps, but pretty plainly not waiting for anything else. Mrs. Thompson was perfectly accustomed to all kinds of men full of all kinds of cranky ways. The point was, to find out just how Mr. Helton's crankiness was different from any other man's, and then get used to it, and let him feel at home. Her father had been cranky, her brothers and uncles had all been set in their ways and none of them alike; and every hired man she'd ever seen had quirks and crotchets of his own. Now here was Mr. Helton, who was a Swede, who wouldn't talk, and who played the harmonica besides.

"They'll be needing something to eat," said Mrs. Thompson in a vague friendly way, "pretty soon. Now I wonder what I ought to be thinking about for supper? Now what do you like to eat, Mr. Helton? We always have plenty of good butter and milk and cream, that's a blessing. Mr. Thompson says we ought to sell all of it, but I say my family comes first." Her little face went all out of shape in a pained blind smile.

"I eat anything," said Mr. Helton, his words wandering up and down.

He *can't* talk, for one thing, thought Mrs. Thompson; it's a shame to keep at him when he don't know the language good. She took a slow step away from the shack, looking back over her shoulder. "We usually have cornbread except on Sundays," she told him. "I suppose in your part of the country you don't get much good cornbread."

Not a word from Mr. Helton. She saw from her eye-corner that he had sat down again, looking at his harmonica, chair tilted. She hoped he would remember it was getting near milking time. As she moved away, he started playing again, the same tune.

Milking time came and went. Mrs. Thompson saw Mr. Helton going back and forth between the cow barn and the milk house. He swung along in an easy lope, shoulders bent, head hanging, the big buckets balancing like a pair of scales at the ends of his bony arms. Mr. Thompson rode in from town sitting straighter than usual, chin in, a towsack full of supplies swung behind the saddle. After a trip to the barn, he came into the kitchen full of good will, and gave Mrs. Thompson a hearty smack on the cheek after dusting her face off with his tough whiskers. He had been to the hotel, that was plain. "Took a look around the premises, Ellie," he shouted. "That Swede sure is grinding out the labor. But he is the closest mouthed feller I ever met up with in all my days. Looks like he's scared he'll crack his jaw if he opens his front teeth."

Mrs. Thompson was stirring up a big bowl of buttermilk cornbread. "You smell like a toper, Mr. Thompson," she said with perfect dignity. "I wish you'd get one of the little boys to bring me in an extra load of firewood. I'm thinking about baking a batch of cookies tomorrow."

Mr. Thompson, all at once smelling the liquor on his own breath, sneaked out, justly rebuked, and brought in the firewood himself. Arthur and Herbert, grubby from thatched head to toes, from skin to shirt, came stamping in yelling for supper. "Go wash your faces and comb your hair," said Mrs. Thompson, automatically. They retired to the porch. Each one put his hand under the pump and wet his forelock, combed it down with his fingers, and returned at once to the kitchen, where all the fair prospects of life were centered. Mrs. Thompson set an extra plate and commanded Arthur, the eldest, eight years old, to call Mr. Helton for supper.

Arthur, without moving from the spot, bawled like a bull calf, "Saaaaaay, Hellllllton, suuuuuupper's ready!" and added in a lower voice, "You big Swede!"

"Listen to me," said Mrs. Thompson, "that's no way to act. Now you go out there and ask him decent, or I'll get your daddy to give you a good licking."

Mr. Helton loomed, long and gloomy, in the doorway. "Sit right there," boomed Mr. Thompson, waving his arm. Mr. Helton swung his square shoes across the kitchen in two steps, slumped onto the bench and sat. Mr. Thompson occupied his chair at the head of the table, the two boys scrambled into place opposite Mr. Helton, and Mrs. Thompson sat at the end nearest the stove. Mrs. Thompson clasped her hands, bowed her head and said aloud hastily, "Lord, for all these and Thy other blessings we thank Thee in Jesus' name, amen," trying to finish before Herbert's rusty little paw reached the nearest dish. Otherwise she would be duty-bound to send him away from the table, and growing children need their meals. Mr. Thompson and Arthur always waited, but Herbert, aged six, was too young to take training yet.

Mr. and Mrs. Thompson tried to engage Mr. Helton in conversation, but it was a failure. They tried first the weather, and then the crops, and then the cows, but Mr. Helton simply did not reply. Mr. Thompson then told something funny he had seen in town. It was about some of the other old grangers at the hotel, friends of his, giving beer to a goat, and the goat's subsequent behavior. Mr. Helton did not seem to hear. Mrs. Thompson laughed dutifully, but she didn't think it was very funny. She had heard it often before, though Mr. Thompson, each time he told it, pretended it had happened that self-same day. It must have happened years ago if it ever happened at all, and it had never been a story that Mrs. Thompson thought suitable for mixed company. The whole thing came of Mr. Thompson's weakness for a dram too much now and then, though he voted for local option at every election. She passed the food to Mr. Helton, who took a helping of everything, but not much, not enough to keep him up to his full powers if he expected to go on working the way he had started.

At last, he took a fair-sized piece of cornbread, wiped his plate up as clean as if it had been licked by a hound dog, stuffed his mouth full, and, still chewing, slid off the bench and started for the door.

"Good night, Mr. Helton," said Mrs. Thompson, and the other Thompsons took it up in a scattered chorus. "Good night, Mr. Helton!"

"Good night," said Mr. Helton's wavering voice grudgingly from the darkness.

"Gude not," said Arthur, imitating Mr. Helton.

"Gude not," said Herbert, the copy-cat.

"You don't do it right," said Arthur. "Now listen to me. Guuuuuude naht," and he ran a hollow scale in a luxury of successful impersonation. Herbert almost went into a fit with joy.

"Now you *stop* that," said Mrs. Thompson. "He can't help the way he talks. You ought to be ashamed of yourselves, both of you, making fun of a poor stranger like that. How'd you like to be a stranger in a strange land?"

"I'd like it," said Arthur. "I think it would be fun."

"They're both regular heathens, Ellie," said Mr. Thompson. "Just plain ignoramuses." He turned the face of awful fatherhood upon his young.

"You're both going to get sent to school next year, and that'll knock some sense into you."

"I'm going to git sent to the 'formatory when I'm old enough," piped up Herbert. "That's where I'm goin'."

"Oh, you are, are you?" asked Mr. Thompson. "Who says so?"

"The Sunday School Supintendant," said Herbert, a bright boy showing off.

"You see?" said Mr. Thompson, staring at his wife. "What did I tell you?" He became a hurricane of wrath. "Get to bed, you two," he roared until his Adam's apple shuddered. "Get now before I take the hide off you!" They got, and shortly from their attic bedroom the sounds of scuffling and snorting and giggling and growling filled the house and shook the kitchen ceiling.

Mrs. Thompson held her head and said in a small uncertain voice, "It's no use picking on them when they're so young and tender. I can't stand it."

"My goodness, Ellie," said Mr. Thompson, "we've got to raise 'em. We can't just let 'em grow up hog wild."

She went on in another tone. "That Mr. Helton seems all right, even if he can't be made to talk. Wonder how he comes to be so far from home."

"Like I said, he isn't no whamper-jaw," said Mr. Thompson, "but he sure knows how to lay out the work. I guess that's the main thing around here. Country's full of fellers trampin' round looking for work."

Mrs. Thompson was gathering up the dishes. She now gathered up Mr. Thompson's plate from under his chin. "To tell you the honest truth," she remarked, "I think it's a mighty good change to have a man round the place who knows how to work and keep his mouth shut. Means he'll keep out of our business. Not that we've got anything to hide, but it's convenient."

"That's a fact," said Mr. Thompson. "Haw, haw," he shouted suddenly. "Means you can do all the talking, huh?"

"The only thing," went on Mrs. Thompson, "is this: he don't eat hearty enough to suit me. I like to see a man set down and relish a good meal. My granma used to say it was no use putting dependence on a man who won't set down and make out his dinner. I hope it won't be that way this time."

"Tell *you* the truth, Ellie," said Mr. Thompson, picking his teeth with a fork and leaning back in the best of good humors, "I always thought your granma was a ter'ble ole fool. She'd just say the first thing that popped into her head and call it God's wisdom."

"My granma wasn't anybody's fool. Nine times out of ten she knew what she was talking about. I always say, the first thing you think is the best thing you can say."

"Well," said Mr. Thompson, going into another shout, "you're so *ree-*

fined about that goat story, you just try speaking out in mixed comp'ny sometime! You just try it. S'pose you happened to be thinking about a hen and a rooster, hey? I reckon you'd shock the Babtist preacher!" He gave her a good pinch on her thin little rump. "No more meat on you than a rabbit," he said, fondly. "Now I like 'em cornfed."

Mrs. Thompson looked at him open-eyed and blushed. She could see better by lamplight. "Why, Mr. Thompson, sometimes I think you're the evilest-minded man that ever lived." She took a handful of hair on the crown of his head and gave it a good, slow pull. "That's to show you how it feels, pinching so hard when you're supposed to be playing," she said, gently.

In spite of his situation in life, Mr. Thompson had never been able to outgrow his deep conviction that running a dairy and chasing after chickens was woman's work. He was fond of saying that he could plow a furrow, cut sorghum, shuck corn, handle a team, build a corn crib, as well as any man. Buying and selling, too, were man's work. Twice a week he drove the spring wagon to market with the fresh butter, a few eggs, fruits in their proper season, sold them, pocketed the change, and spent it as seemed best, being careful not to dig into Mrs. Thompson's pin money.

But from the first the cows worried him, coming up regularly twice a day to be milked, standing there reproaching him with their smug female faces. Calves worried him, fighting the rope and strangling themselves until their eyes bulged, trying to get at the teat. Wrestling with a calf unmanned him, like having to change a baby's diaper. Milk worried him, coming bitter sometimes, drying up, turning sour. Hens worried him, cackling, clucking, hatching out when you least expected it and leading their broods into the barnyard where the horses could step on them; dying of roup and wryneck and getting plagues of chicken lice; laying eggs all over God's creation so that half of them were spoiled before a man could find them, in spite of a rack of nests Mrs. Thompson had set out for them in the feed room. Hens were a blasted nuisance.

Slopping hogs was hired man's work, in Mr. Thompson's opinion. Killing hogs was a job for the boss, but scraping them and cutting them up was for the hired man again; and again woman's proper work was dressing meat, smoking, pickling, and making lard and sausage. All his carefully limited fields of activity were related somehow to Mr. Thompson's feeling for the appearance of things, his own appearance in the sight of God and man. "It don't *look* right," was his final reason for not doing anything he did not wish to do.

It was his dignity and his reputation that he cared about, and there were only a few kinds of work manly enough for Mr. Thompson to undertake with his own hands. Mrs. Thompson, to whom so many forms of work would have been becoming, had simply gone down on him early. He saw, after a while, how short-sighted it had been of him to expect much from Mrs. Thompson; he had fallen in love with her delicate waist and lace-trimmed petticoats and big blue eyes, and, though all those charms had disappeared, she had in the meantime become Ellie to him, not at all the same person as Miss Ellen Bridges, popular Sunday School teacher in the Mountain City First Baptist Church, but his dear wife, Ellie, who was not strong. Deprived as he was, however, of the main support in life which a man might expect in marriage, he had almost without knowing it resigned himself to failure. Head erect, a prompt payer of taxes, yearly subscriber to the preacher's salary, land owner and father of a family, employer, a hearty good fellow among men, Mr. Thompson knew, without putting it into words, that he had been going steadily down hill. God amighty, it did look like somebody around the place might take a rake in hand now and then and clear up the clutter around the barn and the kitchen steps. The wagon shed was so full of broken-down machinery and ragged harness and old wagon wheels and battered milk pails and rotting lumber you could hardly drive in there any more. Not a soul on the place would raise a hand to it, and as for him, he had all he could do with his regular work. He would sometimes in the slack season sit for hours worrying about it, squirting tobacco on the ragweeds growing in a thicket against the wood pile, wondering what a fellow could do, handicapped as he was. He looked forward to the boys growing up soon; he was going to put them through the mill just as his own father had done with him when he was a boy; they were going to learn how to take hold and run the place right. He wasn't going to overdo it, but those two boys were going to earn their salt, or he'd know why. Great big lubbers sitting around whittling! Mr. Thompson sometimes grew quite enraged with them, when imagining their possible future, big lubbers sitting around whittling or thinking about fishing trips. Well, he'd put a stop to that, mighty damn quick.

As the seasons passed, and Mr. Helton took hold more and more, Mr. Thompson began to relax in his mind a little. There seemed to be nothing the fellow couldn't do, all in the day's work and as a matter of course. He got up at five o'clock in the morning, boiled his own coffee and fried his own bacon and was out in the cow lot before Mr. Thompson had even begun to yawn, stretch, groan, roar and thump around looking for his jeans. He milked the cows, kept the milk house, and churned the butter; rounded the hens up and somehow persuaded them to lay in the nests, not under the house and behind the haystacks; he fed them regularly and they hatched out until you couldn't set a foot down for them. Little by little the piles of trash around the barns and house disappeared. He carried buttermilk and corn to the hogs, and curried cockleburs out of the horses' manes. He was gentle with the calves, if a little grim with the cows and hens; judging by his conduct, Mr. Helton had never heard of the difference between man's and woman's work on a farm.

In the second year, he showed Mr. Thompson the picture of a cheese press in a mail order catalogue, and said, "This is a good thing. You buy this, I make cheese." The press was bought and Mr. Helton did make cheese, and it was sold, along with the increased butter and the crates of eggs. Sometimes Mr. Thompson felt a little contemptuous of Mr. Helton's ways. It did seem kind of picayune for a man to go around picking up half a dozen ears of corn that had fallen off the wagon on the way from the field, gathering up fallen fruit to feed to the pigs, storing up old nails and stray parts of machinery, spending good time stamping a fancy pattern on the butter before it went to market. Mr. Thompson, sitting up high on the spring-wagon seat, with the decorated butter in a five-gallon lard can wrapped in wet towsack, driving to town, chirruping to the horses and snapping the reins over their backs, sometimes thought that Mr. Helton was a pretty meeching sort of fellow; but he never gave way to these feelings, he knew a good thing when he had it. It was a fact the hogs were in better shape and sold for more money. It was a fact that Mr. Thompson stopped buying feed, Mr. Helton managed the crops so well. When beef- and hog-slaughtering time came, Mr. Helton knew how to save the scraps that Mr. Thompson had thrown away, and wasn't above scraping guts and filling them with sausages that he made by his own methods. In all, Mr. Thompson had no grounds for complaint. In the third year, he raised Mr. Helton's wages, though Mr. Helton had not asked for a raise. The fourth year, when Mr. Thompson was not only out of debt but had a little cash in the bank, he raised Mr. Helton's wages again, two dollars and a half a month each time.

"The man's worth it, Ellie," said Mr. Thompson, in a glow of self-justification for his extravagance. "He's made this place pay, and I want him to know I appreciate it."

Mr. Helton's silence, the pallor of his eyebrows and hair, his long, glum jaw and eyes that refused to see anything, even the work under his hands, had grown perfectly familiar to the Thompsons. At first, Mrs. Thompson complained a little. "It's like sitting down at the table with a disembodied spirit," she said. "You'd think he'd find something to say, sooner or later."

"Let him alone," said Mr. Thompson. "When he gets ready to talk, he'll talk."

The years passed, and Mr. Helton never got ready to talk. After his work was finished for the day, he would come up from the barn or the milk house or the chicken house, swinging his lantern, his big shoes clumping like pony hoofs on the hard path. They, sitting in the kitchen in the winter, or on the back porch in summer, would hear him drag out his wooden chair, hear the creak of it tilted back, and then for a little while he would play his single tune on one or another of his harmonicas. The harmonicas were in different keys, some lower and sweeter than the others, but the same changeless tune went on, a strange tune, with sudden turns in it, night after night, and sometimes even in the afternoons when Mr. Helton sat down to catch his breath. At first the Thompsons liked it very much, and always stopped to listen. Later there came a time when they were fairly sick of it, and began to wish to each other that he would learn a new one. At last they did not hear it any more, it was as natural as the sound of the wind rising in the evenings, or the cows lowing, or their own voices.

Mrs. Thompson pondered now and then over Mr. Helton's soul. He didn't seem to be a church-goer, and worked straight through Sunday as if it were any common day of the week. "I think we ought to invite him to go to hear Dr. Martin," she told Mr. Thompson. "It isn't very Christian of us not to ask him. He's not a forward kind of man. He'd wait to be asked."

"Let him alone," said Mr. Thompson. "The way I look at it, his religion is every man's own business. Besides, he ain't got any Sunday clothes. He wouldn't want to go to church in them jeans and jumpers of his. I don't know what he does with his money. He certainly don't spend it foolishly."

Still, once the notion got into her head, Mrs. Thompson could not rest until she invited Mr. Helton to go to church with the family next Sunday. He was pitching hay into neat little piles in the field back of the orchard. Mrs. Thompson put on smoked glasses and a sunbonnet and walked all the way down there to speak to him. He stopped and leaned on his pitchfork, listening, and for a moment Mrs. Thompson was almost frightened at his face. The pale eyes seemed to glare past her, the eyebrows frowned, the long jaw hardened. "I got work," he said bluntly, and lifting his pitchfork he turned from her and began to toss the hay. Mrs. Thompson, her feelings hurt, walked back thinking that by now she should be used to Mr. Helton's ways, but it did seem like a man, even a foreigner, could be just a little polite when you gave him a Christian invitation. "He's not polite, that's the only thing I've got against him," she said to Mr. Thompson. "He just can't seem to behave like other people. You'd think he had a grudge against the world," she said. "I sometimes don't know what to make of it."

In the second year something had happened that made Mrs. Thompson uneasy, the kind of thing she could not put into words, hardly into thoughts, and if she had tried to explain to Mr. Thompson it would have sounded worse than it was, or not bad enough. It was that kind of queer thing that seems to be giving a warning, and yet, nearly always nothing comes of it. It was on a hot, still spring day, and Mrs. Thompson had been down to the garden patch to pull some new carrots and green onions and string beans for dinner. As she worked, sunbonnet low over her eyes, putting each kind of vegetable in a pile by itself in her basket, she noticed how neatly Mr. Helton weeded, and how rich the soil was. He had spread it all over with manure from the barns, and worked it in, in the fall, and the vegetables were coming up fine and full. She walked back under the nubbly little fig trees where the unpruned branches leaned almost to the ground, and the thick leaves made a cool screen. Mrs. Thompson was always looking for shade to save her eyes. So she, looking idly about, saw through the screen a sight that struck her as very strange. If it had been a noisy spectacle, it would have been quite natural. It was the silence that struck her. Mr. Helton was shaking Arthur by the shoulders, ferociously, his face most terribly fixed and pale. Arthur's head snapped back and forth and he had not stiffened in resistance, as he did when Mrs. Thompson tried to shake him. His eyes were rather frightened, but surprised, too, probably more surprised than anything else. Herbert stood by meekly, watching. Mr. Helton dropped Arthur, and seized Herbert, and shook him with the same methodical ferocity, the same face of hatred. Herbert's mouth crumpled as if he would cry, but he made no sound. Mr. Helton let him go, turned and strode into the shack, and the little boys ran, as if for their lives, without a word. They disappeared around the corner to the front of the house.

Mrs. Thompson took time to set her basket on the kitchen table, to push her sunbonnet back on her head and draw it forward again, to look in the stove and make certain the fire was going, before she followed the boys. They were sitting huddled together under a clump of chinaberry trees in plain sight of her bedroom window, as if it were a safe place they had discovered.

"What are you doing?" asked Mrs. Thompson.

They looked hang-dog from under their foreheads and Arthur mumbled, "Nothin'."

"Nothing *now,* you mean," said Mrs. Thompson, severely. "Well, I have plenty for you to do. Come right in here this minute and help me fix vegetables. This minute."

They scrambled up very eagerly and followed her close. Mrs. Thompson tried to imagine what they had been up to; she did not like the notion of Mr. Helton taking it on himself to correct her little boys, but she was afraid to ask them for reasons. They might tell her a lie, and she would have to overtake them in it, and whip them. Or she would have to pretend to believe them, and they would get in the habit of lying. Or they might tell her the truth, and it would be something she would have to whip them for. The very thought of it gave her a headache. She supposed she might ask Mr. Helton, but it was not her place to ask. She would wait and tell Mr. Thompson, and let him get at the bottom of it. While her mind ran on, she kept the little boys hopping. "Cut those carrot tops closer, Herbert, you're just being careless. Arthur, stop breaking up the beans so little. They're little enough already. Herbert, you go get an armload of wood. Arthur, you take these onions and wash them under the pump. Herbert, as soon as you're done here, you get a broom and sweep out this kitchen. Arthur, you get a shovel and take up the ashes. Stop picking your nose, Herbert. How often must I tell you? Arthur, you go look in the top drawer of my bureau, left-hand side, and bring me the vaseline for Herbert's nose. Herbert, come here to me. . . ."

They galloped through their chores, their animal spirits rose with activity, and shortly they were out in the front yard again, engaged in a wrestling match. They sprawled and fought, scrambled, clutched, rose and fell shouting, as aimlessly, noisily, monotonously as two puppies. They imitated various animals, not a human sound from them, and their dirty faces were streaked with sweat. Mrs. Thompson, sitting at her window, watched them with baffled pride and tenderness, they were so sturdy and healthy and growing so fast; but uneasily, too, with her pained little smile and the tears rolling from her eyelids that clinched themselves against the sunlight. They were so idle and careless, as if they had no future in this world, and no immortal souls to save, and oh, what had they been up to that Mr. Helton had shaken them, with his face positively dangerous?

In the evening before supper, without a word to Mr. Thompson of the curious fear the sight had caused her, she told him that Mr. Helton had shaken the little boys for some reason. He stepped out to the shack and spoke to Mr. Helton. In five minutes he was back, glaring at his young. "He says them brats been fooling with his harmonicas, Ellie, blowing in them and getting them all dirty and full of spit and they don't play good."

"Did he say all that?" asked Mrs. Thompson. "It doesn't seem possible."

"Well, that's what he meant, anyhow," said Mr. Thompson. "He didn't say it just that way. But he acted pretty worked up about it."

"That's a shame," said Mrs. Thompson, "a perfect shame. Now we've got to do something so they'll remember they mustn't go into Mr. Helton's things."

"I'll tan their hides for them," said Mr. Thompson. "I'll take a calf rope to them if they don't look out."

"Maybe you'd better leave the whipping to me," said Mrs. Thompson. "You haven't got a light enough hand for children."

"That's just what's the matter with them now," shouted Mr. Thompson, "rotten spoiled and they'll wind up in the penitentiary. You don't half whip 'em. Just little love taps. My pa used to knock me down with a stick of stove wood or anything else that came handy."

"Well, that's not saying it's right," said Mrs. Thompson. "I don't hold with that way of raising children. It makes them run away from home. I've seen too much of it."

"I'll break every bone in 'em," said Mr. Thompson, simmering down, "if they don't mind you better and stop being so bull-headed."

"Leave the table and wash your face and hands," Mrs. Thompson commanded the boys, suddenly. They slunk out and dabbled at the pump and slunk in again, trying to make themselves small. They had learned long ago that their mother always made them wash when there was trouble ahead. They looked at their plates. Mr. Thompson opened up on them.

"Well, now, what you got to say for yourselves about going into Mr. Helton's shack and ruining his harmonicas?"

The two little boys wilted, their faces drooped into the grieved hopeless lines of children's faces when they are brought to the terrible bar of blind adult justice; their eyes telegraphed each other in panic, "Now we're really going to catch a licking"; in despair, they dropped their buttered cornbread on their plates, their hands lagged on the edge of the table.

"I ought to break your ribs," said Mr. Thompson, "and I'm a good mind to do it."

"Yes, sir," whispered Arthur, faintly.

"Yes, sir," said Herbert, his lip trembling.

"Now, papa," said Mrs. Thompson in a warning tone. The children did not glance at her. They had no faith in her good will. She had betrayed them in the first place. There was no trusting her. Now she might save them and she might not. No use depending on her.

"Well, you ought to get a good thrashing. You deserve it, don't you, Arthur?"

Arthur hung his head. "Yes, sir."

"And the next time I catch either of you hanging around Mr. Helton's shack, I'm going to take the hide off *both* of you, you hear me, Herbert?"

Herbert mumbled and choked, scattering his cornbread. "Yes, sir."

"Well, now sit up and eat your supper and not another word out of you," said Mr. Thompson, beginning on his own food. The little boys perked up somewhat and started chewing, but every time they looked around they met their parents' eyes, regarding them steadily. There was no telling when they would think of something new. The boys ate warily, trying not to be seen or heard, the cornbread sticking, the buttermilk gurgling, as it went down their gullets.

"And something else, Mr. Thompson," said Mrs. Thompson after a pause. "Tell Mr. Helton he's to come straight to us when they bother him, and not to trouble shaking them himself. Tell him we'll look after that."

"They're so mean," answered Mr. Thompson, staring at them. "It's a wonder he don't just kill 'em off and be done with it." But there was something in the tone that told Arthur and Herbert that nothing more worth worrying about was going to happen this time. Heaving deep sighs, they sat up, reaching for the food nearest them.

"Listen," said Mrs. Thompson, suddenly. The little boys stopped eating. "Mr. Helton hasn't come for his supper. Arthur, go and tell Mr. Helton he's late for supper. Tell him nice, now."

Arthur, miserably depressed, slid out of his place and made for the door, without a word.

There were no miracles of fortune to be brought to pass on a small dairy farm. The Thompsons did not grow rich, but they kept out of the poor house, as Mr. Thompson was fond of saying, meaning he had got a little foothold in spite of Ellie's poor health, and unexpected weather, and strange declines in market prices, and his own mysterious handicaps which weighed him down. Mr. Helton was the hope and the prop of the family, and all the Thompsons became fond of him, or at any rate they ceased to regard him as in any way peculiar, and looked upon him, from a distance they did not know how to bridge, as a good man and a good friend. Mr. Helton went his way, worked, played his tune. Nine years passed. The boys grew up and learned to work. They could not remember the time when Ole Helton hadn't been there: a grouchy cuss, Brother Bones; Mr. Helton, the dairymaid; that Big Swede. If he had heard them, he might have been annoyed at some of the names they called him. But he did not hear them, and besides they meant no harm—or at least such harm as existed was all there, in the names; the boys referred to their father as the Old Man, or the Old Geezer, but not to his face. They lived through by main strength all the grimy, secret, oblique phases of growing up and got past the crisis safely if anyone does. Their parents could see they were good solid boys with hearts of gold in spite of their rough ways. Mr. Thompson was relieved to find that, without knowing how he had done it, he had succeeded in raising a set of boys who were not trifling whittlers. They were such good boys Mr. Thompson began to believe they were born that way, and that he had never spoken a harsh word to them in their lives, much less thrashed them. Herbert and Arthur never disputed his word.

Mr. Helton, his hair wet with sweat, plastered to his dripping forehead, his jumper streaked dark and light blue and clinging to his ribs, was chopping a little firewood. He chopped slowly, struck the ax into the end of the chopping log, and piled the wood up neatly. He then disappeared round the house into his shack, which shared with the wood pile a good shade from a row of mulberry trees. Mr. Thompson was lolling in a swing chair on the front porch, a place he had never liked. The chair was new, and Mrs. Thompson had wanted it on the front porch, though the side porch was the place for it, being cooler; and Mr. Thompson wanted to sit in the chair, so there he was. As soon as the new wore off of it, and Ellie's pride in it was exhausted, he would move it round to the side porch. Meantime the August heat was almost unbearable, the air so thick you could poke a hole in it. The dust was inches thick on everything, though Mr. Helton sprinkled the whole yard regularly every night. He even shot the hose upward and washed the tree tops and the roof of the house. They had laid waterpipes to the kitchen and an outside faucet. Mr. Thompson must have dozed, for he opened his eyes and shut his mouth just in time to save his face before a stranger who had driven up to the front gate. Mr. Thompson stood up, put on his hat, pulled up his jeans, and watched while the stranger tied his team, attached to a light spring wagon, to the hitching post. Mr. Thompson recognized the team and wagon. They were from a livery stable in Buda. While the stranger was opening the gate, a strong gate that Mr. Helton had built and set firmly on its hinges several years back, Mr. Thompson strolled down the path to greet him and find out what in God's world a man's business might be that would bring him out at this time of day, in all this dust and welter.

He wasn't exactly a fat man. He was more like a man who had been fat recently. His skin was baggy and his clothes were too big for him, and he somehow looked like a man who should be fat, ordinarily, but who might have just got over a spell of sickness. Mr. Thompson didn't take to his looks at all, he couldn't say why.

The stranger took off his hat. He said in a loud hearty voice, "Is this Mr. Thompson, Mr. Royal Earle Thompson?"

"That's my name," said Mr. Thompson, almost quietly, he was so taken aback by the free manner of the stranger.

"My name is Hatch," said the stranger, "Mr. Homer T. Hatch, and I've come to see you about buying a horse."

"I reckon you've been misdirected," said Mr. Thompson. "I haven't got a horse for sale. Usually if I've got anything like that to sell," he said, "I tell the neighbors and tack up a little sign on the gate."

The fat man opened his mouth and roared with joy, showing rabbit teeth brown as shoeleather. Mr. Thompson saw nothing to laugh at, for once. The stranger shouted, "That's just an old joke of mine." He caught one of his hands in the other and shook hands with himself heartily. "I always say something like that when I'm calling on a stranger, because I've noticed that when a feller says he's come to buy something nobody takes him for a suspicious character. You see? Haw, haw, haw."

His joviality made Mr. Thompson nervous, because the expression in the man's eyes didn't match the sounds he was making. "Haw, haw," laughed Mr. Thompson obligingly, still not seeing the joke. "Well, that's all wasted on me because I never take any man for a suspicious character 'til he shows hisself to be one. Says or does something," he explained. "Until that happens, one man's as good as another, so far's *I'm* concerned."

"Well," said the stranger, suddenly very sober and sensible, "I ain't come neither to buy nor sell. Fact is, I want to see you about something that's of interest to us both. Yes, sir, I'd like to have a little talk with you, and it won't cost you a cent."

"I guess that's fair enough," said Mr. Thompson, reluctantly. "Come on around the house where there's a little shade."

They went round and seated themselves on two stumps under a chinaberry tree.

"Yes, sir, Homer T. Hatch is my name and America is my nation," said the stranger. "I reckon you must know the name. I used to have a cousin named Jameson Hatch lived up the country a ways."

"Don't think I know the name," said Mr. Thompson. "There's some Hatchers settled somewhere around Mountain City."

"Don't know the old Hatch family," cried the man in deep concern. He seemed to be pitying Mr. Thompson's ignorance. "Why, we came over from Georgia fifty years ago. Been here long yourself?"

"Just all my whole life," said Mr. Thompson, beginning to feel peevish. "And my pa and my grampap before me. Yes, sir, we've been right here all along. Anybody wants to find a Thompson knows where to look for him. My grampap immigrated in 1836."

"From Ireland, I reckon?" said the stranger.

"From Pennsylvania," said Mr. Thompson. "Now what makes you think we came from Ireland?"

The stranger opened his mouth and began to shout with merriment, and he shook hands with himself as if he hadn't met himself for a long time. "Well, what I always says is, a feller's got to come from *somewhere,* ain't he?"

While they were talking, Mr. Thompson kept glancing at the face near him. He certainly did remind Mr. Thompson of somebody, or maybe he really had seen the man himself somewhere. He couldn't just place the features. Mr. Thompson finally decided it was just that all rabbit-teethed men looked alike.

"That's right," acknowledged Mr. Thompson, rather sourly, "but what I always say is, Thompsons have been settled here for so long it don't make much difference any more *where* they come from. Now a course, this is the slack season, and we're all just laying round a little, but nevertheless we've all got our chores to do, and I don't want to hurry you, and so if you've come to see me on business maybe we'd better get down to it."

"As I said, it's not in a way, and again in a way it is," said the fat man. "Now I'm looking for a man named Helton, Mr. Olaf Eric Helton, from North Dakota, and I was told up around the country a ways that I might find him here, and I wouldn't mind having a little talk with him. No, siree, I sure wouldn't mind, if it's all the same to you."

"I never knew his middle name," said Mr. Thompson, "but Mr. Helton is right here, and been here now for going on nine years. He's a mighty steady man, and you can tell anybody I said so."

"I'm glad to hear that," said Mr. Homer T. Hatch. "I like to hear of a feller mending his ways and settling down. Now when I knew Mr. Helton he was pretty wild, yes, sir, wild is what he was, he didn't know his own mind at all. Well, now, it's going to be a great pleasure to me to meet up with an old friend and find him all settled down and doing well by hisself."

"We've all got to be young once," said Mr. Thompson. "It's like the measles, it breaks out all over you, and you're a nuisance to yourself and everybody else, but it don't last, and it usually don't leave no ill effects." He was so pleased with this notion he forgot and broke into a guffaw. The stranger folded his arms over his stomach and went into a kind of fit, roaring until he had tears in his eyes. Mr. Thompson stopped shouting and eyed the stranger uneasily. Now he liked a good laugh as well as any man, but there ought to be a little moderation. Now this feller laughed like a perfect lunatic, that was a fact. And he wasn't laughing because he really thought things were funny, either. He was laughing for reasons of his own. Mr. Thompson fell into a moody silence, and waited until Mr. Hatch settled down a little.

Mr. Hatch got out a very dirty blue cotton bandanna and wiped his eyes. "That joke just about caught me where I live," he said, almost apologetically. "Now I wish I could think up things as funny as that to say. It's a gift. It's . . ."

"If you want to speak to Mr. Helton, I'll go and round him up," said Mr. Thompson, making motions as if he might get up. "He may be in the milk house and he may be setting in his shack this time of day." It was drawing towards five o'clock. "It's right around the corner," he said.

"Oh, well, there ain't no special hurry," said Mr. Hatch. "I've been wanting to speak to him for a good long spell now and I guess a few minutes more won't make no difference. I just more wanted to locate him, like. That's all."

Mr. Thompson stopped beginning to stand up, and unbuttoned one more button of his shirt, and said, "Well, he's here, and he's this kind of man, that if he had any business with you he'd like to get it over. He don't dawdle, that's one thing you can say for him."

Mr. Hatch appeared to sulk a little at these words. He wiped his face with the bandanna and opened his mouth to speak, when round the house there came the music of Mr. Helton's harmonica. Mr. Thompson raised a finger. "There he is," said Mr. Thompson. "Now's your time."

Mr. Hatch cocked an ear towards the east side of the house and listened for a few seconds, a very strange expression on his face.

"I know that tune like I know the palm of my own hand," said Mr. Thompson, "but I never heard Mr. Helton say what it was."

"That's a kind of Scandahoovian song," said Mr. Hatch. "Where I come from they sing it a lot. In North Dakota, they sing it. It says something about starting out in the morning feeling so good you can't hardly stand it, so you drink up all your likker before noon. All the likker, y' understand, that you was saving for the noon lay-off. The words ain't much, but it's a pretty tune. It's a kind of drinking song." He sat there drooping a little, and Mr. Thompson didn't like his expression. It was a satisfied expression, but it was more like the cat that et the canary.

"So far as I know," said Mr. Thompson, "he ain't touched a drop since he's been on the place, and that's nine years this coming September. Yes, sir, nine years, so far as I know, he ain't wetted his whistle once. And that's more than I can say for myself," he said, meekly proud.

"Yes, that's a drinking song," said Mr. Hatch. "I used to play 'Little Brown Jug' on the fiddle when I was younger than I am now," he went on, "but this Helton, he just keeps it up. He just sits and plays it by himself."

"He's been playing it off and on for nine years right here on the place," said Mr. Thompson, feeling a little proprietary.

"And he was certainly singing it as well, fifteen years before that, in North Dakota," said Mr. Hatch. "He used to sit up in a straitjacket, practically, when he was in the asylum—"

"What's that you say?" said Mr. Thompson. "What's that?"

"Shucks, I didn't mean to tell you," said Mr. Hatch, a faint leer of regret in his drooping eyelids. "Shucks, that just slipped out. Funny, now I'd made up my mind I wouldn' say a word, because it would just make a lot of excitement, and what I say is, if a man has lived harmless and quiet for nine years it don't matter if he *is* loony, does it? So long's he keeps quiet and don't do nobody harm."

"You mean they had him in a straitjacket?" asked Mr. Thompson, uneasily. "In a lunatic asylum?"

"They sure did," said Mr. Hatch. "That's right where they had him, from time to time."

"They put my Aunt Ida in one of them things in the State asylum," said Mr. Thompson. "She got vi'lent, and they put her in one of these jackets with long sleeves and tied her to an iron ring in the wall, and Aunt Ida got so wild she broke a blood vessel and when they went to look after her she was dead. I'd think one of them things was dangerous."

"Mr. Helton used to sing his drinking song when he was in a straitjacket," said Mr. Hatch. "Nothing ever bothered him, except if you tried to make him talk. That bothered him, and he'd get vi'lent, like your Aunt Ida. He'd get vi'lent and then they'd put him in the jacket and go off and leave him, and he'd lay there perfickly contented, so far's you could see, singing his song. Then one night he just disappeared. Left, you might say, just went, and nobody ever saw hide or hair of him again. And then I come along and find him here," said Mr. Hatch, "all settled down and playing the same song."

"He never acted crazy to me," said Mr. Thompson. "He always acted like a sensible man, to me. He never got married, for one thing, and he works like a horse, and I bet he's got the first cent I paid him when he landed here, and he don't drink, and he never says a word, much less swear, and he don't waste time runnin' around Saturday nights, and if he's crazy," said Mr. Thompson, "why, I think I'll go crazy myself for a change."

"Haw, ha," said Mr. Hatch, "heh, he, that's good! Ha, ha, ha, I hadn't thought of it jes like that. Yeah, that's right! Let's all go crazy and get rid of our wives and save our money, hey?" He smiled unpleasantly, showing his little rabbit teeth.

Mr. Thompson felt he was being misunderstood. He turned around and motioned toward the open window back of the honeysuckle trellis. "Let's move off down here a little," he said. "I oughta thought of that before." His visitor bothered Mr. Thompson. He had a way of taking the words out of Mr. Thompson's mouth, turning them around and mixing them up until Mr. Thompson didn't know himself what he had said. "My wife's not very strong," said Mr. Thompson. "She's been kind of invalid now goin' on fourteen years. Its mighty tough on a poor man, havin' sickness in the family. She had four operations," he said proudly, "one right after the other, but they didn't do any good. For five years handrunnin', I just turned every nickel I made over to the doctors. Upshot is, she's a mighty delicate woman."

"My old woman," said Mr. Homer T. Hatch, "had a back like a mule, yes, sir. That woman could have moved the barn with her bare hands if she'd ever took the notion. I used to say, it was a good thing she didn't know her own stren'th. She's dead now, though. That kind wear out quicker than the puny ones. I never had much use for a woman always complainin'. I'd get rid of her mighty quick, yes, sir, mighty quick. It's just as you say: a dead loss, keepin' one of 'em up."

This was not at all what Mr. Thompson had heard himself say; he had been trying to explain that a wife as expensive as his was a credit to a man. "She's a mighty reasonable woman," said Mr. Thompson, feeling baffled, "but I wouldn't answer for what she'd say or do if she found out we'd had a lunatic on the place all this time." They had moved away from the window; Mr. Thompson took Mr. Hatch the front way, because if he went the back way they would have to pass Mr. Helton's shack. For some reason he didn't want the stranger to see or talk to Mr. Helton. It was strange, but that was the way Mr. Thompson felt.

Mr. Thompson sat down again, on the chopping log, offering his guest another tree stump. "Now, I mighta got upset myself at such a thing, once," said Mr. Thompson, "but now I *deefy* anything to get me lathered up." He cut himself an enormous plug of tobacco with his horn-handled pocketknife, and offered it to Mr. Hatch, who then produced his own plug and, opening a huge bowie knife with a long blade sharply whetted, cut off a large wad and put it in his mouth. They then compared plugs and both of them were astonished to see how different men's ideas of good chewing tobacco were.

"Now, for instance," said Mr. Hatch, "mine is lighter colored. That's because, for one thing, there ain't any sweetenin' in this plug. I like it dry, natural leaf, medium strong."

"A little sweetenin' don't do no harm so far as I'm concerned," said Mr. Thompson, "but it's got to be mighty little. But with me, now, I want a strong leaf, I want it heavy-cured, as the feller says. There's a man near here, named Williams, Mr. John Morgan Williams, who chews a plug—well, sir, it's black as your hat and soft as melted tar. It fairly drips with molasses, jus' plain molasses, and it chews like licorice. Now, I don't call that a good chew."

"One man's meat," said Mr. Hatch, "is another man's poison. Now, such a chew would simply gag me. I couldn't begin to put it in my mouth."

"Well," said Mr. Thompson, a tinge of apology in his voice, "I jus' barely tasted it myself, you might say. Just took a little piece in my mouth and spit it out again."

"I'm dead sure I couldn't even get that far," said Mr. Hatch. "I like a dry natural chew without any artificial flavorin' of any kind."

Mr. Thompson began to feel that Mr. Hatch was trying to make out he had the best judgment in tobacco, and was going to keep up the argument until he proved it. He began to feel seriously annoyed with the fat man. After all, who was he and where did he come from? Who was he to go around telling other people what kind of tobacco to chew?

"Artificial flavorin'," Mr. Hatch went on, doggedly, "is jes put in to cover up a cheap leaf and make a man think he's gettin' somethin' more than he *is* gettin'. Even a little sweetenin' is a sign of a cheap leaf, you can mark my words."

"I've always paid a fair price for my plug," said Mr. Thompson, stiffly. "I'm not a rich man and I don't go round settin' myself up for one, but I'll say this, when it comes to such things as tobacco, I buy the best on the market."

"Sweetenin', even a little," began Mr. Hatch, shifting his plug and squirting tobacco juice at a dry-looking little rose bush that was having a hard enough time as it was, standing all day in the blazing sun, its roots clenched in the baked earth, "is the sign of—"

"About this Mr. Helton, now," said Mr. Thompson, determinedly, "I don't see no reason to hold it against a man because he went loony once or twice in his lifetime and so I don't expect to take no steps about it. Not a step. I've got nothin' against the man, he's always treated me fair. They's things and people," he went on, " 'nough to drive any man loony. The wonder to me is, more men don't wind up in straitjackets, the way things are going these days and times."

"That's right," said Mr. Hatch, promptly, entirely too promptly, as if he were turning Mr. Thompson's meaning back on him. "You took the words right out of my mouth. There ain't every man in a straitjacket that ought to be there. Ha, ha, you're right all right. You got the idea."

Mr. Thompson sat silent and chewed steadily and stared at a spot on the ground about six feet away and felt a slow muffled resentment climbing from somewhere deep down in him, climbing and spreading all through him. What was this fellow driving at? What was he trying to say? It wasn't so much his words, but his looks and his way of talking: that droopy look in the eye, that tone of voice, as if he was trying to mortify Mr. Thompson about something. Mr. Thompson didn't like it, but he couldn't get hold of it either. He wanted to turn around and shove the fellow off the stump, but it wouldn't look reasonable. Suppose something happened to the fellow when he fell off the stump, just for instance, if he fell on the ax and cut himself, and then someone should ask Mr. Thompson why he shoved him, and what could a man say? It would look mighty funny, it would sound mighty strange to say, Well, him and me fell out over a plug of tobacco. He might just shove him anyhow and then tell people he was a fat man not used to the heat and while he was talking he got dizzy and fell off by himself, or something like that, and it wouldn't be the truth either, because it wasn't the heat and it wasn't the tobacco. Mr. Thompson made up his mind to get the fellow off the place pretty quick, without seeming to be anxious, and watch him sharp till he was out of sight. It doesn't pay to be friendly with strangers from another part of the country. They're always up to something, or they'd stay at home where they belong.

"And they's some people," said Mr. Hatch, "would jus' as soon have a loonatic around their house as not, they can't see no difference between them and anybody else. I always say, if that's the way a man feels, don't care who he associates with, why, why, that's his business, not mine. I don't wanta have a thing to do with it. Now back home in North Dakota, we don't feel that way. I'd like to a seen anybody hiring a loonatic there, aspecially after what he done."

"I didn't understand your home was North Dakota," said Mr. Thompson. "I thought you said Georgia."

"I've got a married sister in North Dakota," said Mr. Hatch, "married a Swede, but a white man if ever I saw one. So I say *we* because we got into a little business together out that way. And it seems like home, kind of."

"What did he do?" asked Mr. Thompson, feeling very uneasy again.

"Oh, nothin' to speak of," said Mr. Hatch, jovially, "jus' went loony one day in the hayfield and shoved a pitchfork right square through his brother, when they was makin' hay. They was goin' to execute him, but they found out he had went crazy with the heat, as the feller says, and so they put him in the asylum. That's all he done. Nothin' to get lathered up about, ha, ha, ha!" he said, and taking out his sharp knife he began to slice off a chew as carefully as if he were cutting cake.

"Well," said Mr. Thompson, "I don't deny that's news. Yes, sir, news. But I still say somethin' must have drove him to it. Some men make you feel like giving 'em a good killing just by lookin' at you. His brother may a been a mean ornery cuss."

"Brother was going to get married," said Mr. Hatch; "used to go courtin' his girl nights. Borrowed Mr. Helton's harmonica to give her a serenade one evenin', and lost it. Brand new harmonica."

"He thinks a heap of his harmonicas," said Mr. Thompson. "Only money he ever spends, now and then he buys hisself a new one. Must have a dozen in that shack, all kinds and sizes."

"Brother wouldn't buy him a new one," said Mr. Hatch, "so Mr. Helton just ups, as I says, and runs his pitchfork through his brother. Now you know he musta been crazy to get all worked up over a little thing like that."

"Sounds like it," said Mr. Thompson, reluctant to agree in anything with this intrusive and disagreeable fellow. He kept thinking he couldn't remember when he had taken such a dislike to a man on first sight.

"Seems to me you'd get pretty sick of hearin' the same tune year in, year out," said Mr. Hatch.

"Well, sometimes I think it wouldn't do no harm if he learned a new one," said Mr. Thompson, "but he don't, so there's nothin' to be done about it. It's a pretty good tune, though."

"One of the Scandahoovians told me what it meant, that's how I come to know," said Mr. Hatch. "Especially that part about getting so gay you jus' go ahead and drink up all the likker you got on hand before noon. It seems like up in them Swede countries a man carries a bottle of wine around with him as a matter of course, at least that's the way I understood it. Those fellers will tell you anything, though—" He broke off and spat.

The idea of drinking any kind of liquor in this heat made Mr. Thompson dizzy. The idea of anybody feeling good on a day like this, for instance, made him tired. He felt he was really suffering from the heat. The fat man looked as if he had grown to the stump; he slumped there in his damp, dark clothes too big for him, his belly slack in his pants, his wide black felt hat pushed off his narrow forehead red with prickly heat. A bottle of good cold beer, now, would be a help, thought Mr. Thompson, remembering the four bottles sitting deep in the pool at the springhouse, and his dry tongue squirmed in his mouth. He wasn't going to offer this man anything, though, not even a drop of water. He wasn't even going to chew any more tobacco with him. He shot out his quid suddenly, and wiped his mouth on the back of his hand, and studied the head near him attentively. The man was no good, and he was there for no good, but what was he up to? Mr. Thompson made up his mind he'd give him a little more time to get his business, whatever it was, with Mr. Helton over, and then if he didn't get off the place he'd kick him off.

Mr. Hatch, as if he suspected Mr. Thompson's thoughts, turned his eyes, wicked and pig-like, on Mr. Thompson. "Fact is," he said, as if he had made up his mind about something, "I might need your help in the little matter I've got on hand, but it won't cost you any trouble. Now, this Mr. Helton here, like I tell you, he's a dangerous escaped loonatic, you might say. Now fact is, in the last twelve years or so I musta rounded up twenty-odd escaped loonatics, besides a couple of escaped convicts that I just run into by accident, like. I don't make a business of it, but if there's a reward, and there usually is a reward, of course, I get it. It amounts to a tidy little sum in the long run, but that ain't the main question. Fact is, I'm for law and order, I don't like to see lawbreakers and loonatics at large. It ain't the place for them. Now I reckon you're bound to agree with me on that, aren't you?"

Mr. Thompson said, "Well, circumstances alters cases, as the feller says. Now, what I know of Mr. Helton, he ain't dangerous, as I told you." Something serious was going to happen, Mr. Thompson could see that. He stopped thinking about it. He'd just let this fellow shoot off his head and then see what could be done about it. Without thinking he got out his knife and plug and started to cut a chew, then remembered himself and put them back in his pocket.

"The law," said Mr. Hatch, "is solidly behind me. Now this Mr. Helton, he's been one of my toughest cases. He's kept my record from being practically one hundred per cent. I knew him before he went loony, and I know the fam'ly, so I undertook to help out rounding him up. Well, sir, he was gone slick as a whistle, for all we knew the man was as good as dead long while ago. Now we might never have caught up with him, but do you know what he did? Well, sir, about two weeks ago his old mother gets a letter from him, and in that letter, what do you reckon she found? Well, it was a check on that little bank in town for eight hundred and fifty dollars, just like that; the letter wasn't nothing much, just said he was sending her a few little savings, she might need something, but there it was, name, postmark, date, everything. The old woman practically lost her mind with joy. She's gettin' childish, and it looked like she kinda forgot that her only living son killed his brother and went loony. Mr. Helton said he was getting along all right, and for her not to tell nobody. Well, natchally, she couldn't keep it to herself, with that check to cash and everything. So that's how I come to know." His feelings got the better of him. "You coulda knocked me down with a feather." He shook hands with himself and rocked, wagging his head, going "Heh, heh," in his throat. Mr. Thompson felt the corners of his mouth turning down. Why, the dirty low-down hound, sneaking around spying into other people's business like that. Collecting blood money, that's what it was! Let him talk!

"Yea, well, that musta been a surprise all right," he said, trying to hold his voice even. "I'd say a surprise."

"Well, siree," said Mr. Hatch, "the more I got to thinking about it, the more I just come to the conclusion that I'd better look into the matter a little, and so I talked to the old woman. She's pretty decrepit, now, half blind and all, but she was all for taking the first train out and going to see her son. I put it up to her square—how she was too feeble for the trip, and all. So, just as a favor to her, I told her for my expenses I'd come down and see Mr. Helton and bring her back all the news about him. She gave me a new shirt she made herself by hand, and a big Swedish kind of cake to bring to him, but I musta mislaid them along the road somewhere. It don't reely matter, though, he prob'ly ain't in any state of mind to appreciate 'em."

Mr. Thompson sat up and turning round on the log looked at Mr. Hatch and asked as quietly as he could, "And now what are you aiming to do? That's the question."

Mr. Hatch slouched up to his feet and shook himself. "Well, I come all prepared for a little scuffle," he said. "I got the handcuffs," he said, "but I don't want no violence if I can help it. I didn't want to say nothing around the countryside, making an uproar. I figured the two of us could overpower him." He reached into his big inside pocket and pulled them out. Handcuffs, for God's sake, thought Mr. Thompson. Coming round on a peaceable afternoon worrying a man, and making trouble, and fishing handcuffs out of his pocket on a decent family homestead, as if it was all in the day's work.

Mr. Thompson, his head buzzing, got up too. "Well," he said, roundly, "I want to tell you I think you've got a mighty sorry job on hand, you sure must be hard up for something to do, and now I want to give you a good piece of advice. You just drop the idea that you're going to come here and make trouble for Mr. Helton, and the quicker you drive that hired rig away from my front gate the better I'll be satisfied."

Mr. Hatch put one handcuff in his outside pocket, the other dangling down. He pulled his hat down over his eyes, and reminded Mr. Thompson of a sheriff, somehow. He didn't seem in the least nervous, and didn't take up Mr. Thompson's words. He said, "Now listen just a minute, it ain't reasonable to suppose that a man like yourself is going to stand in the way of getting an escaped loonatic back to the asylum where he belongs. Now I know it's enough to throw you off, coming sudden like this, but fact is I counted on your being a respectable man and helping me out to see that justice is done. Now a course, if you won't help, I'll have to look around for help somewheres else. It won't look very good to your neighbors that you was harbring an escaped loonatic who killed his own brother, and then you refused to give him up. It will look mighty funny."

Mr. Thompson knew almost before he heard the words that it would look funny. It would put him in a mighty awkward position. He said, "But I've been trying to tell you all along that the man ain't loony now. He's been perfectly harmless for nine years. He's—he's—"

Mr. Thompson couldn't think how to describe how it was with Mr. Helton. "Why, he's been like one of the family," he said, "the best standby a man ever had." Mr. Thompson tried to see his way out. It was a fact Mr. Helton might go loony again any minute, and now this fellow talking around the country would put Mr. Thompson in a fix. It was a terrible position. He couldn't think of any way out. "You're crazy," Mr. Thompson roared suddenly, "you're the crazy one around here, you're crazier than he ever was! You get off this place or I'll handcuff you and turn you over to the law. You're trespassing," shouted Mr. Thompson. "Get out of here before I knock you down!"

He took a step towards the fat man, who backed off, shrinking, "Try it, try it, go ahead!" and then something happened that Mr. Thompson tried hard afterwards to piece together in his mind, and in fact it never did come straight. He saw the fat man with his long bowie knife in his hand, he saw Mr. Helton come round the corner on the run, his long jaw dropped, his arms swinging, his eyes wild. Mr. Helton came in between them, fists doubled up, then stopped short, glaring at the fat man, his big frame seemed to collapse, he trembled like a shied horse; and then the fat man drove at him, knife in one hand, handcuffs in the other. Mr. Thompson saw it coming, he saw the blade going into Mr. Helton's stomach, he knew he had the ax out of the log in his own hands, felt his arms go up over his head and bring the ax down on Mr. Hatch's head as if he were stunning a beef.

Mrs. Thompson had been listening uneasily for some time to the voices going on, one of them strange to her, but she was too tired at first to get up and come out to see what was going on. The confused shouting that rose so suddenly brought her up to her feet and out across the front porch without her slippers, hair half-braided. Shading her eyes, she saw first Mr. Helton, running all stooped over through the orchard, running like a man with dogs after him; and Mr. Thompson supporting himself on the ax handle was leaning over shaking by the shoulder a man Mrs. Thompson had never seen, who lay doubled up with the top of his head smashed and the blood running away in a greasy-looking puddle. Mr. Thompson without taking his hand from the man's shoulder, said in a thick voice, "He killed Mr. Helton, he killed him, I saw him do it. I had to knock him out," he called loudly, "but he won't come to."

Mrs. Thompson said in a faint scream, "Why, yonder goes Mr. Helton," and she pointed. Mr. Thompson pulled himself up and looked where she pointed. Mrs. Thompson sat down slowly against the side of the house and began to slide forward on her face; she felt as if she were drowning, she couldn't rise to the top somehow, and her only thought was she was glad the boys were not there, they were out, fishing at Halifax, oh, God, she was glad the boys were not there.

Mr. and Mrs. Thompson drove up to their barn about sunset. Mr. Thompson handed the reins to his wife, got out to open the big door, and Mrs. Thompson guided old Jim in under the roof. The buggy was gray with dust and age, Mrs. Thompson's face was gray with dust and weariness, and Mr. Thompson's face, as he stood at the horse's head and began unhitching, was gray except for the dark blue of his freshly shaven jaws and chin, gray and blue and caved in, but patient, like a dead man's face.

Mrs. Thompson stepped down to the hard packed manure of the barn floor, and shook out her light flower-sprigged dress. She wore her smoked glasses, and her wide shady leghorn hat with the wreath of exhausted pink and blue forget-me-nots hid her forehead, fixed in a knot of distress.

The horse hung his head, raised a huge sigh and flexed his stiffened legs. Mr. Thompson's words came up muffled and hollow. "Poor ole Jim," he said, clearing his throat, "he looks pretty sunk in the ribs. I guess he's had a hard week." He lifted the harness up in one piece, slid it off and Jim walked out of the shafts halting a little. "Well, this is the last time," Mr. Thompson said, still talking to Jim. "Now you can get a good rest."

Mrs. Thompson closed her eyes behind her smoked glasses. The last time, and high time, and they should never have gone at all. She did not need her glasses any more, now the good darkness was coming down again, but her eyes ran full of tears steadily, though she was not crying, and she felt better with the glasses, safer, hidden away behind them. She took out her handkerchief with her hands shaking as they had been shaking ever since *that day,* and blew her nose. She said, "I see the boys have lighted the lamps. I hope they've started the stove going."

She stepped along the rough path holding her thin dress and starched petticoats around her, feeling her way between the sharp small stones, leaving the barn because she could hardly bear to be near Mr. Thompson, advancing slowly towards the house because she dreaded going there. Life was all one dread, the faces of her neighbors, of her boys, of her husband, the face of the whole world, the shape of her own house in the darkness, the very smell of the grass and the trees were horrible to her. There was no place to go, only one thing to do, bear it somehow—but how? She asked herself that question often. How was she going to keep on living now? Why had she lived at all? She wished now she had died one of those times when she had been so sick, instead of living on for this.

The boys were in the kitchen; Herbert was looking at the funny pictures from last Sunday's newspapers, the Katzenjammer Kids and Happy Hooligan. His chin was in his hands and his elbows on the table, and he was really reading and looking at the pictures, but his face was unhappy. Arthur was building the fire, adding kindling a stick at a time, watching it catch and blaze. His face was heavier and darker than Herbert's, but he was a little sullen by nature; Mrs. Thompson thought, he takes things harder, too. Arthur said, "Hello, Momma," and went on with his work. Herbert swept the papers together and moved over on the bench. They were big boys—fifteen and seventeen, and Arthur as tall as his father. Mrs. Thompson sat down beside Herbert, taking off her hat. She said, "I guess you're hungry. We were late today. We went the Log Hollow road, it's rougher than ever." Her pale mouth drooped with a sad fold on either side.

"I guess you saw the Mannings, then," said Herbert.

"Yes, and the Fergusons, and the Allbrights, and that new family McClellan."

"Anybody say anything?" asked Herbert.

"Nothing much, you know how it's been all along, some of them keeps saying, yes, they know it was a clear case and a fair trial and they say how glad they are your papa came out so well, and all that, some of 'em do, anyhow, but it looks like they don't really take sides with him. I'm about wore out," she said, the tears rolling again from under her dark glasses. "I don't know what good it does, but your papa can't seem to rest unless he's telling how it happened. I don't know."

"I don't think it does any good, not a speck," said Arthur, moving away from the stove. "It just keeps the whole question stirred up in people's minds. Everybody will go round telling what he heard, and the whole thing is going to get worse mixed up than ever. It just makes matters worse. I wish you could get Papa to stop driving round the country talking like that."

"Your papa knows best," said Mrs. Thompson. "You oughtn't to criticize him. He's got enough to put up with without that."

Arthur said nothing, his jaw stubborn. Mr. Thompson came in, his eyes hollowed out and dead-looking, his thick hands gray white and seamed from washing them clean every day before he started out to see the neighbors to tell them his side of the story. He was wearing his Sunday clothes, a thick pepper-and-salt-colored suit with a black string tie.

Mrs. Thompson stood up, her head swimming. "Now you-all get out of the kitchen, it's too hot in here and I need room. I'll get us a little bite of supper, if you'll just get out and give me some room."

They went as if they were glad to go, the boys outside, Mr. Thompson into his bedroom. She heard him groaning to himself as he took off his shoes, and heard the bed creak as he lay down. Mrs. Thompson opened the icebox and felt the sweet coldness flow out of it; she had never expected to have an icebox, much less did she hope to afford to keep it filled with ice. It still seemed like a miracle, after two or three years. There was the food, cold and clean, all ready to be warmed over. She would never have had that icebox if Mr. Helton hadn't happened along one day, just by the strangest luck; so saving, and so managing, so good, thought Mrs. Thompson, her heart swelling until she feared she would faint again, standing there with the door open and leaning her head upon it. She simply could not bear to remember Mr. Helton, with his long sad face and silent ways, who had always been so quiet and harmless, who had worked so hard and helped Mr. Thompson so much, running through the hot fields and woods, being hunted like a mad dog, everybody turning out with ropes and guns and sticks to catch and tie him. Oh, God, said Mrs. Thompson in a long dry moan, kneeling before the icebox and fumbling inside for the dishes, even if they did pile mattresses all over the jail floor and against the walls, and five men there to hold him to keep him from hurting himself any more, he was already hurt too badly, he couldn't have lived anyway. Mr. Barbee, the sheriff, told her about it. He said, well, they didn't aim to harm him but they had to catch him, he was crazy as a loon; he picked up rocks and tried to brain every man that got near him. He had two harmonicas in his jumper pocket, said the sheriff, but they fell out in the scuffle, and Mr. Helton tried to pick 'em up again, and that's when they finally got him. "They *had* to be rough, Miz Thompson, he fought like a wildcat." Yes, thought Mrs. Thompson again with the same bitterness, of course, they had to be rough. They always have to be rough, Mr. Thompson can't argue with a man and get him off the place peaceably; no, she thought, standing up and shutting the icebox, he has to kill somebody, he has to be a murderer and ruin his boys' lives and cause Mr. Helton to be killed like a mad dog.

Her thoughts stopped with a little soundless explosion, cleared and began again. The rest of Mr. Helton's harmonicas were still in the shack, his tune ran in Mrs. Thompson's head at certain times of the day. She missed it in the evenings. It seemed so strange she had never known the name of that song, nor what it meant, until after Mr. Helton was gone. Mrs. Thompson, trembling in the knees, took a drink of water at the sink and poured the red beans into the baking dish, and began to roll the pieces of chicken in flour to fry them. There was a time, she said to herself, when I thought I had neighbors and friends, there was a time when we could hold up our heads, there was a time when my husband hadn't killed a man and I could tell the truth to anybody about anything.

Mr. Thompson, turning on his bed, figured that he had done all he could, he'd just try to let the matter rest from now on. His lawyer, Mr. Burleigh, had told him right at the beginning, "Now you keep calm and collected. You've got a fine case, even if you haven't got witnesses. Your wife must sit in court, she'll be a powerful argument with the jury. You just plead not guilty and I'll do the rest. The trial is going to be a mere formality, you haven't got a thing to worry about. You'll be clean out of this before you know it." And to make talk Mr. Burleigh had got to telling about all the men he knew around the country who for one reason or another had been forced to kill somebody, always in self-defense, and there just wasn't anything to it at all. He even told about how his own father in the old days had shot and killed a man just for setting foot inside his gate when he told him not to. "Sure, I shot the scoundrel," said Mr. Burleigh's father, "in self-defense; I *told* him I'd shoot him if he set his foot in my yard, and he did, and I did." There had been bad blood between them for years, Mr. Burleigh said, and his father had waited a long time to catch the other fellow in the wrong, and when he did he certainly made the most of his opportunity.

"But Mr. Hatch, as I told you," Mr. Thompson had said, "made a pass at Mr. Helton with his bowie knife. That's why I took a hand."

"All the better," said Mr. Burleigh. "That stranger hadn't any right coming to your house on such an errand. Why, hell," said Mr. Burleigh, "that wasn't even manslaughter you committed. So now you just hold your horses and keep your shirt on. And don't say one word without I tell you."

Wasn't even manslaughter. Mr. Thompson had to cover Mr. Hatch with a piece of wagon canvas and ride to town to tell the sheriff. It had been hard on Ellie. When they got back, the sheriff and the coroner and two deputies, they found her sitting beside the road, on a low bridge over a gulley, about half a mile from the place. He had taken her up behind his saddle and got her back to the house. He had already told the sheriff that his wife had witnessed the whole business, and now he had time, getting her to her room and in bed, to tell her what to say if they asked anything. He had left out the part about Mr. Helton being crazy all along, but it came out at the trial. By Mr. Burleigh's advice Mr. Thompson had pretended to be perfectly ignorant; Mr. Hatch hadn't said a word about that. Mr. Thompson pretended to believe that Mr. Hatch had just come looking for Mr. Helton to settle old scores, and the two members of Mr. Hatch's family who had come down to try to get Mr. Thompson convicted didn't get anywhere at all. It hadn't been much of a trial, Mr. Burleigh saw to that. He had charged a reasonable fee, and Mr. Thompson had paid him and felt grateful, but after it was over Mr. Burleigh didn't seem pleased to see him when he got to dropping into the office to talk it over, telling him things that had slipped his mind at first: trying to explain what an ornery low hound Mr. Hatch had been, anyhow. Mr. Burleigh seemed to have lost his interest; he looked sour and upset when he saw Mr. Thompson at the door. Mr. Thompson kept saying to himself that he'd got off, all right, just as Mr. Burleigh had predicted, but, but—

and it was right there that Mr. Thompson's mind stuck, squirming like an angleworm on a fishhook: he had killed Mr. Hatch, and he was a murderer. That was the truth about himself that Mr. Thompson couldn't grasp, even when he said the word to himself. Why, he had not even once *thought* of killing anybody, much less Mr. Hatch, and if Mr. Helton hadn't come out so unexpectedly, hearing the row, why, then—but then, Mr. Helton had come on the run that way to help him. What he couldn't understand was what happened next. He had seen Mr. Hatch go after Mr. Helton with the knife, he had seen the point, blade up, go into Mr. Helton's stomach and slice up like you slice a hog, but when they finally caught Mr. Helton there wasn't a knife scratch on him. Mr. Thompson knew he had the ax in his own hands and felt himself lifting it, but he couldn't remember hitting Mr. Hatch. He couldn't remember it. He couldn't. He remembered only that he had been determined to stop Mr. Hatch from cutting Mr. Helton. If he was given a chance he could explain the whole matter. At the trial they hadn't let him talk. They just asked questions and he answered yes or no, and they never did get to the core of the matter. Since the trial, now, every day for a week he had washed and shaved and put on his best clothes and had taken Ellie with him to tell every neighbor he had that he never killed Mr. Hatch on purpose, and what good did it do? Nobody believed him. Even when he turned to Ellie and said, "You was there, you saw it, didn't you?" and Ellie spoke up, saying, "Yes, that's the truth. Mr. Thompson was trying to save Mr. Helton's life," and he added, "If you don't believe me, you can believe my wife. She won't lie," Mr. Thompson saw something in all their faces that disheartened him, made him feel empty and tired out. They didn't believe he was not a murderer.

Even Ellie never said anything to comfort him. He hoped she would say finally, "I remember now, Mr. Thompson, I really did come round the corner in time to see everything. It's not a lie, Mr. Thompson. Don't you worry." But as they drove together in silence, with the days still hot and dry, shortening for fall, day after day, the buggy jolting in the ruts, she said nothing; they grew to dread the sight of another house, and the people in it: all houses looked alike now, and the people—old neighbors or new—had the same expression when Mr. Thompson told them why he had come and began his story. Their eyes looked as if someone had pinched the eyeball at the back; they shriveled and the light went out of them. Some of them sat with fixed tight smiles trying to be friendly. "Yes, Mr. Thompson, we know how you must feel. It must be terrible for you, Mrs. Thompson. Yes, you know, I've about come to the point where I believe in such a thing as killing in self-defense. Why, certainly, we believe you, Mr. Thompson, why shouldn't we believe you? Didn't you have a perfectly fair and above-board trial? Well, now, natchally, Mr. Thompson, we think you done right."

Mr. Thompson was satisfied they didn't think so. Sometimes the air around him was so thick with their blame he fought and pushed with his fists, and the sweat broke out all over him, he shouted his story in a dust-choked voice, he would fairly bellow at last; "My wife, here, you know her, she was there, she saw and heard it all, if you don't believe me, ask her, she won't lie!" and Mrs. Thompson, with her hands knotted together, aching, her chin trembling, would never fail to say: "Yes, that's right, that's the truth—"

The last straw had been laid on today, Mr. Thompson decided. Tom Allbright, an old beau of Ellie's, why, he had squired Ellie around a whole summer, had come out to meet them when they drove up, and standing there bareheaded had stopped them from getting out. He had looked past them with an embarrassed frown on his face, telling them his wife's sister was there with a raft of young ones, and the house was pretty full and everything upset, or he'd ask them to come in. "We've been thinking of trying to get up to your place one of these days," said Mr. Allbright, moving away trying to look busy, "we've been mighty occupied up here of late." So they had to say, "Well, we just happened to be driving this way," and go on. "The Allbrights," said Mrs. Thompson, "always was fair-weather friends." "They look out for number one, that's a fact," said Mr. Thompson. But it was cold comfort to them both.

Finally Mrs. Thompson had given up. "Let's go home," she said. "Old Jim's tired and thirsty, and we've gone far enough."

Mr. Thompson said, "Well, while we're out this way, we might as well stop at the McClellans'." They drove in, and asked a little cotton-haired boy if his mamma and papa were at home. Mr. Thompson wanted to see them. The little boy stood gazing with his mouth open, then galloped into the house shouting, "Mommer, Popper, come out hyah. That man that kilt Mr. Hatch has come ter see yer!"

The man came out in his sock feet, with one gallus up, the other broken and dangling, and said, "Light down, Mr. Thompson, and come in. The ole woman's washing, but she'll git here." Mrs. Thompson, feeling her way, stepped down and sat in a broken rocking-chair on the porch that sagged under her feet. The woman of the house, barefooted, in a calico wrapper, sat on the edge of the porch, her fat sallow face full of curiosity. Mr. Thompson began, "Well, as I reckon you happen to know, I've had some strange troubles lately, and, as the feller says, it's not the kind of trouble that happens to a man every day in the year, and there's some things I don't want no misunderstanding about in the neighbors' minds, so—" He halted and stumbled forward, and the two listening faces took on a mean look, a greedy, despising look, a look that said plain as day, "My, you must be a purty sorry feller to come round worrying about what *we* think, *we* know you wouldn't be here if you had anybody else to turn to—my, I wouldn't lower myself that much, myself." Mr. Thompson was ashamed of himself, he was suddenly in a rage, he'd like to knock their dirty skunk heads together, the low-down white trash—but he held himself down and went on to the end. "My wife will tell you," he said, and this was the hardest place, because Ellie always without moving a muscle seemed to stiffen as if somebody had threatened to hit her; "ask my wife, she won't lie."

"It's true, I saw it—"

"Well, now," said the man, drily, scratching his ribs inside his shirt, "that sholy is too bad. Well, now, I kaint see what we've got to do with all this here, however. I kaint see no good reason for us to git mixed up in these murder matters, I shore kaint. Whichever way you look at it, it ain't none of my business. However, it's mighty nice of you-all to come around and give us the straight of it, fur we've heerd some mighty queer yarns about it, mighty queer, I golly you couldn't hardly make head ner tail of it."

"Evvybody goin' round shootin' they heads off," said the woman. "Now we don't hold with killin'; the Bible says—"

"Shet yer trap," said the man, "and keep it shet 'r I'll shet it fer yer. Now it shore looks like to me—"

"We mustn't linger," said Mrs. Thompson, unclasping her hands. "We've lingered too long now. It's getting late, and we've far to go." Mr. Thompson took the hint and followed her. The man and the woman lolled against their rickety porch poles and watched them go.

Now lying on his bed, Mr. Thompson knew the end had come. Now, this minute, lying in the bed where he had slept with Ellie for eighteen years; under this roof where he had laid the shingles when he was waiting to get married; there as he was with his whiskers already sprouting since his shave that morning; with his fingers feeling his bony chin, Mr. Thompson felt he was a dead man. He was dead to his other life, he had got to the end of something without knowing why, and he had to make a fresh start, he did not know how. Something different was going to begin, he didn't know what. It was in some way not his business. He didn't feel he was going to have much to do with it. He got up, aching, hollow, and went out to the kitchen where Mrs. Thompson was just taking up the supper.

"Call the boys," said Mrs. Thompson. They had been down to the barn, and Arthur put out the lantern before hanging it on a nail near the door. Mr. Thompson didn't like their silence. They had hardly said a word about anything to him since that day. They seemed to avoid him, they ran the place together as if he wasn't there, and attended to everything without asking him for any advice. "What you boys been up to?" he asked, trying to be hearty. "Finishing your chores?"

"No, sir," said Arthur, "there ain't much to do. Just greasing some axles." Herbert said nothing. Mrs. Thompson bowed her head: "For these and all Thy blessings. . . . Amen," she whispered weakly, and the Thompsons sat there with their eyes down and their faces sorrowful, as if they were at a funeral.

Every time he shut his eyes, trying to sleep, Mr. Thompson's mind started up and began to run like a rabbit. It jumped from one thing to another, trying to pick up a trail here or there that would straighten out what had happened that day he killed Mr. Hatch. Try as he might, Mr. Thompson's mind would not go anywhere that it had not already been, he could not see anything but what he had seen once, and he knew that was not right. If he had not seen straight that first time, then everything about his killing Mr. Hatch was wrong from start to finish, and there was nothing more to be done about it, he might just as well give up. It still seemed to him that he had done, maybe not the right thing, but the only thing he could do, that day, but had he? *Did he have to kill Mr. Hatch?* He had never seen a man he hated more, the minute he laid eyes on him. He knew in his bones the fellow was there for trouble. What seemed so funny now was this: Why hadn't he just told Mr. Hatch to get out before he ever even got in?

Mrs. Thompson, her arms crossed on her breast, was lying beside him, perfectly still, but she seemed awake, somehow. "Asleep, Ellie?"

After all, he might have got rid of him peaceably, or maybe he might have had to overpower him and put those handcuffs on him and turn him over to the sheriff for disturbing the peace. The most they could have done was to lock Mr. Hatch up while he cooled off for a few days, or fine him a little something. He would try to think of things he might have said to Mr. Hatch. Why, let's see, I could just have said, Now look here, Mr. Hatch, I want to talk to you as man to man. But his brain would go empty. What could he have said or done? But if he *could* have done anything else almost except kill Mr. Hatch, then nothing would have happened to Mr. Helton. Mr. Thompson hardly ever thought of Mr. Helton. His mind just skipped over him and went on. If he stopped to think about Mr. Helton he'd never in God's world get anywhere. He tried to imagine how it might all have been, this very night even, if Mr. Helton were still safe and sound out in his shack playing his tune about feeling so good in the morning, drinking up all the wine so you'd feel even better; and Mr. Hatch safe in jail somewhere, mad as hops, maybe, but out of harm's way and ready to listen to reason and to repent of his meanness, the dirty, yellow-livered hound coming around persecuting an innocent man and ruining a whole family that never harmed him! Mr. Thompson felt the veins of his forehead start up, his fists clutched as if they seized an ax handle, the sweat broke out on him, he bounded up from the bed with a yell smothered in his throat, and Ellie started up after him, crying out, "Oh, oh, don't! Don't! Don't!" as if she were having a nightmare. He stood shaking until his bones rattled in him, crying hoarsely, "Light the lamp, light the lamp, Ellie."

Instead, Mrs. Thompson gave a shrill weak scream, almost the same scream he had heard on that day she came around the house when he was standing there with the ax in his hand. He could not see her in the dark, but she was on the bed, rolling violently. He felt for her in horror, and his groping hands found her arms, up, and her own hands pulling her hair straight out from her head, her neck strained back, and the tight screams strangling her. He shouted out for Arthur, for Herbert. "Your mother!" he bawled, his voice cracking. As he held Mrs. Thompson's arms, the boys came tumbling in, Arthur with the lamp above his head. By this light Mr. Thompson saw Mrs. Thompson's eyes, wide open, staring dreadfully at him, the tears pouring. She sat up at sight of the boys, and held out one arm towards them, the hand wagging in a crazy circle, then dropped on her back again, and suddenly went limp. Arthur set the lamp on the table and turned on Mr. Thompson. "She's scared," he said, "she's scared to death." His face was in a knot of rage, his fists were doubled up, he faced his father as if he meant to strike him. Mr. Thompson's jaw fell, he was so surprised he stepped back from the bed. Herbert went to the other side. They stood on each side of Mrs. Thompson and watched Mr. Thompson as if he were a dangerous wild beast. "What did you do to her?" shouted Arthur, in a grown man's voice. "You touch her again and I'll blow your heart out!" Herbert was pale and his cheek twitched, but he was on Arthur's side; he would do what he could to help Arthur.

Mr. Thompson had no fight left in him. His knees bent as he stood, his chest collapsed. "Why, Arthur," he said, his words crumbling and his breath coming short. "She's fainted again. Get the ammonia." Arthur did not move. Herbert brought the bottle, and handed it, shrinking, to his father.

Mr. Thompson held it under Mrs. Thompson's nose. He poured a little in the palm of his hand and rubbed it on her forehead. She gasped and opened her eyes and turned her head away from him. Herbert began a doleful hopeless sniffling. "Mamma," he kept saying, "Mamma, don't die."

"I'm all right," Mrs. Thompson said. "Now don't you worry around. Now Herbert, you mustn't do that. I'm all right." She closed her eyes. Mr. Thompson began pulling on his best pants; he put on his socks and shoes. The boys sat on each side of the bed, watching Mrs. Thompson's face. Mr. Thompson put on his shirt and coat. He said, "I reckon I'll ride over and get the doctor. Don't look like all this fainting is a good sign. Now you just keep watch until I get back." They listened, but said nothing. He said, "Don't you get any notions in your head. I never did your mother any harm in my life, on purpose." He went out, and, looking back, saw Herbert staring at him from under his brows, like a stranger. "You'll know how to look after her," said Mr. Thompson.

Mr. Thompson went through the kitchen. There he lighted the lantern, took a thin pad of scratch paper and a stub pencil from the shelf where the boys kept their schoolbooks. He swung the lantern on his arm and reached into the cupboard where he kept the guns. The shotgun was there to his hand, primed and ready, a man never knows when he may need a shotgun. He went out of the house without looking around, or looking back when he had left it, passed his barn without seeing it, and struck out to the farthest end of his fields, which ran for half a mile to the east. So many blows had been struck at Mr. Thompson and from so many directions he couldn't stop any more to find out where he was hit. He walked on, over plowed ground and over meadow, going through barbed wire fences cautiously, putting his gun through first; he could almost see in the dark, now his eyes were used to it. Finally he came to the last fence; here he sat down, back against a post, lantern at his side, and, with the pad on his knee, moistened the stub pencil and began to write:

"Before Almighty God, the great judge of all before who I am about to appear, I do hereby solemnly swear that I did not take the life of Mr. Homer T. Hatch on purpose. It was done in defense of Mr. Helton. I did not aim to hit him with the ax but only to keep him off Mr. Helton. He aimed a blow at Mr. Helton who was not looking for it. It was my belief at the time that Mr. Hatch would of taken the life of Mr. Helton if I did not interfere. I have told all this to the judge and the jury and they let me off but nobody believes it. This is the only way I can prove I am not a cold blooded murderer like everybody seems to think. If I had been in Mr. Helton's place he would of done the same for me. I still think I done the only thing there was to do. My wife—"

Mr. Thompson stopped here to think a while. He wet the pencil point with the tip of his tongue and marked out the last two words. He sat a while blacking out the words until he had made a neat oblong patch where they had been, and started again:

"It was Mr. Homer T. Hatch who came to do wrong to a harmless man. He caused all this trouble and he deserved to die but I am sorry it was me who had to kill him."

He licked the point of his pencil again, and signed his full name carefully, folded the paper and put it in his outside pocket. Taking off his right shoe and sock, he set the butt of the shotgun along the ground with the twin barrels pointed towards his head. It was very awkward. He thought about this a little, leaning his head against the gun mouth. He was trembling and his head was drumming until he was deaf and blind, but he lay down flat on the earth on his side, drew the barrel under his chin and fumbled for the trigger with his great toe. That way he could work it.

HENRY JAMES

Madame de Mauves

The view from the terrace at Saint-Germain-en-Laye is immense and famous. Paris lies spread before you in dusky vastness, domed and fortified, glittering here and there through her light vapors, and girdled with her silver Seine. Behind you is a park of stately symmetry, and behind that a forest, where you may lounge through turfy avenues and light-checkered glades, and quite forget that you are within half an hour of the boulevards. One afternoon, however, in mid-spring, some five years ago, a young man seated on the terrace had chosen not to forget this. His eyes were fixed in idle wistfulness on the mighty human hive before him. He was fond of rural things, and he had come to Saint-Germain a week before to meet the spring half-way; but though he could boast of a six months' acquaintance with the great city, he never looked at it from his present standpoint without a feeling of painfully unsatisfied curiosity. There were moments when it seemed to him that not to be there just then was to miss some thrilling chapter of experience. And yet his winter's experience had been rather fruitless, and he had closed the book almost with a yawn. Though not in the least a cynic, he was what one may call a disappointed observer; and he never chose the right-hand road without beginning to suspect after an hour's wayfaring that the left would have been the interesting one. He now had a dozen minds to go to Paris for the evening, to dine at the Café Brébant, and to repair afterwards to the Gymnase and listen to the latest exposition of the duties of the injured husband. He would probably have risen to execute this project, if he had not observed a little girl who, wandering along the terrace, had suddenly stopped short and begun to gaze at him with

From *A Passionate Pilgrim and Other Tales* by Henry James, copyright 1875 by James R. Osgood and Company, Boston.

round-eyed frankness. For a moment he was simply amused, for the child's face denoted helpless wonderment; the next he was agreeably surprised. "Why, this is my friend Maggie," he said; "I see you have not forgotten me."

Maggie, after a short parley, was induced to seal her remembrance with a kiss. Invited then to explain her appearance at Saint-Germain, she embarked on a recital in which the general, according to the infantine method, was so fatally sacrificed to the particular, that Longmore looked about him for a superior source of information. He found it in Maggie's mamma, who was seated with another lady at the opposite end of the terrace; so, taking the child by the hand, he led her back to her companions.

Maggie's mamma was a young American lady, as you would immediately have perceived, with a pretty and friendly face and an expensive spring toilet. She greeted Longmore with surprised cordiality, mentioned his name to her friend, and bade him bring a chair and sit with them. The other lady, who, though equally young and perhaps even prettier, was dressed more soberly, remained silent, stroking the hair of the little girl, whom she had drawn against her knee. She had never heard of Longmore, but she now perceived that her companion had crossed the ocean with him, had met him afterwards in travelling, and (having left her husband in Wall Street) was indebted to him for various small services.

Maggie's mamma turned from time to time and smiled at her friend with an air of invitation; the latter smiled back, and continued gracefully to say nothing.

For ten minutes Longmore felt a revival of interest in his interlocutor; then (as riddles are more amusing than commonplaces) it gave way to curiosity about her friend. His eyes wandered; her volubility was less suggestive than the latter's silence.

The stranger was perhaps not obviously a beauty nor obviously an American, but essentially both, on a closer scrutiny. She was slight and fair, and, though naturally pale, delicately flushed, apparently with recent excitement. What chiefly struck Longmore in her face was the union of a pair of beautifully gentle, almost languid gray eyes, with a mouth peculiarly expressive and firm. Her forehead was a trifle more expansive than belongs to classic types, and her thick brown hair was dressed out of the fashion, which was just then very ugly. Her throat and bust were slender, but all the more in harmony with certain rapid, charming movements of the head, which she had a way of throwing back every now and then, with an air of attention and a sidelong glance from her dove-like eyes. She seemed at once alert and indifferent, contemplative and restless; and Longmore very soon discovered that if she was not a brilliant beauty, she was at least an extremely interesting one. This very impression made him magnanimous. He perceived that he had interrupted a confidential conversation, and he judged it discreet to withdraw, having first learned from Maggie's mamma—Mrs. Draper—that she was to take the six-o'clock train back to Paris. He promised to meet her at the station.

He kept his appointment, and Mrs. Draper arrived betimes, accompanied by her friend. The latter, however, made her farewells at the door and drove away again, giving Longmore time only to raise his hat. "Who is she?" he asked with visible ardor, as he brought Mrs. Draper her tickets.

"Come and see me to-morrow at the Hôtel de l'Empire," she answered, "and I will tell you all about her." The force of this offer in making him punctual at the Hôtel de l'Empire Longmore doubtless never exactly measured; and it was perhaps well that he did not, for he found his friend, who was on the point of leaving Paris, so distracted by procrastinating milliners and perjured lingères that she had no wits left for disinterested narrative. "You must find Saint-Germain dreadfully dull," she said, as he was going. "Why won't you come with me to London?"

"Introduce me to Madame de Mauves," he answered, "and Saint-Germain will satisfy me." All he had learned was the lady's name and residence.

"Ah! she, poor woman, will not make Saint-Germain cheerful for you. She's very unhappy."

Longmore's further inquiries were arrested by the arrival of a young lady with a bandbox; but he went away with the promise of a note of introduction, to be immediately despatched to him at Saint-Germain.

He waited a week, but the note never came; and he declared that it was not for Mrs. Draper to complain of her milliner's treachery. He lounged on the terrace and walked in the forest, studied suburban street life, and made a languid attempt to investigate the records of the court of the exiled Stuarts; but he spent most of his time in wondering where Madame de Mauves lived, and whether she never walked on the terrace. Sometimes, he finally discovered; for one afternoon toward dusk he perceived her leaning against the parapet, alone. In his momentary hesitation to approach her, it seemed to him that there was almost a shade of trepidation; but his curiosity was not diminished by the consciousness of this result of a quarter of an hour's acquaintance. She immediately recognized him on his drawing near, with the manner of a person unaccustomed to encounter a confusing variety of faces. Her dress, her expression, were the same as before; her charm was there, like that of sweet music on a second hearing. She soon made conversation easy by asking him for news of Mrs. Draper. Longmore told her that he was daily expecting news, and, after a pause, mentioned the promised note of introduction.

"It seems less necessary now," he said—"for me, at least. But for you—I should have liked you to know the flattering things Mrs. Draper would probably have said about me."

"If it arrives at last," she answered, "you must come and see me and bring it. If it doesn't, you must come without it."

Then, as she continued to linger in spite of the thickening twilight, she explained that she was waiting for her husband, who was to arrive in the train from Paris, and who often passed along the terrace on his way home. Longmore well remembered that Mrs. Draper had pronounced her unhappy, and he found it convenient to suppose that this same husband made her so. Edified by his six months in Paris—"What else is possible," he asked himself, "for a sweet American girl who marries an unclean Frenchman?"

But this tender expectancy of her lord's return undermined his hypothesis, and it received a further check from the gentle eagerness with which she turned and greeted an approaching figure. Longmore beheld in the fading light a stoutish gentleman, on the fair side of forty, in a high light hat, whose countenance, indistinct against the sky, was adorned by a fantastically pointed mustache. M. de Mauves saluted his wife with punctilious gallantry, and having bowed to Longmore, asked her several questions in French. Before taking his proffered arm to walk to their carriage, which was in waiting at the terrace gate, she introduced our hero as a friend of Mrs. Draper, and a fellow-countryman, whom she hoped to see at home. M. de Mauves responded briefly, but civilly, in very fair English, and led his wife away.

Longmore watched him as he went, twisting his picturesque mustache, with a feeling of irritation which he certainly would have been at a loss to account for. The only conceivable cause was the light which M. de Mauves's good English cast upon his own bad French. For reasons involved apparently in the very structure of his being, Longmore found himself unable to speak the language tolerably. He admired and enjoyed it, but the very genius of awkwardness controlled his phraseology. But he reflected with satisfaction that Madame de Mauves and he had a common idiom, and his vexation was effectually dispelled by his finding on his table that evening a letter from Mrs. Draper. It enclosed a short, formal missive to Madame de Mauves, but the epistle itself was copious and confidential. She had deferred writing till she reached London, where for a week, of course, she had found other amusements.

"I think it is these distracting Englishwomen," she wrote, "with their green barege gowns and their white-stitched boots, who have reminded me in self-defense of my graceful friend at Saint-Germain and my promise to introduce you to her. I believe I told you that she was unhappy, and I wondered afterwards whether I had not been guilty of a breach of confidence. But you would have found it out for yourself, and besides, she told me no secrets. She declared she was the happiest creature in the world, and then, poor thing, she burst into tears, and I prayed to be delivered from such happiness. It's the miserable story of an American girl, born to be neither a slave nor a toy, marrying a profligate Frenchman, who believes that a woman must be one or the other. The silliest American woman is too good for the best foreigner, and the poorest of us have moral needs a Frenchman can't appreciate. She was romantic and wilful, and thought Americans were vulgar. Matrimonial felicity perhaps *is* vulgar; but I think nowadays she wishes she were a little less elegant. M. de Mauves cared, of course, for nothing but her money, which he's spending royally on his *menus plaisirs.* I hope you appreciate the compliment I pay you when I recommend you to go and console an unhappy wife. I have never given a man such a proof of esteem, and if you were to disappoint me I should renounce the world. Prove to Madame de Mauves that an American friend may mingle admiration and respect better than a French husband. She avoids society and lives quite alone, seeing no one but a horrible French sister-in-law. Do let me hear that you have drawn some of the sadness from that desperate smile of hers. Make her smile with a good conscience."

These zealous admonitions left Longmore slightly disturbed. He found himself on the edge of a domestic tragedy from which he instinctively recoiled. To call upon Madame de Mauves with his present knowledge seemed a sort of fishing in troubled waters. He was a modest man, and yet he asked himself whether the effect of his attentions might not be to add to her tribulation. A flattering sense of unwonted opportunity, however, made him, with the lapse of time, more confident,—possibly more reckless. It seemed a very inspiring idea to draw the sadness from his fair countrywoman's smile, and at least he hoped to persuade her that there was such a thing as an agreeable American. He immediately called upon her.

2

She had been placed for her education, fourteen years before, in a Parisian convent, by a widowed mamma, fonder of Homburg and Nice than of letting out tucks in the frocks of a vigorously growing daughter. Here, besides various elegant accomplishments,—the art of wearing a train, of composing a bouquet, of presenting a cup of tea,—she acquired a certain turn of the imagination which might have passed for a sign of precocious worldliness. She dreamed of marrying a title,—not for the pleasure of hearing herself called Mme. la Vicomtesse (for which it seemed to her that she should never greatly care), but because she had a romantic belief that the best birth is the guaranty of an ideal delicacy of feeling. Romances are rarely shaped in such perfect good faith, and Euphemia's excuse was in the radical purity of her imag ination. She was profoundly incorruptible, and she cherished this pernicious conceit as if it had been a dogma revealed by a white-winged angel. Even after experience had given her a hundred rude hints, she found it easier to believe in fables, when they had a certain nobleness of meaning, than in well-attested but sordid facts. She believed that a gentleman with a long pedigree must be of necessity a very fine fellow, and that the consciousness of a picturesque family tradition imparts an exquisite tone to the character. *Noblesse oblige,* she thought, as regards yourself, and insures, as regards your wife. She had never spoken to a nobleman in her life, and these convictions were but a matter of transcendent theory. They were the fruit, in part, of the perusal of various ultramontane works of fiction—the only ones admitted to the convent library—in which the hero was always a legitimist vicomte who fought duels by the dozen, but went twice a month to confession; and in part of the perfumed gossip of her companions, many of them *filles de haut lieu,* who in the convent garden, after Sundays at home, depicted their brothers and cousins as Prince Charmings and young Paladins. Euphemia listened and said nothing; she shrouded her visions of matrimony under a coronet in religious mystery. She was not of that type of young lady who is easily induced to declare that her husband must be six feet high and a little near-sighted, part his hair in the middle, and have amber lights in his beard. To her companions she seemed to have a very pallid fancy; and even the fact that she was a sprig of the transatlantic democracy never sufficiently explained her apathy on social questions. She had a mental image of that son of the Crusaders who was to suffer her to adore him, but like many an artist who has produced a masterpiece of idealization, she shrank from exposing it to public criticism. It was the portrait of a gentleman rather ugly than handsome, and rather poor than rich. But his ugliness was to be nobly expressive, and his poverty delicately proud. Euphemia had a fortune of her own, which, at the proper time, after fixing on her in eloquent silence those fine eyes which were to soften the feudal severity of his visage, he was to accept with a world of stifled protestations. One condition alone she was to make,—that his blood should be of the very finest strain. On this she would stake her happiness.

It so chanced that circumstances were to give convincing color to this primitive logic.

Though little of a talker, Euphemia was an ardent listener, and there were moments when she fairly hung upon the lips of Mademoiselle Marie de Mauves. Her intimacy with this chosen schoolmate was, like most intimacies, based on their points of difference. Mademoiselle de Mauves was very positive, very shrewd, very ironical, very French,—everything that Euphemia felt herself unpardonable in not being. During her Sundays *en ville* she had examined the world and judged it, and she imparted her impressions to our attentive heroine with an agreeable mixture of enthusiasm and scepticism. She was moreover a handsome and well-grown person, on whom Euphemia's ribbons and trinkets had a trick of looking better than on their slender proprietress. She had, finally, the supreme merit of being a rigorous example of the virtue of exalted birth, having, as she did, ancestors honorably mentioned by Joinville and Commines, and a stately grandmother with a hooked nose, who came up with her after the holidays from a veritable *castel* in Auvergne. It seemed to Euphemia that these attributes made her friend more at home in the world than if she had been the daughter of even the most prosperous grocer. A certain aristocratic impudence Mademoiselle de Mauves abundantly possessed, and her raids among her friend's finery were quite in the spirit of her baronial ancestors in the twelfth century,—a spirit which Euphemia considered but a large way of understanding friendship,—a freedom from small deference to the world's opinions which would sooner or later justify itself in acts of surprising magnanimity. Mademoiselle de Mauves perhaps enjoyed but slightly that easy attitude toward society which Euphemia envied her. She proved herself later in life such an accomplished schemer that her sense of having further heights to scale must have awakened early. Our heroine's ribbons and trinkets had much to do with the other's sisterly patronage, and her appealing pliancy of character even more; but the concluding motive of Marie's writing to her grand-mamma to invite Euphemia for a three weeks' holiday to the *castel* in Auvergne, involved altogether superior considerations. Mademoiselle de Mauves was indeed at this time seventeen years of age, and presumably capable of general views; and Euphemia, who was hardly less, was a very well-grown subject for experiment, besides being pretty enough almost to pre-assure success. It is a proof of the sincerity of Euphemia's aspirations that the *castel* was not a shock to her faith. It was neither a cheerful nor a luxurious abode, but the young girl found it as delightful as a play. It had battered towers and an empty moat, a rusty drawbridge and a court paved with crooked, grass-grown slabs, over which the antique coach-wheels of the old lady with the hooked nose seemed to awaken the echoes of the seventeenth century. Euphemia was not frightened out of her dream; she had the pleasure of seeing it assume the consistency of a flattering presentiment. She had a taste for old servants, old anecdotes, old furniture, faded household colors, and sweetly stale odors,—musty treasures in which the Château de Mauves abounded. She made a dozen sketches in water-colors, after her conventual pattern; but sentimentally, as one may say, she was forever sketching with a freer hand.

Old Madame de Mauves had nothing severe but her nose, and she seemed to Euphemia, as indeed she was, a graciously venerable relic of a historic order of things. She took a great fancy to the young American, who was ready to sit all day at her feet and listen to anecdotes of the *bon temps* and quotations from the family chronicles. Madame de Mauves was a very honest old woman, and uttered her thoughts with antique plainness. One day, after pushing back Euphemia's shining locks and blinking at her with some tenderness from under her spectacles, she declared, with an energetic shake of the head, that she didn't know what to make of her. And in answer to the young girl's startled blush,—"I should like to advise you," she said, "but you seem to me so all of a piece that I am afraid that if I advise you, I shall spoil you. It's easy to see that you're not one of us. I don't know whether you're better, but you seem to me to listen to the murmur of your own young spirit, rather than to the voice from behind the confessional or to the whisper of opportunity. Young girls, in my day, when they were stupid, were very docile, but when they were clever, were very sly. You're clever enough, I imagine, and yet if I guessed all your secrets at this moment, is there one I should have to frown at? I can tell you a wickeder one than any you have discovered for yourself. If you expect to live in France, and you want to be happy, don't listen too hard to that little voice I just spoke of,—the voice that is neither the curé's nor the world's. You'll fancy it saying things that it won't help your case to hear. They'll make you sad, and when you're sad you'll grow plain, and when you're plain you'll grow bitter, and when you're bitter you'll be very disagreeable. I was brought up to think that a woman's first duty was to please, and the happiest women I've known have been the ones who performed this duty faithfully. As you're not a Catholic, I suppose you can't be a dévote; and if you don't take life as a fifty years' mass, the only way to take it is as a game of skill. Listen: not to lose, you must,—I don't say cheat; but don't be too sure your neighbor won't, and don't be shocked out of your self-possession if he does. Don't lose, my dear; I beseech you, don't lose. Be neither suspicious nor credulous; but if you find your neighbor peeping, don't cry out, but very politely wait your own chance. I've had my *revanche* more than once in my day, but I'm not sure that the sweetest I could take against life as a whole would be to have your blessed innocence profit by my experience."

This was rather awful advice, but Euphemia understood it too little to be either edified or frightened. She sat listening to it very much as she would have listened to the speeches of an old lady in a comedy, whose diction should picturesquely correspond to the pattern of her mantilla and the fashion of her headdress. Her indifference was doubly dangerous, for Madame de Mauves spoke at the prompting of coming events, and her words were the result of a somewhat troubled conscience,—a conscience which told her at once that Euphemia was too tender a victim to be sacrificed to an ambition, and that the prosperity of her house was too precious a heritage to be sacrificed to a scruple. The prosperity in question had suffered repeated and grievous breaches, and the house of De Mauves had been pervaded by the cold comfort of an establishment in which people were obliged to balance dinner-table allusions to feudal ancestors against the absence of side dishes; a state of things the more regrettable as the family was now mainly represented by a gentleman whose appetite was large, and who justly maintained that its historic glories were not established by underfed heroes.

Three days after Euphemia's arrival, Richard de Mauves came down from Paris to pay his respects to his grandmother, and treated our heroine to her first encounter with a gentilhomme in the flesh. On coming in he kissed his grandmother's hand, with a smile which caused her to draw it away with dignity, and set Euphemia, who was standing by, wondering what had happened between them. Her unanswered wonder was but the beginning of a life of bitter perplexity, but the reader is free to know that the smile of M. de Mauves was a reply to a certain postscript affixed by the old lady to a letter promptly addressed to him by her granddaughter, after Euphemia had been admitted to justify the latter's promises. Mademoiselle de Mauves brought her letter to her grandmother for approval, but obtained no more than was expressed in a frigid nod. The old lady watched her with a sombre glance as she proceeded to seal the letter, and suddenly bade her open it again and bring her a pen.

"Your sister's flatteries are all nonsense," she wrote; "the young lady is far too good for you, *mauvais sujet*. If you have a conscience you'll not come and take possession of an angel of innocence."

The young girl, who had read these lines, made up a little face as she redirected the letter; but she laid down her pen with a confident nod, which might have seemed to mean that, to the best of her belief, her brother had not a conscience.

"If you meant what you said," the young man whispered to his grandmother on the first opportunity, "it would have been simpler not to let her send the letter!"

It was perhaps because she was wounded by this cynical insinuation, that Madame de Mauves remained in her own apartment during a greater part of Euphemia's stay, so that the latter's angelic innocence was left entirely to the Baron's mercy. It suffered no worse mischance, however, than to be prompted to intenser communion with itself. M. de Mauves was the hero of the young girl's romance made real, and so completely accordant with this creature of her imagination, that she felt afraid of him, very much as she would have been of a supernatural apparition. He was thirty-five years old,—young enough to suggest possibilities of ardent activity, and old enough to have formed opinions which a simple woman might deem it an intellectual privilege to listen to. He was perhaps a trifle handsomer than Euphemia's rather grim, Quixotic ideal, but a very few days reconciled her to his good looks, as they would have reconciled her to his ugliness. He was quiet, grave, and eminently distinguished. He spoke little, but his speeches, without being sententious, had a certain nobleness of tone which caused them to re-echo in the young girl's ears at the end of the day. He paid her very little direct attention, but his chance words—if he only asked her if she objected to his cigarette—were accompanied by a smile of extraordinary kindness.

It happened that shortly after his arrival, riding an unruly horse, which Euphemia with shy admiration had watched him mount in the castle yard, he was thrown with a violence which, without disparaging his skill, made him for a fortnight an interesting invalid, lounging in the library with a bandaged knee. To beguile his confinement, Euphemia was repeatedly induced to sing to him, which she did with a little natural tremor in her voice, which might have passed for an exquisite refinement of art. He never overwhelmed her with compliments, but he listened with unwandering attention, remembered all her melodies, and sat humming them to himself. While his imprisonment lasted, indeed, he passed hours in her company, and made her feel not unlike some unfriended artist who has suddenly gained the opportunity to devote a fortnight to the study of a great model. Euphemia studied with noiseless diligence what she supposed to be the "character" of M. de Mauves, and the more she looked the more fine lights and shades she seemed to behold in this masterpiece of nature. M. de Mauve's character indeed, whether from a sense of being generously scrutinized, or for reasons which bid graceful defiance to analysis, had never been so amiable; it seemed really to reflect the purity of Euphemia's interpretation of it. There had been nothing especially to admire in the state of mind in which he left Paris,—a hard determination to marry a young girl whose charms might or might not justify his sister's account of them, but who was mistress, at the worst, of a couple of hundred thousand francs a year. He had not counted out sentiment; if she pleased him, so much the better; but he had left a meagre margin for it, and he would hardly have admitted that so excellent a match could be improved by it. He was a placid sceptic, and it was a singular fate for a man who believed in nothing to be so tenderly believed in. What his original faith had been he could hardly have told you; for as he came back to his childhood's home to mend his fortunes by pretending to fall in love, he was a thoroughly perverted creature, and overlaid with more corruptions than a summer day's questioning of his conscience would have released him from. Ten years' pursuit of pleasure, which a bureau full of unpaid bills was all he had to show for, had pretty well stifled the natural lad, whose violent will and generous temper might have been shaped by other circumstances to a result which a romantic imagination might fairly accept as a late-blooming flower of hereditary honor. The Baron's violence had been subdued, and he had learned to be irreproachably polite; but he had lost the edge of his generosity, and his politeness, which in the long run society paid for, was hardly more than a form of luxurious egotism, like his fondness for cambric handkerchiefs, lavender gloves, and other fopperies by which shopkeepers remained out of pocket. In after years he was terribly polite to his wife. He had formed himself, as the phrase was, and the form prescribed to him by the society into which his birth and his tastes introduced him was marked by some peculiar features. That which mainly concerns us is its classification of the fairer half of humanity as objects not essentially different—say from the light gloves one soils in an evening and throws away. To do M. de Mauves justice, he had in the course of time encountered such plentiful evidence of this pliant, glove-like quality in the feminine character, that idealism naturally seemed to him a losing game.

Euphemia, as he lay on his sofa, seemed by no means a refutation; she simply reminded him that very young women are generally innocent, and that this, on the whole, was the most charming stage of their development. Her innocence inspired him with profound respect, and it seemed to him that if he shortly became her husband it would be exposed to a danger the less. Old Madame de Mauves, who flattered herself that in this whole matter she was being laudably rigid, might have learned a lesson from his gallant consideration. For a fortnight the Baron was almost a blushing boy again. He watched from behind the "Figaro," and admired, and held his tongue. He was not in the least disposed toward a flirtation; he had no desire to trouble the waters he proposed to transfuse into the golden cup of matrimony. Sometimes a word, a look, a movement of Euphemia's, gave him the oddest sense of being, or of seeming at least, almost bashful; for she had a way of not dropping her eyes, according to the mysterious virginal mechanism, of not fluttering out of the room when she found him there alone, of treating him rather as a benignant than as a pernicious influence,—a radiant frankness of demeanor, in fine, in spite of an evident natural reserve, which it seemed equally graceless not to make the subject of a compliment and indelicate not to take for granted. In this way there was wrought in the Baron's mind a vague, unwonted resonance of soft impressions, as we may call it, which indicated the transmutation of "sentiment" from a contingency into a fact. His imagination enjoyed it; he was very fond of music, and this reminded him of some of the best he had ever heard. In spite of the bore of being laid up with a lame knee, he was in a better humor than he had known for months; he lay smoking cigarettes and listening to the nightingales, with the comfortable smile of one of his country neighbors whose big ox should have taken the prize at a fair. Every now and then, with an impatient suspicion of the resemblance, he declared that he was pitifully *bête;* but he was under a charm which braved even the supreme penalty of seeming ridiculous. One morning he had half an hour's tête-à-tête with his grandmother's confessor, a soft-voiced old abbé, whom, for reasons of her own, Madame de Mauves had suddenly summoned, and had left waiting in the drawing-room while she rearranged her curls. His reverence, going up to the old lady, assured her that M. le Baron was in a most edifying state of mind, and a promising subject for the operation of grace. This was a pious interpretation of the Baron's momentary good-humor. He had always lazily wondered what priests were good for, and he now remembered, with a sense of especial obligation to the abbé, that they were excellent for marrying people.

A day or two after this he left off his bandages, and tried to walk. He made his way into the garden and hobbled successfully along one of the alleys; but in the midst of his progress he was seized with a spasm of pain which forced him to stop and call for help. In an instant Euphemia came tripping along the path and offered him her arm with the frankest solicitude.

"Not to the house," he said, taking it; "farther on, to the bosquet." This choice was prompted by her having immediately confessed that she had seen him leave the house, had feared an accident, and had followed him on tiptoe.

"Why didn't you join me?" he had asked, giving her a look in which admiration was no longer disguised, and yet felt itself half at the mercy of her replying that a *jeune fille* should not be seen following a gentleman. But it drew a breath which filled its lungs for a long time afterward, when she replied simply that if she had overtaken him he might have accepted her arm out of politeness, whereas she wished to have the pleasure of seeing him walk alone.

The bosquet was covered with an odorous tangle of blossoming vines, and a nightingale overhead was shaking out love-notes with a profuseness which made the Baron consider his own conduct the perfection of propriety.

"In America," he said, "I have always heard that when a man wishes to marry a young girl, he offers himself simply, face to face, without any ceremony,—without parents, and uncles, and cousins sitting round in a circle."

"Why, I believe so," said Euphemia, staring, and too surprised to be alarmed.

"Very well, then," said the Baron, "suppose our bosquet here to be American. I offer you my hand, à l'Américaine. It will make me intensely happy to have you accept it."

Whether Euphemia's acceptance was in the American manner is more than I can say; I incline to think that for fluttering, grateful, trustful, softly-amazed young hearts, there is only one manner all over the world.

That evening, in the little turret chamber which it was her happiness to inhabit, she wrote a dutiful letter to her mamma, and had just sealed it when she was sent for by Madame de Mauves. She found this ancient lady seated in her boudoir, in a lavender satin gown, with all her candles lighted, as if to celebrate her grandson's betrothal. "Are you very happy?" Madame de Mauves demanded, making Euphemia sit down before her.

"I'm almost afraid to say so," said the young girl, "lest I should wake myself up."

"May you never wake up, *belle enfant*," said the old lady, solemnly. "This is the first marriage ever made in our family in this way,—by a Baron de Mauves proposing to a young girl in an arbor, like Jeannot and Jeannette. It has not been our way of doing things, and people may say it wants frankness. My grandson tells me he considers it the perfection of frankness. Very good. I'm a very old woman, and if your differences should ever be as frank as your agreement, I shouldn't like to see them. But I should be sorry to die and think you were going to be unhappy. You can't be, beyond a certain point; because, though in this world the Lord sometimes makes light of our expectations, he never altogether ignores our deserts. But you're very young and innocent, and easy to deceive. There never was a man in the world—among the saints themselves—as good as you believe the Baron. But he's a *galant homme* and a gentleman, and I've been talking to him tonight. To you I want to say this,—that you're to forget the worldly rubbish I talked the other day about frivolous women being happy. It's not the kind of happiness that would suit you. Whatever befalls you, promise me this: to be yourself. The Baron de Mauves will be none the worse for it. Yourself, understand, in spite of everything,—bad precepts and bad examples, bad usage even. Be persistently and patiently yourself, and a De Mauves will do you justice!"

Euphemia remembered this speech in after years, and more than once, wearily closing her eyes, she seemed to see the old woman sitting upright in her faded finery and smiling grimly, like one of the Fates who sees the wheel of fortune turning up her favorite event. But at the moment it seemed to her simply to have the proper gravity of the occasion; this was the way, she supposed, in which lucky young girls were addressed on their engagement by wise old women of quality.

At her convent, to which she immediately returned, she found a letter from her mother, which shocked her far more than the remarks of Madame de Mauves. Who were these people, Mrs. Cleve demanded, who had presumed to talk to her daughter of marriage without asking her leave? Questionable gentlefolk, plainly; the best French people never did such things. Euphemia would return straightway to her convent, shut herself up, and await her own arrival.

It took Mrs. Cleve three weeks to travel from Nice to Paris, and during this time the young girl had no communication with her lover beyond accepting a bouquet of violets, marked with his initials and left by a female friend. "I've not brought you up with such devoted care," she declared to her daughter at their first interview, "to marry a penniless Frenchman. I will take you straight home, and you will please to forget M. de Mauves."

Mrs. Cleve received that evening at her hotel a visit from the Baron which mitigated her wrath, but failed to modify her decision. He had very good manners, but she was sure he had horrible morals; and Mrs. Cleve, who had been a very good-natured censor on her own account, felt a genuine spiritual need to sacrifice her daughter to propriety. She belonged to that large class of Americans who make light of America in familiar discourse, but are startled back into a sense of moral responsibility when they find Europeans taking them at their word. "I know the type, my dear," she said to her daughter with a sagacious nod. "He'll not beat you; sometimes you'll wish he would."

Euphemia remained solemnly silent; for the only answer she felt capable of making her mother was that her mind was too small a measure of things, and that the Baron's "type" was one which it took some mystical illumination to appreciate. A person who confounded him with the common throng of her watering-place acquaintance was not a person to argue with. It seemed to Euphemia that she had no cause to plead; her cause was in the Lord's hands and her lover's.

M. de Mauves had been irritated and mortified by Mrs. Cleve's opposition, and hardly knew how to handle an adversary who failed to perceive that a De Mauves of necessity gave more than he received. But he had obtained information on his return to Paris which exalted the uses of humility. Euphemia's fortune, wonderful to say, was greater than its fame, and in view of such a prize, even a De Mauves could afford to take a snubbing.

The young man's tact, his deference, his urbane insistence, won a concession from Mrs. Cleve. The engagement was to be suspended and her daughter was to return home, be brought out and receive the homage she was entitled to, and which would but too surely take a form dangerous to the Baron's suit. They were to exchange neither letters, nor mementos, nor messages; but if at the end of two years Euphemia had refused offers enough to attest the permanence of her attachment, he should receive an invitation to address her again.

This decision was promulgated in the presence of the parties interested. The Baron bore himself gallantly, and looked at the young girl, expecting some tender protestation. But she only looked at him silently in return, neither weeping, nor smiling, nor putting out her hand. On this they separated; but as the Baron walked away, he declared to himself that, in spite of the confounded two years, he was a very happy fellow,—to have a fiancée who, to several millions of francs, added such strangely beautiful eyes.

How many offers Euphemia refused but scantily concerns us,—and how the Baron wore his two years away. He found that he needed pastimes, and, as pastimes were expensive, he added heavily to the list of debts to be cancelled by Euphemia's millions. Sometimes, in the thick of what he had once called pleasure with a keener conviction than now, he put to himself the case of their failing him after all; and then he remembered that last mute assurance of her eyes, and drew a long breath of such confidence as he felt in nothing else in the world save his own punctuality in an affair of honor.

At last, one morning, he took the express to Havre with a letter of Mrs. Cleve's in his pocket, and ten days later made his bow to mother and daughter in New York. His stay was brief, and he was apparently unable to bring himself to view what Euphemia's uncle, Mr. Butterworth, who gave her away at the altar, called our great experiment in democratic self-government in a serious light. He smiled at everything, and seemed to regard the New World as a colossal *plaisanterie*. It is true that a perpetual smile was the most natural expression of countenance for a man about to marry Euphemia Cleve.

3

Longmore's first visit seemed to open to him so large an opportunity for tranquil enjoyment, that he very soon paid a second, and, at the end of a fortnight, had spent a great many hours in the little drawing-room which Madame de Mauves rarely quitted except to drive or walk in the forest. She lived in an old-fashioned pavilion, between a high-walled court and an excessively artificial garden, beyond whose enclosure you saw a long line of tree-tops. Longmore liked the garden, and in the mild afternoons used to move his chair through the open window to the little terrace which overlooked it, while his hostess sat just within. After a while she came out and wandered through the narrow alleys and beside the thin-spouting fountain, and last introduced him to a little gate in the garden wall, opening upon a lane which led into the forest. Hitherward, more than once, she wandered with him, bareheaded and meaning to go but twenty rods, but always strolling good-naturedly farther, and often taking a generous walk. They discovered a vast deal to talk about, and to the pleasure of finding the hours tread inaudibly away, Longmore was able to add the satisfaction of suspecting that he was a "resource" for Madame de Mauves. He had made her acquaintance with the sense, not altogether comfortable, that she was a woman with a painful secret, and that seeking her acquaintance would be like visiting at a house where there was an invalid who could bear no noise. But he very soon perceived that her sorrow, since sorrow it was, was not an aggressive one; that it was not fond of attitudes and ceremonies, and that her earnest wish was to forget it. He felt that even if Mrs. Draper had not told him she was unhappy, he would have guessed it; and yet he could hardly have pointed to his evidence. It was chiefly negative,—she never alluded to her husband. Beyond this it seemed to him simply that her whole being was pitched on a lower key than harmonious Nature meant; she was like a powerful singer who had lost her high notes. She never drooped nor sighed nor looked unutterable things; she indulged in no dusky sarcasms against fate; she had, in short, none of the coquetry of unhappiness. But Longmore was sure that her gentle gayety was the result of strenuous effort, and that she was trying to interest herself in his thoughts to escape from her own. If she had wished to irritate his curiosity and lead him to take her confidence by storm, nothing could have served her purpose better than this ingenuous reserve. He declared to himself that there was a rare magnanimity in such ardent self-effacement, and that but one woman in ten thousand was capable of merging an intensely personal grief in thankless outward contemplation. Madame de Mauves, he instinctively felt, was not sweeping the horizon for a compensation or a consoler; she had suffered a personal deception which had disgusted her with persons. She was not striving to balance her sorrow with some strongly flavored joy; for the present, she was trying to live with it, peaceably, reputably, and without scandal,—turning the key on it occasionally, as you would on a companion liable to attacks of insanity. Longmore was a man of fine senses and of an active imagination, whose leading-strings had never been slipped. He began to regard his hostess as a figure haunted by a shadow which was somehow her intenser, more authentic self. This hovering mystery came to have for him an extraordinary charm. Her delicate beauty acquired to his eye the serious cast of certain blank-browed Greek statues, and sometimes, when his imagination, more than his ear, detected a vague tremor in the tone in which she attempted to make a friendly question seem to have behind it none of the hollow resonance of absent-mindedness, his marvelling eyes gave her an answer more eloquent, though much less to the point, than the one she demanded.

She gave him indeed much to wonder about, and, in his ignorance, he formed a dozen experimental theories upon the history of her marriage. She had married for love and staked her whole soul on it, of that he was convinced. She had not married a Frenchman to be near Paris and her base of supplies of millinery; he was sure she had seen conjugal happiness in a light of which her present life, with its conveniences for shopping and its moral aridity, was the absolute negation. But by what extraordinary process of the heart—through what mysterious intermission of that moral instinct which may keep pace with the heart, even when that organ is making unprecedented time—had she fixed her affections on an arrogantly frivolous Frenchman? Longmore needed no telling; he knew M. de Mauves was frivolous; it was stamped on his eyes, his nose, his mouth, his carriage. For French women Longmore had but a scanty kindness, or at least (what with him was very much the same thing) but a scanty gallantry; they all seemed to belong to the type of a certain fine lady to whom he had ventured to present a letter of introduction, and whom, directly after his first visit to her, he had set down in his note-book as "metallic." Why should Madame de Mauves have chosen a French woman's lot,—she whose character had a perfume which doesn't belong to even the brightest metals? He asked her one day frankly if it had cost her nothing to transplant herself,—if she was not oppressed with a sense of irreconcilable difference from "all these people." She was silent awhile, and he fancied that she was hesitating as to whether she should resent so unceremonious an allusion to her husband. He almost wished she would; it would seem a proof that her deep reserve of sorrow had a limit.

"I almost grew up here," she said at last, "and it was here for me that those dreams of the future took shape that we all have when we cease to be very young. As matters stand, one may be very American and yet arrange it with one's conscience to live in Europe. My imagination perhaps—I had a little when I was younger—helped me to think I should find happiness here. And after all, for a woman, what does it signify? This is not America, perhaps, about me, but it's quite as little France. France is out there, beyond the garden, in the town, in the forest; but here, close about me, in my room and"—she paused a moment—"in my mind, it's a nameless country of my own. It's not her country," she added, "that makes a woman happy or unhappy."

Madame Clairin, Euphemia's sister-in-law, might have been supposed to have undertaken the graceful task of making Longmore ashamed of his uncivil jottings about her sex and nation. Mademoiselle de Mauves, bringing example to the confirmation of precept, had made a remunerative match and sacrificed her name to the millions of a prosperous and aspiring wholesale druggist,—a gentleman liberal enough to consider his fortune a moderate price for being towed into circles unpervaded by pharmaceutic odors. His system, possibly, was sound, but his own application of it was unfortunate. M. Clairin's head was turned by his good luck. Having secured an aristocratic wife, he adopted an aristocratic vice and began to gamble at the Bourse. In an evil hour he lost heavily and staked heavily to recover himself. But he overtook his loss only by a greater one. Then he let everything go,—his wits, his courage, his probity,—everything that had made him what his ridiculous marriage had so promptly unmade. He walked up the Rue Vivienne one day with his hands in his empty pockets, and stood for half an hour staring confusedly up and down the glittering boulevard. People brushed against him, and half a dozen carriages almost ran over him, until at last a policeman, who had been watching him for some time, took him by the arm and led him gently away. He looked at the man's cocked hat and sword with tears in his eyes; he hoped he was going to interpret to him the wrath of Heaven,—to execute the penalty of his dead-weight of self-abhorrence. But the sergent de ville only stationed him in the embrasure of a door, out of harm's way, and walked away to supervise a financial contest between an old lady and a cabman. Poor M. Clairin had only been married a year, but he had had time to measure the lofty spirit of a De Mauves. When night had fallen, he repaired to the house of a friend and asked for a night's lodging; and as his friend, who was simply his old head bookkeeper and lived in a small way, was put to some trouble to accommodate him,—"You must excuse me," Clairin said, "but I can't go home. I'm afraid of my wife!" Toward morning he blew his brains out. His widow turned the remnants of his property to better account than could have been expected, and wore the very handsomest mourning. It was for this latter reason, perhaps, that she was obliged to retrench at other points and accept a temporary home under her brother's roof.

Fortune had played Madame Clairin a terrible trick, but had found an adversary and not a victim. Though quite without beauty, she had always had what is called the grand air, and her air from this time forward was grander than ever. As she trailed about in her sable furbelows, tossing back her well-dressed head, and holding up her vigilant eye-glass, she seemed to be sweeping the whole field of society and asking herself where she should pluck her revenge. Suddenly she espied it, ready made to her hand, in poor Longmore's wealth and amiability. American dollars and American complaisance had made her brother's fortune; why shouldn't they make hers? She overestimated Longmore's wealth and misinterpreted his amiability; for she was sure that a man could not be so contented without being rich, nor so unassuming without being weak. He encountered her advances with a formal politeness which covered a great deal of unflattering discomposure. She made him feel acutely uncomfortable; and though he was at a loss to conceive how he could be an object of interest to a shrewd Parisienne, he had an indefinable sense of being enclosed in a magnetic circle, like the victim of an incantation. If Madame Clairin could have fathomed his Puritanic soul, she would have laid by her wand and her book and admitted that he was an impossible subject. She gave him a kind of moral chill, and he never mentally alluded to her save as that dreadful woman,—that terrible woman. He did justice to her grand air, but for his pleasure he preferred the small air of Madame de Mauves; and he never made her his bow, after standing frigidly passive for five minutes to one of her gracious overtures to intimacy, without feeling a peculiar desire to ramble away into the forest, fling himself down on the warm grass, and, staring up at the blue sky, forget that there were any women in nature who didn't please like the swaying tree-tops. One day, on his arrival, she met him in the court and told him that her sister-in-law was shut up with a headache, and that his visit must be for her. He followed her into the drawing-room with the best grace at his command, and sat twirling his hat for half an hour. Suddenly he understood her; the caressing cadence of her voice was a distinct invitation to solicit the incomparable honor of her hand. He blushed to the roots of his hair and jumped up with uncontrollable alacrity; then, dropping a glance at Madame Clairin, who sat watching him with hard eyes over the edge of her smile, as it were, perceived on her brow a flash of unforgiving wrath. It was not becoming, but his eyes lingered a moment, for it seemed to illuminate her character. What he saw there frightened him, and he felt himself murmuring, "Poor Madame de Mauves!" His departure was abrupt, and this time he really went into the forest and lay down on the grass.

After this he admired Madame de Mauves more than ever; she seemed a brighter figure, dogged by a darker shadow. At the end of a month he received a letter from a friend with whom he had arranged a tour through the Low Countries, reminding him of his promise to meet him promptly at Brussels. It was only after his answer was posted that he fully measured the zeal with which he had declared that the journey must either be deferred or abandoned,—that he could not possibly leave Saint-Germain. He took a walk in the forest, and asked himself if this was irrevocably true. If it was, surely his duty was to march straight home and pack his trunk. Poor Webster, who, he knew, had counted ardently on this excursion, was an excellent fellow; six weeks ago he would have gone through fire and water to join Webster. It had never been in his books to throw overboard a friend whom he had loved for ten years for a married woman whom for six weeks he had—admired. It was certainly beyond question that he was lingering at Saint-Germain because this admirable married woman was there; but in the midst of all this admiration what had become of prudence? This was the conduct of a man prepared to fall utterly in love. If she was as unhappy as he believed, the love of such a man would help her very little more than his indifference; if she was less so, she needed no help and could dispense with his friendly offices. He was sure, moreover, that if she knew he was staying on her account, she would be extremely annoyed. But this very feeling had much to do with making it hard to go; her displeasure would only enhance the gentle stoicism which touched him to the heart. At moments, indeed, he assured himself that to linger was simply impertinent; it was indelicate to make a daily study of such a shrinking grief. But inclination answered that some day her self-support would fail, and he had a vision of this admirable creature calling vainly for help. He would be her friend, to any length; it was unworthy of both of them to think about consequences. But he was a friend who carried about with him a muttering resentment that he had not known her five years earlier, and a brooding hostility to those who had anticipated him. It seemed one of fortune's most mocking strokes, that she should be surrounded by persons whose only merit was that they threw the charm of her character into radiant relief.

Longmore's growing irritation made it more and more difficult for him to see any other merit than this in the Baron de Mauves. And yet, disinterestedly, it would have been hard to give a name to the portentous vices which such an estimate implied, and there were times when our hero was almost persuaded against his finer judgment that he was really the most considerate of husbands, and that his wife liked melancholy for melancholy's sake. His manners were perfect, his urbanity was unbounded, and he seemed never to address her but, sentimentally speaking, hat in hand. His tone to Longmore (as the latter was perfectly aware) was that of a man of the world to a man not quite of the world; but what it lacked in deference it made up in easy friendliness. "I can't thank you enough for having overcome my wife's shyness," he more than once declared. "If we left her to do as she pleased, she would bury herself alive. Come often, and bring some one else. She'll have nothing to do with my friends, but perhaps she'll accept yours."

The Baron made these speeches with a remorseless placidity very amazing to our hero, who had an innocent belief that a man's head may point out to him the shortcomings of his heart and make him ashamed of them. He could not fancy him capable both of neglecting his wife and taking an almost humorous view of her suffering. Longmore had, at any rate, an exasperating sense that the Baron thought rather less of his wife than more, for that very same fine difference of nature which so deeply stirred his own sympathies. He was rarely present during Longmore's visits, and made a daily journey to Paris, where he had "business," as he once mentioned,--not in the least with a tone of apology. When he appeared, it was late in the evening, and with an imperturbable air of being on the best of terms with every one and everything, which was peculiarly annoying if you happened to have a tacit quarrel with him. If he was a good fellow, he was surely a good fellow spoiled. Something he had, however, which Longmore vaguely envied—a kind of superb positiveness—a manner rounded and polished by the traditions of centuries—an amenity exercised for his own sake and not his neighbors'—which seemed the result of something better than a good conscience—of a vigorous and unscrupulous temperament. The Baron was plainly not a moral man, and poor Longmore, who was, would have been glad to learn the secret of his luxurious serenity. What was it that enabled him, without being a monster with visibly cloven feet, exhaling brimstone, to misprize so cruelly a lovely wife, and to walk about the world with a smile under his mustache? It was the essential grossness of his imagination, which had nevertheless helped him to turn so many neat compliments. He could be very polite, and he could doubtless be supremely impertinent; but he was as unable to draw a moral inference of the finer strain, as a school-boy who has been playing truant for a week to solve a problem in algebra. It was ten to one he didn't know his wife was unhappy; he and his brilliant sister had doubtless agreed to consider their companion a Puritanical little person, of meagre aspirations and slender accomplishments, contented with looking at Paris from the terrace, and, as an especial treat, having a countryman very much like herself to supply her with homely transatlantic gossip. M. de Mauves was tired of his companion: he relished a higher flavor in female society. She was too modest, too simple, too delicate; she had too few arts, too little coquetry, too much charity. M. de Mauves, some day, lighting a cigar, had probably decided she was stupid. It was the same sort of taste, Longmore moralized, as the taste for Gérôme in painting and for M. Gustave Flaubert in literature. The Baron was a pagan and his wife was a Christian, and between them, accordingly, was a gulf. He was by race and instinct a *grand seigneur.* Longmore had often heard of this distinguished social type, and was properly grateful for an opportunity to examine it closely. It had certainly a picturesque boldness of outline, but it was fed from spiritual sources so remote from those of which he felt the living gush in his own soul, that he found himself gazing at it, in irreconcilable antipathy, across a dim historic mist. "I'm a modern *bourgeois,*" he said, "and not perhaps so good a judge of how far a pretty woman's tongue may go at supper without prejudice to her reputation. But I've not met one of the sweetest of women without recognizing her and discovering that a certain sort of character offers better entertainment than Thérésa's songs, sung by a dissipated duchess. Wit for wit, I think mine carries me further." It was easy indeed to perceive that, as became a *grand seigneur,* M. de Mauves had a stock of rigid notions. He would not especially have desired, perhaps, that his wife should compete in amateur operettas with the duchesses in question, chiefly of recent origin; but he held that a gentleman may take his amusement where he finds it, that he is quite at liberty not to find it at home; and that the wife of a De Mauves who should hang her head and have red eyes, and allow herself to make any other response to officious condolence than that her husband's amusements were his own affair, would have forfeited every claim to having her fingertips bowed over and kissed. And yet in spite of these sound principles, Longmore fancied that the Baron was more irritated than gratified by his wife's irreproachable reserve. Did it dimly occur to him that it was self-control and not self-effacement? She was a model to all the inferior matrons of his line, past and to come, and an occasional "scene" from her at a convenient moment would have something reassuring,—would attest her stupidity a trifle more forcibly than her inscrutable tranquillity.

Longmore would have given much to know the principle of her submissiveness, and he tried more than once, but with rather awkward timidity, to sound the mystery. She seemed to him to have been long resisting the force of cruel evidence, and, though she had succumbed to it at last, to have denied herself the right to complain, because if faith was gone her heroic generosity remained. He believed even that she was capable of reproaching herself with having expected too much, and of trying to persuade herself out of her bitterness by saying that her hopes had been illusions and that this was simply—life. "I hate tragedy," she once said to him; "I have a really pusillanimous dread of moral suffering. I believe that—without base concessions—there is always some way of escaping from it. I had almost rather never smile all my life than have a single violent explosion of grief." She lived evidently in nervous apprehension of being fatally convinced,—of seeing to the end of her deception. Longmore, when he thought of this, felt an immense longing to offer her something of which she could be as sure as of the sun in heaven.

4

His friend Webster lost no time in accusing him of the basest infidelity, and asking him what he found at Saint-Germain to prefer to Van Eyck and Memling, Rubens and Rembrandt. A day or two after the receipt of Webster's letter, he took a walk with Madame de Mauves in the forest. They sat down on a fallen log, and she began to arrange into a bouquet the anemones and violets she had gathered. "I have a letter," he said at last, "from a friend whom I some time ago promised to join at Brussels. The time has come,—it has passed. It finds me terribly unwilling to leave Saint-Germain."

She looked up with the candid interest which she always displayed in his affairs, but with no disposition, apparently, to make a personal application of his words. "Saint-Germain is pleasant enough," she said; "but are you doing yourself justice? Won't you regret in future days that instead of travelling and seeing cities and monuments and museums and improving your mind, you sat here—for instance—on a log, pulling my flowers to pieces?"

"What I shall regret in future days," he answered after some hesitation, "is that I should have sat here and not spoken the truth on the matter. I am fond of museums and monuments and of improving my mind, and I'm particularly fond of my friend Webster. But I can't bring myself to leave Saint-Germain without asking you a question. You must forgive me if it's unfortunate, and be assured that curiosity was never more respectful. Are you really as unhappy as I imagine you to be?"

She had evidently not expected his question, and she greeted it with a startled blush. "If I strike you as unhappy," she said, "I have been a poorer friend to you than I wished to be."

"I, perhaps, have been a better friend of yours than you have supposed. I've admired your reserve, your courage, your studied gayety. But I have felt the existence of something beneath them that was more *you*—more you as I wished to know you—than they were; something that I have believed to be a constant sorrow."

She listened with great gravity, but without an air of offence, and he felt that while he had been timorously calculating the last consequences of friendship, she had placidly accepted them. "You surprise me," she said slowly, and her blush still lingered. "But to refuse to answer you would confirm an impression which is evidently already too strong. An unhappiness that one can sit comfortably talking about, is an unhappiness with distinct limitations. If I were examined before a board of commissioners for investigating the felicity of mankind, I'm sure I should be pronounced a very fortunate woman."

There was something delightfully gentle to him in her tone, and its softness seemed to deepen as she continued: "But let me add, with all gratitude for your sympathy, that it's my own affair altogether. It needn't disturb you, Mr. Longmore, for I have often found myself in your company a very contented person."

"You're a wonderful woman," he said, "and I admire you as I never have admired any one. You're wiser than anything I, for one, can say to you; and what I ask of you is not to let me advise or console you, but simply thank you for letting me know you." He had intended no such outburst as this, but his voice rang loud, and he felt a kind of unfamiliar joy as he uttered it.

She shook her head with some impatience. "Let us be friends,—as I supposed we were going to be,—without protestations and fine words. To have you making bows to my wisdom,—that would be real wretchedness. I can dispense with your admiration better than the Flemish painters can,—better than Van Eyck and Rubens, in spite of all their worshippers. Go join your friend,—see everything, enjoy everything, learn everything, and write me an excellent letter, brimming over with your impressions. I'm extremely fond of the Dutch painters," she added with a slight faltering of the voice, which Longmore had noticed once before, and which he had interpreted as the sudden weariness of a spirit self-condemned to play a part.

"I don't believe you care about the Dutch painters at all," he said with an unhesitating laugh. "But I shall certainly write you a letter."

She rose and turned homeward, thoughtfully rearranging her flowers as she walked. Little was said; Longmore was asking himself, with a tremor in the unspoken words, whether all this meant simply that he was in love. He looked at the rooks wheeling against the golden-hued sky, between the tree-tops, but not at his companion, whose personal presence seemed lost in the felicity she had created. Madame de Mauves was silent and grave, because she was painfully disappointed. A sentimental friendship she had not desired; her scheme had been to pass with Longmore as a placid creature with a good deal of leisure which she was disposed to devote to profitable conversation of an impersonal sort. She liked him extremely, and felt that there was something in him to which, when she made up her girlish mind that a needy French baron was the ripest fruit of time, she had done very scanty justice. They went through the little gate in the garden wall and approached the house. On the terrace Madame Clairin was entertaining a friend,—a little elderly gentleman with a white mustache, and an order in his button-hole. Madame de Mauves chose to pass round the house into the court; whereupon her sister-in-law, greeting Longmore with a commanding nod, lifted her eye-glass and stared at them as they went by. Longmore heard the little old gentleman uttering some old-fashioned epigram about "la vieille galanterie Française," and then, by a sudden impulse, he looked at Madame de Mauves and wondered what she was doing in such a world. She stopped before the house, without asking him to come in. "I hope," she said, "you'll consider my advice, and waste no more time at Saint-Germain."

For an instant there rose to his lips some faded compliment about his time not being wasted, but it expired before the simple sincerity of her look. She stood there as gently serious as the angel of disinterestedness, and Longmore felt as if he should insult her by treating her words as a bait for flattery. "I shall start in a day or two," he answered, "but I won't promise you not to come back."

"I hope not," she said simply. "I expect to be here a long time."

"I shall come and say good by," he rejoined; on which she nodded with a smile, and went in.

He turned away, and walked slowly homeward by the terrace. It seemed to him that to leave her thus, for a gain on which she herself insisted, was to know her better and admire her more. But he was in a vague ferment of feeling which her evasion of his question half an hour before had done more to deepen than to allay. Suddenly, on the terrace, he encountered M. de Mauves, who was leaning against the parapet finishing a cigar. The Baron, who, he fancied, had an air of peculiar affability, offered him his fair, plump hand. Longmore stopped; he felt a sudden angry desire to cry out to him that he had the loveliest wife in the world; that he ought to be ashamed of himself not to know it; and that for all his shrewdness he had never looked into the depths of her eyes. The Baron, we know, considered that he had; but there was something in Euphemia's eyes now that was not there five years before. They talked for a while about various things, and M. de Mauves gave a humorous account of his visit to America. His tone was not soothing to Longmore's excited sensibilities. He seemed to consider the country a gigantic joke, and his urbanity only went so far as to admit that it was not a bad one. Longmore was not, by habit, an aggressive apologist for our institutions; but the Baron's narrative confirmed his worst impressions of French superficiality. He had understood nothing, he had felt nothing, he had learned nothing; and our hero, glancing askance at his aristocratic profile, declared that if the chief merit of a long pedigree was to leave one so vaingloriously stupid, he thanked his stars that the Longmores had emerged from obscurity in the present century, in the person of an enterprising lumber merchant. M. de Mauves dwelt of course on that prime oddity of ours,—the liberty allowed to young girls;

and related the history of his researches into the "opportunities" it presented to French noblemen,—researches in which, during a fortnight's stay. he seemed to have spent many agreeable hours. "I am bound to admit," he said, "that in every case I was disarmed by the extreme candor of the young lady, and that they took care of themselves to better purpose than I have seen some mammas in France take care of them." Longmore greeted this handsome concession with the grimmest of smiles, and damned his impertinent patronage.

Mentioning at last that he was about to leave Saint-Germain, he was surprised, without exactly being flattered, by the Baron's quickened attention. "I'm very sorry," the latter cried. "I hoped we had you for the summer." Longmore murmured something civil, and wondered why M. de Mauves should care whether he stayed or went. "You were a diversion to Madame de Mauves," the Baron added. "I assure you I mentally blessed your visits."

"They were a great pleasure to me," Longmore said gravely. "Some day I expect to come back."

"Pray do," and the Baron laid his hand urgently on his arm. "You see I have confidence in you!" Longmore was silent for a moment, and the Baron puffed his cigar reflectively and watched the smoke. "Madame de Mauves," he said at last, "is a rather singular person."

Longmore shifted his position, and wondered whether he was going to "explain" Madame de Mauves.

"Being as you are her fellow-countryman," the Baron went on, "I don't mind speaking frankly. She's just a little morbid,—the most charming woman in the world, as you see, but a little fanciful,—a little *exaltée*. Now you see she has taken this extraordinary fancy for solitude. I can't get her to go anywhere,—to see any one. When my friends present themselves she's polite, but she's freezing. She doesn't do herself justice, and I expect every day to hear two or three of them say to me, 'Your wife's *jolie à croquer:* what a pity she hasn't a little *esprit.*' You must have found out that she has really a great deal. But to tell the whole truth, what she needs is to forget herself. She sits alone for hours poring over her English books and looking at life through that terrible brown fog which they always seem to me to fling over the world. I doubt if your English authors," the Baron continued, with a serenity which Longmore afterwards characterized as sublime, "are very sound reading for young married women. I don't pretend to know much about them; but I remember that, not long after our marriage, Madame de Mauves undertook to read me one day a certain Wordsworth,—a poet highly esteemed, it appears, *chez vous*. It seemed to me that she took me by the nape of the neck and forced my head for half an hour over a basin of *soupe aux choux,* and that one ought to ventilate the drawing-room before any one called. But I suppose you know him,—*ce génie là*. I think my wife never forgave me, and that it was a real shock to her to find she had married a man who had very much the same taste in literature as in cookery. But you're a man of general culture," said the Baron, turning to Longmore and fixing his eyes on the seal on his watch-guard. "You can talk about everything, and I'm sure you like Alfred de Musset as well as Wordsworth. Talk to her about everything, Alfred de Musset included. Bah! I forgot you're going. Come back then as soon as possible and talk about your travels. If Madame de Mauves too would travel for a couple of months, it would do her good. It would enlarge her horizon,"—and M. de Mauves made a series of short nervous jerks with his stick in the air,—"it would wake up her imagination. She's too rigid, you know,—it would show her that one may bend a trifle without breaking." He paused a moment and gave two or three vigorous puffs. Then turning to his companion again, with a little nod and a confidential smile:—"I hope you admire my candor. I wouldn't say all this to one of *us*."

Evening was coming on, and the lingering light seemed to float in the air in faintly golden motes. Longmore stood gazing at these luminous particles; he could almost have fancied them a swarm of humming insects, murmuring as a refrain, "She has a great deal of *esprit*,—she has a great deal of *esprit*." "Yes, she has a great deal," he said mechanically, turning to the Baron. M. de Mauves glanced at him sharply, as if to ask what the deuce he was talking about. "She has a great deal of intelligence," said Longmore, deliberately, "a great deal of beauty, a great many virtues."

M. de Mauves busied himself for a moment in lighting another cigar, and when he had finished, with a return of his confidential smile, "I suspect you of thinking," he said, "that I don't do my wife justice. Take care,—take care, young man; that's a dangerous assumption. In general, a man always does his wife justice. More than justice," cried the Baron with a laugh,—"that we keep for the wives of other men!"

Longmore afterwards remembered it in favor of the Baron's grace of address that he had not measured at this moment the dusky abyss over which it hovered. But a sort of deepening subterranean echo lingered on his spiritual ear. For the present his keenest sensation was a desire to get away and cry aloud that M. de Mauves was an arrogant fool. He bade him an abrupt good-night, which must serve also, he said, as good by.

"Decidedly, then, you go?" said M. de Mauves, almost peremptorily.

"Decidedly."

"Of course you'll come and say good by to Madame de Mauves." His tone implied that the omission would be most uncivil; but there seemed to Longmore something so ludicrous in his taking a lesson in consideration from M. de Mauves, that he burst into a laugh. The Baron frowned, like a man for whom it was a new and most unpleasant sensation to be perplexed. "You're a queer fellow," he murmured, as Longmore turned away, not foreseeing that he would think him a very queer fellow indeed before he had done with him. Longmore sat down to dinner at his hotel with his usual good intentions; but as he was lifting his first glass of wine to his lips, he suddenly fell to musing and set down his wine untasted. His revery lasted long, and when he emerged from it, his fish was cold; but this mattered little, for his appetite was gone. That evening he packed his trunk with a kind of indignant energy. This was so effective that the operation was accomplished before bedtime, and as he was not in the least sleepy, he devoted the interval to writing two letters; one was a short note to Madame de Mauves, which he intrusted to a servant, to be delivered the next morning. He had found it best, he said, to leave Saint-Germain immediately, but he expected to be back in Paris in the early autumn. The other letter was the result of his having remembered a day or two before that he had not yet complied with Mrs. Draper's injunction to give her an account of his impressions of her friend. The present occasion seemed propitious, and he wrote half a dozen pages. His tone, however, was grave, and Mrs. Draper, on receiving them, was slightly disappointed,—she would have preferred a stronger flavor of rhapsody. But what chiefly concerns us is the concluding sentences.

"The only time she ever spoke to me of her marriage," he wrote, "she intimated that it had been a perfect love-match. With all abatements, I suppose most marriages are; but in her case this would mean more, I think, than in that of most women; for her love was an absolute idealization. She believed her husband was a hero of rose-colored romance, and he turns out to be not even a hero of very sad-colored reality. For some time now she has been sounding her mistake, but I don't believe she has touched the bottom of it yet. She strikes me as a person who is begging off from full knowledge,—who has struck a truce with painful truth, and is trying awhile the experiment of living with closed eyes. In the dark she tries to see again the gilding on her idol. Illusion of course is illusion, and one must always pay for it; but there is something truly tragical in seeing an earthly penalty levied on such divine folly as this. As for M. de Mauves, he's a Frenchman to his fingers' ends; and I confess I should dislike him for this if he were a much better man. He can't forgive his wife for having married him too sentimentally and loved him too well; for in some uncorrupted corner of his being he feels, I suppose, that as she saw him, so he ought to have been. It's a perpetual vexation to him that a little American bourgeoise should have fancied him a finer fellow than he is, or than he at all wants to be. He hasn't a glimmering of real acquaintance with his wife; he can't understand the stream of passion flowing so clear and still. To tell the truth, I hardly can myself; but when I see the spectacle I can admire it furiously. M. de Mauves, at any rate, would like to have the comfort of feeling that his wife was as corruptible as himself; and you'll hardly believe me when

I tell you that he goes about intimating to gentlemen whom he deems worthy of the knowledge, that it would be a convenience to him to have them make love to her."

5

On reaching Paris, Longmore straightway purchased a Murray's "Belgium," to help himself to believe that he would start on the morrow for Brussels; but when the morrow came, it occurred to him that, by way of preparation, he ought to acquaint himself more intimately with the Flemish painters in the Louvre. This took a whole morning, but it did little to hasten his departure. He had abruptly left Saint-Germain, because it seemed to him that respect for Madame de Mauves demanded that he should allow her husband no reason to suppose that he had understood him; but now that he had satisfied this immediate need of delicacy, he found himself thinking more and more ardently of Euphemia. It was a poor expression of ardor to be lingering irresolutely on the deserted boulevards, but he detested the idea of leaving Saint-Germain five hundred miles behind him. He felt very foolish, nevertheless, and wandered about nervously, promising himself to take the next train; but a dozen trains started, and Longmore was still in Paris. This sentimental tumult was more than he had bargained for, and, as he looked in the shop windows, he wondered whether it was a "passion." He had never been fond of the word, and had grown up with a kind of horror of what it represented. He had hoped that when he fell in love, he should do it with an excellent conscience, with no greater agitation than a mild general glow of satisfaction. But here was a sentiment compounded of pity and anger, as well as admiration, and bristling with scruples and doubts. He had come abroad to enjoy the Flemish painters and all others; but what fair-tressed saint of Van Eyck or Memling was so appealing a figure as Madame de Mauves? His restless steps carried him at last out of the long villa-bordered avenue which leads to the Bois de Boulogne.

Summer had fairly begun, and the drive beside the lake was empty, but there were various loungers on the benches and chairs, and the great café had an air of animation. Longmore's walk had given him an appetite, and he went into the establishment and demanded a dinner, remarking for the hundredth time, as he observed the smart little tables disposed in the open air, how much better they ordered this matter in France.

"Will monsieur dine in the garden, or in the salon?" asked the waiter. Longmore chose the garden; and observing that a great vine of June roses was trained over the wall of the house, placed himself at a table near by, where the best of dinners was served him on the whitest of linen, in the most shining of porcelain. It so happened that his table was near a window, and that as he sat he could look into a corner of the salon. So it was that his attention rested on a lady seated just within the window, which was open, face to face apparently to a companion who was concealed by the curtain. She was a very pretty woman, and Longmore looked at her as often as was consistent with good manners. After a while he even began to wonder who she was, and to suspect that she was one of those ladies whom it is no breach of good manners to look at as often as you like. Longmore, too, if he had been so disposed, would have been the more free to give her all his attention, that her own was fixed upon the person opposite to her. She was what the French call a *belle brune,* and though our hero, who had rather a conservative taste in such matters, had no great relish for her bold outlines and even bolder coloring, he could not help admiring her expression of basking contentment.

She was evidently very happy, and her happiness gave her an air of innocence. The talk of her friend, whoever he was, abundantly suited her humor, for she sat listening to him with a broad, lazy smile, and interrupted him occasionally, while she crunched her bonbons, with a murmured response, presumably as broad, which seemed to deepen his eloquence. She drank a great deal of champagne and ate an immense number of strawberries, and was plainly altogether a person with an impartial relish for strawberries, champagne, and what she would have called *bêtises.*

They had half finished dinner when Longmore sat down, and he was still in his place when they rose. She had hung her bonnet on a nail above her chair, and her companion passed round the table to take it down for her. As he did so, she bent her head to look at a wine stain on her dress, and in the movement exposed the greater part of the back of a very handsome neck. The gentleman observed it, and observed also, apparently, that the room beyond them was empty; that he stood within eyeshot of Longmore he failed to observe. He stooped suddenly and imprinted a gallant kiss on the fair expanse. Longmore then recognized M. de Mauves. The recipient of this vigorous tribute put on her bonnet, using his flushed smile as a mirror, and in a moment they passed through the garden, on their way to their carriage.

Then, for the first time, M. de Mauves perceived Longmore. He measured with a rapid glance the young man's relation to the open window, and checked himself in the impulse to stop and speak to him. He contented himself with bowing with great gravity as he opened the gate for his companion.

That evening Longmore made a railway journey, but not to Brussels. He had effectually ceased to care about Brussels; the only thing he now cared about was Madame de Mauves. The atmosphere of his mind had had a sudden clearing up; pity and anger were still throbbing there, but they had space to rage at their pleasure, for doubts and scruples had abruptly departed. It was little, he felt, that he could interpose between her resignation and the unsparing harshness of her position; but that little, if it involved the sacrifice of everything that bound him to the tranquil past it seemed to him that he could offer her with a rapture which at last made reflection a woefully halting substitute for faith. Nothing in his tranquil past had given such a zest to consciousness as the sense of tending with all his being to a single aim which bore him company on his journey to Saint-Germain. How to justify his return, how to explain his ardor, troubled him little. He was not sure, even, that he wished to be understood; he wished only to feel that it was by no fault of his that Madame de Mauves was alone with the ugliness of fate. He was conscious of no distinct desire to "make love" to her; if he could have uttered the essence of his longing, he would have said that he wished her to remember that in a world colored gray to her vision by disappointment, there was one vividly honest man. She might certainly have remembered it, however, without his coming back to remind her; and it is not to be denied that, as he packed his valise that evening, he wished immensely to hear the sound of her voice.

He waited the next day till his usual hour of calling,—the late afternoon; but he learned at the door that Madame de Mauves was not at home. The servant offered the information that she was walking in the forest. Longmore went through the garden and out of the little door into the lane, and, after half an hour's vain exploration, saw her coming toward him at the end of a green by-path. As he appeared, she stopped for a moment, as if to turn aside; then recognizing him, she slowly advanced, and he was soon shaking hands with her.

"Nothing has happened," she said, looking at him fixedly. "You're not ill?"

"Nothing, except that when I got to Paris I found how fond I had grown of Saint-Germain."

She neither smiled nor looked flattered; it seemed indeed to Longmore that she was annoyed. But he was uncertain, for he immediately perceived that in his absence the whole character of her face had altered. It told him that something momentous had happened. It was no longer self-contained melancholy that he read in her eyes, but grief and agitation which had lately struggled with that passionate love of peace of which she had spoken to him, and forced it to know that deep experience is never peaceful. She was pale, and she had evidently been shedding tears. He felt his heart beating hard; he seemed now to know her secrets. She continued to look at him with a contracted brow, as if his return had given her a sense of responsibility too great to be disguised by a commonplace welcome. For some moments, as he turned and walked beside her, neither spoke; then abruptly,—"Tell me truly, Mr. Longmore," she said, "why you have come back."

He turned and looked at her with an air which startled her into a certainty of what she had feared. "Because I've learned the real answer to the question I asked you the other day. You're not happy,—you're too good to be happy on the terms offered you. Madame de Mauves," he went on with a gesture which protested against a gesture of her own, "I can't be happy if you're not. I don't care for anything so long as I see such a depth of unconquerable sadness in your eyes. I found during three dreary days in Paris that the thing in the world I most care for is this daily privilege of seeing you. I know it's absolutely brutal to tell you I admire you; it's an insult to you to treat you as if you had complained to me or appealed to me. But such a friendship as I waked up to there"—and he tossed his head toward the distant city—"is a potent force, I assure you; and when forces are compressed they explode. But if you had told me every trouble in your heart, it would have mattered little; I couldn't say more than I must say now,—that if that in life from which you've hoped most has given you least, *my* devoted respect will refuse no service and betray no trust."

She had begun to make marks in the earth with the point of her parasol; but she stopped and listened to him in perfect immobility. Rather, her immobility was not perfect; for when he stopped speaking a faint flush had stolen into her cheek. It told Longmore that she was moved, and his first perceiving it was the happiest instant of his life. She raised her eyes at last, and looked at him with what at first seemed a pleading dread of excessive emotion.

"Thank you—thank you!" she said, calmly enough; but the next moment her own emotion overcame her calmness, and she burst into tears. Her tears vanished as quickly as they came, but they did Longmore a world of good. He had always felt indefinably afraid of her; her being had somehow seemed fed by a deeper faith and a stronger will than his own; but her half-dozen smothered sobs showed him the bottom of her heart, and assured him that she was weak enough to be grateful.

"Excuse me," she said; "I'm too nervous to listen to you. I believe I could have faced an enemy to-day, but I can't endure a friend."

"You're killing yourself with stoicism,—that's my belief," he cried. "Listen to a friend for his own sake, if not for yours. I have never ventured to offer you an atom of compassion, and you can't accuse yourself of an abuse of charity."

She looked about her with a kind of weary confusion which promised a reluctant attention. But suddenly perceiving by the wayside the fallen log on which they had rested a few evenings before, she went and sat down on it in impatient resignation, and looked at Longmore, as he stood silent, watching her, with a glance which seemed to urge that, if she was charitable now, he must be very wise.

"Something came to my knowledge yesterday," he said as he sat down beside her, "which gave me a supreme sense of your moral isolation. You are truth itself, and there is no truth about you. You believe in purity and duty and dignity, and you live in a world in which they are daily belied. I sometimes ask myself with a kind of rage how you ever came into such a world,—and why the perversity of fate never let me know you before."

"I like my 'world' no better than you do, and it was not for its own sake I came into it. But what particular group of people is worth pinning one's faith upon? I confess it sometimes seems to me that men and women are very poor creatures. I suppose I'm romantic. I have a most unfortunate taste for poetic fitness. Life is hard prose, which one must learn to read contentedly. I believe I once thought that all the prose was in America, which was very foolish. What I thought, what I believed, what I expected, when I was an ignorant girl, fatally addicted to falling in love with my own theories, is more than I can begin to tell you now. Sometimes, when I remember certain impulses, certain illusions of those days, they take away my breath, and I wonder my bedazzled visions didn't lead me into troubles greater than any I have now to lament. I had a conviction which you would probably smile at if I were to attempt to express it to you. It was a singular form for passionate faith to take, but it had all of the sweetness and the ardor of passionate faith. It led me to take a great step, and it lies behind me now in the distance like a shadow melting slowly in the light of experience. It has faded, but it has not vanished. Some feelings, I am sure, die only with ourselves; some illusions are as much the condition of our life as our heart-beats. They say that life itself is an illusion,—that this world is a shadow of which the reality is yet to come. Life is all of a piece, then, and there is no shame in being miserably human. As for my 'isolation,' it doesn't greatly matter; it's the fault, in part, of my obstinacy. There have been times when I have been frantically distressed, and, to tell you the truth, wretchedly homesick, because my maid—a jewel of a maid—lied to me with every second breath. There have been moments when I have wished I was the daughter of a poor New England minister, living in a little white house under a couple of elms, and doing all the housework."

She had begun to speak slowly, with an air of effort; but she went on quickly, as if talking were a relief. "My marriage introduced me to people and things which seemed to me at first very strange and then very horrible, and then, to tell the truth, very contemptible. At first I expended a great deal of sorrow and dismay and pity on it all; but there soon came a time when I began to wonder whether it was worth one's tears. If I could tell you the eternal friendships I've seen broken, the inconsolable woes consoled, the jealousies and vanities leading off the dance, you would agree with me that tempers like yours and mine can understand neither such losses nor such compensations. A year ago, while I was in the country, a friend of mine was in despair at the infidelity of her husband; she wrote me a most tragical letter, and on my return to Paris I went immediately to see her. A week had elapsed, and, as I had seen stranger things, I thought she might have recovered her spirits. Not at all; she was still in despair,—but at what? At the conduct, the abandoned, shameless conduct of Mme. de T. You'll imagine, of course, that Mme. de T. was the lady whom my friend's husband preferred to his wife. Far from it; he had never seen her. Who, then, was Mme. de T.? Mme. de T. was cruelly devoted to M. de V. And who was M. de V.? M. de V.—in two words, my friend was cultivating two jealousies at once. I hardly know what I said to her; something, at any rate, that she found unpardonable, for she quite gave me up. Shortly afterward my husband proposed we should cease to live in Paris, and I gladly assented, for I believe I was falling into a state of mind that made me a detestable companion. I should have preferred to go quite into the country, into Auvergne, where my husband has a place. But to him Paris, in some degree, is necessary, and Saint-Germain has been a sort of compromise."

"A sort of compromise!" Longmore repeated. "That's your whole life."

"Its the life of many people, of most people of quiet tastes, and it is certainly better than acute distress. One is at loss theoretically to defend a compromise; but if I found a poor creature clinging to one from day to day, I should think it poor friendship to make him lose his hold." Madame de Mauves had no sooner uttered these words than she smiled faintly, as if to mitigate their personal application.

"Heaven forbid," said Longmore, "that one should do that unless one has something better to offer. And yet I am haunted by a vision of a life in which you should have found no compromises, for they are a perversion of natures that tend only to goodness and rectitude. As I see it, you should have found happiness serene, profound, complete; a *femme de chambre* not a jewel perhaps, but warranted to tell but one fib a day; a society possibly rather provincial, but (in spite of your poor opinion of mankind) a good deal of solid virtue; jealousies and vanities very tame, and no particular iniquities and adulteries. A husband," he added after a moment,—"a husband of your own faith and race and spiritual substance, who would have loved you well."

She rose to her feet, shaking her head. "You are very kind to go to the expense of visions for me. Visions are vain things; we must make the best of the reality."

"And yet," said Longmore, provoked by what seemed the very wantonness of her patience, "the reality, if I'm not mistaken, has very recently taken a shape that keenly tests your philosophy."

She seemed on the point of replying that his sympathy was too zealous; but a couple of impatient tears in his eyes proved that it was founded on a devotion to which it was impossible not to defer. "Philosophy?" she said. "I have none. Thank Heaven!" she cried, with vehemence, "I have none. I believe, Mr. Longmore," she added in a moment, "that I have nothing on earth but a conscience,—it's a good time to tell you so,—nothing but a dogged, clinging, inexpugnable conscience. Does that prove me to be indeed of your faith and race, and have you one for which you can say as much? I don't say it in vanity, for I believe that if my conscience will prevent me from doing anything very base, it will effectually prevent me from doing anything very fine."

"I am delighted to hear it," cried Longmore. "We are made for each other. It's very certain I too shall never do anything fine. And yet I have fancied that in my case this inexpugnable organ you so eloquently describe might be blinded and gagged awhile, in a fine cause, if not turned out of doors. In yours," he went on with the same appealing irony, "is it absolutely invincible?"

But her fancy made no concession to his sarcasm. "Don't laugh at your conscience," she answered gravely; "that's the only blasphemy I know."

She had hardly spoken when she turned suddenly at an unexpected sound, and at the same moment Longmore heard a footstep in an adjacent by-path which crossed their own at a short distance from where they stood.

"It's M. de Mauves," said Euphemia directly, and moved slowly forward. Longmore, wondering how she knew it, had overtaken her by the time her husband advanced into sight. A solitary walk in the forest was a pastime to which M. de Mauves was not addicted, but he seemed on this occasion to have resorted to it with some equanimity. He was smoking a fragrant cigar, and his thumb was thrust into the armhole of his waistcoat, with an air of contemplative serenity. He stopped short with surprise on seeing his wife and her companion, and Longmore considered his surprise impertinent. He glanced rapidly from one to the other, fixed Longmore's eye sharply for a single instant, and then lifted his hat with formal politeness.

"I was not aware," he said, turning to Madame de Mauves, "that I might congratulate you on the return of monsieur."

"You should have known it," she answered gravely, "if I had expected Mr. Longmore's return."

She had become very pale, and Longmore felt that this was a first meeting after a stormy parting. "My return was unexpected to myself," he said. "I came last evening."

M. de Mauves smiled with extreme urbanity. "It's needless for me to welcome you. Madame de Mauves knows the duties of hospitality." And with another bow he continued his walk.

Madame de Mauves and her companion returned slowly home, with few words, but, on Longmore's part at least, many thoughts. The Baron's appearance had given him an angry chill; it was a dusky cloud reabsorbing the light which had begun to shine between himself and his companion.

He watched Euphemia narrowly as they went, and wondered what she had last had to suffer. Her husband's presence had checked her frankness, but nothing indicated that she had accepted the insulting meaning of his words. Matters were evidently at a crisis between them, and Longmore wondered vainly what it was on Euphemia's part that prevented an absolute rupture. What did she suspect?—how much did she know? To what was she resigned?—how much had she forgiven? How, above all, did she reconcile with knowledge, or with suspicion, that ineradicable tenderness of which she had just now all but assured him? "She has loved him once," Longmore said with a sinking of the heart, "and with her to love once is to commit one's being forever. Her husband thinks her too rigid! What would a poet call it?"

He relapsed with a kind of aching impotence into the sense of her being somehow beyond him, unattainable, immeasurable by his own fretful spirit. Suddenly he gave three passionate switches in the air with his cane, which made Madame de Mauves look round. She could hardly have guessed that they meant that where ambition was so vain, it was an innocent compensation to plunge into worship.

Madame de Mauves found in her drawing-room the little elderly Frenchman, M. de Chalumeau, whom Longmore had observed a few days before on the terrace. On this occasion, too, Madame Clairin was entertaining him, but as her sister-in-law came in she surrendered her post and addressed herself to our hero. Longmore, at thirty, was still an ingenuous youth, and there was something in this lady's large coquetry which had the power of making him blush. He was surprised at finding he had not absolutely forfeited her favor by his deportment at their last interview, and a suspicion of her meaning to approach him on another line completed his uneasiness.

"So you've returned from Brussels," she said, "by way of the forest."

"I've not been to Brussels. I returned yesterday from Paris by the only way,—by the train."

Madame Clairin stared and laughed. "I've never known a young man to be so fond of Saint-Germain. They generally declare it's horribly dull."

"That's not very polite to you," said Longmore, who was vexed at his blushes, and determined not to be abashed.

"Ah, what am I?" demanded Madame Clairin, swinging open her fan. "I'm the dullest thing here. They've not had your success with my sister-in-law."

"It would have been very easy to have it. Madame de Mauves is kindness itself."

"To her own countrymen!"

Longmore remained silent; he hated the talk. Madame Clairin looked at him a moment, and then turned her head and surveyed Euphemia, to whom M. de Chalumeau was serving up another epigram, which she was receiving with a slight droop of the head and her eyes absently wandering through the window. "Don't pretend to tell me," she murmured suddenly, "that you're not in love with that pretty woman."

"*Allons donc!*" cried Longmore, in the best French he had ever uttered. He rose the next minute, and took a hasty farewell.

6

He allowed several days to pass without going back; it seemed delicate not to appear to regard his friend's frankness during their last interview as a general invitation. This cost him a great effort, for hopeless passions are not the most deferential; and he had, moreover, a constant fear, that if, as he believed, the hour of supreme "explanations" had come, the magic of her magnanimity might convert M. de Mauves. Vicious men, it was abundantly recorded, had been so converted as to be acceptable to God, and the something divine in Euphemia's temper would sanctify any means she should choose to employ. Her means, he kept repeating, were no business of his, and the essence of his admiration ought to be to respect her freedom; but he felt as if he should turn away into a world out of which most of the joy had departed, if her freedom, after all, should spare him only a murmured "Thank you."

When he called again he found to his vexation that he was to run the gantlet of Madame Clairin's officious hospitality. It was one of the first mornings of perfect summer, and the drawing-room, through the open windows, was flooded with a sweet confusion of odors and bird-notes which filled him with the hope that Madame de Mauves would come out and spend half the day in the forest. But Madame Clairin, with her hair not yet dressed, emerged like a brassy discord in a maze of melody.

At the same moment the servant returned with Euphemia's regrets; she was indisposed and unable to see Mr. Longmore. The young man knew that he looked disappointed, and that Madame Clairin was observing him, and this consciousness impelled her to give him a glance of almost aggressive frigidity. This was apparently what she desired. She wished to throw him off his balance, and, if he was not mistaken, she had the means.

"Put down your hat, Mr. Longmore," she said, "and be polite for once. You were not at all polite the other day when I asked you that friendly question about the state of your heart."

"I have no heart—to talk about," said Longmore, uncompromisingly.

"As well say you've none at all. I advise you to cultivate a little eloquence; you may have use for it. That was not an idle question of mine; I don't ask idle questions. For a couple of months now that you've been coming and going among us, it seems to me that you have had very few to answer of any sort."

"I have certainly been very well treated," said Longmore.

Madame Clairin was silent a moment, and then—"Have you never felt disposed to ask any?" she demanded.

Her look, her tone, were so charged with roundabout meanings that it seemed to Longmore as if even to understand her would savor of dishonest complicity. "What is it you have to tell me?" he asked, frowning and blushing.

Madame Clairin flushed. It is rather hard, when you come bearing yourself very much as the sibyl when she came to the Roman king, to be treated as something worse than a vulgar gossip. "I might tell you, Mr. Longmore," she said, "that you have as bad a *ton* as any young man I ever met. Where have you lived,—what are your ideas? I wish to call your attention to a fact which it takes some delicacy to touch upon. You have noticed, I suppose, that my sister-in-law is not the happiest woman in the world."

Longmore assented with a gesture.

Madame Clairin looked slightly disappointed at his want of enthusiasm. Nevertheless—"You have formed, I suppose," she continued, "your conjectures on the causes of her—dissatisfaction."

"Conjecture has been superfluous. I have seen the causes—or at least a specimen of them—with my own eyes."

"I know perfectly what you mean. My brother, in a single word, is in love with another woman. I don't judge him; I don't judge my sister-in-law. I permit myself to say that in her position I would have managed otherwise. I would have kept my husband's affection, or I would have frankly done without it, before this. But my sister is an odd compound; I don't profess to understand her. Therefore it is, in a measure, that I appeal to you, her fellow-countryman. Of course you'll be surprised at my way of looking at the matter, and I admit that it's a way in use only among people whose family traditions compel them to take a superior view of things." Madame Clairin paused, and Longmore wondered where her family traditions were going to lead her.

"Listen," she went on. "There has never been a De Mauves who has not given his wife the right to be jealous. We know our history for ages back, and the fact is established. It's a shame if you like, but it's something to have a shame with such a pedigree. The De Mauves are real Frenchmen, and their wives—I may say it—have been worthy of them. You may see all their portraits in our Château de Mauves; every one of them an 'injured' beauty, but not one of them hanging her head. Not one of them had the bad taste to be jealous, and yet not one in a dozen was guilty of an escapade,—not one of them was talked about. There's good sense for you! How they managed—go and look at the dusky, faded canvases and pastels, and ask. They were femmes d'esprit. When they had a headache, they put on a little rouge and came to supper as usual; and when they had a heart-ache, they put a little rouge on their hearts. These are fine traditions, and it doesn't seem to me fair that a little American bourgeoise should come in and interrupt them, and should hang her photograph, with her obstinate little *air penché,* in the gallery of our shrewd fine ladies. A De Mauves must be a De Mauves. When she married my brother, I don't suppose she took him for a member of a *societé de bonnes œuvres.* I don't say we're right; who is right? But we're as history has made us, and if any one is to change, it had better be Madame de Mauves herself." Again Madame Clairin paused and opened and closed her fan. "Let her conform!" she said, with amazing audacity.

Longmore's reply was ambiguous; he simply said, "Ah!"

Madame Clairin's pious retrospect had apparently imparted an honest zeal to her indignation. "For a long time," she continued, "my sister has been taking the attitude of an injured woman, affecting a disgust with the world, and shutting herself up to read the 'Imitation.' I've never remarked on her conduct, but I've quite lost patience with it. When a woman with her prettiness lets her husband wander, she deserves her fate. I don't wish you to agree with me—on the contrary; but I call such a woman a goose. She must have bored him to death. What has passed between them for many months needn't concern us; what provocation my sister has had—monstrous, if you wish—what ennui my brother has suffered. It's enough that a week ago, just after you had ostensibly gone to Brussels, something happened to produce an explosion. She found a letter in his pocket—a photograph—a trinket—*que sais-je?* At any rate, the scene was terrible. I didn't listen at the keyhole, and I don't know what was said; but I have reason to believe that my brother was called to account as I fancy none of his ancestors have ever been,—even by injured sweethearts."

Longmore had leaned forward in silent attention with his elbows on his knees, and instinctively he dropped his face into his hands. "Ah, poor woman!" he groaned.

"Voilà!" said Madame Clairin. "You pity her."

"Pity her?" cried Longmore, looking up with ardent eyes and forgetting the spirit of Madame Clairin's narrative in the miserable facts. "Don't you?"

"A little. But I'm not acting sentimentally; I'm acting politically. I wish to arrange things,—to see my brother free to do as he chooses,—to see Euphemia contented. Do you understand me?"

'Very well, I think. You're the most immoral person I've lately had the privilege of conversing with."

Madame Clairin shrugged her shoulders. "Possibly. When was there a great politician who was not immoral?"

"Nay," said Longmore in the same tone. "You're too superficial to be a great politician. You don't begin to know anything about Madame de Mauves."

Madame Clairin inclined her head to one side, eyed Longmore sharply, mused a moment, and then smiled with an excellent imitation of intelligent compassion. "It's not in my interest to contradict you."

"It would be in your interest to learn, Madame Clairin," the young man went on with unceremonious candor, "what honest men most admire in a woman,—and to recognize it when you see it."

Longmore certainly did injustice to her talents for diplomacy, for she covered her natural annoyance at this sally with a pretty piece of irony. "So you *are* in love!" she quietly exclaimed.

Longmore was silent awhile. "I wonder if you would understand me," he said at last, "if I were to tell you that I have for Madame de Mauves the most devoted friendship?"

"You underrate my intelligence. But in that case you ought to exert your influence to put an end to these painful domestic scenes."

"Do you suppose," cried Longmore, "that she talks to me about her domestic scenes?"

Madame Clairin stared. "Then your friendship isn't returned?" And as Longmore turned away, shaking his head,—"Now, at least," she added, "she will have something to tell you. I happen to know the upshot of my brother's last interview with his wife." Longmore rose to his feet as a sort of protest against the indelicacy of the position into which he was being forced; but all that made him tender made him curious, and she caught in his averted eyes an expression which prompted her to strike her blow. "My brother is monstrously in love with a certain person in Paris; of course he ought not to be; but he wouldn't be a De Mauves if he were not. It was this unsanctified passion that spoke. 'Listen, madam,' he cried at last: 'let us live like people who understand life! It's unpleasant to be forced to say such things outright, but you have a way of bringing one down to the rudiments. I'm faithless, I'm heartless, I'm brutal, I'm everything horrible,—it's understood. Take your revenge, console yourself; you're too pretty a woman to have anything to complain of. Here's a handsome young man sighing himself into a consumption for you. Listen to the poor fellow, and you'll find that virtue is none the less becoming for being good-natured. You'll see that it's not after all such a doleful world, and that there is even an advantage in having the most impudent of husbands.' " Madame Clairin paused; Longmore had turned very pale. "You may believe it," she said; "the speech took place in my presence; things were done in order. And now, Mr. Longmore,"—this with a smile which he was too troubled at the moment to appreciate, but which he remembered later with a kind of awe,—"we count upon you!"

"He said this to her, face to face, as you say it to me now?" Longmore asked slowly, after a silence.

"Word for word, and with the greatest politeness."

"And Madame de Mauves—what did she say?"

Madame Clairin smiled again. "To such a speech as that a woman says —nothing. She had been sitting with a piece of needlework, and I think she had not seen her husband since their quarrel the day before. He came in with the gravity of an ambassador, and I'm sure that when he made his *demande en mariage* his manner was not more respectful. He only wanted white gloves!" said Madame Clairin. "Euphemia sat silent a few moments drawing her stitches, and then without a word, without a glance, she walked out of the room. It was just what she should have done!"

"Yes," Longmore repeated, "it was just what she should have done."

"And I, left alone with my brother, do you know what I said?"

Longmore shook his head. "*Mauvais sujet!*" he suggested.

" 'You've done me the honor,' I said, 'to take this step in my presence. I don't pretend to qualify it. You know what you're about, and it's your own affair. But you may confide in my discretion.' Do you think he has had reason to complain of it?" She received no answer; Longmore was slowly turning away and passing his gloves mechanically round the band of his hat. "I hope," she cried, "you're not going to start for Brussels!"

Plainly, Longmore was deeply disturbed, and Madame Clairin might flatter herself on the success of her plea for old-fashioned manners. And yet there was something that left her more puzzled than satisfied in the reflective tone with which he answered, "No, I shall remain here for the present." The processes of his mind seemed provokingly subterranean, and she would have fancied for a moment that he was linked with her sister in some monstrous conspiracy of asceticism.

"Come this evening," she boldly resumed. "The rest will take care of itself. Meanwhile I shall take the liberty of telling my sister-in-law that I have repeated—in short, that I have put you *au fait.*"

Longmore started and colored, and she hardly knew whether he was going to assent or demur. "Tell her what you please. Nothing you can tell her will affect her conduct."

"Voyons! Do you mean to tell me that a woman, young, pretty, sentimental, neglected—insulted, if you will—? I see you don't believe it. Believe simply in your own opportunity! But for heaven's sake, if it's to lead anywhere, don't come back with that *visage de croquemort.* You look as if you were going to bury your heart,—not to offer it to a pretty woman. You're much better when you smile. Come, do yourself justice."

"Yes," he said, "I must do myself justice." And abruptly, with a bow, he took his departure.

7

He felt, when he found himself unobserved, in the open air, that he must plunge into violent action, walk fast and far, and defer the opportunity for thought. He strode away into the forest, swinging his cane, throwing back his head, gazing away into the verdurous vistas, and following the road without a purpose. He felt immensely excited, but he could hardly have said whether his emotion was a pain or a joy. It was joyous as all increase of freedom is joyous; something seemed to have been knocked down across his path; his destiny appeared to have rounded a cape and brought him into sight of an open sea. But his freedom resolved itself somehow into the need of despising all mankind, with a single exception; and the fact of Madame de Mauves inhabiting a planet contaminated by the presence of this baser multitude kept his elation from seeming a pledge of ideal bliss.

But she was there, and circumstance now forced them to be intimate. She had ceased to have what men call a secret for him, and this fact itself brought with it a sort of rapture. He had no prevision that he should "profit," in the vulgar sense, by the extraordinary position into which they had been thrown; it might be but a cruel trick of destiny to make hope a harsher mockery and renunciation a keener suffering. But above all this rose the conviction that she could do nothing that would not deepen his admiration.

It was this feeling that circumstance—unlovely as it was in itself—was to force the beauty of her character into more perfect relief, that made him stride along as if he were celebrating a kind of spiritual festival. He rambled at random for a couple of hours, and found at last that he had left the forest behind him and had wandered into an unfamiliar region. It was a perfectly rural scene, and the still summer day gave it a charm for which its meagre elements but half accounted.

Longmore thought he had never seen anything so characteristically French; all the French novels seemed to have described it, all the French landscapists to have painted it. The fields and trees were of a cool metallic green; the grass looked as if it might stain your trousers, and the foliage your hands. The clear light had a sort of mild grayness; the sunbeams were of silver rather than gold. A great red-roofed, high-stacked farmhouse, with whitewashed walls and a straggling yard, surveyed the high road, on one side, from behind a transparent curtain of poplars. A narrow stream, half choked with emerald rushes and edged with gray aspens, occupied the opposite quarter. The meadows rolled and sloped away gently to the low horizon, which was barely concealed by the continuous line of clipped and marshaled trees. The prospect was not rich, but it had a frank homeliness which touched the young man's fancy. It was full of light atmosphere and diffused sunshine, and if it was prosaic, it was soothing.

Longmore was disposed to walk further, and he advanced along the road beneath the poplars. In twenty minutes he came to a village which straggled away to the right, among orchards and *potagers*. On the left, at a stone's throw from the road, stood a little pink-faced inn, which reminded him that he had not breakfasted, having left home with a prevision of hospitality from Madame de Mauves. In the inn he found a brick-tiled parlor and a hostess in sabots and a white cap, whom, over the omelette she speedily served him,—borrowing license from the bottle of sound red wine which accompanied it,—he assured that she was a true artist. To reward his compliment, she invited him to smoke his cigar in her little garden behind the house.

Here he found a *tonnelle* and a view of ripening crops, stretching down to the stream. The *tonnelle* was rather close, and he preferred to lounge on a bench against the pink wall, in the sun, which was not too hot. Here, as he rested and gazed and mused, he fell into a train of thought which, in an indefinable fashion, was a soft influence from the scene about him. His heart, which had been beating fast for the past three hours, gradually checked its pulses and left him looking at life with a rather more level gaze. The homely tavern sounds coming out through the open windows, the sunny stillness of the fields and crops, which covered so much vigorous natural life, suggested very little that was transcendental, had very little to say about renunciation,—nothing at all about spiritual zeal. They seemed to utter a message from plain ripe nature, to express the unperverted reality of things, to say that the common lot is not brilliantly amusing, and that the part of wisdom is to grasp frankly at experience, lest you miss it altogether. What reason there was for his falling a-wondering after this whether a deeply wounded heart might be soothed and healed by such a scene, it would be difficult to explain; certain it is that, as he sat there, he had a waking dream of an unhappy woman strolling by the slow-flowing stream before him, and pulling down the blossoming boughs in the orchards. He mused and mused, and at last found himself feeling angry that he could not somehow think worse of Madame de Mauves,—or at any rate think otherwise. He could fairly claim that in a sentimental way he asked very little of life,—he made modest demands on passion; why then should his only passion be born to ill-fortune? why should his first—his last—glimpse of positive happiness be so indissolubly linked with renunciation?

It is perhaps because, like many spirits of the same stock, he had in his composition a lurking principle of asceticism to whose authority he had ever paid an unquestioning respect, that he now felt all the vehemence of rebellion. To renounce—to renounce again—to renounce forever—was this all that youth and longing and resolve were meant for? Was experience to be muffled and mutilated, like an indecent picture? Was a man to sit and deliberately condemn his future to be the blank memory of a regret, rather than the long reverberation of a joy? Sacrifice? The word was a trap for minds muddled by fear, an ignoble refuge of weakness. To insist now seemed not to dare, but simply to be, to live on possible terms.

His hostess came out to hang a cloth to dry on the hedge, and, though her guest was sitting quietly enough, she seemed to see in his kindled eyes a flattering testimony to the quality of her wine.

As she turned back into the house, she was met by a young man whom Longmore observed in spite of his preoccupation. He was evidently a member of that jovial fraternity of artists whose very shabbiness has an affinity with the element of picturesqueness and unexpectedness in life which provokes a great deal of unformulated envy among people foredoomed to be respectable.

Longmore was struck first with his looking like a very clever man, and then with his looking like a very happy one. The combination, as it was expressed in his face, might have arrested the attention of even a less cynical philosopher. He had a slouched hat and a blond beard, a light easel under one arm, and an unfinished sketch in oils under the other.

He stopped and stood talking for some moments to the landlady with a peculiarly good-humored smile. They were discussing the possibilities of dinner; the hostess enumerated some very savory ones, and he nodded briskly, assenting to everything. It couldn't be, Longmore thought, that he found such soft contentment in the prospect of lamb chops and spinach and a *tarte à la crème*. When the dinner had been ordered, he turned up his sketch, and the good woman fell a-wondering and looking off at the spot by the stream-side where he made it.

Was it his work, Longmore wondered, that made him so happy? Was a strong talent the best thing in the world? The landlady went back to her kitchen, and the young painter stood as if he were waiting for something, beside the gate which opened upon the path across the fields. Longmore sat brooding and asking himself whether it was better to cultivate an art than to cultivate a passion. Before he had answered the question the painter had grown tired of waiting. He picked up a pebble, tossed it lightly into an upper window, and called, "Claudine!"

Claudine appeared; Longmore heard her at the window, bidding the young man to have patience. "But I'm losing my light," he said; "I must have my shadows in the same place as yesterday."

"Go without me, then," Claudine answered. "I will join you in ten minutes." Her voice was fresh and young; it seemed to say to Longmore that she was as happy as her companion.

"Don't forget the Chénier," cried the young man; and turning away, he passed out of the gate and followed the path across the fields until he disappeared among the trees by the side of the stream. Who was Claudine? Longmore vaguely wondered; and was she as pretty as her voice? Before long he had a chance to satisfy himself; she came out of the house with her hat and parasol, prepared to follow her companion. She had on a pink muslin dress and a little white hat, and she was as pretty as a Frenchwoman needs to be to be pleasing. She had a clear brown skin and a bright dark eye, and a step which seemed to keep time to some slow music, heard only by herself. Her hands were encumbered with various articles which she seemed to intend to carry with her. In one arm she held her parasol and a large roll of needlework, and in the other a shawl and a heavy white umbrella, such as painters use for sketching. Meanwhile she was trying to thrust into her pocket a paper-covered volume which Longmore saw to be the Poems of André Chénier; but in the effort she dropped the large umbrella, and uttered a half-smiling exclamation of disgust. Longmore stepped forward with a bow and picked up the umbrella, and as she, protesting her gratitude, put out her hand to take it, it seemed to him that she was unbecomingly overburdened.

"You have too much to carry," he said; "you must let me help you."

"You're very good, monsieur," she answered. "My husband always forgets something. He can do nothing without his umbrella. He is *d'une étourderie—*"

"You must allow me to carry the umbrella," Longmore said. "It's too heavy for a lady."

She assented, after many compliments to his politeness; and he walked by her side into the meadow. She went lightly and rapidly, picking her steps and glancing forward to catch a glimpse of her husband. She was graceful, she was charming, she had an air of decision and yet of sweetness, and it seemed to Longmore that a young artist would work none the worse for having her seated at his side, reading Chénier's iambics. They were newly married, he supposed, and evidently their path of life had none of the mocking crookedness of some others. They asked little; but what need one ask more than such quiet summer days, with the creature one loves, by a shady stream, with art and books and a wide, unshadowed horizon? To spend such a morning, to stroll back to dinner in the red-tiled parlor of the inn, to ramble away again as the sun got low,—all this was a vision of bliss which floated before him, only to torture him with a sense of the impossible. All Frenchwomen are not coquettes, he remarked, as he kept pace with his companion. She uttered a word now and then, for politeness' sake, but she never looked at him, and seemed not in the least to care that he was a well-favored young man. She cared for nothing but the young artist in the shabby coat and the slouched hat, and for discovering where he had set up his easel.

This was soon done. He was encamped under the trees, close to the stream, and, in the diffused green shade of the little wood, seemed to be in no immediate need of his umbrella. He received a vivacious rebuke, however, for forgetting it, and was informed of what he owed to Longmore's complaisance. He was duly grateful; he thanked our hero warmly, and offered him a seat on the grass. But Longmore felt like a marplot, and lingered only long enough to glance at the young man's sketch, and to see it was a very clever rendering of the silvery stream and the vivid green rushes. The young wife had spread her shawl on the grass at the base of a tree, and meant to seat herself when Longmore had gone, and murmur Chénier's verses to the music of the gurgling river. Longmore looked awhile from one to the other, barely stifled a sigh, bade them good morning, and took his departure.

He knew neither where to go nor what to do; he seemed afloat on the sea of ineffectual longing. He strolled slowly back to the inn, and in the doorway met the landlady coming back from the butcher's with the lamb chops for the dinner of her lodgers.

"Monsieur has made the acquaintance of the *dame* of our young painter," she said with a broad smile,—a smile too broad for malicious meanings. "Monsieur has perhaps seen the young man's picture. It appears that he has a great deal of talent."

"His picture was very pretty," said Longmore, "but his *dame* was prettier still."

"She's a very nice little woman; but I pity her all the more."

"I don't see why she's to be pitied," said Longmore; "they seem a very happy couple."

The landlady gave a knowing nod.

"Don't trust to it, monsieur! Those artists,—*ça n'a pas de principes!* From one day to another he can plant her there! I know them, *allez.* I've had them here very often; one year with one, another year with another."

Longmore was puzzled for a moment. Then, "You mean she's not his wife?" he asked.

She shrugged her shoulders. "What shall I tell you? They are not *des hommes sérieux*, those gentlemen! They don't engage themselves for an eternity. It's none of my business, and I've no wish to speak ill of madame. She's a very nice little woman, and she loves her *jeune homme* to distraction."

"Who is she?" asked Longmore. "What do you know about her?"

"Nothing for certain; but it's my belief that she's better than he. I've even gone so far as to believe that she's a lady,—a true lady,—and that she has given up a great many things for him. I do the best I can for them, but I don't believe she's been obliged all her life to content herself with a dinner of two courses." And she turned over her lamb chops tenderly, as if to say that though a good cook could imagine better things, yet if you could have but one course, lamb chops had much in their favor. "I shall cook them with bread crumbs. *Voilà les femmes, monsieur!*"

Longmore turned away with the feeling that women were indeed a measureless mystery, and that it was hard to say whether there was greater beauty in their strength or in their weakness. He walked back to Saint-Germain, more slowly than he had come, with less philosophic resignation to any event, and more of the urgent egotism of the passion which philosophers call the supremely selfish one. Every now and then the episode of the happy young painter and the charming woman who had given up a great many things for him rose vividly in his mind, and seemed to mock his moral unrest like some obtrusive vision of unattainable bliss.

The landlady's gossip cast no shadow on its brightness; her voice seemed that of the vulgar chorus of the uninitiated, which stands always ready with its gross prose rendering of the inspired passages in human action. Was it possible a man could take *that* from a woman,—take all that lent lightness to that other woman's footstep and intensity to her glance,—and not give her the absolute certainty of a devotion as unalterable as the process of the sun? Was it possible that such a rapturous union had the seeds of trouble,—that the charm of such a perfect accord could be broken by anything but death? Longmore felt an immense desire to cry out a thousand times "No!" for it seemed to him at last that he was somehow spiritually the same as the young painter, and that the latter's companion had the soul of Euphemia de Mauves.

The heat of the sun, as he walked along, became oppressive, and when he re-entered the forest he turned aside into the deepest shade he could find, and stretched himself on the mossy ground at the foot of a great beech. He lay for a while staring up into the verdurous dusk overhead, and trying to conceive Madame de Mauves hastening toward some quiet stream-side where he waited, as he had seen that trusting creature do an hour before. It would be hard to say how well he succeeded; but the effort soothed him rather than excited him, and as he had had a good deal both of moral and physical fatigue, he sank at last into a quiet sleep.

While he slept he had a strange, vivid dream. He seemed to be in a wood, very much like the one on which his eyes had lately closed; but the wood was divided by the murmuring stream he had left an hour before. He was walking up and down, he thought, restlessly and in intense expectation of some momentous event. Suddenly, at a distance, through the trees, he saw the gleam of a woman's dress, and hurried forward to meet her. As he advanced he recognized her, but he saw at the same time that she was on the opposite bank of the river. She seemed at first not to notice him, but when they were opposite each other she stopped and looked at him very gravely and pityingly. She made him no motion that he should cross the stream, but he wished greatly to stand by her side. He knew the water was deep, and it seemed to him that he knew that he should have to plunge, and that he feared that when he rose to the surface she would have disappeared. Nevertheless, he was going to plunge, when a boat turned into the current from above and came swiftly toward them, guided by an oarsman, who was sitting so that they could not see his face. He brought the boat to the bank where Longmore stood; the latter stepped in, and with a few strokes they touched the opposite shore. Longmore got out, and, though he was sure he had crossed the stream, Madame de Mauves was not there. He turned with a kind of agony and saw that now she was on the other bank,—the one he had left. She gave him a grave, silent glance, and walked away up the stream. The boat and the boatman resumed their course, but after going a short distance they stopped, and the boatman turned back and looked at the still divided couple. Then Longmore recognized him,—just as he had recognized him a few days before at the café in the Bois de Boulogne.

8

He must have slept some time after he ceased dreaming, for he had no immediate memory of his dream. It came back to him later, after he had roused himself and had walked nearly home. No great ingenuity was needed to make it seem a rather striking allegory, and it haunted and oppressed him for the rest of the day. He took refuge, however, in his quickened conviction that the only sound policy in life is to grasp unsparingly at happiness; and it seemed no more than one of the vigorous measures dictated by such a policy, to return that evening to Madame de Mauves. And yet when he had decided to do so, and had carefully dressed himself, he felt an irresistible nervous tremor which made it easier to linger at his open window, wondering, with a strange mixture of dread and desire, whether Madame Clairin had told her sister-in-law that she had told him. . . . His presence now might be simply a gratuitous cause of suffering; and yet his absence might seem to imply that it was in the power of circumstances to make them ashamed to meet each other's eyes. He sat a long time with his head in his hands, lost in a painful confusion of hopes and questionings. He felt at moments as if he could throttle Madame Clairin, and yet he could not help asking himself whether it was not possible that she might have done him a service. It was late when he left the hotel, and as he entered the gate of the other house his heart was beating so that he was sure his voice would show it.

The servant ushered him into the drawing-room, which was empty, with the lamp burning low. But the long windows were open, and their light curtains swaying in a soft, warm wind, and Longmore stepped out upon the terrace. There he found Madame de Mauves alone, slowly pacing up and down. She was dressed in white, very simply, and her hair was arranged, not as she usually wore it, but in a single loose coil, like that of a person unprepared for company.

She stopped when she saw Longmore, seemed slightly startled, uttered an exclamation, and stood waiting for him to speak. He looked at her, tried to say something, but found no words. He knew it was awkward, it was offensive, to stand silent, gazing; but he could not say what was suitable, and he dared not say what he wished.

Her face was indistinct in the dim light, but he could see that her eyes were fixed on him, and he wondered what they expressed. Did they warn him, did they plead or did they confess to a sense of provocation? For an instant his head swam; he felt as if it would make all things clear to stride forward and fold her in his arms. But a moment later he was still standing looking at her; he had not moved; he knew that she had spoken, but he had not understood her.

"You were here this morning," she continued, and now, slowly, the meaning of her words came to him. "I had a bad headache and had to shut myself up." She spoke in her usual voice.

Longmore mastered his agitation and answered her without betraying himself: "I hope you are better now."

"Yes, thank you, I'm better—much better."

He was silent a moment, and she moved away to a chair and seated herself. After a pause he followed her and stood before her, leaning against the balustrade of the terrace. "I hoped you might have been able to come out for the morning into the forest. I went alone; it was a lovely day, and I took a long walk."

"It was a lovely day," she said absently, and sat with her eyes lowered, slowly opening and closing her fan. Longmore, as he watched her, felt more and more sure that her sister-in-law had seen her since her interview with him; that her attitude toward him was changed. It was this same something that chilled the ardor with which he had come, or at least converted the dozen passionate speeches which kept rising to his lips into a kind of reverential silence. No, certainly, he could not clasp her to his arms now, any more than some early worshipper could have clasped the marble statue in his temple. But Longmore's statue spoke at last, with a full human voice, and even with a shade of human hesitation. She looked up, and it seemed to him that her eyes shone through the dusk.

"I'm very glad you came this evening," she said. "I have a particular reason for being glad. I half expected you, and yet I thought it possible you might not come."

"As I have been feeling all day," Longmore answered, "it was impossible I should not come. I have spent the day in thinking of you."

She made no immediate reply, but continued to open and close her fan thoughtfully. At last,—"I have something to say to you," she said abruptly. "I want you to know to a certainty that I have a very high opinion of you." Longmore started and shifted his position. To what was she coming? But he said nothing, and she went on.

"I take a great interest in you; there's no reason why I should not say it,—I have a great friendship for you."

He began to laugh; he hardly knew why, unless that this seemed the very mockery of coldness. But she continued without heeding him.

"You know, I suppose, that a great disappointment always implies a great confidence—a great hope?"

"I have hoped," he said, "hoped strongly; but doubtless never rationally enough to have a right to bemoan my disappointment."

"You do yourself injustice. I have such confidence in your reason, that I should be greatly disappointed if I were to find it wanting."

"I really almost believe that you are amusing yourself at my expense," cried Longmore. "My reason? Reason is a mere word! The only reality in the world is *feeling!*"

She rose to her feet and looked at him gravely. His eyes by this time were accustomed to the imperfect light, and he could see that her look was reproachful, and yet that it was beseechingly kind. She shook her head impatiently, and laid her fan upon his arm with a strong pressure.

"If that were so, it would be a weary world. I know your feeling, however, nearly enough. You needn't try to express it. It's enough that it gives me the right to ask a favor of you,—to make an urgent, a solemn request."

"Make it; I listen."

"*Don't disappoint me.* If you don't understand me now, you will to-morrow, or very soon. When I said just now that I had a very high opinion of you, I meant it very seriously. It was not a vain compliment. I believe that there is no appeal one may make to your generosity which can remain long unanswered. If this were to happen,—if I were to find you selfish where I thought you generous, narrow where I thought you large,"—and she spoke slowly, with her voice lingering with emphasis on each of these words,—"vulgar where I thought you rare,—I should think worse of human nature. I should suffer,—I should suffer keenly. I should say to myself in the dull days of the future, 'There was one man who might have done so and so; and he, too, failed.' But this shall not be. You have made too good an impression on me not to make the very best. If you wish to please me forever, there's a way."

She was standing close to him, with her dress touching him, her eyes fixed on his. As she went on her manner grew strangely intense, and she had the singular appearance of a woman preaching reason with a kind of passion. Longmore was confused, dazzled, almost bewildered. The intention of her words was all remonstrance, refusal, dismissal; but her presence there, so close, so urgent, so personal, seemed a distracting contradiction of it. She had never been so lovely. In her white dress, with her pale face and deeply lighted eyes, she seemed the very spirit of the summer night. When she had ceased speaking, she drew a long breath; Longmore felt it on his cheek, and it stirred in his whole being a sudden, rapturous conjecture. Were her words in their soft severity a mere delusive spell, meant to throw into relief her almost ghostly beauty, and was this the only truth, the only reality, the only law?

He closed his eyes and felt that she was watching him, not without pain and perplexity herself. He looked at her again, met her own eyes, and saw a tear in each of them. Then this last suggestion of his desire seemed to die away with a stifled murmur, and her beauty, more and more radiant in the darkness, rose before him as a symbol of something vague which was yet more beautiful than itself.

"I may understand you to-morrow," he said, "but I don't understand you now."

"And yet I took counsel with myself to-day and asked myself how I had best speak to you. On one side, I might have refused to see you at all." Longmore made a violent movement, and she added: "In that case I should have written to you. I might see you, I thought, and simply say to you that there were excellent reasons why we should part, and that I begged this visit should be your last. This I inclined to do; what made me decide otherwise was—simply friendship! I said to myself that I should be glad to remember in future days, not that I had dismissed you, but that you had gone away out of the fulness of your own wisdom."

"The fulness—the fulness!" cried Longmore.

"I'm prepared, if necessary," Madame de Mauves continued after a pause, "to fall back upon my strict right. But, as I said before, I shall be greatly disappointed, if I am obliged to."

"When I hear you say that," Longmore answered, "I feel so angry, so horribly irritated, that I wonder it is not easy to leave you without more words."

"If you should go away in anger, this idea of mine about our parting would be but half realized. No, I don't want to think of you as angry; I don't want even to think of you as making a serious sacrifice. I want to think of you as—"

"As a creature who never has existed,—who never can exist! A creature who knew you without loving you,—who left you without regretting you!"

She turned impatiently away and walked to the other end of the terrace. When she came back, he saw that her impatience had become a cold sternness. She stood before him again, looking at him from head to foot, in deep reproachfulness, almost in scorn. Beneath her glance he felt a kind of shame. He colored; she observed it and withheld something she was about to say. She turned away again, walked to the other end of the terrace, and stood there looking away into the garden. It seemed to him that she had guessed he understood her, and slowly—slowly—half as the fruit of his vague self-reproach,—he did understand her. She was giving him a chance to do gallantly what it seemed unworthy of both of them he should do meanly.

She liked him, she must have liked him greatly, to wish so to spare him, to go to the trouble of conceiving an ideal of conduct for him. With this sense of her friendship,—her strong friendship she had just called it,—Longmore's soul rose with a new flight, and suddenly felt itself breathing a clearer air. The words ceased to seem a mere bribe to his ardor; they were charged with ardor themselves; they were a present happiness. He moved rapidly toward her with a feeling that this was something he might immediately enjoy.

They were separated by two thirds of the length of the terrace, and he had to pass the drawing-room window. As he did so he started with an exclamation. Madame Clairin stood posted there, watching him. Conscious, apparently, that she might be suspected of eavesdropping, she stepped forward with a smile and looked from Longmore to his hostess.

"Such a tête-à-tête as that," she said, "one owes no apology for interrupting. One ought to come in for good manners."

Madame de Mauves turned round, but she answered nothing. She looked straight at Longmore, and her eyes had extraordinary eloquence. He was not exactly sure, indeed, what she meant them to say; but they seemed to say plainly something of this kind: "Call it what you will, what you have to urge upon me is the thing which this woman can best conceive. What I ask of you is something she can't!" They seemed, somehow, to beg him to suffer her to be herself, and to intimate that that self was as little as possible like Madame Clairin. He felt an immense answering desire not to do anything which would seem natural to this lady. He had laid his hat and cane on the parapet of the terrace. He took them up, offered his hand to Madame de Mauves with a simple good night, bowed silently to Madame Clairin, and departed.

9

He went home and without lighting his candle flung himself on his bed. But he got no sleep till morning; he lay hour after hour tossing, thinking, wondering; his mind had never been so active. It seemed to him that Euphemia had laid on him in those last moments an inspiring commission, and that she had expressed herself almost as largely as if she had listened assentingly to an assurance of his love.

It was neither easy nor delightful thoroughly to understand her; but little by little her perfect meaning sank into his mind and soothed it with a sense of opportunity, which somehow stifled his sense of loss. For, to begin with, she meant that she could love him in no degree nor contingency, in no imaginable future. This was absolute; he felt that he could alter it no more than he could transpose the constellations he lay gazing at through his open window. He wondered what it was, in the background of her life, that she grasped so closely: a sense of duty, unquenchable to the end? a love that no offence could trample out? "Good heavens!" he thought, "is the world so rich in the purest pearls of passion, that such tenderness as that can be wasted forever,—poured away without a sigh into bottomless darkness?" Had she, in spite of the detestable present, some precious memory which contained the germ of a shrinking hope? Was she prepared to submit to everything and yet to believe? Was it strength, was it weakness, was it a vulgar fear, was it conviction, conscience, constancy?

Longmore sank back with a sigh and an oppressive feeling that it was vain to guess at such a woman's motives. He only felt that those of Madame de Mauves were buried deep in her soul, and that they must be of some fine temper, not of a base one. He had a dim, overwhelming sense of a sort of invulnerable constancy being the supreme law of her character,—a constancy which still found a foothold among crumbling ruins. "She has loved once," he said to himself as he rose and wandered to his window; "that's forever. Yes, yes,—if she loved again she would be *common.*" He stood for a long time looking out into the starlit silence of the town and the forest, and thinking of what life would have been if *his* constancy had met hers unpledged. But life was this, now, and he must live. It was living keenly to stand there with a petition from such a woman to revolve. He was not to disappoint her, he was to justify a conception which it had beguiled her weariness to shape. Longmore's imagination swelled; he threw back his head and seemed to be looking for Madame de Mauves's conception among the blinking, mocking stars. But it came to him rather on the mild night-wind, as it wandered in over the house-tops which covered the rest of so many heavy human hearts. What she asked he felt that she was asking, not for her own sake (she feared nothing, she needed nothing), but for that of his own happiness and his own character. He must assent to destiny. Why else was he young and strong, intelligent and resolute? He must not give it to her to reproach him with thinking that she had a moment's attention for his love,—to plead, to argue, to break off in bitterness; he must see everything from above, her indifference and his own ardor; he must prove his strength, he must do the handsome thing; he must decide that the handsome thing was to submit to the inevitable, to be supremely delicate, to spare her all pain, to stifle his passion, to ask no compensation, to depart without delay and try to believe that wisdom is its own reward. All this, neither more nor less, it was a matter of friendship with Madame de Mauves to expect of him. And what should he gain by it? He should have pleased her! . . . He flung himself on his bed again, fell asleep at last, and slept till morning.

Before noon the next day he had made up his mind that he would leave Saint-Germain at once. It seemed easier to leave without seeing her, and yet if he might ask a grain of "compensation," it would be five minutes face to face with her. He passed a restless day. Wherever he went he seemed to see her standing before him in the dusky halo of evening, and looking at him with an air of still negation more intoxicating than the most passionate self-surrender. He must certainly go, and yet it was hideously hard. He compromised and went to Paris to spend the rest of the day. He strolled along the boulevards and looked at the shops, sat awhile in the Tuileries gardens and looked at the shabby unfortunates for whom this only was nature and summer; but simply felt, as a result of it all, that it was a very dusty, dreary, lonely world into which Madame de Mauves was turning him away.

In a sombre mood he made his way back to the boulevards and sat down at a table on the great plain of hot asphalt, before a café. Night came on, the lamps were lighted, the tables near him found occupants, and Paris began to wear that peculiar evening look of hers which seems to say, in the flare of windows and theatre doors, and the muffled rumble of swift-rolling carriages, that this is no world for you unless you have your pockets lined and your scruples drugged. Longmore, however, had neither scruples nor desires; he looked at the swarming city for the first time with an easy sense of repaying its indifference. Before long a carriage drove up to the pavement directly in front of him, and remained standing for several minutes without its occupant getting out. It was one of those neat, plain coupés, drawn by a single powerful horse, in which one is apt to imagine a pale, handsome woman, buried among silk cushions, and yawning as she sees the gas-lamps glittering in the gutters. At last the door opened and out stepped M. de Mauves. He stopped and leaned on the window for some time, talking in an excited manner to a person within. At last he gave a nod and the carriage rolled away. He stood swinging his cane and looking up and down the boulevard, with the air of a man fumbling, as one may say, with the loose change of time. He turned toward the café and was apparently, for want of anything better worth his attention, about to seat himself at one of the tables, when he perceived Longmore. He wavered an instant, and then, without a change in his nonchalant gait, strolled toward him with a bow and a vague smile.

It was the first time they had met since their encounter in the forest after Longmore's false start for Brussels. Madame Clairin's revelations, as we may call them, had not made the Baron especially present to his mind; he had another office for his emotions than disgust. But as M. de

Mauves came toward him he felt deep in his heart that he abhorred him. He noticed, however, for the first time, a shadow upon the Baron's cool placidity, and his delight at finding that somewhere at last the shoe pinched *him,* mingled with his impulse to be as exasperatingly impenetrable as possible, enabled him to return the other's greeting with all his own self-possession.

M. de Mauves sat down, and the two men looked at each other across the table, exchanging formal greetings which did little to make their mutual scrutiny seem gracious. Longmore had no reason to suppose that the Baron knew of his sister's revelations. He was sure that M. de Mauves cared very little about his opinions, and yet he had a sense that there was that in his eyes which would have made the Baron change color if keener suspicion had helped him to read it. M. de Mauves did not change color, but he looked at Longmore with a half-defiant intentness, which betrayed at once an irritating memory of the episode in the Bois de Boulogne, and such vigilant curiosity as was natural to a gentleman who had intrusted his "honor" to another gentleman's magnanimity,—or to his artlessness. It would appear that Longmore seemed to the Baron to possess these virtues in rather scantier measure than a few days before; for the cloud deepened on his face, and he turned away and frowned as he lighted a cigar.

The person in the coupé, Longmore thought, whether or not the same person as the heroine of the episode of the Bois de Boulogne, was not a source of unalloyed delight. Longmore had dark blue eyes, of admirable lucidity,—truth-telling eyes which had in his childhood always made his harshest taskmasters smile at his nursery fibs. An observer watching the two men, and knowing something of their relations, would certainly have said that what he saw in those eyes must not a little have puzzled and tormented M. de Mauves. They judged him, they mocked him, they eluded him, they threatened him, they triumphed over him, they treated him as no pair of eyes had ever treated him. The Baron's scheme had been to make no one happy but himself, and here was Longmore already, if looks were to be trusted, primed for an enterprise more inspiring than the finest of his own achievements. Was this candid young barbarian but a *faux bonhomme* after all? He had puzzled the Baron before, and this was once too often.

M. de Mauves hated to seem preoccupied, and he took up the evening paper to help himself to look indifferent. As he glanced over it he uttered some cold commonplace on the political situation, which gave Longmore an easy opportunity of replying by an ironical sally which made him seem for the moment aggressively at his ease. And yet our hero was far from being master of the situation. The Baron's ill-humor did him good, so far as it pointed to a want of harmony with the lady in the coupé; but it disturbed him sorely as he began to suspect that it possibly meant jealousy of himself. It passed through his mind that jealousy is a passion with a double face, and that in some of its moods it bears a plausible likeness to affection. It recurred to him painfully that the Baron might grow ashamed of his political compact with his wife, and he felt that it would be far more tolerable in the future to think of his continued turpitude than of his repentance. The two men sat for half an hour exchanging stinted small-talk, the Baron feeling a nervous need of playing the spy, and Longmore indulging a ferocious relish of his discomfort. These rigid courtesies were interrupted however by the arrival of a friend of M. de Mauves;—a tall, pale, consumptive-looking dandy, who filled the air with the odor of heliotrope. He looked up and down the boulevard wearily, examined the Baron's toilet from head to foot, then surveyed his own in the same fashion, and at last announced languidly that the Duchess was in town! M. de Mauves must come with him to call; she had abused him dreadfully a couple of evenings before,—a sure sign she wanted to see him.

"I depend upon you," said M. de Mauves's friend with an infantine drawl, "to put her *entrain*."

M. de Mauves resisted, and protested that he was *d'une humeur massacrante;* but at last he allowed himself to be drawn to his feet, and stood looking awkwardly—awkwardly for M. de Mauves—at Longmore. "You'll excuse me," he said dryly; "you, too, probably, have occupation for the evening?"

"None but to catch my train," Longmore answered, looking at his watch.

"Ah, you go back to Saint-Germain?"

"In half an hour."

M. de Mauves seemed on the point of disengaging himself from his companion's arm, which was locked in his own; but on the latter uttering some persuasive murmur, he lifted his hat stiffly and turned away.

Longmore packed his trunk the next day with dogged heroism and wandered off to the terrace, to try and beguile the restlessness with which he waited for evening; for he wished to see Madame de Mauves for the last time at the hour of long shadows and pale pink-reflected lights, as he had almost always seen her. Destiny, however, took no account of this humble plea for poetic justice; it was his fortune to meet her on the terrace sitting under a tree, alone. It was an hour when the place was almost empty; the day was warm, but as he took his place beside her a light breeze stirred the leafy edges on the broad circle of shadow in which she sat. She looked at him with candid anxiety, and he immediately told her that he should leave Saint-Germain that evening,—that he must bid her farewell. Her eye expanded and brightened for a moment as he spoke; but she said nothing and turned her glance away toward distant Paris, as it lay twinkling and flashing through its hot exhalations. "I have a request to make of you!" he added. "That you think of me as a man who has felt much and claimed little."

She drew a long breath, which almost suggested pain. "I can't think of you as unhappy. It's impossible. You have a life to lead, you have duties, talents, and interests. I shall hear of your career. And then," she continued after a pause and with the deepest seriousness, "one can't be unhappy through having a better opinion of a friend, instead of a worse."

For a moment he failed to understand her. "Do you mean that there can be varying degrees in my opinion of you?"

She rose and pushed away her chair. "I mean," she said quickly, "that it's better to have done nothing in bitterness,—nothing in passion." And she began to walk.

Longmore followed her, without answering. But he took off his hat and with his pocket-handkerchief wiped his forehead. "Where shall you go? what shall you do?" he asked at last, abruptly.

"Do? I shall do as I've always done,—except perhaps that I shall go for a while to Auvergne."

"I shall go to America. I have done with Europe for the present."

She glanced at him as he walked beside her after he had spoken these words, and then bent her eyes for a long time on the ground. At last, seeing that she was going far, she stopped and put out her hand. "Good by," she said; "may you have all the happiness you deserve!"

He took her hand and looked at her, but something was passing in him that made it impossible to return her hand's light pressure. Something of infinite value was floating past him, and he had taken an oath not to raise a finger to stop it. It was borne by the strong current of the world's great life and not of his own small one. Madame de Mauves disengaged her hand, gathered her shawl, and smiled at him almost as you would do at a child you should wish to encourage. Several moments later he was still standing watching her receding figure. When it had disappeared, he shook himself, walked rapidly back to his hotel, and without waiting for the evening train paid his bill and departed.

Later in the day M. de Mauves came into his wife's drawing-room, where she sat waiting to be summoned to dinner. He was dressed with a scrupulous freshness which seemed to indicate an intention of dining out. He walked up and down for some moments in silence, then rang the bell for a servant, and went out into the hall to meet him. He ordered the carriage to take him to the station, paused a moment with his hand on the knob of the door, dismissed the servant angrily as the latter lingered observing him, re-entered the drawing-room, resumed his restless walk, and at last stepped abruptly before his wife, who had taken up a book. "May I ask the favor," he said with evident effort, in spite of a forced smile of easy courtesy, "of having a question answered?"

"It's a favor I never refused," Madame de Mauves replied.

"Very true. Do you expect this evening a visit from Mr. Longmore?"

"Mr. Longmore," said his wife, "has left Saint-Germain." M. de Mauves started and his smile expired. "Mr. Longmore," his wife continued, "has gone to America."

M. de Mauves stared a moment, flushed deeply, and turned away. Then recovering himself,—"Had anything happened?" he asked. "Had he a sudden call?"

But his question received no answer. At the same moment the servant threw open the door and announced dinner; Madame Clairin rustled in, rubbing her white hands, Madame de Mauves passed silently into the dining-room, and he stood frowning and wondering. Before long he went out upon the terrace and continued his uneasy walk. At the end of a quarter of an hour the servant came to inform him that the carriage was at the door. "Send it away," he said curtly. "I shall not use it." When the ladies had half finished dinner he went in and joined them, with a formal apology to his wife for his tardiness.

The dishes were brought back, but he hardly tasted them; on the other hand, he drank a great deal of wine. There was little talk; what there was, was supplied by Madame Clairin. Twice she saw her brother's eyes fixed on her own, over his wineglass, with a piercing, questioning glance. She replied by an elevation of the eyebrows, which did the office of a shrug of the shoulders. M. de Mauves was left alone to finish his wine; he sat over it for more than an hour, and let the darkness gather about him. At last the servant came in with a letter and lighted a candle. The letter was a telegram, which M. de Mauves, when he had read it, burnt at the candle. After five minutes' meditation, he wrote a message on the back of a visiting-card and gave it to the servant to carry to the office. The man knew quite as much as his master suspected about the lady to whom the telegram was addressed; but its contents puzzled him; they consisted of the single word, "*Impossible.*" As the evening passed without her brother reappearing in the drawing-room, Madame Clairin came to him where he sat, by his solitary candle. He took no notice of her presence for some time; but he was the one person to whom she allowed this license. At last, speaking in a peremptory tone, "The American has gone home at an hour's notice," he said. "What does it mean?"

Madame Clairin now gave free play to the shrug she had been obliged to suppress at the table. "It means that I have a sister-in-law whom I haven't the honor to understand."

He said nothing more, and silently allowed her to depart, as if it had been her duty to provide him with an explanation and he was disgusted with her levity. When she had gone, he went into the garden and walked up and down, smoking. He saw his wife sitting alone on the terrace, but remained below strolling along the narrow paths. He remained a long time. It became late and Madame de Mauves disappeared. Toward midnight he dropped upon a bench, tired, with a kind of angry sigh. It was sinking into his mind that he, too, did not understand Madame Clairin's sister-in-law.

Longmore was obliged to wait a week in London for a ship. It was very hot, and he went out for a day to Richmond. In the garden of the hotel at which he dined he met his friend Mrs. Draper, who was staying there. She made eager inquiry about Madame de Mauves, but Longmore at first, as they sat looking out at the famous view of the Thames, parried her questions and confined himself to small-talk. At last she said she was afraid he had something to conceal; whereupon, after a pause, he asked her if she remembered recommending him, in the letter she sent to him at Saint-Germain, to draw the sadness from her friend's smile. "The last I saw of her was her smile," said he,—"when I bade her good by."

"I remember urging you to 'console' her," Mrs. Draper answered, "and I wondered afterwards whether—a model of discretion as you are—I hadn't given you rather foolish advice."

"She has her consolation in herself," he said; "she needs none that any one else can offer her. That's for troubles for which—be it more, be it less—our own folly has to answer. Madame de Mauves has not a grain of folly left."

"Ah, don't say that!" murmured Mrs. Draper. "Just a little folly is very graceful."

Longmore rose to go, with a quick nervous movement. "Don't talk of grace," he said, "till you have measured her reason."

For two years after his return to America he heard nothing of Madame de Mauves. That he thought of her intently, constantly, I need hardly say: most people wondered why such a clever young man should not "devote" himself to something; but to himself he seemed absorbingly occupied. He never wrote to her; he believed that she preferred it. At last he heard that Mrs. Draper had come home, and he immediately called on her. "Of course," she said after the first greetings, "you are dying for news of Madame de Mauves. Prepare yourself for something strange. I heard from her two or three times during the year after your return. She left Saint-Germain and went to live in the country, on some old property of her husband's. She wrote me very kind little notes, but I felt somehow that—in spite of what you said about 'consolation'—they were the notes of a very sad woman. The only advice I could have given her was to leave her wretch of a husband and come back to her own land and her own people. But this I didn't feel free to do, and yet it made me so miserable not to be able to help her that I preferred to let our correspondence die a natural death. I had no news of her for a year. Last summer, however, I met at Vichy a clever young Frenchman whom I accidentally learned to be a friend of Euphemia's lovely sister-in-law, Madame Clairin. I lost no time in asking him what he knew about Madame de Mauves,—a countrywoman of mine and an old friend. 'I congratulate you on possessing her friendship,' he answered. 'That's the charming little woman who killed her husband.' You may imagine that I promptly asked for an explanation, and he proceeded to relate to me what he called the whole story. M. de Mauves had *fait quelques folies*, which his wife had taken absurdly to heart. He had repented and asked her forgiveness, which she had inexorably refused. She was very pretty, and severity, apparently, suited her style; for whether or no her husband had been in love with her before, he fell madly in love with her now. He was the proudest man in France, but he had begged her on his knees to be readmitted to favor. All in vain! She was stone, she was ice, she was outraged virtue. People noticed a great change in him: he gave up society, ceased to care for anything, looked shockingly. One fine day they learned that he had blown out his brains. My friend had the story of course from Madame Clairin."

Longmore was strongly moved, and his first impulse after he had recovered his composure was to return immediately to Europe. But several years have passed, and he still lingers at home. The truth is, that in the midst of all the ardent tenderness of his memory of Madame de Mauves, he has become conscious of a singular feeling,—a feeling for which awe would be hardly too strong a name.

THOMAS MANN

Tonio Kröger

The winter sun, poor ghost of itself, hung milky and wan behind layers of cloud above the huddled roofs of the town. In the gabled streets it was wet and windy and there came in gusts a sort of soft hail, not ice, not snow.

School was out. The hosts of the released streamed over the paved court and out at the wrought-iron gate, where they broke up and hastened off right and left. Elder pupils held their books in a strap high on the left shoulder and rowed, right arm against the wind, towards dinner. Small people trotted gaily off, splashing the slush with their feet, the tools of learning rattling amain in their walrus-skin satchels. But one and all pulled off their caps and cast down their eyes in awe before the Olympian hat and ambrosial beard of a master moving homewards with measured stride. . . .

"Ah, there you are at last, Hans," said Tonio Kröger. He had been waiting a long time in the street and went up with a smile to the friend he saw coming out of the gate in talk with other boys and about to go off with them. . . . "What?" said Hans, and looked at Tonio. "Right-oh! We'll take a little walk, then."

Tonio said nothing and his eyes were clouded. Did Hans forget, had he only just remembered that they were to take a walk together today? And he himself had looked forward to it with almost incessant joy.

"Well, good-bye, fellows," said Hans Hansen to his comrades. "I'm taking a walk with Kröger." And the two turned to their left, while the others sauntered off in the opposite direction.

Hans and Tonio had time to take a walk after school because in neither of their families was dinner served before four o'clock. Their fathers were prominent business men, who held public office and were of consequence in the town. Hans's people had owned for some generations the big wood-yards down by the river, where powerful machine-saws hissed and spat and cut up timber; while Tonio was the son of Consul Kröger, whose grain-sacks with the firm name in great black letters you might see any day driven through the streets; his large, old ancestral home was the finest house in all the town. The two friends had to keep taking off their hats to their many acquaintances; some folk did not even wait for the fourteen-year-old lads to speak first, as by rights they should.

Both of them carried their satchels across their shoulders and both were well and warmly dressed: Hans in a short sailor jacket, with the wide blue collar of his sailor suit turned out over shoulders and back, and Tonio in a belted grey overcoat. Hans wore a Danish sailor cap with black ribbons, beneath which streamed a shock of straw-coloured hair. He was uncommonly handsome and well built, broad in the shoulders and narrow in the hips, with keen, far-apart, steel-blue eyes; while beneath Tonio's round fur cap was a brunette face with the finely chiselled features of the south; the dark eyes, with delicate shadows and too heavy lids, looked dreamily and a little timorously on the world. Tonio's walk was idle and uneven, whereas the other's slim legs in their black stockings moved with an elastic, rhythmic tread.

Tonio did not speak. He suffered. His rather oblique brows were drawn together in a frown, his lips were rounded to whistle, he gazed into space with his head on one side. Posture and manner were habitual.

Suddenly Hans shoved his arm into Tonio's, with a sideways look—he knew very well what the trouble was. And Tonio, though he was silent for the next few steps, felt his heart soften.

"I hadn't forgotten, you see, Tonio," Hans said, gazing at the pavement, "I only thought it wouldn't come off today because it was so wet and windy. But I don't mind that at all, and it's jolly of you to have waited. I thought you had gone home, and I was cross. . . ."

Everything in Tonio leaped and jumped for joy at the words.

"All right; let's go over the wall," he said with a quaver in his voice. "Over the Millwall and the Holstenwall, and I'll go as far as your house with you, Hans. Then I'll have to walk back alone, but that doesn't matter; next time you can go round my way."

At bottom he was not really convinced by what Hans said; he quite knew the other attached less importance to this walk than he did himself. Yet he saw Hans was sorry for his remissness and willing to be put in a position to ask pardon, a pardon that Tonio was far indeed from withholding.

The truth was, Tonio loved Hans Hansen, and had already suffered much on his account. He who loves the more is the inferior and must suffer; in this hard and simple fact his fourteen-year-old soul had already been instructed by life; and he was so organized that he received such experiences consciously, wrote them down as it were inwardly, and even, in a certain way, took pleasure in them, though without ever letting them mould his conduct, indeed, or drawing any practical advantage from them. Being what he was, he found this knowledge far more important and far more interesting than the sort they made him learn in school; yes, during his lesson hours in the vaulted Gothic classrooms he was mainly occupied in feeling his way about among these intuitions of his and penetrating them. The process gave him the same kind of satisfaction as that he felt when he moved about in his room with his violin—for he played the violin—and made the tones, brought out as softly as ever he knew how, mingle with the plashing of the fountain that leaped and danced down there in the garden beneath the branches of the old walnut tree.

The fountain, the old walnut tree, his fiddle, and away in the distance the North Sea, within sound of whose summer murmurings he spent his holidays—these were the things he loved, within these he enfolded his spirit, among these things his inner life took its course. And they were all things whose names were effective in verse and occurred pretty frequently in the lines Tonio Kröger sometimes wrote.

The fact that he had a note-book full of such things, written by himself, leaked out through his own carelessness and injured him no little with the masters as well as among his fellows. On the one hand, Consul Kröger's son found their attitude both cheap and silly, and despised his schoolmates and his masters as well, and in his turn (with extraordinary penetration) saw through and disliked their personal weaknesses and bad breeding. But then, on the other hand, he himself felt his verse-making extravagant and out of place and to a certain extent agreed with those who considered it an unpleasing occupation. But that did not enable him to leave off.

As he wasted his time at home, was slow and absent-minded at school, and always had bad marks from the masters, he was in the habit of bringing home pitifully poor reports, which troubled and angered his father, a tall, fastidiously dressed man, with thoughtful blue eyes, and always a wild flower in his buttonhole. But for his mother, she cared nothing about the reports—Tonio's beautiful black-haired mother, whose name was Consuelo, and who was so absolutely different from the other ladies in the town, because father had brought her long ago from some place far down on the map.

Tonio loved his dark, fiery mother, who played the piano and mandolin so wonderfully, and he was glad his doubtful standing among men did not distress her. Though at the same time he found his father's annoyance a more dignified and respectable attitude and despite his scoldings understood him very well, whereas his mother's blithe indifference always seemed just a little wanton. His thoughts at times would run something like this: "It is true enough that I am what I am and will not and cannot alter: heedless, self-willed, with my mind on things nobody else thinks of. And so it is right they should scold and punish me and not smother things all up with kisses and music. After all, we are not gypsies living in a green wagon; we're respectable people, the family of Consul Kröger." And not seldom he would think: "Why is it I am different, why do I fight everything, why am I at odds with the masters and like a stranger among the other boys? The good scholars, and the solid majority—they don't find the masters funny, they don't write verses, their thoughts are all about things that people do think about and can talk about out loud. How regular and comfortable they must feel, knowing that everybody knows just where they stand! It must be nice! But what is the matter with me, and what will be the end of it all?

These thoughts about himself and his relation to life played an important part in Tonio's love for Hans Hansen. He loved him in the first place because he was handsome; but in the next because he was in every respect his own opposite and foil. Hans Hansen was a capital scholar, and a jolly chap to boot, who was head at drill, rode and swam to perfection, and lived in the sunshine of popularity. The masters were almost tender with him, they called him Hans and were partial to him in every way; the other pupils curried favour with him; even grown people stopped him on the street, twitched the shock of hair beneath his Danish sailor cap, and said: "Ah, here you are, Hans Hansen, with your pretty blond hair! Still head of the school? Remember me to your father and mother, that's a fine lad!"

Such was Hans Hansen; and ever since Tonio Kröger had known him, from the very minute he set eyes on him, he had burned inwardly with a heavy, envious longing. "Who else has blue eyes like yours, or lives in such friendliness and harmony with all the world? You are always spending your time with some right and proper occupation. When you have done your prep you take your riding-lesson, or make things with a fret-saw; even in the holidays, at the seashore, you row and sail and swim all the time, while I wander off somewhere and lie down in the sand and stare at the strange and mysterious changes that whisk over the face of the sea. And all that is why your eyes are so clear. To be like you . . ."

He made no attempt to be like Hans Hansen, and perhaps hardly even seriously wanted to. What he did ardently, painfully want was that just as he was, Hans Hansen should love him; and he wooed Hans Hansen in his own way, deeply, lingeringly, devotedly, with a melancholy that gnawed and burned more terribly than all the sudden passion one might have expected from his exotic looks.

And he wooed not in vain. Hans respected Tonio's superior power of putting certain difficult matters into words; moreover, he felt the lively presence of an uncommonly strong and tender feeling for himself; he was grateful for it, and his response gave Tonio much happiness—though also many pangs of jealousy and disillusion over his futile efforts to establish a communion of spirit between them. For the queer thing was that Tonio, who after all envied Hans Hansen for being what he was, still kept on trying to draw him over to his own side; though of course he could succeed in this at most only at moments and superficially. . . .

"I have just been reading something so wonderful and splendid . . ." he said. They were walking and eating together out of a bag of fruit toffees they had bought at Iverson's sweet-shop in Mill Street for ten pfennigs. "You must read it, Hans, it is Schiller's *Don Carlos* . . . I'll lend it you if you like. . . ."

"Oh, no," said Hans Hansen, "you needn't, Tonio, that's not anything for me. I'll stick to my horse books. There are wonderful cuts in them, let me tell you. I'll show them to you when you come to see me. They are instantaneous photography—the horse in motion; you can see him trot and canter and jump, in all positions, that you never can get to see in life, because they happen so fast. . . ."

"In all positions?" asked Tonio politely. "Yes, that must be great. But about *Don Carlos*—it is beyond anything you could possibly dream of. There are places in it that are so lovely they make you jump . . . as though it were an explosion—"

"An explosion?" asked Hans Hansen. "What sort of an explosion?"

"For instance, the place where the king has been crying because the marquis betrayed him . . . but the marquis did it only out of love for the prince, you see, he sacrifices himself for his sake. And the word comes out of the cabinet into the antechamber that the king has been weeping. 'Weeping? The king been weeping?' All the courtiers are fearfully upset, it goes through and through you, for the king has always been so frightfully stiff and stern. But it is so easy to understand why he cried, and I feel sorrier for him than for the prince and the marquis put together. He is always so alone, nobody loves him, and then he thinks he has found one man, and then *he* betrays him. . . ."

Hans Hansen looked sideways into Tonio's face, and something in it must have won him to the subject, for suddenly he shoved his arm once more into Tonio's and said:

"How had he betrayed him, Tonio?"

Tonio went on.

"Well," he said, "you see all the letters for Brabant and Flanders—"

"There comes Irwin Immerthal," said Hans.

Tonio stopped talking. If only the earth would open and swallow Immerthal up! "Why does he have to come disturbing us? If he only doesn't go with us all the way and talk about the riding-lessons!" For Irwin Immerthal had riding-lessons too. He was the son of the bank president and lived close by, outside the city wall. He had already been home and left his bag, and now he walked towards them through the avenue. His legs were crooked and his eyes like slits.

"'lo, Immerthal," said Hans. "I'm taking a little walk with Kröger. . . ."

"I have to go into town on an errand," said Immerthal. "But I'll walk a little way with you. Are those fruit toffees you've got? Thanks, I'll have a couple. Tomorrow we have our next lesson, Hans." He meant the riding-lesson.

"What larks!" said Hans. "I'm going to get the leather gaiters for a present, because I was top lately in our papers."

"You don't take riding-lessons, I suppose, Kröger?" asked Immerthal, and his eyes were only two gleaming cracks.

"No . . ." answered Tonio, uncertainly.

"You ought to ask your father," Hans Hansen remarked, "so you could have lessons too, Kröger."

"Yes . . ." said Tonio. He spoke hastily and without interest; his throat had suddenly contracted, because Hans had called him by his last name. Hans seemed conscious of it too, for he said by way of explanation: "I call you Kröger because your first name is so crazy. Don't mind my saying so, I can't do with it all. Tonio—why, what sort of name is that? Though of course I know it's not your fault in the least."

"No, they probably called you that because it sounds so foreign and sort of something special," said Immerthal, obviously with intent to say just the right thing.

Tonio's mouth twitched. He pulled himself together and said:

"Yes, it's a silly name—Lord knows I'd rather be called Heinrich or Wilhelm. It's all because I'm named after my mother's brother Antonio. She comes from down there, you know. . . ."

There he stopped and let the others have their say about horses and saddles. Hans had taken Immerthal's arm; he talked with a fluency that *Don Carlos* could never have roused in him. . . . Tonio felt a mounting desire to weep pricking his nose from time to time; he had hard work to control the trembling of his lips.

Hans could not stand his name—what was to be done? He himself was called Hans, and Immerthal was called Irwin; two good, sound, familiar names, offensive to nobody. And Tonio was foreign and queer. Yes, there was always something queer about him, whether he would or no, and he was alone, the regular and usual would none of him; although after all he was no gypsy in a green wagon, but the son of Consul Kröger, a member of the Kröger family. But why did Hans call him Tonio as long as they were alone and then feel ashamed as soon as anybody else was by? Just now he had won him over, they had been close together, he was sure. "How had he betrayed him, Tonio?" Hans asked, and took his arm. But he had breathed easier directly Immerthal came up, he had dropped him like a shot, even gratuitously taunted him with his outlandish name. How it hurt to have to see through all this! . . . Hans Hansen did like him a little, when they were alone, that he knew. But let a third person come, he was ashamed, and offered up his friend. And again he was alone. He thought of King Philip. The king had wept. . . .

"Goodness, I have to go," said Irwin Immerthal. "Good-bye, and thanks for the toffee." He jumped upon a bench that stood by the way, ran along it with his crooked legs, jumped down, and trotted off.

"I like Immerthal," said Hans, with emphasis. He had a spoilt and arbitrary way of announcing his likes and dislikes, as though graciously pleased to confer them like an order on this person and that. . . . He went on talking about the riding-lessons where he had left off. Anyhow, it was not very much farther to his house; the walk over the walls was not a long one. They held their caps and bent their heads before the strong, damp wind that rattled and groaned in the leafless trees. And Hans Hansen went on talking, Tonio throwing in a forced yes or no from time to time. Hans talked eagerly, had taken his arm again; but the contact gave Tonio no pleasure. The nearness was only apparent, not real; it meant nothing. . . .

They struck away from the walls close to the station, where they saw a train puff busily past, idly counted the coaches, and waved to the man who was perched on top of the last one bundled in a leather coat. They stopped in front of the Hansen villa on the Lindenplatz, and Hans went into detail about what fun it was to stand on the bottom rail of the garden gate and let it swing on its creaking hinges. After that they said good-bye.

"I must go in now," said Hans. "Good-bye, Tonio. Next time I'll take you home, see if I don't."

"Good-bye, Hans," said Tonio. "It was a nice walk."

They put out their hands, all wet and rusty from the garden gate. But as Hans looked into Tonio's eyes, he bethought himself, a look of remorse came over his charming face.

"And I'll read *Don Carlos* pretty soon, too," he said quickly. "That bit about the king in his cabinet must be nuts." Then he took his bag under his arm and ran off through the front garden. Before he disappeared he turned and nodded once more.

And Tonio went off as though on wings. The wind was at his back; but it was not the wind alone that bore him along so lightly.

Hans would read *Don Carlos,* and then they would have something to talk about, and neither Irwin Immerthal nor another could join in. How well they understood each other! Perhaps—who knew?—some day he might even get Hans to write poetry! . . . No, no, that he did not ask. Hans must not become like Tonio, he must stop just as he was, so strong and bright, everybody loved him as he was, and Tonio most of all. But it would do him no harm to read *Don Carlos.* . . . Tonio passed under the squat old city gate, along by the harbour, and up the steep, wet, windy, gabled street to his parents' house. His heart beat richly: longing was awake in it, and a gentle envy; a faint contempt, and no little innocent bliss.

Ingeborg Holm, blonde little Inge, the daughter of Dr. Holm, who lived on Market Square opposite the tall old Gothic fountain with its manifold spires—she it was Tonio Kröger loved when he was sixteen years old.

Strange how things come about! He had seen her a thousand times; then one evening he saw her again; saw her in a certain light, talking with a friend in a certain saucy way, laughing and tossing her head; saw her lift her arm and smooth her back hair with her schoolgirl hand, that was by no means particularly fine or slender, in such a way that the thin white sleeve slipped down from her elbow; heard her speak a word or two, a quite indifferent phrase, but with a certain intonation, with a warm ring in her voice; and his heart throbbed with ecstasy, far stronger than that he had once felt when he looked at Hans Hansen long ago, when he was still a little, stupid boy.

That evening he carried away her picture in his eye: the thick blond plait, the longish, laughing blue eyes, the saddle of pale freckles across the nose. He could not go to sleep for hearing that ring in her voice; he tried in a whisper to imitate the tone in which she had uttered the commonplace phrase, and felt a shiver run through and through him. He knew by experience that this was love. And he was accurately aware that love would surely bring him much pain, affliction, and sadness, that it would certainly destroy his peace, filling his heart to overflowing with melodies which would be no good to him because he would never have the time or tranquillity to give them permanent form. Yet he received this love with joy, surrendered himself to it, and cherished it with all the strength of his being; for he knew that love made one vital and rich, and he longed to be vital and rich, far more than he did to work tranquilly on anything to give it permanent form.

Tonio Kröger fell in love with merry Ingeborg Holm in Frau Consul Hustede's drawing-room on the evening when it was emptied of furniture for the weekly dancing-class. It was a private class, attended only by members of the first families; it met by turns in the various parental houses to receive instruction from Knaak, the dancing-master, who came from Hamburg expressly for the purpose.

François Knaak was his name, and what a man he was! "*J'ai l'honneur de me vous représenter,*" he would say, "*mon nom est Knaak. . . .* This is not said during the bowing, but after you have finished and are standing up straight again. In a low voice, but distinctly. Of course one does not need to introduce oneself in French every day in the week, but if you can do it correctly and faultlessly in French you are not likely to make a mistake when you do it in German." How marvellously the silky black frock-coat fitted his chubby hips! His trouser-legs fell down in soft folds upon his patent-leather pumps with their wide satin bows, and his brown eyes glanced about him with languid pleasure in their own beauty.

All this excess of self-confidence and good form was positively overpowering. He went trippingly—and nobody tripped like him, so elastically, so weavingly, rockingly, royally—up to the mistress of the house, made a bow, waited for a hand to be put forth. This vouchsafed, he gave murmurous voice to his gratitude, stepped buoyantly back, turned on his left foot, swiftly drawing the right one backwards on its toe-tip, and moved away, with his hips shaking.

When you took leave of a company you must go backwards out at the door; when you fetched a chair, you were not to shove it along the floor or clutch it by one leg; but gently, by the back, and set it down without a sound. When you stood, you were not to fold your hands on your tummy or seek with your tongue the corners of your mouth. If you did, Herr Knaak had a way of showing you how it looked that filled you with disgust for that particular gesture all the rest of your life.

This was deportment. As for dancing, Herr Knaak was, if possible, even more of a master at that. The salon was emptied of furniture and lighted by a gas-chandelier in the middle of the ceiling and candles on the mantel-shelf. The floor was strewn with talc, and the pupils stood about in a dumb semicircle. But in the next room, behind the portières, mothers and aunts sat on plush-upholstered chairs and watched Herr Knaak through their lorgnettes, as in little springs and hops, curtsying slightly, the hem of his frock-coat held up on each side by two fingers, he demonstrated the single steps of the mazurka. When he wanted to dazzle his audience completely he would suddenly and unexpectedly spring from the ground, whirling his two legs about each other with bewildering swiftness in the air, as it were trilling with them, and then, with a subdued bump, which nevertheless shook everything within him to its depths, returned to earth.

"What an unmentionable monkey!" thought Tonio Kröger to himself. But he saw the absorbed smile on jolly little Inge's face as she followed Herr Knaak's movements; and that, though not that alone, roused in him something like admiration of all this wonderfully controlled corporeality. How tranquil, how imperturbable was Herr Knaak's gaze! His eyes did not plumb the depth of things to the place where life becomes complex and melancholy; they knew nothing save that they were beautiful brown eyes. But that was just why his bearing was so proud. To be able to walk like that, one must be stupid; then one was loved, then one was lovable. He could so well understand how it was that

Inge, blonde, sweet little Inge, looked at Herr Knaak as she did. But would never a girl look at him like that?

Oh, yes, there would, and did. For instance, Magdalena Vermehren, Attorney Vermehren's daughter, with the gentle mouth and the great, dark, brilliant eyes, so serious and adoring. She often fell down in the dance; but when it was "ladies' choice" she came up to him; she knew he wrote verses and twice she had asked him to show them to her. She often sat at a distance, with drooping head, and gazed at him. He did not care. It was Inge he loved, blonde, jolly Inge, who most assuredly despised him for his poetic effusions . . . he looked at her, looked at her narrow blue eyes full of fun and mockery, and felt an envious longing; to be shut away from her like this, to be forever strange—he felt it in his breast, like a heavy, burning weight.

"First couple *en avant,*" said Herr Knaak; and no words can tell how marvellously he pronounced the nasal. They were to practise the quadrille, and to Tonio Kröger's profound alarm he found himself in the same set with Inge Holm. He avoided her where he could, yet somehow was forever near her; kept his eyes away from her person and yet found his gaze ever on her. There she came, tripping up hand-in-hand with red-headed Ferdinand Matthiessen; she flung back her braid, drew a deep breath, and took her place opposite Tonio. Herr Heinzelmann, at the piano, laid bony hands upon the keys, Herr Knaak waved his arm, the quadrille began.

She moved to and fro before his eyes, forwards and back, pacing and swinging; he seemed to catch a fragrance from her hair or the folds of her thin white frock, and his eyes grew sadder and sadder. "I love you, dear, sweet Inge," he said to himself, and put into his words all the pain he felt to see her so intent upon the dance with not a thought of him. Some lines of an exquisite poem by Storm came into his mind: "I would sleep, but thou must dance." It seemed against all sense, and most depressing, that he must be dancing when he was in love. . . .

"First couple *en avant,*" said Herr Knaak; it was the next figure. "*Compliment! Moulinet des dames! Tour de main!*" and he swallowed the silent *e* in the "*de,*" with quite indescribable ease and grace.

"Second couple *en avant!*" This was Tonio Kröger and his partner. "*Compliment!*" And Tonio Kröger bowed. "*Moulinet des dames!*" And Tonio Kröger, with bent head and gloomy brows, laid his hand on those of the four ladies, on Ingeborg Holm's hand, and danced the *moulinet.*

Roundabout rose a tittering and laughing. Herr Knaak took a ballet pose conventionally expressive of horror. "Oh, dear! Oh, dear!" he cried. "Stop! Stop! Kröger among the ladies! *En arrière,* Fräulein Kröger, step back, *fi donc!* Everybody else understood it but you. Shoo! Get out! Get away!" He drew out his yellow silk handkerchief and flapped Tonio Kröger back to his place.

Everyone laughed, the girls and the boys and the ladies beyond the portières; Herr Knaak had made something too utterly funny out of the little episode, it was as amusing as a play. But Herr Heinzelmann at the piano sat and waited, with a dry, business-like air, for a sign to go on; he was hardened against Herr Knaak's effects.

Then the quadrille went on. And the intermission followed. The parlourmaid came clinking in with a tray of wine-jelly glasses, the cook followed in her wake with a load of plum-cake. But Tonio Kröger stole away. He stole out into the corridor and stood there, his hands behind his back, in front of a window with the blind down. He never thought that one could not see through the blind and that it was absurd to stand there as though one were looking out.

For he was looking within, into himself, the theatre of so much pain and longing. Why, why was he here? Why was he not sitting by the window in his own room, reading Storm's *Immensee* and lifting his eyes to the twilight garden outside, where the old walnut tree moaned? That was the place for him! Others might dance, others bend their fresh and lively minds upon the pleasure in hand! . . . But no, no, after all, his place was here, where he could feel near Inge, even although he stood lonely and aloof, seeking to distinguish the warm notes of her voice amid the buzzing, clattering, and laughter within. Oh, lovely Inge, blonde Inge of the narrow, laughing blue eyes! So lovely and laughing as you are one can only be if one does not read *Immensee* and never tries to write things like it. And that was just the tragedy!

Ah, she *must* come! She *must* notice where he had gone, must feel how he suffered! She must slip out to him, even pity must bring her, to lay her hand on his shoulder and say: "Do come back to us, ah, don't be sad—I love you, Tonio." He listened behind him and waited in frantic suspense. But not in the least. Such things did not happen on this earth.

Had she laughed at him too like all the others? Yes, she had, however gladly he would have denied it for both their sakes. And yet it was only because he had been so taken up with her that he had danced the *moulinet des dames*. Suppose he had—what did that matter? Had not a magazine accepted a poem of his a little while ago—even though the magazine had failed before his poem could be printed? The day was coming when he would be famous, when they would print everything he wrote; and *then* he would see if that made any impression on Inge Holm! No, it would make no impression at all; that was just it. Magdalena Vermehren, who was always falling down in the dances, yes, she would be impressed. But never Ingeborg Holm, never blue-eyed, laughing Inge. So what was the good of it?

Tonio Kröger's heart contracted painfully at the thought. To feel stirring within you the wonderful and melancholy play of strange forces and to be aware that those others you yearn for are blithely inaccessible to all that moves you—what a pain is this! And yet! He stood there aloof and alone, staring hopelessly at a drawn blind and making, in his distraction, as though he could look out. But yet he was happy. For he lived. His heart was full; hotly and sadly it beat for thee, Ingeborg Holm, and his soul embraced thy blonde, simple, pert, commonplace little personality in blissful self-abnegation.

Often after that he stood thus, with burning cheeks, in lonely corners, whither the sound of the music, the tinkling of glasses and fragrance of flowers came but faintly, and tried to distinguish the ringing tones of thy voice amid the distant happy din; stood suffering for thee—and still was happy! Often it angered him to think that he might talk with Magdalena Vermehren, who always fell down in the dance. She understood him, she laughed or was serious in the right places; while Inge the fair, let him sit never so near her, seemed remote and estranged, his speech not being her speech. And still—he was happy. For happiness, he told himself, is not in being loved—which is a satisfaction of the vanity and mingled with disgust. Happiness is in loving, and perhaps in snatching fugitive little approaches to the beloved object. And he took inward note of this thought, wrote it down in his mind; followed out all its implications and felt it to the depths of his soul.

"Faithfulness," thought Tonio Kröger. "Yes, I will be faithful, I will love thee, Ingeborg, as long as I live!" He said this in the honesty of his intentions. And yet a still small voice whispered misgivings in his ear: after all, he had forgotten Hans Hansen utterly, even though he saw him every day! And the hateful, the pitiable fact was that this still, small, rather spiteful voice was right: time passed and the day came when Tonio Kröger was no longer so unconditionally ready as once he had been to die for the lively Inge, because he felt in himself desires and powers to accomplish in his own way a host of wonderful things in this world.

And he circled with watchful eye the sacrificial altar, where flickered the pure, chaste flame of his love; knelt before it and tended and cherished it in every way, because he so wanted to be faithful. And in a little while, unobservably, without sensation or stir, it went out after all.

But Tonio Kröger still stood before the cold altar, full of regret and dismay at the fact that faithfulness was impossible upon this earth. Then he shrugged his shoulders and went his way.

He went the way that go he must, a little idly, a little irregularly, whistling to himself, gazing into space with his head on one side; and if he went wrong it was because for some people there is no such thing as a right way. Asked what in the world he meant to become, he gave various answers, for he was used to say (and had even already written it) that he bore within himself the possibility of a thousand ways of life, together with the private conviction that they were all sheer impossibilities.

Even before he left the narrow streets of his native city, the threads that bound him to it had gently loosened. The old Kröger family gradually declined, and some people quite rightly considered Tonio Kröger's own existence and way of life as one of the signs of decay. His father's mother, the head of the family, had died, and not long after his own father followed, the tall, thoughtful, carefully dressed gentleman with the field-flower in his buttonhole. The great Kröger house, with all its stately tradition, came up for sale, and the firm was dissolved. Tonio's mother, his beautiful, fiery mother, who played the piano and mandolin so wonderfully and to whom nothing mattered at all, she married again after a year's time; married a musician, moreover, a virtuoso with an Italian name, and went away with him into remote blue distances. Tonio Kröger found this a little irregular, but who was he to call her to order, who wrote poetry himself and could not even give an answer when asked what he meant to do in life?

And so he left his native town and its tortuous, gabled streets with the damp wind whistling through them; left the fountain in the garden and the ancient walnut tree, familiar friends of his youth; left the sea too, that he loved so much, and felt no pain to go. For he was grown up and sensible and had come to realize how things stood with him; he looked down on the lowly and vulgar life he had led so long in these surroundings.

He surrendered utterly to the power that to him seemed the highest on earth, to whose service he felt called, which promised him elevation and honours: the power of intellect, the power of the Word, that lords it with a smile over the unconscious and inarticulate. To this power he surrendered with all the passion of youth, and it rewarded him with all it had to give, taking from him inexorably, in return, all that it is wont to take.

It sharpened his eyes and made him see through the large words which puff out the bosoms of mankind; it opened for him men's souls and his own, made him clairvoyant, showed him the inwardness of the world and the ultimate behind men's words and deeds. And all that he saw could be put in two words: the comedy and the tragedy of life.

And then, with knowledge, its torment and its arrogance, came solitude; because he could not endure the blithe and innocent with their darkened understanding, while they in turn were troubled by the sign on his brow. But his love of the word kept growing sweeter and sweeter, and his love of form; for he used to say (and had already said it in writing) that knowledge of the soul would unfailingly make us melancholy if the pleasures of expression did not keep us alert and of good cheer.

He lived in large cities and in the south, promising himself a luxuriant ripening of his art by southern suns; perhaps it was the blood of his mother's race that drew him thither. But his heart being dead and loveless, he fell into adventures of the flesh, descended into the depths of lust and searing sin, and suffered unspeakably thereby. It might have been his father in him, that tall, thoughtful, fastidiously dressed man with the wild flower in his buttonhole, that made him suffer so down there in the south; now and again he would feel a faint, yearning memory of a certain joy that was of the soul; once it had been his own, but now, in all his joys, he could not find it again.

Then he would be seized with disgust and hatred of the senses; pant after purity and seemly peace, while still he breathed the air of art, the tepid, sweet air of permanent spring, heavy with fragrance where it breeds and brews and burgeons in the mysterious bliss of creation. So for all result he was flung to and fro forever between two crass extremes: between icy intellect and scorching sense, and what with his pangs of conscience led an exhausting life, rare, extraordinary, excessive, which at bottom he, Tonio Kröger, despised. "What a labyrinth!" he sometimes thought. "How could I possibly have got into all these fantastic adventures? As though I had a wagonful of travelling gypsies for my ancestors!"

But as his health suffered from these excesses, so his artistry was sharpened; it grew fastidious, precious, *raffiné,* morbidly sensitive in questions of tact and taste, rasped by the banal. His first appearance in print elicited much applause; there was joy among the elect, for it was a good and workmanlike performance, full of humour and acquaintance with pain. In no long time his name—the same by which his masters had reproached him, the same he had signed to his earliest verses on the walnut tree and the fountain and the sea, those syllables compact of the north and the south, that good middle-class name with the exotic twist to it—became a synonym for excellence; for the painful thoroughness of the experiences he had gone through, combined with a tenacious ambition and a persistent industry, joined battle with the irritable fastidiousness of his taste and under grinding torments issued in work of a quality quite uncommon.

He worked, not like a man who works that he may live, but as one who is bent on doing nothing but work; having no regard for himself as a human being but only as a creator; moving about grey and unobtrusive among his fellows like an actor without his make-up, who counts for nothing as soon as he stops representing something else. He worked withdrawn out of sight and sound of the small fry, for whom he felt nothing but contempt, because to them a talent was a social asset like another; who, whether they were poor or not, went about ostentatiously shabby or else flaunted startling cravats, all the time taking jolly good care to amuse themselves, to be artistic and charming without the smallest notion of the fact that good work only comes out under pressure of a bad life; that he who lives does not work; that one must die to life in order to be utterly a creator.

"Shall I disturb you?" asked Tonio Kröger on the threshold of the atelier. He held his hat in his hand and bowed with some ceremony, although Lisabeta Ivanovna was a good friend of his, to whom he told all his troubles.

"Mercy on you, Tonio Kröger! Don't be so formal," answered she, with her lilting intonation. "Everybody knows you were taught good manners in your nursery." She transferred her brush to her left hand, that held the palette, reached him her right, and looked him in the face, smiling and shaking her head.

"Yes, but you are working," he said. "Let's see. Oh, you've been getting on," and he looked at the colour-sketches leaning against chairs at both sides of the easel and from them to the large canvas covered with a square linen mesh, where the first patches of colour were beginning to appear among the confused and schematic lines of the charcoal sketch.

This was in Munich, in a back building in Schellingstrasse, several storeys up. Beyond the wide window facing the north were blue sky, sunshine, birds twittering; the young sweet breath of spring streaming through an open pane mingled with the smells of paint and fixative. The afternoon light, bright golden, flooded the spacious emptiness of the atelier; it made no secret of the bad flooring or the rough table under the window, covered with little bottles, tubes, and brushes; it illumined the unframed studies on the unpapered walls, the torn silk screen that shut off a charmingly furnished little living-corner near the door; it shone upon the inchoate work on the easel, upon the artist and the poet there before it.

She was about the same age as himself—slightly past thirty. She sat there on a low stool, in her dark-blue apron, and leant her chin in her hand. Her brown hair, compactly dressed, already a little grey at the sides, was parted in the middle and waved over the temples, framing a sensitive, sympathetic, dark-skinned face, which was Slavic in its facial structure, with flat nose, strongly accentuated cheek-bones, and little bright black eyes. She sat there measuring her work with her head on one side and her eyes screwed up; her features were drawn with a look of misgiving, almost of vexation.

He stood beside her, his right hand on his hip, with the other furiously twirling his brown moustache. His dress, reserved in cut and a soothing shade of grey, was punctilious and dignified to the last degree. He was whistling softly to himself, in the way he had, and his slanting brows were gathered in a frown. The dark-brown hair was parted with severe correctness, but the laboured forehead beneath showed a nervous twitching, and the chiselled southern features were sharpened as though they had been gone over again with a graver's tool. And yet the mouth—how gently curved it was, the chin how softly formed! . . . After a little he drew his hand across his brow and eyes and turned away.

"I ought not to have come," he said.

"And why not, Tonio Kröger?"

"I've just got up from my desk, Lisabeta, and inside my head it looks just the way it does on this canvas. A scaffolding, a faint first draft smeared with corrections and a few splotches of colour; yes, and I come up here and see the same thing. And the same conflict and contradiction in the air," he went on, sniffing, "that has been torturing me at home. It's extraordinary. If you are possessed by an idea, you find it expressed everywhere, you even *smell* it. Fixative and the breath of spring; art and—what? Don't say nature, Lisabeta, 'nature' isn't exhausting. Ah, no, I ought to have gone for a walk, though it's doubtful if it would have made me feel better. Five minutes ago, not far from here, I met a man I know, Adalbert, the novelist. 'God damn the spring!' says he in the aggressive way he has. 'It is and always has been the most ghastly time of the year. Can you get hold of a single sensible idea, Kröger? Can you sit still and work out even the smallest effect, when your blood tickles till it's positively indecent and you are teased by a whole host of irrelevant sensations that when you look at them turn out to be unworkable trash? For my part, I am going to a café. A café is neutral territory, the change of the seasons doesn't affect it; it represents, so to speak, the detached and elevated sphere of the literary man, in which one is only capable of refined ideas.' And he went into the café . . . and perhaps I ought to have gone with him."

Lisabeta was highly entertained.

"I like that, Tonio Kröger. That part about the indecent tickling is good. And he is right too, in a way, for spring is really not very conducive to work. But now listen. Spring or no spring, I will just finish this little place—work out this little effect, as your friend Adalbert would say. Then we'll go into the 'salon' and have tea, and you can talk yourself out, for I can perfectly well see you are too full for utterance. Will you just compose yourself somewhere—on that chest, for instance, if you are not afraid for your aristocratic garments—"

"Oh, leave my clothes alone, Lisabeta Ivanovna! Do you want me to go about in a ragged velveteen jacket or a red waistcoat? Every artist is as bohemian as the deuce, inside! Let him at least wear proper clothes and behave outwardly like a respectable being. No, I am not too full for utterance," he said as he watched her mixing her paints. "I've told you, it is only that I have a problem and a conflict, that sticks in my mind and disturbs me at my work. . . . Yes, what was it we were just saying? We were talking about Adalbert, the novelist, that stout and forthright man. 'Spring is the most ghastly time of the year,' says he, and goes into a café. A man has to know what he needs, eh? Well, you see he's not the only one; the spring makes me nervous, too; I get dazed with the triflingness and sacredness of the memories and feelings it evokes; only that I don't succeed in looking down on it; for the truth is it makes me ashamed; I quail before its sheer naturalness and triumphant youth. And I don't know whether I should envy Adalbert or despise him for his ignorance. . . .

"Yes, it is true; spring is a bad time for work; and why? Because we are feeling too much. Nobody but a beginner imagines that he who creates must feel. Every real and genuine artist smiles at such naïve blunders as that. A melancholy enough smile, perhaps, but still a smile. For what an artist talks about is never the main point; it is the raw material, in and for itself indifferent, out of which, with bland and serene mastery, he creates the work of art. If you care too much about what you have to say, if your heart is too much in it, you can be pretty sure of making a mess. You get pathetic, you wax sentimental; something dull and doddering, without roots or outlines, with no sense of humour—something tiresome and banal grows under your hand, and you get nothing out of it but apathy in your audience and disappointment and misery in yourself. For so it is, Lisabeta; feeling, warm, heartfelt feeling, is always banal and futile; only the irritations and icy ecstasies of the artist's corrupted nervous system are artistic. The artist must be unhuman, extra-human; he must stand in a queer aloof relationship to our humanity; only so is he in a position, I ought to say only so would he be tempted, to represent it, to present it, to portray it to good effect. The very gift of style, of form and expression, is nothing else than this cool and fastidious attitude towards humanity; you might say there has to be this impoverishment and devastation as a preliminary condition. For sound natural feeling, say what you like, has no taste. It is all up with the artist as soon as he becomes a man and begins to feel. Adalbert knows that; that's why he betook himself to the café, the neutral territory—God help him!"

"Yes, God help him, Batuschka," said Lisabeta, as she washed her hands in a tin basin. "You don't need to follow his example."

"No, Lisabeta, I am not going to; and the only reason is that I am now and again in a position to feel a little ashamed of the springtime of my art. You see sometimes I get letters from strangers, full of praise and thanks and admiration from people whose feelings I have touched. I read them and feel touched myself at these warm if ungainly emotions I have called up; a sort of pity steals over me at this naïve enthusiasm; and I positively blush at the thought of how these good people would freeze up if they were to get a look behind the scenes. What they, in their innocence, cannot comprehend is that a properly constituted, healthy, decent man never writes, acts, or composes—all of which does not hinder me from using his admiration for my genius to goad myself on; nor from taking it in deadly earnest and aping the airs of a great man. Oh, don't talk to me, Lisabeta. I tell you I am sick to death of depicting humanity without having any part or lot in it. . . . Is an artist a male, anyhow? Ask the females! It seems to me we artists are all of us something like those unsexed papal singers . . . we sing like angels; but—"

"Shame on you, Tonio Kröger. But come to tea. The water is just on the boil, and here are some *papyros.* You were talking about singing soprano, do go on. But really you ought to be ashamed of yourself. If I did not know your passionate devotion to your calling and how proud you are of it—"

"Don't talk about 'calling,' Lisabeta Ivanovna. Literature is not a calling, it is a curse, believe me! When does one begin to feel the curse? Early, horribly early. At a time when one ought by rights still to be living in peace and harmony with God and the world. It begins by your feeling yourself set apart, in a curious sort of opposition to the nice, regular people; there is a gulf of ironic sensibility, of knowledge, scepticism, disagreement, between you and the others; it grows deeper and deeper, you realize that you are alone; and from then on any *rapprochement* is simply hopeless! What a fate! That is, if you still have enough heart, enough warmth of affections, to feel how frightful it is! . . . Your self-consciousness is kindled, because you among thousands feel the sign on your brow and know that everyone else sees it. I once knew an actor, a man of genius, who had to struggle with a morbid self-consciousness and instability. When he had no rôle to play, nothing to represent, this man, consummate artist but impoverished human being, was overcome by an exaggerated consciousness of his ego. A genuine artist—not one who has taken up art as a profession like another, but artist foreordained and damned—you can pick out, without boasting very sharp perceptions, out of a group of men. The sense of being set apart and not belonging, of being known and observed, something both regal and incongruous shows in his face. You might see something of the same sort on the features of a prince walking through a crowd in ordinary clothes. But no civilian clothes are any good here, Lisabeta. You can disguise yourself, you can dress up like an attaché or a lieutenant of the guard on leave; you hardly need to give a glance or speak a word before everyone knows you are not a human being, but something else: something queer, different, inimical.

"But what is it, to be an artist? Nothing shows up the general human dislike of thinking, and man's innate craving to be comfortable, better than his attitude to this question. When these worthy people are affected by a work of art, they say humbly that that sort of thing is a 'gift.' And because in their innocence they assume that beautiful and uplifting results must have beautiful and uplifting causes, they never dream that the 'gift' in question is a very dubious affair and rests upon extremely sinister foundations. Everybody knows that artists are 'sensitive' and easily wounded; just as everybody knows that ordinary people, with a normal bump of self-confidence, are not. Now you see, Lisabeta, I cherish at the bottom of my soul all the scorn and suspicion of the artist gentry—translated into terms of the intellectual—that my upright old forbears there on the Baltic would have felt for any juggler or mountebank that entered their houses. Listen to this. I know a banker, grey-haired business man, who has a gift for writing stories. He employs this gift in his idle hours, and some of his stories are of the first rank. But despite—I say despite—this excellent gift his withers are by no means unwrung: on the contrary, he has had to serve a prison sentence, on anything but trifling grounds. Yes, it was actually first *in prison* that he became conscious of his gift, and his experiences as a convict are the main theme in all his works. One might be rash enough to conclude that a man has to be at home in some kind of jail in order to become a poet. But can you escape the suspicion that the source and essence of his being an artist had less to do with his life in prison than they had with the reasons that *brought him there?* A banker who writes—that is a rarity, isn't it? But a banker who isn't a criminal, who is irreproachably respectable, and yet writes—he doesn't exist. Yes, you are laughing, and yet I am more than half serious. No problem, none in the world, is more tormenting than this of the artist and his human aspect. Take the most miraculous case of all, take the most typical and therefore the most powerful of artists, take such a morbid and profoundly equivocal work as *Tristan and Isolde,* and look at the effect it has on a healthy young man of thoroughly normal feelings. Exaltation, encouragement, warm, downright enthusiasm, perhaps incitement to 'artistic' creation of his own. Poor young dilettante! In us artists it looks fundamentally different from what he wots of, with his 'warm heart' and 'honest enthusiasm.' I've seen women and youths go mad over artists . . . and I *knew* about them . . . ! The origin, the accompanying phenomena, and the conditions of the artist life—good Lord, what I haven't observed about them, over and over!"

"Observed, Tonio Kröger? If I may ask, only 'observed'?"

He was silent, knitting his oblique brown brows and whistling softly to himself.

"Let me have your cup, Tonio. The tea is weak. And take another cigarette. Now, you perfectly know that you are looking at things as they do not necessarily have to be looked at. . . ."

"That is Horatio's answer, dear Lisabeta. ' 'Twere to consider too curiously, to consider so.' "

"I mean, Tonio Kröger, that one can consider them just exactly as well from another side. I am only a silly painting female, and if I can contradict you at all, if I can defend your own profession a little against you, it is not by saying anything new, but simply by reminding you of some things you very well know yourself: of the purifying and healing influence of letters, the subduing of the passions by knowledge and eloquence; literature as the guide to understanding, forgiveness, and love, the redeeming power of the word, literary art as the noblest manifestation of the human mind, the poet as the most highly developed of human beings, the poet as saint. Is it to consider things not curiously enough, to consider them so?"

"You may talk like that, Lisabeta Ivanovna, you have a perfect right. And with reference to Russian literature, and the works of your poets, one can really worship them; they really come close to being that elevated literature you are talking about. But I am not ignoring your objections, they are part of the things I have in my mind today. . . . Look at me, Lisabeta. I don't look any too cheerful, do I? A little old and tired and pinched, eh? Well, now to come back to the 'knowledge.' Can't you imagine a man, born orthodox, mild-mannered, well-meaning, a bit sentimental, just simply over-stimulated by his psychological clairvoyance, and going to the dogs? Not to let the sadness of the world unman you; to read, mark, learn, and put to account even the most torturing things and to be of perpetual good cheer, in the sublime consciousness of moral superiority over the horrible invention of existence—yes, thank you! But despite all the joys of expression once in a while the thing gets on your nerves. '*Tout comprendre c'est tout pardonner.*' I don't know about that. There is something I call being sick of knowledge, Lisabeta: when it is enough for you to see through a thing in order to be sick to death of it, and not in the least in a forgiving mood. Such was the case of Hamlet the Dane, that typical literary man. He knew what it meant to be called to knowledge without being born to it. To see things clear, if even through your tears, to recognize, notice, observe—and have to put it all down with a smile, at the very moment when hands are clinging, and lips meeting, and the human gaze is blinded with feeling—it is infamous, Lisabeta, it is indecent, outrageous—but what good does it do to be outraged?

"Then another and no less charming side of the thing, of course, is your ennui, your indifferent and ironic attitude towards truth. It is a fact that there is no society in the world so dumb and hopeless as a circle of literary people who are hounded to death as it is. All knowledge is old and tedious to them. Utter some truth that it gave you considerable youthful joy to conquer and possess—and they will all chortle at you for your naïveté. Oh, yes, Lisabeta, literature is a wearing job. In human society, I do assure you, a reserved and sceptical man can be taken for stupid, whereas he is really only arrogant and perhaps lacks courage. So much for 'knowledge.' Now for the 'Word.' It isn't so much a matter of the 'redeeming power' as it is of putting your emotions on ice and serving them up chilled! Honestly, don't you think there's a good deal of cool cheek in the prompt and superficial way a writer can get rid of his feelings by turning them into literature? If your heart is too full, if you are overpowered with the emotions of some sweet or exalted moment—nothing simpler! Go to the literary man, he will put it all straight for you instanter. He will analyse and formulate your affair, label it and express it and discuss it and polish it off and make you indifferent to it for time and eternity—and not charge you a farthing. You will go home quite relieved, cooled off, enlightened; and wonder what it was all about and why you were so mightily moved. And will you seriously enter the lists in behalf of this vain and frigid charlatan? What is uttered, so runs this *credo,* is finished and done with. If the whole world could be expressed, it would be saved, finished and done. . . . Well and good. But I am not a nihilist—"

"You are not a—" said Lisabeta. . . . She was lifting a teaspoonful of tea to her mouth and paused in the act to stare at him.

"Come, come, Lisabeta, what's the matter? I say I am not a nihilist, with respect, that is, to lively feeling. You see, the literary man does not understand that life may go on living, unashamed, even after it has been expressed and therewith finished. No matter how much it has been redeemed by becoming literature, it keeps right on sinning—for all action is sin in the mind's eye—

"I'm nearly done, Lisabeta. Please listen. I love life—this is an admission. I present it to you, you may have it. I have never made it to anyone else. People say—people have even written and printed—that I hate life, or fear or despise or abominate it. I liked to hear this, it has always flattered me; but that does not make it true. I love life. You smile; and I know why, Lisabeta. But I implore you not to take what I am saying for literature. Don't think of Cæsar Borgia or any drunken philosophy that has him for a standard-bearer. He is nothing to me, your Cæsar Borgia. I have no opinion of him, and I shall never comprehend how one can honour the extraordinary and dæmonic as an ideal. No, life as the eternal antinomy of mind and art does not represent itself to us as a vision of savage greatness and ruthless beauty; we who are set apart and different do not conceive it as, like us, unusual; it is the normal, respectable, and admirable that is the kingdom of our longing: life, in all its seductive banality! That man is very far from being an artist, my dear, whose last and deepest enthusiasm is the *raffiné,* the eccentric and satanic; who does not know a longing for the innocent, the simple, and the living, for a little friendship, devotion, familiar human happiness—the gnawing, surreptitious hankering, Lisabeta, for the bliss of the commonplace. . . .

"A genuine human friend. Believe me, I should be proud and happy to possess a friend among men. But up to now all the friends I have had have been dæmons, kobolds, impious monsters, and spectres dumb with excess of knowledge—that is to say literary men.

"I may be standing upon some platform, in some hall in front of people who have come to listen to me. And I find myself looking round among my hearers, I catch myself secretly peering about the auditorium, and all the while I am thinking who it is that has come here to listen to me, whose grateful applause is in my ears, with whom my art is making me one. . . . I do not find what I seek, Lisabeta, I find the herd. The same old community, the same old gathering of early Christians, so to speak: people with fine souls in uncouth bodies, people who are always falling down in the dance, if you know what I mean; the kind to whom poetry serves as a sort of mild revenge on life. Always and only the poor and suffering, never any of the others, the blue-eyed ones, Lisabeta—they do not need mind. . . .

"And, after all, would it not be a lamentable lack of logic to want it otherwise? It is against all sense to love life and yet bend all the powers you have to draw it over to your own side, to the side of finesse and melancholy and the whole sickly aristocracy of letters. The kingdom of art increases and that of health and innocence declines on this earth. What there is left of it ought to be carefully preserved; one ought not to tempt people to read poetry who would much rather read books about the instantaneous photography of horses.

"For, after all, what more pitiable sight is there than life led astray by art? We artists have a consummate contempt for the dilettante, the man who is leading a living life and yet thinks he can be an artist too if he gets the chance. I am speaking from personal experience, I do assure you. Suppose I am in a company in a good house, with eating and drinking going on, and plenty of conversation and good feeling; I am glad and grateful to be able to lose myself among good regular people for a while. Then all of a sudden—I am thinking of something that actually happened—an officer gets up, a lieutenant, a stout, good-looking chap, whom I could never have believed guilty of any conduct unbecoming his uniform, and actually in good set terms asks the company's permission to read some verses of his own composition. Everybody looks disconcerted, they laugh and tell him to go on, and he takes them at their word and reads from a sheet of paper he has up to now been hiding in his coat-tail pocket—something about love and music, as deeply felt as it is inept. But I ask you: a lieutenant! A man of the world! He surely did not need to. . . . Well, the inevitable result is long faces, silence, a little artificial applause, everybody thoroughly uncomfortable. The first sensation I am conscious of is guilt—I feel partly responsible for the disturbance this rash youth has brought upon the company; and no wonder, for I, as a member of the same guild, am a target for some of the unfriendly glances. But next minute I realize something else: this man for whom just now I felt the greatest respect has suddenly sunk in my eyes. I feel a benevolent pity. Along with some other brave and good-natured gentlemen I go up and speak to him. 'Congratulations, Herr Lieutenant,'

I say, 'that is a very pretty talent you have. It was charming.' And I am within an ace of clapping him on the shoulder. But is that the way one is supposed to feel towards a lieutenant—benevolent? . . . It was his own fault. There he stood, suffering embarrassment for the mistake of thinking that one may pluck a single leaf from the laurel tree of art without paying for it with his life. No, there I go with my colleague, the convict banker—but don't you find, Lisabeta, that I have quite a Hamlet-like flow of oratory today?"

"Are you done, Tonio Kröger?"

"No. But there won't be any more."

"And quite enough too. Are you expecting a reply?"

"Have you one ready?"

"I should say. I have listened to you faithfully, Tonio, from beginning to end, and I will give you the answer to everything you have said this afternoon and the solution of the problem that has been upsetting you. Now: the solution is that you, as you sit there, are, quite simply, a bourgeois."

"Am I?" he asked a little crestfallen.

"Yes; that hits you hard, it must. So I will soften the judgment just a little. You are a bourgeois on the wrong path, a bourgeois *manqué*."

Silence. Then he got up resolutely and took his hat and stick.

"Thank you, Lisabeta Ivanovna; now I can go home in peace. I am expressed."

Towards autumn Tonio Kröger said to Lisabeta Ivanovna:

"Well, Lisabeta, I think I'll be off. I need a change of air. I must get away, out into the open."

"Well, well, well, little Father! Does it please your Highness to go down to Italy again?"

"Oh, get along with your Italy, Lisabeta. I'm fed up with Italy, I spew it out of my mouth. It's a long time since I imagined I could belong down there. Art, eh? Blue-velvet sky, ardent wine, the sweets of sensuality. In short, I don't want it—I decline with thanks. The whole *bellezza* business makes me nervous. All those frightfully animated people down there with their black animal-like eyes; I don't like them either. These Romance peoples have no soul in their eyes. No, I'm going to take a trip to Denmark."

"To Denmark?"

"Yes. I'm quite sanguine of the results. I happen never to have been there, though I lived all my youth so close to it. Still I have always known and loved the country. I suppose I must have this northern tendency from my father, for my mother was really more for the *bellezza*, in so far, that is, as she cared very much one way or the other. But just take the books that are written up there, that clean, meaty, whimsical Scandinavian literature, Lisabeta, there's nothing like it, I love it. Or take the Scandinavian meals, those incomparable meals, which can only be digested in strong sea air (I don't know whether I can digest them in any sort of air); I know them from my home too, because we ate that way up there. Take even the names, the given names that people rejoice in up north; we have a good many of them in my part of the country too: Ingeborg, for instance, isn't it the purest poetry—like a harp-tone? And then the sea—up there it's the Baltic! . . . In a word, I am going, Lisabeta. I want to see the Baltic again and read the books and hear the names on their native heath; I want to stand on the terrace at Kronberg, where the ghost appeared to Hamlet, bringing despair and death to that poor, noble-souled youth. . . ."

"How are you going, Tonio, if I may ask? What route are you taking?"

"The usual one," he said, shrugging his shoulders, and blushed perceptibly. "Yes, I shall touch my—my point of departure, Lisabeta, after thirteen years, and that may turn out rather funny."

She smiled.

"That is what I wanted to hear, Tonio Kröger. Well, be off, then, in God's name. Be sure to write to me, do you hear? I shall expect a letter full of your experiences in—Denmark."

And Tonio Kröger travelled north. He travelled in comfort (for he was wont to say that anyone who suffered inwardly more than other people had a right to a little outward ease); and he did not stay until the towers of the little town he had left rose up in the grey air. Among them he made a short and singular stay.

The dreary afternoon was merging into evening when the train pulled into the narrow, reeking shed, so marvellously familiar. The volumes of thick smoke rolled up to the dirty glass roof and wreathed to and fro there in long tatters, just as they had, long ago, on the day when Tonio Kröger, with nothing but derision in his heart, had left his native town.—He arranged to have his luggage sent to his hotel and walked out of the station.

There were the cabs, those enormously high, enormously wide black cabs drawn by two horses, standing in a rank. He did not take one, he only looked at them, as he looked at everything: the narrow gables, and the pointed towers peering above the roofs close at hand; the plump, fair, easy-going populace, with their broad yet rapid speech. And a nervous laugh mounted in him, mysteriously akin to a sob.—He walked on, slowly, with the damp wind constantly in his face, across the bridge, with the mythological statues on the railings, and some distance along the harbour.

Good Lord, how tiny and close it all seemed! The comical little gabled streets were climbing up just as of yore from the port to the town! And on the ruffled waters the smoke-stacks and masts of the ships dipped gently in the wind and twilight. Should he go up that next street, leading, he knew, to a certain house? No, tomorrow. He was too sleepy. His head was heavy from the journey, and slow, vague trains of thought passed through his mind.

Sometimes in the past thirteen years, when he was suffering from indigestion, he had dreamed of being back home in the echoing old house in the steep, narrow street. His father had been there too, and reproached him bitterly for his dissolute manner of life, and this, each time, he had found quite as it should be. And now the present refused to distinguish itself in any way from one of those tantalizing dream-fabrications in which the dreamer asks himself if this be delusion or reality and is driven to decide for the latter, only to wake up after all in the end. . . . He paced through the half-empty streets with his head inclined against the wind, moving as though in his sleep in the direction of the hotel, the first hotel in the town, where he meant to sleep. A bow-legged man, with a pole at the end of which burned a tiny fire, walked before him with a rolling, seafaring gait and lighted the gas-lamps.

What was at the bottom of this? What was it burning darkly beneath the ashes of his fatigue, refusing to burst out into a clear blaze? Hush, hush, only no talk. Only don't make words! He would have liked to go on so, for a long time, in the wind, through the dusky, dreamily familiar streets—but everything was so little and close together here. You reached your goal at once.

In the upper town there were arc-lamps, just lighted. There was the hotel with the two black lions in front of it; he had been afraid of them as a child. And there they were, still looking at each other as though they were about to sneeze; only they seemed to have grown much smaller Tonio Kröger passed between them into the hotel.

As he came on foot, he was received with no great ceremony. There was a porter, and a lordly gentleman dressed in black, to do the honours; the latter, shoving back his cuffs with his little fingers, measured him from the crown of his head to the soles of his boots, obviously with intent to place him, to assign him to his proper category socially and hierarchically speaking and then mete out the suitable degree of courtesy. He seemed not to come to any clear decision and compromised on a moderate display of politeness. A mild-mannered waiter with yellow-white side-whiskers, in a dress suit shiny with age, and rosettes on his soundless shoes, led him up two flights into a clean old room furnished in patriarchal style. Its windows gave on a twilit view of courts and gables, very mediæval and picturesque, with the fantastic bulk of the old church close by. Tonio Kröger stood awhile before this window;

then he sat down on the wide sofa, crossed his arms, drew down his brows, and whistled to himself.

Lights were brought and his luggage came up. The mild-mannered waiter laid the hotel register on the table, and Tonio Kröger, his head on one side, scrawled something on it that might be taken for a name, a station, and a place of origin. Then he ordered supper and went on gazing into space from his sofa-corner. When it stood before him he let it wait long untouched, then took a few bites and walked up and down an hour in his room, stopping from time to time and closing his eyes. Then he very slowly undressed and went to bed. He slept long and had curiously confused and ardent dreams.

It was broad day when he woke. Hastily he recalled where he was and got up to draw the curtains; the pale-blue sky, already with a hint of autumn, was streaked with frayed and tattered cloud; still, above his native city the sun was shining.

He spent more care than usual upon his toilette, washed and shaved and made himself fresh and immaculate as though about to call upon some smart family where a well-dressed and flawless appearance was *de rigueur;* and while occupied in this wise he listened to the anxious beating of his heart.

How bright it was outside! He would have liked better a twilight air like yesterday's, instead of passing through the streets in the broad sunlight, under everybody's eye. Would he meet people he knew, be stopped and questioned and have to submit to be asked how he had spent the last thirteen years? No, thank goodness, he was known to nobody here; even if anybody remembered him, it was unlikely he would be recognized—for certainly he had changed in the meantime! He surveyed himself in the glass and felt a sudden sense of security behind his mask, behind his work-worn face, that was older than his years. . . . He sent for breakfast, and after that he went out; he passed under the disdainful eye of the porter and the gentleman in black, through the vestibule and between the two lions, and so into the street.

Where was he going? He scarcely knew. It was the same as yesterday. Hardly was he in the midst of this long-familiar scene, this stately conglomeration of gables, turrets, arcades, and fountains, hardly did he feel once more the wind in his face, that strong current wafting a faint and pungent aroma from far-off dreams, than the same mistiness laid itself like a veil about his senses. . . . The muscles of his face relaxed, and he looked at men and things with a look grown suddenly calm. Perhaps right there, on that street corner, he might wake up after all. . . .

Where was he going? It seemed to him the direction he took had a connection with his sad and strangely rueful dreams of the night. . . . He went to Market Square, under the vaulted arches of the Rathaus, where the butchers were weighing out their wares red-handed, where the tall old Gothic fountain stood with its manifold spires. He paused in front of a house, a plain narrow building, like many another, with a fretted baroque gable; stood there lost in contemplation. He read the plate on the door, his eyes rested a little while on each of the windows. Then slowly he turned away.

Where did he go? Towards home. But he took a roundabout way outside the walls—for he had plenty of time. He went over the Millwall and over the Holstenwall, clutching his hat, for the wind was rushing and moaning through the trees. He left the wall near the station, where he saw a train puffing busily past, idly counted the coaches, and looked after the man who sat perched upon the last. In the Lindenplatz he stopped at one of the pretty villas, peered long into the garden and up at the windows, lastly conceived the idea of swinging the gate to and fro upon its hinges till it creaked. Then he looked awhile at his moist, rust-stained hand and went on, went through the squat old gate, along the harbour, and up the steep, windy street to his parents' house.

It stood aloof from its neighbours, its gable towering above them; grey and sombre, as it had stood these three hundred years; and Tonio Kröger read the pious, half-illegible motto above the entrance. Then he drew a long breath and went in.

His heart gave a throb of fear, lest his father might come out of one of the doors on the ground floor, in his office coat, with the pen behind his ear, and take him to task for his excesses. He would have found the reproach quite in order; but he got past unchidden. The inner door was ajar, which appeared to him reprehensible though at the same time he felt as one does in certain broken dreams, where obstacles melt away of themselves, and one presses onward in marvellous favour with fortune. The wide entry, paved with great square flags, echoed to his tread. Opposite the silent kitchen was the curious projecting structure, of rough boards, but cleanly varnished, that had been the servants' quarters. It was quite high up and could only be reached by a sort of ladder from the entry. But the great cupboards and carven presses were gone. The son of the house climbed the majestic staircase, with his hand on the white-enamelled, fret-work balustrade. At each step he lifted his hand, and put it down again with the next as though testing whether he could call back his ancient familiarity with the stout old railing. . . . But at the landing of the entresol he stopped. For on the entrance door was a white plate; and on it in black letters he read: "Public Library."

"Public Library?" thought Tonio Kröger. What were either literature or the public doing here? He knocked . . . heard a "Come in," and obeying it with gloomy suspense gazed upon a scene of most unhappy alteration.

The storey was three rooms deep, and all the doors stood open. The walls were covered nearly all the way up with long rows of books in uniform bindings, standing in dark-coloured bookcases. In each room a poor creature of a man sat writing behind a sort of counter. The farthest two just turned their heads, but the nearest got up in haste and, leaning with both hands on the table, stuck out his head, pursed his lips, lifted his brows, and looked at the visitor with eagerly blinking eyes.

"I beg pardon," said Tonio Kröger without turning his eyes from the book-shelves. "I am a stranger here, seeing the sights. So this is your Public Library? May I examine your collection a little?"

"Certainly, with pleasure," said the official, blinking still more violently. "It is open to everybody. . . . Pray look about you. Should you care for a catalogue?"

"No, thanks," answered Tonio Kröger, "I shall soon find my way about." And he began to move slowly along the walls, with the appearance of studying the rows of books. After a while he took down a volume, opened it, and posted himself at the window.

This was the breakfast-room. They had eaten here in the morning instead of in the big dining-room upstairs, with its white statues of gods and goddesses standing out against the blue walls. . . . Beyond there had been a bedroom, where his father's mother had died—only after a long struggle, old as she was, for she had been of a pleasure-loving nature and clung to life. And his father too had drawn his last breath in the same room: that tall, correct, slightly melancholy and pensive gentleman with the wild flower in his buttonhole. . . . Tonio had sat at the foot of his death-bed, quite given over to unutterable feelings of love and grief. His mother had knelt at the bedside, his lovely, fiery mother, dissolved in hot tears; and after that she had withdrawn with her artist into the far blue south. . . . And beyond still, the small third room, likewise full of books and presided over by a shabby man—that had been for years on end his own. Thither he had come after school and a walk—like today's; against that wall his table had stood with the drawer where he had kept his first clumsy, heartfelt attempts at verse. . . . The walnut tree . . . a pang went through him. He gave a sidewise glance out at the window. The garden lay desolate, but there stood the old walnut tree where it used to stand, groaning and creaking heavily in the wind. And Tonio Kröger let his gaze fall upon the book he had in his hands, an excellent piece of work, and very familiar. He followed the black lines of print, the paragraphs, the flow of words that flowed with so much art, mounting in the ardour of creation to a certain climax and effect and then as artfully breaking off. . . .

"Yes, that was well done," he said; put back the book and turned away. Then he saw that the functionary still stood bolt-upright, blinking with a mingled expression of zeal and misgiving.

"A capital collection, I see," said Tonio Kröger. "I have already quite a good idea of it. Much obliged to you. Good-bye." He went out; but it was a poor exit, and he felt sure the official would stand there perturbed and blinking for several minutes.

He felt no desire for further researches. He had been home. Strangers were living upstairs in the large rooms behind the pillared hall; the top of the stairs was shut off by a glass door which used not to be there, and on the door was a plate. He went away, down the steps, across the echoing corridor, and left his parental home. He sought a restaurant, sat down in a corner, and brooded over a heavy, greasy meal. Then he returned to his hotel.

"I am leaving," he said to the fine gentleman in black. "This afternoon." And he asked for his bill, and for a carriage to take him down to the harbour where he should take the boat for Copenhagen. Then he went up to his room and sat there stiff and still, with his cheek on his hand, looking down on the table before him with absent eyes. Later he paid his bill and packed his things. At the appointed hour the carriage was announced and Tonio Kröger went down in travel array.

At the foot of the stairs the gentleman in black was waiting.

"Beg pardon," he said, shoving back his cuffs with his little fingers. . . . "Beg pardon, but we must detain you just a moment. Herr Seehaase, the proprietor, would like to exchange two words with you. A matter of form. . . . He is back there. . . . If you will have the goodness to step this way. . . . It is *only* Herr Seehaase, the proprietor."

And he ushered Tonio Kröger into the background of the vestibule. . . . There, in fact, stood Herr Seehaase. Tonio Kröger recognized him from old time. He was small, fat, and bow-legged. His shaven side-whisker was white, but he wore the same old low-cut dress coat and little velvet cap embroidered in green. He was not alone. Beside him, at a little high desk fastened into the wall, stood a policeman in a helmet, his gloved right hand resting on a document in coloured inks; he turned towards Tonio Kröger with his honest, soldierly face as though he expected Tonio to sink into the earth at his glance.

Tonio Kröger looked at the two and confined himself to waiting.

"You came from Munich?" the policeman asked at length in a heavy, good-natured voice.

Tonio Kröger said he had.

"You are going to Copenhagen?"

"Yes, I am on the way to a Danish seashore resort."

"Seashore resort? Well, you must produce your papers," said the policeman. He uttered the last word with great satisfaction.

"Papers . . . ?" He had no papers. He drew out his pocketbook and looked into it; but aside from notes there was nothing there but some proof-sheets of a story which he had taken along to finish reading. He hated relations with officials and had never got himself a passport. . . .

"I am sorry," he said, "but I don't travel with papers."

"Ah!" said the policeman. "And what might be your name?"

Tonio replied.

"Is that a fact?" asked the policeman, suddenly erect, and expanding his nostrils as wide as he could. . . .

"Yes, that is a fact," answered Tonio Kröger.

"And what are you, anyhow?"

Tonio Kröger gulped and gave the name of his trade in a firm voice. Herr Seehaase lifted his head and looked him curiously in the face.

"H'm," said the policeman. "And you give out that you are not identical with an individdle named"—he said "individdle" and then, referring to his document in coloured inks, spelled out an involved, fantastic name which mingled all the sounds of all the races—Tonio Kröger forgot it next minute—"of unknown parentage and unspecified means," he went on, "wanted by the Munich police for various shady transactions, and probably in flight towards Denmark?"

"Yes, I give out all that, and more," said Tonio Kröger, wriggling his shoulders. The gesture made a certain impression.

"What? Oh, yes, of course," said the policeman. "You say you can't show any papers—"

Herr Seehaase threw himself into the breach.

"It is only a formality," he said pacifically, "nothing else. You must bear in mind the official is only doing his duty. If you could only identify yourself somehow—some document . . ."

They were all silent. Should he make an end of the business, by reveal- to Herr Seehaase that he was no swindler without specified means, no gypsy in a green wagon, but the son of the late Consul Kröger, a member of the Kröger family? No, he felt no desire to do that. After all, were not these guardians of civic order within their right? He even agreed with them—up to a point. He shrugged his shoulders and kept quiet.

"What have you got, then?" asked the policeman. "In your portfoly, I mean?"

"Here? Nothing. Just a proof-sheet," answered Tonio Kröger.

"Proof-sheet? What's that? Let's see it."

And Tonio Kröger handed over his work. The policeman spread it out on the shelf and began reading. Herr Seehaase drew up and shared it with him. Tonio Kröger looked over their shoulders to see what they read. It was a good moment, a little effect he had worked out to a perfection. He had a sense of self-satisfaction.

"You see," he said, "there is my name. I wrote it, and it is going to be published, you understand."

"All right, that will answer," said Herr Seehaase with decision, gathered up the sheets and gave them back. "That will have to answer, Petersen," he repeated crisply, shutting his eyes and shaking his head as though to see and hear no more. "We must not keep the gentleman any longer. The carriage is waiting. I implore you to pardon the little inconvenience, sir. The officer has only done his duty, but I told him at once he was on the wrong track. . . ."

"Indeed!" thought Tonio Kröger.

The officer seemed still to have his doubts; he muttered something else about individdle and document. But Herr Seehaase, overflowing with regrets, led his guest through the vestibule, accompanied him past the two lions to the carriage, and himself, with many respectful bows, closed the door upon him. And then the funny, high, wide old cab rolled and rattled and bumped down the steep, narrow street to the quay.

And such was the manner of Tonio Kröger's visit to his ancestral home.

Night fell and the moon swam up with silver gleam as Tonio Kröger's boat reached the open sea. He stood at the prow wrapped in his cloak against a mounting wind, and looked beneath into the dark going and coming of the waves as they hovered and swayed and came on, to meet with a clap and shoot erratically away in a bright gush of foam.

He was lulled in a mood of still enchantment. The episode at the hotel, their wanting to arrest him for a swindler in his own home, had cast him down a little, even although he found it quite in order—in a certain way. But after he came on board he had watched, as he used to do as a boy with his father, the lading of goods into the deep bowels of the boat, amid shouts of mingled Danish and Plattdeutsch; not only boxes and bales, but also a Bengal tiger and a polar bear were lowered in cages with stout iron bars. They had probably come from Hamburg and were destined for a Danish menagerie. He had enjoyed these distractions. And as the boat glided along between flat river-banks he quite forgot Officer Petersen's inquisition; while all the rest—his sweet, sad, rueful dreams of the night before, the walk he had taken, the walnut tree—had welled up again in his soul. The sea opened out and he saw in the distance the beach where he as a lad had been let to listen to the ocean's summer dreams; saw the flashing of the lighthouse tower and the lights of the Kurhaus where he and his parents had lived. . . . The Baltic! He bent his head to the strong salt wind; it came sweeping on, it enfolded him, made him faintly giddy and a little deaf; and in that mild confusion of the senses all memory of evil, of anguish and error, effort and exertion of the will, sank away into joyous oblivion and were gone. The roaring, foaming, flapping, and slapping all about him came to his ears like the groan and rustle of an old walnut tree, the creaking of a garden gate. . . . More and more the darkness came on.

"The stars! Oh, by Lord, look at the stars!" a voice suddenly said, with a heavy singsong accent that seemed to come out of the inside of a tun. He recognized it. It belonged to a young man with red-blond hair who had been Tonio Kröger's neighbour at dinner in the salon. His dress was very simple, his eyes were red, and he had the moist and chilly look of a person who has just bathed. With nervous and self-conscious movements he had taken unto himself an astonishing quantity of lobster omelet. Now he leaned on the rail beside Tonio Kröger and looked up at the skies, holding his chin between thumb and forefinger. Beyond a doubt he was in one of those rare and festal and edifying moods that cause the barriers between man and man to fall; when the heart opens even to the stranger, and the mouth utters that which otherwise it would blush to speak. . . .

"Look, by dear sir, just look at the stars. There they stahd and glitter; by goodness, the whole sky is full of theb! And I ask you, when you stahd ahd look up at theb, ahd realize that bany of theb are a huddred tibes larger thad the earth, how does it bake you feel? Yes, we have idvehted the telegraph and the telephode and all the triuphs of our bodern tibes. But whed we look up there, after all we have to recogdize and uhderstad that we are worbs, biserable worbs, ahd dothing else. Ab I right, sir, or ab I wrog? Yes, we are worbs," he answered himself, and nodded meekly and abjectly in the direction of the firmament.

"Ah, no, he has no literature in his belly," thought Tonio Kröger. And he recalled something he had lately read, an essay by a famous French writer on cosmological and psychological philosophies, a very delightful *causerie.*

He made some sort of reply to the young man's feeling remarks, and they went on talking, leaning over the rail, and looking into the night with its movement and fitful lights. The young man, it seemed, was a Hamburg merchant on his holiday.

"Y'ought to travel to Copedhagen on the boat, thigks I, and so here I ab, and so far it's been fide. But they shouldn't have given us the lobster obelet, sir, for it's going to be storby—the captain said so hibself—and that's do joke with indigestible food like that in your stobach. . . ."

Tonio Kröger listened to all this engaging artlessness and was privately drawn to it.

"Yes," he said, "all the food up here is too heavy. It makes one lazy and melancholy."

"Belancholy?" repeated the young man, and looked at him, taken aback. Then he asked, suddenly: "You are a stradger up here, sir?"

"Yes, I come from a long way off," answered Tonio Kröger vaguely, waving his arm.

"But you're right," said the youth; "Lord kdows you are right about the belancholy. I am dearly always belancholy, but specially on evedings like this when there are stars in the sky." And he supported his chin again with thumb and forefinger.

"Surely this man writes verses," thought Tonio Kröger; "business man's verses, full of deep feeling and single-mindedness."

Evening drew on. The wind had grown so violent as to prevent them from talking. So they thought they would sleep a bit, and wished each other good-night.

Tonio Kröger stretched himself out on the narrow cabin bed, but he found no repose. The strong wind with its sharp tang had power to rouse him; he was strangely restless with sweet anticipations. Also he was violently sick with the motion of the ship as she glided down a steep mountain of wave and her screw vibrated as in agony, free of the water. He put on all his clothes again and went up to the deck.

Clouds raced across the moon. The sea danced. It did not come on in full-bodied, regular waves; but far out in the pale and flickering light the water was lashed, torn, and tumbled; leaped upward like great licking flames; hung in jagged and fantastic shapes above dizzy abysses, where the foam seemed to be tossed by the playful strength of colossal arms and flung upward in all directions. The ship had a heavy passage; she lurched and stamped and groaned through the welter; and far down in her bowels the tiger and the polar bear voiced their acute discomfort. A man in an oilskin, with the hood drawn over his head and a lantern strapped to his chest, went straddling painfully up and down the deck. And at the stern, leaning far out, stood the young man from Hamburg suffering the worst. "Lord!" he said, in a hollow, quavering voice, when he saw Tonio Kröger. "Look at the uproar of the elebents, sir!" But he could say no more—he was obliged to turn hastily away.

Tonio Kröger clutched at a taut rope and looked abroad into the arrogance of the elements. His exultation outvied storm and wave; within himself he chanted a song to the sea, instinct with love of her: "O thou wild friend of my youth, Once more I behold thee—" But it got no further, he did not finish it. It was not fated to receive a final form nor in tranquillity to be welded to a perfect whole. For his heart was too full. . . .

Long he stood; then stretched himself out on a bench by the pilot-house and looked up at the sky, where stars were flickering. He even slept a little. And when the cold foam splashed his face it seemed in his half-dreams like a caress.

Perpendicular chalk-cliffs, ghostly in the moonlight, came in sight. They were nearing the island of Möen. Then sleep came again, broken by salty showers of spray that bit into his face and made it stiff. . . . When he really roused, it was broad day, fresh and palest grey, and the sea had gone down. At breakfast he saw the young man from Hamburg again, who blushed rosy-red for shame of the poetic indiscretions he had been betrayed into by the dark, ruffled up his little red-blond moustache with all five fingers, and called out a brisk and soldierly good-morning—after that he studiously avoided him.

And Tonio Kröger landed in Denmark. He arrived in Copenhagen, gave tips to everybody who laid claim to them, took a room at a hotel, and roamed the city for three days with an open guide-book and the air of an intelligent foreigner bent on improving his mind. He looked at the king's New Market and the "Horse" in the middle of it, gazed respectfully up the columns of the Frauenkirch, stood long before Thorwaldsen's noble and beautiful statuary, climbed the round tower, visited castles, and spent two lively evenings in the Tivoli. But all this was not exactly what he saw.

The doors of the houses—so like those in his native town, with open-work gables of baroque shape—bore names known to him of old; names that had a tender and precious quality, and withal in their syllables an accent of plaintive reproach, of repining after the lost and gone. He walked, he gazed, drawing deep, lingering draughts of moist sea air; and everywhere he saw eyes as blue, hair as blond, faces as familiar, as those that had visited his rueful dreams the night he had spent in his native town. There in the open street it befell him that a glance, a ringing word, a sudden laugh would pierce him to his marrow.

He could not stand the bustling city for long. A restlessness, half memory and half hope, half foolish and half sweet, possessed him; he was moved to drop this rôle of ardently inquiring tourist and lie somewhere, quite quietly, on a beach. So he took ship once more and travelled under a cloudy sky, over a black water, northwards along the coast of Seeland towards Helsingör. Thence he drove, at once, by carriage, for three-quarters of an hour, along and above the sea, reaching at length his ultimate goal, the little white "bath-hotel" with green blinds. It stood surrounded by a settlement of cottages, and its shingled turret tower looked out on the beach and the Swedish coast. Here he left the carriage, took possession of the light room they had ready for him, filled shelves and presses with his kit, and prepared to stop awhile.

It was well on in September; not many guests were left in Aalsgaard. Meals were served on the ground floor, in the great beamed dining-room, whose lofty windows led out upon the veranda and the sea. The landlady presided, an elderly spinster with white hair and faded eyes, a faint colour in her cheek and a feeble twittering voice. She was forever arranging her red hands to look well upon the tablecloth. There was a short-necked old gentleman, quite blue in the face, with a grey sailor beard; a fish-dealer he was, from the capital, and strong at the German. He seemed entirely congested and inclined to apoplexy; breathed in short gasps, kept putting his beringed first finger to one nostril, and snorting violently to get a passage of air through the other. Notwithstanding, he addressed himself constantly to the whisky-bottle, which stood at his place at luncheon and dinner, and breakfast as well. Besides him the company consisted only of three tall American youths with their governor or tutor, who kept adjusting his glasses in unbroken silence. All day long he played football with his charges, who had narrow, taciturn faces and reddish-yellow hair parted in the middle. "Please pass the *wurst,*" said one. "That's not *wurst,* it's *schinken,*" said the other, and this was the extent of their conversation, as the rest of the time they sat there dumb, drinking hot water.

Tonio Kröger could have wished himself no better table-companions. He revelled in the peace and quiet, listened to the Danish palatals, the clear and the clouded vowels in which the fish-dealer and the landlady desultorily conversed; modestly exchanged views with the fish-dealer on the state of the barometer, and then left the table to go through the veranda and onto the beach once more, where he had already spent long, long morning hours.

Sometimes it was still and summery there. The sea lay idle and smooth, in stripes of blue and russet and bottle-green, played all across with glittering silvery lights. The seaweed shrivelled in the sun and the jelly-fish lay steaming. There was a faintly stagnant smell and a whiff of tar from the fishing-boat against which Tonio Kröger leaned, so standing that he had before his eyes not the Swedish coast but the open horizon, and in his face the pure, fresh breath of the softly breathing sea.

Then grey, stormy days would come. The waves lowered their heads like bulls and charged against the beach; they ran and ramped high up the sands and left them strewn with shining wet sea-grass, driftwood, and mussels. All abroad beneath an overcast sky extended ranges of billows, and between them foaming valleys palely green; but above the spot where the sun hung behind the cloud a patch like white velvet lay on the sea.

Tonio Kröger stood wrapped in wind and tumult, sunk in the continual dull, drowsy uproar that he loved. When he turned away it seemed suddenly warm and silent all about him. But he was never unconscious of the sea at his back; it called, it lured, it beckoned him. And he smiled.

He went landward, by lonely meadow-paths, and was swallowed up in the beech-groves that clothed the rolling landscape near and far. Here he sat down on the moss, against a tree, and gazed at the strip of water he could see between the trunks. Sometimes the sound of surf came on the wind—a noise like boards collapsing at a distance. And from the tree-tops over his head a cawing—hoarse, desolate, forlorn. He held a book on his knee, but did not read a line. He enjoyed profound forgetfulness, hovered disembodied above space and time; only now and again his heart would contract with a fugitive pain, a stab of longing and regret, into whose origin he was too lazy to inquire.

Thus passed some days. He could not have said how many and had no desire to know. But then came one on which something happened; happened while the sun stood in the sky and people were about; and Tonio Kröger, even, felt no vast surprise.

The very opening of the day had been rare and festal. Tonio Kröger woke early and suddenly from his sleep, with a vague and exquisite alarm; he seemed to be looking at a miracle, a magic illumination. His room had a glass door and balcony facing the sound; a thin white gauze curtain divided it into living- and sleeping-quarters, both hung with delicately tinted paper and furnished with an airy good taste that gave them a sunny and friendly look. But now to his sleep-drunken eyes it lay bathed in a serene and roseate light, and unearthly brightness that gilded walls and furniture and turned the gauze curtain to radiant pink cloud. Tonio Kröger did not at once understand. Not until he stood at the glass door and looked out did he realize that this was the sunrise.

For several days there had been clouds and rain; but now the sky was like a piece of pale-blue silk, spanned shimmering above sea and land, and shot with light from red and golden clouds. The sun's disk rose in splendour from a crisply glittering sea that seemed to quiver and burn beneath it. So began the day. In a joyous daze Tonio Kröger flung on his clothes, and breakfasting in the veranda before everybody else, swam from the little wooden bath-house some distance out into the sound, then walked for an hour along the beach. When he came back, several omnibuses were before the door, and from the dining-room he could see people in the parlour next door where the piano was, in the veranda, and on the terrace in front; quantities of people sitting at little tables enjoying beer and sandwiches amid lively discourse. There were whole families, there were old and young, there were even a few children.

At second breakfast—the table was heavily laden with cold viands, roast, pickled, and smoked—Tonio Kröger inquired what was going on.

"Guests," said the fish-dealer. "Tourists and ball-guests from Helsingör. Lord help us, we shall get no sleep this night! There will be dancing and music, and I fear me it will keep up till late. It is a family reunion, a sort of celebration and excursion combined; they all subscribe to it and take advantage of the good weather. They came by boat and bus and they are having breakfast. After that they go on with their drive, but at night they will all come back for a dance here in the hall. Yes, damn it, you'll see we shan't get a wink of sleep."

"Oh, it will be a pleasant change," said Tonio Kröger.

After that there was nothing more said for some time. The landlady arranged her red fingers on the cloth, the fish-dealer blew through his nostril, the Americans drank hot water and made long faces.

Then all at once a thing came to pass: *Hans Hansen and Ingeborg Holm walked through the room.*

Tonio Kröger, pleasantly fatigued after his swim and rapid walk, was leaning back in his chair and eating smoked salmon on toast; he sat facing the veranda and the ocean. All at once the door opened and the two entered hand-in-hand—calmly and unhurried. Ingeborg, blonde Inge, was dressed just as she used to be at Herr Knaak's dancing-class. The light flowered frock reached down to her ankles and it had a tulle fichu draped with a pointed opening that left her soft throat free. Her hat hung by its ribbons over her arm. She, perhaps, was a little more grown up than she used to be, and her wonderful plait of hair was wound round her head; but Hans Hansen was the same as ever. He wore his sailor overcoat with gilt buttons, and his wide blue sailor collar lay across his shoulders and back; the sailor cap with its short ribbons he was dangling carelessly in his hand. Ingeborg's narrow eyes were turned away; perhaps she felt shy before the company at table. But Hans Hansen turned his head straight towards them, and measured one after another defiantly with his steel-blue eyes; challengingly, with a sort of contempt. He even dropped Ingeborg's hand and swung his cap harder than ever, to show what manner of man he was. Thus the two, against the silent, blue-dyed sea, measured the length of the room and passed through the opposite door into the parlour.

This was at half past eleven in the morning. While the guests of the house were still at table the company in the veranda broke up and went away by the side door. No one else came into the dining-room. The guests could hear them laughing and joking as they got into the omnibuses, which rumbled away one by one. . . . "So they are coming back?" asked Tonio Kröger.

"That they are," said the fish-dealer. "More's the pity. They have ordered music, let me tell you—and my room is right above the dining-room."

"Oh, well, it's a pleasant change," repeated Tonio Kröger. Then he got up and went away.

That day he spent as he had the others, on the beach and in the wood, holding a book on his knee and blinking in the sun. He had but one thought; they were coming back to have a dance in the hall, the fish-dealer had promised they would; and he did nothing but be glad of this, with a sweet and timorous gladness such as he had not felt through all these long dead years. Once he happened, by some chance association, to think of his friend Adalbert, the novelist, the man who had known what he wanted and betaken himself to the café to get away from the spring. Tonio Kröger shrugged his shoulders at the thought of him.

Luncheon was served earlier than usual, also supper, which they ate in the parlour because the dining-room was being got ready for the ball, and the whole house flung in disorder for the occasion. It grew dark; Tonio Kröger sitting in his room heard on the road and in the house the sounds of approaching festivity. The picnickers were coming back; from Helsingör, by bicycle and carriage, new guests were arriving; a fiddle and a nasal clarinet might be heard practising down in the dining-room. Everything promised a brilliant ball. . . .

Now the little orchestra struck up a march, he could hear the notes, faint but lively. The dancing opened with a polonaise. Tonio Kröger sat for a while and listened. But when he heard the march-time go over into a waltz he got up and slipped noiselessly out of his room.

From his corridor it was possible to go by the side stairs to the side entrance of the hotel and thence to the veranda without passing through a room. He took this route, softly and stealthily as though on forbidden paths, feeling along through the dark, relentlessly drawn by this stupid jigging music, that now came up to him loud and clear.

The veranda was empty and dim, but the glass door stood open into the hall, where shone two large oil lamps, furnished with bright reflectors. Thither he stole on soft feet; and his skin prickled with the thievish pleasure of standing unseen in the dark and spying on the dancers there in the brightly lighted room. Quickly and eagerly he glanced about for the two whom he sought. . . .

Even though the ball was only half an hour old, the merriment seemed in full swing; however, the guests had come hither already warm and merry, after a whole day of carefree, happy companionship. By bending forward a little, Tonio Kröger could see into the parlour from where he was. Several old gentlemen sat there smoking, drinking, and playing cards; others were with their wives on the plush-upholstered chairs in the foreground watching the dance. They sat with their knees apart and their hands resting on them, puffing out their cheeks with a prosperous air; the mothers, with bonnets perched on their parted hair, with their hands folded over their stomachs and their heads on one side, gazed into the whirl of dancers. A platform had been erected on the long side of the hall, and on it the musicians were doing their utmost. There was even a trumpet, that blew with a certain caution, as though afraid of its own voice, and yet after all kept breaking and cracking. Couples were dipping and circling about, others walked arm-in-arm up and down the room. No one wore ballroom clothes; they were dressed as for an outing in the summertime: the men in countrified suits which were obviously their Sunday wear; the girls in light-coloured frocks with bunches of field-flowers in their bodices. Even a few children were there, dancing with each other in their own way, even after the music stopped. There was a long-legged man in a coat with a little swallow-tail, a provincial lion with an eye-glass and frizzed hair, a post-office clerk or some such thing; he was like a comic figure stepped bodily out of a Danish novel; and he seemed to be the leader and manager of the ball. He was everywhere at once, bustling, perspiring, officious, utterly absorbed; setting down his feet, in shiny, pointed, military half-boots, in a very artificial and involved manner, toes first; waving his arms to issue an order, clapping his hands for the music to begin; here, there, and everywhere, and glancing over his shoulder in pride at his great bow of office, the streamers of which fluttered grandly in his rear.

Yes, there they were, those two, who had gone by Tonio Kröger in the broad light of day; he saw them again—with a joyful start he recognized them almost at the same moment. Here was Hans Hansen by the door, quite close; his legs apart, a little bent over, he was eating with circumspection a large piece of sponge-cake, holding his hand cupwise under his chin to catch the crumbs. And there by the wall sat Ingeborg Holm, Inge the fair; the post-office clerk was just mincing up to her with an exaggerated bow and asking her to dance. He laid one hand on his back and gracefully shoved the other into his bosom. But she was shaking her head in token that she was a little out of breath and must rest awhile, whereat the post-office clerk sat down by her side.

Tonio Kröger looked at them both, these two for whom he had in time past suffered love—at Hans and Ingeborg. They were Hans and Ingeborg not so much by virtue of individual traits and similarity of costume as by similarity of race and type. This was the blond, fair-haired breed of the steel-blue eyes, which stood to him for the pure, the blithe, the untroubled in life; for a virginal aloofness that was at once both simple and full of pride. . . . He looked at them. Hans Hansen was standing there in his sailor suit, lively and well built as ever, broad in the shoulders and narrow in the hips; Ingeborg was laughing and tossing her head in a certain high-spirited way she had; she carried her hand, a schoolgirl hand, not at all slender, not at all particularly aristocratic, to the back of her head in a certain manner so that the thin sleeve fell away from her elbow—and suddenly such a pang of home-sickness shook his breast that involuntarily he drew farther back into the darkness lest someone might see his features twitch.

"Had I forgotten you?" he asked. "No, never. Not thee, Hans, not thee, Inge the fair! It was always you I worked for; when I heard applause I always stole a look to see if you were there. . . . Did you read *Don Carlos*, Hans Hansen, as you promised me at the garden gate? No, don't read it! I do not ask it any more. What have you to do with a king who weeps for loneliness? You must not cloud your clear eyes or make them dreamy and dim by peering into melancholy poetry. . . . To be like you! To begin again, to grow up like you, regular like you, simple and normal and cheerful, in conformity and understanding with God and man, beloved of the innocent and happy. To take you, Ingeborg Holm, to wife, and have a son like you, Hans Hansen—to live free from the curse of knowledge and the torment of creation, live and praise God in blessed mediocrity! Begin again? But it would do no good. It would turn out the same—everything would turn out the same as it did before. For some go of necessity astray, because for them there is no such thing as a right path."

The music ceased; there was a pause in which refreshments were handed round. The post-office assistant tripped about in person with a trayful of herring salad and served the ladies; but before Ingeborg Holm he even went down on one knee as he passed her the dish, and she blushed for pleasure.

But now those within began to be aware of a spectator behind the glass door; some of the flushed and pretty faces turned to measure him with hostile glances; but he stood his ground. Ingeborg and Hans looked at him too, at almost the same time, both with that utter indifference in their eyes that looks so like contempt. And he was conscious too of a gaze resting on him from a different quarter; turned his head and met with his own the eyes that had sought him out. A girl stood not far off, with a fine, pale little face—he had already noticed her. She had not danced much, she had few partners, and he had seen her sitting there against the wall, her lips closed in a bitter line. She was standing alone now too; her dress was a thin light stuff, like the others, but beneath the transparent frock her shoulders showed angular and poor, and the thin neck was thrust down so deep between those meagre shoulders that as she stood there motionless she might almost be thought a little deformed. She was holding her hands in their thin mitts across her flat breast, with the fingertips touching; her head was drooped, yet she was looking up at Tonio Kröger with black swimming eyes. He turned away. . . .

Here, quite close to him, were Ingeborg and Hans. He had sat down beside her—she was perhaps his sister—and they ate and drank together surrounded by other rosy-cheeked folk; they chattered and made merry, called to each other in ringing voices, and laughed aloud. Why could he not go up and speak to them? Make some trivial remark to him or her, to which they might at least answer with a smile? It would make him happy—he longed to do it; he would go back more satisfied to his room if he might feel he had established a little contact with them. He thought out what he might say; but he had not the courage to say it. Yes, this too was just as it had been: they would not understand him, they would listen like strangers to anything he was able to say. For their speech was not his speech.

It seemed the dance was about to begin again. The leader developed a comprehensive activity. He dashed hither and thither, adjuring everybody to get partners; helped the waiters to push chairs and glasses out of the way, gave orders to the musicians, even took some awkward people by the shoulders and shoved them aside. . . . What was coming? They formed squares of four couples each. . . . A frightful memory brought the colour to Tonio Kröger's cheeks. They were forming for a quadrille.

The music struck up, the couples bowed and crossed over. The leader called off; he called off—Heaven save us—in French! And pronounced the nasals with great distinction. Ingeborg Holm danced close by, in the set nearest the glass door. She moved to and fro before him, forwards and back, pacing and turning; he caught a waft from her hair or the thin stuff of her frock, and it made him close his eyes with the old, familiar feeling, the fragrance and bitter-sweet enchantment he had faintly felt in all these days, that now filled him utterly with irresistible sweetness. And what was the feeling? Longing, tenderness? Envy? Self-contempt? . . . *Moulinet des dames!* "Did you laugh, Ingeborg the blonde, did you laugh at me when I disgraced myself by dancing the *moulinet*? And would you still laugh today even after I have become something like a famous man? Yes, that you would, and you would be right to laugh. Even if I in my own person had written the nine symphonies and *The World as Will and Idea* and painted the Last Judgment, you would still be eternally right to laugh. . . ." As he looked at her he thought of a line of verse once so familiar to him, now long forgotten: "I would sleep, but thou must dance." How well he knew it, that melancholy northern mood it evoked—its heavy inarticulateness. To sleep. . . . To long to be allowed to live the life of simple feeling, to rest sweetly and passively in feeling alone, without compulsion to act and achieve—and yet to be forced to dance, dance the cruel and perilous sword-dance of art; without even being allowed to forget the melancholy conflict within oneself; to be forced to dance, the while one loved. . . .

A sudden wild extravagance had come over the scene. The sets had broken up, the quadrille was being succeeded by a galop, and all the couples were leaping and gliding about. They flew past Tonio Kröger to a maddeningly quick tempo, crossing, advancing, retreating, with quick, breathless laughter. A couple came rushing and circling towards Tonio Kröger; the girl had a pale, refined face and lean, high shoulders. Suddenly, directly in front of him, they tripped and slipped and stumbled. . . . The pale girl fell, so hard and violently it almost looked dangerous; and her partner with her. He must have hurt himself badly, for he quite forgot her, and, half rising, began to rub his knee and grimace; while she, quite dazed, it seemed, still lay on the floor. Then Tonio Kröger came forward, took her gently by the arms, and lifted her up. She looked dazed, bewildered, wretched; then suddenly her delicate face flushed pink.

"*Tak, O, mange tak!*" she said, and gazed up at him with dark, swimming eyes.

"You should not dance any more, Fräulein," he said gently. Once more he looked round at *them*, at Ingeborg and Hans, and then he went out, left the ball and the veranda and returned to his own room.

He was exhausted with jealousy, worn out with the gaiety in which he had had no part. Just the same, just the same as it had always been. Always with burning cheeks he had stood in his dark corner and suffered for you, you blond, you living, you happy ones! And then quite simply gone away. Somebody *must* come now! Ingeborg *must* notice he had gone, must slip after him, lay a hand on his shoulder and say: "Come back and be happy. I love you!" But she came not at all. No, such things did not happen. Yes, all was as it had been, and he too was happy, just as he had been. For his heart was alive. But between that past and this present what had happened to make him become that which he now was? Icy desolation, solitude: mind, and art, forsooth!

He undressed, lay down, put out the light. Two names he whispered into his pillow, the few chaste northern syllables that meant for him his true and native way of love, of longing and happiness; that meant to him life and home, meant simple and heartfelt feeling. He looked back on the years that had passed. He thought of the dreamy adventures of the senses, nerves, and mind in which he had been involved; saw himself eaten up with intellect and introspection, ravaged and paralysed by insight, half worn out by the fevers and frosts of creation, helpless and in anguish of conscience between two extremes, flung to and fro between austerity and lust; *raffiné*, impoverished, exhausted by frigid and artificially heightened ecstasies; erring, forsaken, martyred, and ill—and sobbed with nostalgia and remorse.

Here in his room it was still and dark. But from below life's lulling, trivial waltz-rhythm came faintly to his ears.

Tonio Kröger sat up in the north, composing his promised letter to his friend Lisabeta Ivanovna.

"Dear Lisabeta down there in Arcady, whither I shall shortly return," he wrote: "Here is something like a letter, but it will probably disappoint you, for I mean to keep it rather general. Not that I have nothing to tell; for indeed, in my way, I have had experiences; for instance, in my native town they were even going to arrest me . . . but of that by word of mouth. Sometimes now I have days when I would rather state things in general terms than go on telling stories.

"You probably still remember, Lisabeta, that you called me a *bourgeois*, a *bourgeois manqué*? You called me that in an hour when, led on by other confessions I had previously let slip, I confessed to you my love of life, or what I call life. I ask myself if you were aware how very close you came to the truth, how much my love of 'life' is one and the same thing as my being a *bourgeois*. This journey of mine has given me much occasion to ponder the subject.

"My father, you know, had the temperament of the north: solid, reflective, puritanically correct, with a tendency to melancholia. My mother, of indeterminate foreign blood, was beautiful, sensuous, naïve, passionate, and careless at once, and, I think, irregular by instinct. The mixture was no doubt extraordinary and bore with it extraordinary dangers. The issue of it, a *bourgeois* who strayed off into art, a bohemian who feels nostalgic yearnings for respectability, an artist with a bad conscience. For surely it is my *bourgeois* conscience makes me see in the artist life, in all irregularity and all genius, something profoundly suspect, profoundly disreputable, that fills me with this lovelorn *faiblesse* for the simple and good, the comfortably normal, the average unendowed respectable human being.

"I stand between two worlds. I am at home in neither, and I suffer in consequence. You artists call me a *bourgeois,* and the *bourgeois* try to arrest me. . . . I don't know which makes me feel worse. The *bourgeois* are stupid; but you adorers of the beautiful, who call me phlegmatic and without aspirations, you ought to realize that there is a way of being an artist that goes so deep and is so much a matter of origins and destinies that no longing seems to it sweeter and more worth knowing than longing after the bliss of the commonplace.

"I admire those proud, cold beings who adventure upon the paths of great and dæmonic beauty and despise 'mankind'; but I do not envy them. For if anything is capable of making a poet of a literary man, it is my *bourgeois* love of the human, the living and usual. It is the source of all warmth, goodness, and humour; I even almost think it is itself that love of which it stands written that one may speak with the tongues of men and of angels and yet having it not is as sounding brass and tinkling cymbals.

"The work I have so far done is nothing or not much—as good as nothing. I will do better, Lisabeta—this is a promise. As I write, the sea whispers to me and I close my eyes. I am looking into a world unborn and formless, that needs to be ordered and shaped; I see into a whirl of shadows of human figures who beckon to me to weave spells to redeem them: tragic and laughable figures and some that are both together—and to these I am drawn. But my deepest and secretest love belongs to the blond and blue-eyed, the fair and living, the happy, lovely, and commonplace.

"Do not chide this love, Lisabeta; it is good and fruitful. There is longing in it, and a gentle envy; a touch of contempt and no little innocent bliss."

WILLIAM FAULKNER

The Bear

There was a man and a dog too this time. Two beasts, counting Old Ben, the bear, and two men, counting Boon Hogganbeck, in whom some of the same blood ran which ran in Sam Fathers, even though Boon's was a plebeian strain of it and only Sam and Old Ben and the mongrel Lion were taintless and incorruptible.

He was sixteen. For six years now he had been a man's hunter. For six years now he had heard the best of all talking. It was of the wilderness, the big woods, bigger and older than any recorded document:—of white man fatuous enough to believe he had bought any fragment of it, of Indian ruthless enough to pretend that any fragment of it had been his to convey; bigger than Major de Spain and the scrap he pretended to, knowing better; older than old Thomas Sutpen of whom Major de Spain had had it and who knew better; older even than old Ikkemotubbe, the Chickasaw chief, of whom old Sutpen had had it and who knew better in his turn. It was of the men, not white nor black nor red but men, hunters, with the will and hardihood to endure and the humility and skill to survive, and the dogs and the bear and deer juxtaposed and reliefed against it, ordered and compelled by and within the wilderness in the ancient and unremitting contest according to the ancient and immitigable rules which voided all regrets and brooked no quarter;—the best game of all, the best of all breathing and forever the best of all listening, the voices quiet and weighty and deliberate for retrospection and recollection and exactitude among the concrete trophies—the racked guns and the heads and skins—in the libraries of town houses or the offices of plantation houses or (and best of all) in the camps themselves where the intact and still-warm meat yet hung, the men who had slain it sitting before the burning logs on hearths when there were houses and hearths or about the smoky blazing of piled wood in front of stretched tarpaulins when there were not. There was always a bottle present, so that it would seem to him that those fine fierce instants of heart and brain and courage and wiliness and speed were concentrated and distilled into that brown liquor which not women, nor boys and children, but only hunters drank, drinking not of the blood they spilled but some condensation of the wild immortal spirit, drinking it moderately, humbly even, not with the pagan's base and baseless hope of acquiring thereby the virtues of cunning and strength and speed but in salute to them. Thus it seemed to him on this December morning not only natural but actually fitting that this should have begun with whisky.

He realized later that it had begun long before that. It had already begun on that day when he first wrote his age in two ciphers and his cousin McCaslin brought him for the first time to the camp, the big woods, to earn for himself from the wilderness the name and state of hunter provided he in his turn were humble and enduring enough. He had already inherited then, without ever having seen it, the big old bear with one trap-ruined foot that in an area almost a hundred miles square had earned for himself a name, a definite designation like a living man:—the long legend of corn-cribs broken down and rifled, of shoats and grown pigs and even calves carried bodily into the woods and devoured and traps and deadfalls overthrown and dogs mangled and slain and shotgun and even rifle shots delivered at point-blank range yet with no more effect than so many peas blown through a tube by a child—a corridor of wreckage and destruction beginning back before the boy was born, through which sped, not fast but rather with the ruthless and irresistible deliberation of a locomotive, the shaggy tremendous shape. It ran in his knowledge before he ever saw it. It loomed and towered in his dreams before he even saw the unaxed woods where it left its crooked print, shaggy, tremendous, red-eyed, not malevolent but just big, too big for the dogs which tried to bay it, for the horses which tried to ride it down, for the men and the bullets they fired into it; too big for the very country which was its constricting scope. It was as if the boy had already divined what his senses and intellect had not encompassed yet: that doomed wilderness whose edges were being constantly and punily gnawed at by men with plows and axes who feared it because it was wilderness, men myriad and nameless even to one another in the land where the old bear had earned a name, and through which ran not even a mortal beast but an anachronism indomitable and invincible out of an old dead time, a phantom, epitome and apotheosis of the old wild life which the little puny humans swarmed and hacked at in a fury of abhorrence and fear like pygmies about the ankles of a drowsing elephant;—the old bear, solitary, indomitable, and alone; widowered childless and absolved of mortality—old Priam reft of his old wife and outlived all his sons.

Still a child, with three years then two years then one year yet before he too could make one of them, each November he would watch the wagon containing the dogs and the bedding and food and guns and his cousin McCaslin and Tennie's Jim and Sam Fathers too until Sam moved to the camp to live, depart for the Big Bottom, the big woods. To him, they were going not to hunt bear and deer but to keep yearly rendezvous with the bear which they did not even intend to kill. Two weeks later they would return, with no trophy, no skin. He had not expected it. He had not even feared that it might be in the wagon this time with the other skins and heads. He did not even tell himself that in three years or two years or one year more he would be present and that it might even be his gun. He believed that only after he had served his apprenticeship in the woods which would prove him worthy to be a hunter, would he even be permitted to distinguish the crooked print, and that even then for two November weeks he would merely make another minor one, along with his cousin and Major de Spain and General Compson and Walter Ewell and Boon and the dogs which feared to bay it and the shotguns and rifles which failed even to bleed it, in the yearly pageant-rite of the old bear's furious immortality.

His day came at last. In the surrey with his cousin and Major de Spain and General Compson he saw the wilderness through a slow drizzle of November rain just above the ice point as it seemed to him later he always saw it or at least always remembered it—the tall and endless wall of dense November woods under the dissolving afternoon and the year's death, sombre, impenetrable (he could not even discern yet how, at what point they could possibly hope to enter it even though he knew that Sam Fathers was waiting there with the wagon), the surrey moving through the skeleton stalks of cotton and corn in the last of open country, the last trace of man's puny gnawing at the immemorial flank, until, dwarfed by that perspective into an almost ridiculous diminishment, the surrey itself seemed to have ceased to move (this too to be completed later, years later, after he had grown to a man and had seen the sea) as a solitary small boat hangs in lonely immobility, merely tossing up and down, in the infinite waste of the ocean while the water and then the apparently impenetrable land which it nears without appreciable progress, swings slowly and opens the widening inlet which is the anchorage. He entered it. Sam was waiting, wrapped in a quilt on the wagon seat behind the patient and steaming mules. He entered his novitiate to the true wilderness with Sam beside him as he had begun his apprenticeship in miniature to manhood after the rabbits and such with Sam beside him, the two of them wrapped in the damp, warm, negro-rank quilt, while the wilderness closed behind his entrance as it had opened momentarily to accept him, opening before his advancement as it closed behind his progress, no fixed path the wagon followed but a channel non-existent ten yards ahead of it and ceasing to exist ten yards after it had passed, the wagon progressing not by its own volition but by attrition of their intact yet fluid circumambience, drowsing, earless, almost lightless.

It seemed to him that at the age of ten he was witnessing his own birth. It was not even strange to him. He had experienced it all before, and not merely in dreams. He saw the camp—a paintless six-room bungalow set on piles above the spring high-water—and he knew already how it was going to look. He helped in the rapid orderly disorder of their establishment in it and even his motions were familiar to him, foreknown. Then for two weeks he ate the coarse, rapid food—the shapeless sour bread, the wild strange meat, venison and bear and turkey and coon which he had never tasted before—which men ate, cooked by men who were hunters first and cooks afterward; he slept in harsh sheetless blankets as hunters slept. Each morning the gray of dawn found him and Sam Fathers on the stand, the crossing, which had been allotted him. It was the poorest one, the most barren. He had expected that; he had not dared yet to hope even to himself that he would even hear the running dogs this first time. But he did hear them. It was on the third morning—a murmur, sourceless, almost indistinguishable, yet he knew what it was although he had never before heard that many dogs running at once, the murmur swelling into separate and distinct voices until he could call the five dogs which his cousin owned from among the others. "Now," Sam said, "slant your gun up a little and draw back the hammers and then stand still."

But it was not for him, not yet. The humility was there; he had learned that. And he could learn the patience. He was only ten, only one week. The instant had passed. It seemed to him that he could actually see the deer, the buck, smoke-colored, elongated with speed, vanished, the woods, the gray solitude still ringing even when the voices of the dogs had died away; from far away across the sombre woods and the gray half-liquid morning there came two shots. "Now let your hammers down," Sam said.

He did so. "You knew it too," he said.

"Yes," Sam said. "I want you to learn how to do when you didn't shoot. It's after the chance for the bear or the deer has done already come and gone that men and dogs get killed."

"Anyway, it wasn't him," the boy said. "It wasn't even a bear. It was just a deer."

"Yes," Sam said, "it was just a deer."

Then one morning, it was in the second week, he heard the dogs again. This time before Sam even spoke he readied the too-long, too-heavy, man-sized gun as Sam had taught him, even though this time he knew the dogs and the deer were coming less close than ever, hardly within hearing even. They didn't sound like any running dogs he had ever heard before even. Then he found that Sam, who had taught him first of all to cock the gun and take position where he could see best in all directions and then never to move again, had himself moved up beside him. "There," he said. "Listen." The boy listened, to no ringing chorus strong and fast on a free scent but a moiling yapping an octave too high and with something more than indecision and even abjectness in it which he could not yet recognize, reluctant, not even moving very fast, taking a long time to pass out of hearing, leaving even then in the air that echo of thin and almost human hysteria, abject, almost humanly grieving, with this time nothing ahead of it, no sense of a fleeing unseen smoke-colored shape. He could hear Sam breathing at his shoulder. He saw the arched curve of the old man's inhaling nostrils.

"It's Old Ben!" he cried, whispering.

Sam didn't move save for the slow gradual turning of his head as the voices faded on and the faint steady rapid arch and collapse of his nostrils. "Hah," he said. "Not even running. Walking."

"But up here!" the boy cried. "Way up here!"

"He do it every year," Sam said. "Once. Ash and Boon say he comes up here to run the other little bears away. Tell them to get to hell out of here and stay out until the hunters are gone. Maybe." The boy no longer heard anything at all, yet still Sam's head continued to turn gradually and steadily until the back of it was toward him. Then it turned back and looked down at him—the same face, grave, familiar, expressionless until it smiled, the same old man's eyes from which as he watched there faded slowly a quality darkly and fiercely lambent, passionate and proud. "He dont care no more for bears than he does for dogs or men neither. He come to see who's here, who's new in camp this year, whether he can shoot or not, can stay or not. Whether we got the dog yet that can bay and hold him until a man gets there with a gun. Because he's the head bear. He's the man." It faded, was gone; again they were the eyes as he had known them all his life. "He'll let them follow him to the river. Then he'll send them home. We might as well go too; see how they look when they get back to camp."

The dogs were there first, ten of them huddled back under the kitchen, himself and Sam squatting to peer back into the obscurity where they crouched, quiet, the eyes rolling and luminous, vanishing, and no sound, only that effluvium which the boy could not quite place yet, of something more than dog, stronger than dog and not just animal, just beast even. Because there had been nothing in front of the abject and painful yapping except the solitude, the wilderness, so that when the eleventh hound got back about mid-afternoon and he and Tennie's Jim held the passive and still trembling bitch while Sam daubed her tattered ear and raked shoulder with turpentine and axle-grease, it was still no living creature but only the wilderness which, leaning for a moment, had patted lightly once her temerity. "Just like a man," Sam said. "Just like folks. Put off as long as she could having to be brave, knowing all the time that sooner or later she would have to be brave once so she could keep on calling herself a dog, and knowing beforehand what was going to happen when she done it."

He did not know just when Sam left. He only knew that he was gone. For the next three mornings he rose and ate breakfast and Sam was not waiting for him. He went to his stand alone; he found it without help now and stood on it as Sam had taught him. On the third morning he heard the dogs again, running strong and free on a true scent again, and he readied the gun as he had learned to do and heard the hunt sweep past on since he was not ready yet, had not deserved other yet in just one short period of two weeks as compared to all the long life which he had already dedicated to the wilderness with patience and humility; he heard the shot again, one shot, the single clapping report of Walter Ewell's rifle. By now he could not only find his stand and then return to camp without guidance, by using the compass his cousin had given him he reached Walter, waiting beside the buck and the moiling of dogs over the cast entrails before any of the others except Major de Spain and Tennie's Jim on the horses, even before Uncle Ash arrived with the one-eyed wagon-mule which did not mind the smell of blood or even, so they said, of bear.

It was not Uncle Ash on the mule. It was Sam, returned. And Sam was waiting when he finished his dinner and, himself on the one-eyed mule and Sam on the other one of the wagon team, they rode for more than three hours through the rapid shortening sunless afternoon, following no path, no trail even that he could discern, into a section of country he had never seen before. Then he understood why Sam had made him ride the one-eyed mule which would not spook at the smell of blood, of wild animals. The other one, the sound one, stopped short and tried to whirl and bolt even as Sam got down, jerking and wrenching at the rein while Sam held it, coaxing it forward with his voice since he did not dare risk hitching it, drawing it forward while the boy dismounted from the marred one which would stand. Then, standing beside Sam in the thick great gloom of ancient woods and the winter's dying afternoon, he looked quietly down at the rotted log scored and gutted with claw-marks and, in the wet earth beside it, the print of the enormous warped two-toed foot. Now he knew what he had heard in the hounds' voices in the woods that morning and what he had smelled when he peered under the kitchen where they huddled. It was in him too, a little different because they were brute beasts and he was not, but only a little different—an eagerness, passive; an abjectness, a sense of his own fragility and impotence against the timeless woods, yet without doubt or dread; a flavor like brass in the sudden run of saliva in his mouth, a hard sharp constriction either in his brain or his stomach, he could not tell which and it did not matter; he knew only that for the first time he realized that the bear which had run in his listening and loomed in his dreams since before he could remember and which therefore must have existed in the listening and the dreams of his cousin and Major de Spain and even old General Compson before they began to remember in their turn, was a mortal animal and that they had departed for the camp each November with no actual intention of slaying it, not because it could not be slain but because so far they had no actual hope of being able to. "It will be tomorrow," he said.

"You mean we will try tomorrow," Sam said. "We aint got the dog yet."

"We've got eleven," he said. "They ran him Monday."

"And you heard them," Sam said. "Saw them too. We aint got the dog yet. It wont take but one. But he aint there. Maybe he aint nowhere. The only other way will be for him to run by accident over somebody that had a gun and knowed how to shoot it."

"That wouldn't be me," the boy said. "It would be Walter or Major or—"

"It might," Sam said. "You watch close tomorrow. Because he's smart. That's how come he has lived this long. If he gets hemmed up and has got to pick out somebody to run over, he will pick out you."

"How?" he said. "How will he know. . . ." He ceased. "You mean he already knows me, that I aint never been to the big bottom before, aint had time to find out yet whether I . . ." He ceased again, staring at Sam; he said humbly, not even amazed: "It was me he was watching. I dont reckon he did need to come but once."

"You watch tomorrow," Sam said. "I reckon we better start back. It'll be long after dark now before we get to camp."

The next morning they started three hours earlier than they had ever done. Even Uncle Ash went, the cook, who called himself by profession a camp cook and who did little else save cook for Major de Spain's hunting and camping parties, yet who had been marked by the wilderness from simple juxtaposition to it until he responded as they all did, even the boy who until two weeks ago had never even seen the wilderness, to a hound's ripped ear and shoulder and the print of a crooked foot in a patch of wet earth. They rode. It was too far to walk: the boy and Sam and Uncle Ash in the wagon with the dogs, his cousin and Major de Spain and General Compson and Boon and Walter and Tennie's Jim riding double on the horses; again the first gray light found him, as on that first morning two weeks ago, on the stand where Sam had placed and left him. With the gun which was too big for him, the breech-loader which did not even belong to him but to Major de Spain and which he had fired only once, at a stump on the first day to learn the recoil and how to reload it with the paper shells, he stood against a big gum tree beside a little bayou whose black still water crept without motion out of a cane-brake, across a small clearing and into the cane again, where, invisible, a bird, the big woodpecker called Lord-to-God by negroes, clattered at a dead trunk. It was a stand like any other stand, dissimilar only in incidentals to the one where he had stood each morning for two weeks; a territory new to him yet no less familiar than that other one which after two weeks he had come to believe he knew a little—the same solitude, the same loneliness through which frail and timorous man had merely passed without altering it, leaving no mark nor scar, which looked exactly as it must have looked when the first ancestor of Sam Fathers' Chickasaw predecessors crept into it and looked about him, club or stone axe or bone arrow drawn and ready, different only because, squatting at the edge of the kitchen, he had smelled the dogs huddled and cringing beneath it and saw the raked ear and side of the bitch that, as Sam had said, had to be brave once in order to keep on calling herself a dog, and saw yesterday in the earth beside the gutted log, the print of the living foot. He heard no dogs at all. He never did certainly hear them. He only heard the drumming of the woodpecker stop short off, and knew that the bear was looking at him. He never saw it. He did not know whether it was facing him from the cane or behind him. He did not move, holding the useless gun which he knew now he would never fire at it, now or ever, tasting in his saliva that taint of brass which he had smelled in the huddled dogs when he peered under the kitchen.

Then it was gone. As abruptly as it had stopped, the woodpecker's dry hammering set up again, and after a while he believed he even heard the dogs—a murmur, scarce a sound even, which he had probably been hearing for a time, perhaps a minute or two, before he remarked it, drifting into hearing and then out again, dying away. They came nowhere near him. If it was dogs he heard, he could not have sworn to it; if it was a bear they ran, it was another bear. It was Sam himself who emerged from the cane and crossed the bayou, the injured bitch following at heel as a bird dog is taught to walk. She came and crouched against his leg, trembling. "I didn't see him," he said. "I didn't, Sam."

"I know it," Sam said. "He done the looking. You didn't hear him neither, did you?"

"No," the boy said. "I—"

"He's smart," Sam said. "Too smart." Again the boy saw in his eyes that quality of dark and brooding lambence as Sam looked down at the bitch trembling faintly and steadily against the boy's leg. From her raked shoulder a few drops of fresh blood clung like bright berries. "Too big. We aint got the dog yet. But maybe some day."

Because there would be a next time, after and after. He was only ten. It seemed to him that he could see them, the two of them, shadowy in the limbo from which time emerged and became time: the old bear absolved of mortality and himself who shared a little of it. Because he recognised now what he had smelled in the huddled dogs and tasted in his own saliva, recognised fear as a boy, a youth, recognises the existence of love and passion and experience which is his heritage but not yet his patrimony, from entering by chance the presence or perhaps even merely the bedroom of a woman who has loved and been loved by many men. *So I will have to see him,* he thought, without dread or even hope. *I will have to look at him.* So it was in June of the next summer. They were at the camp again, celebrating Major de Spain's and General Compson's birthdays. Although the one had been born in September and the other in the depth of winter and almost thirty years earlier, each June the two of them and McCaslin and Boon and Walter Ewell (and the boy too from now on) spent two weeks at the camp, fishing and shooting squirrels and turkey and running coons and wildcats with the dogs at night. That is, Boon and the negroes (and the boy too now) fished and shot squirrels and ran the coons and cats, because the proven hunters, not only Major de Spain and old General Compson (who spent those two weeks sitting in a rocking chair before a tremendous iron pot of Brunswick stew, stirring and tasting, with Uncle Ash to quarrel with about how he was making it and Tennie's Jim to pour whisky into the tin dipper from which he drank it), but even McCaslin and Walter Ewell who were still young enough, scorned such other than shooting the wild gobblers with pistols for wagers or to test their marksmanship.

That is, his cousin McCaslin and the others thought he was hunting squirrels. Until the third evening he believed that Sam Fathers thought so too. Each morning he would leave the camp right after breakfast. He had his own gun now, a new breech-loader, a Christmas gift; he would own and shoot it for almost seventy years, through two new pairs of barrels and locks and one new stock, until all that remained of the original gun was the silver-inlaid trigger-guard with his and McCaslin's engraved names and the date in 1878. He found the tree beside the little bayou where he had stood that morning. Using the compass he ranged from that point; he was teaching himself to be better than a fair woodsman without even knowing he was doing it. On the third day he even found the gutted log where he had first seen the print. It was almost completely crumbled now, healing with unbelievable speed, a passionate and almost visible relinquishment, back into the earth from which the tree had grown. He ranged the summer woods now, green with gloom, if anything actually dimmer than they had been in November's gray dissolution, where even at noon the sun fell only in windless dappling upon the earth which never completely dried and which crawled with snakes—moccasins and watersnakes and rattlers, themselves the color of the dappled gloom so that he would not always see them until they moved; returning to camp later and later and later, first day, second day, passing in the twilight of the third evening the little log pen enclosing the log barn where Sam was putting up the stock for the night. "You aint looked right yet," Sam said.

He stopped. For a moment he didn't answer. Then he said peacefully, in a peaceful rushing burst, as when a boy's miniature dam in a little brook gives way: "All right. Yes. But how? I went to the bayou. I even found that log again. I—"

"I reckon that was all right. Likely he's been watching you. You never saw his foot?"

"I . . ." the boy said. "I didn't . . . I never thought . . ."

"It's the gun," Sam said. He stood beside the fence, motionless, the old man, son of a negro slave and a Chickasaw chief, in the battered and faded overalls and the frayed five-cent straw hat which had been the badge of the negro's slavery and was now the regalia of his freedom. The camp—the clearing, the house, the barn and its tiny lot with which Major de Spain in his turn had scratched punily and evanescently at the wilderness—faded in the dusk, back into the immemorial darkness of the woods. *The gun,* the boy thought. *The gun.* "You will have to choose," Sam said.

He left the next morning before light, without breakfast, long before Uncle Ash would wake in his quilts on the kitchen floor and start the fire. He had only the compass and a stick for the snakes. He could go almost a mile before he would need to see the compass. He sat on a log, the invisible compass in his hand, while the secret night-sounds which had ceased at his movements, scurried again and then fell still for good and the owls ceased and gave over to the waking day birds and there was light in the gray wet woods and he could see the compass. He went fast yet still quietly, becoming steadily better and better as a woodsman without yet having time to realise it; he jumped a doe and a fawn, walked them out of the bed, close enough to see them—the crash of undergrowth, the white scut, the fawn scudding along behind her, faster than he had known it could have run. He was hunting right, upwind, as Sam had taught him, but that didn't matter now. He had left the gun, by his own will and relinquishment he had accepted not a gambit, not a choice, but a condition in which not only the bear's heretofore inviolable anonymity but all the ancient rules and balances of hunter and hunted had been abrogated. He would not even be afraid, not even in the moment when the fear would take him completely: blood, skin, bowels, bones, memory from the long time before it even became his memory—all save that thin clear quenchless lucidity which alone differed him from this bear and from all the other bears and bucks he would follow during almost seventy years, to which Sam had said: "Be scared. You cant help that. But dont be afraid. Aint nothing in the woods going to hurt you if you dont corner it or it dont smell that you are afraid. A bear or a deer has got to be scared of a coward the same as a brave man has got to be."

By noon he was far beyond the crossing on the little bayou, farther into the new and alien country than he had ever been, travelling now not only by the compass but by the old, heavy, biscuit-thick silver watch which had been his father's. He had left the camp nine hours ago; nine hours from now, dark would already have been an hour old. He stopped, for the first time since he had risen from the log when he could see the compass face at last, and looked about, mopping his sweating face on his sleeve. He had already relinquished, of his will, because of his need, in humility and peace and without regret, yet apparently that had not been enough, the leaving of the gun was not enough. He stood for a moment—a child, alien and lost in the green and soaring gloom of the markless wilderness. Then he relinquished completely to it. It was the watch and the compass. He was still tainted. He removed the linked chain of the one and the looped thong of the other from his overalls and hung them on a bush and leaned the stick beside them and entered it.

When he realised he was lost, he did as Sam had coached and drilled him: made a cast to cross his backtrack. He had not been going very fast for the last two or three hours, and he had gone even less fast since he left the compass and watch on the bush. So he went slower still now, since the tree could not be very far; in fact, he found it before he really expected to and turned and went to it. But there was no bush beneath it, no compass nor watch, so he did next as Sam had coached and drilled him: made this next circle in the opposite direction and much larger, so that the pattern of the two of them would bisect his track somewhere, but crossing no trace nor mark anywhere of his feet or any feet, and now he was going faster though still not panicked, his heart beating a little more rapidly but strong and steady enough, and this time it was not even the tree because there was a down log beside it which he had never seen before and beyond the log a little swamp, a seepage of moisture somewhere between earth and water, and he did what Sam had coached and drilled him as the next and the last, seeing as he sat down on the log the crooked print, the warped indentation in the wet ground which while he looked at it continued to fill with water until it was level full and the water began to overflow and the sides of the print began to dissolve away. Even as he looked up he saw the next one, and, moving, the one beyond it; moving, not hurrying, running, but merely keeping pace with them as they appeared before him as though they were being shaped out of thin air just one constant pace short of where he would lose them forever and be lost forever himself, tireless, eager, without doubt or dread, panting a little above the strong rapid little hammer of his heart, emerging suddenly into a little glade, and the wilderness coalesced. It rushed, soundless, and solidified—the tree, the bush, the compass and the watch glinting where a ray of sunlight touched them. Then he saw the bear. It did not emerge, appear: it was just there, immobile, fixed in the green and windless noon's hot dappling, not as big as he had dreamed it but as big as he had expected, bigger, dimensionless against the dappled obscurity, looking at him. Then it moved. It crossed the glade without haste, walking for an instant into the sun's full glare and out of it, and stopped again and looked back at him across one shoulder. Then it was gone. It didn't walk into the woods. It faded, sank back into the wilderness without motion as he had watched a fish, a huge old bass, sink back into the dark depths of its pool and vanish without even any movement of its fins.

2

So he should have hated and feared Lion. He was thirteen then. He had killed his buck and Sam Fathers had marked his face with the hot blood, and in the next November he killed a bear. But before that accolade he had become as competent in the woods as many grown men with the same experience. By now he was a better woodsman than most grown men with more. There was no territory within twenty-five miles of the camp that he did not know—bayou, ridge, landmark trees and path; he could have led anyone direct to any spot in it and brought him back. He knew game trails that even Sam Fathers had never seen; in the third fall he found a buck's bedding-place by himself and unbeknown to his cousin he borrowed Walter Ewell's rifle and lay in wait for the buck at dawn and killed it when it walked back to the bed as Sam had told him how the old Chickasaw fathers did.

By now he knew the old bear's footprint better than he did his own, and not only the crooked one. He could see any one of the three sound prints and distinguish it at once from any other, and not only because of its size. There were other bears within that fifty miles which left tracks almost as large, or at least so near that the one would have appeared larger only by juxtaposition. It was more than that. If Sam Fathers had been his mentor and the backyard rabbits and squirrels his kindergarten, then the wilderness the old bear ran was his college and the old male bear itself, so long unwifed and childless as to have become its own ungendered progenitor, was his alma mater.

He could find the crooked print now whenever he wished, ten miles or five miles or sometimes closer than that, to the camp. Twice while on stand during the next three years he heard the dogs strike its trail and once even jump it by chance, the voices high, abject, almost human in their hysteria. Once, still-hunting with Walter Ewell's rifle, he saw it cross a long corridor of down timber where a tornado had passed. It rushed through rather than across the tangle of trunks and branches as a locomotive would, faster than he had ever believed it could have moved, almost as fast as a deer even because the deer would have spent most of that distance in the air; he realised then why it would take a dog not only of abnormal courage but size and speed too ever to bring it to bay.

He had a little dog at home, a mongrel, of the sort called fyce by negroes, a ratter, itself not much bigger than a rat and possessing that sort of courage which had long since stopped being bravery and had become foolhardiness. He brought it with him one June and, timing them as if they were meeting an appointment with another human being, himself carrying the fyce with a sack over its head and Sam Fathers with a brace of the hounds on a rope leash, they lay downwind of the trail and actually ambushed the bear. They were so close that it turned at bay although he realised later this might have been from surprise and amazement at the shrill and frantic uproar of the fyce. It turned at bay against the trunk of a big cypress, on its hind feet; it seemed to the boy that it would never stop rising, taller and taller, and even the two hounds seemed to have taken a kind of desperate and despairing courage from the fyce. Then he realised that the fyce was actually not going to stop. He flung the gun down and ran. When he overtook and grasped the shrill, frantically pinwheeling little dog, it seemed to him that he was directly under the bear. He could smell it, strong and hot and rank. Sprawling, he looked up where it loomed and towered over him like a thunderclap. It was quite familiar, until he remembered: this was the way he had used to dream about it.

Then it was gone. He didn't see it go. He knelt, holding the frantic fyce with both hands, hearing the abased wailing of the two hounds drawing further and further away, until Sam came up, carrying the gun. He laid it quietly down beside the boy and stood looking down at him. "You've done seed him twice now, with a gun in your hands," he said. "This time you couldn't have missed him."

The boy rose. He still held the fyce. Even in his arms it continued to yap frantically, surging and straining toward the fading sound of the hounds like a collection of live-wire springs. The boy was panting a little. "Neither could you," he said. "You had the gun. Why didn't you shoot him?"

Sam didn't seem to have heard. He put out his hand and touched the little dog in the boy's arms which still yapped and strained even though the two hounds were out of hearing now. "He's done gone," Sam said. "You can slack off and rest now, until next time." He stroked the little dog until it began to grow quiet under his hand. "You's almost the one we wants," he said. "You just aint big enough. We aint got that one yet. He will need to be just a little bigger than smart, and a little braver than either." He withdrew his hand from the fyce's head and stood looking into the woods where the bear and the hounds had vanished. "Somebody is going to, some day."

"I know it," the boy said. "That's why it must be one of us. So it wont be until the last day. When even he dont want it to last any longer."

So he should have hated and feared Lion. It was in the fourth summer, the fourth time he had made one in the celebration of Major de Spain's and General Compson's birthday. In the early spring Major de Spain's mare had foaled a horse colt. One evening when Sam brought the horses and mules up to stable them for the night, the colt was missing and it was all he could do to get the frantic mare into the lot. He had thought at first to let the mare lead him back to where she had become separated from the foal. But she would not do it. She would not even feint toward any particular part of the woods or even in any particular direction. She merely ran, as if she couldn't see, still frantic with terror. She whirled and ran at Sam once, as if to attack him in some ultimate desperation, as if she could not for the moment realise that he was a man and a long-familiar one. He got her into the lot at last. It was too dark by that time to back-track her, to unravel the erratic course she had doubtless pursued.

He came to the house and told Major de Spain. It was an animal, of course, a big one, and the colt was dead now, wherever it was. They all knew that. "It's a panther," General Compson said at once. "The same one. That doe and fawn last March." Sam had sent Major de Spain word of it when Boon Hogganbeck came to the camp on a routine visit to see how the stock had wintered—the doe's throat torn out, and the beast had run down the helpless fawn and killed it too.

"Sam never did say that was a panther," Major de Spain said. Sam said nothing now, standing behind Major de Spain where they sat at supper, inscrutable, as if he were just waiting for them to stop talking so he could go home. He didn't even seem to be looking at anything. "A panther might jump a doe, and he wouldn't have much trouble catching the fawn afterward. But no panther would have jumped that colt with the dam right there with it. It was Old Ben," Major de Spain said. "I'm disappointed in him. He has broken the rules. I didn't think he would have done that. He has killed mine and McCaslin's dogs, but that was all right. We gambled the dogs against him; we gave each other warning. But now he has come into my house and destroyed my property, out of season too. He broke the rules. It was Old Ben, Sam." Still Sam said nothing, standing there until Major de Spain should stop talking. "We'll back-track her tomorrow and see," Major de Spain said.

Sam departed. He would not live in the camp; he had built himself a little hut something like Joe Baker's, only stouter, tighter, on the bayou a quarter-mile away, and a stout log crib where he stored a little corn for the shoat he raised each year. The next morning he was waiting when they waked. He had already found the colt. They did not even wait for breakfast. It was not far, not five hundred yards from the stable—the three-months' colt lying on its side, its throat torn out and the entrails and one ham partly eaten. It lay not as if it had been dropped but as if it had been struck and hurled, and no cat-mark, no claw-mark where a panther would have gripped it while finding its throat. They read the tracks where the frantic mare had circled and at last rushed in with that same ultimate desperation with which she had whirled on Sam Fathers yesterday evening, and the long tracks of dead and terrified running and those of the beast which had not even rushed at her when she advanced but had merely walked three or four paces toward her until she broke, and General Compson said, "Good God, what a wolf!"

Still Sam said nothing. The boy watched him while the men knelt, measuring the tracks. There was something in Sam's face now. It was neither exultation nor joy nor hope. Later, a man, the boy realised what it had been, and that Sam had known all the time what had made the tracks and what had torn the throat out of the doe in the spring and killed the fawn. It had been foreknowledge in Sam's face that morning. *And he was glad,* he told himself. *He was old. He had no children, no people, none of his blood anywhere above earth that he would ever meet again. And even if he were to, he could not have touched it, spoken to it, because for seventy years now he had had to be a negro. It was almost over now and he was glad.*

They returned to camp and had breakfast and came back with guns and the hounds. Afterward the boy realised that they also should have known then what killed the colt as well as Sam Fathers did. But that was neither the first nor the last time he had seen men rationalise from and even act upon their misconceptions. After Boon, standing astride the colt, had whipped the dogs away from it with his belt, they snuffed at the tracks. One of them, a young dog hound without judgment yet, bayed once, and they ran for a few feet on what seemed to be a trail. Then they stopped, looking back at the men, eager enough, not baffled, merely questioning, as if they were asking "Now what?" Then they rushed back to the colt, where Boon, still astride it, slashed at them with the belt.

"I never knew a trail to get cold that quick," General Compson said.

"Maybe a single wolf big enough to kill a colt with the dam right there beside it dont leave scent," Major de Spain said.

"Maybe it was a hant," Walter Ewell said. He looked at Tennie's Jim. "Hah, Jim?"

Because the hounds would not run it, Major de Spain had Sam hunt out and find the tracks a hundred yards farther on and they put the dogs on it again and again the young one bayed and not one of them realised then that the hound was not baying like a dog striking game but was merely bellowing like a country dog whose yard has been invaded. General Compson spoke to the boy and Boon and Tennie's Jim: to the squirrel hunters. "You boys keep the dogs with you this morning. He's probably hanging around somewhere, waiting to get his breakfast off the colt. You might strike him."

But they did not. The boy remembered how Sam stood watching them as they went into the woods with the leashed hounds—the Indian face in which he had never seen anything until it smiled except that faint arching of the nostrils on that first morning when the hounds had found Old Ben. They took the hounds with them on the next day, though when they reached the place where they hoped to strike a fresh trail, the carcass of the colt was gone. Then on the third morning Sam was waiting again, this time until they had finished breakfast. He said, "Come." He led them to his house, his little hut, to the corn-crib beyond it. He had removed the corn and had made a deadfall of the door, baiting it with the colt's carcass; peering between the logs, they saw an animal almost the color of a gun or pistol barrel, what little time they had to examine its color or shape. It was not crouched nor even standing. It was in motion, in the air, coming toward them—a heavy body crashing with tremendous force against the door so that the thick door jumped and clattered in its frame, the animal, whatever it was, hurling itself against the door again seemingly before it could have touched the floor and got a new purchase to spring from. "Come away," Sam said, "fore he break his neck." Even when they retreated the heavy and measured crashes continued, the stout door jumping and clattering each time, and still no sound from the beast itself—no snarl, no cry.

"What in hell's name is it?" Major de Spain said.

"It's a dog," Sam said, his nostrils arching and collapsing faintly and steadily and that faint, fierce milkiness in his eyes again as on that first morning when the hounds had struck the old bear. "It's the dog."

"*The* dog?" Major de Spain said.

"That's gonter hold Old Ben."

"Dog the devil," Major de Spain said. "I'd rather have Old Ben himself in my pack than that brute. Shoot him."

"No," Sam said.

"You'll never tame him. How do you ever expect to make an animal like that afraid of you?"

"I dont want him tame," Sam said; again the boy watched his nostrils and the fierce milky light in his eyes. "But I almost rather he be tame than scared, of me or any man or any thing. But he wont be neither, of nothing."

"Then what are you going to do with it?"

"You can watch," Sam said.

Each morning through the second week they would go to Sam's crib. He had removed a few shingles from the roof and had put a rope on the colt's carcass and had drawn it out when the trap fell. Each morning they would watch him lower a pail of water into the crib while the dog hurled itself tirelessly against the door and dropped back and leaped again. It never made any sound and there was nothing frenzied in the act but only a cold and grim indomitable determination. Toward the end of the week it stopped jumping at the door. Yet it had not weakened appreciably and it was not as if it had rationalised the fact that the door was not going to give. It was as if for that time it simply disdained to jump any longer. It was not down. None of them had ever seen it down. It stood, and they could see it now—part mastiff, something of Airedale and something of a dozen other strains probably, better than thirty inches at the shoulders and weighing as they guessed almost ninety pounds, with cold yellow eyes and a tremendous chest and over all that strange color like a blued gun-barrel.

Then the two weeks were up. They prepared to break camp. The boy begged to remain and his cousin let him. He moved into the little hut with Sam Fathers. Each morning he watched Sam lower the pail of water into the crib. By the end of that week the dog was down. It would rise and half stagger, half crawl to the water and drink and collapse again. One morning it could not even reach the water, could not raise its forequarters even from the floor. Sam took a short stick and prepared to enter the crib. "Wait," the boy said. "Let me get the gun—"

"No," Sam said. "He cant move now." Nor could it. It lay on its side while Sam touched it, its head and the gaunted body, the dog lying motionless, the yellow eyes open. They were not fierce and there was nothing of petty malevolence in them, but a cold and almost impersonal malignance like some natural force. It was not even looking at Sam nor at the boy peering at it between the logs.

Sam began to feed it again. The first time he had to raise its head so it could lap the broth. That night he left a bowl of broth containing lumps of meat where the dog could reach it. The next morning the bowl was empty and the dog was lying on its belly, its head up, the cold yellow eyes watching the door as Sam entered, no change whatever in the cold yellow eyes and still no sound from it even when it sprang, its aim and co-ordination still bad from weakness so that Sam had time to strike it down with the stick and leap from the crib and slam the door as the dog, still without having had time to get its feet under it to jump again seemingly, hurled itself against the door as if the two weeks of starving had never been.

At noon that day someone came whooping through the woods from the direction of the camp. It was Boon. He came and looked for a while between the logs, at the tremendous dog lying again on its belly, its head up, the yellow eyes blinking sleepily at nothing: the indomitable and unbroken spirit. "What we better do," Boon said, "is to let that son of a bitch go and catch Old Ben and run him on the dog." He turned to the boy his weather-reddened and beetling face. "Get your traps together. Cass says for you to come on home. You been in here fooling with that horse-eating varmint long enough."

Boon had a borrowed mule at the camp; the buggy was waiting at the edge of the bottom. He was at home that night. He told McCaslin about it. "Sam's going to starve him again until he can go in and touch him. Then he will feed him again. Then he will starve him again, if he has to."

"But why?" McCaslin said. "What for? Even Sam will never tame that brute."

"We dont want him tame. We want him like he is. We just want him to find out at last that the only way he can get out of that crib and stay out of it is to do what Sam or somebody tells him to do. He's the dog that's going to stop Old Ben and hold him. We've already named him. His name is Lion."

Then November came at last. They returned to the camp. With General Compson and Major de Spain and his cousin and Walter and Boon he stood in the yard among the guns and bedding and boxes of food and watched Sam Fathers and Lion come up the lane from the lot—the Indian, the old man in battered overalls and rubber boots and a worn sheepskin coat and a hat which had belonged to the boy's father; the tremendous dog pacing gravely beside him. The hounds rushed out to meet them and stopped, except the young one which still had but little of judgment. It ran up to Lion, fawning. Lion didn't snap at it. He didn't even pause. He struck it rolling and yelping for five or six feet with a blow of one paw as a bear would have done and came on into the yard and stood, blinking sleepily at nothing, looking at no one, while Boon said, "Jesus. Jesus.—Will he let me touch him?"

"You can touch him," Sam said. "He dont care. He dont care about nothing or nobody."

The boy watched that too. He watched it for the next two years from that moment when Boon touched Lion's head and then knelt beside him, feeling the bones and muscles, the power. It was as if Lion were a woman—or perhaps Boon was the woman. That was more like it—the big, grave, sleepy-seeming dog which, as Sam Fathers said, cared about no man and no thing; and the violent, insensitive, hard-faced man with his touch of remote Indian blood and the mind almost of a child. He watched Boon take over Lion's feeding from Sam and Uncle Ash both. He would see Boon squatting in the cold rain beside the kitchen while Lion ate. Because Lion neither slept nor ate with the other dogs though none of them knew where he did sleep until in the second November, thinking until then that Lion slept in his kennel beside Sam Fathers' hut, when the boy's cousin McCaslin said something about it to Sam by sheer chance and Sam told him. And that night the boy and Major de Spain and McCaslin with a lamp entered the back room where Boon slept—the little, tight, airless room rank with the smell of Boon's unwashed body and his wet hunting-clothes—where Boon, snoring on his back, choked and waked and Lion raised his head beside him and looked back at them from his cold, slumbrous yellow eyes.

"Damn it, Boon," McCaslin said. "Get that dog out of here. He's got to run Old Ben tomorrow morning. How in hell do you expect him to smell anything fainter than a skunk after breathing you all night?"

"The way I smell aint hurt my nose none that I ever noticed," Boon said.

"It wouldn't matter if it had," Major de Spain said. "We're not depending on you to trail a bear. Put him outside. Put him under the house with the other dogs."

Boon began to get up. "He'll kill the first one that happens to yawn or sneeze in his face or touches him."

"I reckon not," Major de Spain said. "None of them are going to risk yawning in his face or touching him either, even asleep. Put him outside. I want his nose right tomorrow. Old Ben fooled him last year. I dont think he will do it again."

Boon put on his shoes without lacing them; in his long soiled underwear, his hair still tousled from sleep, he and Lion went out. The others returned to the front room and the poker game where McCaslin's and Major de Spain's hands waited for them on the table. After a while McCaslin said, "Do you want me to go back and look again?"

"No," Major de Spain said. "I call," he said to Walter Ewell. He spoke to McCaslin again. "If you do, dont tell me. I am beginning to see the first sign of my increasing age: I dont like to know that my orders have been disobeyed, even when I knew when I gave them that they would be.—A small pair," he said to Walter Ewell.

"How small?" Walter said.

"Very small," Major de Spain said.

And the boy, lying beneath his piled quilts and blankets waiting for sleep, knew likewise that Lion was already back in Boon's bed, for the rest of that night and the next one and during all the nights of the next November and the next one. He thought then: *I wonder what Sam thinks. He could have Lion with him, even if Boon is a white man. He could ask Major or McCaslin either. And more than that. It was Sam's hand that touched Lion first and Lion knows it.* Then he became a man and he knew that too. It had been all right. That was the way it should have been. Sam was the chief, the prince; Boon, the plebeian, was his huntsman. Boon should have nursed the dogs.

On the first morning that Lion led the pack after Old Ben, seven strangers appeared in the camp. They were swampers: gaunt, malaria-ridden men appearing from nowhere, who ran trap-lines for coons or perhaps farmed little patches of cotton and corn along the edge of the bottom, in clothes but little better than Sam Fathers' and nowhere near as good as Tennie's Jim's, with worn shotguns and rifles, already squatting patiently in the cold drizzle in the side yard when day broke. They had a spokesman; afterward Sam Fathers told Major de Spain how all during the past summer and fall they had drifted into the camp singly or in pairs and threes, to look quietly at Lion for a while and then go away: "Mawnin, Major. We heerd you was aimin to put that ere blue dawg on that old two-toed bear this mawnin. We figgered we'd come up and watch, if you dont mind. We wont do no shooting, lessen he runs over us."

"You are welcome," Major de Spain said. "You are welcome to shoot. He's more your bear than ours."

"I reckon that aint no lie. I done fed him enough cawn to have a sheer in him. Not to mention a shoat three years ago."

"I reckon I got a sheer too," another said. "Only it aint in the bear." Major de Spain looked at him. He was chewing tobacco. He spat. "Hit was a heifer calf. Nice un too. Last year. When I finally found her, I reckon she looked about like that colt of yourn looked last June."

"Oh," Major de Spain said. "Be welcome. If you see game in front of my dogs, shoot it."

Nobody shot Old Ben that day. No man saw him. The dogs jumped him within a hundred yards of the glade where the boy had seen him that day in the summer of his eleventh year. The boy was less than a quarter-mile away. He heard the jump but he could distinguish no voice among the dogs that he did not know and therefore would be Lion's, and he thought, believed, that Lion was not among them. Even the fact that they were going much faster than he had ever heard them run behind Old Ben before and that the high thin note of hysteria was missing now from their voices was not enough to disabuse him. He didn't comprehend until that night, when Sam told him that Lion would never cry on a trail. "He gonter growl when he catches Old Ben's throat," Sam said. "But he aint gonter never holler, no more than he ever done when he was jumping at that two-inch door. It's that blue dog in him. What you call it?"

"Airedale," the boy said.

Lion was there; the jump was just too close to the river. When Boon returned with Lion about eleven that night, he swore that Lion had stopped Old Ben once but that the hounds would not go in and Old Ben broke away and took to the river and swam for miles down it and he and Lion went down one bank for about ten miles and crossed and came up the other but it had begun to get dark before they struck any trail where Old Ben had come up out of the water, unless he was still in the water when he passed the ford where they crossed. Then he fell to cursing the hounds and ate the supper Uncle Ash had saved for him and went off to bed and after a while the boy opened the door of the little stale room thunderous with snoring and the great grave dog raised its head from Boon's pillow and blinked at him for a moment and lowered its head again.

When the next November came and the last day, the day which it was now becoming traditional to save for Old Ben, there were more than a dozen strangers waiting. They were not all swampers this time. Some of them were townsmen, from other county seats like Jefferson, who had heard about Lion and Old Ben and had come to watch the great blue dog keep his yearly rendezvous with the old two-toed bear. Some of them didn't even have guns and the hunting-clothes and boots they wore had been on a store shelf yesterday.

This time Lion jumped Old Ben more than five miles from the river and bayed and held him and this time the hounds went in, in a sort of desperate emulation. The boy heard them; he was that near. He heard Boon whooping; he heard the two shots when General Compson delivered both barrels, one containing five buckshot, the other a single ball, into the bear from as close as he could force his almost unmanageable horse. He heard the dogs when the bear broke free again. He was running now; panting, stumbling, his lungs bursting, he reached the place where General Compson had fired and where Old Ben had killed two of the hounds. He saw the blood from General Compson's shots, but he could go no further. He stopped, leaning against a tree for his breathing to ease and his heart to slow, hearing the sound of the dogs as it faded on and died away.

In camp that night—they had as guests five of the still terrified strangers in new hunting coats and boots who had been lost all day until Sam Fathers went out and got them—he heard the rest of it: how Lion had stopped and held the bear again but only the one-eyed mule which did not mind the smell of wild blood would approach and Boon was riding the mule and Boon had never been known to hit anything. He shot at the bear five times with his pump gun, touching nothing, and Old Ben killed another hound and broke free once more and reached the river and was gone. Again Boon and Lion hunted as far down one bank as they dared. Too far; they crossed in the first of dusk and dark overtook them within a mile. And this time Lion found the broken trail, the blood perhaps, in the darkness where Old Ben had come up out of the water, but Boon had him on a rope, luckily, and he got down from the mule and fought Lion hand-to-hand until he got him back to camp. This time Boon didn't even curse. He stood in the door, muddy, spent, his huge gargoyle's face tragic and still amazed. "I missed him," he said. "I was in twenty-five feet of him and I missed him five times."

"But we have drawn blood," Major de Spain said. "General Compson drew blood. We have never done that before."

"But I missed him," Boon said. "I missed him five times. With Lion looking right at me."

"Never mind," Major de Spain said. "It was a damned fine race. And we drew blood. Next year we'll let General Compson or Walter ride Katie, and we'll get him."

Then McCaslin said, "Where is Lion, Boon?"

"I left him at Sam's," Boon said. He was already turning away. "I aint fit to sleep with him."

So he should have hated and feared Lion. Yet he did not. It seemed to him that there was a fatality in it. It seemed to him that something, he didn't know what, was beginning; had already begun. It was like the last act on a set stage. It was the beginning of the end of something, he didn't know what except that he would not grieve. He would be humble and proud that he had been found worthy to be a part of it too or even just to see it too.

3

It was December. It was the coldest December he had ever remembered. They had been in camp four days over two weeks, waiting for the weather to soften so that Lion and Old Ben could run their yearly race. Then they would break camp and go home. Because of these unforeseen additional days which they had had to pass waiting on the weather, with nothing to do but play poker, the whisky had given out and he and Boon were being sent to Memphis with a suitcase and a note from Major de Spain to Mr Semmes, the distiller, to get more. That is, Major de Spain and McCaslin were sending Boon to get the whisky and sending him to see that Boon got back with it or most of it or at least some of it.

Tennie's Jim waked him at three. He dressed rapidly, shivering, not so much from the cold because a fresh fire already boomed and roared on the hearth, but in that dead winter hour when the blood and the heart are slow and sleep is incomplete. He crossed the gap between house and kitchen, the gap of iron earth beneath the brilliant and rigid night where dawn would not begin for three hours yet, tasting, tongue palate and to the very bottom of his lungs the searing dark, and entered the kitchen, the lamp-lit warmth where the stove glowed, fogging the windows, and where Boon already sat at the table at breakfast, hunched over his plate, almost in his plate, his working jaws blue with stubble and his face innocent of water and his coarse, horse-mane hair innocent of comb—the quarter Indian, grandson of a Chickasaw squaw, who on occasion resented with his hard and furious fists the intimation of one single drop of alien blood and on others, usually after whisky, affirmed with the same fists and the same fury that his father had been the full-blood Chickasaw and even a chief and that even his mother had been only half white. He was four inches over six feet; he had the mind of a child, the heart of a horse, and little hard shoe-button eyes without depth or meanness or generosity or viciousness or gentleness or anything else, in the ugliest face the boy had ever seen. It looked like somebody had found a walnut a little larger than a football and with a machinist's hammer had shaped features into it and then painted it, mostly red; not Indian red but a fine bright ruddy color which whisky might have had something to do with but which was mostly just happy and violent out-of-doors, the wrinkles in it not the residue of the forty years it had survived but from squinting into the sun or into the gloom of cane-brakes where game had run, baked into it by the camp fires before which he had lain trying to sleep on the cold November or December ground while waiting for daylight so he could rise and hunt again, as though time were merely something he walked through as he did through air, aging him no more than air did. He was brave, faithful, improvident and unreliable; he had neither profession job nor trade and owned one vice and one virtue: whisky, and that absolute and unquestioning fidelity to Major de Spain and the boy's cousin McCaslin. "Sometimes I'd call them both virtues," Major de Spain said once. "Or both vices," McCaslin said.

He ate his breakfast, hearing the dogs under the kitchen, wakened by the smell of frying meat or perhaps by the feet overhead. He heard Lion once, short and peremptory, as the best hunter in any camp has only to speak once to all save the fools, and none other of Major de Spain's and McCaslin's dogs were Lion's equal in size and strength and perhaps even in courage, but they were not fools; Old Ben had killed the last fool among them last year.

Tennie's Jim came in as they finished. The wagon was outside. Ash decided he would drive them over to the log-line where they would flag the outbound log-train and let Tennie's Jim wash the dishes. The boy knew why. It would not be the first time he had listened to old Ash badgering Boon.

It was cold. The wagon wheels banged and clattered on the frozen ground; the sky was fixed and brilliant. He was not shivering, he was shaking, slow and steady and hard, the food he had just eaten still warm and solid inside him while his outside shook slow and steady around it as though his stomach floated loose. "They wont run this morning," he said. "No dog will have any nose today."

"Cep Lion," Ash said. "Lion dont need no nose. All he need is a bear." He had wrapped his feet in towsacks and he had a quilt from his pallet bed on the kitchen floor drawn over his head and wrapped around him until in the thin brilliant starlight he looked like nothing at all that the boy had ever seen before. "He run a bear through a thousand-acre icehouse. Catch him too. Them other dogs dont matter because they aint going to keep up with Lion nohow, long as he got a bear in front of him."

"What's wrong with the other dogs?" Boon said. "What the hell do you know about it anyway? This is the first time you've had your tail out of that kitchen since we got here except to chop a little wood."

"Aint nothing wrong with them," Ash said. "And long as it's left up to them, aint nothing going to be. I just wish I had knowed all my life how to take care of my health good as them hounds knows."

"Well, they aint going to run this morning," Boon said. His voice was harsh and positive. "Major promised they wouldn't until me and Ike get back."

"Weather gonter break today. Gonter soft up. Rain by night." Then Ash laughed, chuckled, somewhere inside the quilt which concealed even his face. "Hum up here, mules!" he said, jerking the reins so that the mules leaped forward and snatched the lurching and banging wagon for several feet before they slowed again into their quick, short-paced, rapid plodding. "Sides, I like to know why Major need to wait on you. It's Lion he aiming to use. I aint never heard tell of you bringing no bear nor no other kind of meat into this camp."

Now Boon's going to curse Ash or maybe even hit him, the boy thought. But Boon never did, never had; the boy knew he never would even though four years ago Boon had shot five times with a borrowed pistol at a negro on the street in Jefferson, with the same result as when he had shot five times at Old Ben last fall. "By God," Boon said, "he aint going to put Lion or no other dog on nothing until I get back tonight. Because he promised me. Whip up them mules and keep them whipped up. Do you want me to freeze to death?"

They reached the log-line and built a fire. After a while the log-train came up out of the woods under the paling east and Boon flagged it. Then in the warm caboose the boy slept again while Boon and the conductor and brakeman talked about Lion and Old Ben as people later would talk about Sullivan and Kilrain and, later still, about Dempsey and Tunney. Dozing, swaying as the springless caboose lurched and clattered, he would hear them still talking, about the shoats and calves Old Ben had killed and the cribs he had rifled and the traps and deadfalls he had wrecked and the lead he probably carried under his hide—Old Ben, the two-toed bear in a land where bears with trap-ruined feet had been called Two-Toe or Three-Toe or Cripple-Foot for fifty years, only Old Ben was an extra bear (the head bear, General Compson called him) and so had earned a name such as a human man could have worn and not been sorry.

They reached Hoke's at sunup. They emerged from the warm caboose in their hunting clothes, the muddy boots and stained khaki and Boon's blue unshaven jowls. But that was all right. Hoke's was a sawmill and commissary and two stores and a loading-chute on a sidetrack from the main line, and all the men in it wore boots and khaki too. Presently the Memphis train came. Boon bought three packages of popcorn-and-molasses and a bottle of beer from the news butch and the boy went to sleep again to the sound of his chewing.

But in Memphis it was not all right. It was as if the high buildings and the hard pavements, the fine carriages and the horse cars and the men in starched collars and neckties made their boots and khaki look a little rougher and a little muddier and made Boon's beard look worse and more unshaven and his face look more and more like he should never have brought it out of the woods at all or at least out of reach of Major de Spain or McCaslin or someone who knew it and could have said, "Dont be afraid. He wont hurt you." He walked through the station, on the slick floor, his face moving as he worked the popcorn out of his teeth with his tongue, his legs spraddled and stiff in the hips as if he were walking on buttered glass, and that blue stubble on his face like the filings from a new gun-barrel. They passed the first saloon. Even through the closed doors the boy could seem to smell the sawdust and the reek of old drink. Boon began to cough. He coughed for something less than a minute. "Damn this cold," he said. "I'd sure like to know where I got it."

"Back there in the station," the boy said.

Boon had started to cough again. He stopped. He looked at the boy. "What?" he said.

"You never had it when we left camp nor on the train either." Boon looked at him, blinking. Then he stopped blinking. He didn't cough again. He said quietly:

"Lend me a dollar. Come on. You've got it. If you ever had one, you've still got it. I dont mean you are tight with your money because you aint. You just dont never seem to ever think of nothing you want. When I was sixteen a dollar bill melted off of me before I even had time to read the name of the bank that issued it." He said quietly: "Let me have a dollar, Ike."

"You promised Major. You promised McCaslin. Not till we get back to camp."

"All right," Boon said in that quiet and patient voice. "What can I do on just one dollar? You aint going to lend me another."

"You're damn right I aint," the boy said, his voice quiet too, cold with rage which was not at Boon, remembering: Boon snoring in a hard chair in the kitchen so he could watch the clock and wake him and McCaslin and drive them the seventeen miles in to Jefferson to catch the train to Memphis; the wild, never-bridled Texas paint pony which he had persuaded McCaslin to let him buy and which he and Boon had bought at auction for four dollars and seventy-five cents and fetched home wired between two gentle old mares with pieces of barbed wire and which had never even seen shelled corn before and didn't even know what it was unless the grains were bugs maybe and at last (he was ten and Boon had been ten all his life) Boon said the pony was gentled and with a towsack over its head and four negroes to hold it they backed it into an old two-wheeled cart and hooked up the gear and he and Boon got up and Boon said, "All right, boys. Let him go" and one of the negroes—it was Tennie's Jim—snatched the towsack off and leaped for his life and they lost the first wheel against a post of the open gate only at that moment Boon caught him by the scruff of the neck and flung him into the roadside ditch so he only saw the rest of it in fragments: the other wheel as it slammed through the side gate and crossed the back yard and leaped up onto the gallery and scraps of the cart here and there along the road and Boon vanishing rapidly on his stomach in the leaping and spurting dust and still holding the reins until they broke too and two days later they finally caught the pony seven miles away still wearing the hames and the headstall of the bridle around its neck like a duchess with two necklaces at one time. He gave Boon the dollar.

"All right," Boon said. "Come on in out of the cold."

"I aint cold," he said

"You can have some lemonade."

"I dont want any lemonade."

The door closed behind him. The sun was well up now. It was a brilliant day, though Ash had said it would rain before night. Already it was warmer; they could run tomorrow. He felt the old lift of the heart, as pristine as ever, as on the first day; he would never lose it, no matter how old in hunting and pursuit: the best, the best of all breathing, the humility and the pride. He must stop thinking about it. Already it seemed to him that he was running, back to the station, to the tracks themselves: the first train going south, he must stop thinking about it. The street was busy. He watched the big Norman draft horses, the Percherons; the trim carriages from which the men in the fine overcoats and the ladies rosy in furs descended and entered the station. (They were still next door to it but one.) Twenty years ago his father had ridden into Memphis as a member of Colonel Sartoris' horse in Forrest's command, up Main street and (the tale told) into the lobby of the Gayoso Hotel where the Yankee officers sat in the leather chairs spitting into the tall bright cuspidors and then out again, scot-free—

The door opened behind him. Boon was wiping his mouth on the back of his hand. "All right," he said. "Let's go tend to it and get the hell out of here."

They went and had the suitcase packed. He never knew where or when Boon got the other bottle. Doubtless Mr Semmes gave it to him. When they reached Hoke's again at sundown, it was empty. They could get a return train to Hoke's in two hours; they went straight back to the station as Major de Spain and then McCaslin had told Boon to do and then ordered him to do and had sent the boy along to see that he did. Boon took the first drink from his bottle in the washroom. A man in a uniform cap came to tell him he couldn't drink there and looked at Boon's face once and said nothing. The next time he was pouring into his water glass beneath the edge of a table in the restaurant when the manager (she was a woman) did tell him he couldn't drink there and he went back to the washroom. He had been telling the negro waiter and all the other people in the restaurant who couldn't help but hear him and who had never heard of Lion and didn't want to, about Lion and Old Ben. Then he happened to think of the zoo. He had found out that there was another train to Hoke's at three oclock and so they would spend the time at the zoo and take the three oclock train until he came back from the washroom for the third time. Then they would take the first train back to camp, get Lion and come back to the zoo where, he said, the bears were fed on ice cream and lady fingers and he would match Lion against them all.

So they missed the first train, the one they were supposed to take, but he got Boon onto the three oclock train and they were all right again, with Boon not even going to the washroom now but drinking in the aisle and talking about Lion and the men he buttonholed no more daring to tell Boon he couldn't drink there than the man in the station had dared.

When they reached Hoke's at sundown, Boon was asleep. The boy waked him at last and got him and the suitcase off the train and he even persuaded him to eat some supper at the sawmill commissary. So he was all right when they got in the caboose of the log-train to go back into the woods, with the sun going down red and the sky already overcast and the ground would not freeze tonight. It was the boy who slept now, sitting behind the ruby stove while the springless caboose jumped and clattered and Boon and the brakeman and the conductor talked about Lion and Old Ben because they knew what Boon was talking about because this was home. "Overcast and already thawing," Boon said. "Lion will get him tomorrow."

It would have to be Lion, or somebody. It would not be Boon. He had never hit anything bigger than a squirrel that anybody ever knew, except the negro woman that day when he was shooting at the negro man. He was a big negro and not ten feet away but Boon shot five times with the pistol he had borrowed from Major de Spain's negro coachman and the negro he was shooting at outed with a dollar-and-a-half mail-order pistol and would have burned Boon down with it only it never went off, it just went snicksnicksnicksnicksnick five times and Boon still blasting away and he broke a plate-glass window that cost McCaslin forty-five dollars and hit a negro woman who happened to be passing in the leg only Major de Spain paid for that; he and McCaslin cut cards, the plate-glass window against the negro woman's leg. And the first day on stand this year, the first morning in camp, the buck ran right over Boon; he heard Boon's old pump gun go whow. whow. whow. whow. whow. and then his voice: "God damn, here he comes! Head him! Head him!" and when he got there the buck's tracks and the five exploded shells were not twenty paces apart.

There were five guests in camp that night from Jefferson: Mr Bayard Sartoris and his son and General Compson's son and two others. And the next morning he looked out the window, into the gray thin drizzle of daybreak which Ash had predicted, and there they were, standing and squatting beneath the thin rain, almost two dozen of them who had fed Old Ben corn and shoats and even calves for ten years, in their worn hats and hunting coats and overalls which any town negro would have thrown away or burned and only the rubber boots strong and sound, and the worn and blueless guns, and some even without guns. While they ate breakfast a dozen more arrived, mounted and on foot: loggers from the camp thirteen miles below and sawmill men from Hoke's and the only gun among them that one which the log-train conductor carried: so that when they went into the woods this morning Major de Spain led a party almost as strong, excepting that some of them were not armed, as some he had led in the last darkening days of '64 and '65. The little yard would not hold them. They overflowed it, into the lane where Major de Spain sat his mare while Ash in his dirty apron thrust the greasy cartridges into his carbine and passed it up to him and the great grave blue dog stood at his stirrup not as a dog stands but as a horse stands, blinking his sleepy topaz eyes at nothing, deaf even to the yelling of the hounds which Boon and Tennie's Jim held on leash.

"We'll put General Compson on Katie this morning," Major de Spain said. "He drew blood last year; if he'd had a mule then that would have stood, he would have—"

"No," General Compson said. "I'm too old to go helling through the woods on a mule or a horse or anything else any more. Besides, I had my chance last year and missed it. I'm going on a stand this morning. I'm going to let that boy ride Katie."

"No, wait," McCaslin said. "Ike's got the rest of his life to hunt bears in. Let somebody else—"

"No," General Compson said. "I want Ike to ride Katie. He's already a better woodsman than you or me either and in another ten years he'll be as good as Walter."

At first he couldn't believe it, not until Major de Spain spoke to him. Then he was up, on the one-eyed mule which would not spook at wild blood, looking down at the dog motionless at Major de Spain's stirrup, looking in the gray streaming light bigger than a calf, bigger than he knew it actually was—the big head, the chest almost as big as his own, the blue hide beneath which the muscles flinched or quivered to no touch since the heart which drove blood to them loved no man and no thing, standing as a horse stands yet different from a horse which infers only weight and speed while Lion inferred not only courage and all else that went to make up the will and desire to pursue and kill, but endurance, the will and desire to endure beyond all imaginable limits of flesh in order to overtake and slay. Then the dog looked at him. It moved its head and looked at him across the trivial uproar of the hounds, out of the yellow eyes as depthless as Boon's, as free as Boon's of meanness or generosity or gentleness or viciousness. They were just cold and sleepy. Then it blinked, and he knew it was not looking at him and never had been, without even bothering to turn its head away.

That morning he heard the first cry. Lion had already vanished while

Sam and Tennie's Jim were putting saddles on the mule and horse which had drawn the wagon and he watched the hounds as they crossed and cast, snuffing and whimpering, until they too disappeared. Then he and Major de Spain and Sam and Tennie's Jim rode after them and heard the first cry out of the wet and thawing woods not two hundred yards ahead, high, with that abject, almost human quality he had come to know, and the other hounds joining in until the gloomed woods rang and clamored. They rode then. It seemed to him that he could actually see the big blue dog boring on, silent, and the bear too: the thick, locomotive-like shape which he had seen that day four years ago crossing the blow-down, crashing on ahead of the dogs faster than he had believed it could have moved, drawing away even from the running mules. He heard a shotgun, once. The woods had opened, they were going fast, the clamor faint and fading on ahead; they passed the man who had fired—a swamper, a pointing arm, a gaunt face, the small black orifice of his yelling studded with rotten teeth.

He heard the changed note in the hounds' uproar and two hundred yards ahead he saw them. The bear had turned. He saw Lion drive in without pausing and saw the bear strike him aside and lunge into the yelling hounds and kill one of them almost in its tracks and whirl and run again. Then they were in a streaming tide of dogs. He heard Major de Spain and Tennie's Jim shouting and the pistol sound of Tennie's Jim's leather thong as he tried to turn them. Then he and Sam Fathers were riding alone. One of the hounds had kept on with Lion though. He recognised its voice. It was the young hound which even a year ago had had no judgment and which, by the lights of the other hounds anyway, still had none. *Maybe that's what courage is,* he thought. "Right," Sam said behind him. "Right. We got to turn him from the river if we can."

Now they were in cane: a brake. He knew the path through it as well as Sam did. They came out of the undergrowth and struck the entrance almost exactly. It would traverse the brake and come out onto a high open ridge above the river. He heard the flat clap of Walter Ewell's rifle, then two more. "No," Sam said. "I can hear the hound. Go on."

They emerged from the narrow roofless tunnel of snapping and hissing cane, still galloping, onto the open ridge below which the thick yellow river, reflectionless in the gray and streaming light, seemed not to move. Now he could hear the hound too. It was not running. The cry was a high frantic yapping and Boon was running along the edge of the bluff, his old gun leaping and jouncing against his back on its sling made of a piece of cotton plow-line. He whirled and ran up to them, wild-faced, and flung himself onto the mule behind the boy. "That damn boat!" he cried. "It's on the other side! He went straight across! Lion was too close to him! That little hound too! Lion was so close I couldn't shoot! Go on!" he cried, beating his heels into the mule's flanks. "Go on!"

They plunged down the bank, slipping and sliding in the thawed earth, crashing through the willows and into the water. He felt no shock, no cold, he on one side of the swimming mule, grasping the pommel with one hand and holding his gun above the water with the other, Boon opposite him. Sam was behind them somewhere, and then the river, the water about them, was full of dogs. They swam faster than the mules; they were scrabbling up the bank before the mules touched bottom. Major de Spain was whooping from the bank they had just left and, looking back, he saw Tennie's Jim and the horse as they went into the water.

Now the woods ahead of them and the rain-heavy air were one uproar. It rang and clamored; it echoed and broke against the bank behind them and reformed and clamored and rang until it seemed to the boy that all the hounds which had ever bayed game in this land were yelling down at him. He got his leg over the mule as it came up out of the water. Boon didn't try to mount again. He grasped one stirrup as they went up the bank and crashed through the undergrowth which fringed the bluff and saw the bear, on its hind feet, its back against a tree while the bellowing hounds swirled around it and once more Lion drove in, leaping clear of the ground.

This time the bear didn't strike him down. It caught the dog in both arms, almost loverlike, and they both went down. He was off the mule now. He drew back both hammers of the gun but he could see nothing but moiling spotted houndbodies until the bear surged up again. Boon was yelling something, he could not tell what; he could see Lion still clinging to the bear's throat and he saw the bear, half erect, strike one of the hounds with one paw and hurl it five or six feet and then, rising and rising as though it would never stop, stand erect again and begin to rake at Lion's belly with its forepaws. Then Boon was running. The boy saw the gleam of the blade in his hand and watched him leap among the hounds, hurdling them, kicking them aside as he ran, and fling himself astride the bear as he had hurled himself onto the mule, his legs locked around the bear's belly, his left arm under the bear's throat where Lion clung, and the glint of the knife as it rose and fell.

It fell just once. For an instant they almost resembled a piece of statuary: the clinging dog, the bear, the man astride its back, working and probing the buried blade. Then they went down, pulled over backward by Boon's weight, Boon underneath. It was the bear's back which reappeared first but at once Boon was astride it again. He had never released the knife and again the boy saw the almost infinitesimal movement of his arm and shoulder as he probed and sought; then the bear surged erect, raising with it the man and the dog too, and turned and still carrying the man and the dog it took two or three steps toward the woods on its hind feet as a man would have walked and crashed down. It didn't collapse, crumple. It fell all of a piece, as a tree falls, so that all three of them, man dog and bear, seemed to bounce once.

He and Tennie's Jim ran forward. Boon was kneeling at the bear's head. His left ear was shredded, his left coat sleeve was completely gone, his right boot had been ripped from knee to instep; the bright blood thinned in the thin rain down his leg and hand and arm and down the side of his face which was no longer wild but was quite calm. Together they prized Lion's jaws from the bear's throat. "Easy, goddamn it," Boon said. "Cant you see his guts are all out of him?" He began to remove his coat. He spoke to Tennie's Jim in that calm voice: "Bring the boat up. It's about a hundred yards down the bank there. I saw it." Tennie's Jim rose and went away. Then, and he could not remember if it had been a call or an exclamation from Tennie's Jim or if he had glanced up by chance, he saw Tennie's Jim stooping and saw Sam Fathers lying motionless on his face in the trampled mud.

The mule had not thrown him. He remembered that Sam was down too even before Boon began to run. There was no mark on him whatever and when he and Boon turned him over, his eyes were open and he said something in that tongue which he and Joe Baker had used to speak together. But he couldn't move. Tennie's Jim brought the skiff up; they could hear him shouting to Major de Spain across the river. Boon wrapped Lion in his hunting coat and carried him down to the skiff and they carried Sam down and returned and hitched the bear to the one-eyed mule's saddle-bow with Tennie's Jim's leash-thong and dragged him down to the skiff and got him into it and left Tennie's Jim to swim the horse and the two mules back across. Major de Spain caught the bow of the skiff as Boon jumped out and past him before it touched the bank. He looked at Old Ben and said quietly: "Well." Then he walked into the water and leaned down and touched Sam and Sam looked up at him and said something in that old tongue he and Joe Baker spoke. "You dont know what happened?" Major de Spain said.

"No, sir," the boy said. "It wasn't the mule. It wasn't anything. He was off the mule when Boon ran in on the bear. Then we looked up and he was lying on the ground." Boon was shouting at Tennie's Jim, still in the middle of the river.

"Come on, goddamn it!" he said. "Bring me that mule!"

"What do you want with a mule?" Major de Spain said.

Boon didn't even look at him. "I'm going to Hoke's to get the doctor," he said in that calm voice, his face quite calm beneath the steady thinning of the bright blood.

"You need a doctor yourself," Major de Spain said. "Tennie's Jim—"

"Damn that," Boon said. He turned on Major de Spain. His face was still calm, only his voice was a pitch higher. "Cant you see his goddamn guts are all out of him?"

"Boon!" Major de Spain said. They looked at one another. Boon was a good head taller than Major de Spain; even the boy was taller now than Major de Spain.

"I've got to get the doctor," Boon said. "His goddamn guts—"

"All right," Major de Spain said. Tennie's Jim came up out of the water. The horse and the sound mule had already scented Old Ben; they surged and plunged all the way up to the top of the bluff, dragging Tennie's Jim with them, before he could stop them and tie them and come back. Major de Spain unlooped the leather thong of his compass from his buttonhole and gave it to Tennie's Jim. "Go straight to Hoke's," he said. "Bring Doctor Crawford back with you. Tell him there are two men to be looked at. Take my mare. Can you find the road from here?"

"Yes, sir," Tennie's Jim said.

"All right," Major de Spain said. "Go on." He turned to the boy. "Take the mules and the horse and go back and get the wagon. We'll go on down the river in the boat to Coon bridge. Meet us there. Can you find it again?"

"Yes, sir," the boy said.

"All right. Get started."

He went back to the wagon. He realised then how far they had run. It was already afternoon when he put the mules into the traces and tied the horse's lead-rope to the tail-gate. He reached Coon bridge at dusk. The skiff was already there. Before he could see it and almost before he could see the water he had to leap from the tilting wagon, still holding the reins, and work around to where he could grasp the bit and then the ear of the plunging sound mule and dig his heels and hold it until Boon came up the bank. The rope of the led horse had already snapped and it had already disappeared up the road toward camp. They turned the wagon around and took the mules out and he led the sound mule a hundred yards up the road and tied it. Boon had already brought Lion up to the wagon and Sam was sitting up in the skiff now and when they raised him he tried to walk, up the bank and to the wagon and he tried to climb into the wagon but Boon did not wait; he picked Sam up bodily and set him on the seat. Then they hitched Old Ben to the one-eyed mule's saddle again and dragged him up the bank and set two skid-poles into the open tail-gate and got him into the wagon and he went and got the sound mule and Boon fought it into the traces, striking it across its hard hollow-sounding face until it came into position and stood trembling. Then the rain came down, as though it had held off all day waiting on them.

They returned to camp through it, through the streaming and sightless dark, hearing long before they saw any light the horn and the spaced shots to guide them. When they came to Sam's dark little hut he tried to stand up. He spoke again in the tongue of the old fathers; then he said clearly: "Let me out. Let me out."

"He hasn't got any fire," Major said. "Go on!" he said sharply.

But Sam was struggling now, trying to stand up. "Let me out, master," he said. "Let me go home."

So he stopped the wagon and Boon got down and lifted Sam out. He did not wait to let Sam try to walk this time. He carried him into the hut and Major de Spain got light on a paper spill from the buried embers on the hearth and lit the lamp and Boon put Sam on his bunk and drew off his boots and Major de Spain covered him and the boy was not there, he was holding the mules, the sound one which was trying again to bolt since when the wagon stopped Old Ben's scent drifted forward again along the streaming blackness of air, but Sam's eyes were probably open again in that profound look which saw further than them or the hut, further than the death of a bear and the dying of a dog. Then they went on, toward the long wailing of the horn and the shots which seemed each to linger intact somewhere in the thick streaming air until the next spaced report joined and blended with it, to the lighted house, the bright streaming windows, the quiet faces as Boon entered, bloody and quite calm, carrying the bundled coat. He laid Lion, blood coat and all, on his stale sheetless pallet bed which not even Ash, as deft in the house as a woman, could ever make smooth.

The sawmill doctor from Hoke's was already there. Boon would not let the doctor touch him until he had seen to Lion. He wouldn't risk giving Lion chloroform. He put the entrails back and sewed him up without it while Major de Spain held his head and Boon his feet. But he never tried to move. He lay there, the yellow eyes open upon nothing while the quiet men in the new hunting clothes and in the old ones crowded into the little airless room rank with the smell of Boon's body and garments, and watched. Then the doctor cleaned and disinfected Boon's face and arm and leg and bandaged them and, the boy in front with a lantern and the doctor and McCaslin and Major de Spain and General Compson following, they went to Sam Fathers' hut. Tennie's Jim had built up the fire; he squatted before it, dozing. Sam had not moved since Boon had put him in the bunk and Major de Spain had covered him with the blankets, yet he opened his eyes and looked from one to another of the faces and when McCaslin touched his shoulder and said, "Sam. The doctor wants to look at you," he even drew his hands out of the blanket and began to fumble at his shirt buttons until McCaslin said, "Wait. We'll do it." They undressed him. He lay there—the copper-brown, almost hairless body, the old man's body, the old man, the wild man not even one generation from the woods, childless, kinless, peopleless—motionless, his eyes open but no longer looking at any of them, while the doctor examined him and drew the blankets up and put the stethoscope back into his bag and snapped the bag and only the boy knew that Sam too was going to die.

"Exhaustion," the doctor said. "Shock maybe. A man his age swimming rivers in December. He'll be all right. Just make him stay in bed for a day or two. Will there be somebody here with him?"

"There will be somebody here," Major de Spain said.

They went back to the house, to the rank little room where Boon still sat on the pallet bed with Lion's head under his hand while the men, the ones who had hunted behind Lion and the ones who had never seen him before today, came quietly in to look at him and went away. Then it was dawn and they all went out into the yard to look at Old Ben, with his eyes open too and his lips snarled back from his worn teeth and his mutilated foot and the little hard lumps under his skin which were the old bullets (there were fifty-two of them, buckshot rifle and ball) and the single almost invisible slit under his left shoulder where Boon's blade had finally found his life. Then Ash began to beat on the bottom of the dishpan with a heavy spoon to call them to breakfast and it was the first time he could remember hearing no sound from the dogs under the kitchen while they were eating. It was as if the old bear, even dead there in the yard, was a more potent terror still than they could face without Lion between them.

The rain had stopped during the night. By midmorning the thin sun appeared, rapidly burning away mist and cloud, warming the air and the earth; it would be one of those windless Mississippi December days which are a sort of Indian summer's Indian summer. They moved Lion out to the front gallery, into the sun. It was Boon's idea. "Goddamn it," he said, "he never did want to stay in the house until I made him. You know that." He took a crowbar and loosened the floor boards under his pallet bed so it could be raised, mattress and all, without disturbing Lion's position, and they carried him out to the gallery and put him down facing the woods.

Then he and the doctor and McCaslin and Major de Spain went to Sam's hut. This time Sam didn't open his eyes and his breathing was so quiet, so peaceful that they could hardly see that he breathed. The doctor didn't even take out his stethoscope nor even touch him. "He's all right," the doctor said. "He didn't even catch cold. He just quit."

"Quit?" McCaslin said.

"Yes. Old people do that sometimes. Then they get a good night's sleep or maybe it's just a drink of whisky, and they change their minds."

They returned to the house. And then they began to arrive—the swamp-dwellers, the gaunt men who ran trap-lines and lived on quinine and coons and river water, the farmers of little corn- and cotton-patches along the bottom's edge whose fields and cribs and pig-pens the old bear had rifled, the loggers from the camp and the sawmill men from Hoke's and the town men from further away than that, whose hounds the old bear had slain and traps and deadfalls he had wrecked and whose lead he carried. They came up mounted and on foot and in wagons, to enter the yard and look at him and then go on to the front where Lion lay, filling the little yard and overflowing it until there were almost a hundred of them squatting and standing in the warm and drowsing sunlight, talking quietly of hunting, of the game and the dogs which ran it, of hounds and bear and deer and men of yesterday vanished from the earth, while from time to time the great blue dog would open his eyes, not as if he were listening to them but as though to look at the woods for a moment before closing his eyes again, to remember the woods or to see that they were still there. He died at sundown.

Major de Spain broke camp that night. They carried Lion into the woods, or Boon carried him that is, wrapped in a quilt from his bed, just as he had refused to let anyone else touch Lion yesterday until the doctor got there; Boon carrying Lion, and the boy and General Compson and Walter and still almost fifty of them following with lanterns and lighted pine-knots—men from Hoke's and even further, who would have to ride out of the bottom in the dark, and swampers and trappers who would have to walk even, scattering toward the little hidden huts where they lived. And Boon would let nobody else dig the grave either and lay Lion in it and cover him and then General Compson stood at the head of it while the blaze and smoke of the pine-knots streamed away among the winter branches and spoke as he would have spoken over a man. Then they returned to camp. Major de Spain and McCaslin and Ash had rolled and tied all the bedding. The mules were hitched to the wagon and pointed out of the bottom and the wagon was already loaded and the stove in the kitchen was cold and the table was set with scraps of cold food and bread and only the coffee was hot when the boy ran into the kitchen where Major de Spain and McCaslin had already eaten. "What?" he cried. "What? I'm not going."

"Yes," McCaslin said, "we're going out tonight. Major wants to get on back home."

"No!" he said. "I'm going to stay."

"You've got to be back in school Monday. You've already missed a week more than I intended. It will take you from now until Monday to catch up. Sam's all right. You heard Doctor Crawford. I'm going to leave Boon and Tennie's Jim both to stay with him until he feels like getting up."

He was panting. The others had come in. He looked rapidly and almost frantically around at the other faces. Boon had a fresh bottle. He upended it and started the cork by striking the bottom of the bottle with the heel of his hand and drew the cork with his teeth and spat it out and drank. "You're damn right you're going back to school," Boon said. "Or I'll burn the tail off of you myself if Cass dont, whether you are sixteen or sixty. Where in hell do you expect to get without education? Where would Cass be? Where in hell would I be if I hadn't never went to school?"

He looked at McCaslin again. He could feel his breath coming shorter and shorter and shallower and shallower, as if there were not enough air in the kitchen for that many to breathe. "This is just Thursday. I'll come home Sunday night on one of the horses. I'll come home Sunday, then. I'll make up the time I lost studying Sunday night, McCaslin," he said, without even despair.

"No, I tell you," McCaslin said. "Sit down here and eat your supper. We're going out to—"

"Hold up, Cass," General Compson said. The boy did not know General Compson had moved until he put his hand on his shoulder. "What is it, bud?" he said.

"I've got to stay," he said. "I've got to."

"All right," General Compson said. "You can stay. If missing an extra week of school is going to throw you so far behind you'll have to sweat to find out what some hired pedagogue put between the covers of a book, you better quit altogether.—And you shut up, Cass," he said, though McCaslin had not spoken. "You've got one foot straddled into a farm and the other foot straddled into a bank; you aint even got a good hand-hold where this boy was already an old man long before you damned Sartorises and Edmondses invented farms and banks to keep yourselves from having to find out what this boy was born knowing and fearing too maybe but without being afraid, that could go ten miles on a compass because he wanted to look at a bear none of us had ever got near enough to put a bullet in and looked at the bear and came the ten miles back on the compass in the dark; maybe by God that's the why and the wherefore of farms and banks.—I reckon you still aint going to tell what it is?"

But still he could not. "I've got to stay," he said.

"All right," General Compson said. "There's plenty of grub left. And you'll come home Sunday, like you promised McCaslin? Not Sunday night: Sunday."

"Yes, sir," he said

"All right," General Compson said. "Sit down and eat, boys," he said. "Let's get started. It's going to be cold before we get home."

They ate. The wagon was already loaded and ready to depart; all they had to do was to get into it. Boon would drive them out to the road, to the farmer's stable where the surrey had been left. He stood beside the wagon, in silhouette on the sky, turbaned like a Paythan and taller than any there, the bottle tilted. Then he flung the bottle from his lips without even lowering it, spinning and glinting in the faint starlight, empty. "Them that's going," he said, "get in the goddamn wagon. Them that aint, get out of the goddamn way." The others got in. Boon mounted to the seat beside General Compson and the wagon moved, on into the obscurity until the boy could no longer see it, even the moving density of it amid the greater night. But he could still hear it, for a long while: the slow, deliberate banging of the wooden frame as it lurched from rut to rut. And he could hear Boon even when he could no longer hear the wagon. He was singing, harsh, tuneless, loud.

That was Thursday. On Saturday morning Tennie's Jim left on McCaslin's woods-horse which had not been out of the bottom one time now in six years, and late that afternoon rode through the gate on the spent horse and on to the commissary where McCaslin was rationing the tenants and the wage-hands for the coming week, and this time McCaslin forestalled any necessity or risk of having to wait while Major de Spain's surrey was being horsed and harnessed. He took their own, and with Tennie's Jim already asleep in the back seat he drove in to Jefferson and waited while Major de Spain changed to boots and put on his overcoat, and they drove the thirty miles in the dark of that night and at daybreak on Sunday morning they swapped to the waiting mare and mule and as the sun rose they rode out of the jungle and onto the low ridge where they had buried Lion: the low mound of unannealed earth where Boon's spade-marks still showed, and beyond the grave the platform of freshly cut saplings bound between four posts and the blanket-wrapped bundle upon the platform and Boon and the boy squatting between the platform and the grave until Boon, the bandage removed, ripped from his head so that the long scoriations of Old Ben's claws resembled crusted tar in the sunlight, sprang up and threw down upon them with the old gun with which he had never been known to hit anything although McCaslin was already off the mule, kicked both feet free of the irons and vaulted down before the mule had stopped, walking toward Boon.

"Stand back," Boon said. "By God, you wont touch him. Stand back, McCaslin." Still McCaslin came on, fast yet without haste.

"Cass!" Major de Spain said. Then he said, "Boon! You, Boon!" and he was down too and the boy rose too, quickly, and still McCaslin came on not fast but steady and walked up to the grave and reached his hand steadily out, quickly yet still not fast, and took hold the gun by the middle so that he and Boon faced one another across Lion's grave, both holding the gun. Boon's spent indomitable amazed and frantic face almost a head higher than McCaslin's beneath the black scoriations of beast's claws and then Boon's chest began to heave as though there were not enough air in all the woods, in all the wilderness, for all of them, for him and anyone else, even for him alone.

"Turn it loose, Boon," McCaslin said.

"You damn little spindling—" Boon said. "Dont you know I can take it away from you? Dont you know I can tie it around your neck like a damn cravat?"

"Yes," McCaslin said. "Turn it loose, Boon."

"This is the way he wanted it. He told us. He told us exactly how to do it. And by God you aint going to move him. So we did it like he said, and I been sitting here ever since to keep the damn wildcats and varmints away from him and by God—" Then McCaslin had the gun, downslanted while he pumped the slide, the five shells snicking out of it so fast that the last one was almost out before the first one touched the ground and McCaslin dropped the gun behind him without once having taken his eyes from Boon's.

"Did you kill him, Boon?" he said. Then Boon moved. He turned, he moved like he was still drunk and then for a moment blind too, one hand out as he blundered toward the big tree and seemed to stop walking before he reached the tree so that he plunged, fell toward it, flinging up both hands and catching himself against the tree and turning until his back was against it, backing with the tree's trunk his wild spent scoriated face and the tremendous heave and collapse of his chest, McCaslin following, facing him again, never once having moved his eyes from Boon's eyes. "Did you kill him, Boon?"

"No!" Boon said. "No!"

"Tell the truth," McCaslin said. "I would have done it if he had asked me to." Then the boy moved. He was between them, facing McCaslin; the water felt as if it had burst and sprung not from his eyes alone but from his whole face, like sweat.

"Leave him alone!" he cried. "Goddamn it! Leave him alone!"

4

then he was twenty-one. He could say it, himself and his cousin juxtaposed not against the wilderness but against the tamed land which was to have been his heritage, the land which old Carothers McCaslin his grandfather had bought with white man's money from the wild men whose grandfathers without guns hunted it, and tamed and ordered or believed he had tamed and ordered it for the reason that the human beings he held in bondage and in the power of life and death and removed the forest from it and in their sweat scratched the surface of it to a depth of perhaps fourteen inches in order to grow something out of it which had not been there before and which could be translated back into the money he who believed he had bought it had had to pay to get it and hold it and a reasonable profit too: and for which reason old Carothers McCaslin, knowing better, could raise his children, his descendants and heirs, to believe the land was his to hold and bequeath since the strong and ruthless man has a cynical foreknowledge of his own vanity and pride and strength and a contempt for all his get: just as, knowing better, Major de Spain had his fragment of that wilderness which was bigger and older than any recorded deed: just as, knowing better, old Thomas Sutpen, from whom Major de Spain had had his fragment for money: just as Ikkemotubbe, the Chickasaw chief, from whom Thomas Sutpen had had the fragment for money or rum or whatever it was, knew in his turn that not even a fragment of it had been his to relinquish or sell

not against the wilderness but against the land, not in pursuit and lust but in relinquishment, and in the commissary as it should have been, not the heart perhaps but certainly the solar-plexus of the repudiated and relinquished: the square, galleried, wooden building squatting like a portent above the fields whose laborers it still held in thrall, '65 or no, and placarded over with advertisements for snuff and cures for chills and salves and potions manufactured and sold by white men to bleach the pigment and straighten the hair of negroes that they might resemble the very race which for two hundred years had held them in bondage and from which for another hundred years not even a bloody civil war would have set them completely free

himself and his cousin amid the old smells of cheese and salt meat and kerosene and harness, the ranked shelves of tobacco and overalls and bottled medicine and thread and plow-bolts, the barrels and kegs of flour and meal and molasses and nails, the wall pegs dependant with plow-lines and plow-collars and hames and trace-chains, and the desk and the shelf above it on which rested the ledgers in which McCaslin recorded the slow outward trickle of food and supplies and equipment which returned each fall as cotton made and ginned and sold (two threads frail as truth and impalpable as equators yet cable-strong to bind for life them who made the cotton to the land their sweat fell on), and the older ledgers clumsy and archaic in size and shape, on the yellowed pages of which were recorded in the faded hand of his father Theophilus and his uncle Amodeus during the two decades before the Civil War, the manumission in title at least of Carothers McCaslin's slaves.

"Relinquish," McCaslin said. "Relinquish. You, the direct male descendant of him who saw the opportunity and took it, bought the land, took the land, got the land no matter how, held it to bequeath, no matter how, out of the old grant, the first patent, when it was a wilderness of wild beasts and wilder men, and cleared it, translated it into something to bequeath to his children, worthy of bequeathment for his descendants' ease and security and pride and to perpetuate his name and accomplishments. Not only the male descendant but the only and last descendant in the male line and in the third generation, while I am not only four generations from old Carothers, I derived through a woman and the very McCaslin in my name is mine only by sufferance and courtesy and my grandmother's pride in what that man accomplished whose legacy and monument you think you can repudiate." and he

"I cant repudiate it. It was never mine to repudiate. It was never Father's and Uncle Buddy's to bequeath me to repudiate because it was never Grandfather's to bequeath them to bequeath me to repudiate because it was never old Ikkemotubbe's to sell to Grandfather for bequeathment and repudiation. Because it was never Ikkemotubbe's fathers' fathers' to bequeath Ikkemotubbe to sell to Grandfather or any man because on the instant when Ikkemotubbe discovered, realized, that he could sell it for money, on that instant it ceased ever to have been his forever, father to father to father, and the man who bought it bought nothing."

"Bought nothing?" and he

"Bought nothing. Because He told in the Book how He created the earth, made it and looked at it and said it was all right, and then He made man. He made the earth first and peopled it with dumb creatures, and then He created man to be His overseer on the earth and to hold suzerainty over the earth and the animals on it in His name, not to hold for himself and his descendants inviolable title forever, generation after generation, to the oblongs and squares of the earth, but to hold the earth mutual and intact in the communal anonymity of brotherhood, and all the fee He asked was pity and humility and sufferance and endurance and the sweat of his face for bread. And I know what you are going to say," he said: "That nevertheless Grandfather–" and McCaslin

"–did own it. And not the first. Not alone and not the first since, as your Authority states, man was dispossessed of Eden. Nor yet the second and still not alone, on down through the tedious and shabby chronicle of His chosen sprung from Abraham, and of the sons of them who dispossessed Abraham, and of the five hundred years during which half the known world and all it contained was chattel to one city as this plantation and all the life it contained was chattel and revokeless thrall to this commissary store and those ledgers yonder during your grandfather's life, and the next thousand years while men fought over the fragments of that collapse until at last even the fragments were exhausted and men snarled over the gnawed bones of the old world's worthless evening until an accidental egg discovered to them a new hemisphere. So let me say it: That nevertheless and notwithstanding old Carothers did own it. Bought it, got it, no matter; kept it, held it, no matter; bequeathed it: else why do you stand here relinquishing and repudiating? Held it, kept it for fifty years until you could repudiate it, while He–this Arbiter, this Architect, this Umpire–condoned–or did He? looked down and saw–or did He? Or at least did nothing: saw, and could not, or did not see; saw, and would not, or perhaps He would not see–perverse, impotent, or blind: which?" and he

"Dispossessed." and McCaslin

"What?" and he

"Dispossessed. Not impotent: He didn't condone; not blind, because He watched it. And let me say it. Dispossessed of Eden. Dispossessed of Canaan, and those who dispossessed him dispossessed him dispossessed, and the five hundred years of absentee landlords in the Roman bagnios, and the thousand years of wild men from the northern woods who dispossessed them and devoured their ravished substance ravished in turn again and then snarled in what you call the old world's worthless twilight over the old world's gnawed bones, blasphemous in His name until He used a simple egg to discover to them a new world where a nation of people could be founded in humility and pity and sufferance and pride of one to another. And Grandfather did own the land nevertheless and notwithstanding because He permitted it, not impotent and not condoning and not blind because He ordered and watched it. He saw the land already accursed even as Ikkemotubbe and Ikkemotubbe's father old Issetibbeha and old Issetibbeha's fathers too held it, already tainted even before any white man owned it by what Grandfather and his kind, his fathers, had brought into the new land which He had vouchsafed them out of pity and sufferance, on condition of pity and humility and sufferance and endurance, from that old world's corrupt and worthless twilight as though in the sailfuls of the old world's tainted wind which drove the ships—" and McCaslin

"Ah."

"—and no hope for the land anywhere so long as Ikkemotubbe and Ikkemotubbe's descendants held it in unbroken succession. Maybe He saw that only by voiding the land for a time of Ikkemotubbe's blood and substituting for it another blood, could He accomplish His purpose. Maybe He knew already what that other blood would be, maybe it was more than justice that only the white man's blood was available and capable to raise the white man's curse, more than vengeance when—" and McCaslin

"Ah."

"—when He used the blood which had brought in the evil to destroy the evil as doctors use fever to burn up fever, poison to slay poison. Maybe He chose Grandfather out of all of them He might have picked. Maybe He knew that Grandfather himself would not serve His purpose because Grandfather was born too soon too, but that Grandfather would have descendants, the right descendants; maybe He had foreseen already the descendants Grandfather would have, maybe He saw already in Grandfather the seed progenitive of the three generations He saw it would take to set at least some of His lowly people free—" and McCaslin

"The sons of Ham. You who quote the Book: the sons of Ham." and he

"There are some things He said in the Book, and some things reported of Him that He did not say. And I know what you will say now: That if truth is one thing to me and another thing to you, how will we choose which is truth? You dont need to choose. The heart already knows. He didn't have His Book written to be read by what must elect and choose, but by the heart, not by the wise of the earth because maybe they dont need it or maybe the wise no longer have any heart, but by the doomed and lowly of the earth who have nothing else to read with but the heart.

Because the men who wrote His Book for Him were writing about truth and there is only one truth and it covers all things that touch the heart." and McCaslin

"So these men who transcribed His Book for Him were sometime liars." and he

"Yes. Because they were human men. They were trying to write down the heart's truth out of the heart's driving complexity, for all the complex and troubled hearts which would beat after them. What they were trying to tell, what He wanted said, was too simple. Those for whom they transcribed His words could not have believed them. It had to be expounded in the everyday terms which they were familiar with and could comprehend, not only those who listened but those who told it too, because if they who were that near to Him as to have been elected from among all who breathed and spoke language to transcribe and relay His words, could comprehend truth only through the complexity of passion and lust and hate and fear which drives the heart, what distance back to truth must they traverse whom truth could only reach by word-of-mouth?" and McCaslin

"I might answer that, since you have taken to proving your points and disproving mine by the same text, I dont know. But I dont say that, because you have answered yourself: No time at all if, as you say, the heart knows truth, the infallible and unerring heart. And perhaps you are right, since although you admitted three generations from old Carothers to you, there were not three. There were not even completely two. Uncle Buck and Uncle Buddy. And they not the first and not alone. A thousand other Bucks and Buddies in less than two generations and sometimes less than one in this land which so you claim God created and man himself cursed and tainted. Not to mention 1865." and he

"Yes. More men than Father and Uncle Buddy," not even glancing toward the shelf above the desk, nor did McCaslin. They did not need to. To him it was as though the ledgers in their scarred cracked leather bindings were being lifted down one by one in their fading sequence and spread open on the desk or perhaps upon some apocryphal Bench, or even Altar or perhaps before the Throne Itself for a last perusal and contemplation and refreshment of the Allknowledgeable before the yellowed pages and the brown thin ink in which was recorded the injustice and a little at least of its amelioration and restitution faded back forever into the anonymous communal original dust

the yellowed pages scrawled in fading ink by the hand first of his grandfather and then of his father and uncle, bachelors up to and past fifty and then sixty, the one who ran the plantation and the farming of it and the other who did the housework and the cooking and continued to do it even after his twin married and the boy himself was born

the two brothers who as soon as their father was buried moved out of the tremendously-conceived, the almost barnlike edifice which he had not even completed, into a one-room log cabin which the two of them built themselves and added other rooms to while they lived in it, refusing to allow any slave to touch any timber of it other than the actual raising into place the logs which two men alone could not handle, and domiciled all the slaves in the big house some of the windows of which were still merely boarded up with odds and ends of plank or with the skins of bear and deer nailed over the empty frames: each sundown the brother who superintended the farming would parade the negroes as a first sergeant dismisses a company, and herd them willynilly, man woman and child, without question protest or recourse, into the tremendous abortive edifice scarcely yet out of embryo, as if even old Carothers McCaslin had paused aghast at the concrete indication of his own vanity's boundless conceiving: he would call his mental roll and herd them in and with a hand-wrought nail as long as a flenching-knife and suspended from a short deer-hide thong attached to the door-jamb for that purpose, he would nail to the door of that house which lacked half its windows and had no hinged back door at all, so that presently and for fifty years afterward, when the boy himself was big to hear and remember it, there was in the land a sort of folk-tale: of the countryside all night long full of skulking McCaslin slaves dodging the moonlit roads and the Patrol-riders to visit other plantations, and of the unspoken gentlemen's agreement between the two white men and the two dozen black ones that, after the white man had counted them and driven the home-made nail into the front door at sundown, neither of the white men would go around behind the house and look at the back door, provided that all the negroes were behind the front one when the brother who drove it drew out the nail again at daybreak

the twins who were identical even in their handwriting, unless you had specimens side by side to compare, and even when both hands appeared on the same page (as often happened, as if, long since past any oral intercourse, they had used the diurnally advancing pages to conduct the unavoidable business of the compulsion which had traversed all the waste wilderness of North Mississippi in 1830 and '40 and singled them out to drive) they both looked as though they had been written by the same perfectly normal ten-year-old boy, even to the spelling, except that the spelling did not improve as one by one the slaves which Carothers McCaslin had inherited and purchased—Roscius and Phoebe and Thucydides and Eunice and their descendants, and Sam Fathers and his mother for both of whom he had swapped an underbred trotting gelding to old Ikkemotubbe, the Chickasaw chief from whom he had likewise bought the land, and Tennie Beauchamp whom the twin Amodeus had won from a neighbor in a poker-game, and the anomaly calling itself Percival Brownlee which the twin Theophilus had purchased, neither he nor his brother ever knew why apparently, from Bedford Forrest while he was still only a slave-dealer and not yet a general (It was a single page, not long and covering less than a year, not seven months in fact, begun in the hand which the boy had learned to distinguish as that of his father:

> *Percavil Brownly 26yr Old. cleark @ Bookepper. bought from N.B.Forest at Cold Water 3 Mar 1856 $265. dolars*

and beneath that, in the same hand:

> *5 mar 1856 No bookepper any way Cant read. Can write his Name but I already put that down My self Says he can Plough but dont look like it to Me. sent to Feild to day Mar 5 1856*

and the same hand:

> *6 Mar 1856 Cant plough either Says he aims to be a Precher so may be he can lead live stock to Crick to Drink*

and this time it was the other, the hand which he now recognized as his uncle's when he could see them both on the same page:

> *Mar 23th 1856 Cant do that either Except one at a Time Get shut of him*

then the first again:

> *24 Mar 1856 Who in hell would buy him*

then the second:

> *19th of Apr 1856 Nobody You put yourself out of Market at Cold Water two months ago I never said sell him Free him*

the first:

> *22 Apr 1856 Ill get it out of him*

the second:

> *Jun 13th 1856 How $1 per yr 265$ 265 yrs Wholl sign his Free paper*

then the first again:

> *1 Oct 1856 Mule josephine Broke Leg   shot Wrong stall wrong niger wrong everything $100. dolars*

and the same:

> *2 Oct 1856 Freed Debit McCaslin @ McCaslin $265. dolars*

then the second again:

Oct 3th Debit Theophilus McCaslin Niger 265$ Mule 100$ 365$ He hasnt gone yet Father should be here

then the first:

3 Oct 1856 Son of a bitch wont leave What would father done

the second:

29th of Oct 1856 Renamed him

the first:

31 Oct 1856 Renamed him what

the second:

Chrstms 1856 Spintrius

) took substance and even a sort of shadowy life with their passions and complexities too as page followed page and year year; all there, not only the general and condoned injustice and its slow amortization but the specific tragedy which had not been condoned and could never be amortized; the new page and the new ledger, the hand which he could now recognise at first glance as his father's:

Father dide Lucius Quintus Carothers McCaslin, Callina 1772 Missippy 1837. Dide and burid 27 June 1837

Roskus. rased by Granfather in Callina Dont know how old. Freed 27 June 1837 Dont want to leave. Dide and Burid 12 Jan 1841

Fibby Roskus Wife. bought by granfather in Callina says Fifty Freed 27 June 1837 Dont want to leave. Dide and burd 1 Aug 1849

Thucydus Roskus @ Fibby Son born in Callina 1779. Refused 10acre peace fathers Will 28 Jun 1837 Refused Cash offer $200. dolars from A. @ T. McCaslin 28 Jun 1837 Wants to stay and work it out

and beneath this and covering the next five pages and almost that many years, the slow, day-by-day accruement of the wages allowed him and the food and clothing—the molasses and meat and meal, the cheap durable shirts and jeans and shoes, and now and then a coat against rain and cold —charged against the slowly yet steadily mounting sum of balance (and it would seem to the boy that he could actually see the black man, the slave whom his white owner had forever manumitted by the very act from which the black man could never be free so long as memory lasted, entering the commissary, asking permission perhaps of the white man's son to see the ledger-page which he could not even read, not even asking for the white man's word, which he would have had to accept for the reason that there was absolutely no way under the sun for him to test it, as to how the account stood, how much longer before he could go and never return, even if only as far as Jefferson seventeen miles away), on to the double pen-stroke closing the final entry:

3 Nov 1841 By Cash to Thucydus McCaslin $200. dolars Set Up blaksmith in J. Dec 1841 Dide and burid in J 17 feb 1854

Eunice Bought by Father in New Orleans 1807 $650. dolars. Marrid to Thucydus 1809 Drownd in Crick Cristmas Day 1832

and then the other hand appeared, the first time he had seen it in the ledger to distinguish it as his uncle's, the cook and housekeeper whom even McCaslin, who had known him and the boy's father for sixteen years before the boy was born, remembered as sitting all day long in the rocking chair from which he cooked the food, before the kitchen fire on which he cooked it:

June 21th 1833 Drownd herself

and the first:

23 Jun 1833 Who in hell ever heard of a niger drownding him self

and the second, unhurried, with a complete finality; the two identical entries might have been made with a rubber stamp save for the date:

Aug 13th 1833 Drownd herself

and he thought *But why? But why?* He was sixteen then. It was neither the first time he had been alone in the commissary nor the first time he had taken down the old ledgers familiar on their shelf above the desk ever since he could remember. As a child and even after nine and ten and eleven, when he had learned to read, he would look up at the scarred and cracked backs and ends but with no particular desire to open them, and though he intended to examine them someday because he realized that they probably contained a chronological and much more comprehensive though doubtless tedious record than he would ever get from any other source, not alone of his own flesh and blood but of all his people, not only the whites but the black ones too, who were as much a part of his ancestry as his white progenitors, and of the land which they had all held and used in common and fed from and on and would continue to use in common without regard to color or titular ownership, it would only be on some idle day when he was old and perhaps even bored a little, since what the old books contained would be after all these years fixed immutably, finished, unalterable, harmless. Then he was sixteen. He knew what he was going to find before he found it. He got the commissary key from McCaslin's room after midnight while McCaslin was asleep and with the commissary door shut and locked behind him and the forgotten lantern stinking anew the rank dead icy air, he leaned above the yellowed page and thought not Why drowned herself, but thinking what he believed his father had thought when he found his brother's first comment: Why did Uncle Buddy think she had drowned herself? finding, beginning to find on the next succeeding page what he knew he would find, only this was still not it because he already knew this:

> *Tomasina called Tomy Daughter of Thucydus @ Eunice Born 1810 dide in Child bed June 1833 and Burd. Yr stars fell*

nor the next:

> *Turl Son of Thucydus @ Eunice Tomy born Jun 1833 yr stars fell Fathers will*

and nothing more, no tedious recording filling this page of wages, day by day, and food and clothing charged against them, no entry of his death and burial because he had outlived his white half-brothers and the books which McCaslin kept did not include obituaries: just *Fathers will* and he had seen that too: old Carothers' bold cramped hand far less legible than his sons' even and not much better in spelling, who while capitalizing almost every noun and verb, made no effort to punctuate or construct whatever, just as he made no effort either to explain or obfuscate the thousand-dollar legacy to the son of an unmarried slave-girl, to be paid only at the child's coming-of-age, bearing the consequence of the act of which there was still no definite incontrovertible proof that he acknowledged, not out of his own substance, but penalizing his sons with it, charging them a cash forfeit on the accident of their own paternity; not even a bribe for silence toward his own fame since his fame would suffer only after he was no longer present to defend it, flinging almost contemptuously, as he might a cast-off hat or pair of shoes, the thousand dollars which could have had no more reality to him under those conditions than it would have to the negro, the slave who would not even see it until he came of age, twenty-one years too late to begin to learn what money was. *So I reckon that was cheaper than saying My son to a nigger,* he thought. *Even if My son wasn't but just two words. But there must have been love,* he thought. *Some sort of love. Even what he would have called love: not just an afternoon's or a night's spittoon.* There was the old man, old, within five years of his life's end, long a widower and, since his sons were not only bachelors but were approaching middleage, lonely in the house and doubtless even bored since his plantation was established now and functioning and there was enough money now, too much of it probably for a man whose vices even apparently remained below his means; there was the girl, husbandless and young, only twenty-three when the child was born: perhaps he had sent for her at first out of loneliness, to have a young voice and movement in the house, summoned her, bade her mother send her each morning to sweep the floors and make the beds and the mother acquiescing since that was probably already understood, already planned: the only child of a couple who were not field hands and who held themselves something above the other slaves, not alone for that reason but because the husband and his father and mother too had been inherited by the white man from his father, and the white man himself had travelled three hundred miles and better to New Orleans in a day when men travelled by horseback or steamboat, and bought the girl's mother as a wife for him

and that was all. The old frail pages seemed to turn of their own accord even while he thought, *His own daughter His own daughter. No. No Not even him,* back to that one where the white man (not even a widower then) who never went anywhere, any more than his sons in their time ever did, and who did not need another slave, had gone all the way to New Orleans and bought one. And Tomey's Terrel was still alive when the boy was ten years old and he knew from his own observation and memory that there had already been some white in Tomey's Terrel's blood before his father gave him the rest of it; and looking down at the yellowed page spread beneath the yellow glow of the lantern smoking and stinking in that rank chill midnight room fifty years later, he seemed to see her actually walking into the icy creek on that Christmas day six months before her daughter's and her lover's (*Her first lover's,* he thought. *Her first*) child was born, solitary, inflexible, griefless, ceremonial, in formal and succinct repudiation of grief and despair, who had already had to repudiate belief and hope

that was all. He would never need look at the ledgers again nor did he; the yellowed pages in their fading and implacable succession were as much a part of his consciousness and would remain so forever, as the fact of his own nativity:

> *Tennie Beauchamp 21yrs Won by Amodeus McCaslin from Hubert Beauchamp Esqre Posible Strait against three Treys in sigt Not called 1859 Marrid to Tomys Turl 1859*

and no date of freedom because her freedom, as well as that of her first surviving child, derived not from Buck and Buddy McCaslin in the commissary but from a stranger in Washington, and no date of death and burial, not only because McCaslin kept no obituaries in his books, but because in this year 1883 she was still alive and would remain so to see a grandson by her last surviving child:

Amodeus McCaslin Beauchamp Son of tomys Turl @ Tennie Beauchamp 1859 dide 1859

then his uncle's hand entire, because his father was now a member of the cavalry command of that man whose name as a slave-dealer he could not even spell: and not even a page and not even a full line:

Dauter Tomes Turl and tenny 1862

and not even a line and not even a sex and no cause given though the boy could guess it because McCaslin was thirteen then and he remembered how there was not always enough to eat in more places than Vicksburg:

Child of tomes Turl and Tenny 1863

and the same hand again and this one lived, as though Tennie's perseverance and the fading and diluted ghost of old Carothers' ruthlessness had at last conquered even starvation: and clearer, fuller, more carefully written and spelled than the boy had yet seen it, as if the old man, who should have been a woman to begin with, trying to run what was left of the plantation in his brother's absence in the intervals of cooking and caring for himself and the fourteen-year-old orphan, had taken as an omen for renewed hope the fact that this nameless inheritor of slaves was at least remaining alive long enough to receive a name:

James Thucydus Beauchamp Son of Tomes Turl and Tenny Beauchamp Born 29th december 1864 and both Well Wanted to call him Theophilus but Tride Amodeus McCaslin and Callina McCaslin and both dide so Disswaded Them Born at Two clock A,m, both Well

but no more, nothing; it would be another two years yet before the boy, almost a man now, would return from the abortive trip into Tennessee with the still-intact third of old Carothers' legacy to his negro son and his descendants, which as the three surviving children established at last one by one their apparent intention of surviving, their white half-uncles had increased to a thousand dollars each, conditions permitting, as they came of age, and completed the page himself as far as it would even be completed when that day was long passed beyond which a man born in 1864 (or 1867 either, when he himself saw light) could have expected or himself hoped or even wanted to be still alive; his own hand now, queerly enough resembling neither his father's nor his uncle's nor even McCaslin's, but like that of his grandfather's save for the spelling:

> *Vanished sometime on night of his twenty-first birthday Dec 29 1885. Traced by Isaac McCaslin to Jackson Tenn. and there lost. His third of legacy $1000.00 returned to McCaslin Edmonds Trustee this day Jan 12 1886*

but not yet: that would be two years yet, and now his father's again, whose old commander was now quit of soldiering and slave-trading both; once more in the ledger and then not again, and more illegible than ever, almost indecipherable at all from the rheumatism which now crippled him and almost completely innocent now even of any sort of spelling as well as punctuation, as if the four years during which he had followed the sword of the only man ever breathing who ever sold him a negro, let alone beat him in a trade, had convinced him not only of the vanity of faith and hope but of orthography too:

> *Miss sophonsiba b dtr t t @ t 1869*

but not of belief and will because it was there, written, as McCaslin had told him, with the left hand, but there in the ledger one time more and then not again, for the boy himself was a year old, and when Lucas was born six years later, his father and uncle had been dead inside the same twelve-months almost five years; his own hand again, who was there and saw it, 1886, she was just seventeen, two years younger than himself, and he was in the commissary when McCaslin entered out of the first of dusk and said, "He wants to marry Fonsiba," like that: and he looked past McCaslin and saw the man, the stranger, taller than McCaslin and wearing better clothes than McCaslin and most of the other white men the boy knew habitually wore, who entered the room like a white man and stood in it like a white man, as though he had let McCaslin precede him into it not because McCaslin's skin was white but simply because McCaslin lived there and knew the way, and who talked like a white man too, looking at him past McCaslin's shoulder rapidly and keenly once and then no more, without further interest, as a mature and contained white man not impatient but just pressed for time might have looked. "Marry Fonsiba?" he cried. "Marry Fonsiba?" and then no more either, just watching and listening while McCaslin and the negro talked:

"To live in Arkansas, I believe you said."

"Yes. I have property there. A farm."

"Property? A farm? You own it?"

"Yes."

"You dont say Sir, do you?"

"To my elders, yes."

"I see. You are from the North."

"Yes. Since a child."

"Then your father was a slave."

"Yes. Once."

"Then how do you own a farm in Arkansas?"

"I have a grant. It was my father's. From the United States. For military service."

"I see," McCaslin said. "The Yankee army."

"The United States army," the stranger said; and then himself again, crying it at McCaslin's back:

"Call aunt Tennie! I'll go get her! I'll—" But McCaslin was not even including him; the stranger did not even glance back toward his voice, the two of them speaking to one another again as if he were not even there:

"Since you seem to have it all settled," McCaslin said, "why have you bothered to consult my authority at all?"

"I dont," the stranger said. "I acknowledge your authority only so far as you admit your responsibility toward her as a female member of the family of which you are the head. I dont ask your permission. I——"

"That will do!" McCaslin said. But the stranger did not falter. It was neither as if he were ignoring McCaslin nor as if he had failed to hear him. It was as though he were making, not at all an excuse and not exactly a justification, but simply a statement which the situation absolutely required and demanded should be made in McCaslin's hearing whether McCaslin listened to it or not. It was as if he were talking to himself, for himself to hear the words spoken aloud. They faced one another, not close yet at slightly less than foils' distance, erect, their voices not raised, not impactive, just succinct:

"—I inform you, notify you in advance as chief of her family. No man of honor could do less. Besides, you have, in your way, according to your lights and upbringing——"

"That's enough, I said," McCaslin said. "Be off this place by full dark. Go." But for another moment the other did not move, contemplating McCaslin with that detached and heatless look, as if he were watching reflected in McCaslin's pupils the tiny image of the figure he was sustaining.

"Yes," he said. "After all, this is your house. And in your fashion you have. . . . But no matter. You are right. This is enough." He turned back toward the door; he paused again but only for a second, already moving while he spoke: "Be easy. I will be good to her." Then he was gone.

"But how did she ever know him?" the boy cried. "I never even heard of him before! And Fonsiba, that's never been off this place except to go to church since she was born——"

"Ha," McCaslin said. "Even their parents dont know until too late how seventeen-year-old girls ever met the men who marry them too, if they are lucky." And the next morning they were both gone, Fonsiba too. McCaslin never saw her again, nor did he, because the woman he found at last, five months later, was no one he had ever known. He carried a third of the three-thousand-dollar fund in gold in a money-belt, as when he had vainly traced Tennie's Jim into Tennessee a year ago. They—the man—had left an address of some sort with Tennie, and three months later a letter came, written by the man although McCaslin's wife, Alice, had taught Fonsiba to read and write too a little. But it bore a different postmark from the address the man had left with Tennie, and he travelled by rail as far as he could and then by contracted stage and then by a hired livery rig and then by rail again for a distance: an experienced traveller by now and an experienced bloodhound too, and a successful one this time because he would have to be; as the slow interminable empty muddy December miles crawled and crawled and night followed night in hotels, in roadside taverns of rough logs and containing little else but a bar, and in the cabins of strangers, and the hay of lonely barns, in none of which he dared undress because of his secret golden girdle like that of a disguised one of the Magi travelling incognito and not even hope to draw him but only determination and desperation, he would tell himself: *I will have to find her. I will have to. We have already lost one of them. I will have to find her this time.* He did. Hunched in the slow and icy rain, on a spent hired horse splashed to the chest and higher, he saw it—a single log edifice with a clay chimney, which seemed in process of being flattened by the rain to a nameless and valueless rubble of dissolution in that roadless and even pathless waste of unfenced fallow and wilderness jungle—no barn, no stable, not so much as a hen-coop: just a log cabin built by hand and no clever hand either, a meagre pile of clumsily-cut firewood sufficient for about one day and not even a gaunt hound to come bellowing out from under the house when he rode up—a farm only in embryo, perhaps a good farm, maybe even a plantation someday, but not now, not for years yet and only then with labor, hard and enduring and unflagging work and sacrifice; he shoved open the crazy kitchen door in its awry frame and entered an icy gloom where not even a fire for cooking burned, and after another moment saw, crouched into the wall's angle behind a crude table, the coffee-colored face which he had known all his life but knew no more, the body which had been born within a hundred yards of the room that he was born in and in which some of his own blood ran, but which was now completely inheritor of generation after generation to whom an unannounced white man on a horse was a white man's hired Patroller wearing a pistol sometimes and a blacksnake whip always; he entered the next room, the only other room the cabin owned, and found, sitting in a rocking chair before the hearth, the man himself, reading—sitting there in the only chair in the house, before that miserable fire for which there was not wood sufficient to last twenty-four hours, in the same ministerial clothing in which he had entered the commissary five months ago and a pair of gold-framed spectacles which, when he looked up and then rose to his feet, the boy saw did not even contain lenses, reading a book in the midst of that desolation, that muddy waste fenceless and even pathless and without even a walled shed for stock to stand beneath: and over all, permeant, clinging to the man's very clothing and exuding from his skin itself, that rank stink of baseless and imbecile delusion, that boundless rapacity and folly, of the carpet-bagger followers of victorious armies.

"Dont you see?" he cried. "Dont you see? This whole land, the whole South, is cursed, and all of us who derive from it, whom it ever suckled, white and black both, lie under the curse? Granted that my people brought the curse onto the land: maybe for that reason their descendants alone can—not resist it, not combat it—maybe just endure and outlast it until the curse is lifted. Then your peoples' turn will come because we have forfeited ours. But not now. Not yet. Dont you see?"

The other stood now, the unfrayed garments still ministerial even if not quite so fine, the book closed upon one finger to keep the place, the lensless spectacles held like a music master's wand in the other workless hand while the owner of it spoke his measured and sonorous imbecility of the boundless folly and the baseless hope: "You're wrong. The curse you whites brought into this land has been lifted. It has been voided and discharged. We are seeing a new era, an era dedicated, as our founders intended it, to freedom, liberty and equality for all, to which this country will be the new Canaan——"

"Freedom from what? From work? Canaan?" He jerked his arm, comprehensive, almost violent: whereupon it all seemed to stand there about them, intact and complete and visible in the drafty, damp, heatless, negro-stale negro-rank sorry room—the empty fields without plow or seed to work them, fenceless against the stock which did not exist within or without the walled stable which likewise was not there. "What corner of Canaan is this?"

"You are seeing it at a bad time. This is winter. No man farms this time of year."

"I see. And of course her need for food and clothing will stand still while the land lies fallow."

"I have a pension," the other said. He said it as a man might say *I have grace* or *I own a gold mine*. "I have my father's pension too. It will arrive on the first of the month. What day is this?"

"The eleventh," he said. "Twenty days more. And until then?"

"I have a few groceries in the house from my credit account with the merchant in Midnight who banks my pension check for me. I have executed to him a power of attorney to handle it for me as a matter of mutual—"

"I see. And if the groceries dont last the twenty days?"

"I still have one more hog."

"Where?"

"Outside," the other said. "It is customary in this country to allow stock to range free during the winter for food. It comes up from time to time.

But no matter if it doesn't; I can probably trace its footprints when the need——"

"Yes!" he cried. "Because no matter: you still have the pension check. And the man in Midnight will cash it and pay himself out of it for what you have already eaten and if there is any left over, it is yours. And the hog will be eaten by then or you still cant catch it, and then what will you do?"

"It will be almost spring then," the other said. "I am planning in the spring——"

"It will be January," he said. "And then February. And then more than half of March—" and when he stopped again in the kitchen she had not moved, she did not even seem to breathe or to be alive except her eyes watching him; when he took a step toward her it was still not movement because she could have retreated no further: only the tremendous, fathomless, ink-colored eyes in the narrow, thin, too thin, coffee-colored face watching him without alarm, without recognition, without hope. "Fonsiba," he said. "Fonsiba. Are you all right?"

"I'm free," she said. Midnight was a tavern, a livery stable, a big store (that would be where the pension check banked itself as a matter of mutual elimination of bother and fret, he thought) and a little one, a saloon and a blacksmith shop. But there was a bank there too. The president (the owner, for all practical purposes) of it was a translated Mississippian who had been one of Forrest's men too: and his body lightened of the golden belt for the first time since he left home eight days ago, with pencil and paper he multiplied three dollars by twelve months and divided it into one thousand dollars; it would stretch that way over almost twenty-eight years and for twenty-eight years at least she would not starve, the banker promising to send the three dollars himself by a trusty messenger on the fifteenth of each month and put it into her actual hand, and he returned home and that was all because in 1874 his father and his uncle were both dead and the old ledgers never again came down from the shelf above the desk to which his father had returned them for the last time that day in 1869. But he could have completed it:

> *Lucas Quintus Carothers McCaslin Beauchamp. Last surviving son and child of Tomey's Terrel and Tennie Beauchamp. March 17, 1874*

except that there was no need: not *Lucius Quintus* @c @c @c, but *Lucas Quintus,* not refusing to be called Lucius, because he simply eliminated that word from the name; not denying, declining the name itself, because he used three quarters of it; but simply taking the name and changing, altering it, making it no longer the white man's but his own, by himself composed, himself selfprogenitive and nominate, by himself ancestored, as, for all the old ledgers recorded to the contrary, old Carothers himself was and that was all: 1874 the boy; 1888 the man, repudiated denied and free; 1895 and husband but no father, unwidowered but without a wife, and found long since that no man is ever free and probably could not bear it if he were; married then and living in Jefferson in the little new jerry-built bungalow which his wife's father had given them: and one morning Lucas stood suddenly in the doorway of the room where he was reading the Memphis paper and he looked at the paper's dateline and thought *It's his birthday. He's twenty-one today* and Lucas said: "Whar's the rest of that money old Carothers left? I wants it. All of it."

that was all: and McCaslin

"More men than that one Buck and Buddy to fumble-heed that truth so mazed for them that spoke it and so confused for them that heard yet still there was 1865": and he

"But not enough. Not enough of even Father and Uncle Buddy to fumble-heed in even three generations not even three generations fathered by Grandfather not even if there had been nowhere beneath His sight any but Grandfather and so He would not even have needed to elect and choose. But He tried and I know what you will say. That having Himself created them He could have known no more of hope than He could have pride and grief, but He didn't hope He just waited because He had made them: not just because He had set them alive and in motion but because He had already worried with them so long: worried with them so long because He had seen how in individual cases they were capable of anything, any height or depth remembered in mazed incomprehension out of heaven where hell was created too and so He must admit them or else admit his equal somewhere and so be no longer God and therefore must accept responsibility for what He Himself had done in order to live with Himself in His lonely and paramount heaven. And He probably knew it was vain but He had created them and knew them capable of all things because He had shaped them out of the primal Absolute which contained all and had watched them since in their individual exaltation and baseness and they themselves not knowing why nor how nor even when: until at last He saw that they were all Grandfather all of them and that even from them the elected and chosen the best the very best He could expect (not hope mind: not hope) would be Bucks and Buddies and not even enough of them and in the third generation not even Bucks and Buddies but—" and McCaslin

"Ah": and he

"Yes. If He could see Father and Uncle Buddy in Grandfather He must have seen me too. —an Isaac born into a later life than Abraham's and repudiating immolation: fatherless and therefore safe declining the altar because maybe this time the exasperated Hand might not supply the kid—" and McCaslin

"Escape": and he

"All right. Escape.—Until one day He said what you told Fonsiba's husband that afternoon here in this room: *This will do. This is enough:* not in exasperation or rage or even just sick to death as you were sick that day: just *This is enough* and looked about for one last time, for one time more since He had created them, upon this land this South for which He had done so much with woods for game and streams for fish and deep rich soil for seed and lush springs to sprout it and long summers to mature it and serene falls to harvest it and short mild winters for men and animals and saw no hope anywhere and looked beyond it where hope should have been, where to East North and West lay illimitable that whole hopeful continent dedicated as a refuge and sanctuary of liberty and freedom from what you called the old world's worthless evening and saw the rich descendants of slavers, females of both sexes, to whom the black they shrieked of was another specimen another example like the Brazilian macaw brought home in a cage by a traveller, passing resolutions about horror and outrage in warm and air-proof halls: and the thundering cannonade of politicians earning votes and the medicine-shows of pulpiteers earning Chatauqua fees, to whom the outrage and the injustice were as much abstractions as Tariff or Silver or Immortality and who employed the very shackles of its servitude and the sorry rags of its regalia as they did the other beer and banners and mottoes, redfire and brimstone and sleight-of-hand and musical handsaws: and the whirling wheels which manufactured for a profit the pristine replacements of the shackles and shoddy garments as they wore out and spun the cotton and made the gins which ginned it and the cars and ships which hauled it, and the men who ran the wheels for that profit and established and collected the taxes it was taxed with and the rates for hauling it and the commissions for selling it: and He could have repudiated them since they were his creation now and forever more throughout all their generations until not only that old world from which He had rescued them but this new one too which He had revealed and led them to as a sanctuary and refuge were become the same worthless tideless rock cooling in the last crimson evening except that out of all that empty sound and bootless fury one silence, among that loud and moiling all of them just one simple enough to believe that horror and outrage were first and last simply horror and outrage and crude enough to act upon that, illiterate and had no words for talking or perhaps was just busy and had no time to, one out of them all who did not bother Him with cajolery and adjuration then pleading then threat and had not even bothered to inform Him in advance what he was about so that a lesser than He might have even missed the simple act of lifting the long ancestral musket down from the deerhorns above the door, whereupon He said *My name is Brown too* and the other *So is mine* and He *Then mine or yours cant be because I am against it* and the other *So am I* and He triumphantly *Then where are you going with that gun?* and the other told him in one sentence one word and He: amazed: Who knew neither hope nor pride nor grief *But your Association, your Committee, your Officers. Where are your Minutes, your Motions, your Parliamentary Procedures?* and the other *I aint against them. They are all right I reckon for them that have the time. I am just against the weak because they are niggers being held in bondage by the strong just because they are white.* So He turned once more to this land which He still intended to save because He had done so much for it—" and McCaslin

"What?" and he

"—to these people He was still committed to because they were his creations—" and McCaslin

"Turned back to us? His face to us?" and he

"—whose wives and daughters at least made soups and jellies for them when they were sick, and carried the trays through the mud and the winter too into the stinking cabins and sat in the stinking cabins and kept fires going until crises came and passed, but that was not enough: and when they were very sick had them carried into the big house itself into the company room itself maybe and nursed them there which the white man would have done too for any other of his cattle that was sick but at least the man who hired one from a livery wouldn't have and still that was not enough: so that He said and not in grief either Who had made them and so could know no more of grief than He could of pride or hope: *Apparently they can learn nothing save through suffering, remember nothing save when underlined in blood—*" and McCaslin

"Ashby on an afternoon's ride, to call on some remote maiden cousins of his mother or maybe just acquaintances of hers, comes by chance upon a minor engagement of outposts and dismounts and with his crimson-lined cloak for target leads a handful of troops he never saw before against an entrenched position of backwoods-trained riflemen. Lee's battle-order, wrapped maybe about a handful of cigars and doubtless thrown away when the last cigar was smoked, found by a Yankee Intelligence officer on the floor of a saloon behind the Yankee lines after Lee had already divided his forces before Sharpsburg. Jackson on the Plank Road, already rolled up the flank which Hooker believed could not be turned and, waiting only for night to pass to continue the brutal and incessant slogging which would fling that whole wing back into Hooker's lap where he sat on a front gallery in Chancellorsville drinking rum toddies and telegraphing Lincoln that he had defeated Lee, is shot from among a whole covey of minor officers and in the blind night by one of his own patrols, leaving as next by seniority Stuart, that gallant man born apparently already horsed and sabred and already knowing all there was to know about war except the slogging and brutal stupidity of it: and that same Stuart off raiding Pennsylvania hen-roosts when Lee should have known of all of Meade just where Hancock was on Cemetery Ridge: and Longstreet too at Gettysburg and that same Longstreet shot out of saddle by his own men in the dark by mistake just as Jackson was. His face to us? His face to us?" and he

"How else have made them fight? Who else but Jacksons and Stuarts and Ashbys and Morgans and Forrests?—the farmers of the central and middle-west, holding land by the acre instead of the tens or maybe even the hundreds, farming it themselves and to no single crop of cotton or tobacco or cane, owning no slaves and needing and wanting none, and already looking toward the Pacific coast, not always as long as two generations there and having stopped where they did stop only through the fortuitous mischance that an ox died or a wagon-axle broke. And the New England mechanics who didn't even own land and measured all things by the weight of water and the cost of turning wheels, and the narrow fringe of traders and shipowners still looking backward across the Atlantic and attached to the continent only by their counting-houses. And those who should have had the alertness to see: the wildcat manipulators of mythical wilderness townsites; and the astuteness to rationalise: the bankers who held the mortgages on the land which the first were only waiting to abandon, and on the railroads and steamboats to carry them still further west, and on the factories and the wheels and the rented tenements those who ran them lived in; and the leisure and scope to comprehend and fear in time and even anticipate. the Boston-bred (even when not born in Boston) spinster descendants of long lines of similarly-bred and likewise spinster aunts and uncles whose hands knew no callus except that of the indicting pen, to whom the wilderness itself began at the top of tide and who looked, if at anything other than Beacon Hill, only toward heaven—not to mention all the loud rabble of the camp-followers of pioneers: the bellowing of politicians, the mellifluous choiring of self-styled men of God, the—" and McCaslin

"Here, here. Wait a minute". and he

"Let me talk now. I'm trying to explain to the head of my family something which I have got to do which I dont quite understand myself, not in justification of it but to explain it if I can. I could say I dont know why I must do it but that I do know I have got to because I have got myself to have to live with for the rest of my life and all I want is peace to do it in. But you are the head of my family. More. I knew a long time ago that I would never have to miss my father, even if you are just finding out that you have missed your son—the drawers of bills and the shavers of notes and the schoolmasters and the self-ordained to teach and lead and all that horde of the semi-literate with a white shirt but no change for it, with one eye on themselves and watching each other with the other one. Who else could have made them fight: could have struck them so aghast with fear and dread as to turn shoulder to shoulder and face one way and even stop talking for a while and even after two years of it keep them still so wrung with terror that some among them would seriously propose moving their very capital into a foreign country lest it be ravaged and pillaged by a people whose entire white male population would have little more than filled any one of their larger cities: except Jackson in the Valley and three separate armies trying to catch him and none of them ever knowing whether they were just retreating from a battle or just running into one, and Stuart riding his whole command entirely around the biggest single armed force this continent ever saw in order to see what it looked like from behind and Morgan leading a cavalry charge against a stranded man-of-war. Who else could have declared a war against a power with ten times the area and a hundred times the men and a thousand times the resources, except men who could believe that all necessary to conduct a successful war was not acumen nor shrewdness nor politics nor diplomacy nor money nor even integrity and simple arithmetic, but just love of land and courage——"

"And an unblemished and gallant ancestry and the ability to ride a horse," McCaslin said. "Dont leave that out." It was evening now, the tranquil sunset of October mazy with windless woodsmoke. The cotton was long since picked and ginned, and all day now the wagons loaded with gathered corn moved between field and crib, processional across the enduring land. "Well, maybe that's what He wanted. At least, that's what He got." This time there was no yellowed procession of fading and harmless ledger-pages. This was chronicled in a harsher book, and McCaslin, fourteen and fifteen and sixteen, had seen it and the boy himself had inherited it as Noah's grandchildren had inherited the Flood although they had not been there to see the deluge: that dark corrupt and bloody time while three separate peoples had tried to adjust not only to one another but to the new land which they had created and inherited too and must live in for the reason that those who had lost it were no less free to quit it than those who had gained it were:—those upon whom freedom and equality had been dumped overnight and without warning or preparation or any training in how to employ it or even just endure it and who misused it, not as children would nor yet because they had been so long in bondage and then so suddenly freed, but misused it as human beings always misuse freedom, so that he thought *Apparently there is a wisdom beyond even that learned through suffering necessary for a man to distinguish between liberty and license;* those who had fought for four years and lost to preserve a condition under which that franchisement was anomaly and paradox, not because they were opposed to freedom as freedom but for the old reasons for which man (not the generals and politicians but man) has always fought and died in wars: to preserve a status quo or to establish a better future one to endure for his children; and lastly, as if that were not enough for bitterness and hatred and fear, that third race even more alien to the people whom they resembled in pigment and in whom even the same blood ran, than to the people whom they did not,—that race threefold in one and alien even among themselves save for a single fierce will for rapine and pillage, composed of the sons of middleaged Quartermaster lieutenants and Army sutlers and contractors in military blankets and shoes and transport mules, who followed the battles they themselves had not fought and inherited the conquest they themselves had not helped to gain, sanctioned and protected even if not blessed, and left their bones and in another generation would be engaged in a fierce economic competition of small sloven farms with the black men they were supposed to have freed and the white descendants of fathers who had owned no slaves anyway whom they were supposed to have disinherited and in the third generation would be back once more in the little lost county seats as barbers and garage mechanics and deputy sheriffs and mill- and gin-hands and power-plant firemen, leading, first in mufti then later in an actual formalized regalia of hooded sheets and passwords and fiery Christian symbols, lynching mobs against the race their ancestors had come to save: and of all that other nameless horde of speculators in human misery, manipulators of money and politics and land, who follow catastrophe and are their own protection as grasshoppers are and need no blessing and sweat no plow or axe-helve and batten and vanish and leave no bones, just as they derived apparently from no ancestry, no mortal flesh, no act even of passion or even of lust: and the Jew who came without protection too, since after two thousand years he had got out of the habit of being or needing it, and solitary, without even the solidarity of the locusts and in this a sort of courage since he had come thinking not in terms of simple pillage but in terms of his great-grandchildren, seeking yet some place to establish them to endure even though forever alien: and unblessed: a pariah about the face of the Western earth which twenty centuries later was still taking revenge on him for the fairy tale with which he had conquered it. McCaslin had actually seen it, and the boy even at almost eighty would never be able to distinguish certainly between what he had seen and what had been told him: a lightless and gutted and empty land where women crouched with the huddled children behind locked doors and men armed in sheets and masks rode the silent roads and the bodies of white and black both, victims not so much of hate as of desperation and despair, swung from lonely limbs: and men shot dead in polling-booths with the still wet pen in one hand and the unblotted ballot in the other: and a United States marshal in Jefferson who signed his official papers with a crude cross, an ex-slave called Sickymo, not at all because his ex-owner was a doctor and apothecary but because, still a slave, he would steal his master's grain alcohol and dilute it with water and peddle it in pint bottles from a cache beneath the roots of a big sycamore tree behind the drug store, who had attained his high office because his half-white sister was the concubine of the Federal A.P.M.: and this time McCaslin did not even say Look but merely lifted one hand, not even pointing, not even specifically toward the shelf of ledgers but toward the desk, toward the corner where it sat beside the scuffed patch on the floor where two decades of heavy shoes had stood while the white man at the desk added and multiplied and subtracted. And again he did not need to look because he had seen this himself and, twenty-three years after the Surrender and twenty-four after the Proclamation, was still watching it: the ledgers, new ones now and filled rapidly, succeeding one another rapidly and containing more names than old Carothers or even his father and Uncle Buddy had ever dreamed of; new names and new faces to go with them, among which the old names and faces that even his father and uncle would have recognized, were lost, vanished—Tomey's Terrel dead, and even the tragic and miscast Percival Brownlee, who couldn't keep books and couldn't farm either, found his true niche at last, reappeared in 1862 during the boy's father's absence and had apparently been living on the plantation for at least a month before his uncle found out about it, conducting impromptu revival meetings among negroes, preaching and leading the singing also in his high sweet true soprano voice and disappeared again on foot and at top speed, not behind but ahead of a body of raiding Federal horse and reappeared for the third and last time in the entourage of a travelling Army paymaster, the two of them passing through Jefferson in a surrey at the exact moment when the boy's father (it was 1866) also happened to be crossing the Square, the surrey and its occupants traversing rapidly that quiet and bucolic scene and even in that fleeting moment and to others beside the boy's father giving an illusion of flight and illicit holiday like a man on an excursion during his wife's absence with his wife's personal maid, until Brownlee glanced up and saw his late co-master and gave him one defiant female glance and then broke again, leaped from the surrey and disappeared this time for good and it was only by chance that McCaslin, twenty years later, heard of him again, an old man now and quite fat, as the well-to-do proprietor of a select New Orleans brothel; and Tennie's Jim gone, nobody knew where, and Fonsiba in Arkansas with her three dollars each month and the scholar-husband with his lensless spectacles and frock coat and his plans for the spring; and only Lucas was left, the baby, the last save himself of old Carothers' doomed and fatal blood which in the male derivation seemed to destroy all it touched, and even he was repudiating and at least hoping to escape it;—Lucas, the boy of fourteen whose name would not even appear for six years yet among those rapid pages in the bindings new and dustless too since McCaslin lifted them down daily now to write into them the continuation of that record which two hundred years had not been enough to complete, and another hundred would not be enough to discharge; that chronicle which was a whole land in miniature, which multiplied and compounded was the entire South, twenty-three years after surrender and twenty-four from emancipation—that slow trickle of molasses and meal and meat, of shoes and straw hats and overalls, of plow-lines and collars and heel-bolts and buckheads and clevises, which returned each fall as cotton—the two threads frail as truth and impalpable as equators yet cable-strong to bind for life them who made the cotton to the land their sweat fell on: and he

"Yes. Binding them for a while yet, a little while yet. Through and beyond that life and maybe through and beyond the life of that life's sons and maybe even through and beyond that of the sons of those sons. But not always, because they will endure. They will outlast us because they are—" it was not a pause, barely a falter even, possibly appreciable only to himself, as if he couldn't speak even to McCaslin, even to explain his repudiation, that which to him too, even in the act of escaping (and maybe this was the reality and the truth of his need to escape), was heresy: so that even in escaping he was taking with him more of that evil and unregenerate old man who could summon, because she was his property, a human being because she was old enough and female, to his widower's house and get a child on her and then dismiss her because she was of an inferior race, and then bequeath a thousand dollars to the infant because he would be dead then and wouldn't have to pay it, than even he had feared. "Yes. He didn't want to. He had to. Because they will endure. They are better than we are. Stronger than we are. Their vices are vices aped from white men or that white men and bondage have taught them: improvidence and intemperance and evasion—not laziness: evasion: of what white men had set them to, not for their aggrandisement or even comfort but his own—" and McCaslin

"All right. Go on: Promiscuity. Violence. Instability and lack of control. Inability to distinguish between mine and thine—" and he

"How distinguish, when for two hundred years mine did not even exist for them?" and McCaslin

"All right. Go on. And their virtues—" and he

"Yes. Their own. Endurance—" and McCaslin

"So have mules": and he

"—and pity and tolerance and forbearance and fidelity and love of children—" and McCaslin

"So have dogs": and he

"—whether their own or not or black or not. And more: what they got not only not from white people but not even despite white people because they had it already from the old free fathers a longer time free than us because we have never been free—" and it was in McCaslin's eyes too, he had only to look at McCaslin's eyes and it was there, that summer twilight seven years ago, almost a week after they had returned from the camp before he discovered that Sam Fathers had told McCaslin: an old bear, fierce and ruthless not just to stay alive but ruthless with the fierce pride of liberty and freedom, jealous and proud enough of liberty and freedom to see it threatened not with fear nor even alarm but almost with joy, seeming deliberately to put it into jeopardy in order to savor it and keep his old strong bones and flesh supple and quick to defend and preserve it; an old man, son of a negro slave and an Indian king, inheritor on the one hand of the long chronicle of a people who had learned humility through suffering and learned pride through the endurance which survived the suffering, and on the other side the chronicle of a people even longer in the land than the first, yet who now existed there only in the solitary brotherhood of an old and childless negro's alien blood and the wild and invincible spirit of an old bear; a boy who wished to learn humility and pride in order to become skillful and worthy in the woods but found himself becoming so skillful so fast that he feared he would never become worthy, because he had not learned humility and pride though he had tried, until one day an old man, who could not have defined either led him as though by the hand to where an old bear and a little mongrel dog showed him that, by possessing one thing other, he would possess them both; and a little dog, nameless and mongrel and many-fathered, grown yet weighing less than six pounds, who couldn't be dangerous because there was nothing anywhere much smaller, not fierce because that would have been called just noise, not humble because it was already too near the ground to genuflect, and not proud because it would not have been close enough for anyone to discern what was casting that shadow and which didn't even know it was not going to heaven since they had already decided it had no immortal soul, so that all it could be was brave, even though they would probably call that too just noise. *"And you didn't shoot," McCaslin said. "How close were you?"*

"I don't know," he said. "There was a big wood tick just inside his off hind leg. I saw that. But I didn't have the gun then."

"But you didn't shoot when you had the gun," McCaslin said. "Why?" But McCaslin didn't wait, rising and crossing the room, across the pelt of the bear he had killed two years ago and the bigger one McCaslin had killed before he was born, to the bookcase beneath the mounted head of his first buck, and returned with the book and sat down again and opened it. "Listen," he said. He read the five stanzas aloud and closed the book on his finger and looked up. "All right," he said. "Listen," and read again, but only one stanza this time and closed the book and laid it on the table. "She cannot fade, though thou hast not thy bliss," McCaslin said: "Forever wilt thou love, and she be fair."

"He's talking about a girl," he said.

"He had to talk about something," McCaslin said. Then he said, "He was talking about truth. Truth is one. It doesn't change. It covers all things which touch the heart—honor and pride and pity and justice and courage and love. Do you see now?" He didn't know. Somehow it had seemed simpler than that, simpler than somebody talking in a book about a young man and a girl he would never need to grieve over because he could never approach any nearer and would never have to get any further away. He had heard about an old bear and finally got big enough to hunt it and he hunted it four years and at last met it with a gun in his hands and he didn't shoot. Because a little dog—But he could have shot long before the fyce covered the twenty yards to where the bear waited, and Sam Fathers could have shot at any time during the interminable minute while Old Ben stood on his hind legs over them. . . . He ceased. McCaslin watched

him, still speaking, the voice, the words as quiet as the twilight itself was: "Courage and honor and pride, and pity and love of justice and of liberty. They all touch the heart, and what the heart holds to becomes truth, as far as we know truth. Do you see now?"

and he could still hear them, intact in this twilight as in that one seven years ago, no louder still because they did not need to be because they would endure: and he had only to look at McCaslin's eyes beyond the thin and bitter smiling, the faint lip-lift which would have had to be called smiling;—his kinsman, his father almost, who had been born too late into the old time and too soon for the new, the two of them juxtaposed and alien now to each other against their ravaged patrimony, the dark and ravaged fatherland still prone and panting from its etherless operation:

"Habet then.—So this land is, indubitably, of and by itself cursed": and he

"Cursed": and again McCaslin merely lifted one hand, not even speaking and not even toward the ledgers: so that, as the stereopticon condenses into one instantaneous field the myriad minutiae of its scope, so did that slight and rapid gesture establish in the small cramped and cluttered twilit room not only the ledgers but the whole plantation in its mazed and intricate entirety—the land, the fields and what they represented in terms of cotton ginned and sold, the men and women whom they fed and clothed and even paid a little cash money at Christmas-time in return for the labor which planted and raised and picked and ginned the cotton, the machinery and mules and gear with which they raised it and their cost and upkeep and replacement—that whole edifice intricate and complex and founded upon injustice and erected by ruthless rapacity and carried on even yet with at times downright savagery not only to the human beings but the valuable animals too, yet solvent and efficient and, more than that: not only still intact but enlarged, increased; brought still intact by McCaslin, himself little more than a child then, through and out of the debacle and chaos of twenty years ago where hardly one in ten survived, and enlarged and increased and would continue so, solvent and efficient and intact and still increasing so long as McCaslin and his McCaslin successors lasted, even though their surnames might not even be Edmonds then: and he

"Habet too. Because that's it: not the land, but us. Not only the blood, but the name too; not only its color but its designation: Edmonds, white, but, a female line, could have no other but the name his father bore; Beauchamp, the elder line and the male one, but, black, could have had any name he liked and no man would have cared, except the name his father bore who had no name—" and McCaslin

"And since I know too what you know I will say now, once more let me say it: And one other, and in the third generation too, and the male, the eldest, the direct and sole and white and still McCaslin even, father to son to son—" and he

"I am free": and this time McCaslin did not even gesture, no inference of fading pages, no postulation of the stereoptic whole, but the frail and iron thread strong as truth and impervious as evil and longer than life itself and reaching beyond record and patrimony both to join him with the lusts and passions, the hopes and dreams and griefs, of bones whose names while still fleshed and capable even old Carothers' grandfather had never heard: and he:

"And of that too": and McCaslin

"Chosen, I suppose (I will concede it) out of all your time by Him, as you say Buck and Buddy were from theirs. And it took Him a bear and an old man and four years just for you. And it took you fourteen years to reach that point and about that many, maybe more, for Old Ben, and more than seventy for Sam Fathers. And you are just one. How long then? How long?" and he

"It will be long. I have never said otherwise. But it will be all right because they will endure—" and McCaslin

"And anyway, you will be free.—No, not now nor ever, we from them nor they from us. So I repudiate too. I would deny even if I knew it were true. I would have to. Even you can see that I could do no else. I am what I am; I will be always what I was born and have always been. And more than me. More than me, just as there were more than Buck and Buddy in what you called His first plan which failed": and he

"And more than me": and McCaslin

"No. Not even you. Because mark. You said how on that instant when Ikkemotubbe realised that he could sell the land to Grandfather, it ceased forever to have been his. All right; go on: Then it belonged to Sam Fathers, old Ikkemotubbe's son. And who inherited from Sam Fathers, if not you? co-heir perhaps with Boon, if not of his life maybe, at least of his quitting it?" and he

"Yes. Sam Fathers set me free."

and Isaac McCaslin, not yet Uncle Ike, a long time yet before he would be uncle to half a county and still father to none, living in one small cramped fireless rented room in a Jefferson boardinghouse where petit juries were domiciled during court terms and itinerant horse- and mule-traders stayed, with his kit of brand-new carpenter's tools and the shotgun McCaslin had given him with his name engraved in silver and old General Compson's compass (and, when the General died, his silver-mounted horn too) and the iron cot and mattress and the blankets which he would take each fall into the woods for more than sixty years and the bright tin coffee-pot

there had been a legacy, from his Uncle Hubert Beauchamp, his godfather, that bluff burly roaring childlike man from whom Uncle Buddy had won Tomey's Terrel's wife Tennie in the poker-game in 1859—"posible strait against three Treys in sigt Not called"—; no pale sentence or paragraph scrawled in cringing fear of death by a weak and trembling hand as a last desperate sop flung backward at retribution, but a Legacy, a Thing, possessing weight to the hand and bulk to the eye and even audible: a silver cup filled with gold pieces and wrapped in burlap and sealed with his godfather's ring in the hot wax, which (intact still) even before his Uncle Hubert's death and long before his own majority, when it would be his, had become not only a legend but one of the family lares. After his father's and his Uncle Hubert's sister's marriage they moved back into the big house, the tremendous cavern which old Carothers had started and never finished, cleared the remaining negroes out of it and with his mother's dowry completed it, at least the rest of the windows and doors and moved into it, all of them save Uncle Buddy who declined to leave the cabin he and his twin had built, the move being the bride's notion and more than just a notion and none ever to know if she really wanted to live in the big house or if she knew beforehand that Uncle Buddy would refuse to move: and two weeks after his birth in 1867, the first time he and his mother came down stairs one night, and the silver cup sitting on the cleared dining-room table beneath the bright lamp and while his mother and his father and McCaslin and Tennie (his nurse: carrying him)—all of them again but Uncle Buddy—watched, his Uncle Hubert rang one by one into the cup the bright and glinting mintage and wrapped it into the burlap envelope and heated the wax and sealed it and carried it back home with him where he lived alone now without even his sister either to hold him down as McCaslin said or to try to raise him up as Uncle Buddy said, and (dark times then in Mississippi) Uncle Buddy said most of the niggers gone and the ones that didn't go even Hub Beauchamp could not have wanted: but the dogs remained and Uncle Buddy said Beauchamp fiddled while Nero fox-hunted

they would go and see it there; at last his mother would prevail and they would depart in the surrey, once more all save Uncle Buddy and McCaslin to keep Uncle Buddy company, until one winter Uncle Buddy began to fail and from then on it was himself, beginning to remember now, and his mother and Tennie and Tomey's Terrel to drive: the twenty-two miles into the next county, the twin gateposts on one of which McCaslin could remember the half-grown boy blowing a fox-horn at breakfast dinner and supper-time and jumping down to open to any passer who happened to hear it but where there were no gates at all now, the shabby and overgrown entrance to what his mother still insisted that people call Warwick because her brother was if truth but triumphed and justice but prevailed the rightful earl of it, the paintless house which outwardly did not change but which on the inside seemed each time larger because he was too little to realize then that there was less and less in it of the fine furnishings, the rosewood and mahogany and walnut which for him had never existed anywhere anyway save in his mother's tearful lamentations and the occasional piece small enough to be roped somehow onto the rear or the top of the carriage on their return (And he remembered this, he had seen it: an instant, a flash, his mother's soprano "Even my dress! Even my dress!" loud and outraged in the barren unswept hall; a face young and female and even lighter in color than Tomey's Terrel's for an instant in a closing door; a swirl, a glimpse of the silk gown and the flick and glint of an ear-ring: an apparition rapid and tawdry and illicit, yet somehow even to the child, the infant still almost, breathless and exciting and evocative: as though, like two limpid and pellucid streams meeting, the child which he still was had made serene and absolute and perfect rapport and contact through that glimpsed nameless illicit hybrid female flesh with the boy which had existed at that stage of inviolable and immortal adolescence in his uncle for almost sixty years; the dress, the face, the ear-rings gone in that same aghast flash and his uncle's voice: "She's my cook! She's my new cook! I had to have a cook, didn't I?" then the uncle himself, the face alarmed and aghast too yet still innocently and somehow even indomitably of a boy, they retreating in their turn now, back to the front gallery, and his uncle again, pained and still amazed, in a sort of desperate resurgence if not of courage at least of self-assertion: "They're free now; They're folks too just like we are!" and his mother: "That's why! That's why! My mother's house! Defiled! Defiled!" and his uncle: "Damn it, Sibbey, at least give her time to pack her grip": then over, finished, the loud uproar and all, himself and Tennie and he remembered Tennie's inscrutable face at the broken shutterless window of the bare room which had once been the parlor while they watched, hurrying down the lane at a stumbling trot, the routed compounder of his uncle's uxory: the back, the nameless face which he had seen only for a moment, the once-hooped dress ballooning and flapping below a man's overcoat, the worn heavy carpet-bag jouncing and banging against her knee, routed and in retreat true enough and in the empty lane, solitary, young-looking, and forlorn, yet withal still exciting and evocative and wearing still the silken banner captured inside the very citadel of respectability, and unforgettable.)

the cup, the sealed inscrutable burlap, sitting on the shelf in the locked closet, Uncle Hubert unlocking the door and lifting it down and passing it from hand to hand: his mother, his father, McCaslin and even Tennie, insisting that each take it in turn and heft it for weight and shake it again to prove the sound, Uncle Hubert himself standing spraddled before the cold unswept hearth in which the very bricks themselves were crumbling into a litter of soot and dust and mortar and the droppings of chimney-sweeps, still roaring and still innocent and still indomitable: and for a long time he believed nobody but himself had noticed that his uncle now put the cup only into his hands, unlocked the door and lifted it down and put it into his hands and stood over him until he had shaken it obediently until it sounded then took it from him and locked it back into the closet before anyone else could have offered to touch it, and even later, when competent not only to remember but to rationalise, he could not say what it was or even if it had been anything because the parcel was still heavy and still rattled, not even when, Uncle Buddy dead and his father, at last and after almost seventy-five years in bed after the sun rose, said: "Go get that damn cup. Bring that damn Hub Beauchamp too if you have to": because it still rattled though his uncle no longer put it even into his hands now but carried it himself from one to the other, his mother, McCaslin, Tennie, shaking it before each in turn, saying: "Hear it? Hear it?" his face still innocent, not quite baffled but only amazed and not very amazed and still indomitable: and, his father and Uncle Buddy both gone now, one day without reason or any warning the almost completely empty house in which his uncle and Tennie's ancient and quarrelsome great-grandfather (who claimed to have seen Lafayette and McCaslin said in another ten years would be remembering God) lived, cooked and slept in one single room, burst into peaceful conflagration, a tranquil instantaneous sourceless unanimity of combustion, walls floors and roof: at sunup it stood where his uncle's father had built it sixty years ago, at sundown the four blackened and smokeless chimneys rose from a light white powder of ashes and a few charred ends of planks which did not even appear to have been very hot: and out of the last of evening, the last one of the twenty-two miles, on the old white mare which was the last of that stable which McCaslin remembered, the two old men riding double up to the sister's door, the one wearing his fox-horn on its braided deerhide thong and the other carrying the burlap parcel wrapped in a shirt, the tawny wax-daubed shapeless lump sitting again and on an almost identical shelf and his uncle holding the half-opened door now, his hand not only on the knob but one foot against it and the key waiting in the other hand, the face urgent and still not baffled but still and even indomitably not very amazed and himself standing in the half-opened door looking quietly up at the burlap shape become almost three times its original height and a good half less than its original thickness and turning away and he would remember not his mother's look this time nor yet Tennie's inscrutable expression but McCaslin's dark and aquiline face grave insufferable and bemused: then one night they waked him and fetched him still half-asleep into the lamp light, the smell of medicine which was familiar by now in that room and the smell of something else which he had not smelled before and knew at once and would never forget, the pillow, the worn and ravaged face from which looked out still the boy innocent and immortal and amazed and urgent, looking at him and trying to tell him until McCaslin moved and leaned over the bed and drew from the top of the night shirt the big iron key on the greasy cord which suspended it, the eyes saying Yes Yes Yes now, and cut the cord and unlocked the closet and brought the parcel to the bed, the eyes still trying to tell him even when he took the parcel so that was still not it, the hands still clinging to the parcel even while relinquishing it, the eyes more urgent than ever trying to tell him but they never did; and he was ten and his mother was dead too and McCaslin said, "You are almost half-way now. You might as well open it": and he: "No. He said twenty-one": and he was twenty-one and McCaslin shifted the bright lamp to the center of the cleared dining-room table and set the parcel beside it and laid his open knife beside the parcel and stood back with that expression of old grave intolerant and repudiating and he lifted it, the burlap lump which fifteen years ago had changed its shape completely overnight, which shaken gave forth a thin weightless not-quite-musical curiously muffled clatter, the bright knife-blade hunting amid the mazed intricacy of string, the knobby gouts of wax bearing his uncle's Beauchamp seal rattling onto the table's polished top and, standing amid the collapse of burlap folds, the unstained tin coffee-pot still brand new, the handful of copper coins and now he knew what had given them the muffled sound: a collection of minutely folded scraps of paper sufficient almost for a rat's nest, of good linen bond, of the crude ruled paper such as negroes use, of raggedly-torn ledger-pages and the margins of newspapers and once the paper label from a new pair of overalls, all dated and all signed, beginning with the first one not six months after they had watched him seal the silver cup into the burlap on this same table in this same room by the light even of this same lamp almost twenty-one years ago:

> *I owe my Nephew Isaac Beauchamp McCaslin five (5) pieces Gold which I.O.U constitues My note of hand with Interest at 5 percent*
>
> *Hubert Fitz-Hubert Beauchamp*
>
> *at Warwick 27 Nov 1867*

and he: "Anyway he called it Warwick": once at least, even if no more. But there was more:

> *Isaac 24 Dec 1867 I.O.U. 2 pieces Gold H.Fh.B. I.O.U. Isaac 1 piece Gold 1 Jan 1868 H.Fh.B.*

then five again then three then one then one then a long time and what dream, what dreamed splendid recoup, not of any injury or betrayal of trust because it had been merely a loan: nay, a partnership:

> *I.O.U. Beauchamp McCaslin or his heirs twenty-five (25) pieces Gold This & All preceding constituting My notes of hand at twenty (20) percentum compounded annually. This date of 19th January 1873*
>
> *Beauchamp*

no location save that in time and signed by the single not name but word as the old proud earl himself might have scrawled Nevile: and that made forty-three and he could not remember himself of course but the legend had it at fifty, which balanced: one: then one: then one: then one and then the last three and then the last chit, dated after he came to live in the house with them and written in the shaky hand not of a beaten old man because he had never been beaten to know it but of a tired old man maybe and even at that tired only on the outside and still indomitable, the simplicity of the last one the simplicity not of resignation but merely of amazement, like a simple comment or remark, and not very much of that:

One silver cup. Hubert Beauchamp

and McCaslin: "So you have plenty of coppers anyway. But they are still not old enough yet to be either rarities or heirlooms. So you will have to take the money": except that he didn't hear McCaslin, standing quietly beside the table and looking peacefully at the coffee-pot and the pot sitting one night later on the mantel above what was not even a fireplace in the little cramped icelike room in Jefferson as McCaslin tossed the folded banknotes onto the bed and, still standing (there was nowhere to sit save on the bed) did not even remove his hat and overcoat: and he

"As a loan. From you. This one": and McCaslin

"You cant. I have no money that I can lend to you. And you will have to go to the bank and get it next month because I wont bring it to you": and he could not hear McCaslin now either, looking peacefully at McCaslin, his kinsman, his father almost yet no kin now as, at the last, even fathers and sons are no kin: and he

"It's seventeen miles, horseback and in the cold. We could both sleep here": and McCaslin

"Why should I sleep here in my house when you wont sleep yonder in yours?" and gone, and he looking at the bright rustless unstained tin and thinking and not for the first time, how much it takes to compound a man (Isaac McCaslin for instance) and of the devious intricate choosing yet unerring path that man's (Isaac McCaslin's for instance) spirit takes among all that mass to make him at last what he is to be, not only to the astonishment of them (the ones who sired the McCaslin who sired his father and Uncle Buddy and their sister, and the ones who sired the Beauchamp who sired his Uncle Hubert and his Uncle Hubert's sister) who believed they had shaped him, but to Isaac McCaslin too

as a loan and used it though he would not have had to: Major de Spain offered him a room in his house as long as he wanted it and asked nor would ever ask any question, and old General Compson more than that, to take him into his own room, to sleep in half of his own bed and more than Major de Spain because he told him baldly why: "You sleep with me and before this winter is out, I'll know the reason. You'll tell me. Because I dont believe you just quit. It looks like you just quit but I have watched you in the woods too much and I dont believe you just quit even if it does look damn like it": using it as a loan, paid his board and rent for a month and bought the tools, not simply because he was good with his hands because he had intended to use his hands and it could have been with horses, and not in mere static and hopeful emulation of the Nazarene as the young gambler buys a spotted shirt because the old gambler won in one yesterday, but (without the arrogance of false humility and without the false humbleness of pride, who intended to earn his bread, didn't especially want to earn it but had to earn it and for more than just bread) because if the Nazarene had found carpentering good for the life and ends He had assumed and elected to serve, it would be all right too for Isaac McCaslin even though Isaac McCaslin's ends, although simple enough in their apparent motivation, were and would be always incomprehensible to him, and his life, invincible enough in its needs, if he could have helped himself, not being the Nazarene, he would not have chosen it: and paid it back. He had forgotten the thirty dollars which McCaslin would put into the bank in his name each month, fetched it in to him and flung it onto the bed that first one time but no more; he had a partner now or rather he was the partner: a blasphemous profane clever old dipsomaniac who had built blockade-runners in Charleston in '62 and '63 and had been a ship's carpenter since and appeared in Jefferson two years ago, nobody knew from where nor why, and spent a good part of his time since recovering from delirium tremens in the jail; they had put a new roof on the stable of the bank's president and (the old man in jail again still celebrating that job) he went to the bank to collect for it and the president said, "I should borrow from you instead of paying you": and it had been seven months now and he remembered for the first time, two-hundred-and-ten dollars, and this was the first job of any size and when he left the bank the account stood at two-twenty, two-forty to balance, only twenty dollars more to go, then it did balance though by then the total had increased to three hundred and thirty and he said, "I will transfer it now": and the president said, "I cant do that McCaslin told me not to. Haven't you got another initial you could use and open another account?" but that was all right, the coins the silver and the bills as they accumulated knotted into a handkerchief and the coffee-pot wrapped in an old shirt as when Tennie's great-grandfather had fetched it from Warwick eighteen years ago, in the bottom of the iron-bound trunk which old Carothers had brought from Carolina and his landlady said, "Not even a lock! And you dont even lock your door, not even when you leave!" and himself looking at her as peacefully as he had looked at McCaslin that first night in this same room, no kin to him at all yet more than kin as those who serve you even for pay are your kin and those who injure you are more than brother or wife

and he had the wife now; got the old man out of jail and fetched him to the rented room and sobered him by superior strength, did not even remove his own shoes for twenty-four hours, got him up and got food into him and they built the barn this time from the ground up and he married her: an only child, a small girl yet curiously bigger than she seemed at first, solider perhaps, with dark eyes and a passionate heart-shaped face, who had time even on that farm to watch most of the day while he sawed timbers to the old man's measurements: and she: "Papa told me about you. That farm is really yours, isn't it?" and he

"And McCaslin's": and she

"Was there a will leaving half of it to him?" and he

"There didn't need to be a will. His grandmother was my father's sister. We were the same as brothers": and she

"You are the same as second cousins and that's all you ever will be. But I dont suppose it matters": and they were married, they were married and it was the new country, his heritage too as it was the heritage of all, out of the earth, beyond the earth yet of the earth because his too was of the earth's long chronicle, his too because each must share with another in order to come into it, and in the sharing they become one: for that while, one: for that little while at least, one: indivisible, that while at least irrevocable and unrecoverable, living in a rented room still but for just a little while and that room wall-less and topless and floorless in glory for him to leave each morning and return to at night; her father already owned the lot in town and furnished the material and he and his partner would build it, her dowry from one: her wedding-present from three, she not to know it until the bungalow was finished and ready to be moved into and he never knew who told her, not her father and not his partner and not even in drink though for a while he believed that, himself coming home from work and just time to wash and rest a moment before going down to supper, entering no rented cubicle since it would still partake of glory even after they would have grown old and lost it: and he saw her face then, just before she spoke: "Sit down": the two of them sitting on the bed's edge, not even touching yet, her face strained and terrible, her voice a passionate and expiring whisper of immeasurable promise: "I love you. You know I love you. When are we going to move?" and he

"I didn't—I didn't know—Who told you—" the hot fierce palm clapped over his mouth, crushing his lips into his teeth, the fierce curve of fingers digging into his cheek and only the palm slacked off enough for him to answer:

"The farm. Our farm. Your farm": and he

"I——" then the hand again, finger and palm, the whole enveloping weight of her although she still was not touching him save the hand, the voice: "No! No!" and the fingers themselves seeming to follow through the cheek the impulse to speech as it died in his mouth, then the whisper, the breath again, of love and of incredible promise, the palm slackening again to let him answer:

"When?" and he

"I——" then she was gone, the hand too, standing, her back to him and her head bent, the voice so calm now that for an instant it seemed no voice of hers that he ever remembered: "Stand up and turn your back and shut your eyes": and repeated before he understood and stood himself with his eyes shut and heard the bell ring for supper below stairs and the calm voice again: "Lock the door": and he did so and leaned his forehead against the cold wood, his eyes closed, hearing his heart and the sound he had begun to hear before he moved until it ceased and the bell rang again below stairs and he knew it was for them this time and he heard the bed and turned and he had never seen her naked before, he had asked her to once, and why: that he wanted to see her naked because he loved her and he wanted to see her looking at him naked because he loved her but after that he never mentioned it again, even turning his face when she put the nightgown on over her dress to undress at night and putting the dress on over the gown to remove it in the morning and she would not let him get into bed beside her until the lamp was out and even in the heat of summer she would draw the sheet up over them both before she would let him turn to her: and the landlady came up the stairs up the hall and rapped on the door and then called their names but she didn't move, lying still on the bed outside the covers, her face turned away on the pillow, listening to nothing, thinking of nothing, not of him anyway he thought: then the landlady went away and she said, "Take off your clothes": her head still turned away, looking at nothing, thinking of nothing, waiting for nothing, not even him, her hand moving as though with volition and vision of its own, catching his wrist at the exact moment when he paused beside the bed so that he never paused but merely changed the direction of moving, downward now, the hand drawing him and she moved at last, shifted, a movement one single complete inherent not practiced and one time older than man, looking at him now, drawing him still downward with the one hand down and down and he neither saw nor felt it shift, palm flat against his chest now and holding him away with the same apparent lack of any effort or any need for strength, and not looking at him now, she didn't need to, the chaste woman, the wife, already looked upon all the men who ever rutted and now her whole body had changed, altered, he had never seen it but once and now it was not even the one he had seen but composite of all woman-flesh since man that ever of its own will reclined on its back and opened, and out of it somewhere, without any movement of lips even, the dying and invincible whisper: "Promise": and he

"Promise?"

"The farm." He moved. He had moved, the hand shifting from his chest once more to his wrist, grasping it, the arm still lax and only the light increasing pressure of the fingers as though arm and hand were a piece of wire cable with one looped end, only the hand tightening as he pulled against it. "No," he said. "No": and she was not looking at him still but not like the other but still the hand: "No, I tell you. I wont. I cant. Never": and still the hand and he said, for the last time, he tried to speak clearly and he knew it was still gently and he thought, *She already knows more than 1 with all the man-listening in camps where there was nothing to read ever even heard of. They are born already bored with what a boy approaches only at fourteen and fifteen with blundering and aghast trembling:* "I cant. Not ever. Remember": and still the steady and invincible hand and he said Yes and he thought, *She is lost. She was born lost. We were all born lost* then he stopped thinking and even saying Yes, it was like nothing he had ever dreamed, let alone heard in mere man-talking until after a no-time he returned and lay spent on the insatiate immemorial beach and again with a movement one time more, older than man, she turned and freed herself and on their wedding night she had cried and he thought she was crying now at first, into the tossed and wadded pillow and the cachinnation: "And that's all. That's all from me. If this dont get you that son you talk about, it wont be mine": lying on her side, her back to the empty rented room, laughing and laughing

5

He went back to the camp one more time before the lumber company moved in and began to cut the timber. Major de Spain himself never saw it again. But he made them welcome to use the house and hunt the land whenever they liked, and in the winter following the last hunt when Sam Fathers and Lion died, General Compson and Walter Ewell invented a plan to corporate themselves, the old group, into a club and lease the camp and the hunting privileges of the woods—an invention doubtless of the somewhat childish old General but actually worthy of Boon Hogganbeck himself. Even the boy, listening, recognised it for the subterfuge it was: to change the leopard's spots when they could not alter the leopard, a baseless and illusory hope to which even McCaslin seemed to subscribe for a while, that once they had persuaded Major de Spain to return to the camp he might revoke himself, which even the boy knew he would not do. And he did not. The boy never knew what occurred when Major de Spain declined. He was not present when the subject was broached and McCaslin never told him. But when June came and the time for the double birthday celebration there was no mention of it and when November came no one spoke of using Major de Spain's house and he never knew whether or not Major de Spain knew they were going on the hunt though without doubt old Ash probably told him: he and McCaslin and General Compson (and that one was the General's last hunt too) and Walter and Boon and Tennie's Jim and old Ash loaded two wagons and drove two days and almost forty miles beyond any country the boy had ever seen before and lived in tents for the two weeks. And the next spring they heard (not from Major de Spain) that he had sold the timber-rights to a Memphis lumber company and in June the boy came to town with McCaslin one Saturday and went to Major de Spain's office—the big, airy, book-lined, second-storey room with windows at one end opening upon the shabby hinder purlieus of stores and at the other a door giving onto the railed balcony above the Square, with its curtained alcove where sat a cedar water-bucket and a sugar-bowl and spoon and tumbler and a wicker-covered demijohn of whisky, and the bamboo-and-paper punkah swinging back and forth above the desk while old Ash in a tilted chair beside the entrance pulled the cord.

"Of course," Major de Spain said. "Ash will probably like to get off in the woods himself for a while, where he wont have to eat Daisy's cooking. Complain about it, anyway. Are you going to take anybody with you?"

"No sir," he said, "I thought that maybe Boon--" For six months now Boon had been town-marshal at Hoke's; Major de Spain had compounded with the lumber company—or perhaps compromised was closer, since it was the lumber company who had decided that Boon might be better as a town-marshal than head of a logging gang.

"Yes," Major de Spain said. "I'll wire him today. He can meet you at Hoke's. I'll send Ash on by the train and they can take some food in and all you will have to do will be to mount your horse and ride over."

"Yes sir," he said. "Thank you." And he heard his voice again. He didn't know he was going to say it yet he did know, he had known it all the time: "Maybe if you . . ." His voice died. It was stopped, he never knew how because Major de Spain did not speak and it was not until his voice ceased that Major de Spain moved, turned back to the desk and the papers spread on it and even that without moving because he was sitting at the desk with a paper in his hand when the boy entered, the boy standing there looking down at the short plumpish gray-haired man in sober fine broadcloth and an immaculate glazed shirt whom he was used to seeing in boots and muddy corduroy, unshaven, sitting the shaggy powerful long-hocked mare with the worn Winchester carbine across the saddlebow and the great blue dog standing motionless as bronze at the stirrup, the two of them in that last year and to the boy anyway coming to resemble one another somehow as two people competent for love or for business who have been in love or in business together for a long time sometimes do. Major de Spain did not look up again.

"No. I will be too busy. But good luck to you. If you have it, you might bring me a young squirrel."

"Yes sir," he said. "I will."

He rode his mare, the three-year-old filly he had bred and raised and broken himself. He left home a little after midnight and six hours later, without even having sweated her, he rode into Hoke's, the tiny log-line junction which he had always thought of as Major de Spain's property too although Major de Spain had merely sold the company (and that many years ago) the land on which the sidetracks and loading-platforms and the commissary store stood, and looked about in shocked and grieved amazement even though he had had forewarning and had believed himself prepared: a new planing-mill already half completed which would cover two or three acres and what looked like miles and miles of stacked steel rails red with the light bright rust of newness and of piled crossties sharp with creosote, and wire corrals and feeding-troughs for two hundred mules at least and the tents for the men who drove them; so that he arranged for the care and stabling of his mare as rapidly as he could and did not look any more, mounted into the log-train caboose with his gun and climbed into the cupola and looked no more save toward the wall of wilderness ahead within which he would be able to hide himself from it once more anyway.

Then the little locomotive shrieked and began to move: a rapid churning of exhaust, a lethargic deliberate clashing of slack couplings traveling backward along the train, the exhaust changing to the deep slow clapping bites of power as the caboose too began to move and from the cupola he watched the train's head complete the first and only curve in the entire line's length and vanish into the wilderness, dragging its length of train behind it so that it resembled a small dingy harmless snake vanishing into weeds, drawing him with it too until soon it ran once more at its maximum clattering speed between the twin walls of unaxed wilderness as of old. It had been harmless once. Not five years ago Walter Ewell had shot a six-point buck from this same moving caboose, and there was the story of the half-grown bear: the train's first trip in to the cutting thirty miles away, the bear between the rails, its rear end elevated like that of a playing puppy while it dug to see what sort of ants or bugs they might contain or perhaps just to examine the curious symmetrical squared barkless logs which had appeared apparently from nowhere in one endless mathematical line overnight, still digging until the driver on the braked engine not fifty feet away blew the whistle at it, whereupon it broke frantically and took the first tree it came to: an ash sapling not much bigger than a man's thigh and climbed as high as it could and clung there, its head ducked between its arms as a man (a woman perhaps) might have done while the brakeman threw chunks of ballast at it, and when the engine returned three hours later with the first load of outbound logs the bear was halfway down the tree and once more scrambled back up as high as it could and clung again while the train passed and was still there when the engine went in again in the afternoon and still there when it came back out at dusk; and Boon had been in Hoke's with the wagon after a barrel of flour that noon when the train-crew told about it and Boon and Ash, both twenty years younger then, sat under the tree all that night to keep anybody from shooting it and the next morning Major de Spain had the log-train held at Hoke's and just before sundown on the second day, with not only Boon and Ash but Major de Spain and General Compson and Walter and McCaslin, twelve then, watching, it came down the tree after almost thirty-six hours without even water and McCaslin told him how for a minute they thought it was going to stop right there at the barrow-pit where they were standing and drink, how it looked at the water and paused and looked at them and at the water again, but did not, gone, running, as bears run, the two sets of feet, front and back, tracking two separate though parallel courses.

It had been harmless then. They would hear the passing log-train sometimes from the camp; sometimes, because nobody bothered to listen for it or not. They would hear it going in, running light and fast, the light clatter of the trucks, the exhaust of the diminutive locomotive and its shrill peanut-parcher whistle flung for one petty moment and absorbed by the brooding and inattentive wilderness without even an echo. They would hear it going out, loaded, not quite so fast now yet giving its frantic and toylike illusion of crawling speed, not whistling now to conserve steam, flinging its bitten laboring miniature puffing into the immemorial woodsface with frantic and bootless vainglory, empty and noisy and puerile, carrying to no destination or purpose sticks which left nowhere any scar or stump as the child's toy loads and transports and unloads its dead sand and rushes back for more, tireless and unceasing and rapid yet never quite so fast as the Hand which plays with it moves the toy burden back to load the toy again. But it was different now. It was the same train, engine cars and caboose, even the same enginemen brakeman and conductor to whom Boon, drunk then sober then drunk again then fairly sober once more all in the space of fourteen hours, had bragged that day two years ago about what they were going to do to Old Ben tomorrow, running with its same illusion of frantic rapidity between the same twin walls of impenetrable and impervious woods, passing the old landmarks, the old game crossings over which he had trailed bucks wounded and not wounded and more than once seen them, anything but wounded, bot out of the woods and up and across the embankment which bore the rails and ties then down and into the woods again as the earth-bound supposedly move but crossing as arrows travel, groundless, elongated, three times its actual length and even paler, different in color, as if there were a point between immobility and absolute motion where even mass chemically altered, changing without pain or agony not only in bulk and shape but in color too, approaching the color of wind, yet this time it was as though the train (and not only the train but himself, not only his vision which had seen it and his memory which remembered it but his clothes too, as garments carry back into the clean edgeless blowing of air the lingering effluvium of a sick-room or of death) had brought with it into the doomed wilderness even before the actual axe the shadow and portent of the new mill not even finished yet and the rails and ties which were not even laid; and he knew now what he had known as soon as he saw Hoke's this morning but had not yet thought into words: why Major de Spain had not come back, and that after this time he himself, who had had to see it one time other, would return no more.

Now they were near. He knew it before the engine-driver whistled to warn him. Then he saw Ash and the wagon, the reins without doubt wrapped once more about the brake-lever as within the boy's own memory Major de Spain had been forbidding him for eight years to do, the train slowing, the slackened couplings jolting and clashing again from car to car, the caboose slowing past the wagon as he swung down with his gun, the conductor leaning out above him to signal the engine, the caboose still slowing, creeping, although the engine's exhaust was already slatting in mounting tempo against the unechoing wilderness, the crashing of drawbars once more traveling backward along the train, the caboose picking up speed at last. Then it was gone. It had not been. He could no longer hear it. The wilderness soared, musing, inattentive, myriad, eternal, green; older than any mill-shed, longer than any spur-line. "Mr Boon here yet?" he said.

"He beat me in," Ash said. "Had the wagon loaded and ready for me at Hoke's yistiddy when I got there and setting on the front steps at camp last night when I got in. He already been in the woods since fo daylight this morning. Said he gwine up to the Gum Tree and for you to hunt up that way and meet him." He knew where that was: a single big sweet-gum just outside the woods, in an old clearing; if you crept up to it very quietly this time of year and then ran suddenly into the clearing, sometimes you caught as many as a dozen squirrels in it, trapped, since there was no other tree near they could jump to. So he didn't get into the wagon at all.

"I will," he said.

"I figured you would," Ash said, "I fotch you a box of shells." He passed the shells down and began to unwrap the lines from the brake-pole.

"How many times up to now do you reckon Major has told you not to do that?" the boy said.

"Do which?" Ash said. Then he said: "And tell Boon Hogganbeck dinner gonter be on the table in a hour and if yawl want any to come on and eat it."

"In an hour?" he said. "It aint nine oclock yet." He drew out his watch and extended it face-toward Ash. "Look." Ash didn't even look at the watch.

"That's town time. You aint in town now. You in the woods."

"Look at the sun then."

"Nemmine the sun too," Ash said. "If you and Boon Hogganbeck want any dinner, you better come on in and get it when I tole you. I aim to get done in that kitchen because I got my wood to chop. And watch your feet. They're crawling."

"I will," he said.

Then he was in the woods, not alone but solitary; the solitude closed about him, green with summer. They did not change, and, timeless, would not, any more than would the green of summer and the fire and rain of fall and the iron cold and sometimes even snow

the day, the morning when he killed the buck and Sam marked his face with its hot blood, they returned to camp and he remembered old Ash's blinking and disgruntled and even outraged disbelief until at last McCaslin had had to affirm the fact that he had really killed it: and that night Ash sat snarling and unapproachable behind the stove so that Tennie's Jim had to serve the supper and waked them with breakfast already on the table the next morning and it was only half-past one oclock and at last out of Major de Spain's angry cursing and Ash's snarling and sullen rejoinders the fact emerged that Ash not only wanted to go into the woods and shoot a deer also but he intended to and Major de Spain said, "By God, if we dont let him we will probably have to do the cooking from now on": and Walter Ewell said, "Or get up at midnight to eat what Ash cooks": and since he had already killed his buck for this hunt and was not to shoot again unless they needed meat, he offered his gun to Ash until Major de Spain took command and allotted that gun to Boon for the day and gave Boon's unpredictable pump gun to Ash, with two buckshot shells but Ash said, "I got shells": and showed them, four: one buck, one of number three shot for rabbits, two of bird-shot and told one by one their history and their origin and he remembered not Ash's face alone but Major de Spain's and Walter's and General Compson's too, and Ash's voice: "Shoot? In course they'll shoot! Genl Cawmpson guv me this un"—the buckshot—"right outen the same gun he kilt that big buck with eight years ago. And this un"—it was the rabbit shell: triumphantly—"is oldern thisyer boy!" And that morning he loaded the gun himself, reversing the order: the bird-shot, the rabbit, then the buck so that the buckshot would feed first into the chamber, and himself without a gun, he and Ash walked beside Major de Spain's and Tennie's Jim's horses and the dogs (that was the snow) until they cast and struck, the sweet strong cries ringing away into the muffled falling air and gone almost immediately, as if the constant and unmurmuring flakes had already buried even the unformed echoes beneath their myriad and weightless falling, Major de Spain and Tennie's Jim gone too, whooping on into the woods; and then it was all right, he knew as plainly as if Ash had told him that Ash had now hunted his deer and that even his tender years had been forgiven for having killed one, and they turned back toward home through the falling snow—that is, Ash said, "Now whut?" and he said, "This way"—himself in front because, although they were less than a mile from camp, he knew that Ash, who had spent two weeks of his life in the camp each year for the last twenty, had no idea whatever where they were, until quite soon the manner in which Ash carried Boon's gun was making him a good deal more than just nervous and he made Ash walk in front, striding on, talking now, an old man's garrulous monologue beginning with where he was at the moment then of the woods and of camping in the woods and of eating in camps then of eating then of cooking it and of his wife's cooking then briefly of his old wife and almost at once and at length of a new light-colored woman who nursed next door to Major de Spain's and if she didn't watch out who she was switching her tail at he would show her how old was an old man or not if his wife just didn't watch him all the time, the two of them in a game trail through a dense brake of cane and brier which would bring them out within a quarter-mile of camp, approaching a big fallen tree-trunk lying athwart the path and just as Ash, still talking, was about to step over it the bear, the yearling, rose suddenly beyond the log, sitting up, its forearms against its chest and its wrists limply arrested as if it had been surprised in the act of covering its face to pray: and after a certain time Ash's gun yawed jerkily up and he said, "You haven't got a shell in the barrel yet. Pump it": but the gun already snicked and he said, "Pump it. You haven't got a shell in the barrel yet": and Ash pumped the action and in a certain time the gun steadied again and snicked and he said, "Pump it": and watched the buckshot shell jerk, spinning heavily, into the cane. This is the rabbit shot: he thought and the gun snicked and he thought: The next is bird-shot: and he didn't have to say Pump it; he cried, "Dont shoot! Dont shoot!" but that was already too late too, the light dry vicious snick! before he could speak and the bear turned and dropped to all-fours and then was gone and there was only the log, the cane, the velvet and constant snow and Ash said, "Now whut?" and he said, "This way. Come on": and began to back away down the path and Ash said, "I got to find my shells": and he said, "Goddamn it, goddamn it, come on": but Ash leaned the gun against the log and returned and stooped and fumbled among the cane roots until he came back and stooped and found the shells and they rose and at that moment the gun, untouched, leaning against the log six feet away and for that while even forgotten by both of them, roared, bellowed and flamed, and ceased: and he carried it now, pumped out the last mummified shell and gave that one also to Ash and, the action still open, himself carried the gun until he stood it in the corner behind Boon's bed at the camp

—; summer, and fall, and snow, and wet and sap rife spring in their ordered immortal sequence, the deathless and immemorial phases of the mother who had shaped him if any had toward the man he almost was, mother and father both to the old man born of a negro slave and a Chickasaw chief who had been his spirit's father if any had, whom he had revered and harkened to and loved and lost and grieved: and he would marry someday and they too would own for their brief while that brief unsubstanced glory which inherently of itself cannot last and hence why glory: and they would, might, carry even the remembrance of it into the time when flesh no longer talks to flesh because memory at least does last: but still the woods would be his mistress and his wife.

He was not going toward the Gum Tree. Actually he was getting farther from it. Time was and not so long ago either when he would not have been allowed here without someone with him, and a little later, when he had begun to learn how much he did not know, he would not have dared be here without someone with him, and later still, beginning to ascertain, even if only dimly, the limits of what he did not know, he could have attempted and carried it through with a compass, not because of any increased belief in himself but because McCaslin and Major de Spain and Walter and General Compson too had taught him at last to believe the compass regardless of what it seemed to state. Now he did not even use the compass but merely the sun and that only subconsciously, yet he could have taken a scaled map and plotted at any time to within a hundred feet of where he actually was; and sure enough, at almost the exact moment when he expected it, the earth began to rise faintly, he passed one of the four concrete markers set down by the lumber company's surveyor to establish the four corners of the plot which Major de Spain had reserved out of the sale, then he stood on the crest of the knoll itself, the four corner-markers all visible now, blanched still even beneath the winter's weathering, lifeless and shockingly alien in that place where dissolution itself was a seething turmoil of ejaculation tumescence conception and birth, and death did not even exist. After two winters' blanketings of leaves and the flood-waters of two springs, there was no trace of the two graves any more at all. But those who would have come this far to find them would not need headstones but would have found them as Sam Fathers himself had taught him to find such: by bearings on trees: and did, almost the first thrust of the hunting knife finding (but only to see if it was still there) the round tin box manufactured for axle-grease and containing now Old Ben's dried mutilated paw, resting above Lion's bones.

He didn't disturb it. He didn't even look for the other grave where he and McCaslin and Major de Spain and Boon had laid Sam's body, along with his hunting horn and his knife and his tobacco-pipe, that Sunday morning two years ago; he didn't have to. He had stepped over it, perhaps on it. But that was all right. *He probably knew I was in the woods this morning long before I got here,* he thought, going on to the tree which had supported one end of the platform where Sam lay when McCaslin and Major de Spain found them—the tree, the other axle-grease tin nailed to the trunk, but weathered, rusted, alien too yet healed already into the wilderness' concordant generality, raising no tuneless note, and empty, long since empty of the food and tobacco he had put into it that day, as empty of that as it would presently be of this which he drew from his pocket—the twist of tobacco, the new bandanna handkerchief, the small paper sack of the peppermint candy which Sam had used to love; that gone too, almost before he had turned his back, not vanished but merely translated into the myriad life which printed the dark mold of these secret and sunless places with delicate fairy tracks, which, breathing and biding and immobile, watched him from beyond every twig and leaf until he moved, moving again, walking on; he had not stopped, he had only paused, quitting the knoll which was no abode of the dead because there was no death, not Lion and not Sam: not held fast in earth but free in earth and not in earth but of earth, myriad yet undiffused of every myriad part, leaf and twig and particle, air and sun and rain and dew and night, acorn oak and leaf and acorn again, dark and dawn and dark and dawn again in their immutable progression and, being myriad, one: and Old Ben too, Old Ben too; they would give him his paw back even, certainly they would give him his paw back: then the long challenge and the long chase, no heart to be driven and outraged, no flesh to be mauled and bled— Even as he froze himself, he seemed to hear Ash's parting admonition. He could even hear the voice as he froze, immobile, one foot just taking his weight, the toe of the other just lifted behind him, not breathing, feeling again and as always the sharp shocking inrush from when Isaac McCaslin long yet was not, and so it was fear all right but not fright as he looked down at it. It had not coiled yet and the buzzer had not sounded either, only one thick rapid contraction, one loop cast sideways as though merely for purchase from which the raised head might start slightly backward, not in fright either, not in threat quite yet, more than six feet of it, the head raised higher than his knee and less than his knee's length away, and old, the once-bright markings of its youth dulled now to a monotone concordant too with the wilderness it crawled and lurked: the old one, the ancient and accursed about the earth, fatal and solitary and he could smell it now: the thin sick smell of rotting cucumbers and something else which had no name, evocative of all knowledge and an old weariness and of pariah-hood and of death. At last it moved. Not the head. The elevation of the head did not change as it began to glide away from him, moving erect yet off the perpendicular as if the head and that elevated third were complete and all: an entity walking on two feet and free of all laws of mass and balance and should have been because even now he could not quite believe that all that shift and flow of shadow behind that walking head could have been one snake: going and then gone; he put the other foot down at last and didn't know it, standing with one hand raised as Sam had stood that afternoon six years ago when Sam led him into the wilderness and showed him and he ceased to be a child, speaking the old tongue which Sam had spoken that day without premeditation either: "Chief," he said: "Grandfather."

He couldn't tell when he first began to hear the sound, because when he became aware of it, it seemed to him that he had been already hearing it for several seconds—a sound as though someone were hammering a gun-barrel against a piece of railroad iron, a sound loud and heavy and not rapid yet with something frenzied about it, as the hammerer were not only a strong man and an earnest one but a little hysterical too. Yet it couldn't be on the log-line because, although the track lay in that direction, it was at least two miles from him and this sound was not three hundred yards away. But even as he thought that, he realised where the sound must be coming from: whoever the man was and whatever he was doing, he was somewhere near the edge of the clearing where the Gum Tree was and where he was to meet Boon. So far, he had been hunting as he advanced, moving slowly and quietly and watching the ground and the trees both. Now he went on, his gun unloaded and the barrel slanted up and back to facilitate its passage through brier and undergrowth, approaching as it grew louder and louder that steady savage somehow queerly hysterical beating of metal on metal, emerging from the woods, into the old clearing, with the solitary gum tree directly before him. At first glance the tree seemed to be alive with frantic squirrels. There appeared to be forty or fifty of them leaping and darting from branch to branch until the whole tree had become one green maelstrom of mad leaves, while from time to time, singly or in twos and threes, squirrels would dart down the trunk then whirl without stopping and rush back up again as though sucked violently back by the vacuum of their fellows' frenzied vortex. Then he saw Boon, sitting, his back against the trunk, his head bent, hammering furiously at something on his lap. What he hammered with was the barrel of his dismembered gun, what he hammered at was the breech of it. The rest of the gun lay scattered about him in a half-dozen pieces while he bent over the piece on his lap his scarlet and streaming walnut face, hammering the disjointed barrel against the gun-breech with the frantic abandon of a madman. He didn't even look up to see who it was. Still hammering, he merely shouted back at the boy in a hoarse strangled voice:

"Get out of here! Dont touch them! Dont touch a one of them! They're mine!"

JOSEPH CONRAD

Heart of Darkness

The *Nellie*, a cruising yawl, swung to her anchor without a flutter of the sails, and was at rest. The flood had made, the wind was nearly calm, and being bound down the river, the only thing for it was to come to and wait for the turn of the tide.

The sea-reach of the Thames stretched before us like the beginning of an interminable waterway. In the offing the sea and the sky were welded together without a joint, and in the luminous space the tanned sails of the barges drifting up with the tide seemed to stand still in red clusters of canvas sharply peaked, with gleams of varnished sprits. A haze rested on the low shores that ran out to sea in vanishing flatness. The air was dark above Gravesend, and farther back still seemed condensed into a mournful gloom, brooding motionless over the biggest, and the greatest, town on earth.

The Director of Companies was our captain and our host. We four affectionately watched his back as he stood in the bows looking to seaward. On the whole river there was nothing that looked half so nautical. He resembled a pilot, which to a seaman is trustworthiness personified. It was difficult to realize his work was not out there in the luminous estuary, but behind him, within the brooding gloom.

Between us there was, as I have already said somewhere, the bond of the sea. Besides holding our hearts together through long periods of separation, it had the effect of making us tolerant of each other's yarns—and even convictions. The Lawyer—the best of old fellows—had, because of his many years and many virtues, the only cushion on deck, and was lying on the only rug. The Accountant had brought out already a box of dominoes,

From *Youth and Two Other Stories* by Joseph Conrad, copyright 1903, 1925, by Doubleday, Doran and Company, Inc.

and was toying architecturally with the bones. Marlow sat cross-legged right aft, leaning against the mizzen-mast. He had sunken cheeks, a yellow complexion, a straight back, an ascetic aspect, and, with his arms dropped, the palms of hands outwards, resembled an idol. The director, satisfied the anchor had good hold, made his way aft and sat down amongst us. We exchanged a few words lazily. Afterwards there was silence on board the yacht. For some reason or other we did not begin that game of dominoes. We felt meditative, and fit for nothing but placid staring. The day was ending in a serenity of still and exquisite brilliance. The water shone pacifically; the sky, without a speck, was a benign immensity of unstained light; the very mist on the Essex marshes was like a gauzy and radiant fabric, hung from the wooded rises inland, and draping the low shores in diaphanous folds. Only the gloom to the west, brooding over the upper reaches, became more somber every minute, as if angered by the approach of the sun.

And at last, in its curved and imperceptible fall, the sun sank low, and from glowing white changed to a dull red without rays and without heat, as if about to go out suddenly, stricken to death by the touch of that gloom brooding over a crowd of men.

Forthwith a change came over the waters, and the serenity became less brilliant but more profound. The old river in its broad reach rested unruffled at the decline of day, after ages of good service done to the race that peopled its banks, spread out in the tranquil dignity of a waterway leading to the uttermost ends of the earth. We looked at the venerable stream not in the vivid flush of a short day that comes and departs forever, but in the august light of abiding memories. And indeed nothing is easier for a man who has, as the phrase goes, "followed the sea" with reverence and affection, than to evoke the great spirit of the past upon the lower reaches of the Thames. The tidal current runs to and fro in its unceasing service, crowded with memories of men and ships it had borne to the rest of home or to the battles of the sea. It had known and served all the men of whom the nation is proud, from Sir Francis Drake to Sir John Franklin, knights all, titled and untitled—the knights-errant of the sea. It had borne all the ships whose names are like jewels flashing in the night of time, from the *Golden Hind* returning with her round flanks full of treasure, to be visited by the Queen's Highness and thus pass out of the gigantic tale, to the *Erebus* and *Terror*, bound on other conquests—and that never returned. It had known the ships and the men. They had sailed from Deptford, from Greenwich, from Erith—the adventurers and the settlers; kings' ships and the ships of men on 'Change; captains, admirals, the dark "interlopers" of the Eastern trade, and the commissioned "generals" of East India fleets. Hunters for gold or pursuers of fame, they all had gone out on that stream, bearing the sword, and often the torch, messengers of the might within the land, bearers of a spark from the sacred fire. What greatness had not floated on the ebb of that river into the mystery of an unknown earth! . . . The dreams of men, the seed of commonwealths, the germs of empires.

The sun set; the dusk fell on the stream, and lights began to appear along the shore. The Chapman lighthouse, a three-legged thing erect on a mud-flat, shone strongly. Lights of ships moved in the fairway—a great stir of lights going up and going down. And farther west on the upper reaches the place of the monstrous town was still marked ominously on the sky, a brooding gloom in sunshine, a lurid glare under the stars.

"And this also," said Marlow suddenly, "has been one of the dark places on the earth."

He was the only man of us who still "followed the sea." The worst that could be said of him was that he did not represent his class. He was a seaman, but he was a wanderer, too, while most seamen lead, if one may so express it, a sedentary life. Their minds are of the stay-at-home order, and their home is always with them—the ship; and so is their country—the sea. One ship is very much like another, and the sea is always the same. In the immutability of their surroundings the foreign shores, the foreign faces, the changing immensity of life, glide past, veiled not by a sense of mystery but by a slightly disdainful ignorance; for there is nothing mysterious to a seaman unless it be the sea itself, which is the mistress of his existence and as inscrutable as Destiny. For the rest, after his hours of work, a casual stroll or a casual spree on shore suffices to unfold for him the secret of a whole continent, and generally he finds the secret not worth knowing. The yarns of seamen have a direct simplicity, the whole meaning of which lies within the shell of a cracked nut. But Marlow was not typical (if his propensity to spin yarns be excepted), and to him the meaning of an episode was not inside like a kernel but outside, enveloping the tale which brought it out only as a glow brings out a haze, in the likeness of one of these misty halos that sometimes are made visible by the spectral illumination of moonshine.

His remark did not seem at all surprising. It was just like Marlow. It was accepted in silence. No one took the trouble to grunt even; and presently he said, very slow—

"I was thinking of very old times, when the Romans first came here, nineteen hundred years ago—the other day. . . . Light came out of this river since—you say Knights? Yes; but it is like a running blaze on a plain, like a flash of lightning in the clouds. We live in the flicker—may it last as long as the old earth keeps rolling! But darkness was here yesterday. Imagine the feelings of a commander of a fine—what d'ye call 'em?—trireme in the Mediterranean, ordered suddenly to the north; run overland across the Gauls in a hurry; put in charge of one of these craft the legionaries—a wonderful lot of handy men they must have been, too—used to build, apparently by the hundred, in a month or two, if we may believe what we read. Imagine him here—the very end of the world, a sea the color of lead, a sky the color of smoke, a kind of ship about as rigid as a concertina—and going up this river with stores, or orders, or what you like. Sand-banks, marshes, forests, savages,—precious little to eat fit for a civilized man, nothing but Thames water to drink. No Falernian wine here, no going ashore. Here and there a military camp lost in a wilderness, like a needle in a bundle of hay—cold, fog, tempests, disease, exile, and death,—death skulking in the air, in the water, in the bush. They must have been dying like flies here. Oh, yes—he did it. Did it very well, too, no doubt, and without thinking much about it either, except afterwards to brag of what he had gone through in his time, perhaps. They were men enough to face the darkness. And perhaps he was cheered by keeping his eye on a chance of promotion to the fleet at Ravenna by and by, if he had good friends in Rome and survived the awful climate. Or think of a decent young citizen in a toga—perhaps too much dice, you know—coming out here in the train of some prefect, or tax-gatherer, or trader even, to mend his fortunes. Land in a swamp, march through the woods, and in some inland post feel the savagery, the utter savagery, had closed round him,—all that mysterious life of the wilderness that stirs in the forest, in the jungles, in the hearts of wild men. There's no initiation either into such mysteries. He has to live in the midst of the incomprehensible, which is also detestable. And it has a fascination, too, that goes to work upon him. The fascination of the abomination—you know, imagine the growing regrets, the longing to escape, the powerless disgust, the surrender, the hate."

He paused.

"Mind," he began again, lifting one arm from the elbow, the palm of the hand outwards, so that, with his legs folded before him, he had the pose of a Buddha preaching in European clothes and without a lotus-flower—"Mind, none of us would feel exactly like this. What saves us is efficiency—the devotion to efficiency. But these chaps were not much account, really. They were no colonists; their administration was merely a squeeze, and nothing more, I suspect. They were conquerors, and for that you want only brute force—nothing to boast of, when you have it, since your strength is just an accident arising from the weakness of others. They grabbed what they could get for the sake of what was to be got. It was just robbery with violence, aggravated murder on a great scale, and men going at it blind—as is very proper for those who tackle a darkness. The conquest of the earth, which mostly means the taking it away from those who have a different complexion or slightly flatter noses than ourselves, is not a pretty thing when you look into it too much. What redeems it is the idea only. An idea at the back of it; not a sentimental pretense but an idea; and an unselfish belief in the idea—something you can set up, and bow down before, and offer a sacrifice to. . . ."

He broke off. Flames glided in the river, small green flames, red flames, white flames, pursuing, overtaking, joining, crossing each other—then separating slowly or hastily. The traffic of the great city went on in the deepening night upon the sleepless river. We looked on, waiting patiently—there was nothing else to do till the end of the flood; but it was only after a long silence, when he said, in a hesitating voice, "I suppose you fellows remember I did once turn fresh-water sailor for a bit," that we knew we were fated, before the ebb began to run, to hear one of Marlow's inconclusive experiences.

"I don't want to bother you much with what happened to me personally," he began, showing in this remark the weakness of many tellers of tales who seem so often unaware of what their audience would best like to hear; "yet to understand the effect of it on me you ought to know how I got out there, what I saw, how I went up that river to the place where I first met the poor chap. It was the farthest point of navigation and the culminating point of my experience. It seemed somehow to throw a kind of light on everything about me—and into my thoughts. It was somber enough, too—and pitiful—not extraordinary in any way—not very clear either. No, not very clear. And yet it seemed to throw a kind of light.

"I had then, as you remember, just returned to London after a lot of Indian Ocean, Pacific, China Seas—a regular dose of the East—six years or so, and I was loafing about, hindering you fellows in your work and invading your homes, just as though I had got a heavenly mission to civilize you. It was very fine for a time, but after a bit I did get tired of resting. Then I began to look for a ship—I should think the hardest work on earth. But the ships wouldn't even look at me. And I got tired of that game, too.

"Now when I was a little chap I had a passion for maps. I would look for hours at South America, or Africa, or Australia, and lose myself in all the glories of exploration. At that time there were many blank spaces on the earth, and when I saw one that looked particularly inviting on a map (but they all look that) I would put my finger on it and say, When I grow up I will go there. The North Pole was one of these places, I remember. Well, I haven't been there yet, and shall not try now. The glamour's off. Other places were scattered about the Equator, and in every sort of latitude all over the two hemispheres. I have been in some of them, and . . . well, we won't talk about that. But there was one yet—the biggest, the most blank, so to speak—that I had a hankering after.

"True, by this time it was not a blank space any more. It had got filled since my childhood with rivers and lakes and names. It had ceased to be a blank space of delightful mystery—a white patch for a boy to dream gloriously over. It had become a place of darkness. But there was in it one river especially, a mighty big river, that you could see on the map, resembling an immense snake uncoiled, with its head in the sea, its body at rest curving afar over a vast country, and its tail lost in the depths of the land. And as I looked at the map of it in a shop-window, it fascinated me as a snake would a bird—a silly little bird. Then I remembered there was a big concern, a Company for trade on that river. Dash it all! I thought to myself, they can't trade without using some kind of craft on that lot of fresh water—steamboats! Why shouldn't I try to get charge of one? I went on along Fleet Street, but could not shake off the idea. The snake had charmed me.

"You understand it was a Continental concern, that Trading society; but I have a lot of relations living on the Continent, because it's cheap and not so nasty as it looks, they say.

"I am sorry to own I began to worry them. This was already a fresh departure for me. I was not used to getting things that way, you know. I always went my own road and on my own legs where I had a mind to go. I wouldn't have believed it of myself; but, then—you see—I felt somehow I must get there by hook or by crook. So I worried them. The men said 'My dear fellow,' and did nothing. Then—would you believe it?—I tried the women. I, Charlie Marlow, set the women to work—to get a job. Heavens! Well, you see, the notion drove me. I had an aunt, a dear enthusiastic soul. She wrote: 'It will be delightful. I am ready to do anything, anything for you. It is a glorious idea. I know the wife of a very high personage in the Administration, and also a man who has lots of influence with,' etc., etc. She was determined to make no end of fuss to get me appointed skipper of a river steamboat, if such was my fancy.

"I got my appointment—of course; and I got it very quick. It appears the Company had received news that one of their captains had been killed in a scuffle with the natives. This was my chance, and it made me the more anxious to go. It was only months and months afterwards, when I made the attempt to recover what was left of the body, that I heard the original quarrel arose from a misunderstanding about some hens. Yes, two black hens. Fresleven—that was the fellow's name, a Dane—thought himself wronged somehow in the bargain, so he went ashore and started to hammer the chief of the village with a stick. Oh, it didn't surprise me in the least to hear this, and at the same time to be told that Fresleven was the gentlest, quietest creature that ever walked on two legs. No doubt he was; but he had been a couple of years already out there engaged in the noble cause, you know, and he probably felt the need at last of asserting his self-respect in some way. Therefore he whacked the old nigger mercilessly, while a big crowd of his people watched him, thunderstruck, till some man—I was told the chief's son—in desperation at hearing the old chap yell, made a tentative jab with a spear at the white man—and of course it went quite easy between the shoulder blades. Then the whole population cleared into the forest, expecting all kinds of calamities to happen, while, on the other hand, the steamer Fresleven commanded left also in a bad panic, in charge of the engineer, I believe. Afterwards nobody seemed to trouble much about Fresleven's remains, till I got out and stepped into his shoes. I couldn't let it rest, though; but when an opportunity offered at last to meet my predecessor, the grass growing through his ribs was tall enough to hide his bones. They were all there. The supernatural being had not been touched after he fell. And the village was de serted, the huts gaped black, rotting, all askew within the fallen enclosures. A calamity had come to it, sure enough. The people had vanished. Mad terror had scattered them, men, women, and children, through the bush, and they had never returned. What became of the hens I don't know either. I should think the cause of progress got them, anyhow. However, through this glorious affair I got my appointment, before I had fairly begun to hope for it.

"I flew around like mad to get ready, and before forty-eight hours I was crossing the Channel to show myself to my employers, and sign the contract. In a very few hours I arrived in a city that always makes me think of a whited sepulcher. Prejudice no doubt. I had no difficulty in finding the Company's offices. It was the biggest thing in the town, and everybody I met was full of it. They were going to run an over-sea empire, and make no end of coin by trade.

"A narrow and deserted street in deep shadow, high houses, innumerable windows with venetian blinds, a dead silence, grass sprouting between the stones, imposing carriage archways right and left, immense double doors standing ponderously ajar. I slipped through one of these cracks, went up a swept and ungarnished staircase, as arid as a desert, and opened the first door I came to. Two women, one fat and the other slim, sat on straw-bottomed chairs, knitting black wool. The slim one got up and walked straight at me—still knitting with downcast eyes—and only just as I began to think of getting out of her way, as you would for a somnambulist, stood still, and looked up. Her dress was as plain as an umbrella-cover, and she turned round without a word and preceded me into a waiting-room. I gave my name, and looked about. Deal table in the middle, plain chairs all around the walls, on one end a large shining map, marked with all the colors of a rainbow. There was a vast amount of red—good to see at any time, because one knows that some real work is done in there, a deuce of a lot of blue, a little green, smears of orange, and, on the East Coast, a purple patch, to show where the jolly pioneers of progress drink the jolly lager-beer. However, I wasn't going into any of these. I was going into the yellow. Dead in the center. And the river was there—fascinating—deadly—like a snake. Ough! A door opened, a white-haired secretarial head, but wearing a compassionate expression, appeared, and a skinny forefinger beckoned me into the sanctuary. Its light was dim, and a heavy writing-desk squatted in the middle. From behind that structure came out an impression of pale plumpness in a frock-coat. The great man himself. He was five feet six, I should judge, and had his grip on the handle-end of ever so many millions. He shook hands, I fancy, murmured vaguely, was satisfied with my French. *Bon voyage.*

"In about forty-five seconds I found myself again in the waiting-room with the compassionate secretary, who, full of desolation and sympathy, made me sign some document. I believe I undertook amongst other things not to disclose any trade secrets. Well, I am not going to.

"I began to feel slightly uneasy. You know I am not used to such ceremonies, and there was something ominous in the atmosphere. It was just as though I had been let into some conspiracy—I don't know—something not quite right; and I was glad to get out. In the outer room the two women knitted black wool feverishly. People were arriving, and the younger one was walking back and forth introducing them. The old one sat on her chair. Her flat cloth slippers were propped up on a foot-warmer, and a cat reposed on her lap. She wore a starched white affair on her head, had a wart on one cheek, and silver-rimmed spectacles hung on the tip of her nose. She glanced at me above the glasses. The swift and indifferent placidity of that look troubled me. Two youths with foolish and cheery countenances were being piloted over, and she threw at them the same quick glance of unconcerned wisdom. She seemed to know all about them and about me, too. An eerie feeling came over me. She seemed uncanny and fateful. Often far away there I thought of these two, guarding the door of Darkness, knitting black wool as for a warm pall, one introducing, introducing continuously to the unknown, the other scrutinizing the cheery and foolish faces with unconcerned old eyes. *Ave!* Old knitter of black wool. *Morituri te salutant.* Not many of those she looked at ever saw her again—not half, by a long way.

"There was yet a visit to the doctor. 'A simple formality,' assured me the secretary, with an air of taking an immense part in all my sorrows. Accordingly a young chap wearing his hat over the left eyebrow, some clerk I suppose,—there must have been clerks in the business, though the house was as still as a house in a city of the dead—came from somewhere upstairs, and led me forth. He was shabby and careless, with inkstains on the sleeves of his jacket, and his cravat was large and billowy, under a chin shaped like the toe of an old boot. It was a little too early for the doctor, so I proposed a drink, and thereupon he developed a vein of joviality. As we sat over our vermouths he glorified the Company's business, and by and by I expressed casually my surprise at him not going out there. He became very cool and collected all at once. 'I am not such a fool as I look, quoth Plato to his disciples,' he said sententiously, emptied his glass with great resolution, and we rose.

"The old doctor felt my pulse, evidently thinking of something else the while. 'Good, good for there,' he mumbled, and then with a certain eagerness asked me whether I would let him measure my head. Rather surprised, I said Yes, when he produced a thing like calipers and got the dimensions back and front and every way, taking notes carefully. He was an unshaven little man in a threadbare coat like a gaberdine, with his feet in slippers, and I thought him a harmless fool. 'I always ask leave, in the interests of science, to measure the crania of those going out there,' he said. 'And when they come back, too?' I asked. 'Oh, I never see them,' he remarked; 'and, moreover, the changes take place inside, you know.' He smiled, as if at some quiet joke. 'So you are going out there. Famous.

Interesting, too.' He gave me a searching glance, and made another note. 'Ever any madness in your family?' he asked, in a matter-of-fact tone. I felt very annoyed. 'Is that question in the interests of science, too?' 'It would be,' he said, without taking notice of my irritation, 'interesting for science to watch the mental changes of individuals, on the spot, but . . .' 'Are you an alienist?' I interrupted. 'Every doctor should be—a little,' answered that original, imperturbably. 'I have a little theory which you Messieurs who go out there must help me to prove. This is my share in the advantages my country shall reap from the possession of such a magnificent dependency. The mere wealth I leave to others. Pardon my questions, but you are the first Englishman coming under my observation . . .' I hastened to assure him I was not in the least typical. 'If I were,' said I, 'I wouldn't be talking like this with you.' 'What you say is rather profound, and probably erroneous,' he said, with a laugh. 'Avoid irritation more than exposure to the sun. Adieu. How do you English say, eh? Good-by. Ah! Good-by. Adieu. In the tropics one must before everything keep calm.' . . . He lifted a warning forefinger. . . . *'Du calme, du calme. Adieu.'*

"One thing more remained to do—say good-by to my excellent aunt. I found her triumphant. I had a cup of tea—the last decent cup of tea for many days—and in a room that most soothingly looked just as you would expect a lady's drawing-room to look, we had a long quiet chat by the fireside. In the course of these confidences it became quite plain to me I had been represented to the wife of the high dignitary, and goodness knows to how many more people besides, as an exceptional and gifted creature—a piece of good fortune for the Company—a man you don't get hold of every day. Good heavens! and I was going to take charge of a two-penny-half-penny river-steamboat with a penny whistle attached! It appeared, however, I was also one of the Workers, with a capital—you know. Something like an emissary of light, something like a lower sort of apostle. There had been a lot of such rot let loose in print and talk just about that time, and the excellent woman, living right in the rush of all that humbug, got carried off her feet. She talked about 'weaning those ignorant millions from their horrid ways,' till, upon my word, she made me quite uncomfortable. I ventured to hint that the Company was run for profit.

" 'You forget, dear Charlie, that the laborer is worthy of his hire,' she said, brightly. It's queer how out of touch with truth women are. They live in a world of their own, and there has never been anything like it, and never can be. It is too beautiful altogether, and if they were to set it up it would go to pieces before the first sunset. Some confounded fact we men have been living contentedly with ever since the day of creation would start up and knock the whole thing over.

"After this I got embraced, told to wear flannel, be sure to write often, and so on—and I left. In the street—I don't know why—a queer feeling came to me that I was an impostor. Odd thing that I, who used to clear out for any part of the world at twenty-four hours' notice, with less thought than most men give to the crossing of a street, had a moment—I won't say of hesitation, but of startled pause, before this commonplace affair. The best way I can explain it to you is by saying that, for a second or two, I felt as though, instead of going to the center of a continent, I were about to set off for the center of the earth.

"I left in a French steamer, and she called in every blamed port they have out there, for, as far as I could see, the sole purpose of landing soldiers and custom-house officers. I watched the coast. Watching a coast as it slips by the ship is like thinking about an enigma. There it is before you—smiling, frowning, inviting, grand, mean, insipid, or savage, and always mute with an air of whispering, Come and find out. This one was almost featureless, as if still in the making, with an aspect of monotonous grimness. The edge of a colossal jungle, so dark-green as to be almost black, fringed with white surf, ran straight, like a ruled line, far, far away along a blue sea whose glitter was blurred by a creeping mist. The sun was fierce, the land seemed to glisten and drip with steam. Here and there grayish-whitish specks showed up clustered inside the white surf, with a flag flying above them perhaps. Settlements some centuries old, and still no bigger than pinheads on the untouched expanse of their background. We pounded along, stopped, landed soldiers; went on, landed custom-house clerks to levy toll in what looked like a God-forsaken wilderness, with a tin shed and a flag-pole lost in it; landed more soldiers—to take care of the custom-house clerks, presumably. Some, I heard, got drowned in the surf; but whether they did or not, nobody seemed particularly to care. They were just flung out there, and on we went. Every day the coast looked the same, as though we had not moved; but we passed various places—trading places—with names like Gran' Bassam, Little Popo; names that seemed to belong to some sordid farce acted in front of a sinister backcloth. The idleness of a passenger, my isolation amongst all these men with whom I had no point of contact, the oily and languid sea, the uniform somberness of the coast, seemed to keep me away from the truth of things, within the toil of a mournful and senseless delusion. The voice of the surf heard now and then was a positive pleasure, like the speech of a brother. It was something natural, that had its reason, that had a meaning. Now and then a boat from the shore gave one a momentary contact with reality. It was paddled by black fellows. You could see from afar the white of their eyeballs glistening. They shouted, sang; their bodies streamed with perspiration; they had faces like grotesque masks—these chaps; but they had bone, muscle, a wild vitality, an intense energy of movement, that was as natural and true as the surf along their coast. They wanted no excuse for being there. They were a great comfort to look at. For a time I would feel I belonged still to a world of straightforward facts; but the feeling would not last long. Something would turn up to scare it away. Once, I remember, we came upon a man-of-war anchored off the coast. There wasn't even a shed there, and she was shelling the bush. It appears the French had one of their wars going on thereabouts. Her ensign dropped limp like a rag; the muzzles of the long six-inch guns stuck out all over the low hull; the greasy, slimy swell swung her up lazily and let her down, swaying her thin masts. In the empty immensity of earth, sky, and water, there she was, incomprehensible, firing into a continent. Pop, would go one of the six-inch guns; a small flame would dart and vanish, a little white smoke would disappear, a tiny projectile would give a feeble screech—and nothing happened. Nothing could happen. There was a touch of insanity in the proceeding, a sense of lugubrious drollery in the sight; and it was not dissipated by somebody on board assuring me earnestly there was a camp of natives—he called them enemies!—hidden out of sight somewhere.

"We gave her her letters (I heard the men in that lonely ship were dying of fever at the rate of three a day) and went on. We called at some more places with farcical names, where the merry dance of death and trade goes on in a still and earthy atmosphere as of an overheated catacomb; all along the formless coast bordered by dangerous surf, as if Nature herself had tried to ward off intruders; in and out of rivers, streams of death in life, whose banks were rotting into mud, whose waters, thickened into slime, invaded the contorted mangroves, that seemed to writhe at us in the extremity of an impotent despair. Nowhere did we stop long enough to get a particularized impression, but the general sense of vague and oppressive wonder grew upon me. It was like a weary pilgrimage amongst hints for nightmares.

"It was upward of thirty days before I saw the mouth of the big river. We anchored off the seat of the government. But my work would not begin till some two hundred miles farther on. So as soon as I could I made a start for a place thirty miles higher up.

"I had my passage on a little sea-going steamer. Her captain was a Swede, and knowing me for a seaman, invited me on the bridge. He was a young man, lean, fair, and morose, with lanky hair and a shuffling gait. As we left the miserable little wharf, he tossed his head contemptuously at the shore. 'Been living there?' he asked. I said, 'Yes.' 'Fine lot these government chaps—are they not?' he went on, speaking English with great precision and considerable bitterness. 'It is funny what some people will do for a few francs a month. I wonder what becomes of that kind when it goes up-country?' I said to him I expected to see that soon. 'So-o-o!' he exclaimed. He shuffled athwart, keeping one eye ahead vigilantly. 'Don't be too sure,' he continued. 'The other day I took up a man who hanged himself on the road. He was a Swede, too.' 'Hanged himself! Why, in God's name?' I cried. He kept on looking out watchfully. 'Who knows? The sun was too much for him, or the country perhaps.'

"At last we opened a reach. A rocky cliff appeared, mounds of turned-up earth by the shore, houses on a hill, others with iron roofs, amongst a waste of excavations, or hanging to the declivity. A continuous noise of the rapids above hovered over this scene of inhabited devastation. A lot of people, mostly black and naked, moved about like ants. A jetty projected into the river. A blinding sunlight drowned all this at times in a sudden recrudescence of glare. 'There's your Company's station,' said the Swede, pointing to three wooden barrack-like structures on the rocky slope. 'I will send your things up. Four boxes did you say? So. Farewell.'

"I came upon a boiler wallowing in the grass, then found a path leading up the hill. It turned aside for the boulders, and also for an undersized railway-truck lying there on its back with its wheels in the air. One was off. The thing looked as dead as the carcass of some animal. I came upon more pieces of decaying machinery, a stack of rusty rails. To the left a clump of trees made a shady spot, where dark things seemed to stir feebly. I blinked, the path was steep. A horn tooted to the right, and I saw the black people run. A heavy and dull detonation shook the ground, a puff of smoke came out of the cliff, and that was all. No change appeared on the face of the rock. They were building a railway. The cliff was not in the way or anything; but this objectless blasting was all the work going on.

"A slight clinking behind me made me turn my head. Six black men advanced in a file, toiling up the path. They walked erect and slow, balancing small baskets full of earth on their heads, and the clink kept time with their footsteps. Black rags were wound round their loins, and the short ends behind waggled to and fro like tails. I could see every rib, the joints of their limbs were like knots in a rope; each had an iron collar on his neck, and all were connected together with a chain whose bights swung between them, rhythmically clinking. Another report from the cliff made me think suddenly of that ship of war I had seen firing into a continent. It was the same kind of ominous voice; but these men could by no stretch of imagination be called enemies. They were called criminals, and the outraged law, like the bursting shells, had come to them, an insoluble mystery from the sea. All their meager breasts panted together, the violently dilated nostrils quivered, the eyes stared stonily up-hill. They passed me within six inches, without a glance, with that complete, deathlike indifference of unhappy savages. Behind this raw matter one of the reclaimed, the product of the new forces at work, strolled despondently, carrying a rifle by its middle. He had a uniform jacket with one button off, and seeing a white man on the path, hoisted his weapon to his shoulder with alacrity. This was simple prudence, white men being so much alike at a distance that he could not tell who I might be. He was speedily reassured, and with a large, white, rascally grin, and a glance at his charge, seemed to take me into partnership in his exalted trust. After all, I also was a part of the great cause of these high and just proceedings.

"Instead of going up, I turned and descended to the left. My idea was to let that chain-gang get out of sight before I climbed the hill. You know I am not particularly tender; I've had to strike and to fend off. I've had to resist and to attack sometimes—that's only one way of resisting—without counting the exact cost, according to the demands of such sort of life as I had blundered into. I've seen the devil of violence, and the devil of greed, and the devil of hot desire; but, by all the stars! these were strong, lusty, red-eyed devils, that swayed and drove men—men, I tell you. But as I stood on this hillside, I foresaw that in the blinding sunshine of that land I would become acquainted with a flabby, pretending, weak-eyed devil of a rapacious and pitiless folly. How insidious he could be, too, I was only to find out several months later and a thousand miles farther. For a moment I stood appalled, as though by a warning. Finally I descended the hill, obliquely, towards the trees I had seen.

"I avoided a vast artificial hole somebody had been digging on the slope, the purpose of which I found it impossible to divine. It wasn't a quarry or a sandpit, anyhow. It was just a hole. It might have been connected with the philanthropic desire of giving the criminals something to do. I don't know. Then I nearly fell into a very narrow ravine, almost no more than a scar in the hillside. I discovered that a lot of imported drainage-pipes for the settlement had been tumbled in there. There wasn't one that was not broken. It was a wanton smashup. At last I got under the trees. My purpose was to stroll into the shade for a moment; but no sooner within than it seemed to me I had stepped into the gloomy circle of some Inferno. The rapids were near, and an uninterrupted, uniform, headlong, rushing noise filled the mournful stillness of the grove, where not a breath stirred, not a leaf moved, with a mysterious sound—as though the tearing pace of the launched earth had suddenly become audible.

"Black shapes crouched, lay, sat between the trees leaning against the trunks, clinging to the earth, half coming out, half effaced within the dim light, in all the attitudes of pain, abandonment, and despair. Another mine on the cliff went off, followed by a slight shudder of the soil under my feet. The work was going on. The work! And this was the place where some of the helpers had withdrawn to die.

"They were dying slowly—it was very clear. They were not enemies, they were not criminals, they were nothing earthly now,—nothing but black shadows of disease and starvation, lying confusedly in the greenish gloom. Brought from all the recesses of the coast in all the legality of time contracts, lost in uncongenial surroundings, fed on unfamiliar food, they sickened, became inefficient, and were then allowed to crawl away and rest. These moribund shapes were free as air—and nearly as thin. I began to distinguish the gleam of the eyes under the trees. Then, glancing down, I saw a face near my hand. The black bones reclined at full length with one shoulder against the tree, and slowly the eyelids rose and the sunken eyes looked up at me, enormous and vacant, a kind of blind, white flicker in the depths of the orbs, which died out slowly. The man seemed young—almost a boy—but you know with them it's hard to tell. I found nothing else to do but to offer him one of my good Swede's ship's biscuits I had in my pocket. The fingers closed slowly on it and held—there was no other movement and no other glance. He had tied a bit of white worsted round his neck— Why? Where did he get it? Was it a badge—an ornament—a charm—a propitiatory act? Was there any idea at all connected with it? It looked startling round his black neck, this bit of white thread from beyond the seas.

"Near the same tree two more bundles of acute angles sat with their legs drawn up. One, with his chin propped on his knees, stared at nothing, in an intolerable and appalling manner: his brother phantom rested its forehead, as if overcome with a great weariness; and all about others were scattered in every pose of contorted collapse, as in some picture of a massacre or a pestilence. While I stood horror-struck, one of these creatures rose to his hands and knees, and went off on all-fours towards the river to drink. He lapped out of his hand, then sat up in the sunlight, crossing his shins in front of him, and after a time let his wooly head fall on his breastbone.

"I didn't want any more loitering in the shade, and I made haste towards the station. When near the buildings I met a white man, in such an unexpected elegance of get-up that in the first moment I took him for a sort of vision. I saw a high starched collar, white cuffs, a light alpaca jacket, snowy trousers, a clean necktie, and varnished boots. No hat. Hair parted, brushed, oiled, under a green-lined parasol held in a big white hand. He was amazing, and had a penholder behind his ear.

"I shook hands with this miracle, and I learned he was the Company's chief accountant, and that all the bookkeeping was done at this station. He had come out for a moment, he said, 'to get a breath of fresh air.' The expression sounded wonderfully odd, with its suggestion of sedentary desk-life. I wouldn't have mentioned the fellow to you at all, only it was from his lips that I first heard the name of the man who is so indissolubly connected with the memories of that time. Moreover, I respected the fellow. Yes; I respected his collars, his vast cuffs, his brushed hair. His appearance was certainly that of a hairdresser's dummy; but in the great demoralization of the land he kept up his appearance. That's backbone. His starched collars and got-up shirt-fronts were achievements of character. He had been out nearly three years; and, later, I could not help asking him how he managed to sport such linen. He had just the faintest blush, and said modestly, 'I've been teaching one of the native women about the station. It was difficult. She had a distaste for the work.' Thus this man had verily accomplished something. And he was devoted to his books, which were in apple-pie order.

"Everything else in the station was in a muddle,—heads, things, buildings. Strings of dusty niggers with splay feet arrived and departed; a stream of manufactured goods, rubbishy cottons, beads, and brass-wire sent into the depths of darkness, and in return came a precious trickle of ivory.

"I had to wait in the station for ten days—an eternity. I lived in a hut in the yard, but to be out of the chaos I would sometimes get into the accountant's office. It was built of horizontal planks, and so badly put together that, as he bent over his high desk, he was barred from neck to heels with narrow strips of sunlight. There was no need to open the big shutter to see. It was hot there, too; big flies buzzed fiendishly, and did not sting, but stabbed. I sat generally on the floor, while, of faultless appearance (and even slightly scented), perching on a high stool, he wrote, he wrote. Sometimes he stood up for exercise. When a trucklebed with a sick man (some invalid agent from up-country) was put in there, he exhibited a gentle annoyance. 'The groans of this sick person,' he said, 'distract my attention. And without that it is extremely difficult to guard against clerical errors in this climate.'

"One day he remarked, without lifting his head, 'In the interior you will no doubt meet Mr. Kurtz.' On my asking who Mr. Kurtz was, he said he was a first-class agent; and seeing my disappointment at this information, he added slowly, laying down his pen, 'He is a very remarkable person.' Further questions elicited from him that Mr. Kurtz was at present in charge of a trading post, a very important one, in the true ivory-country, at 'the very bottom of there. Sends in as much ivory as all the others put together. . . .' He began to write again. The sick man was too ill to groan. The flies buzzed in a great peace.

"Suddenly there was a growing murmur of voices and a great tramping of feet. A caravan had come in. A violent babble of uncouth sounds burst out on the other side of the planks. All the carriers were speaking together, and in the midst of the uproar the lamentable voice of the chief agent was heard 'giving it up' tearfully for the twentieth time that day. . . . He rose slowly. 'What a frightful row,' he said. He crossed the room gently to look at the sick man, and returning, said to me, 'He does not hear.' 'What! Dead?' I asked, startled. 'No, not yet,' he answered, with great composure. Then, alluding with a toss of the head to the tumult in the station-yard, 'When one has got to make correct entries, one comes to hate those savages—hate them to the death.' He remained thoughtful for a moment. 'When you see Mr. Kurtz,' he went on, 'tell him for me that everything here'—he glanced at the desk—'is very satisfactory. I don't like to write to him—with those messengers of ours you never know who may get hold of your letter—at that Central Station.' He stared at me for a moment with his mild, bulging eyes. 'Oh, he will go far, very far,' he began again. 'He will be a somebody in the Administration before long. They, above—the Council in Europe, you know—mean him to be.'

"He turned to his work. The noise outside had ceased, and presently in going out I stopped at the door. In the steady buzz of flies the homeward-bound agent was lying flushed and insensible; the other, bent over his books, was making correct entries of perfectly correct transactions; and fifty feet below the doorstep I could see the still tree-tops of the grove of death.

"Next day I left that station at last, with a caravan of sixty men, for a two-hundred-mile tramp.

"No use telling you much about that. Paths, paths, everywhere; a stamped-in network of paths spreading over the empty land, through long grass, through burnt grass, through thickets, down and up chilly ravines, up and down stony hills ablaze with heat; and a solitude, a solitude, nobody, not a hut. The population had cleared out a long time ago. Well, if a lot of mysterious niggers armed with all kinds of fearful weapons suddenly took to traveling on the road between Deal and Gravesend, catching the yokels right and left to carry heavy loads for them, I fancy every farm and cottage thereabouts would get empty very soon. Only here the dwellings were gone, too. Still I passed through several abandoned villages. There's something pathetically childish in the ruins of grass walls. Day after day, with the stamp and shuffle of sixty pair of bare feet behind me, each pair under a sixty-pound load. Camp, cook, sleep, strike camp, march. Now and then a carrier dead in harness, at rest in the long grass near the path, with an empty water-gourd and his long staff lying by his side. A great silence around and above. Perhaps on some quiet night the tremor of far-off drums, sinking, swelling, a tremor vast, faint; a sound weird, appealing, suggestive, and wild—and perhaps with as profound a meaning as the sound of bells in a Christian country. Once a white man in an unbuttoned uniform, camping on the path with an armed escort of lank Zanzibaris, very hospitable and festive—not to say drunk. Was looking after the upkeep of the road, he declared. Can't say I saw any road or any upkeep, unless the body of a middle-aged Negro, with a bullet-hole in the forehead, upon which I absolutely stumbled three miles farther on, may be considered as a permanent improvement. I had a white companion, too, not a bad chap, but rather too fleshy and with the exasperating habit of fainting on the hot hillsides, miles away from the least bit of shade and water. Annoying, you know, to hold your own coat like a parasol over a man's head while he is coming-to. I couldn't help asking him once what he meant by coming there at all. 'To make money, of course. What do you think?' he said, scornfully. Then he got fever, and had to be carried in a hammock slung under a pole. As he weighed sixteen stone I had no end of rows with the carriers. They jibbed, ran away, sneaked off with their loads in the night—quite a mutiny. So, one evening, I made a speech in English with gestures, not one of which was lost to the sixty pairs of eyes before me, and the next morning I started the hammock off in front all right. An hour afterwards I came upon the whole concern wrecked in a bush—man, hammock, groans, blankets, horrors. The heavy pole had skinned his poor nose. He was very anxious for me to kill somebody, but there wasn't the shadow of a carrier near. I remembered the old doctor—'It would be interesting for science to watch the mental changes of individuals, on the spot.' I felt I was becoming scientifically interesting. However, all that is to no purpose. On the fifteenth day I came in sight of the big river again, and hobbled into the Central Station. It was on a backwater surrounded by scrub and forest, with a pretty border of smelly mud on one side, and on the three others enclosed by a crazy fence of rushes. A neglected gap was all the gate it had, and the first glance at the place was enough to let you see the flabby devil was running that show. White men with long staves in their hands appeared languidly from amongst the buildings, strolling up to take a look at me, and then retired out of sight somewhere. One of them, a stout, excitable chap with black mustaches, informed me with great volubility and many digressions, as soon as I told him who I was, that my steamer was at the bottom of the river. I was thunderstruck. What, how, why? Oh, it was 'all right.' The 'manager himself' was there. All quite correct. 'Everybody had behaved splendidly! splendidly!'—'you must,' he said in agitation, 'go and see the general manager at once. He is waiting!'

"I did not see the real significance of that wreck at once. I fancy I see it now, but I am not sure—not at all. Certainly the affair was too stupid—when I think of it—to be altogether natural. Still. . . . But at the moment it presented itself simply as a confounded nuisance. The steamer was sunk. They had started two days before in a sudden hurry up the river with the manager on board, in charge of some volunteer skipper, and before they had been out three hours they tore the bottom out of her on stones, and she sank near the south bank. I asked myself what I was to do there, now my boat was lost. As a matter of fact, I had plenty to do in fishing my command out of the river. I had to set about it the very next day. That, and the repairs when I brought the pieces to the station, took some months.

"My first interview with the manager was curious. He did not ask me to sit down after my twenty-mile walk that morning. He was commonplace in complexion, in feature, in manners, and in voice. He was of middle size and of ordinary build. His eyes, of the usual blue, were perhaps remarkably cold, and he certainly could make his glance fall on one as trenchant and heavy as an ax. But even at these times the rest of his person seemed to disclaim the intention. Otherwise there was only an indefinable, faint expression of his lips, something stealthy—a smile—not a smile—I remember it, but I can't explain. It was unconscious, this smile was, though just after he had said something it got intensified for an instant. It came at the end of his speeches like a seal applied on the words to make the meaning of the commonest phrase appear absolutely inscrutable. He was a common trader, from his youth up employed in these parts—nothing more. He was obeyed, yet he inspired neither love nor fear, nor even respect. He inspired uneasiness. That was it! Uneasiness. Not a definite mistrust—just uneasiness—nothing more. You have no idea how effective such a . . . a . . . faculty can be. He had no genius for organizing, for initiative, or for order even. That was evident in such things as the deplorable state of the station. He had no learning, and no intelligence. His position had come to him—why? Perhaps because he was never ill. . . . He had served three terms of three years out there. . . . Because triumphant health in the general rout of constitutions is a kind of power in itself. When he went home on leave he rioted on a large scale—pompously. Jack ashore—with a difference—in externals only. This one could gather from his casual talk. He originated nothing, he could keep the routine going—that's all. But he was great. He was great by this little thing that it was impossible to tell what could control such a man. He never gave that secret away. Perhaps there was nothing within him. Such a suspicion made one pause—for out there there were no external checks. Once when various tropical diseases had laid low almost every 'agent' in the station, he was heard to say, 'Men who come out here should have no entrails.' He sealed the utterance with that smile of his, as though it had been a door opening into a darkness he had in his keeping. You fancied you had seen things—but the seal was on. When annoyed at meal-times by the constant quarrels of the white men about precedence, he ordered an immense round table to be made, for which a special house had to be built. This was the station's mess-room. Where he sat was the first place—the rest were nowhere. One felt this to be his unalterable conviction. He was neither civil nor uncivil. He was quiet. He allowed his 'boy' an overfed young Negro from the coast—to treat the white men, under his very eyes, with provoking insolence.

"He began to speak as soon as he saw me. I had been very long on the road. He could not wait. Had to start without me. The up-river stations had to be relieved. There had been so many delays already that he did not know who was dead and who was alive, and how they got on—and so on, and so on. He paid no attention to my explanations, and, playing with a stick of sealing-wax, repeated several times that the situation was 'very grave, very grave.' There were rumors that a very important station was in jeopardy, and its chief, Mr. Kurtz, was ill. Hoped it was not true. Mr. Kurtz was . . . I felt weary and irritable. Hang Kurtz, I thought. I interrupted him by saying I had heard of Mr. Kurtz on the coast. 'Ah! So they talk of him down there,' he murmured to himself. Then he began again, assuring me Mr. Kurtz was the best agent he had, an exceptional man, of the greatest importance to the Company; therefore I could understand his anxiety. He was, he said, 'very, very uneasy.' Certainly he fidgeted on his chair a good deal, exclaimed, 'Ah, Mr. Kurtz!' broke the stick of sealing-wax and seemed dumfounded by the accident. Next thing he wanted to know 'how long it would take to . . .' I interrupted him again. Being hungry, you know, and kept on my feet too, I was getting savage. 'How can I tell?' I said. 'I haven't even seen the wreck yet—some months, no doubt.' All this talk seemed to me so futile. 'Some months,' he said. 'Well, let us say three months before we can make a start. Yes. That ought to do the affair.' I flung out of his hut (he lived all alone in a clay hut with a sort of veranda) muttering to myself my opinion of him. He was a chattering idiot. Afterwards I took it back when it was borne in upon me startlingly with what extreme nicety he had estimated the time requisite for the 'affair.'

"I went to work the next day, turning, so to speak, my back on that station. In that way only it seemed to me I could keep my hold on the redeeming facts of life. Still, one must look about sometimes; and then I saw this station, these men strolling aimlessly about in the sunshine of the yard. I asked myself sometimes what it all meant. They wandered here and there with their absurd long staves in their hands, like a lot of faithless pilgrims bewitched inside a rotten fence. The word 'ivory' rang in the air, was whispered, was sighed. You would think they were praying to it. A taint of imbecile rapacity blew through it all, like a whiff from some corpse. By Jove! I've never seen anything so unreal in my life. And outside, the silent wilderness surrounding this cleared speck on the earth struck me as something great and invincible, like evil or truth, waiting patiently for the passing away of this fantastic invasion.

"Oh, these months! Well, never mind. Various things happened. One evening a grass shed full of calico, cotton prints, beads, and I don't know what else, burst into a blaze so suddenly that you would have thought the earth had opened to let an avenging fire consume all that trash. I was smoking my pipe quietly by my dismantled steamer, and saw them all cutting capers in the light, with their arms lifted high, when the stout man with mustaches came tearing down to the river, a tin pail in his hand, assured me that everybody was 'behaving splendidly, splendidly,' dipped about a quart of water and tore back again. I noticed there was a hole in the bottom of his pail.

"I strolled up. There was no hurry. You see the thing had gone off like a box of matches. It had been hopeless from the very first. The flame had leaped high, driven everybody back, lighted up everything—and collapsed. The shed was already a heap of embers glowing fiercely. A nigger was being beaten near by. They said he had caused the fire in some way; be that as it may, he was screeching most horribly. I saw him, later, for several days, sitting in a bit of shade looking very sick and trying to recover himself: afterwards he arose and went out—and the wilderness without a sound took him into its bosom again. As I approached the glow from the dark I found myself at the back of two men, talking. I heard the name of Kurtz pronounced, then the words, 'take advantage of this unfortunate accident.' One of the men was the manager. I wished him a good evening. 'Did you ever see anything like it—eh? it is incredible,' he said, and walked off. The other man remained. He was a first-class agent, young, gentlemanly, a bit reserved, with a forked little beard and a hooked nose. He was standoffish with the other agents, and they on their side said he was the manager's spy upon them. As to me, I had hardly ever spoken to him before. We got into talk, and by and by we strolled away from the hissing ruins. Then he asked me to his room, which was in the main building of the station. He struck a match, and I perceived that this young aristocrat had not only a silver-mounted dressing-case but also a whole candle all to himself. Just at that time the manager was the only man supposed to have any right to candles. Native mats covered the clay walls; a collection of spears, assegais, shields, knives was hung up in trophies. The business intrusted to this fellow was the making of bricks—so I had been informed; but there wasn't a fragment of a brick anywhere in the station, and he had been there more than a year—waiting. It seems he could not make bricks without something, I don't know what—straw, maybe. Anyway, it could not be found there, and as it was not likely to be sent from Europe, it did not appear clear to me what he was waiting for. An act of special creation perhaps. However, they were all waiting—all the sixteen or twenty pilgrims of them—for something; and upon my word it did not seem an uncongenial occupation, from the way they took it, though the only thing that ever came to them was disease—as far as I could see. They beguiled the time by back-biting and intriguing against each other in a foolish kind of way. There was an air of plotting about that station, but nothing came of it, of course. It was as unreal as everything else—as the philanthropic pretense of the whole concern, as their talk, as their government, as their show of work. The only real feeling was a desire to get appointed to a trading-post where ivory was to be had, so that they could earn percentages. They intrigued and slandered and hated each other only on that account,—but as to effectually lifting a little finger —oh, no. By heavens! there is something after all in the world allowing one man to steal a horse while another must not look at a halter. Steal a horse straight out. Very well. He has done it. Perhaps he can ride. But there is a way of looking at a halter that would provoke the most charitable of saints into a kick.

"I had no idea why he wanted to be sociable, but as we chatted in there it suddenly occurred to me the fellow was trying to get at something—in fact, pumping me. He alluded constantly to Europe, to the people I was supposed to know there—putting leading questions as to my acquaintances in the sepulchral city, and so on. His little eyes glittered like mica discs—with curiosity—though he tried to keep up a bit of superciliousness. At first I was astonished, but very soon I became awfully curious to see what he would find out from me. I couldn't possibly imagine what I had in me to make it worth his while. It was very pretty to see how he baffled himself, for in truth my body was full only of chills, and my head had nothing in it but that wretched steamboat business. It was evident he took me for a perfectly shameless prevaricator. At last he got angry, and, to conceal a movement of furious annoyance, he yawned. I rose. Then I noticed a small sketch in oils, on a panel, representing a woman, draped and blindfolded, carrying a lighted torch. The background was somber—almost black. The movement of the woman was stately, and the effect of the torch-light on the face was sinister.

"It arrested me, and he stood by civilly, holding an empty half-pint champagne bottle (medical comforts) with the candle stuck in it. To my question he said Mr. Kurtz had painted this—in this very station more than a year ago—while waiting for means to go to his trading-post. 'Tell me, pray,' said I, 'who is this Mr. Kurtz?'

" 'The chief of the Inner Station,' he answered in a short tone, looking away. 'Much obliged,' I said, laughing. 'And you are the brickmaker of the Central Station. Everyone knows that.' He was silent for a while. 'He is a prodigy,' he said at last. 'He is an emissary of pity, and science, and progress, and devil knows what else. We want,' he began to declaim suddenly, 'for the guidance of the cause intrusted to us by Europe, so to speak, higher intelligence, wide sympathies, a singleness of purpose.' 'Who says that?' I asked. 'Lots of them,' he replied. 'Some even write that; and so *he* comes here, a special being, as you ought to know.' 'Why ought I to know?' I interrupted, really surprised. He paid no attention. 'Yes. Today he is chief of the best station, next year he will be assistant-manager, two years more and . . . but I daresay you know what he will be in two years' time. You are of the new gang—the gang of virtue. The same people who sent him specially also recommended you. Oh, don't say no. I've my own eyes to trust.' Light dawned upon me. My dear aunt's influential acquaintances were producing an unexpected effect upon that young man. I nearly burst into a laugh. 'Do you read the Company's confidential correspondence?' I asked. He hadn't a word to say. It was great fun. 'When Mr. Kurtz,' I continued, severely, 'is General Manager, you won't have the opportunity.'

"He blew the candle out suddenly, and we went outside. The moon had risen. Black figures strolled about listlessly, pouring water on the glow, whence proceeded a sound of hissing; steam ascended in the moonlight, the beaten nigger groaned somewhere. 'What a row the brute makes!' said the indefatigable man with the mustaches, appearing near us. 'Serves him right. Transgression—punishment—bang! Pitiless, pitiless. That's the only way. This will prevent all conflagrations for the future. I was just telling the manager. . . .' He noticed my companion, and became crestfallen all at once. 'Not in bed yet,' he said, with a kind of servile heartiness; 'it's so natural. Ha! Danger—agitation.' He vanished. I went on to the river-side, and the other followed me. I heard a scathing murmur at my ear, 'Heap of muffs—go to.' The pilgrims could be seen in knots gesticulating, discussing. Several had still their staves in their hands. I verily believe they took these sticks to bed with them. Beyond the fence the forest stood up spectrally in the moonlight, and through the dim stir, through the faint sounds of that lamentable courtyard, the silence of the land went home to one's very heart—its mystery, its greatness, the amazing reality of its concealed life. The hurt nigger moaned feebly somewhere near by, and then fetched a deep sigh that made me mend my pace away from there. I felt a hand introducing itself under my arm. 'My dear sir,' said the fellow, 'I don't want to be misunderstood, and especially by you, who will see Mr. Kurtz long before I can have that pleasure. I wouldn't like him to get a false idea of my disposition. . . .'

"I let him run on, this papier-mâché Mephistopheles, and it seemed to me that if I tried I could poke my forefinger through him, and would find nothing inside but a little loose dirt, maybe. He, don't you see, had been planning to be assistant-manager by and by under the present man, and I could see that the coming of that Kurtz had upset them both not a little. He talked precipitately, and I did not try to stop him. I had my shoulders against the wreck of my steamer, hauled up on the slope like a carcass of some big river animal. The smell of mud, of primeval mud, by Jove! was in my nostrils, the high stillness of primeval forest was before my eyes; there were shiny patches on the black creek. The moon had spread over everything a thin layer of silver—over the rank grass, over the mud, upon the wall of matted vegetation standing higher than the wall of a temple, over the great river I could see through a somber gap glittering, glittering, as it flowed broadly by without a murmur. All this was great, expectant, mute, while the man jabbered about himself. I wondered whether the stillness on the face of the immensity looking at us two were meant as an appeal or as a menace. What were we who had strayed in here? Could we handle that dumb thing, or would it handle us? I felt how big, how confoundedly big, was that thing that couldn't talk, and perhaps was deaf as well. What was in there? I could see a little ivory coming out from there, and I had heard Mr. Kurtz was in there. I had heard enough about it, too—God knows! Yet somehow it didn't bring any image with it—no more than if I had been told an angel or a fiend was in there. I believed it in the same way one of you might believe there are inhabitants in the planet Mars. I knew once a Scotch sailmaker who was certain, dead sure, there were people in Mars. If you asked him for some idea how they looked and behaved, he would get shy and mutter something about 'walking on all-fours.' If you as much as smiled, he would—though a man of sixty—offer to fight you. I would not have gone so far as to fight for Kurtz, but I went for him near enough to a lie. You know I hate, detest, and can't bear a lie, not because I am straighter than the rest of us, but simply because it appalls me. There is a taint of death, a flavor of mortality in lies—which is exactly what I hate and detest in the world—what I want to forget. It makes me miserable and sick, like biting something rotten would do. Temperament, I suppose. Well, I went near enough to it by letting the young fool there believe anything he liked to imagine as to my influence in Europe. I became in an instant as much of a pretense as the rest of the bewitched pilgrims. This simply because I had a notion it somehow would be of help to that Kurtz whom at the time I did not see—you understand. He was just a word for me. I did not see the man in the name any more than you do. Do you see him? Do you see the story? Do you see anything? It seems to me I am trying to tell you a dream—making a vain attempt, because no relation of a dream can convey the dream-sensation, that commingling of absurdity, surprise, and bewilderment in a tremor of struggling revolt, that notion of being captured by the incredible which is of the very essence of dreams. . . ."

He was silent for a while.

". . . No, it is impossible; it is impossible to convey the life-sensation of any given epoch of one's existence—that which makes its truth, its meaning—its subtle and penetrating essence. It is impossible. We live, as we dream—alone. . . ."

He paused again as if reflecting, then added—

"Of course in this you fellows see more than I could then. You see me, whom you know. . . ."

It had become so pitch dark that we listeners could hardly see one another. For a long time already he, sitting apart, had been no more to us than a voice. There was not a word from anybody. The others might have been asleep, but I was awake. I listened, I listened on the watch for the sentence, for the word, that would give me the clew to the faint uneasiness inspired by this narrative that seemed to shape itself without human lips in the heavy night-air of the river.

". . . Yes—I let him run on," Marlow began again, "and think what he pleased about the powers that were behind me. I did! And there was nothing behind me! There was nothing but that wretched, old, mangled steamboat I was leaning against, while he talked fluently about 'the necessity for every man to get on.' 'And when one comes out here, you conceive, it is not to gaze at the moon.' Mr. Kurtz was a 'universal genius,' but even a genius would find it easier to work with 'adequate tools—intelligent men.' He did not make bricks—why, there was a physical impossibility in the way—as I was well aware; and if he did secretarial work for the manager, it was because 'no sensible man rejects wantonly the confidence of his superiors.' Did I see it? I saw it. What more did I want? What I really wanted was rivets, by heaven! Rivets. To get on with the work—to stop the hole. Rivets I wanted. There were cases of them down at the coast—cases—piled up—burst—split! You kicked a loose rivet at every second step in that station yard on the hillside. Rivets had rolled into the grove of death. You could fill your pockets with rivets for the trouble of stooping down—and there wasn't one rivet to be found where it was wanted. We had plates that would do, but nothing to fasten them with. And every week the messenger, a lone Negro, letter-bag on shoulder and staff in hand, left our station for the coast. And several times a week a coast caravan came in with trade goods—ghastly glazed calico that made you shudder only to look at it; glass beads, valued about a penny a quart, confounded spotted cotton handkerchiefs. And no rivets. Three carriers could have brought all that was wanted to set that steamboat afloat.

"He was becoming confidential now, but I fancy my unresponsive attitude must have exasperated him at last, for he judged it necessary to inform me he feared neither God nor devil, let alone any mere man. I said I could see that very well, but what I wanted was a certain quantity of rivets—and rivets were what really Mr. Kurtz wanted, if he had only known it. Now letters went to the coast every week. . . . 'My dear sir,' he cried, 'I write from dictation.' I demanded rivets. There was a way—for an intelligent man. He changed his manner; became very cold, and suddenly began to talk about a hippopotamus; wondered whether sleeping on board the steamer (I stuck to my salvage night and day) I wasn't disturbed. There was an old hippo that had the bad habit of getting out on the bank and roaming at night over the station grounds. The pilgrims used to turn out in a body and empty every rifle they could lay hands on at him. Some even had sat up o' nights for him. All this energy was wasted, though. 'That animal has a charmed life,' he said; 'but you can say this only of brutes in this country. No man—you apprehend me?—no man here bears a charmed life.' He stood there for a moment in the moonlight with his delicate hooked nose set a little askew, and his mica eyes glittering without a wink, then, with a curt good night, he strode off. I could see he was disturbed and considerably puzzled, which made me feel more hopeful than I had been for days. It was a great comfort to turn from that chap to my influential friend, the battered, twisted, ruined, tin-pot steamboat. I clambered on board. She rang under my feet like an empty Huntley & Palmer biscuit-tin kicked along a gutter; she was nothing so solid in make, and rather less pretty in shape, but I had expended enough hard work on her to make me love her. No influential friend would have served me better. She had given me a chance to come out a bit—to find out what I could do. No, I don't like work. I had rather laze about and think of all the fine things that can be done. I don't like work—no man does—but I like what is in the work,—the chance to find yourself. Your own reality—for yourself, not for others—what no other man can ever know. They can only see the mere show, and never can tell what it really means.

"I was not surprised to see somebody sitting aft, on the deck, with his legs dangling over the mud. You see I rather chummed with the few mechanics there were in that station, whom the other pilgrims naturally despised—on account of their imperfect manners, I suppose. This was the foreman—a boiler-maker by trade—a good worker. He was a lank, bony, yellow-faced man, with big intense eyes. His aspect was worried, and his head was as bald as the palm of my hand; but his hair in falling seemed to have stuck to his chin, and had prospered in the new locality, for his beard hung down to his waist. He was a widower with six young children (he had left them in charge of a sister of his to come out there), and the passion of his life was pigeon-flying. He was an enthusiast and a connoisseur. He would rave about pigeons. After work hours he used sometimes to come over from his hut for a talk about his children and his pigeons; at work, when he had to crawl in the mud under the bottom of the steamboat, he would tie up that beard of his in a kind of white serviette he brought for the purpose. It had loops to go over his ears. In the evening he could be seen squatted on the bank rinsing that wrapper in the creek with great care, then spreading it solemnly on a bush to dry.

"I slapped him on the back and shouted, 'We shall have rivets!' He scrambled to his feet exclaiming, 'No! Rivets!' as though he couldn't believe his ears. Then in a low voice, 'You . . . eh?' I don't know why we behaved like lunatics. I put my finger to the side of my nose and nodded mysteriously. 'Good for you!' he cried, snapped his fingers above his head, lifting one foot. I tried a jig. We capered on the iron deck. A frightful clatter came out of that hulk, and the virgin forest on the other bank of the creek sent it back in a thundering roll upon the sleeping station. It must have made some of the pilgrims sit up in their hovels. A dark figure obscured the lighted doorway of the manager's hut, vanished, then, a second or so after, the doorway itself vanished, too. We stopped, and the silence driven away by the stamping of our feet flowed back again from the recesses of the land. The great wall of vegetation, an exuberant and entangled mass of trunks, branches, leaves, boughs, festoons, motionless in the moonlight, was like a rioting invasion of soundless life, a rolling wave of plants, piled up, crested, ready to topple over the creek, to sweep every little man of us out of his little existence. And it moved not. A deadened burst of mighty splashes and snorts reached us from afar, as though an ichthyosaurus had been taking a bath of glitter in the great river. 'After all,' said the boiler-maker in a reasonable tone, 'why shouldn't we get the rivets?' Why not, indeed! I did not know of any reason why we shouldn't. 'They'll come in three weeks,' I said, confidently.

"But they didn't. Instead of rivets there came an invasion, an infliction, a visitation. It came in sections during the next three weeks, each section headed by a donkey carrying a white man in new clothes and tan shoes, bowing from that elevation right and left to the impressed pilgrims. A quarrelsome band of footsore sulky niggers trod on the heels of the donkeys; a lot of tents, campstools, tin boxes, white cases, brown bales would be shot down in the courtyard, and the air of mystery would deepen a little over the muddle of the station. Five such installments came, with their absurd air of disorderly flight with the loot of innumerable outfit shops and provision stores, that, one would think, they were lugging, after a raid, into the wilderness for equitable division. It was an inextricable mess of things decent in themselves but that human folly made look like the spoils of thieving.

"This devoted band called itself the Eldorado Exploring Expedition, and I believe they were sworn to secrecy. Their talk, however, was the talk of sordid buccaneers: it was reckless without hardihood, greedy without audacity, and cruel without courage; there was not an atom of foresight or of serious intention in the whole batch of them, and they did not seem aware these things are wanted for the work of the world. To tear treasure out of the bowels of the land was their desire, with no more moral purpose at the back of it than there is in burglars breaking into a safe. Who paid the expenses of the noble enterprise I don't know; but the uncle of our manager was leader of the lot.

"In exterior he resembled a butcher in a poor neighborhood, and his eyes had a look of sleepy cunning. He carried his fat paunch with ostentation on his short legs, and during the time his gang infested the station spoke to no one but his nephew. You could see these two roaming about all day long with their heads close together in an everlasting confab.

"I had given up worrying myself about the rivets. One's capacity for that kind of folly is more limited than you would suppose. I said Hang!—and let things slide. I had plenty of time for meditation, and now and then I would give some thought to Kurtz. I wasn't very interested in him. No. Still, I was curious to see whether this man, who had come out equipped with moral ideas of some sort, would climb to the top after all and how he would set about his work when there."

2

"One evening as I was lying flat on the deck of my steamboat, I heard voices approaching—and there were the nephew and the uncle strolling along the bank. I laid my head on my arm again, and had nearly lost myself in a doze, when somebody said in my ear, as it were: 'I am as harmless as a little child, but I don't like to be dictated to. Am I the manager—or am I not? I was ordered to send him there. It's incredible.' . . . I became aware that the two were standing on the shore alongside the forepart of the steamboat, just below my head. I did not move; it did not occur to me to move: I was sleepy. 'It *is* unpleasant,' grunted the uncle. 'He has asked the Administration to be sent there,' said the other, 'with the idea of showing what he could do; and I was instructed accordingly. Look at the influence that man must have. Is it not frightful?' They both agreed it was frightful, then made several bizarre remarks: 'Make rain and fine weather—one man—the Council—by the nose'—bits of absurd sentences that got the better of my drowsiness, so that I had pretty near the whole of my wits about me when the uncle said, 'The climate may do away with this difficulty for you. Is he alone there?' 'Yes,' answered the manager; 'he sent his assistant down the river with a note to me in these terms: "Clear this poor devil out of the country, and don't bother sending more of that sort. I had rather be alone than have the kind of men you can dispose of with me." It was more than a year ago. Can you imagine such impudence!' 'Anything since then?' asked the other, hoarsely. 'Ivory,' jerked the nephew; 'lots of it—prime sort—lots—most annoying, from him.' 'And with that?' questioned the heavy rumble. 'Invoice,' was the reply fired out, so to speak. Then silence. They had been talking about Kurtz.

"I was broad awake by this time, but, lying perfectly at ease, remained still, having no inducement to change my position. 'How did that ivory come all this way?' growled the elder man, who seemed very vexed. The other explained that it had come with a fleet of canoes in charge of an English half-caste clerk Kurtz had with him; that Kurtz had apparently intended to return himself, the station being by that time bare of goods and stores, but after coming three hundred miles, had suddenly decided to go back, which he started to do alone in a small dugout with four paddlers, leaving the half-caste to continue down the river with the ivory. The two fellows there seemed astounded at anybody attempting such a thing. They were at a loss for an adequate motive. As to me, I seemed to see Kurtz for the first time. It was a distinct glimpse: the dugout, four paddling savages, and the lone white man turning his back suddenly on the headquarters, on relief, on thoughts of home—perhaps; setting his face towards the depths of the wilderness, towards his empty and desolate station. I did not know the motive. Perhaps he was just simply a fine fellow who stuck to his work for its own sake. His name, you understand, had not been pronounced once. He was 'that man.' The half-caste, who, as far as I could see, had conducted a difficult trip with great prudence and pluck, was invariably alluded to as 'that scoundrel.' The 'scoundrel' had reported that the 'man' had been very ill—had recovered imperfectly. . . . The two below me moved away then a few paces, and strolled back and forth at some little distance. I heard: 'Military post—doctor—two hundred miles—quite alone now—unavoidable delays—nine months—no news—strange rumors.' They approached again, just as the manager was saying, 'No one, as far as I know, unless a species of wandering trader—a pestilential fellow, snapping ivory from the natives.' Who was it they were talking about now? I gathered in snatches that this was some man supposed to be in Kurtz's district, and of whom the manager did not approve. 'We will not be free from unfair competition till one of these fellows is hanged for an example,' he said. 'Certainly,' grunted the other; 'get him hanged! Why not? Anything—anything can be done in this country. That's what I say; nobody here, you understand, *here*, can endanger your position. And why? You stand the climate—you outlast them all. The danger is in Europe; but there before I left I took care to—' They moved off and whispered, then their voices rose again. 'The extraordinary series of delays is not my fault. I did my best.' The fat man sighed. 'Very sad.' 'And the pestiferous absurdity of his talk,' continued the other; 'he bothered me enough when he was here. "Each station should be like a beacon on the road towards better things, a center for trade, of course, but also for humanizing, improving, instructing." Conceive you—that ass! And he wants to be manager! No, it's—' Here he got choked by excessive indignation, and I lifted my head the least bit. I was surprised to see how near they were—right under me. I could have spat upon their hats. They were looking on the ground, absorbed in thought. The manager was switching his leg with a slender twig: his sagacious relative lifted his head. 'You have been well since you came out this time?' he asked. The other gave a start. 'Who? I? Oh! Like a charm—like a charm. But the rest—oh, my goodness! All sick. They die so quick, too, that I haven't the time to send them out of the country—it's incredible!' 'H'm. Just so,' grunted the uncle. 'Ah! my boy, trust to this—I say, trust to this.' I saw him extend his short flipper of an arm for a gesture that took in the forest, the creek, the mud, the river,—seemed to beckon with a dishonoring flourish before the sunlit face of the land a treacherous appeal to the lurking death, to the hidden evil, to the profound darkness of its heart. It was so startling that I leaped to my feet and looked back at the edge of the forest, as though I had expected an answer of some sort to that black display of confidence. You know the foolish notions that come to one sometimes. The high stillness confronted these two figures with its ominous patience, waiting for the passing away of a fantastic invasion.

"They swore aloud together—out of sheer fright, I believe—then pretending not to know anything of my existence, turned back to the station. The sun was low; and leaning forward side by side, they seemed to be tugging painfully uphill their two ridiculous shadows of unequal length, that trailed behind them slowly over the tall grass without bending a single blade.

"In a few days the Eldorado Expedition went into the patient wilderness, that closed upon it as the sea closes over a diver. Long afterwards the news came that all the donkeys were dead. I know nothing as to the fate of the less valuable animals. They, no doubt, like the rest of us, found what they deserved. I did not inquire. I was then rather excited at the prospect of meeting Kurtz very soon. When I say very soon I mean it comparatively. It was just two months from the day we left the creek when we came to the bank below Kurtz's station.

"Going up that river was like traveling back to the earliest beginnings of the world, when vegetation rioted on the earth and the big trees were kings. An empty stream, a great silence, an impenetrable forest. The air was warm, thick, heavy, sluggish. There was no joy in the brilliance of sunshine. The long stretches of the waterway ran on, deserted, into the gloom of overshadowed distances. On silvery sandbanks hippos and alligators sunned themselves side by side. The broadening waters flowed through a mob of wooded islands; you lost your way on that river as you would in a desert, and butted all day long against shoals, trying to find the channel, till you thought yourself bewitched and cut off forever from everything you had known once—somewhere—far away—in another existence perhaps. There were moments when one's past came back to one, as it will sometimes when you have not a moment to spare to yourself; but it came in the shape of an unrestful and noisy dream, remembered with wonder amongst the overwhelming realities of this strange world of plants, and water, and silence. And this stillness of life did not in the least resemble a peace. It was the stillness of an implacable force brooding over an inscrutable intention. It looked at you with a vengeful aspect. I got used to it afterwards; I did not see it any more; I had no time. I had to keep guessing at the channel; I had to discern, mostly by inspiration, the signs of hidden banks; I watched for sunken stones; I was learning to clap my teeth smartly before my heart flew out, when I shaved by a fluke some infernal sly old snag that would have ripped the life out of the tin-pot steamboat and drowned all the pilgrims; I had to keep a lookout for the signs of dead wood we could cut up in the night for next day's steaming. When you have to attend to things of that sort, to the mere incidents of the surface, the reality—the reality, I tell you—fades. The inner truth is hidden—luckily, luckily. But I felt it all the same; I felt often its mysterious stillness watching me at my monkey tricks, just as it watches you fellows performing on your respective tight-ropes for—what is it? half-a-crown a tumble—"

"Try to be civil, Marlow," growled a voice, and I knew there was at least one listener awake besides myself.

"I beg your pardon. I forgot the heartache which makes up the rest of the price. And indeed what does the price matter, if the trick be well done? You do your tricks very well. And I didn't do badly either, since I managed not to sink that steamboat on my first trip. It's a wonder to me yet. Imagine a blindfolded man set to drive a van over a bad road. I sweated and shivered over that business considerably, I can tell you. After all, for a seaman, to scrape the bottom of the thing that's supposed to float all the time under his care is the unpardonable sin. No one may know of it, but you never forget the thump—eh? A blow on the very heart. You remember it, you dream of it, you wake up at night and think of it—years after—and go hot and cold all over. I don't pretend to say that steamboat floated all the time. More than once she had to wade for a bit, with twenty cannibals splashing around and pushing. We had enlisted some of these chaps on the way for a crew. Fine fellows—cannibals—in their place. They were men one could work with, and I am grateful to them. And, after all, they did not eat each other before my face: they had brought along a provision of hippo-meat which went rotten, and made the mystery of the wilderness stink in my nostrils. Phoo! I can sniff it now. I had the manager on board and three or four pilgrims with their staves—all complete. Sometimes we came upon a station close by the bank, clinging to the skirts of the unknown, and the white men rushing out of a tumble-down hovel, with great gestures of joy and surprise and welcome, seemed very strange—had the appearance of being held there captive by a spell. The word ivory would ring in the air for a while—and on we went again into the silence, along empty reaches, round the still bends, between the high walls of our winding way, reverberating in hollow claps the ponderous beat of the stern-wheel. Trees, trees, millions of trees, massive, immense, running up high; and at their foot, hugging the bank against the stream, crept the little begrimed steamboat, like a sluggish beetle crawling on the floor of a lofty portico. It made you feel very small, very lost, and yet it was not altogether depressing, that feeling. After all, if you were small, the grimy beetle crawled on—which was just what you wanted it to do. Where the pilgrims imagined it crawled to I don't know. To some place where they expected to get something, I bet! For me it crawled towards Kurtz—exclusively; but when the steam-pipes started leaking we crawled very slow. The reaches opened before us and closed behind, as if the forest had stepped leisurely across the water to bar the way for our return. We penetrated deeper and deeper into the heart of darkness. It was very quiet there. At night sometimes the roll of drums behind the curtain of trees would run up the river and remain sustained faintly, as if hovering in the air high over our heads, till the first break of day. Whether it meant war, peace, or prayer we could not tell. The dawns were heralded by the descent of a chill stillness; the wood-cutters slept, their fires burned low; the snapping of a twig would make you start. We were wanderers on a prehistoric earth, on an earth that wore the aspect of an unknown planet. We could have fancied ourselves the first of men taking possession of an accursed inheritance, to be subdued at the cost of profound anguish and of excessive toil. But suddenly, as we struggled round a bend, there would be a glimpse of rush walls, of peaked grass-roofs, a burst of yells, a whirl of black limbs, a mass of hands clapping, of feet stamping, of bodies swaying, of eyes rolling, under the droop of heavy and motionless foliage. The steamer toiled along slowly on the edge of a black and incomprehensible frenzy. The prehistoric man was cursing us, praying to us, welcoming us—who could tell? We were cut off from the comprehension of our surroundings; we glided past like phantoms, wondering and secretly appalled, as sane men would be before an enthusiastic outbreak in a madhouse. We could not understand because we were too far and could not remember, because we were traveling in the night of first ages, of those ages that are gone, leaving hardly a sign—and no memories.

"The earth seemed unearthly. We are accustomed to look upon the shackled form of a conquered monster, but there—there you could look at a thing monstrous and free. It was unearthly, and the men were— No, they were not inhuman. Well, you know, that was the worst of it—this suspicion of their not being inhuman. It would come slowly to one. They howled and leaped, and spun, and made horrid faces; but what thrilled you was just the thought of their humanity—like yours—the thought of your remote kinship with this wild and passionate uproar. Ugly. Yes, it was ugly enough; but if you were man enough you would admit to yourself that there was in you just the faintest trace of a response to the terrible frankness of that noise, a dim suspicion of there being a meaning in it which you—you so remote from the night of first ages—could comprehend. And why not? The mind of man is capable of anything—because everything is in it, all the past as well as all the future. What was there after all? Joy, fear, sorrow, devotion, valor, rage—who can tell?—but truth—truth stripped of its cloak of time. Let the fool gape and shudder—the man knows, and can look on without a wink. But he must at least be as much of a man as these on the shore. He must meet that truth with his own true stuff—with his own inborn strength. Principles won't do. Acquisitions, clothes, pretty rags—rags that would fly off at the first good shake. No; you want a deliberate belief. An appeal to me in this fiendish row—is there? Very well; I hear; I admit, but I have a voice, too, and for good or evil mine is the speech that cannot be silenced. Of course, a fool, what with sheer fright and fine sentiments, is always safe. Who's that grunting? You wonder I didn't go ashore for a howl and a dance? Well, no—I didn't. Fine sentiments, you say? Fine sentiments, be hanged! I had no time. I had to mess about with white-lead and strips of woolen blanket helping to put bandages on those leaky steam-pipes—I tell you. I had to watch the steering, and circumvent those snags, and get the tin-pot along by hook or by crook. There was surface-truth enough in these things to save a wiser man. And between whiles I had to look after the savage who was fireman. He was an improved specimen; he could fire up a vertical boiler. He was there below me, and, upon my word, to look at him was as edifying as seeing a dog in a parody of breeches and a feather hat, walking on his hind-legs. A few months of training had done for that really fine chap. He squinted at the steam-gauge and at the water-gauge with an evident effort of intrepidity—and he had filed teeth, too, the poor devil, and the wool of his pate shaved into queer patterns, and three ornamental scars on each of his cheeks. He ought to have been clapping his hands and stamping his feet on the bank, instead of which he was hard at work, a thrall to strange witchcraft, full of improving knowledge. He was useful because he had been instructed; and what he knew was this—that should the water in that transparent thing disappear, the evil spirit inside the boiler would get angry through the greatness of his thirst, and take a terrible vengeance. So he sweated and fired up and watched the glass fearfully (with an impromptu charm, made of rags, tied to his arm, and a piece of polished bone, as big as a watch, stuck flatways through his lower lip), while the wooden banks slipped past us slowly, the short noise was left behind, the interminable miles of silence—and we crept on, towards Kurtz. But the snags were thick, the water was treacherous and shallow, the boiler seemed indeed to have a sulky devil in it, and thus neither that fireman nor I had any time to peer into our creepy thoughts.

"Some fifty miles below the Inner Station we came upon a hut of reeds, an inclined and melancholy pole, with the unrecognizable tatters of what had been a flag of some sort flying from it, and a neatly stacked woodpile. This was unexpected. We came to the bank, and on the stack of firewood found a flat piece of board with some faded pencil-writing on it. When deciphered it said: 'Wood for you. Hurry up. Approach cautiously.' There was a signature, but it was illegible—not Kurtz—a much longer word. 'Hurry up.' Where? Up the river? 'Approach cautiously.' We had not done so. But the warning could not have been meant for the place where it could be only found after approach. Something was wrong above. But what—and how much? That was the question. We commented adversely upon the imbecility of that telegraphic style. The bush around said nothing, and would not let us look very far, either. A torn curtain of red twill hung in the doorway of the hut, and flapped sadly in our faces. The dwelling was dismantled; but we could see a white man had lived there not very long ago. There remained a rude table—a plank on two posts; a heap of rubbish reposed in a dark corner, and by the door I picked up a book. It had lost its covers, and the pages had been thumbed into a state of extremely dirty softness; but the back had been lovingly stitched afresh with white cotton thread, which looked clean yet. It was an extraordinary find. Its title was, *An Inquiry into some Points of Seamanship,* by a man Towser, Towson—some such name—Master in his Majesty's Navy. The matter looked dreary reading enough, with illustrative diagrams and repulsive tables of figures, and the copy was sixty years old. I handled this amazing antiquity with the greatest possible tenderness, lest it should dissolve in my hands. Within, Towson or Towser was inquiring earnestly into the breaking strain of ships' chains and tackle, and other such matters. Not a very enthralling book; but at the first glance you could see there a singleness of intention, an honest concern for the right way of going to work, which made these humble pages, thought out so many years ago, luminous with another than a professional light. The simple old sailor, with his talk of chains and purchases, made me forget the jungle and the pilgrims in a delicious sensation of having come upon something unmistakably real. Such a book being there was wonderful enough; but still more astounding were the notes penciled in the margin, and plainly referring to the text. I couldn't believe my eyes! They were in cipher! Yes, it looked like cipher. Fancy a man lugging with him a book of that description into this nowhere and studying it—and making notes—in cipher at that! It was an extravagant mystery.

"I had been dimly aware for some time of a worrying noise, and when I lifted my eyes I saw the woodpile was gone, and the manager, aided by all the pilgrims, was shouting at me from the river-side. I slipped the book into my pocket. I assure you to leave off reading was like tearing myself away from the shelter of an old and solid friendship.

"I started the lame engine ahead. 'It must be this miserable trader—this intruder,' exclaimed the manager, looking back malevolently at the place we had left. 'He must be English,' I said. 'It will not save him from getting into trouble if he is not careful,' muttered the manager darkly. I observed with assumed innocence that no man was safe from trouble in this world.

"The current was more rapid now, the steamer seemed at her last gasp, the stern-wheel flopped languidly, and I caught myself listening on tiptoe for the next beat of the boat, for in sober truth I expected the wretched thing to give up every moment. It was like watching the last flickers of a life. But still we crawled. Sometimes I would pick out a tree a little way ahead to measure our progress towards Kurtz by, but I lost it invariably before we got abreast. To keep the eyes so long on one thing was too much for human patience. The manager displayed a beautiful resignation. I fretted and fumed and took to arguing with myself whether or no I would talk openly with Kurtz; but before I could come to any conclusion it occurred to me that my speech or my silence, indeed any action of mine, would be a mere futility. What did it matter what anyone knew or ignored? What did it matter who was manager? One gets sometimes such a flash of insight. The essentials of this affair lay deep under the surface, beyond my reach, and beyond my power of meddling.

"Towards the evening of the second day we judged ourselves about eight miles from Kurtz's station. I wanted to push on; but the manager looked grave, and told me the navigation up there was so dangerous that it would be advisable, the sun being very low already, to wait where we were till next morning. Moreover, he pointed out that if the warning to approach cautiously were to be followed, we must approach in daylight—not at dusk, or in the dark. This was sensible enough. Eight miles meant three hours' steaming for us, and I could also see suspicious ripples at the upper end of the reach. Nevertheless, I was annoyed beyond expression at the delay, and most unreasonably, too, since one night more could not matter much after so many months. As we had plenty of wood, and caution was the word, I brought up in the middle of the stream. The reach was narrow, straight, with high sides like a railway cutting. The dusk came gliding into it long before the sun had set. The current ran smooth and swift, but a dumb immobility sat on the banks. The living trees, lashed together by the creepers and every living bush of the undergrowth, might have been changed into stone, even to the slenderest twig, to the lightest leaf. It was not sleep—it seemed unnatural, like a state of trance. Not the faintest sound of any kind could be heard. You looked on amazed, and began to suspect yourself of being deaf—then the night came suddenly, and struck you blind as well. About three in the morning some large fish leaped, and the loud splash made me jump as though a gun had been fired. When the sun rose there was a white fog, very warm and clammy, and more blinding than the night. It did not shift or drive; it was just there, standing all round you like something solid. At eight or nine, perhaps, it lifted as a shutter lifts. We had a glimpse of the towering multitude of trees, of the immense matted jungle, with the blazing little ball of the sun hanging over it—all perfectly still—and then the white shutter came down again, smoothly, as if sliding in greased grooves. I ordered the chain, which we had begun to heave in, to be paid out again. Before it stopped running with a muffled rattle, a cry, a very loud cry, as of infinite desolation, soared slowly in the opaque air. It ceased. A complaining clamor, modulated in savage discords, filled our ears. The sheer unexpectedness of it made my hair stir under my cap. I don't know how it struck the others: to me it seemed as though the mist itself had screamed, so suddenly, and apparently from all sides at once, did this tumultuous and mournful uproar arise. It culminated in a hurried outbreak of almost intolerably excessive shrieking, which stopped short, leaving us stiffened in a variety of silly attitudes, and obstinately listening to the nearly as appalling and excessive silence. 'Good God! What is the meaning—' stammered at my elbow one of the pilgrims,—a little fat man, with sandy hair and red whiskers, who wore side-spring boots, and pink pajamas tucked into his socks. Two others remained open-mouthed a whole minute, then dashed into the little cabin, to rush out incontinently and stand darting scared glances, with Winchesters at 'ready' in their hands. What we could see was just the steamer we were on, her outlines blurred as though she had been on the point of dissolving, and a misty strip of water, perhaps two feet broad, around her—and that was all. The rest of the world was nowhere, as far as our eyes and ears were concerned. Just nowhere. Gone, disappeared; swept off without leaving a whisper or a shadow behind.

"I went forward, and ordered the chain to be hauled in short, so as to be ready to trip the anchor and move the steamboat at once if necessary. 'Will they attack?' whispered an awed voice. 'We will be all butchered in this fog,' murmured another. The faces twitched with the strain, the hands trembled slightly, the eyes forgot to wink. It was very curious to see the contrast of expressions of the white men and of the black fellows of our crew, who were as much strangers to that part of the river as we, though their homes were only eight hundred miles away. The whites, of course, greatly discomposed, had besides a curious look of being painfully shocked by such an outrageous row. The others had an alert, naturally interested expression; but their faces were essentially quiet, even those of the one or two who grinned as they hauled at the chain. Several exchanged short, grunting phrases, which seemed to settle the matter to their satisfaction. Their headman, a young, broad-chested black, severely draped in dark-blue fringed cloths, with fierce nostrils and his hair all done up artfully in oily ringlets, stood near me. 'Aha!' I said, just for good fellowship's sake. 'Catch 'im,' he snapped, with a bloodshot widening of his eyes and a flash of sharp teeth—'catch 'im. Give 'im to us.' 'To you, eh?' I asked; 'what would you do with them?' 'Eat 'im!' he said, curtly, and, leaning his elbow on the rail, looked out into the fog in a dignified and profoundly pensive attitude. I would no doubt have been properly horrified, had it not occurred to me that he and his chaps must be very hungry: that they must have been growing increasingly hungry for at least this month past. They had been engaged for six months (I don't think a single one of them had any clear idea of time, as we at the end of countless ages have. They still belonged to the beginnings of time—had no inherited experience to teach them as it were), and of course, as long as there was a piece of paper written over in accordance with some farcical law or other made down the river, it didn't enter anybody's head to trouble how they would live. Certainly they had brought with them some rotten hippo-meat, which couldn't have lasted very long, anyway, even if the pilgrims hadn't, in the midst of a shocking hullabaloo, thrown a considerable quantity of it overboard. It looked like a high-handed proceeding; but it was really a case of legitimate self-defense. You can't breathe dead hippo waking, sleeping, and eating, and at the same time keep your precarious grip on existence. Besides that, they had given them every week three pieces of brass wire, each about nine inches long; and the theory was they were to buy their provisions with that currency in riverside villages. You can see how *that* worked. There were either no villages, or the people were hostile, or the director, who like the rest of us fed out of tins, with an occasional old he-goat thrown in, didn't want to stop the steamer for some more or less recondite reason. So, unless they swallowed the wire itself, or made loops of it to snare the fishes with, I don't see what good their extravagant salary could be to them. I must say it was paid with a regularity worthy of a large and honorable trading company. For the rest, the only thing to eat—though it didn't look eatable in the least—I saw in their possession was a few lumps of some stuff like half-cooked dough, of a dirty lavender color, they kept wrapped in leaves, and now and then swallowed a piece of, but so small that it seemed done more for the looks of the thing than for any serious purpose of sustenance. Why in the name of all the gnawing devils of hunger they didn't go for us—they were thirty to five—and have a good tuck-in for once, amazes me now when I think of it. They were big powerful men, with not much capacity to weigh the consequences, with courage, with strength, even yet, though their skins were no longer glossy and their muscles no longer hard. And I saw that something restraining, one of those human secrets that baffle probability, had come into play there. I looked at them with a swift quickening of interest—not because it occurred to me I might be eaten by them before very long, though I own to you that just then I perceived—in a new light, as it were—how unwholesome the pilgrims looked, and I hoped, yes, I positively hoped, that my aspect was not so—what shall I say?—so—unappetizing: a touch of fantastic vanity which fitted well with the dream-sensation that pervaded all my days at that time.

Perhaps I had a little fever, too. One can't live with one's finger everlastingly on one's pulse. I had often 'a little fever,' or a little touch of other things—the playful paw-strokes of the wilderness, the preliminary trifling before the more serious onslaught which came in due course. Yes; I looked at them as you would on any human being, with a curiosity of their impulses, motives, capacities, weaknesses, when brought to the test of an inexorable physical necessity. Restraint! What possible restraint? Was it superstition, disgust, patience, fear—or some kind of primitive honor? No fear can stand up to hunger, no patience can wear it out, disgust simply does not exist where hunger is; and as to superstition, beliefs, and what you may call principles, they are less than chaff in a breeze. Don't you know the devilry of lingering starvation, its exasperating torment, its black thoughts, its somber and brooding ferocity? Well, I do. It takes a man all his inborn strength to fight hunger properly. It's really easier to face bereavement, dishonor, and the perdition of one's soul—than this kind of prolonged hunger. Sad, but true. And these chaps, too, had no earthly reason for any kind of scruple. Restraint! I would just as soon have expected restraint from a hyena prowling amongst the corpses of a battlefield. But there was the fact facing me—the fact dazzling, to be seen, like the foam on the depths of the sea, like a ripple on an unfathomable enigma, a mystery greater—when I thought of it—than the curious, inexplicable note of desperate grief in this savage clamor that had swept by us on the river-bank, behind the blind whiteness of the fog.

"Two pilgrims were quarreling in hurried whispers as to which bank. 'Left.' 'No, no; how can you? Right, right, of course.' 'It is very serious,' said the manager's voice behind me; 'I would be desolated if anything should happen to Mr. Kurtz before we came up.' I looked at him, and had not the slightest doubt he was sincere. He was just the kind of man who would wish to preserve appearances. That was his restraint. But when he muttered something about going on at once, I did not even take the trouble to answer him. I knew, and he knew, that it was impossible. Were we to let go our hold of the bottom, we would be absolutely in the air—in space. We wouldn't be able to tell where we were going to—whether up or down stream, or across—till we fetched against one bank or the other, —and then we wouldn't know at first which it was. Of course I made no move. I had no mind for a smashup. You couldn't imagine a more deadly place for a shipwreck. Whether drowned at once or not, we were sure to perish speedily in one way or another. 'I authorize you to take all the risks,' he said, after a short silence. 'I refuse to take any,' I said, shortly; which was just the answer he expected, though its tone might have surprised him. 'Well, I must defer to your judgment. You are captain,' he said, with marked civility. I turned my shoulder to him in sign of my appreciation, and looked into the fog. How long would it last? It was the most hopeless lookout. The approach to this Kurtz grubbing for ivory in the wretched bush was beset by as many dangers as though he had been an enchanted princess sleeping in a fabulous castle. 'Will they attack, do you think?' asked the manager, in a confidential tone.

"I did not think they would attack, for several obvious reasons. The thick fog was one. If they left the bank in their canoes they would get lost in it, as we would be if we attempted to move. Still, I had also judged the jungle of both banks quite impenetrable—and yet eyes were in it, eyes that had seen us. The river-side bushes were certainly very thick; but the undergrowth behind was evidently penetrable. However, during the short lift I had seen no canoes anywhere in the reach—certainly not abreast of the steamer. But what made the idea of attack inconceivable to me was the nature of the noise—of the cries we had heard. They had not the fierce character boding immediate hostile intention. Unexpected, wild, and violent as they had been, they had given me an irresistible impression of sorrow. The glimpse of the steamboat had for some reason filled those savages with unrestrained grief. The danger, if any, I expounded, was from our proximity to a great human passion let loose. Even extreme grief may ultimately vent itself in violence—but more generally takes the form of apathy. . . .

"You should have seen the pilgrims stare! They had no heart to grin, or even to revile me: but I believe they thought me gone mad—with fright, maybe. I delivered a regular lecture. My dear boys, it was no good bothering. Keep a look-out? Well, you may guess I watched the fog for the signs of lifting as a cat watches a mouse; but for anything else our eyes were of no more use to us than if we had been buried miles deep in a heap of cotton-wool. It felt like it, too—choking, warm, stifling. Besides, all I said, though it sounded extravagant, was absolutely true to fact. What we afterwards alluded to as an attack was really an attempt at repulse. The action was very far from being aggressive—it was not even defensive, in the usual sense: it was undertaken under the stress of desperation, and in its essence was purely protective.

"It developed itself, I should say, two hours after the fog lifted, and its commencement was at a spot, roughly speaking, about a mile and a half below Kurtz's station. We had just floundered and flopped round a bend, when I saw an islet, a mere grassy hummock of bright green, in the middle of the stream. It was the only thing of the kind; but as we opened the reach more, I perceived it was the head of a long sandbank, or rather of a chain of shallow patches stretching down the middle of the river. They were discolored, just awash, and the whole lot was seen just under the water, exactly as a man's backbone is seen running down the middle of his back under the skin. Now, as far as I did see, I could go to the right or to the left of this. I didn't know either channel, of course. The banks looked pretty well alike, the depth appeared the same; but as I had been informed the station was on the west side, I naturally headed for the western passage.

"No sooner had we fairly entered it than I became aware it was much narrower than I had supposed. To the left of us there was the long uninterrupted shoal, and to the right a high, steep bank heavily overgrown with bushes. Above the bush the trees stood in serried ranks. The twigs overhung the current thickly, and from distance to distance a large limb of some tree projected rigidly over the stream. It was then well on in the afternoon, the face of the forest was gloomy, and a broad strip of shadow had already fallen on the water. In this shadow we steamed up—very slowly, as you may imagine. I sheered her well inshore—the water being deepest near the bank, as the sounding-pole informed me.

"One of my hungry and forbearing friends was sounding in the bows just below me. This steamboat was exactly like a decked scow. On the deck, there were two little teak-wood houses, with doors and windows. The boiler was in the fore-end, and the machinery right astern. Over the whole there was a light roof, supported on stanchions. The funnel projected through that roof, and in front of the funnel a small cabin built of light planks served for a pilot-house. It contained a couch, two campstools, a loaded Martini-Henry leaning in one corner, a tiny table, and the steering-wheel. It had a wide door in front and a broad shutter at each side. All these were always thrown open, of course. I spent my days perched up there on the extreme fore-end of that roof, before the door. At night I slept, or tried to, on the couch. An athletic black belonging to some coast tribe, and educated by my poor predecessor, was the helmsman. He sported a pair of brass earrings, wore a blue cloth wrapper from the waist to the ankles, and thought all the world of himself. He was the most unstable kind of fool I had ever seen. He steered with no end of a swagger while you were by; but if he lost sight of you, he became instantly the prey of an abject funk, and would let that cripple of a steamboat get the upper hand of him in a minute.

"I was looking down at the sounding pole, and feeling much annoyed to see at each try a little more of it stick out of that river, when I saw my poleman give up the business suddenly, and stretch himself flat on the deck, without even taking the trouble to haul his pole in. He kept hold on it though, and it trailed in the water. At the same time the fireman, whom I could also see below me, sat down abruptly before his furnace and ducked his head. I was amazed. Then I had to look at the river mighty quick, because there was a snag in the fairway. Sticks, little sticks, were flying about—thick: they were whizzing before my nose, dropping below me, striking behind me against my pilot-house. All this time the river, the shore, the woods, were very quiet—perfectly quiet. I could only hear the heavy splashing thump of the stern-wheel and the patter of these things. We cleared the snag clumsily. Arrows, by Jove! We were being shot at! I stepped in quickly to close the shutter on the land-side. That fool-helmsman, his hands on the spokes, was lifting his knees high, stamping his feet, champing his mouth, like a reined-in horse. Confound him! And we were staggering within ten feet of the bank. I had to lean right out to swing the heavy shutter, and I saw a face amongst the leaves on the level with my own, looking at me very fierce and steady; and then suddenly, as though a veil had been removed from my eyes, I made out, deep in the tangled gloom, naked breasts, arms, legs, glaring eyes,—the bush was swarming with human limbs in movement, glistening, of bronze color. The twigs shook, swayed, and rustled, the arrows flew out of them, and then the shutter came to. 'Steer her straight,' I said to the helmsman. He held his head rigid, face forward; but his eyes rolled, he kept on lifting and setting down his feet gently, his mouth foamed a little. 'Keep quiet!' I said in a fury. I might just as well have ordered a tree not to sway in the wind. I darted out. Below me there was a great scuffle of feet on the iron deck; confused exclamations; a voice screamed, 'Can you turn back?' I caught sight of a V-shaped ripple on the water ahead. What? Another snag! A fusillade burst out under my feet. The pilgrims had opened with their Winchesters, and were simply squirting lead into that bush. A deuce of a lot of smoke came up and drove slowly forward. I swore at it. Now I couldn't see the ripple or the snag either. I stood in the doorway, peering, and the arrows came in swarms. They might have been poisoned, but they looked as though they wouldn't kill a cat. The bush began to howl. Our wood-cutters raised a warlike whoop; the report of a rifle just at my back deafened me. I glanced over my shoulder, and the pilot-house was yet full of noise and smoke when I made a dash at the wheel. The fool-nigger had dropped everything to throw the shutter open and let off that Martini-Henry. He stood before the wide opening, glaring, and I yelled at him to come back, while I straightened the sudden twist out of that steamboat. There was no room to turn even if I had wanted to, the snag was somewhere very near ahead in that confounded smoke, there was no time to lose, so I just crowded her into the bank—right into the bank, where I knew the water was deep.

"We tore slowly along the overhanging bushes in a whirl of broken twigs and flying leaves. The fusillade below stopped short, as I had foreseen it would when the squirts got empty. I threw my head back to a glinting whizz that traversed the pilot-house, in at one shutter-hole and out at the other. Looking past that mad helmsman, who was shaking the empty rifle and yelling at the shore, I saw vague forms of men running bent double, leaping, gliding, distinct, incomplete, evanescent. Something big appeared in the air before the shutter, the rifle went overboard, and the man stepped back swiftly, looked at me over his shoulder in an extraordinary, profound, familiar manner, and fell upon my feet. The side of his head hit the wheel twice, and the end of what appeared a long cane clattered round and knocked over a little campstool. It looked as though after wrenching that thing from somebody ashore he had lost his balance in the effort. The thin smoke had blown away, we were clear of the snag, and looking ahead I could see that in another hundred yards or so I would be free to sheer off, away from the bank; but my feet felt so very warm and wet that I had to look down. The man had rolled on his back and stared straight up at me; both his hands clutched that cane. It was the shaft of a spear that, either thrown or lunged through the opening, had caught him in the side just below the ribs; the blade had gone in out of sight, after making a frightful gash; my shoes were full; a pool of blood lay very still, gleaming dark-red under the wheel; his eyes shone with an amazing luster. The fusillade burst out again. He looked at me anxiously, gripping the spear like something precious, with an air of being afraid I would try to take it away from him. I had to make an effort to free my eyes from his gaze and attend to steering. With one hand I felt above my head for the line of the steam-whistle, and jerked out screech after screech hurriedly. The tumult of angry and warlike yells was checked instantly, and then from the depths of the woods went out such a tremulous and prolonged wail of mournful fear and utter despair as may be imagined to follow the flight of the last hope from the earth. There was a great commotion in the bush; the shower of arrows stopped, a few dropping shots rang out sharply—then silence, in which the languid beat of the stern-wheel came plainly to my ears. I put the helm hard a-starboard at the moment when the pilgrim in pink pajamas, very hot and agitated, appeared in the doorway. 'The manager sends me—' he began in an official tone, and stopped short. 'Good God!' he said, glaring at the wounded man.

"We two whites stood over him, and his lustrous and inquiring glance enveloped us both. I declare it looked as though he would presently put to us some question in an understandable language; but he died without uttering a sound, without moving a limb, without twitching a muscle. Only in the very last moment, as though in response to some sign we could not see, to some whisper we could not hear, he frowned heavily, and that frown gave to his black death-mask an inconceivably somber, brooding, and menacing expression. The luster of inquiring glance faded swiftly into vacant glassiness. 'Can you steer?' I asked the agent eagerly. He looked very dubious; but I made a grab at his arm, and he understood at once I meant him to steer whether or no. To tell you the truth, I was morbidly anxious to change my shoes and socks. 'He is dead,' murmured the fellow, immensely impressed. 'No doubt about it,' said I tugging like mad at the shoe-laces. 'And by the way, I suppose Mr. Kurtz is dead as well by this time.'

"For the moment that was the dominant thought. There was a sense of extreme disappointment, as though I had found out I had been striving after something altogether without a substance. I couldn't have been more disgusted if I had traveled all this way for the sole purpose of talking with Mr. Kurtz. Talking with . . . I flung one shoe overboard, and became aware that that was exactly what I had been looking forward to—a talk with Kurtz. I made the strange discovery that I had never imagined him as doing, you know, but as discoursing. I didn't say to myself, 'Now I will never see him,' or 'Now I will never shake him by the hand,' but, 'Now I will never hear him.' The man presented himself as a voice. Not of course that I did not connect him with some sort of action. Hadn't I been told in all the tones of jealousy and admiration that he had collected, bartered, swindled, or stolen more ivory than all the other agents together? That was not the point. The point was in his being a gifted creature, and that of all his gifts the one that stood out pre-eminently, that carried with it a sense of real presence, was his ability to talk, his words—the gift of expression, the bewildering, the illuminating, the most exalted and the most contemptible, the pulsating stream of light, or the deceitful flow from the heart of an impenetrable darkness.

"The other shoe went flying unto the devil-god of that river. I thought, by Jove! it's all over. We are too late; he has vanished—the gift has vanished, by means of some spear, arrow, or club. I will never hear that chap speak after all,—and my sorrow had a startling extravagance of emotion, even such as I had noticed in the howling sorrow of these savages in the bush. I couldn't have felt more lonely desolation somehow, had I been robbed of a belief or had missed my destiny in life. . . . Why do you sigh in this beastly way, somebody? Absurd? Well, absurd. Good Lord! mustn't a man ever— Here, give me some tobacco." . . .

There was a pause of profound stillness, then a match flared, and Marlow's lean face appeared, worn, hollow, with downward folds and drooped eyelids, with an aspect of concentrated attention; and as he took vigorous draws at his pipe, it seemed to retreat and advance out of the night in the regular flicker of the tiny flame. The match went out.

"Absurd!" he cried. "This is the worst of trying to tell. . . . Here you all are, each moored with two good addresses, like a hulk with two anchors, a butcher round one corner, a policeman round another, excellent appetites, and temperature normal—you hear—normal from year's end to year's end. And you say, Absurd! Absurd be—exploded! Absurd! My dear boys, what can you expect from a man who out of sheer nervousness had just flung overboard a pair of new shoes! Now I think of it, it is amazing I did not shed tears. I am, upon the whole, proud of my fortitude. I was cut to the quick at the idea of having lost the inestimable privilege of listening to the gifted Kurtz. Of course I was wrong. The privilege was waiting for me. Oh, yes, I heard more than enough. And I was right, too. A voice. He was very little more than a voice. And I heard—him—it—this voice—other voices—all of them were so little more than voices—and the memory of that time itself lingers around me, impalpable, like a dying vibration of one immense jabber, silly, atrocious, sordid, savage, or simply mean, without any kind of sense. Voices, voices —even the girl herself—now—"

He was silent for a long time.

"I laid the ghost of his gifts at last with a lie," he began, suddenly. "Girl! What? Did I mention a girl? Oh, she is out of it—completely. They—the women I mean—are out of it—should be out of it. We must help them to stay in that beautiful world of their own, lest ours gets worse. Oh, she had to be out of it. You should have heard the disinterred body of Mr. Kurtz saying, 'My Intended.' You would have perceived directly then how completely she was out of it. And the lofty frontal bone of Mr. Kurtz! They say the hair goes on growing sometimes, but this—ah—specimen, was impressively bald. The wilderness had patted him on the head, and, behold, it was like a ball—an ivory ball; it had caressed him, and—lo!—he had withered; it had taken him, loved him, embraced him, got into his veins, consumed his flesh, and sealed his soul to its own by the inconceivable ceremonies of some devilish initiation. He was its spoiled and pampered favorite. Ivory? I should think so. Heaps of it, stacks of it. The old mud shanty was bursting with it. You would think there was not a single tusk left either above or below the ground in the whole country. 'Mostly fossil,' the manager had remarked, disparagingly. It was no more fossil than I am; but they call it fossil when it is dug up. It appears these niggers do bury the tusks sometimes—but evidently they couldn't bury this parcel deep enough to save the gifted Mr. Kurtz from his fate. We filled the steamboat with it, and had to pile a lot on the deck. Thus he could see and enjoy as long as he could see, because the appreciation of this favor had remained with him to the last. You should have heard him say, 'My ivory.' Oh, yes, I heard him. 'My Intended, my ivory, my station, my river, my—' everything belonged to him. It made me hold my breath in expectation of hearing the wilderness burst into a prodigious peal of laughter that would shake the fixed stars in their places. Everything belonged to him—but that was a trifle. The thing was to know what he belonged to, how many powers of darkness claimed him for their own. That was the reflection that made you creepy all over. It was impossible—it was not good for one either—trying to imagine. He had taken a high seat amongst the devils of the land—I mean literally. You can't understand. How could you?—with solid pavement under your feet, surrounded by kind neighbors ready to cheer you or to fall on you, stepping delicately between the butcher and the policeman, in the holy terror of scandal and gallows and lunatic asylums—how can you imagine what particular region of the first ages a man's untrammeled feet may take him into by the way of solitude—utter solitude without a policeman—by the way of silence—utter silence, where no warning voice of a kind neighbor can be heard whispering of public opinion? These little things make all the great difference. When they are gone you must fall back upon your own innate strength, upon your own capacity for faithfulness. Of course you may be too much of a fool to go wrong—too dull even to know you are being assaulted by the powers of darkness. I take it, no fool ever made a bargain for his soul with the devil: the fool is too much of a fool, or the devil too much of a devil—I don't know which. Or you may be such a thunderingly exalted creature as to be altogether deaf and blind to anything but heavenly sights and sounds. Then the earth for you is only a standing place—and whether to be like this is your loss or your gain I won't pretend to say. But most of us are neither one nor the other. The earth for us is a place to live in, where we must put up with sights, with sounds, with smells, too, by Jove!—breathe dead hippo, so to speak, and not be contaminated. And there, don't you see? your strength comes in, the faith in your ability for the digging of unostentatious holes to bury the stuff in—your power of devotion, not to yourself, but to an obscure, back-breaking business. And that's difficult enough. Mind, I am not trying to excuse or even explain—I am trying to account to myself for—for—Mr. Kurtz—for the shade of Mr. Kurtz. This initiated wraith from the back of Nowhere honored me with its amazing confidence before it vanished altogether. This was because it could speak English to me. The original Kurtz had been educated partly in England, and—as he was good enough to say himself—his sympathies were in the right place. His mother was half-English, his father was half-French. All Europe contributed to the making of Kurtz; and by and by I learned that, most appropriately, the International Society for the Suppression of Savage Customs had intrusted him with the making of a report, for its future guidance. And he had written it, too. I've seen it. I've read it. It was eloquent, vibrating with eloquence, but too high-strung, I think. Seventeen pages of close writing he had found time for! But this must have been before his—let us say—nerves, went wrong, and caused him to preside at certain midnight dances ending with unspeakable rites, which—as far as I reluctantly gathered from what I heard at various times—were offered up to him—do you understand?—to Mr. Kurtz himself. But it was a beautiful piece of writing. The opening paragraph, however, in the light of later information, strikes me now as ominous. He began with the argument that we whites, from the point of development we had arrived at, 'must necessarily appear to them [savages] in the nature of supernatural beings—we approach them with the might as of a deity,' and so on, and so on. 'By the simple exercise of our will we can exert a power for good practically unbounded,' etc., etc. From that point he soared and took me with him. The peroration was magnificent, though difficult to remember, you know. It gave me the notion of an exotic Immensity ruled by an august Benevolence. It made me tingle with enthusiasm. This was the unbounded power of eloquence—of words—of burning noble words. There were no practical hints to interrupt the magic current of phrases, unless a kind of note at the foot of the last page, scrawled evidently much later, in an unsteady hand, may be regarded as the exposition of a method. It was very simple, and at the end of that moving appeal to every altruistic sentiment it blazed at you, luminous and terrifying, like a flash of lightning in a serene sky: 'Exterminate all the brutes!' The curious part was that he had apparently forgotten all about that valuable postscriptum, because, later on, when he in a sense came to himself, he repeatedly entreated me to take good care of 'my pamphlet' (he called it), as it was sure to have in the future a good influence upon his career. I had full information about all these things, and, besides, as it turned out, I was to have the care of his memory. I've done enough for it to give me the indisputable right to lay it, if I choose, for an everlasting rest in the dustbin of progress, amongst all the sweepings and, figuratively speaking, all the dead cats of civilization. But then, you see, I can't choose. He won't be forgotten. Whatever he was, he was not common. He had the power to charm or frighten rudimentary souls into an aggravated witch-dance in his honor; he could also fill the small souls of the pilgrims with bitter misgivings: he had one devoted friend at least, and he had conquered one soul in the world that was neither rudimentary nor tainted with self-seeking. No; I can't forget him, though I am not prepared to affirm the fellow was exactly worth the life we lost in getting to him. I missed my late helmsman awfully,—I missed him even while his body was still lying in the pilot-house. Perhaps you will think it passing strange this regret for a savage who was no more account than a grain of sand in a black Sahara. Well, don't you see, he had done something, he had steered; for months I had him at my back—a help—an instrument. It was a kind of partnership. He steered for me—I had to look after him, I worried about his deficiencies, and thus a subtle bond had been created, of which I only became aware when it was suddenly broken. And the intimate profundity of that look he gave me when he received his hurt remains to this day in my memory—like a claim of distant kinship affirmed in a supreme moment.

"Poor fool! If he had only left that shutter alone. He had no restraint, no restraint—just like Kurtz—a tree swayed by the wind. As soon as I had put on a dry pair of slippers, I dragged him out, after first jerking the spear out of his side, which operation I confess I performed with my eyes shut tight. His heels leaped together over the little door-step; his shoulders were pressed to my breast; I hugged him from behind desperately. Oh! he was heavy, heavy; heavier than any man on earth, I should imagine. Then without more ado I tipped him overboard. The current snatched him as though he had been a wisp of grass, and I saw the body roll over twice before I lost sight of it forever. All the pilgrims and the manager were then congregated on the awning-deck about the pilot-house, chattering at each other like a flock of excited magpies, and there was a scandalized murmur at my heartless promptitude. What they wanted to keep that body hanging about for I can't guess. Embalm it, maybe. But I had also heard another, and a very ominous, murmur on the deck below. My friends the wood-cutters were likewise scandalized, and with a better show of reason—though I admit that the reason itself was quite inadmissible. Oh, quite! I had made up my mind that if my late helmsman was to be eaten, the fishes alone should have him. He had been a very second-rate helmsman while alive, but now he was dead he might have become a first-class temptation, and possibly cause some startling trouble. Besides, I was anxious to take the wheel, the man in pink pajamas showing himself a hopeless duffer at the business.

"This I did directly the simple funeral was over. We were going half-speed, keeping right in the middle of the stream, and I listened to the talk about me. They had given up Kurtz, they had given up the station; Kurtz was dead, and the station had been burnt—and so on—and so on. The red-haired pilgrim was beside himself with the thought that at least this poor Kurtz had been properly avenged. 'Say! We must have made a glorious slaughter of them in the bush. Eh? What do you think? Say?' He positively danced, the bloodthirsty little gingery beggar. And he had nearly fainted when he saw the wounded man! I could not help saying, 'You made a glorious lot of smoke, anyhow.' I had seen, from the way the tops of the bushes rustled and flew, that almost all the shots had gone too high. You can't hit anything unless you take aim and fire from the shoulder; but these chaps fired from the hip with their eyes shut. The retreat, I maintained—and I was right—was caused by the screeching of the steam-whistle. Upon this they forgot Kurtz, and began to howl at me with indignant protests.

"The manager stood by the wheel murmuring confidentially about the necessity of getting well away down the river before dark at all events, when I saw in the distance a clearing on the river-side and the outlines of some sort of building. 'What's this?' I asked. He clapped his hands in wonder. 'The station!' he cried. I edged in at once, still going half-speed.

"Through my glasses I saw the slope of a hill interspersed with rare trees and perfectly free from undergrowth. A long decaying building on the summit was half buried in the high grass; the large holes in the peaked roof gaped black from afar; the jungle and the woods made a background. There was no enclosure or fence of any kind; but there had been one apparently, for near the house half-a-dozen slim posts remained in a row, roughly trimmed, and with their upper ends ornamented with round carved balls. The rails, or whatever there had been between, had disappeared. Of course the forest surrounded all that. The river-bank was clear, and on the water-side I saw a white man under a hat like a cart-wheel beckoning persistently with his whole arm. Examining the edge of the forest above and below, I was almost certain I could see movements—human forms gliding here and there. I steamed past prudently, then stopped the engines and let her drift down. The man on the shore began to shout, urging us to land. 'We have been attacked,' screamed the manager. 'I know—I know. It's all right,' yelled back the other, as cheerful as you please. 'Come along. It's all right. I am glad.'

"His aspect reminded me of something I had seen—something funny I had seen somewhere. As I maneuvered to get alongside, I was asking myself, 'What does this fellow look like?' Suddenly I got it. He looked like a harlequin. His clothes had been made of some stuff that was brown holland probably, but it was covered with patches all over, with bright patches, blue, red, and yellow,—patches on the back, patches on the front, patches on elbows, on knees; colored binding around his jacket, scarlet edging at the bottom of his trousers; and the sunshine made him look extremely gay and wonderfully neat withal, because you could see how beautifully all this patching had been done. A beardless, boyish face, very fair, no features to speak of, nose peeling, little blue eyes, smiles and frowns chasing each other over that open countenance like sunshine and shadow on a wind-swept plain. 'Look out, captain!' he cried; 'there's a snag lodged in here last night.' What! Another snag? I confess I swore shamefully. I had nearly holed my cripple, to finish off that charming trip. The harlequin on the bank turned his little pug-nose up to me. 'You English?' he asked, all smiles. 'Are you?' I shouted from the wheel. The smiles vanished, and he shook his head as if sorry for my disappointment. Then he brightened up. 'Never mind!' he cried, encouragingly. 'Are we in time?' I asked. 'He is up there,' he replied, with a toss of the head up the hill, and becoming gloomy all of a sudden. His face was like the autumn sky, overcast one moment and bright the next.

"When the manager, escorted by the pilgrims, all of them armed to the teeth, had gone to the house this chap came on board. 'I say, I don't like this. These natives are in the bush,' I said. He assured me earnestly it was all right. 'They are simple people,' he added; 'well, I am glad you came. It took me all my time to keep them off.' 'But you said it was all right,' I cried. 'Oh, they meant no harm,' he said; and as I stared he corrected himself, 'Not exactly.' Then vivaciously, 'My faith, your pilot-house wants a clean-up!' In the next breath he advised me to keep enough steam on the boiler to blow the whistle in case of any trouble. 'One good screech will do more for you than all your rifles. They are simple people,' he repeated. He rattled away at such a rate he quite overwhelmed me. He seemed to be trying to make up for lots of silence, and actually hinted, laughing, that such was the case. 'Don't you talk with Mr. Kurtz?' I said. 'You don't talk with that man—you listen to him,' he exclaimed with severe exaltation. 'But now—' He waved his arm, and in the twinkling of an eye was in the uttermost depths of despondency. In a moment he came up again with a jump, possessed himself of both my hands, shook them continuously, while he gabbled: 'Brother sailor . . . honor . . . pleasure . . . delight . . . introduce myself . . . Russian . . . son of an arch-priest . . . Government of Tambov. . . . What? Tobacco! English tobacco; the excellent English tobacco! Now, that's brotherly. Smoke? Where's a sailor that does not smoke?'

"The pipe soothed him, and gradually I made out he had run away from school, had gone to sea in a Russian ship; ran away again; served some time in English ships; was now reconciled with the arch-priest. He made a point of that. 'But when one is young one must see things, gather experience, ideas; enlarge the mind.' 'Here!' I interrupted. 'You can never tell! Here I met Mr. Kurtz,' he said, youthfully solemn and reproachful. I held my tongue after that. It appears he had persuaded a Dutch trading-house on the coast to fit him out with stores and goods, and had started for the interior with a light heart, and no more idea of what would happen to him than a baby. He had been wandering about that river for nearly two years alone, cut off from everybody and everything. 'I am not so young as I look. I am twenty-five,' he said. 'At first old Van Shuyten would tell me to go to the devil,' he narrated with keen enjoyment; 'but I stuck to him, and talked and talked, till at last he got afraid I would talk the hind-leg off his favorite dog, so he gave me some cheap things and a few guns, and told me he hoped he would never see my face again. Good old Dutchman, Van Shuyten. I've sent him one small lot of ivory a year ago, so that he can't call me a little thief when I get back. I hope he got it. And for the rest I don't care. I had some wood stacked for you. That was my old house. Did you see?'

"I gave him Towson's book. He made as though he would kiss me, but restrained himself. 'The only book I had left, and I thought I had lost it,' he said, looking at it ecstatically. 'So many accidents happen to a man going about alone, you know. Canoes get upset sometimes—and sometimes you've got to clear out so quick when the people get angry.' He thumbed the pages. 'You made notes in Russian?' I asked. He nodded. 'I thought they were written in cipher,' I said. He laughed, then became serious. 'I had lots of trouble to keep these people off,' he said. 'Did they want to kill you?' I asked. 'Oh, no!' he cried, and checked himself. 'Why did they attack us?' I pursued. He hesitated, then said shamefacedly, 'They don't want him to go.' 'Don't they?' I said, curiously. He nodded a nod full of mystery and wisdom. 'I tell you,' he cried, 'this man has enlarged my mind.' He opened his arms wide, staring at me with his little blue eyes that were perfectly round."

3

"I looked at him, lost in astonishment. There he was before me, in motley, as though he had absconded from a troupe of mimes, enthusiastic, fabulous. His very existence was improbable, inexplicable, and altogether bewildering. He was an insoluble problem. It was inconceivable how he had existed, how he had succeeded in getting so far, how he had managed to remain—why he did not instantly disappear. 'I went a little farther,' he said, 'then still a little farther—till I had gone so far that I don't know how I'll ever get back. Never mind. Plenty time. I can manage. You take Kurtz away quick—quick—I tell you.' The glamour of youth enveloped his parti-colored rags, his destitution, his loneliness, the essential desolation of his futile wanderings. For months—for years—his life hadn't been worth a day's purchase; and there he was gallantly, thoughtlessly alive, to all appearance indestructible solely by the virtue of his few years and of his unreflecting audacity. I was seduced into something like admiration—like envy. Glamour urged him on, glamour kept him unscathed. He surely wanted nothing from the wilderness but space to breathe in and to push on through. His need was to exist, and to move onwards at the greatest possible risk, and with a maximum of privation. If the absolutely pure, uncalculating, unpractical spirit of adventure had ever ruled a human being, it ruled this be-patched youth. I almost envied him the possession of this modest and clear flame. It seemed to have consumed all thought of self so completely, that even while he was talking to you, you forgot that it was he—the man before your eyes—who had gone through these things. I did not envy him his devotion to Kurtz, though. He had not meditated over it. It came to him and he accepted it with a sort of eager fatalism. I must say that to me it appeared about the most dangerous thing in every way he had come upon so far.

"They had come together unavoidably, like two ships becalmed near each other, and lay rubbing sides at last. I suppose Kurtz wanted an audience, because on a certain occasion, when encamped in the forest, they had talked all night, or more probably Kurtz had talked. 'We talked of everything,' he said, quite transported at the recollection. 'I forgot there was such a thing as sleep. The night did not seem to last an hour. Everything! Everything! . . . Of love, too.' 'Ah, he talked to you of love!' I said, much amused. 'It isn't what you think,' he cried, almost passionately. 'It was in general. He made me see things—things.'

"He threw his arms up. We were on deck at the time, and the headman of my wood-cutters, lounging near by, turned upon him his heavy and glittering eyes. I looked around, and I don't know why, but I assure you that never, never before, did this land, this river, this jungle, the very arch of this blazing sky, appear to me so hopeless and so dark, so impenetrable to human thought, so pitiless to human weakness. 'And, ever since, you have been with him, of course?' I said.

"On the contrary. It appears their intercourse had been very much broken by various causes. He had, as he informed me proudly, managed to nurse Kurtz through two illnesses (he alluded to it as you would to some risky feat), but as a rule Kurtz wandered alone far in the depths of the forest. 'Very often coming to this station, I had to wait days and days before he would turn up,' he said. 'Ah, it was worth waiting for!—sometimes.' 'What was he doing? exploring or what?' I asked. 'Oh, yes, of course'; he had discovered lots of villages, a lake, too—he did not know exactly in what direction; it was dangerous to inquire too much—but mostly his expeditions had been for ivory. 'But he had no goods to trade with by that time,' I objected. 'There's a good lot of cartridges left even yet,' he answered, looking away. 'To speak plainly, he raided the country,' I said. He nodded. 'Not alone, surely!' He muttered something about the villages round that lake. 'Kurtz got the tribe to follow him, did he?' I suggested. He fidgeted a little. 'They adored him,' he said. The tone of these words was so extraordinary that I looked at him searchingly. It was curious to see his mingled eagerness and reluctance to speak of Kurtz. The man filled his life, occupied his thoughts, swayed his emotions. 'What can you expect?' he burst out; 'he came to them with thunder and lightning, you know—and they had never seen anything like it—and very terrible. He could be very terrible. You can't judge Mr. Kurtz as you would an ordinary man. No, no, no! Now—just to give you an idea—I don't mind telling you, he wanted to shoot me, too, one day—but I don't judge him.' 'Shoot you!' I cried. 'What for?' 'Well, I had a small lot of ivory the chief of that village near my house gave me. You see I used to shoot game for them. Well, he wanted it, and wouldn't hear reason. He declared he would shoot me unless I gave him the ivory and then cleared out of the country, because he could do so, and had a fancy for it, and there was nothing on earth to prevent him killing whom he jolly well pleased. And it was true, too. I gave him the ivory. What did I care! But I didn't clear out. No, no. I couldn't leave him. I had to be careful, of course, till we got friendly again for a time. He had his second illness then. Afterwards I had to keep out of the way; but I didn't mind. He was living for the most part in those villages on the lake. When he came down to the river, sometimes he would take to me, and sometimes it was better for me to be careful. This man suffered too much. He hated all this, and somehow he couldn't get away. When I had a chance I begged him to try and leave while there was time; I offered to go back with him. And he would say yes, and then he would remain; go off on another ivory hunt; disappear for weeks; forget himself amongst these people—forget himself—you know.' 'Why! he's mad,' I said. He protested indignantly. Mr. Kurtz couldn't be mad. If I had heard him talk, only two days ago, I wouldn't dare hint at such a thing. . . . I had taken up my binoculars while we talked, and was looking at the shore, sweeping the limit of the forest at each side and at the back of the house. The consciousness of there being people in that bush, so silent, so quiet—as silent and quiet as the ruined house on the hill—made me uneasy. There was no sign on the face of nature of this amazing tale that was not so much told as suggested to me in desolate exclamations, completed by shrugs, in interrupted phrases, in hints ending in deep sighs. The woods were unmoved, like a mask—heavy, like the closed door of a prison—they looked with their air of hidden knowledge, of patient expectation, of unapproachable silence. The Russian was explaining to me that it was only lately that Mr. Kurtz had come down to the river, bringing along with him all the fighting men of that lake tribe. He had been absent for several months—getting himself adored, I suppose—and had come down unexpectedly, with the intention to all appearance of making a raid either across the river or down stream. Evidently the appetite for more ivory had got the better of the—what shall I say?—less material aspirations. However he had got much worse suddenly. 'I heard he was lying helpless, and so I came up—took my chance,' said the Russian. 'Oh, he is bad, very bad.' I directed my glass to the house. There were no signs of life, but there was the ruined roof, the long mud wall peeping above the grass, with three little square window-holes, no two of the same size; all this brought within reach of my hand, as it were. And then I made a brusque movement, and one of the remaining posts of that vanished fence leaped up in the field of my glass. You remember I told you I had been struck at the distance by certain attempts at ornamentation, rather remarkable in the ruinous aspect of the place. Now I had suddenly a nearer view, and its first result was to make me throw my head back as if before a blow. Then I went carefully from post to post with my glass, and I saw my mistake. These round knobs were not ornamental but symbolic; they were expressive and puzzling, striking and disturbing—food for thought and also for vultures if there had been any looking down from the sky; but at all events for such ants as were industrious enough to ascend the pole. They would have been even more impressive, those heads on the stakes, if their faces had not been turned to the house. Only one, the first I had made out, was facing my way. I was not so shocked as you may think. The start back I had given was really nothing but a movement of surprise. I had expected to see a knob of wood there, you know. I returned deliberately to the first I had seen—and there it was, black, dried, sunken, with closed eyelids,—a head that seemed to sleep at the top of that pole, and with the shrunken dry lips showing a narrow white line of the teeth, was smiling, too, smiling continuously at some endless and jocose dream of that eternal slumber.

"I am not disclosing any trade secrets. In fact, the manager said afterwards that Mr. Kurtz's methods had ruined the district. I have no opinion on that point, but I want you clearly to understand that there was nothing exactly profitable in these heads being there. They only showed that Mr. Kurtz lacked restraint in the gratification of his various lusts, that there was something wanting in him—some small matter which, when the pressing need arose, could not be found under his magnificent eloquence. Whether he knew of this deficiency himself I can't say. I think the knowledge came to him at last—only at the very last. But the wilderness had found him out early, and had taken on him a terrible vengeance for the fantastic invasion. I think it had whispered to him things about himself which he did not know, things of which he had no conception till he took counsel with this great solitude—and the whisper had proved irresistibly fascinating. It echoed loudly within him because he was hollow at the core. . . . I put down the glass, and the head that had appeared near enough to be spoken to seemed at once to have leaped away from me into inaccessible distance.

"The admirer of Mr. Kurtz was a bit crestfallen. In a hurried indistinct voice he began to assure me he had not dared to take these—say, symbols—down. He was not afraid of the natives; they would not stir till Mr. Kurtz gave the word. His ascendancy was extraordinary. The camps of these people surrounded the place, and the chiefs came every day to see him. They would crawl. . . . 'I don't want to know anything of the ceremonies used when approaching Mr. Kurtz,' I shouted. Curious, this feeling that came over me that such details would be more intolerable than those heads drying on the stakes under Mr. Kurtz's windows. After all, that was only a savage sight, while I seemed at one bound to have been transported into some lightless region of subtle horrors, where pure, uncomplicated savagery was a positive relief, being something that had a right to exist—obviously—in the sunshine. The young man looked at me with surprise. I suppose it did not occur to him that Mr. Kurtz was no idol of mine. He forgot I hadn't heard any of these splendid monologues on, what was it? on love, justice, conduct of life—or what not. If it had come to crawling before Mr. Kurtz, he crawled as much as the veriest savage of them all. I had no idea of the conditions, he said: these heads were the heads of rebels. I shocked him excessively by laughing. Rebels! What would be the next definition I was to hear? There had been enemies, criminals, workers—and these were rebels. Those rebellious heads looked very subdued to me on their sticks. 'You don't know how such a life tries a man like Kurtz,' cried Kurtz's last disciple. 'Well, and you?' I said. 'I! I! I am a simple man. I have no great thoughts. I want nothing from anybody. How can you compare me to . . . ?' His feelings were too much for speech, and suddenly he broke down. 'I don't understand,' he groaned. 'I've been doing my best to keep him alive, and that's enough. I had no hand in all this. I have no abilities. There hasn't been a drop of medicine or a mouthful of invalid food for months here. He was shamefully abandoned. A man like this, with such ideas. Shamefully! Shamefully! I—I—haven't slept for the last ten nights. . . .'

"His voice lost itself in the calm of the evening. The long shadows of the forest had slipped downhill while we talked, had gone far beyond the ruined hovel, beyond the symbolic row of stakes. All this was in the gloom, while we down there were yet in the sunshine, and the stretch of the river abreast of the clearing glittered in a still and dazzling splendor, with a murky and overshadowed bend above and below. Not a living soul was seen on the shore. The bushes did not rustle.

"Suddenly round the corner of the house a group of men appeared, as though they had come up from the ground. They waded waist-deep in the grass, in a compact body, bearing an improvised stretcher in their midst. Instantly, in the emptiness of the landscape, a cry arose whose shrillness pierced the still air like a sharp arrow flying straight to the very heart of the land; and, as if by enchantment, streams of human beings—of naked human beings—with spears in their hands, with bows, with shields, with wild glances and savage movements, were poured into the clearing by the dark-faced and pensive forest. The bushes shook, the grass swayed for a time, and then everything stood still in attentive immobility.

"'Now, if he does not say the right thing to them we are all done for,' said the Russian at my elbow. The knot of men with the stretcher had stopped, too, halfway to the steamer, as if petrified. I saw the man on the stretcher sit up, lank and with an uplifted arm, above the shoulders of the bearers. 'Let us hope that the man who can talk so well of love in general will find some particular reason to spare us this time,' I said. I resented bitterly the absurd danger of our situation, as if to be at the mercy of that atrocious phantom had been a dishonoring necessity. I could not hear a sound, but through my glasses I saw the thin arm extended commandingly, the lower jaw moving, the eyes of that apparition shining darkly far in its bony head that nodded with grotesque jerks. Kurtz—Kurtz—that means short in German—don't it? Well, the name was as true as everything else in his life—and death. He looked at least seven feet long. His covering had fallen off, and his body emerged from it pitiful and appalling as from a winding-sheet. I could see the cage of his ribs all astir, the bones of his arm waving. It was as though an animated image of death carved out of old ivory had been shaking its hand with menaces at a motionless crowd of men made of dark and glittering bronze. I saw him open his mouth wide—it gave him a weirdly voracious aspect, as though he had wanted to swallow all the air, all the earth, all the men before him. A deep voice reached me faintly. He must have been shouting. He fell back suddenly. The stretcher shook as the bearers staggered forward again, and almost at the same time I noticed that the crowd of savages was vanishing without any perceptible movement of retreat, as if the forest that had ejected these things so suddenly had drawn them in again as the breath is drawn in a long aspiration.

"Some of the pilgrims behind the stretcher carried his arms—two shotguns, a heavy rifle, and a light revolver-carbine—the thunderbolts of that pitiful Jupiter. The manager bent over him murmuring as he walked beside his head. They laid him down in one of the little cabins—just a room for a bedplace and a campstool or two, you know. We had brought his belated correspondence, and a lot of torn envelopes and open letters littered his bed. His hand roamed feebly amongst these papers. I was struck by the fire of his eyes and the composed languor of his expression. It was not so much the exhaustion of disease. He did not seem in pain. This shadow looked satiated and calm, as though for the moment it had had its fill of all the emotions.

"He rustled one of the letters, and looking straight in my face said, 'I am glad.' Somebody had been writing to him about me. These special recommendations were turning up again. The volume of tone he emitted without effort, almost without the trouble of moving his lips, amazed me. A voice! a voice! It was grave, profound, vibrating, while the man did not seem capable of a whisper. However, he had enough strength in him—factitious no doubt—to very nearly make an end of us, as you shall hear directly.

"The manager appeared silently in the doorway; I stepped out at once and he drew the curtain after me. The Russian, eyed curiously by the pilgrims, was staring at the shore. I followed the direction of his glance.

"Dark human shapes could be made out in the distance, flitting indistinctly against the gloomy border of the forest, and near the river two bronze figures, leaning on tall spears, stood in the sunlight under fantastic headdresses of spotted skins, war-like and still in statuesque repose. And from right to left along the lighted shore moved a wild and gorgeous apparition of a woman.

"She walked with measured steps, draped in striped and fringed cloths, treading the earth proudly, with a slight jingle and flash of barbarous ornaments. She carried her head high; her hair was done in the shape of a helmet; she had brass leggings to the knee, brass wire gauntlets to the elbow, a crimson spot on her tawny cheek, innumerable necklaces of glass beads on her neck; bizarre things, charms, gifts of witch-men, that hung about her, glittered and trembled at every step. She must have had the value of several elephant tusks upon her. She was savage and superb, wild-eyed and magnificent; there was something ominous and stately in her deliberate progress. And in the hush that had fallen suddenly upon the whole sorrowful land, the immense wilderness, the colossal body of the fecund and mysterious life seemed to look at her, pensive, as though it had been looking at the image of its own tenebrous and passionate soul.

"She came abreast of the steamer, stood still, and faced us. Her long shadow fell to the water's edge. Her face had a tragic and fierce aspect of wild sorrow and of dumb pain mingled with the fear of some struggling, half-shaped resolve. She stood looking at us without a stir, and like the wilderness itself, with an air of brooding over an inscrutable purpose. A whole minute passed, and then she made a step forward. There was a low jingle, a glint of yellow metal, a sway of fringed draperies, and she stopped as if her heart had failed her. The young fellow by my side growled. The pilgrims murmured at my back. She looked at us all as if her life had depended upon the unswerving steadiness of her glance. Suddenly she opened her bared arms and threw them up rigid above her head, as though in an uncontrollable desire to touch the sky, and at the same time the swift shadows darted out on the earth, swept around on the river, gathering the steamer into a shadowy embrace. A formidable silence hung over the scene.

"She turned away slowly, walked on, following the bank, and passed into the bushes to the left. Once only her eyes gleamed back at us in the dusk of the thickets before she disappeared.

"'If she had offered to come aboard I really think I would have tried to shoot her,' said the man of patches, nervously. 'I have been risking my life every day for the last fortnight to keep her out of the house. She got in one day and kicked up a row about those miserable rags I picked up in the storeroom to mend my clothes with. I wasn't decent. At least it must have been that, for she talked like a fury to Kurtz for an hour, pointing at me now and then. I don't understand the dialect of this tribe. Luckily for me, I fancy Kurtz felt too ill that day to care, or there would have been mischief. I don't understand. . . . No—it's too much for me. Ah, well, it's all over now.'

"At this moment I heard Kurtz's deep voice behind the curtain: 'Save me!—save the ivory, you mean. Don't tell me. Save *me!* Why, I've had to save you. You are interrupting my plans now. Sick! Sick! Not so sick as you would like to believe. Never mind. I'll carry my ideas out yet—I will return. I'll show you what can be done. You with your little peddling notions—you are interfering with me. I will return. I . . .'

"The manager came out. He did me the honor to take me under the arm and lead me aside. 'He is very low, very low,' he said. He considered it necessary to sigh, but neglected to be consistently sorrowful. 'We have done all we could for him—haven't we? But there is no disguising the fact, Mr. Kurtz has done more harm than good to the Company. He did not see the time was not ripe for vigorous action. Cautiously, cautiously—that's my principle. We must be cautious yet. The district is closed to us for a time. Deplorable! Upon the whole, the trade will suffer. I don't deny there is a remarkable quantity of ivory—mostly fossil. We must save it, at all events—but look how precarious the position is—and why? Because the method is unsound.' 'Do you,' said I, looking at the shore, 'call it "unsound method"?' 'Without doubt,' he exclaimed, hotly. 'Don't you?' . . . 'No method at all,' I murmured after a while. 'Exactly,' he exulted. 'I anticipated this. Shows a complete want of judgment. It is my duty to point it out in the proper quarter.' 'Oh,' said I, 'that fellow—what's his name?—the brickmaker, will make a readable report for you.' He appeared confounded for a moment. It seemed to me I had never breathed an atmosphere so vile, and I turned mentally to Kurtz for relief—positively for relief. 'Nevertheless I think Mr. Kurtz is a remarkable man,' I said with emphasis. He started, dropped on me a cold heavy glance, said very quietly, 'he *was*,' and turned his back on me. My hour of favor was over; I found myself lumped along with Kurtz as a partisan of methods for which the time was not ripe: I was unsound! Ah! but it was something to have at least a choice of nightmares.

"I had turned to the wilderness really, not to Mr. Kurtz, who, I was ready to admit, was as good as buried. And for a moment it seemed to me as if I also were buried in a vast grave full of unspeakable secrets. I felt an intolerable weight oppressing my breast, the smell of the damp earth, the unseen presence of victorious corruption, the darkness of an impenetrable night. . . . The Russian tapped me on the shoulder. I heard him mumbling and stammering something about 'brother seaman—couldn't conceal—knowledge of matters that would affect Mr. Kurtz's reputation.' I waited. For him evidently Mr. Kurtz was not in his grave; I suspect that for him Mr. Kurtz was one of the immortals. 'Well!' said I at last, 'speak out. As it happens, I am Mr. Kurtz's friend—in a way.'

"He stated with a good deal of formality that had we not been 'of the same profession,' he would have kept the matter to himself without regard to consequences. He suspected there was an active ill will towards him on the part of these white men that— 'You are right,' I said, remembering a certain conversation I had overheard. 'The manager thinks you ought to be hanged.' He showed a concern at this intelligence which amused me at first. 'I had better get out of the way quietly,' he said, earnestly. 'I can do no more for Kurtz now, and they would soon find some excuse. What's to stop them? There's a military post three hundred miles from here.' 'Well, upon my word,' said I, 'perhaps you had better go if you have any friends amongst the savages near by.' 'Plenty,' he said. 'They are simple people—and I want nothing, you know.' He stood biting his lip, then: 'I don't want any harm to happen to these whites here, but of course I was thinking of Mr. Kurtz's reputation—but you are a brother seaman and—' 'All right,' said I, after a time. 'Mr. Kurtz's reputation is safe with me.' I did not know how truly I spoke.

"He informed me, lowering his voice, that it was Kurtz who had ordered the attack to be made on the steamer. 'He hated sometimes the idea of being taken away—and then again . . . But I don't understand these matters. I am a simple man. He thought it would scare you away—that you would give it up, thinking him dead. I could not stop him. Oh, I had an awful time of it this last month.' 'Very well,' I said. 'He is all right now.' 'Ye-e-es,' he muttered, not very convinced apparently. 'Thanks,' said I; 'I shall keep my eyes open.' 'But quiet—eh?' he urged, anxiously. 'It would be awful for his reputation if anybody here—' I promised a complete discretion with great gravity. 'I have a canoe and three black fellows waiting not very far. I am off. Could you give me a few Martini-Henry cartridges?' I could, and did, with proper secrecy. He helped himself, with a wink at me, to a handful of my tobacco. 'Between sailors—you know—good English tobacco.' At the door of the pilot-house he turned round—'I say, haven't you a pair of shoes you could spare?' He raised one leg. 'Look.' The soles were tied with knotted strings sandalwise under his bare feet. I rooted out an old pair, at which he looked with admiration before tucking them under his left arm. One of his pockets (bright red) was bulging with cartridges, from the other (dark blue) peeped 'Towson's Inquiry,' etc., etc. He seemed to think himself excellently well equipped for a renewed encounter with the wilderness. 'Ah! I'll never, never meet such a man again. You ought to have heard him recite poetry—his own, too, it was, he told me. Poetry!' He rolled his eyes at the recollection of these delights. 'Oh, he enlarged my mind!' 'Good-by,' said I. He shook hands and vanished in the night. Sometimes I ask myself whether I had ever really seen him—whether it was possible to meet such a phenomenon! . . .

"When I woke up shortly after midnight his warning came to my mind with its hint of danger that seemed, in the starred darkness, real enough to make me get up for the purpose of having a look round. On the hill a big fire burned, illuminating fitfully a crooked corner of the station-house. One of the agents with a picket of a few of our blacks, armed for the purpose, was keeping guard over the ivory; but deep within the forest, red gleams that wavered, that seemed to sink and rise from the ground amongst confused columnar shapes of intense blackness, showed the exact position of the camp where Mr. Kurtz's adorers were keeping their uneasy vigil. The monotonous beating of a big drum filled the air with muffled shocks and a lingering vibration. A steady droning sound of many men chanting each to himself some weird incantation came out from the black, flat wall of the woods as the humming of bees comes out of a hive, and had a strange narcotic effect upon my half-awake senses. I believe I dozed off leaning over the rail, till an abrupt burst of yells, an overwhelming outbreak of a pent-up and mysterious frenzy, woke me up in a bewildered wonder. It was cut short all at once, and the low droning went on with an effect of audible and soothing silence. I glanced casually into the little cabin. A light was burning within, but Mr. Kurtz was not there.

"I think I would have raised an outcry if I had believed my eyes. But I didn't believe them at first—the thing seemed so impossible. The fact is I was completely unnerved by a sheer blank fright, pure abstract terror, unconnected with any distinct shape of physical danger. What made this emotion so overpowering was—how shall I define it?—the moral shock I received, as if something altogether monstrous, intolerable to thought and odious to the soul, had been thrust upon me unexpectedly. This lasted of course the merest fraction of a second, and then the usual sense of commonplace, deadly danger, the possibility of a sudden onslaught and massacre, or something of the kind, which I saw impending, was positively welcome and composing. It pacified me, in fact, so much, that I did not raise an alarm.

"There was an agent buttoned up inside an ulster and sleeping on a chair on deck within three feet of me. The yells had not awakened him; he snored very slightly; I left him to his slumbers and leaped ashore. I did not betray Mr. Kurtz—it was ordered I should never betray him—it was written I should be loyal to the nightmare of my choice. I was anxious to deal with this shadow by myself alone,—and to this day I don't know why I was so jealous of sharing with anyone the peculiar blackness of that experience.

"As soon as I got on the bank I saw a trail—a broad trail through the grass.

I remember the exultation with which I said to myself, 'He can't walk—he is crawling on all-fours—I've got him.' The grass was wet with dew. I strode rapidly with clenched fists. I fancy I had some vague notion of falling upon him and giving him a drubbing. I don't know. I had some imbecile thoughts. The knitting old woman with the cat obtruded herself upon my memory as a most improper person to be sitting at the other end of such an affair. I saw a row of pilgrims squirting lead in the air out of Winchesters held to the hip. I thought I would never get back to the steamer, and imagined myself living alone and unarmed in the woods to an advanced age. Such silly things—you know. And I remember I confounded the beat of the drum with the beating of my heart, and was pleased at its calm regularity.

"I kept to the track though—then stopped to listen. The night was very clear; a dark blue space, sparkling with dew and starlight, in which black things stood very still. I thought I could see a kind of motion ahead of me. I was strangely cocksure of everything that night. I actually left the track and ran in a wide semicircle (I verily believe chuckling to myself) so as to get in front of that stir, of that motion I had seen—if indeed I had seen anything. I was circumventing Kurtz as though it had been a boyish game.

"I came upon him, and, if he had not heard me coming, I would have fallen over him, too, but he got up in time. He rose, unsteady, long, pale, indistinct, like a vapor exhaled by the earth, and swayed slightly, misty and silent before me; while at my back the fires loomed between the trees, and the murmur of many voices issued from the forest. I had cut him off cleverly; but when actually confronting him I seemed to come to my senses, I saw the danger in its right proportion. It was by no means over yet. Suppose he began to shout? Though he could hardly stand, there was still plenty of vigor in his voice. 'Go away—hide yourself,' he said, in that profound tone. It was very awful. I glanced back. We were within thirty yards from the nearest fire. A black figure stood up, strode on long black legs, waving long black arms, across the glow. It had horns—antelope horns, I think—on its head. Some sorcerer, some witch man, no doubt: it looked fiend-like enough. 'Do you know what you are doing?' I whispered. 'Perfectly,' he answered, raising his voice for that single word: it sounded to me far off and yet loud, like a hail through a speaking-trumpet. If he makes a row we are lost, I thought to myself. This clearly was not a case for fisticuffs, even apart from the very natural aversion I had to beat that Shadow—this wandering and tormented thing. 'You will be lost,' I said—'utterly lost.' One gets sometimes such a flash of inspiration, you know. I did say the right thing, though indeed he could not have been more irretrievably lost than he was at this very moment, when the foundations of our intimacy were being laid—to endure—to endure—even to the end—even beyond.

" 'I had immense plans,' he muttered irresolutely. 'Yes,' said I; 'but if you try to shout I'll smash your head with—' There was not a stick or a stone near. 'I will throttle you for good,' I corrected myself. 'I was on the threshold of great things,' he pleaded, in a voice of longing, with a wistfulness of tone that made my blood run cold. 'And now for this stupid scoundrel—' 'Your success in Europe is assured in any case,' I affirmed, steadily. I did not want to have the throttling of him, you understand—and indeed it would have been very little use for any practical purpose. I tried to break the spell—the heavy, mute spell of the wilderness—that seemed to draw him to its pitiless breast by the awakening of forgotten and brutal instincts, by the memory of gratified and monstrous passions. This alone, I was convinced, had driven him out to the edge of the forest, to the bush, towards the gleam of fires, the throb of drums, the drone of weird incantations; this alone had beguiled his unlawful soul beyond the bounds of permitted aspirations. And, don't you see, the terror of the position was not in being knocked on the head—though I had a very lively sense of that danger, too—but in this, that I had to deal with a being to whom I could not appeal in the name of anything high or low. I had, even like the niggers, to invoke him—himself—his own exalted and incredible degradation. There was nothing either above or below him, and I knew it. He had kicked himself loose of the earth. Confound the man! he had kicked the very earth to pieces. He was alone, and I before him did not know whether I stood on the ground or floated in the air. I've been telling you what we said—repeating the phrases we pronounced—but what's the good? They were common everyday words—the familiar, vague sounds exchanged on every waking day of life. But what of that? They had behind them, to my mind, the terrific suggestiveness of words heard in dreams, of phrases spoken in nightmares. Soul! If anybody had ever struggled with a soul, I am the man. And I wasn't arguing with a lunatic either. Believe me or not, his intelligence was perfectly clear—concentrated, it is true, upon himself with horrible intensity, yet clear; and therein was my only chance—barring, of course, the killing him there and then, which wasn't so good, on account of unavoidable noise. But his soul was mad. Being alone in the wilderness, it had looked within itself, and, by heavens! I tell you, it had gone mad. I had—for my sins, I suppose—to go through the ordeal of looking into it myself. No eloquence could have been so withering to one's belief in mankind as his final burst of sincerity. He struggled with himself, too. I saw it,—I heard it. I saw the inconceivable mystery of a soul that knew no restraint, no faith, and no fear, yet struggling blindly with itself. I kept my head pretty well; but when I had him at last stretched on the couch, I wiped my forehead, while my legs shook under me as though I had carried half a ton on my back down that hill. And yet I had only supported him, his bony arm clasped round my neck—and he was not much heavier than a child.

"When next day we left at noon, the crowd, of whose presence behind the curtain of trees I had been acutely conscious all the time, flowed out of the woods again, filled the clearing, covered the slope with a mass of naked, breathing, quivering, bronze bodies. I steamed up a bit, then swung downstream, and two thousand eyes followed the evolutions of the splashing, thumping, fierce river-demon beating the water with its terrible tail and breathing black smoke into the air. In front of the first rank, along the river, three men, plastered with bright red earth from head to foot, strutted to and fro restlessly. When we came abreast again, they faced the river, stamped their feet, nodded their horned heads, swayed their scarlet bodies; they shook towards the fierce river-demon a bunch of black feathers, a mangy skin with a pendent tail—something that looked like a dried gourd; they shouted periodically together strings of amazing words that resembled no sounds of human language; and the deep murmurs of the crowd, interrupted suddenly, were like the responses of some satanic litany.

"We had carried Kurtz into the pilot-house: there was more air there. Lying on the couch, he stared through the open shutter. There was an eddy in the mass of human bodies, and the woman with helmeted head and tawny cheeks rushed out to the very brink of the stream. She put out her hands, shouted something, and all that wild mob took up the shout in a roaring chorus of articulated, rapid, breathless utterance.

" 'Do you understand this?' I asked.

"He kept on looking out past me with fiery, longing eyes, with a mingled expression of wistfulness and hate. He made no answer, but I saw a smile, a smile of indefinable meaning, appear on his colorless lips that a moment after twitched convulsively. 'Do I not?' he said slowly, gasping, as if the words had been torn out of him by a supernatural power.

"I pulled the string of the whistle, and I did this because I saw the pilgrims on deck getting out their rifles with an air of anticipating a jolly lark. At the sudden screech there was a movement of abject terror through that wedged mass of bodies. 'Don't! don't you frighten them away,' cried someone on deck disconsolately. I pulled the string time after time. They broke and ran, they leaped, they crouched, they swerved, they dodged the flying terror of the sound. The three red chaps had fallen flat, face down on the shore, as though they had been shot dead. Only the barbarous and superb woman did not so much as flinch, and stretched tragically her bare arms after us over the somber and glittering river.

"And then that imbecile crowd down on the deck started their little fun, and I could see nothing more for smoke.

"The brown current ran swiftly out of the heart of darkness, bearing us down towards the sea with twice the speed of our upward progress; and Kurtz's life was running swiftly, too, ebbing, ebbing out of his heart into the sea of inexorable time. The manager was very placid, he had no vital anxieties now, he took us both in with a comprehensive and satisfied glance: the 'affair' had come off as well as could be wished. I saw the time approaching when I would be left alone of the party of 'unsound method.' The pilgrims looked upon me with disfavor. I was, so to speak, numbered with the dead. It is strange how I accepted this unforeseen partnership, this choice of nightmares forced upon me in the tenebrous land invaded by these mean and greedy phantoms.

"Kurtz discoursed. A voice! a voice! It rang deep to the very last. It survived his strength to hide in the magnificent folds of eloquence the barren darkness of his heart. Oh, he struggled! he struggled! The wastes of his weary brain were haunted by shadowy images now—images of wealth and fame revolving obsequiously round his unextinguishable gift of noble and lofty expression. My Intended, my station, my career, my ideas—these were the subjects for the occasional utterances of elevated sentiments. The shade of the original Kurtz frequented the bedside of the hollow sham, whose fate it was to be buried presently in the mold of primeval earth. But both the diabolic love and the unearthly hate of the mysteries it had penetrated fought for the possession of that soul satiated with primitive emotions, avid of lying fame, of sham distinction, of all the appearances of success and power.

"Sometimes he was contemptibly childish. He desired to have kings meet him at railway stations on his return from some ghastly Nowhere, where he intended to accomplish great things. 'You show them you have in you something that is really profitable, and then there will be no limits to the recognition of your ability,' he would say. 'Of course you must take care of the motives—right motives—always.' The long reaches that were like one and the same reach, monotonous bends that were exactly alike, slipped past the steamer with their multitude of secular trees looking patiently after this grimy fragment of another world, the forerunner of change, of conquest, of trade, of massacres, of blessings. I looked ahead—piloting. 'Close the shutter,' said Kurtz suddenly one day: 'I can't bear to look at this.' I did so. There was a silence. 'Oh, but I will wring your heart yet!' he cried at the invisible wilderness.

"We broke down—as I had expected—and had to lie up for repairs at the head of an island. This delay was the first thing that shook Kurtz's confidence. One morning he gave me a packet of papers and a photograph—the lot tied together with a shoestring. 'Keep this for me,' he said. 'This noxious fool' (meaning the manager) 'is capable of prying into my boxes when I am not looking.' In the afternoon I saw him. He was lying on his back with closed eyes, and I withdrew quietly, but I heard him mutter, 'Live rightly, die, die. . . .' I listened. There was nothing more. Was he rehearsing some speech in his sleep, or was it a fragment of a phrase from some newspaper article? He had been writing for the papers and meant to do so again, 'for the furthering of my ideas. It's a duty.'

"His was an impenetrable darkness. I looked at him as you peer down at a man who is lying at the bottom of a precipice where the sun never shines. But I had not much time to give him, because I was helping the engine-driver to take to pieces the leaky cylinders, to straighten a bent connecting-rod, and in other such matters. I lived in an infernal mess of rust, filings, nuts, bolts, spanners, hammers, ratchet-drills—things I abominate, because I don't get on with them. I tended the little forge we fortunately had aboard; I toiled wearily in a wretched scrap-heap—unless I had the shakes too bad to stand.

"One evening coming in with a candle I was startled to hear him say a little tremulously, 'I am lying here in the dark waiting for death.' The light was within a foot of his eyes. I forced myself to murmur, 'Oh, nonsense!' and stood over him as if transfixed.

"Anything approaching the change that came over his features I have never seen before, and hope never to see again. Oh, I wasn't touched. I was fascinated. It was as though a veil had been rent. I saw on that ivory face the expression of somber pride, of ruthless power, of craven terror—of an intense and hopeless despair. Did he live his life again in every detail of desire, temptation, and surrender during that supreme moment of complete knowledge? He cried in a whisper at some image, at some vision—he cried out twice, a cry that was no more than a breath—

" 'The horror! The horror!'

"I blew the candle out and left the cabin. The pilgrims were dining in the mess-room, and I took my place opposite the manager, who lifted his eyes to give me a questioning glance, which I successfully ignored. He leaned back, serene, with that peculiar smile of his sealing the unexpressed depths of his meanness. A continuous shower of small flies streamed upon the lamp, upon the cloth, upon our hands and faces. Suddenly the manager's boy put his insolent black head in the doorway, and said in a tone of scathing contempt—

" 'Mistah Kurtz—he dead.'

"All the pilgrims rushed out to see. I remained, and went on with my dinner. I believe I was considered brutally callous. However, I did not eat much. There was a lamp in there—light, don't you know—and outside it was so beastly, beastly dark. I went no more near the remarkable man who had pronounced a judgment upon the adventures of his soul on this earth. The voice was gone. What else had been there? But I am of course aware that next day the pilgrims buried something in a muddy hole.

"And then they very nearly buried me.

"However, as you see, I did not go to join Kurtz there and then. I did not. I remained to dream the nightmare out to the end, and to show my loyalty to Kurtz once more. Destiny. My destiny! Droll thing life is—that mysterious arrangement of merciless logic for a futile purpose. The most you can hope from it is some knowledge of yourself—that comes too late—a crop of unextinguishable regrets. I have wrestled with death. It is the most unexciting contest you can imagine. It takes place in an impalpable grayness, with nothing underfoot, with nothing around, without spectators, without clamor, without glory, without the great desire of victory, without the great fear of defeat, in a sickly atmosphere of tepid skepticism, without much belief in your own right, and still less in that of your adversary. If such is the form of ultimate wisdom, then life is a greater riddle than some of us think it to be. I was within a hair's breadth of the last opportunity for pronouncement, and I found with humiliation that probably I would have nothing to say. This is the reason why I affirm that Kurtz was a remarkable man. He had something to say. He said it. Since I had peeped over the edge myself, I understand better the meaning of his stare, that could not see the flame of the candle, but was wide enough to embrace the whole universe, piercing enough to penetrate all the hearts that beat in the darkness. He had summed up—he had judged. 'The horror!' He was a remarkable man. After all, this was the expression of some sort of belief; it had candor, it had conviction, it had a vibrating note of revolt in its whisper, it had the appalling face of a glimpsed truth—the strange commingling of desire and hate. And it is not my own extremity I remember best—a vision of grayness without form filled with physical pain, and a careless contempt for the evanescence of all things—even of this pain itself. No! It is his extremity that I seem to have lived through. True, he had made that last stride, he had stepped over the edge, while I had been permitted to draw back my hesitating foot. And perhaps in this is the whole difference; perhaps all the wisdom, and all truth, and all sincerity, are just compressed into that inappreciable moment of time in which we step over the threshold of the invisible. Perhaps! I like to think my summing-up would not have been a word of careless contempt. Better his cry—much better. It was an affirmation, a moral victory paid for by innumerable defeats, by abominable terrors, by abominable satisfactions. But it was a victory! That is why I have remained loyal to Kurtz to the last, and even beyond, when a long time after I heard once more, not his own voice, but the echo of his magnificent eloquence thrown to me from a soul as translucently pure as a cliff of crystal.

"No, they did not bury me, though there is a period of time which I remember mistily, with a shuddering wonder, like a passage through some inconceivable world that had no hope in it and no desire. I found myself back in the sepulchral city resenting the sight of people hurrying through the streets to filch a little money from each other, to devour their infamous cookery, to gulp their unwholesome beer, to dream their insignificant and silly dreams. They trespassed upon my thoughts. They were intruders whose knowledge of life was to me an irritating pretense, because I felt so sure they could not possibly know the things I knew. Their bearing, which was simply the bearing of commonplace individuals going about their business in the assurance of perfect safety, was offensive to me like the outrageous flauntings of folly in the face of a danger it is unable to comprehend. I had no particular desire to enlighten them, but I had some difficulty in restraining myself from laughing in their faces, so full of stupid importance. I daresay I was not very well at that time. I tottered about the streets—there were various affairs to settle—grinning bitterly at perfectly respectable persons. I admit my behavior was inexcusable, but then my temperature was seldom normal in these days. My dear aunt's endeavors to 'nurse up my strength' seemed altogether beside the mark. It was not my strength that wanted nursing, it was my imagination that wanted soothing. I kept the bundle of papers given me by Kurtz, not knowing exactly what to do with it. His mother had died lately, watched over, as I was told, by his Intended. A clean-shaved man, with an official manner and wearing gold-rimmed spectacles, called on me one day and made inquiries, at first circuitous, afterwards suavely pressing, about what he was pleased to denominate certain 'documents.' I was not surprised, because I had had two rows with the manager on the subject out there. I had refused to give up the smallest scrap out of that package, and I took the same attitude with the spectacled man. He became darkly menacing at last, and with much heat argued that the Company had the right to every bit of information about its 'territories.' And said he, 'Mr. Kurtz's knowledge of unexplored regions must have been necessarily extensive and peculiar—owing to his great abilities and to the deplorable circumstances in which he had been placed: therefore—' I assured him Mr. Kurtz's knowledge, however extensive, did not bear upon the problems of commerce or administration. He invoked then the name of science. 'It would be an incalculable loss if,' etc., etc. I offered him the report on the 'Suppression of Savage Customs,' with the postscriptum torn off. He took it up eagerly, but ended by sniffing at it with an air of contempt. 'This is not what we had a right to expect,' he remarked. 'Expect nothing else,' I said. 'There are only private letters.' He withdrew upon some threat of legal proceedings, and I saw him no more; but another fellow, calling himself Kurtz's cousin, appeared two days later, and was anxious to hear all the details about his dear relative's last moments. Incidentally he gave me to understand that Kurtz had been essentially a great musician. 'There was the making of an immense success,' said the man, who was an organist, I believe, with lank gray hair flowing over a greasy coat-collar. I had no reason to doubt his statement; and to this day I am unable to say what was Kurtz's profession, whether he ever had any—which was the greatest of his talents. I had taken him for a painter who wrote for the papers, or else for a journalist who could paint—but even the cousin (who took snuff during the interview) could not tell me what he had been—exactly. He was a universal genius—on that point I agreed with the old chap, who thereupon blew his nose noisily into a large cotton handkerchief and withdrew in senile agitation, bearing off some family letters and memoranda without importance. Ultimately a journalist anxious to know something of the fate of his 'dear colleague' turned up. This visitor informed me Kurtz's proper sphere ought to have been politics 'on the popular side.' He had furry straight eyebrows, bristly hair cropped short, an eye-glass on a broad ribbon, and, becoming expansive, confessed his opinion that Kurtz really couldn't write a bit—'but heavens! how that man could talk. He electrified large meetings. He had faith—don't you see?—he had the faith. He could get himself to believe anything—anything. He would have been a splendid leader of an extreme party.' 'What party?' I asked. 'Any party,' answered the other. 'He was an—an—extremist.' Did I not think so? I assented. Did I know, he asked, with a sudden flash of curiosity, 'what it was that had induced him to go out there?' 'Yes,' said I, and forthwith handed him the famous Report for publication, if he thought fit. He glanced through it hurriedly, mumbling all the time, judged 'it would do,' and took himself off with this plunder.

"Thus I was left at last with a slim packet of letters and the girl's portrait. She struck me as beautiful—I mean she had a beautiful expression. I know that the sunlight can be made to lie, too, yet one felt that no manipulation of light and pose could have conveyed the delicate shade of truthfulness upon those features. She seemed ready to listen without mental reservation, without suspicion, without a thought for herself. I concluded I would go and give her back her portrait and those letters myself. Curiosity? Yes; and also some other feeling perhaps. All that had been Kurtz's had passed out of my hands: his soul, his body, his station, his plans, his ivory, his career. There remained only his memory and his Intended—and I wanted to give that up, too, to the past, in a way—to surrender personally all that remained of him with me to that oblivion which is the last word of our common fate. I don't defend myself. I had no clear perception of what it was I really wanted. Perhaps it was an impulse of unconscious loyalty, or the fulfillment of one of those ironic necessities that lurk in the facts of human existence. I don't know. I can't tell. But I went.

"I thought his memory was like the other memories of the dead that accumulate in every man's life—a vague impress on the brain of shadows that had fallen on it in their swift and final passage; but before the high and ponderous door, between the tall houses of a street as still and decorous as a well-kept alley in a cemetery, I had a vision of him on the stretcher, opening his mouth voraciously, as if to devour all the earth with all its mankind. He lived then before me; he lived as much as he had ever lived—a shadow insatiable of splendid appearances, of frightful realities; a shadow darker than the shadow of the night, and draped nobly in the folds of a gorgeous eloquence. The vision seemed to enter the house with me—the stretcher, the phantom-bearers, the wild crowd of obedient worshipers, the gloom of the forests, the glitter of the reach between the murky bends, the beat of the drum, regular and muffled like the beating of a heart—the heart of a conquering darkness. It was a moment of triumph for the wilderness, an invading and vengeful rush which, it seemed to me, I would have to keep back alone for the salvation of another soul. And the memory of what I had heard him say afar there, with the horned shapes stirring at my back, in the glow of fires, within the patient woods, those broken phrases came back to me, were heard again in their ominous and terrifying simplicity. I remembered his abject pleading, his abject threats, the colossal scale of his vile desires, the meanness, the torment, the tempestuous anguish of his soul. And later on I seemed to see his collected languid manner, when he said one day, 'This lot of ivory now is really mine. The Company did not pay for it. I collected it myself at a very great personal risk. I am afraid they will try to claim it as theirs though. H'm. It is a difficult case. What do you think I ought to do—resist? Eh? I want no more than justice.' . . . He wanted no more than justice—no more than justice. I rang the bell before a mahogany door on the first floor, and while I waited he seemed to stare at me out of the glassy panel —stare with that wide and immense stare embracing, condemning, loathing all the universe. I seemed to hear the whispered cry, 'The horror! The horror!'

"The dusk was falling. I had to wait in a lofty drawing-room with three long windows from floor to ceiling that were like three luminous and bedraped columns. The bent gilt legs and backs of the furniture shone in indistinct curves. The tall marble fireplace had a cold and monumental whiteness. A grand piano stood massively in a corner; with dark gleams on the flat surfaces like a somber and polished sarcophagus. A high door opened—closed. I rose.

"She came forward, all in black, with a pale head, floating towards me in the dusk. She was in mourning. It was more than a year since his death, more than a year since the news came; she seemed as though she would remember and mourn forever. She took both my hands in hers and murmured, 'I had heard you were coming.' I noticed she was not very young —I mean not girlish. She had a mature capacity for fidelity, for belief, for suffering. The room seemed to have grown darker, as if all the sad light of the cloudy evening had taken refuge on her forehead. This fair hair, this pale visage, this pure brow, seemed surrounded by an ashy halo from which the dark eyes looked out at me. Their glance was guileless, profound, confident, and trustful. She carried her sorrowful head as though she were proud of that sorrow, as though she would say, I—I alone know how to mourn him as he deserves. But while we were still shaking hands, such a look of awful desolation came upon her face that I perceived she was one of those creatures that are not the playthings of Time. For her he had died only yesterday. And, by Jove! the impression was so powerful that for me, too, he seemed to have died only yesterday—nay, this very minute. I saw her and him in the same instant of time—his death and her sorrow—I saw her sorrow in the very moment of his death. Do you understand? I saw them together—I heard them together. She had said, with a deep catch of the breath, 'I have survived,' while my strained ears seemed to hear distinctly, mingled with her tone of despairing regret, the summing up whisper of his eternal condemnation. I asked myself what I was doing there, with a sensation of panic in my heart as though I had blundered into a place of cruel and absurd mysteries not fit for a human being to behold. She motioned me to a chair. We sat down. I laid the packet gently on the little table, and she put her hand over it. . . . 'You knew him well,' she murmured, after a moment of mourning silence.

"'Intimacy grows quickly out there,' I said. 'I knew him as well as it is possible for one man to know another.'

"'And you admired him,' she said. 'It was impossible to know him and not to admire him. Was it?'

"'He was a remarkable man,' I said, unsteadily. Then before the appealing fixity of her gaze, that seemed to watch for more words on my lips, I went on, 'It was impossible not to—'

"'Love him,' she finished eagerly, silencing me into an appalled dumbness. 'How true! how true! But when you think that no one knew him so well as I! I had all his noble confidence. I knew him best.'

"'You knew him best,' I repeated. And perhaps she did. But with every word spoken the room was growing darker, and only her forehead, smooth and white, remained illumined by the unextinguishable light of belief and love.

"'You were his friend,' she went on. 'His friend,' she repeated, a little louder. 'You must have been, if he had given you this, and sent you to me. I feel I can speak to you—and oh! I must speak. I want you—you have heard his last words—to know I have been worthy of him. . . . It is not pride. . . . Yes! I am proud to know I understood him better than anyone on earth—he told me so himself. And since his mother died I have had no one—no one—to—to—'

"I listened. The darkness deepened. I was not even sure he had given me the right bundle. I rather suspect he wanted me to take care of another batch of his papers which, after his death, I saw the manager examining under the lamp. And the girl talked, easing her pain in the certitude of my sympathy; she talked as thirsty men drink. I had heard that her engagement with Kurtz had been disapproved by her people. He wasn't rich enough or something. And indeed I don't know whether he had not been a pauper all his life. He had given me some reason to infer that it was his impatience of comparative poverty that drove him out there.

"'. . . Who was not his friend who had heard him speak once?' she was saying. 'He drew men towards him by what was best in them.' She looked at me with intensity. 'It is the gift of the great,' she went on, and the sound of her low voice seemed to have the accompaniment of all the other sounds, full of mystery, desolation, and sorrow, I had ever heard—the ripple of the river, the soughing of the trees swayed by the wind, the murmurs of the crowds, the faint ring of incomprehensible words cried from afar, the whisper of a voice speaking from beyond the threshold of an eternal darkness. 'But you have heard him! You know!' she cried.

" 'Yes, I know,' I said with something like despair in my heart, but bowing my head before the faith that was in her, before that great and saving illusion that shone with an unearthly glow in the darkness, in the triumphant darkness from which I could not have defended her—from which I could not even defend myself.

" 'What a loss to me—to us!'—she corrected herself with beautiful generosity; then added in a murmur, 'To the world.' By the last gleams of twilight I could see the glitter of her eyes, full of tears—of tears that would not fall.

" 'I have been very happy—very fortunate—very proud,' she went on. 'Too fortunate. Too happy for a little while. And now I am unhappy for—for life.'

"She stood up; her fair hair seemed to catch all the remaining light in a glimmer of gold. I rose, too.

" 'And of all this,' she went on, mournfully, 'of all his promise, and of all his greatness, of his generous mind, of his noble heart, nothing remains—nothing but a memory. You and I—'

" 'We shall always remember him,' I said, hastily.

" 'No!' she cried. 'It is impossible that all this should be lost—that such a life should be sacrificed to leave nothing—but sorrow. You know what vast plans he had. I knew of them, too—I could not perhaps understand—but others knew of them. Something must remain. His words, at least, have not died.'

" 'His words will remain,' I said.

" 'And his example,' she whispered to herself. 'Men looked up to him—his goodness shone in every act. His example—

" 'True,' I said; 'his example, too. Yes, his example. I forgot that.'

" 'But I do not. I cannot—I cannot believe—not yet. I cannot believe that I shall never see him again, that nobody will see him again, never, never, never.'

"She put out her arms as if after a retreating figure, stretching them black and with clasped pale hands across the fading and narrow sheen of the window. Never see him! I saw him clearly enough then. I shall see this eloquent phantom as long as I live, and I shall see her, too, a tragic and familiar Shade, resembling in this gesture another one, tragic also, and bedecked with powerless charms, stretching bare brown arms over the glitter of the infernal stream, the stream of darkness. She said suddenly very low, 'He died as he lived.'

His end,' said I, with dull anger stirring in me, 'was in every way worthy of his life.'

" 'And I was not with him,' she murmured. My anger subsided before a feeling of infinite pity.

" 'Everything that could be done—' I mumbled.

" 'Ah, but I believed in him more than anyone on earth—more than his own mother, more than—himself. He needed me! Me! I would have treasured every sigh, every word, every sign, every glance.'

"I felt like a chill grip on my chest. 'Don't,' I said, in a muffled voice.

" 'Forgive me. I—I have mourned so long in silence—in silence. . . . You were with him—to the last? I think of his loneliness. Nobody near to understand him as I would have understood. Perhaps no one to hear. . . .'

" 'To the very end,' I said, shakily. 'I heard his very last words. . . .' I stopped in a fright.

" 'Repeat them,' she murmured in a heart-broken tone. 'I want—I want—something—something—to—live with.'

"I was on the point of crying at her, 'Don't you hear them?' The dusk was repeating them in a persistent whisper all around us, in a whisper that seemed to swell menacingly like the first whisper of a rising wind. 'The horror! The horror!'

" 'His last word—to live with,' she insisted. 'Don't you understand I loved him—I loved him—I loved him!'

"I pulled myself together and spoke slowly.

" 'The last word he pronounced was—your name.'

"I heard a light sigh and then my heart stood still, stopped dead short by an exulting and terrible cry, by the cry of inconceivable triumph and of unspeakable pain. 'I knew it—I was sure!' . . . She knew. She was sure. I heard her weeping; she had hidden her face in her hands. It seemed to me that the house would collapse before I could escape, that the heavens would fall upon my head. But nothing happened. The heavens do not fall for such a trifle. Would they have fallen, I wonder, if I had rendered Kurtz that justice which was his due? Hadn't he said he wanted only justice? But I couldn't. I could not tell her. It would have been too dark—too dark altogether. . . ."

Marlow ceased, and sat apart, indistinct and silent, in the pose of a meditating Buddha. Nobody moved for a time. "We have lost the first of the ebb," said the Director, suddenly. I raised my head. The offing was barred by a black bank of clouds, and the tranquil waterway leading to the uttermost ends of the earth flowed somber under an overcast sky—seemed to lead into the heart of an immense darkness.

F R A N Z   K A F K A

Metamorphosis

As Gregor Samsa awoke one morning from a troubled dream, he found himself changed in his bed to some monstrous kind of vermin.

He lay on his back, which was as hard as armor plate, and, raising his head a little, he could see the arch of his great, brown belly, divided by bowed corrugations. The bedcover was slipping helplessly off the summit of the curve, and Gregor's legs, pitiably thin compared with their former size, fluttered helplessly before his eyes.

"What has happened?" he thought. It was no dream. His room, a real man's room—though rather small—lay quiet within its four familiar walls. Over the table, where a collection of cloth samples was scattered—Samsa was a commercial traveler—hung the picture that he had recently cut from an illustrated paper and had put in a pretty gilded frame. This picture showed a lady sitting very upright, wearing a small fur hat and a fur boa; she offered to the gaze a heavy muff into which her arm was thrust up to the elbow.

Gregor looked toward the window; rain could be heard falling on the panes; the foggy weather made him sad. "How would it be if I go to sleep again for awhile and forget all this stupidity?" he thought; but it was absolutely impossible, for he was used to sleeping on the right side and in his present plight he could not get into that position. However hard he tried to throw himself violently on his side, he always turned over on his back with a little swinging movement. He tried a hundred times, closing his eyes so that he should not see the trembling of his legs, and he did not give up until he felt in his side a slight but deep pain, never before experienced.

Reprinted by permission of Schocken Books, Inc. Translated by A. L. Lloyd.

"God!" he thought, "What a job I've chosen. Traveling day in, day out. A much more worrying occupation than working in the office! And apart from business itself, this plague of traveling: the anxieties of changing trains, the irregular, inferior meals, the ever changing faces, never to be seen again, people with whom one has no chance to be friendly. To hell with it all!" He felt a little itch above his stomach and wriggled nearer to the bedpost, dragging himself slowly on his back so that he might more easily raise his head; and he saw, just where he was itching, a few little white points, whose purpose he could not guess at; he tried to scratch the place with one of his feet but he had to draw it back quickly, for the contact made him shudder coldly.

He returned to his former position. He said to himself: "Nothing is more degrading than always to have to rise so early. A man must have his sleep. Other travelers can live like harem women. When I return to the hotel in the morning to enter my orders, I find these gentlemen still at breakfast. I'd like to see what my boss would say if I tried it; I should be sacked immediately. Who knows if that wouldn't be a good thing, after all! If I didn't hold back because of my parents, I would have given notice long ago; I would have gone to the boss and I wouldn't have minced matters. He would have fallen from his desk. That's a funny thing; to sit on a desk so as to speak to one's employees from such a height, especially when one is hard of hearing and people must come close! Still, all hope is not lost; once I have got together the money my parents owe him—that will be in about five or six years—I shall certainly do it. Then I'll take the big step! Meanwhile, I must get up, for my train goes at five."

He looked at the alarm clock which was ticking on the chest. "My God!" he thought; it was half-past six; quarter to seven was not far off. Hadn't the alarm gone? From the bed it could be seen that the little hand was set at four, right enough; the alarm had sounded. But had he been able to sleep calmly through that furniture-shattering din? Calmly, no; his sleep had not been calm; but he had slept only the sounder for that. What should he do now?

The next train went at seven; to catch it he must hurry madly, and his collection of samples was not packed; besides, he himself did not feel at all rested nor inclined to move. And even if he did catch the train, his employer's anger was inevitable, since the firm's errand boy would have been waiting at the five o'clock train and would have notified the firm of his lapse. He was just a toady to his boss, a stupid and servile boy. Supposing Gregor pretended to be ill? But that would be very tiresome, and suspicious, too, for during the four years he had been with the firm he had never had the slightest illness. The manager would come with the Health Insurance doctor; he would reproach his parents for their son's idleness and would cut short any objections by giving the doctor's arguments that no people are sick, only idle. And would he be so far wrong, in such a case? Gregor felt in very good fettle, apart from his unnecessary need for more sleep after such a long night; he even had an unusually keen appetite.

Just as he was quickly turning these thoughts over in his mind without being able to decide to leave the bed—while the alarm clock struck a quarter to seven—he heard a cautious knock on his door, close by his bed's head.

"Gregor," someone called—it was his mother—"It is a quarter to seven. Didn't you want to catch the train?"

What a soft voice! Gregor trembled as he heard his own voice reply. It was unmistakably his former voice, but with it could be heard, as if from below, a painful whining, which only allowed the words their real shape for a moment, immediately to confuse their sound so that one wondered if one had really heard aright. Gregor would have liked to answer fully and to give an explanation but, in these circumstances, he contented himself by saying, "Yes, yes, thank you, mother. I am just getting up." No doubt the door prevented her from judging the change in Gregor's voice, for the explanation reassured his mother, who went away, shuffling in her slippers. But because of this little dialogue the other members of the family had become aware that, contrary to custom, Gregor was still in the house, and his father started to knock on one of the side doors, softly, but with his fists.

"Gregor, Gregor," he cried, "what is the matter?" And, after a moment, in a warning tone, "Gregor! Gregor!"

At the other side door, the young man's sister softly called, "Gregor, aren't you well? Do you need anything?"

"I am getting ready," said Gregor, answering both sides and forcing himself to pronounce carefully and to separate each word with a long pause, to keep a natural voice.

His father went back to breakfast, but the sister still whispered, "Gregor, open the door, I beg you." But Gregor had no intention of answering this request; on the contrary, he complimented himself on having learned the habit of always locking his door, as if in a hotel.

He would get up quietly, without being bothered by anyone; he would dress, and, above all, he would have breakfast; then would come the time to reflect, for he felt it was not in bed that a reasonable solution could be found. He recalled how often an unusual position adopted in bed had resulted in slight pains which proved imaginary as soon as he arose, and Gregor was curious to see his present hallucination gradually dissolve. As for the change in his voice, his private opinion was that it was the prelude to some serious quinsy, the occupational malady of travelers.

He had no difficulty in turning back the coverlet; he needed only to blow himself up a little, and it fell of its own accord. But beyond that he was impeded by his tremendous girth. To get up, he needed arms and hands; but he had only numerous little legs, in perpetual vibration, over which he had no control. Before he could bend one leg, he first had to stretch it out; and when at last he had performed the desired movement, all the other legs worked uncontrollably, in intensely painful agitation. "I must not stay uselessly in bed," said Gregor to himself.

To get his body out of bed, he first tried moving the hind part. But unfortunately this hind part, which he had not yet seen, and of which he could form no very precise idea, went so slowly it proved to be very difficult to move; he summoned all his strength to throw himself forward but, ill-calculating his course, he hurled himself violently against one of the bedposts, and the searing pain he felt showed that the lower part of his body was without doubt the most sensitive.

He then tried to start with the fore part of his body and cautiously turned his head toward the side of the bed. In this he succeeded quite easily, and the rest of his body, despite its weight and size, followed the direction of his head. But when his head left the bed and was hanging in mid-air, he was afraid to continue any further; if he were to fall in this position, it would be a miracle if he did not crack his head; and this was no moment to lose his senses—better to stay in bed.

But when, panting after his efforts, he again found himself stretched out just as before, when he saw his little legs struggling more wildly than ever, despairing of finding any means of bringing peace and order into this chaotic procedure, he once again realized that he absolutely could not stay in bed and that it was perfectly reasonable to sacrifice everything to the slightest chance of getting out. At the same time he did not forget that cool and wise reflection would be far better than desperate resolutions. Ordinarily, at such moments he turned his eyes to the window to gain encouragement and hope. But this day the fog prevented him from seeing the other side of the street; the window gave him neither confidence nor strength. "Seven o'clock already," he said as he listened once more to the sound of the alarm clock. "Seven o'clock already, and the fog has got no thinner!" He lay back again for a moment, breathing weakly, as though, in the complete silence, he could calmly await the return to his normal self.

Then he said, "Before a quarter past it is absolutely essential for me to be up. In any case, someone will be sent from the office to ask for me before then, for the place opens at seven." And he began to rock on his back in order to get his whole body out of bed in one movement. In this manner he would be able to protect his head by raising it sharply as he fell. His back seemed to be hard; nothing would be risked by falling on it to the floor; his only fear was that the noise of his fall, which must surely resound through the whole house, might arouse terror, or, at the very least, uneasiness. However, that would have to be risked.

When Gregor had half his body out of bed—the new method seemed more like a game than a task, for he had only to swing himself on his back—he began to think how easily he could have got up if only he had had a little assistance. Two strong people—he thought of his father and the servant girl—would have been quite enough; they would have needed only to pass their arms under his round back, raise it from the bed, quickly lean forward with their burden, and then wait carefully till he had completed the operation of settling himself on the ground, where he hoped his feet would at last find a way of working together. But even if the doors had not been closed, would it have been wise for him to call for help? At this idea, despite his misery, he could not repress a smile.

Now he had progressed so far that, by sharply accentuating his swinging movement, he felt he was nearly losing his balance; he would have to take a serious decision, for in five minutes it would be a quarter to eight—but suddenly there was a knock at the front door.

"Someone from the office," he said to himself, and he felt his blood run cold, while his little legs quickened their saraband. For a moment all was quiet.

"They're not going to the door," thought Gregor, in an access of absurd hope. But of course the maid, with a firm tread, went to the door and opened it. Gregor needed to hear only the caller's first words of greeting to know immediately who it was—the manager himself. Why was Gregor, particularly, condemned to work for a firm where the worst was suspected at the slightest inadvertence of the employees? Were the employees, without exception, all scoundrels? Was there among their number not one devoted, faithful servant, who, if it did so happen that by chance he missed a few hours work one morning, might have found himself so numbed with remorse that he just could not leave his bed? Would it not have been enough to send some apprentice to put things right—if, in any case, it was necessary to make inquiries at all—instead of the manager himself having to come, in order to let the whole innocent family know that the clearing-up of so suspicious an affair could only be entrusted to a person of his importance? These thoughts so irritated Gregor that he swung himself out of bed with all his might. This made a loud thud, but not the terrible crash that he had feared. The carpet somewhat softened the blow, and Gregor's back was more elastic than he had thought, and so his act was not accompanied by any din. Only his head had been slightly hurt. Gregor had not raised it enough, and it had been knocked in the fall. He turned over a little to rub it on the carpet, in pain and anger.

"Something fell in there just then," cried the manager, in the room on the left. Gregor tried to imagine his employer's face if such a mishap had occurred to him; for such a thing was possible, he had to admit. But, as if in brutal reply, the manager began pacing up and down in the next room, making his patent-leather boots creak.

And in the other room on the right, Gregor's sister whispered to warn her brother, "Gregor, the manager is here."

"I know," said Gregor to himself, but he dared not raise his voice enough for his sister to hear.

"Gregor," said his father in the room on the left, "the manager has come to find out why you didn't catch the early train. We don't know what to say. He wants to speak to you personally. So please open the door. I'm sure he will be kind enough to excuse the untidiness of your room."

"Good morning, good morning, Mr. Samsa," interrupted the manager, cordial and brisk.

"He is not well," said his mother to the manager, while his father went on shouting through the door. "Believe me, he is not well, sir. How else could Gregor have missed the train? The boy thinks of nothing but his work! It makes me upset to see how he never goes out after supper; do you know he's just spent a whole week here and been at home every evening! He sits down with us at the table and stays there, quietly reading the paper or studying his timetables. His greatest indulgence is to do a little fretwork. Just lately he made a small picture frame. It was finished in two or three evenings, and you'd be surprised how pretty it is; it is hanging up in his room. As soon as Gregor opens his door, you will be able to see it. I am so glad you came, sir, because without you we would never have got Gregor to open his door, he is so obstinate; and surely he must be ill, even though he denied it this morning."

"I am just coming," said Gregor slowly and carefully, but he continued to lie still, so as not to miss a word of the conversation.

"I can offer no other suggestion," declared the manager. "Let us only hope it is nothing serious. However, we businessmen must often—fortunately or not, as you will—get on with our jobs and ignore our little indispositions."

"Well, can the manager come in now?" asked his father impatiently, rapping on the door again.

"No," said Gregor. In the room on the left there was a painful silence; in that on the right the sister began to sob.

Why did she not go to the others? Possibly she had only just got out of bed and was not yet dressed. And why did she weep? Because he did not get up to let the manager in, because he risked losing his position, and because the boss would once more worry his parents about their old debts? These were misplaced troubles! Gregor was still there and had not the slightest intention of letting his family down. At this very moment he was stretched out on the carpet, and nobody seeing him in this state could seriously have demanded that he should let the manager enter his room. But it was not on account of this slight impoliteness—for which in normal times he could easily have made his excuses later—that Gregor would be dismissed. And he thought it would be more reasonable, just now, to leave him alone rather than to upset him with tears and speeches. But it was just this uncertainty which was making the others uneasy and which excused their behavior.

"Herr Samsa," now cried the manager, raising his voice, "What is the matter? You barricade yourself in your room, you don't answer yes or no, you needlessly upset your parents, and you neglect your professional duties in an unheard-of manner. I am speaking in the name of your employer and of your parents, and I beg you seriously to give us a satisfactory explanation immediately. I am astonished, astonished! I took you for a quiet, reasonable young man, and here you suddenly give yourself airs, behaving in an absolutely fantastic manner! The head of the firm, speaking to me this morning in your absence, suggested an explanation which I rejected; he mentioned the samples which were entrusted to you a while ago. I gave him my word of honor that this had nothing to do with the affair, but now that I have been witness to your obstinacy, I can assure you, Herr Samsa, that it deprives me of any wish to defend you. Your job is by no means safe! I had intended to tell you this in private but, since you oblige me to waste my time here for nothing, I see no reason for keeping quiet before your parents. I'd have you know that lately your work has been far from satisfactory; we realize, of course, that the time of the year is not propitious for big business, but you must understand, Herr Samsa, that a period with no business at all should not and can not be tolerated!"

Gregor was beside himself; in his anxiety he forgot everything else. "But, sir," he cried, "I will open the door immediately. I will open it. I felt a little ill; a slight giddiness prevented me from getting up. I am still in bed. But I feel better already. I am just getting up. Only a moment's patience. I am not quite so well as I thought. But I am all right, really. How can it be that illness should take one so quickly? Only yesterday I felt quite well, my parents can tell you; and then last evening I had a slight symptom. They must have noticed it. Why didn't I let them know at the office! But then, one always thinks one will be able to get rid of an illness without staying at home. Please, sir, spare my parents. The complaints you made just now are really without any foundation. No one has even suggested them before. Perhaps you have not seen the last orders I sent in. I will leave on the eight-o'clock train; these few moments of rest have done me a great deal of good. Please don't stay, sir, I shall be at the office immediately; and please inform the director of what has happened and put in a good word for me."

And while Gregor hastily cried these words, scarcely realizing what he said, he had, with an ease due to his previous exertions, approached the chest of drawers, against which he now tried to raise himself. He wanted to open the door; he wanted to be seen and to speak with the manager. He was curious to know what impression he would make on these people who were so imperiously demanding his presence. If he frightened them, that would be reassuring, for he would stop being cross-questioned and be left in peace. If they took everything quietly, then he, too, need not be alarmed. And if he hurried he might still catch the eight-o'clock train. The chest was polished, and Gregor slipped on it several times but, by a supreme effort, he managed to get upright. He paid no attention to the pains in his stomach, though they were hurting him. He let himself drop forward onto the top of a near-by chair and clung there with his little legs. Then, finding himself master of his body, he stayed very quiet in order to listen to what the manager had to say.

"Did you understand a word of what he said?" the manager asked the parents. "Is he trying to make fools of us?"

"Good heavens," cried the mother, already in tears. "Perhaps he is seriously ill, and here we are torturing him all this while! Grete! Grete!" she called.

"Mother!" cried the daughter from the other side. They were separated by Gregor's room.

"Fetch a doctor immediately. Gregor is ill. A doctor, quickly! Did you hear him speak?"

"It was an animal's voice," said the manager; after the cries of the women, his voice seemed curiously gentle.

"Anna, Anna!" shouted the father through the hall into the kitchen, clapping his hands. "Get a locksmith, quick!" And already the two young girls—how could his sister have dressed so soon?—ran along the corridor with rustling skirts and opened the front door. No one heard the door close; no doubt it had been left open, as is the custom in houses to which a great misfortune has come.

However, Gregor had become calmer. Doubtless they had not understood his words, though they had seemed clear enough to him, clearer, indeed, than the first time; perhaps his ears were becoming more accustomed to the sounds. But at least they were obliged to realize that his case was not normal, and they were ready, now, to help him. The assurance and resourcefulness with which the first steps had been taken comforted him considerably. He felt himself integrated into human society once again, and, without differentiating between them, he hoped for great and surprising things from the locksmith and the doctor. To clear his throat for the decisive conversation which he would have to hold soon, he coughed a little, but as quietly as possible, for he feared that even his cough might not sound human. Meanwhile, in the next room, it had become quiet. Perhaps his parents were sitting at table in a secret conference with the manager; perhaps everyone was leaning against the door, listening.

Gregor made his way slowly toward it with the chair; then he abandoned the chair and flung himself at the door, holding himself erect against the woodwork—for the bottoms of his feet secreted a sticky substance—and he rested a moment from his efforts. After this, he tried to turn the key in the lock with his mouth. Unfortunately, it seemed he had no proper teeth. How could he take hold of the key? In compensation, instead of teeth he possessed a pair of very strong mandibles and succeeded in seizing the key in the lock, regardless of the pain this caused him; a brownish liquid flowed out of his mouth, spread over the lock and dropped to the floor.

"Listen!" said the manager in the next room. "He is just turning the key."

This was valuable encouragement for Gregor; he would have liked his father, his mother, everybody, to start calling to him, "Courage, Gregor, go on, push hard!" And, with the idea that everyone was following his efforts with passionate attention, he clutched the key with all the power of his jaws until he was nearly unconscious. Following the progress of the turning key, he twisted himself around the lock, hanging on by his mouth, and, clinging to the key, pressed it down again, whenever it slipped, with all the weight of his body. The clear click of the lock as it snapped back awoke Gregor from his momentary coma.

"I have dispensed with the locksmith," he thought, and sighed and leaned his head against the handle to open one panel of the double doors completely.

This method, the only possible one, prevented the others from seeing him for some time, even with the door open. Still erect, he had to grope his way round the door with great caution in order not to spoil his entry by falling flat on his back; so he was concentrating toward this end, with all his attention absorbed by the maneuver, when he heard the manager utter a sonorous, "Oh!" such as the roaring of the wind produces, and saw him—he was just by the door—press his hand over his open mouth and slowly stagger back as if some invisible and intensely powerful force were driving him from the spot. His mother—who, despite the presence of the manager, was standing by with her hair in curlers, still disordered by sleep—began to look at the father, clasping her hands; then she made two steps toward Gregor and fell backward into the family circle in the midst of a confusion of skirts which spread around her, while her face, falling on her breast, was concealed from sight. The father clenched his fists with a menacing air, as if to beat Gregor back into his room; then he looked around the dining room in perplexity, covered his eyes with his hand, and wept with great sobs which shook his powerful chest.

Gregor did not enter the room; he stood against the closed half of the double doors, allowing only a part of his body to be seen, while, above, he turned his head to one side to see what would happen. Meanwhile, it had grown much lighter; on either side of the street a part of the long, dark building opposite could clearly be seen—it was a hospital, with regular windows startlingly pitting its façade; it was still raining, but in great separate drops which fell to the ground, one by one. The breakfast crockery was spread all over the table, for breakfast was the most important meal of the day for Gregor's father; he would prolong it for hours while he read various newspapers. On the wall hung a photograph of Gregor in lieutenant's uniform, taken while he was in military service; he was smiling; his hand lay on the hilt of his sword. By his expression, he seemed happy to be alive; by his gesture, he appeared to command respect for his rank. The living-room door was ajar, and, as the front door was also open, the balcony and the first steps of the stairway could just be seen.

"Now," said Gregor, and he realized that he was the only one to have kept calm, "Now I will get dressed, collect my samples, and go. Will you, will you let me go? Surely you can now see, sir, that I am not obstinate, that I do mean to work; commercial traveling is tiresome, I admit, but without it I cannot live. Where are you going, sir? To the office? Yes? Will you give them a faithful account of what has happened? After all, anyone might find for a moment that they were incapable of resuming their work, but that's just a good opportunity to review the work they have been doing, and to bear in mind that, once the obstacle is removed, they will be able to return with twice the heart. I owe so much to the director, as you know very well. I have my parents and my sister to consider. I am in an awkward position, but I shall return to work. Only, please do not make things more difficult for me; they are hard enough as it is. Take my part at the office. I know only too well they don't like travelers. They think we earn our money too easily, that we lead too grand a life. I realize that the present situation doesn't encourage the removal of this prejudice; but you, sir, the manager, can judge the circumstances better than the rest of the staff, better than the director himself—though this is between ourselves—for in his executive capacity he is often easily misled by an employee's prejudice. You know quite well that the traveler, who is hardly ever in the office the whole year round, is often the victim of scandal, of a chance, undeserved complaint against which he is powerless to defend himself, for he does not even know that he is being accused; he only learns of it as he returns, exhausted, at the end of his trip, when the sad consequences of an affair, whose circumstances he can no longer recall, painfully confront him. Please, sir, don't leave me without a word to show that you think all this at least a little reasonable."

But, at Gregor's first words, the manager had turned away and only glanced back, with snarling lips, over his trembling shoulder. During Gregor's speech, he had not stood still for a moment; instead, he had retreated furtively, step by step, toward the door—always keeping Gregor in sight—as if some secret law forbade him to leave the room. He had already reached the hall and, as he took the very last step out of the living room, one would have thought the floor was burning his shoes, so sharply did he spring. Then he stretched his hand toward the balustrade, as if some unearthly deliverance awaited him at the foot of the stairs.

Gregor realized that, if he were to keep his job, on no account must the manager be allowed to leave in this condition. Unfortunately, his parents did not realize the position very clearly; they had for so long held the idea that Gregor was settled in the firm for life and were so taken up with their present troubles that they had little thought for such a contingency. But Gregor had more foresight. The manager must be stopped, calmed, convinced, and finally won over. The future of Gregor and of his family depended on it! If only his sister were there! She had understood, she had actually begun to weep while Gregor still lay quietly on his back. And the manager, who liked women, would have listened to her; he would have let himself be guided by her; she would have closed the door and would have proved to him, in the hall, how unreasonable his terror was. But she was not there; Gregor himself must manage this affair. And without even considering whether he would ever be able to return to work, nor whether his speech had been understood, he let go of the doorpost to glide through the opening and overtake the manager (who was clutching the balustrade with both hands in a ridiculous manner), vainly sought for a foothold, and, uttering a cry, he fell, with his frail little legs crumpled beneath him.

Suddenly, for the first time that whole morning, he experienced a feeling of physical well-being; his feet were on firm ground; he noticed with joy that his legs obeyed him wonderfully and were even eager to carry him wherever he might wish. But while, under the nervous influence of his need for haste, he hesitated on the spot, not far from his mother, he saw her suddenly jump, fainting though she seemed to be, and throw her arms about with outspread fingers, crying, "Help, for God's sake, help!" She turned her head, the better to see Gregor; then, in flagrant contradiction, she began to retreat madly, having forgotten that behind her stood the table, still laden with breakfast things. She staggered against it and sat down suddenly, like one distraught, regardless of the fact that, at her elbow, the overturned coffeepot was making a pool of coffee on the carpet.

"Mother, mother," whispered Gregor, looking up at her. The manager had quite gone out of his mind. Seeing the coffee spilling, Gregor could not prevent himself from snapping his jaws several times in the air, as if he were eating. Thereupon his mother again began to shriek and quickly jumped up from the table and fell into the arms of the father, who had rushed up behind her. But Gregor had no time to bother about them. The manager was already on the stairs; with his chin on the balustrade, he was looking back for the last time.

Gregor summoned all his courage to try to bring him back; the manager must have suspected something of the sort, for he leaped several steps at a single bound and disappeared with a cry of, "Huh!" which resounded in the hollow of the stair well. This flight had the unfortunate effect of causing Gregor's father—who till now had remained master of himself—to lose his head completely; instead of running after the manager, or at least not interfering with Gregor in his pursuit, he seized in his right hand the manager's walking stick, which had been left behind on a chair with his overcoat and hat, took up in his left a newspaper from the table, and began stamping his feet and brandishing the newspaper and the cane to drive Gregor back into his room. Gregor's prayers were unavailing, were not even understood; he had turned to his father a supplicating head, but, meek though he showed himself, his father merely stamped all the louder. In the dining room, despite the cold, the mother had opened the window wide and was leaning out as far as possible, pressing her face in her hands. A great rush of air swept the space between the room and the stairway; the curtains billowed, the papers rustled, and a few sheets flew over the carpet. But the father pursued Gregor pitilessly, whistling and whooping like a savage, and Gregor, who was not used to walking backward, progressed but slowly.

Had he been able to turn around, he could have reached his room quickly, but he feared to make his father impatient by the slowness of his turning and feared also that at any moment he might receive a mortal blow on his head or on his back from this menacing stick. Soon Gregor had no choice; for he realized with terror that when he was going backward he was not master of his direction and, still fearfully watching the attitude of his father out of the corner of his eye, he began his turning movement as quickly as possible, which was really only very slowly. Perhaps his father realized his good intention for, instead of hindering this move, he guided him from a little distance away, helping Gregor with the tip of the stick. If only he had left off that insupportable whistling! Gregor was completely losing his head. He had nearly completed his turn when, bewildered by the din, he mistook his direction and began to go back to his former position. When at last, to his great joy, he found himself facing the half-opened double doors, he discovered that his body was too big to pass through without hurt. Naturally, it never occurred to his father, in his present state, to open the other half of the double doors in order to allow Gregor to pass. He was dominated by the one fixed idea that Gregor should be made to return to his room as quickly as possible. He would never have entertained the long-winded performance which Gregor would have needed to rear up and pass inside. Gregor heard him storming behind him, no doubt to urge him through as though there were no obstacle in his path; the hubbub no longer sounded like the voice of one single father. Now was no time to play, and Gregor—come what may—hurled himself into the doorway. There he lay, jammed in a slanting position, his body raised up on one side and his flank crushed by the door jamb, whose white paint was now covered with horrible brown stains. He was caught fast and could not free himself unaided; on one side his little legs fluttered in the air, on the other they were painfully pressed under his body; then his father gave him a tremendous blow from behind with the stick. Despite the pain, this was almost a relief; he was lifted bodily into the middle of the room and fell, bleeding thickly. The door was slammed by a thrust of the stick, and then, at last, all was still.

2

It was dusk when Gregor awoke from his heavy, deathlike sleep. Even had he not been disturbed, he would doubtless soon have awakened, for he felt he had had his fill of rest and sleep; however, he seemed to have been awakened by the cautious, furtive noise of a key turning in the lock of the hall door. The reflection of the electric tramway lay dimly here and there about the ceiling and on the upper parts of the furniture, but below, where Gregor was, it was dark. Slowly he dragged himself toward the door to ascertain what had happened and fumbled around clumsily with his feelers, whose use he was at last learning to appreciate. His left side seemed to him to be one long, irritating scar, and he limped about on his double set of legs. One of his legs had been seriously injured during the morning's events—it was a miracle that only one should be hurt—and it dragged lifelessly behind.

When he reached the door, he realized what had attracted him: the smell of food. For there was a bowl of sweetened milk in which floated little pieces of bread. He could have laughed with delight, his appetite had grown so since morning; he thrust his head up to the eyes in the milk. But he drew it back quickly; his painful left side gave him some difficulty, for he could only eat by convulsing his whole body and snorting; also, he could not bear the smell of milk, which once had been his favorite drink and which his sister had no doubt prepared for this special reason. He turned from the bowl in disgust and dragged himself to the middle of the room.

The gas was lit in the dining room; he could see it through the cracks of the door. Now was the time when, ordinarily, his father would read aloud to his family from the evening paper, but this time Gregor heard nothing. Perhaps this traditional reading, which his sister always retailed to him in her conversation and in her letters, had not lapsed entirely from the customs of the household. But everywhere was still, and yet surely someone was in the room.

"What a quiet life my family has led," thought Gregor, staring before him in the darkness, and he felt very proud, for it was to him that his parents and his sister owed so placid a life in so nice a flat. What would happen now, if this peace, this satisfaction, this well-being should end in terror and disaster? In order to dissipate such gloomy thoughts, Gregor began to take a little exercise and crawled back and forth over the floor.

Once during the evening he saw the door on the left open slightly, and once it was the door on the right; someone had wished to enter but had found the task too risky. Gregor resolved to stop by the dining-room door and to entice the hesitant visitor as best he might or at least to see who it was; but the door never opened again, and Gregor waited in vain That morning, when the door had been locked, everyone had tried to invade his room; but now that they had succeeded in opening it no one came to see him; they had even locked his doors on the outside.

Not till late was the light extinguished, and Gregor could guess that his parents and his sister had been waiting till then, for he heard them all go off on tiptoe. Now no one would come to him till the morning, and so he would have the necessary time to reflect on the ordering of his new life; but his great room, in which he was obliged to remain flat on his stomach on the floor, frightened him in a way that he could not understand—for he had lived in it for the past five years—and, with a half-involuntary action of which he was a little ashamed, he hastily slid under the couch; he soon found that here his back was a little crushed and he could not raise his head; he only regretted that his body was too large to go entirely under the couch.

He spent the whole night there, sometimes in a half-sleep from which the pangs of hunger would wake him with a start, sometimes ruminating on his misfortune and his vague hopes, always concluding that his duty was to remain docile and to try to make things bearable for his family, whatever unpleasantness the situation might impose upon them.

Early in the morning he had a chance to test the strength of his new resolutions; it was still almost dark; his sister, already half dressed, opened the hall door and looked in curiously. She did not see Gregor at once but when she perceived him under the sofa—"Heavens, he must be somewhere; he can't have flown away!"—she was overcome by an unmanageable terror and rushed off, slamming the door. Then, repenting her gesture, she opened it again and entered on tiptoe, as if it were the room of a stranger or one seriously ill. Gregor stretched his head out from the side of the sofa and watched her. Would she notice that he had left the milk, and not from lack of appetite? Would she bring him something which suited his taste better? If she did not do so of her own accord, he would rather have died of hunger than draw her attention to these things, despite his overwhelming desire to rush out of his hiding place, to throw himself at his sister's feet, and to beg for something to eat. But suddenly the sister saw the full bowl in astonishment. A little milk had been spilled around it; using a piece of paper, she took up the bowl without touching it and carried it off to the kitchen. Gregor waited anxiously to see what she would bring him in its place and racked his brains to guess. But he had never realized to what lengths his sister's kindness would go. In order to discover her brother's likes, she brought a whole choice of eatables spread on an old newspaper. There were half-rotted stumps of vegetables, the bones of yesterday's dinner covered with a thick white sauce, a few currants and raisins, some almonds, some cheese that Gregor, a few days before, had declared uneatable, a stale loaf, a piece of salted bread and butter, and another without salt. Besides this she brought back the bowl which had become so important to Gregor. This time it was filled with water, and, guessing that her brother would not like to eat before her, she very kindly retired, closing and locking the door to show him that he might eat in peace. Now that his meal was ready, Gregor felt all his legs trembling. His wounds seemed cured, for he felt not the slightest hindrance, and he was astonished to remember that when he had been human and had cut his finger slightly only a few months ago, it had pained him for several days after.

"Have I become less sensitive?" he wondered; but already he had begun sucking at the cheese, which had suddenly and imperiously attracted him above all the other food. Gluttonously he swallowed in turn the cheese, the vegetables, and the sauce, his eyes moist with satisfaction; as to the fresh things, he wanted none of them; their smell repelled him, and, in order to eat, he separated them from the others.

When he had finished and was idly making up his mind to return to his place, his sister slowly began to turn the key in the lock to give him the signal for retreat. He was very frightened, though he was half asleep, and hurried to reach the sofa. It needed great determination to remain beneath it during the time, however short, that his sister was in the room; his heavy meal had so swollen his body that he could scarcely breathe in his retreat. Between two fits of suffocation he saw, with his eyes filled with tears, that his sister, intending no harm, was sweeping up the remains of his meal with the very things that he had not touched, as if he needed them no more; she put the refuse into a bucket, which she covered with a wooden lid and hastily carried away. Hardly had she turned the handle before Gregor struggled out from his hiding place to expand his body to its proper size.

So he was fed each day; in the morning, before his parents and the maid were awake, and in the afternoon, when lunch was over and while his parents were taking their nap and the maid had been provided with some task or other by his sister. Certainly they did not wish Gregor to die of hunger but perhaps they preferred to know nothing about his meals except by hearsay—they could not have borne to see him—perhaps, also, in order to diminish their disgust, his sister was taking pains to spare them the slightest trouble. He must realize that they, too, had their share of misfortune.

Gregor never learned what excuses they had made to rid themselves of the doctor and the locksmith, for, as no one attempted to understand him, no one, not even his sister, imagined that he could understand them. He had to be content, when she came into his room, to listen to her invoking the saints between her sighs. It was only much later, when Grete had become somewhat accustomed to the new situation—to which she never really became reconciled—that Gregor would occasionally overhear an expression which showed some kindness or allowed him to guess at such a meaning. When he had eaten all the food off the newspaper she would say, "He liked what I brought today"; at other times, when he had no appetite—and lately this had become more frequent—she would say, almost sadly, "Now he has left it all."

But even if he could learn no news directly, Gregor overheard a good deal of what was said in the dining room; as soon as he heard anyone speak, he would hurry to the most propitious door and press his whole body close against it. At first, especially, there was little conversation which did not bear more or less directly on his predicament. For two whole days, the mealtimes were given over to deliberating on the new attitude which must be maintained toward Gregor; even between meals they spoke mostly on the same theme, for now at least two members of the household always remained at home, each one fearing to remain alone and, particularly, to leave Gregor unwatched.

It was not very clear how much the maid knew of what had happened, but, on the very first day, she had fallen on her knees and begged his mother to let her go; and a quarter of an hour later she had left the house in tearful gratitude, as if her release were the greatest evidence of the kindness she had met with in the house; and of her own accord she took a long and boring oath never to reveal the secret to anyone. Now his sister and his mother had to look after the cooking; this entailed little trouble, for the appetite of the Samsa family had gone. Occasionally Gregor would hear one member of the family vainly exhorting another to eat. The reply was always the same: "Thank you, I have had enough," or some such phrase. Perhaps, also, they did not drink. Often his sister would ask her father if he would like some beer; she would cheerfully offer to fetch it, or, faced with her father's silence, she would say, to remove any scruples on his part, that the landlady could go for it, but her father would always reply with a loud, "No!" and nothing more would be said.

In the course of the very first day, the father had clearly explained their precise financial situation to his wife and daughter. From time to time he would get up from the table and hunt for some paper or account book in his Wertheim safe, which he had saved from the crash when his business had failed five years before. He could be heard opening the complicated locks of the safe and closing it again after he had taken out what he sought. Ever since he became a prisoner, nothing had given Gregor such pleasure as these financial explanations. He had always imagined that his father had been unable to save a penny from the ruins of his business; in any case, his father had never said anything to undeceive him, and Gregor had never questioned him upon the matter; he had done all he could to help his family to forget as quickly as possible the disaster which had plunged them into such despair.

He had set to work with splendid ardor; in less than no time, from being a junior clerk he had been promoted to the position of traveler, with all the benefits of such a post; and his successes were suddenly transformed into hard cash which could be spread on the table before the surprised and delighted eyes of his family. Those were happy times—they had never since recovered such a sense of delight, though Gregor now earned enough to feed the whole Samsa family. Everyone had grown accustomed to it, his family as much as himself; they took the money gratefully, he gave it willingly, but the act was accompanied by no remarkable effusiveness. Only his sister had remained particularly affectionate toward Gregor, and it was his secret plan to have her enter the conservatory next year regardless of the considerable cost of such an enterprise, which he would try to meet in some way; for, unlike him, Grete was very fond of music and wished to take up the study of the violin. This matter of the conservatory recurred often in the brief conversations between Gregor and his sister, whenever Gregor had a few days to spend with his family; they hardly ever spoke of it except as a dream impossible to realize; his parents did not much like the innocent allusions to the subject, but Gregor thought very seriously of it and had promised himself that he would solemnly announce his plan next Christmas eve.

It was ideas of this kind, ideas completely unsuited to his present situation, which now passed constantly through Gregor's mind while he held himself pressed erect against the door, listening. He would get so tired that he could no longer hear anything; then he would let himself go and allow his head to fall against the door; but he would draw it back immediately, for the slightest noise was noticed in the dining room and would be followed by an interval of silence.

"What can he be doing now?" his father would say after a moment's pause, turning, no doubt, toward the door; the interrupted conversation would only gradually be resumed.

His father was often obliged to repeat his explanations in order to recall forgotten details or to make them understood by his wife, who did not always grasp them the first time. Gregor thus learned, by what the father said, that, despite all their misfortunes, his parents had been able to save a certain amount from their former property—little enough, it is true, but it had been augmented, to some extent, by interest. Also, they had not spent all the money that Gregor, keeping only a few shillings for himself, had handed over to his family each week, enabling them to gather together a little capital. Behind his door, Gregor nodded his head in approval; he was so happy at this unexpected foresight and thrift. Doubtless, with these savings his father could have more rapidly paid off the debt he had contracted to Gregor's employer, which would have brought nearer the date of Gregor's release; but under the circumstances it was much better that his father had acted as he had.

Unfortunately this money was not quite sufficient to enable the family to live on its interest; it would last a year, perhaps two, but no more. It was a sum which must not be touched, which must be kept for a case of urgent necessity. As for money on which to live, that would have to be earned. Now, despite his good health, the father was nevertheless an old man who had ceased to work five years before and who could not be expected to entertain any foolish hopes of getting employment; during these five years of retirement—his first holiday in a life entirely devoted to work and unsuccess—he had become very fat and moved with great difficulty. And the old mother would not be able to earn much, suffering as she did from asthma, for even now it was an effort for her to get about the house; she passed a good deal of her time each day lying on the sofa, panting and wheezing under the open window. And was the breadwinner to be the sister, who was still but a child, seventeen years old, so suited to the life she had led till then, nicely dressed, getting plenty of sleep, helping in the house, taking part in a few harmless little entertainments, and playing her violin? Whenever the conversation fell on this topic, Gregor left the door and lay on the leather sofa, whose coolness was so soothing to his body, burning as it was with anxiety and shame.

Often he lay all night, sleepless, and hearing no sound for hours on end save the creak of the leather as he turned. Or, uncomplainingly, he would push his armchair toward the window, crawl up on it, and, propped on the seat, he would lean against the window, not so much to enjoy the view as to recall the sense of release he once used to feel whenever he looked across the pavements; for now he was daily becoming more short-sighted, he could not even make out the hospital opposite, which he had cursed when he was human because he could see it all too clearly; and had he not known so well that he was living in Charlottenstrasse, a quiet but entirely urban street, he might have thought his window gave out on a desert, where the gray of the sky and the gray of the earth merged indistinguishably together. His attentive sister had only to see the armchair by the window twice to understand; from then on, each time she tidied the room she would push the armchair to the window, and would always leave its lower half open.

If only Gregor had been able to speak to his sister, to thank her for all she was doing for him, he could have borne her services easier; but as it was, they pained and embarrassed him. Grete naturally tried to hide any appearance of blame or trouble regarding the situation, and as time went on she played her part even better, but she could not prevent her brother from realizing his predicament more and more clearly. Each time she entered his room, it was terrible for Gregor. Hardly had she entered, when, despite the pains she always took to spare the others the sight of its interior, she would not even take time to shut the door but would run to the window, open it hastily with a single push, as if to escape imminent suffocation, and would stand there for a minute, however cold it might be, breathing deeply. Twice a day she terrified Gregor with this rush and clatter; he shrank trembling under the couch the whole time; he knew his sister would have spared him this had she been able to stand being in the room with him with the window shut.

One day—it must have been a month after Gregor's change, and his sister had no grounds for astonishment at his appearance—she came a little earlier than usual and found him looking out of the window, motionless and in such a position as to inspire terror. If she had not liked to enter, that would not have surprised Gregor, for his position prevented her from opening the window. But not only would she not enter; she sprang back, slammed the door, and locked it; a stranger might have thought that Gregor was lying in wait for his sister, to attack her. Naturally he hid himself under the couch immediately, but he had to wait till midday for Grete's return, and, when she did come, she appeared unusually troubled. He realized that his appearance was still disgusting to the poor girl, that it would always be so, and that she must fiercely resist her own impulse to flee the moment she caught sight of the tiniest part of Gregor's body protruding from under the sofa. To spare her this sight, he took a sheet on his back, dragged it to the sofa—a task which occupied some hours—and spread it in such a way that his sister could see nothing under the sofa, even if she stooped. Had she found this precaution unnecessary, she would have taken the sheet away, for she guessed that Gregor did not so completely shut himself away for pleasure; but she left the sheet where it lay, and Gregor, prudently parting the curtain with his head to see what impression this new arrangement had made upon his sister, thought he detected a look of gratitude in her face.

During the first fortnight his parents had not been able to bring themselves to enter his room, and he often heard them praising the zeal of his sister, whom they had regarded, so far, as a useless young girl and of whom they had often complained. But now, both his father and mother would wait quite frequently outside Gregor's door while his sister was tidying the room, and scarcely had she come out again before they would make her tell them in detail exactly how she had found the room, what Gregor had eaten, and, in detail, what he was doing at that moment; they would ask her, too, if there were the slightest signs of improvement. His mother seemed impatient to see Gregor, but the father and sister restrained her with argument to which she listened very attentively and with which she wholly agreed. Later, however, they had to use force, and when his mother began to cry, "Let me go to Gregor! My poor boy! Don't you understand that I must see him!" Gregor thought that perhaps it would be as well if his mother did come in, not every day, of course, but perhaps once a week; she would understand things better than his sister, who was but a child, for all her courage, and had perhaps taken on such a difficult task out of childish lightheartedness.

Gregor's wish to see his mother was soon realized. Gregor avoided showing himself at the window during the day, out of consideration to his parents; but his restricted walks around the floor did not fully compensate him for this self-denial, nor could he bear to lie still for long, even during the night; he took no more pleasure in eating, and it soon became his habit to distract himself by walking—around the room, back and forth along the walls, and across the ceiling, on which he would hang; it was quite a different matter from walking across the floor. His breathing became freer, a light, swinging motion went through his body, and he felt so elated that now and then, to his own surprise, he would let himself go and fall to the floor. But by now, knowing better how to manage his body, he succeeded in rendering these falls harmless. His sister soon noticed his new pastime, for he left sticky marks here and there in his track, and Grete took it into her head to help him in his walks by removing all the furniture likely to be a hindrance, particularly the chest and the desk. Unfortunately, she was not strong enough to manage this on her own and dared not ask the help of her father; as for the maid, she certainly would have refused, for if this sixteen-year-old child had worked bravely since the former cook had left, it was on condition that she could stay continually barricaded in the kitchen, whose doors she would only open on special demand. So there was nothing else for it; Grete would have to enlist the mother's help one day when the father was away.

The mother gladly consented, but her exclamations of joy were hushed before Gregor's door. The sister first made sure that everything was in order in the room; then she allowed the mother to enter. In his great haste, Gregor had pulled the sheet down further than usual, and the many folds in which it fell gave the scene the air of a still life. This time he refrained from peeping under the sheet to spy on his mother but he was delighted to have her near.

"You may come in; he is not in sight," said his sister; and, taking her mother by the hand, she led her into the room. Then Gregor heard the two frail women struggling to remove the heavy old chest; the sister undertook the hardest part of the task, despite the warnings of her mother, who feared she might do herself some harm. It took a long time. They had been struggling with the chest for four hours when the mother declared that it might be best to leave it where it was, that it was too heavy for them, that they would not finish moving it before the father returned, and that, with the chest in the middle of the room, Gregor would be considerably impeded in his movements, and, finally, who knew whether he might not be displeased by the removal of his furniture?

The mother thought he would be; the sight of the bare walls struck cold at her heart; might Gregor not feel the same, having long grown so accustomed to the furniture, and would he not feel forsaken in his empty room? "Isn't it a fact," said the mother in a low voice—she had spoken in whispers ever since she entered the room, so that Gregor whose hiding place she had not yet discovered, might not overhear, not so much what she was saying—for she was persuaded that he could not understand—but the very sound of her voice. "Isn't it a fact that when we remove the furniture, we seem to imply that we are giving up all hope of seeing him cured and are wickedly leaving him to his fate? I think it would be better to keep the room just as it was before, so that Gregor will find nothing changed when he comes back to us and will be able the more easily to forget what has happened meanwhile."

Hearing his mother's words, Gregor realized how these two monotonous months, in the course of which nobody had addressed a word to him, must have affected his mind; he could not otherwise explain his desire for an empty room. Did he really wish to allow this warm, comfortable room with its genial furniture to be transformed into a cavern in which, in rapid and complete forgetfulness of his human past, he might exercise his right to crawl all over the walls? It seemed he was already so near to forgetting; and it had required nothing less than his mother's voice, which he had not heard for so long, to rouse him. Nothing should be removed, everything must stay as it is, he could not bear to forego the good influence of his furniture, and, if it prevented him from indulging his crazy impulses, then so much the better.

Unfortunately, his sister was not of this opinion; she had become accustomed to assume authority over her parents where Gregor was concerned—this was not without cause—and now the mother's remarks were enough to make her decide to remove not only the desk and the chest—which till now had been their only aim—but all the other furniture as well, except the indispensable sofa. This was not the result of mere childish bravado, nor the outcome of that new feeling of self-confidence which she had just acquired so unexpectedly and painfully. No, she really believed that Gregor had need of plenty of room for exercise and that, as far as she could see, he never used the furniture. Perhaps, also, the romantic character of girls of her age was partly responsible for her decision, a sentiment which strove to satisfy itself on every possible occasion and which now drove her to dramatize her brother's situation to such an extent so that she could devote herself to Gregor even more passionately than hitherto; for in a room over whose bare walls Gregor reigned alone, no one but Grete dare enter and stay.

She did not allow herself to be turned from her resolve by her mother, made irresolute by the oppressive atmosphere of the room, and who did not hesitate now to remove the chest as best she could. Gregor could bear to see the chest removed, at a pinch, but the desk must stay. And hardly had the women left the room, panting as they pushed the chest, than Gregor put out his head to examine the possibilities of making a prudent and tactful appearance. But unfortunately it was his mother who returned first, while Grete, in the side room, her arms around the chest, was rocking it from side to side without being able to settle it in position. The mother was not used to the sight of Gregor; it might give her a serious shock. Terrified, he hastened to retreat to the other end of the sofa, but he could not prevent the sheet from fluttering slightly, which immediately attracted his mother's attention. She stopped short, stood stockstill for a moment, then hurried back to Grete.

Gregor assured himself that nothing extraordinary was happening—

they were merely removing a few pieces of furniture—but the coming and going of the women, their little cries, the scraping of the furniture over the floor, seemed to combine in such an excruciating din that, however much he withdrew his head, contracted his legs, and pressed himself to the ground, he had to admit that he could not bear this torture much longer. They were emptying his room, taking away from him all that he loved; they had already removed the chest in which he kept his saw and his fret-work outfit; now they were shifting his desk, which had stood so solid and fast to the floor all the time it was in use, that desk on which he had written his lessons while he was at the commercial school, at the secondary school, even at the preparatory school. However, he could no longer keep pace with their intentions, for so absent minded had he become he had almost forgotten their existence, now that fatigue had quietened them and the clatter of the weary feet could no longer be heard.

So he came out—the women were only leaning against the desk in the next room, recovering their breath—and he found himself so bewildered that he changed his direction four times; he really could not decide what he should first salvage—when suddenly he caught sight of the picture of the woman in furs which assumed tremendous importance on the bare wall; he hastily climbed up and pressed himself against the glass, which stuck to his burning belly and refreshed him delightfully. This picture, at least, which Gregor entirely covered, should not be snatched away from him by anyone. He turned his head toward the dining-room door to observe the women as they returned.

They had had but a short rest and were already coming back; Grete's arm was round her mother's waist, supporting her.

"Well, what shall we take now?" said Grete, and she looked around. Her eyes met those of Gregor on the wall. If she succeeded in keeping her presence of mind, it was only for her mother's sake, toward whom she leaned her head to prevent her from seeing anything and said, a little too quickly and with a trembling voice, "Come, wouldn't it be better to go back to the living room for a minute?" The girl's intention was clear to Gregor: she wished to put her mother in a safe place and then to drive him from the wall. Well, let her try! He lay over his picture, and he would not let it go. He would rather leap into his sister's face.

But Grete had merely disquieted her mother; now she turned, saw the gigantic brown stain spread over the wallpaper and, before she realized that it was Gregor she was seeing, she cried, "O God! O God!" in a screaming, raucous voice, fell on the sofa with outspread arms in a gesture of complete renunciation, and gave no further sign of life. "You, Gregor!" cried the sister, raising her fist and piercing Gregor with a look. It was the first word she had addressed to him directly ever since his metamorphosis. Then she ran to get some smelling salts from the dining room to rouse her mother from her swoon. Gregor decided to help—there was still time to save the picture—alas, he found he had stuck fast to the glass and had to make a violent effort to detach himself; then he hurried into the dining room as if able to give his sister some good advice, but he was obliged to content himself with remaining passively behind her while she rummaged among the bottles, and he frightened her so terribly when she turned around that a bottle fell and broke on the floor, a splinter wounded Gregor in the face, and a corrosive medicine flowed round his feet; then Grete hastily grabbed up all the bottles she could carry and rushed in to her mother, slamming the door behind her with her foot. Now Gregor was shut out from his mother, who perhaps was nearly dead through his fault; he dared not open the door lest he drive away his sister, who must stay by his mother; so there was nothing to do but wait, and, gnawed by remorse and distress, he began to wander over the walls, the furniture, and the ceiling so rapidly that everything began to spin around him, till in despair he fell heavily on to the middle of the huge table.

A moment passed; Gregor lay stretched there, around all was still; perhaps that was a good sign. But suddenly he heard a knock. The maid was naturally barricaded in her kitchen; Grete herself must go to the door. His father had returned.

"What has happened?" were his first words; no doubt Grete's expression had explained everything.

The girl replied in a stifled voice—probably she leaned her face against her father's breast—"Mother fainted, but she is better now. Gregor has got out."

"I was waiting for that," said the father, "I told you all along, but you women will never listen."

Gregor realized by these words that his father had misunderstood Grete's brief explanation and imagined that his son had broken loose in some reprehensible way. There was no time to explain. Gregor had to find some way of pacifying his father, so he quickly crawled to the door of his room and pressed himself against it for his father to see, as he came in, how he had every intention of returning to his own room immediately and that it was not at all necessary to drive him back with violence; one had only to open the door and he would quickly withdraw.

But his father was in no mood to notice these fine points. As he entered he cried, "Ah!" in a tone at once of joy and anger; Gregor turned his head away from the door and lifted it toward his father. He was astonished. He had never imagined his father as he stood before him now; it is true that for some time now he had neglected to keep himself acquainted with the events of the house, preferring to devote himself to his new mode of existence, and he had therefore been unaware of a certain change of character in his family. And yet—and yet, was that really his father? Was it really the same man who once had lain wearily in bed when Gregor had been leaving on his journeys, who met him, on his return, in his nightshirt, seated in an armchair out of which he could not even lift himself, throwing his arms high to show how pleased he was? Was this that same old man who, on the rare walks which the family would take together, two or three Sundays a year and on special holidays, would hobble between Gregor and his mother, while they walked slower and slower for him, as he, covered with an old coat, carefully set his stick before him and prudently worked his way forward; and yet, despite their slowness, he would be obliged to stop, whenever he wished to say anything, and call his escort back to him? How upstanding he had become since then!

Now he was wearing a blue uniform with gold buttons, without a single crease, just as you see the employees of banking houses wearing; above the big, stiff collar his double chin spread its powerful folds; under his bristly eyebrows the watchful expression of his black eyes glittered young and purposefully; his white hair, ordinarily untidy, had been carefully brushed till it shone. He threw on to the sofa his cap, ornamented with the gilded monogram of some bank, making it describe the arc of a circle across the room, and, with his hands in his trouser pockets, the long flaps of his coat turned back, he walked toward Gregor with a menacing air. He himself did not know what he was going to do; however, he raised his feet very high, and Gregor, astonished at the enormous size of the soles of his boots, took care to remain still, for he knew that, from the first day of his metamorphosis, his father had held the view that the greatest severity was the only attitude to take up toward Gregor. Then he began to beat a retreat before his father's approach, halting when the other stopped and beginning again at his father's slightest move. In this way they walked several times round the room without any decisive result; it did not even take on the appearance of a pursuit, so slow was their pace.

Gregor was provisionally keeping to the floor; he feared that if his father saw him climbing about the walls or rushing across the ceiling, he might take this maneuver for some refinement of bad behavior. However, he had to admit that he could not go on much longer in this way; in the little time his father needed to take a step, Gregor had to make a whole series of gymnastic movements and, as he had never had good lungs, he now began to pant and wheeze; he tried to recover his breath quickly in order to gather all his strength for a supreme effort, scarcely daring to open his eyes, so stupefied that he could think of no other way to safety than by pursuing his present course; he had already forgotten that the walls were at his disposal, and the carefully carved furniture, all covered with festoons of plush and lace as it was. Suddenly something flew sharply by him, fell to the ground, and rolled away. It was an apple, carelessly thrown; a second one flew by. Paralyzed with terror, Gregor stayed still. It was useless to continue his course, now that his father had decided to bombard him. He had emptied the bowls of fruit on the sideboard, filled his pockets, and now threw apple after apple, without waiting to take aim.

These little red apples rolled about the floor as if electrified, knocking against each other. One lightly-thrown apple struck Gregor's back and fell off without doing any harm, but the next one literally pierced his flesh. He tried to drag himself a little further away, as if a change of position could relieve the shattering agony he suddenly felt, but he seemed to be nailed fast to the spot and stretched his body helplessly, not knowing what to do. With his last, hopeless glance, he saw his door opened suddenly, and, in front of his sister, who was shouting at the top of her voice, his mother came running in, in her petticoat, for his sister had partly undressed her that she might breathe easier in her swoon. And his mother, who ran to the father, losing her skirts one by one, stumbled forward, thrust herself against her husband, embraced him, pressed him to her, and, with her hands clasped at the back of his neck—already Gregor could see no more—begged him to spare Gregor's life.

3

The apple which no one dared draw from Gregor's back remained embedded in his flesh as a palpable memory, and the grave wound which he now had borne for a month seemed to have reminded his father that Gregor, despite his sad and terrible change, remained none the less a member of the family and must not be treated as an enemy; on the contrary, duty demanded that disgust should be overcome and Gregor be given all possible help.

His wound had made him lose, irremediably, no doubt, much of his agility; now, merely to cross his room required a long, long time, as if he were an aged invalid; his walks across the walls could no longer be considered. But this aggravation of his state was largely compensated for, in his opinion, by the fact that now, every evening, the dining-room door was left open; for two hours he would wait for this. Lying in the darkness of his room, invisible to the diners, he could observe the whole family gathered round the table in the lamplight, and he could, by common consent, listen to all they had to say—it was much better than before.

It must be admitted that they no longer held those lively conversations of which, in former times, he had always thought with such sadness as he crept into his damp bed in some little hotel room. Most of the time, now, they discussed nothing in particular after dinner. The father would soon settle himself to doze in his armchair; the mother and daughter would bid each other be silent; the mother, leaning forward in the light, would sew at some fine needlework for a lingerie shop, and the sister, who had obtained a job as a shop assistant, would study shorthand or French in the hope of improving her position. Now and then the father would wake up and, as if he did not know that he had been asleep, would say to his wife, "How late you are sewing tonight!" and would fall off to sleep again, while the mother and sister would exchange a tired smile.

By some capricious obstinacy, the father always refused to take off his uniform, even at home; his dressing gown hung unused in the wardrobe, and he slept in his armchair in full livery, as if to keep himself always ready to carry out some order; even in his own home he seemed to await his superior's voice. Moreover, the uniform had not been new when it was issued to him and now each day it became more shabby, despite the care which the two women devoted to it; and Gregor often spent the evening staring dully at this coat, so spotted and stained, whose polished buttons always shone so brightly, and in which the old man slept, uncomfortably but peacefully.

As soon as the clock struck ten, the mother, in a low voice, tried to rouse her husband and to encourage him to go to bed, as it was impossible to get proper sleep in such a position, and he must sleep normally before returning to work at six the next morning. But, with the obstinacy which had characterized him ever since he had obtained his position at the bank, he would stay at the table although he regularly dropped off to sleep, and thus it would become more and more difficult to induce him to change his armchair for the bed. The mother and sister might insist with their little warnings; he stayed there just the same, slowly nodding his head, his eyes shut tight, and would not get up. The mother might shake him by the wrist, might whisper endearments in his ear; the daughter might abandon her work to assist her mother, but all in vain. The old man would merely sink deeper in his chair. At last the two women would have to take him under the arms to make him open his eyes; then he would look at each in turn and say, "What a life! Is this the hard-earned rest of my old days?" and, leaning on the two women, he would rise painfully, as if he were a tremendous weight, and would allow himself to be led to the door by his wife and daughter; then he would wave them off and continue alone, while the mother and sister, the one quickly throwing down her pen, the other her needle, would run after him to help.

Who in the overworked and overtired family had time to attend to Gregor, except for his most pressing needs? The household budget was ever more and more reduced; at last the maid was dismissed. In her place, a gigantic charwoman with bony features and white hair, which stood up all around her head, came, morning and evening, to do the harder work. The rest was done by the mother, over and above her interminable mending and darning. It even happened that they were obliged to sell various family trinkets which formerly had been worn proudly by the mother and sister at ceremonies and festivals, as Gregor discovered one evening when he heard them discussing the price they hoped to get. But their most persistent complaints were about this flat, which was so much larger than they needed and which had now become too expensive for the family purse; they could not leave, they said, for they could not imagine how Gregor could be moved. Alas, Gregor understood that it was not really he who was the chief obstacle to this removal, for he might easily have been transported in a large wooden box pierced with a few air holes. No, what particularly prevented the family from changing their residence was their own despair, the idea that they had been stricken by such a misfortune as had never before occurred in the family or within the circle of their acquaintances.

Of all the deprivations which the world imposes on poor people, not one had been spared them; the father took his day-time meals with the lesser employees of the bank, the mother was killing herself mending the linen of strangers, the sister ran here and there behind her counter at the customers' bidding; but the family had energy for nothing further. It seemed to poor Gregor that his wound reopened whenever his mother and sister, returning from putting the father to bed, would leave their work in disorder and bring their chairs nearer to each other, till they were sitting almost cheek to cheek; then the mother would say, pointing to Gregor's room, "Close the door, Grete," and he would once more be left in darkness, while, outside, the two women mingled their tears or, worse, sat at the table staring with dry eyes.

These days and nights brought Gregor no sleep. From time to time he thought of taking the family affairs in hand, as he once used, the very next time the door was opened; at the end of a long perspective of time he dimly saw in his mind his employer and the manager, the clerks and apprentices, the porter with his narrow ideas, two or three acquaintances from other offices, a provincial barmaid—a fleeting but dear memory—and a cashier in a hat shop, whom he had pursued earnestly but too slowly; they passed through his mind in confusion, mingled with unknown and forgotten faces; but none of them could bring help to him or his family; nothing was to be gained from them. He was pleased to be able to dismiss them from his mind but now he no longer cared what happened to his family; on the contrary, he only felt enraged because they neglected to tidy his room, and, though nothing imaginable could excite his appetite, he began making involved plans for a raid on the larder, with a view to taking such food as he had a right to, even if he was not hungry. Nowadays his sister no longer tried to guess what might please him; she made a hasty appearance twice a day, in the morning and in the afternoon, before going to her shop, and pushed a few scraps of food into the room with her foot; in the evening, without even bothering to see whether he had touched his meal or whether he had left it entirely—and this was usually the case—she would sweep up the remains with a whisk of the broom.

As for tidying up the room, which Grete now did in the evenings, it could not have been done in a more hasty manner. Great patches of dirt streaked the wall, little heaps of dust and ordure lay here and there about the floor. At first Gregor would place himself in the filthiest places whenever his sister appeared, so that this might seem a reproach to her. But he could have stayed there for weeks, and still Grete would not have altered her conduct; she saw the dirt as well as he but she had finally decided to take no further trouble. This did not prevent her from taking even more jealous care than ever to insure that no other member of the family should presume on her right to the tidying of the room.

Once the mother undertook to give Gregor's room a great cleaning which required several buckets of water, and this deluge deeply upset poor Gregor, crouched under his sofa in bitter immobility—but the mother's punishment soon came. Hardly had the sister, coming home in the evening, noticed the difference in Gregor's room, than, feeling deeply offended, she ran crying and screaming into the dining room, despite the appeal of her mother, who raised her hands in supplication; the father, who was quietly seated at table, leaped up, astonished but powerless to pacify her. Then he, too, became agitated; shouting, he began to attack the mother, on the one hand, for not leaving the care and cleaning of Gregor's room to the girl and, on the other hand, he forbade his daughter ever again to dare to clean it; the mother tried to draw the old man, quivering with anger as he was, into the bedroom; the daughter, shaken with sobs, was banging on the table with her little fists, while Gregor loudly hissed with rage to think that no one had the decency or consideration to close the door and thus spare him the sight of all this trouble and uproar.

But even if the sister, tired out by her work in the shop, could not bother to look after Gregor as carefully as hitherto, she could still have arranged that he should not be neglected without necessarily calling on the aid of her mother, for there was always the charwoman. This old woman, whose bony frame had helped her out of worse trouble during her long life, could not really be said to feel any disgust with Gregor. Though she was not inquisitive, she had opened his door one day and had stood with her hands folded over her stomach, astonished at the sight of Gregor, who began to trot here and there in his alarm, though she had no thought of chasing him. From that day, morning and evening, the old woman never lost an opportunity of opening the door a little to peer into the room.

At first she would call Gregor to make him come out, crying in a familiar tone, "Come on, you old cockroach!" or, "Hey, look at the old cockroach!" To such invitations Gregor would not respond; instead he remained motionless beneath his sofa as if the door had not been opened.

If they had only ordered the charwoman to clean his room out each day instead of allowing her to go on teasing and upsetting him! Early one morning, when heavy rain—perhaps a sign of approaching spring—beat on the roofs, Gregor was so annoyed by the old woman as she began to bait him again that he suddenly turned on her, in a somewhat cumbersome and uncertain manner, it must be admitted, but with every intention of attacking her. She was not at all frightened of him; there was a chair by the door; she took it up and brandished it, opening wide her mouth with the obvious intention of not closing it until she had brought the chair down with a crash on Gregor's back. "Ah, is that all?" she asked, seeing him return to his former position, and she quietly put the chair back in its place.

Nowadays Gregor hardly ate at all. When, by some chance, he passed by his scraps, he would amuse himself by taking a piece of food in his mouth and keeping it there for hours, usually spitting it out in the end. At first he had thought that his loss of appetite was due to the misery into which the state of his room had plunged him; no doubt this was a mistake, for he had soon become reconciled to the squalor of his surroundings. His family had got into the habit of piling into his room whatever could not be accommodated elsewhere, and this meant a great deal, now that one of the rooms had been let to three lodgers. They were very earnest and serious men; all three had thick beards—as Gregor saw one day when he was peering through a crack in the door—and they were fanatically tidy; they insisted on order, not only in their own room, but also, now that they were living here, throughout the whole household, and especially in the kitchen.

They had brought with them all that they needed, and this rendered superfluous a great many things about the house which could neither be sold nor thrown away, and which were now all stacked in Gregor's room, as were the ash bucket and the rubbish bin. Everything that seemed for the moment useless would be dumped in Gregor's room by the charwoman, who was always in a breathless hurry to get through her work; he would just have time to see a hand brandishing some unwanted utensil, and then the door would slam again. Perhaps the old woman intended to return and find the objects she so carelessly relegated here when she needed them and had time to search; or perhaps she meant to throw them all away some day, but in actual fact they stayed in the room, on the very spot where they had first fallen, so that Gregor was obliged to pick his way among the rubbish to make a place for himself—a game for which his taste began to grow, in spite of the appalling misery and fatigue which followed these peregrinations, leaving him paralyzed for hours. As the lodgers sometimes dined at home in the living room, the door of this room would be shut on certain evenings; however, Gregor no longer attached any importance to this; for some while, now, he had ceased to profit by those evenings when the family would open the door and he would remain shrinking in the darkest corner of his room, where the family could not see him.

One day the woman forgot to close the dining-room door, and it was still ajar when the lodgers came in and lit the gas. They sat down at table in the places that previously had been occupied by the father, the mother, and Gregor; each unfolded his napkin and took up his knife and fork. Soon the mother appeared in the doorway with a plate of meat; the sister followed her, carrying a dish of potatoes. When their meal had been set before them, the lodgers leaned over to examine it, and the one who was seated in the middle and who appeared to have some authority over the others, cut a piece of meat as it lay on the dish to ascertain whether it was tender or whether he should send it back to the kitchen. He seemed satisfied, however, and the two women, who had been anxiously watching, gave each other a smile of relief.

The family itself lived in the kitchen. However, the father, before going into the kitchen, always came into the dining room and bowed once with his cap in his hand, then made his way around the table. The boarders rose together and murmured something in their beards. Once they were alone, they began to eat in silence. It seemed curious to Gregor that he could hear the gnashing of their teeth above all the clatter of cutlery; it was as if they wanted to prove to him that one must have real teeth in order to eat properly, and that the best mandibles in the world were but an unsatisfactory substitute. "I am hungry," thought Gregor sadly, "but not for these things. How these lodgers can eat! And in the meantime I might die, for all they care."

He could not remember hearing his sister play since the arrival of the lodgers; but this evening the sound of the violin came from the kitchen. The lodgers had just finished their meal; the middle one had brought a newspaper and had given a page to each of the others; now they all three read, leaning back in their chairs and smoking. The sound of the violin attracted their attention, and they rose and walked on tiptoe toward the hall door, where they halted and remained very close together.

Apparently they had been heard in the kitchen, for the father cried, "Does the violin upset you gentlemen? We'll stop it immediately."

"On the contrary," said the man in the middle. "Would Fräulein Samsa not like to come in and play to us here in the dining room, where it is much nicer and more comfortable?"

"Oh, thank you," said the father, as if he were the violinist.

The gentlemen walked back across the room and waited. Soon the father came in with the music stand, the mother with the sheets of music, and the sister with the violin. The sister calmly prepared to play; her parents, who had never before let their rooms, were exaggeratedly polite to the boarders and were afraid to seem presumptuous by sitting in their own chairs; the father leaned against the door, his right hand thrust between two buttons of his livery coat; but one of the gentlemen offered the mother a chair, in which she finally sat, not daring to move from her corner throughout the performance.

The girl now began to play, while her father and mother, from either side, watched the movement of her hands. Attracted by the music, Gregor had crawled forward a little and had thrust his head into the room. He was no longer astonished that nowadays he had entirely lost that consideration for others, that anxiety to cause no trouble that once had been his pride. Yet never had he more reason to remain hidden, for now, because of the dirt that lay about his room, flying up at the slightest movement, he was always covered with dust and fluff, with ends of cotton and hairs, and with morsels of stale food, which stuck to his back or to his feet and which he trailed after him wherever he went; his apathy had grown too great for him to bother anymore about cleaning himself several times a day by lying on his back and rubbing himself on the carpet, as once he used to do. And this filthy state did not prevent him from crawling over the spotless floor without a moment's shame.

So far, no one had noticed him. The family was too absorbed by the music of the violin, and the lodgers, who had first stood with their hands in their pockets, very close to the music stand—which disturbed the sister a great deal as she was obliged to see their image dancing amid the notes—had at last retired toward the window, where they stood speaking together half aloud, with lowered heads, under the anxious gaze of the father, who was watching attentively. It had become only too evident that they had been deceived in their hopes of hearing some beautiful violin piece, or at least some amusing little tune; it seemed that what the girl was playing bored them and that now they only tolerated her out of politeness. By the way in which they puffed the smoke of their cigars, by the energy with which they blew it toward the ceiling through the mouth or the nose, one could guess how fidgety they were becoming. And the sister was playing so nicely. Her face leaning to one side, her glance followed the score carefully and sadly. Gregor crawled forward a little more and put his head as near as possible to the floor to meet her gaze. Could it be that he was only an animal, when music moved him so? It seemed to him to open a way toward that unknown nourishment he so longed for. He resolved to creep up to his sister and to pull at her dress, to make her understand that she must come with him, for no one here would appreciate her music as much as he. He would never let her out of his room—at least, while he lived—for once, his horrible shape would serve him some useful purpose; he would be at all doors at once, repulsing intruders with his raucous breath; but his sister would not be forced to stay there; she must live with him of her own accord; she would sit by him on the sofa, hearing what he had to say; then he would tell her in confidence that he had firmly intended to send her to the Conservatory and had planned to let everyone know last Christmas—was Christmas really past?—without listening to any objections, had his misfortune not overtaken him too soon. His sister, moved by this explanation, would surely burst into tears, and Gregor, climbing up on her shoulder, would kiss her neck; this would be all the easier, for she had worn neither collar nor ribbon ever since she had been working in the shop.

"Herr Samsa," cried the middle lodger, and he pointed at Gregor, who slowly came into the room. The violin was suddenly silenced, the middle lodger turned to his friends, grinning and shaking his head, then once more he stared at Gregor. The father seemed to consider it more urgent to reassure the lodgers than to drive his son from the room, though the lodgers did not seem to be at all upset by the spectacle; in fact, Gregor seemed to amuse them more highly than did the violin. The father hurried forward and, with outstretched arms, tried to drive them into their room, hiding Gregor from them with his body. Now they began to be really upset, but it is not known whether this was on account of the father's action or because they had been living with such a monstrous neighbor as Gregor without being made aware of it. They demanded explanations, waving their arms in the air; and, fidgeting nervously with their beards, they retreated toward their own door. Meanwhile the sister had recovered from the distress that the sudden interruption of her music had caused her; after remaining a moment completely at a loss, with the violin and the bow hanging from her helpless hands, following the score with her eyes as if she were still playing, she suddenly came back to life, laid the violin in her mother's lap—the mother sat suffocating in her chair, her lungs working violently—and rushed into the next room, toward which the lodgers were rapidly retreating before Herr Samsa's onslaught. One could see how quickly, under Grete's practised hand, pillows and covers were set in order on the beds. The lodgers had not yet reached the room when their beds were already prepared, and Grete had slipped out. The father seemed so possessed by his strange fury that he had quite forgotten the respect due to lodgers.

He drove them to the door of the room, where the middle lodger suddenly came to a stop, stamping thunderously on the floor. "I wish to inform you," said this man, raising his hand and looking around for the two women, "that in view of the disgusting circumstances which govern this family and this house"—and here he spat quickly on the carpet—"I hereby immediately give up my room. Naturally, you will not get a penny for the time I have been living here; on the contrary, I am considering whether I should not claim compensation from you, damages which should easily be awarded in any court of law; it is a matter about which I shall inquire, believe me." He was silent and stared into space, as if awaiting something. Accordingly, his two friends also spoke up: "We, too, give our notice." Thereupon the gentleman in the middle seized the door handle, and they went inside. The door closed with a crash.

The father stumbled toward his chair, put his trembling hands upon the arms, and let himself drop into it; he looked exactly as if he were settling himself for his customary evening nap, but the way his head drooped heavily from side to side showed that he was thinking of something other than sleep. All this time Gregor had stayed still on the spot where he had surprised the lodgers. He felt completely paralyzed with bewilderment at the checking of his plans—perhaps, also, with weakness due to his prolonged fasting. He feared that the whole household would fall upon him immediately; he foresaw the precise moment when this catastrophe would happen, and now he waited. Even the violin did not frighten him as it fell with a clatter from the trembling fingers of his mother, who until now had held it in her lap.

"My dear parents," said his sister, who beat with her hand on the table by way of introduction. "Things cannot go on like this. Even if you do not realize it, I can see it quite clearly. I will not mention my brother's name when I speak of this monster here; I merely want to say: we must find some means of getting rid of it. We have done all that is humanly possible to care for it, to put up with it; I believe that nobody could reproach us in the least."

"She's a thousand times right," said the father. But the mother, who had not yet recovered her breath, coughed helplessly behind her hand, her eyes haggard.

The sister hurried toward her mother and held her forehead. Grete's words seemed to have made up the father's mind, for now he sat up in his armchair and fidgeted with his cap among the dishes on the table, from which the lodgers' meal had not yet been cleared; from time to time he stared at Gregor.

"We must find a way of getting rid of it," repeated the sister, now speaking only to her father, for her mother, shaken by her coughing, could hear nothing. "It will bring you both to the grave. I can see it coming. When people have to work all day, as we must, we cannot bear this eternal torture each time we come home at night. I can stand it no longer." And she wept so bitterly that her tears fell on her mother's face, who wiped them off with a mechanical movement of her hand.

"But what can we do, child?" said the father in a pitiful voice. It was surprising to see how well he understood his daughter.

The sister merely shrugged her shoulders as a sign of the perplexity which, during her tears, had replaced her former assurance.

"If he could only understand us," said the father in a half-questioning tone, but the sister, through her tears, made a violent gesture with her hand as a sign that this was not to be thought of.

"If only he could understand us," repeated the father—and he shut his eyes as he spoke, as if to show that he agreed with the sister that such a thing was quite impossible. "If only he could understand us, perhaps there would be some way of coming to an agreement. But as it is . . ."

"It must go!" cried the sister. "That's the only way out. You must get the idea out of your head that this is Gregor. We have believed that for too long, and that is the cause of all our unhappiness. How could it be Gregor? If it were really he, he would long ago have realized that he could not live with human beings and would have gone off on his own accord. I haven't a brother any longer, but we can go on living and can honor his memory. In his place we have this monster that pursues us and drives away our lodgers; perhaps it wants the whole flat to itself, to drive us out into the streets. Look, father, look!" she suddenly screamed, "it's beginning again!" And in an access of terror, which Gregor could not understand, she let go her mother so suddenly that she bounced in the seat of the armchair; it seemed as if the sister would rather sacrifice her mother than stay near Gregor; she hastily took refuge behind her father, who was very upset by her behavior and now stood up, spreading his arms to protect her.

But Gregor had no thought of frightening anyone, least of all his sister. He had merely started to turn around in order to go back to his room; but it must be realized that this looked very alarming, for his weakness obliged him to assist his difficult turning movement with his head, which he raised and lowered many times, clutching at the carpet with his mandibles. At last he ceased and stared at the family. It seemed they realized his good intentions. They were watching him in mute sadness. The mother lay in her armchair, her outstretched legs pressed tightly together, her eyes nearly closed with fatigue; the father and sister were sitting side by side, and the girl's arm was round her father's neck.

"Now, perhaps, they will let me turn," thought Gregor, and he once more set about his task. He could not repress a sigh of weariness; he was obliged to rest from time to time. However, no one hurried him; they left him entirely alone. When he had completed his turn, he immediately beat a retreat, crawling straight ahead. He was astonished at the distance which separated him from his room; he did not realize that this was due merely to his weak state and that a little before he could have covered the distance without noticing it. His family did not disturb him by a single cry, a single exclamation; but this he did not even notice, so necessary was it to concentrate all his will on getting back to his room. It was only when he had at long last reached his door that he thought of turning his head, not completely, because his neck had become very stiff, but sufficiently to reassure himself that nothing had changed behind him; only his sister was not standing up. His last look was toward his mother, who, by this time, was fast asleep.

Hardly was he in his room before the door was slammed, locked, and double bolted. So sudden was the crash that Gregor's legs gave way. It was his sister who had rushed to the door. She had stood up so as to be ready immediately and at the right moment had run forward so lightly that he had not heard her come; as she turned the key in the lock, she cried to her parents, "At last!"

"What now?" asked Gregor, looking around himself in the darkness. He soon discovered that he could not move. This did not surprise him in the least; it seemed to him much more remarkable that such frail legs had hitherto been able to bear his weight. Now he experienced a feeling of relative comfort. True, his whole body ached, but it seemed that these aches became less and less until finally they disappeared. Even the rotted apple embedded in his back hardly hurt him now; no more did the inflammation of the surrounding parts, covered with fine dust, cause him any further discomfort. He thought of his family in tender solicitude. He realized that he must go, and his opinion on this point was even more firm, if possible, than that of his sister. He lay in this state of peaceful and empty meditation till the clock struck the third morning hour. He saw the landscape grow lighter through the window; then, against his will, his head fell forward and his last feeble breath streamed from his nostrils.

When the charwoman arrived early in the morning—and though she had often been forbidden to do so, she always slammed the door so loudly in her vigor and haste that once she was in the house it was impossible to get any sleep—she did not at first notice anything unusual as she paid her customary morning visit to Gregor. She imagined that he was deliberately lying motionless in order to play the role of an "injured party," as she herself would say—she deemed him capable of such refinements; as she had a long broom in her hand, she tried to tickle him from the doorway. Meeting with little success, she grew angry; she gave him one or two hard pushes, and it was only when his body moved unresistingly before her thrusts that she became curious. She quickly realized what had happened, opened her eyes wide, and whistled in astonishment, but she did not stay in the room; she ran to the bedroom, opened the door, and loudly shouted into the darkness, "Come and look! He's stone dead! He's lying there, absolutely dead as a doornail!"

Herr and Frau Samsa sat up in their bed and tried to calm each other; the old woman had frightened them so much and they did not realize the sense of her message immediately. But now they hastily scrambled out of bed, Herr Samsa on one side, his wife on the other; Herr Samsa put the coverlet over his shoulders, Frau Samsa ran out, clad only in her nightdress; and it was thus that they rushed into Gregor's room. Meanwhile, the dining-room door was opened—Grete had been sleeping there since the arrival of the lodgers—she was fully dressed, as if she had not slept all night, and the pallor of her face seemed to bear witness to her sleeplessness.

"Dead?" said Frau Samsa, staring at the charwoman with a questioning look, though she could see as much for herself without further examination.

"I should say so," said the charwoman, and she pushed Gregor to one side with her broom, to support her statement. Frau Samsa made a movement as if to hold back the broom, but she did not complete her gesture.

"Well," said Herr Samsa, "we can thank God for that!" He crossed himself and signed the three women to do likewise.

Grete, whose eyes had never left the corpse, said, "Look how thin he was! It was such a long time since he had eaten anything. His meals used to come out of the room just as they were taken in." And, indeed, Gregor's body was quite flat and dry; this could be seen more easily now that he was no longer supported on his legs and there was nothing to deceive one's sight.

"Come with us a moment, Grete!" said Frau Samsa with a sad smile, and Grete followed her parents into their bedroom, not without turning often to gaze at the corpse. The charwoman closed the door and opened the French windows. Despite the early hour, the fresh morning air had a certain warmth. It was already the end of March.

The three lodgers came out of their room and gazed around in astonishment for their breakfast; they had been forgotten. "Where is our breakfast?" the middle lodger petulantly demanded of the old woman. But she merely laid her finger to her mouth and signed them, with a mute and urgent gesture, to follow her into Gregor's room. So they entered and stood around Gregor's corpse, with their hands in the pockets of their rather shabby coats, in the midde of the room already bright with sunlight.

Then the bedroom door opened and Herr Samsa appeared in his uniform with his wife on one arm, his daughter on the other. All seemed to have been weeping, and from time to time Grete pressed her face against her father's arm.

"Leave my house immediately!" said Herr Samsa, and he pointed to the door, while the women still clung to his arms.

Somewhat disconcerted, the middle lodger said with a timid smile, "Whatever do you mean?"

The two others clasped their hands behind their backs and kept on rubbing their palms together, as if they were expecting some great dispute which could only end in triumph for them.

"I mean exactly what I say!" answered Herr Samsa and, in line with the two women, he marched straight at the lodger. The latter, however, stood quietly in his place, his eyes fixed on the floor, as if reconsidering what he should do.

"Well, then, we will go," he said at last, raising his eyes to Herr Samsa as if searching, in a sudden access of humility, for some slight approval of his resolution.

Herr Samsa merely nodded several times, opening his eyes very wide. Thereupon the lodger walked away with big strides and soon reached the anteroom; his two friends, who for some while had ceased wringing their hands, now bounded after him, as if afraid Herr Samsa might reach the door before them and separate them from their leader. Once they had gained the hall, they took down their hats from the pegs, grabbed their sticks from the umbrella stand, bowed silently, and left the flat.

With a suspicion which, it appears, was quite unjustified, Herr Samsa ran out onto the landing after them with the women and leaned over the balustrade to watch the three men as they slowly, but steadily, descended the interminable stairway, disappearing once as they reached a certain point on each floor, and then, after a few seconds, coming into view again. As they went farther down the staircase, so the Samsa family's interest diminished, and when they had been met and passed by a butcher's boy who came proudly up the stairs with his basket on his head, Herr Samsa and the women quickly left the landing and went indoors again with an air of relief.

They decided to spend the whole day resting; perhaps they might take a walk in the country; they had earned a respite and needed it urgently. And so they sat down to the table to write three letters of excuse: Herr Samsa to the manager of the Bank, Frau Samsa to her employer, and Grete to the head of her department at the shop. The charwoman came in while they were writing and announced that her work was done and that she was going. The three writers at first merely nodded their heads, without raising their eyes, but, as the old woman did not leave, they eventually laid down their pens and looked crossly at her.

"Well?" asked Herr Samsa. The charwoman was standing in the doorway, smiling as if she had some very good news to tell them but which she would not impart till she had been begged to. The little ostrich feather which stood upright on her hat and which had always annoyed Herr Samsa so much ever since the old woman had entered their service, now waved lightly in all directions.

"Well, what is it?" asked Frau Samsa, toward whom the old woman had always shown so much more respect than to the others.

"Well . . ." she replied, and she laughed so much she could hardly speak for some while. "Well, you needn't worry about getting rid of that thing in there, I have fixed it already."

Frau Samsa and Grete leaned over the table as if to resume their letter-writing; Herr Samsa, noticing that the woman was about to launch forth into a detailed explanation, cut her short with a peremptory gesture of his outstretched hand. Then, prevented from speaking, she suddenly remembered that she was in a great hurry and, crying, "Goodbye, everyone," in a peevish tone, she half turned and was gone in a flash, savagely slamming the door behind her.

"This evening we must sack her," declared Herr Samsa; but neither his wife nor his daughter answered; the old woman had not been able to disturb their newly won tranquillity. They arose, went to the window, and stood there, with their arms around each other; Herr Samsa, turning toward them in his armchair, stared at them for a moment in silence. Then he cried, "Come, come, it's all past history now; you can start paying a little attention to me." The women immediately hurried to him, kissed him, and sat down to finish their letters.

Then they all left the apartment together, a thing they had been unable to do for many months past, and they boarded a tram which would take them some way into the country. There were no other passengers in the compartment, which was warm and bright in the sun. Casually leaning back in their seats, they began to discuss their future. On careful reflection, they decided that things were not nearly so bad as they might have been, for—and this was a point they had not hitherto realized—they had all three found really interesting occupations which looked even more promising in the future. They decided to effect what really should be the greatest improvement as soon as possible. That was to move from the flat they occupied at present. They would take a smaller, cheaper flat, but one more practical, and especially in a better neighborhood than the present one, which Gregor had chosen. Hearing their daughter speak in more and more lively tones, Herr and Frau Samsa noticed almost together that, during this affair, Grete had blossomed into a fine strapping girl, despite the make-up which made her cheeks look pale. They became calmer; almost unconsciously they exchanged glances; it occurred to both of them that it would soon be time for her to find a husband. And it seemed to them that their daughter's gestures were a confirmation of these new dreams of theirs, an encouragement for their good intentions, when, at the end of the journey, the girl rose before them and stretched her young body.

MARK TWAIN

The Mysterious Stranger

A ROMANCE

It was in 1590—winter. Austria was far away from the world, and asleep; it was still the Middle Ages in Austria, and promised to remain so forever. Some even set it away back centuries upon centuries and said that by the mental and spiritual clock it was still the Age of Belief in Austria. But they meant it as a compliment, not a slur, and it was so taken, and we were all proud of it. I remember it well, although I was only a boy; and I remember, too, the pleasure it gave me.

Yes, Austria was far from the world, and asleep, and our village was in the middle of that sleep, being in the middle of Austria. It drowsed in peace in the deep privacy of a hilly and woodsy solitude where news from the world hardly ever came to disturb its dreams, and was infinitely content. At its front flowed the tranquil river, its surface painted with cloud-forms and the reflections of drifting arks and stone-boats; behind it rose the woody steeps to the base of the lofty precipice; from the top of the precipice frowned a vast castle, its long stretch of towers and bastions mailed in vines; beyond the river, a league to the left, was a tumbled expanse of forest-clothed hills cloven by winding gorges where the sun never penetrated; and to the right a precipice overlooked the river, and between it and the hills just spoken of lay a far-reaching plain dotted with little homesteads nested among orchards and shade trees.

The whole region for leagues around was the hereditary property of a prince, whose servants kept the castle always in perfect condition for occupancy, but neither he nor his family came there oftener than once in five years. When they came it was as if the lord of the world had arrived, and had brought all the glories of its kingdoms along; and when they went they left a calm behind which was like the deep sleep which follows an orgy.

Eseldorf was a paradise for us boys. We were not overmuch pestered with schooling. Mainly we were trained to be good Christians; to revere the Virgin, the Church, and the saints above everything. Beyond these matters we were not required to know much; and, in fact, not allowed to. Knowledge was not good for the common people, and could make them discontented with the lot which God had appointed for them, and God would not endure discontentment with His plans. We had two priests. One of them, Father Adolf, was a very zealous and strenuous priest, much considered.

There may have been better priests, in some ways, than Father Adolf, but there was never one in our commune who was held in more solemn and awful respect. This was because he had absolutely no fear of the Devil. He was the only Christian I have ever known of whom that could be truly said. People stood in deep dread of him on that account; for they thought that there must be something supernatural about him, else he could not be so bold and so confident. All men speak in bitter disapproval of the Devil but they do it reverently, not flippantly; but Father Adolf's way was very different; he called him by every name he could lay his tongue to, and it made every one shudder that heard him; and often he would even speak of him scornfully and scoffingly; then the people crossed themselves and went quickly out of his presence, fearing that something fearful might happen.

Father Adolf had actually met Satan face to face more than once, and defied him. This was known to be so. Father Adolf said it himself. He never made any secret of it, but spoke it right out. And that he was speaking true there was proof in at least one instance, for on that occasion he quarreled with the enemy, and intrepidly threw his bottle at him; and there, upon the wall of his study, was the ruddy splotch where it struck and broke.

But it was Father Peter, the other priest, that we all loved best and were sorriest for. Some people charged him with talking around in conversation that God was all goodness and would find a way to save all his poor human children. It was a horrible thing to say, but there was never any absolute proof that Father Peter said it; and it was out of character for him to say it, too, for he was always good and gentle and truthful. He wasn't charged with saying it in the pulpit, where all the congregation could hear and testify, but only outside, in talk; and it is easy for enemies to manufacture *that.* Father Peter had an enemy and a very powerful one, the astrologer who lived in a tumbled old tower up the valley, and put in his night studying the stars. Every one knew he could foretell wars and famines, though that was not so hard, for there was always a war and generally a famine somewhere. But he could also read any man's life through the stars in a big book he had, and find lost property, and every one in the village except Father Peter stood in awe of him. Even Father Adolf, who had defied the Devil, had a wholesome respect for the astrologer when he came through our village wearing his tall, pointed hat and his long, flowing robe with stars on it, carrying his big book and a staff which was known to have magic power. The bishop himself sometimes listened to the astrologer, it was said, for, besides studying the stars and prophesying, the astrologer made a great show of piety, which would impress the bishop, of course.

But Father Peter took no stock in the astrologer. He denounced him openly as a charlatan—a fraud with no valuable knowledge of any kind, or powers beyond those of an ordinary and rather inferior human being, which naturally made the astrologer hate Father Peter and wish to ruin him. It was the astrologer, as we all believed, who originated the story about Father Peter's shocking remark and carried it to the bishop. It was said that Father Peter had made the remark to his niece, Marget, though Marget denied it and implored the bishop to believe her and spare her old uncle from poverty and disgrace. But the bishop wouldn't listen. He suspended Father Peter indefinitely, though he wouldn't go so far as to excommunicate him on the evidence of only one witness; and now Father Peter had been out a couple of years, and our other priest, Father Adolf, had his flock.

Those had been hard years for the old priest and Marget. They had been favorites, but of course that changed when they came under the shadow of the bishop's frown. Many of their friends fell away entirely, and the rest became cool and distant. Marget was a lovely girl of eighteen when the trouble came, and she had the best head in the village, and the most in it. She taught the harp, and earned all her clothes and pocket money by her own industry. But her scholars fell off one by one now; she was forgotten when there were dances and parties among the youth of the village; the young fellows stopped coming to the house, all except Wilhelm Meidling—and he could have been spared; she and her uncle were sad and forlorn in their neglect and disgrace, and the sunshine was gone out of their lives. Matters went worse and worse, all through the two years. Clothes were wearing out, bread was harder and harder to get. And now, at last, the very end was come. Solomon Isaacs had lent all the money he was willing to put on the house, and gave notice that to-morrow he would foreclose.

2

Three of us boys were always together, and had been so from the cradle, being fond of one another from the beginning, and this affection deepened as the years went on—Nikolaus Bauman, son of the principal judge of the local court; Seppi Wohlmeyer, son of the keeper of the principal inn, the "Golden Stag," which had a nice garden, with shade trees reaching down to the riverside, and pleasure boats for hire; and I was the third—Theodor Fischer, son of the church organist, who was also leader of the village musicians, teacher of the violin, composer, tax-collector of the commune, sexton, and in other ways a useful citizen, and respected by all. We knew the hills and the woods as well as the birds knew them; for we were always roaming them when we had leisure—at least, when we were not swimming or boating or fishing, or playing on the ice or sliding down hill.

And we had the run of the castle park, and very few had that. It was because we were pets of the oldest servingman in the castle—Felix Brandt; and often we went there, nights, to hear him talk about old times and strange things, and to smoke with him (he taught us that) and to drink coffee; for he had served in the wars, and was at the siege of Vienna; and there, when the Turks were defeated and driven away, among the captured things were bags of coffee, and the Turkish prisoners explained the character of it and how to make a pleasant drink out of it, and now he always kept coffee by him, to drink himself and also to astonish the ignorant with. When it stormed he kept us all night; and while it thundered and lightened outside he told us about ghosts and horrors of every kind, and of battles and murders and mutilations, and such things, and made it pleasant and cozy inside; and he told these things from his own experience largely. He had seen many ghosts in his time, and witches and enchanters, and once he was lost in a fierce storm at midnight in the mountains, and by the glare of the lightning had seen the Wild Huntsman rage on the blast with his specter dogs chasing after him through the driving cloud-rack. Also he had seen an incubus once, and several times he had seen the great bat that sucks the blood from the necks of people while they are asleep, fanning them softly with its wings and so keeping them drowsy till they die.

He encouraged us not to fear supernatural things, such as ghosts, and said they did no harm, but only wandered about because they were lonely and distressed and wanted kindly notice and compassion; and in time we learned not to be afraid, and even went down with him in the night to the haunted chamber in the dungeons of the castle. The ghost appeared only once, and it went by very dim to the sight and floated noiseless through the air, and then disappeared; and we scarcely trembled, he had taught us so well. He said it came up sometimes in the night and woke him by passing its clammy hand over his face, but it did him no hurt; it only wanted sympathy and notice. But the strangest thing was that he had seen angels—actual angels out of heaven—and had talked with them. They had no wings, and wore clothes, and talked and looked and acted just like any natural person, and you would never know them for angels except for the wonderful things they did which a mortal could not do, and the way they suddenly disappeared while you were talking with them, which was also a thing which no mortal could do. And he said they were pleasant and cheerful, not gloomy and melancholy, like ghosts.

It was after that kind of a talk one May night that we got up next morning and had a good breakfast with him and then went down and crossed the bridge and went away up into the hills on the left to a woody hill-top which was a favorite place of ours, and there we stretched out on the grass in the shade to rest and smoke and talk over these strange things, for they were in our minds yet, and impressing us. But we couldn't smoke, because we had been heedless and left our flint and steel behind

Soon there came a youth strolling toward us through the trees, and he sat down and began to talk in a friendly way, just as if he knew us. But we did not answer him, for he was a stranger and we were not used to strangers and were shy of them. He had new and good clothes on, and was handsome and had a winning face and a pleasant voice, and was easy and graceful and unembarrassed, not slouchy and awkward and diffident, like other boys. We wanted to be friendly with him, but didn't know how to begin. Then I thought of the pipe, and wondered if it would be taken as kindly meant if I offered it to him. But I remembered that we had no fire, so I was sorry and disappointed. But he looked up bright and pleased, and said:

"Fire? Oh, that is easy; I will furnish it."

I was so astonished I couldn't speak, for I had not said anything. He took the pipe and blew his breath on it, and the tobacco glowed red, and spirals of blue smoke rose up. We jumped up and were going to run, for that was natural; and we did run a few steps, although he was yearningly pleading for us to stay, and giving us his word that he would not do us any harm, but only wanted to be friends with us and have company. So we stopped and stood, and wanted to go back, being full of curiosity and wonder, but afraid to venture. He went on coaxing, in his soft, persuasive way; and when we saw that the pipe did not blow up and nothing happened, our confidence returned by little and little, and presently our curiosity got to be stronger than our fear, and we ventured back—but slowly, and ready to fly at any alarm.

He was bent on putting us at ease, and he had the right art; one could not remain doubtful and timorous where a person was so earnest and simple and gentle, and talked so alluringly as he did; no, he won us over, and it was not long before we were content and comfortable and chatty, and glad we had found this new friend. When the feeling of constraint was all gone we asked him how he had learned to do that strange thing, and he said he hadn't learned it at all; it came natural to him—like other things—other curious things.

"What ones?"

"Oh, a number; I don't know how many."

"Will you let us see you do them?"

"Do—please!" the others said.

"You won't run away again?"

"No—indeed we won't. Please do. Won't you?"

"Yes, with pleasure; but you mustn't forget your promise, you know."

We said we wouldn't, and he went to a puddle and came back with water in a cup which he had made out of a leaf, and blew upon it and threw it out, and it was a lump of ice the shape of the cup. We were astonished and charmed, but not afraid any more; we were very glad to be there, and asked him to go on and do some more things. And he did. He said he would give us any kind of fruit we liked, whether it was in season or not. We all spoke at once:

"Orange!"

"Apple!"

"Grapes!"

"They are in your pockets," he said, and it was true. And they were of the best, too, and we ate them and wished we had more, though none of us said so.

"You will find them where those came from," he said, "and everything else your appetites call for; and you need not name the thing you wish; as long as I am with you, you have only to wish and find."

And he said true. There was never anything so wonderful and so interesting. Bread, cakes, sweets, nuts—whatever one wanted, it was there. He ate nothing himself, but sat and chatted, and did one curious thing after another to amuse us. He made a tiny toy squirrel out of clay, and it ran up a tree and sat on a limb overhead and barked down at us. Then he made a dog that was not much larger than a mouse, and it treed the squirrel and danced about the tree, excited and barking, and was as alive as any dog could be. It frightened the squirrel from tree to tree and followed it up until both were out of sight in the forest. He made birds out of clay and set them free, and they flew away, singing.

At last I made bold to ask him to tell us who he was.

"An angel," he said, quite simply, and set another bird free and clapped his hands and made it fly away.

A kind of awe fell upon us when we heard him say that, and we were afraid again; but he said we need not be troubled, there was no occasion for us to be afraid of an angel, and he liked us, anyway. He went on chatting as simply and unaffectedly as ever; and while he talked he made a crowd of little men and women the size of your finger, and they went diligently to work and cleared and leveled off a space a couple of yards square in the grass and began to build a cunning little castle in it, the women mixing the mortar and carrying it up the scaffoldings in pails on their heads, just as our work-women have always done, and the men laying the courses of masonry—five hundred of these toy people swarming briskly about and working diligently and wiping the sweat off their faces as natural as life. In the absorbing interest of watching those five hundred little people make the castle grow step by step and course by course, and take shape and symmetry, that feeling of awe soon passed away and we were quite comfortable and at home again. We asked if we might make some people, and he said yes, and told Seppi to make some cannon for the walls, and told Nikolaus to make some halberdiers with breastplates and greaves and helmets, and I was to make some cavalry, with horses, and in allotting these tasks he called us by our names, but did not say how he knew them. Then Seppi asked him what his own name was, and he said, tranquilly, "Satan," and held out a chip and caught a little woman on it who was falling from the scaffolding and put her back where she belonged, and said, "She is an idiot to step backward like that and not notice what she is about."

It caught us suddenly, that name did, and our work dropped out of our hands and broke to pieces—a cannon, a halberdier, and a horse. Satan laughed, and asked what was the matter. I said, "Nothing, only it seemed a strange name for an angel." He asked why.

"Because it's—it's—well, it's his name, you know."

"Yes—he is my uncle."

He said it placidly, but it took our breath for a moment and made our hearts beat. He did not seem to notice that, but mended our halberdiers and things with a touch, handing them to us finished, and said, "Don't you remember?—he was an angel himself, once."

"Yes—it's true," said Seppi; "I didn't think of that."

"Before the Fall he was blameless."

"Yes," said Nikolaus, "he was without sin."

"It is a good family—ours," said Satan; "there is not a better. He is the only member of it that has ever sinned."

I should not be able to make any one understand how exciting it all was. You know that kind of quiver that trembles around through you when you are seeing something so strange and enchanting and wonderful that it is just a fearful joy to be alive and look at it; and you know how you gaze, and your lips turn dry and your breath comes short, but you wouldn't be anywhere but there, not for the world. I was bursting to ask one question—I had it on my tongue's end and could hardly hold it back—but I was ashamed to ask it; it might be a rudeness. Satan set an ox down that he had been making and smiled up at me and said:

"It wouldn't be a rudeness, and I should forgive it if it was. Have I seen him? Millions of times. From the time that I was a little child a thousand years old I was his second favorite among the nursery angels of our blood and lineage—to use a human phrase—yes, from that time until the Fall, eight thousand years, measured as you count time."

"Eight—thousand!"

"Yes." He turned to Seppi, and went on as if answering something that was in Seppi's mind. "Why, naturally I look like a boy, for that is what I am. With us what you call time is a spacious thing; it takes a long stretch of it to grow an angel to full age." There was a question in my mind, and he turned to me and answered it, "I am sixteen thousand years old—counting as you count." Then he turned to Nikolaus and said: "No, the Fall did not affect me nor the rest of the relationship. It was only he that I was named for who ate of the fruit of the tree and then beguiled the man and the woman with it. We others are still ignorant of sin; we are not able to commit it; we are without blemish, and shall abide in that estate always. We—" Two of the little workmen were quarreling, and in buzzing little bumblebee voices they were cursing and swearing at each other; now came blows and blood; then they locked themselves together in a life-and-death struggle. Satan reached out his hand and crushed the life out of them with his fingers, threw them away, wiped the red from his fingers on his handkerchief, and went on talking where he had left off: "We cannot do wrong; neither have we any disposition to do it, for we do not know what it is."

It seemed a strange speech, in the circumstances, but we barely noticed that, we were so shocked and grieved at the wanton murder he had committed—for murder it was, that was its true name, and it was without palliation or excuse, for the men had not wronged him in any way. It made us miserable, for we loved him, and had thought him so noble and so beautiful and gracious, and had honestly believed he was an angel; and to have him do this cruel thing—ah, it lowered him so, and we had had such pride in him. He went right on talking, just as if nothing had happened, telling about his travels and the interesting things he had seen in the big worlds of our solar system and of other solar systems far away in the remoteness of space, and about the customs of the immortals that inhabit them, somchow fascinating us, enchanting us, charming us in spite of the pitiful scene that was now under our eyes, for the wives of the little dead men had found the crushed and shapeless bodies and were crying over them, and sobbing and lamenting, and a priest was kneeling there with his hands crossed upon his breast, praying; and crowds and crowds of pitying friends were massed about them, reverently uncovered, with their bare heads bowed, and many with the tears running down—a scene which Satan paid no attention to until the small noise of the weeping and praying began to annoy him, then he reached out and took the heavy board seat out of our swing and brought it down and mashed all those people into the earth just as if they had been flies, and went on talking just the same.

An angel, and kill a priest! An angel who did not know how to do wrong, and yet destroys in cold blood hundreds of helpless poor men and women who had never done him any harm! It made us sick to see that awful deed, and to think that none of those poor creatures was prepared except the priest, for none of them had ever heard a mass or seen a church. And we were witnesses; we had seen these murders done and it was our duty to tell, and let the law take its course.

But he went on talking right along, and worked his enchantments upon us again with that fatal music of his voice. He made us forget everything; we could only listen to him, and love him, and be his slaves, to do with us as he would. He made us drunk with the joy of being with him, and of looking into the heaven of his eyes, and of feeling the ecstasy that thrilled along our veins from the touch of his hand.

3

The Stranger had seen everything, he had been everywhere, he knew everything, and he forgot nothing. What another must study, he learned at a glance; there were no difficulties for him. And he made things live before you when he told about them. He saw the world made; he saw Adam created; he saw Samson surge against the pillars and bring the temple down in ruins about him; he saw Caesar's death; he told of the daily life in heaven; he had seen the damned writhing in the red waves of hell; and he made us see all these things, and it was as if we were on the spot and looking at them with our own eyes. And we felt them, too, but there was no sign that they were anything to him beyond mere entertainments. Those visions of hell, those poor babes and women and girls and lads and men shrieking and supplicating in anguish —why, we could hardly bear it, but he was as bland about it as if it had been so many imitation rats in an artificial fire.

And always when he was talking about men and women here on the earth and their doings—even their grandest and sublimest—we were secretly ashamed, for his manner showed that to him they and their doings were of paltry poor consequence; often you would think he was talking about flies, if you didn't know. Once he even said, in so many words, that our people down here were quite interesting to him, notwithstanding they were so dull and ignorant and trivial and conceited, and so diseased and rickety and such a shabby, poor, worthless lot all around. He said it in a quite matter-of-course way and without bitterness, just as a person might talk about bricks or manure or any other thing that was of no consequence and hadn't feelings. I could see he meant no offense, but in my thoughts I set it down as not very good manners.

"Manners!" he said. "Why, it is merely the truth, and truth is good manners; manners are a fiction. The castle is done. Do you like it?"

Any one would have been obliged to like it. It was lovely to look at, it was so shapely and fine, and so cunningly perfect in all its particulars, even to the little flags waving from the turrets. Satan said we must put the artillery in place now, and station the halberdiers and display the cavalry. Our men and horses were a spectacle to see, they were so little like what they were intended for; for, of course, we had no art in making such things. Satan said they were the worst he had seen; and when he touched them and made them alive, it was just ridiculous the way they acted, on account of their legs not being of uniform lengths. They reeled and sprawled around as if they were drunk, and endangered everybody's lives around them, and finally fell over and lay helpless and kicking. It made us all laugh, though it was a shameful thing to see. The guns were charged with dirt, to fire a salute, but they were so crooked and so badly made that they all burst when they went off, and killed some of the gunners and crippled the others. Satan said we would have a storm now, and an earthquake, if we liked, but we must stand off a piece, out of danger. We wanted to call the people away, too, but he said never mind them; they were of no consequence, and we could make more, some time or other, if we needed them.

A small storm-cloud began to settle down black over the castle, and the miniature lightning and thunder began to play, and the ground to quiver, and the wind to pipe and wheeze, and the rain to fall, and all the people flocked into the castle for shelter. The cloud settled down blacker and blacker, and one could see the castle only dimly through it; the lightning blazed out flash upon flash and pierced the castle and set it on fire, and the flames shone out red and fierce through the cloud, and the people came flying out, shrieking, but Satan brushed them back, paying no attention to our begging and crying and imploring; and in the midst of the howling of the wind and volleying of the thunder the magazine blew up, the earthquake rent the ground wide, and the castle's wreck and ruin tumbled into the chasm, which swallowed it from sight, and closed upon it, with all that innocent life, not one of the five hundred poor creatures escaping. Our hearts were broken; we could not keep from crying.

"Don't cry," Satan said; "they were of no value."

"But they are gone to hell!"

"Oh, it is no matter; we can make plenty more."

It was of no use to try to move him; evidently he was wholly without feelings and could not understand. He was full of bubbling spirits, and as gay as if this were a wedding instead of a fiendish massacre. And he was bent on making us feel as he did, and of course his magic accomplished his desire. It was no trouble to him; he did whatever he pleased with us. In a little while we were dancing on that grave, and he was playing to us on a strange, sweet instrument which he took out of his pocket; and the music—but there is no music like that, unless perhaps in heaven, and that was where he brought it from, he said. It made one mad, for pleasure; and we could not take our eyes from him, and the looks that went out of our eyes came from our hearts, and their dumb speech was worship. He brought the dance from heaven, too, and the bliss of paradise was in it.

Presently he said he must go away on an errand. But we could not bear the thought of it, and clung to him, and pleaded with him to stay; and that pleased him, and he said so, and said he would not go yet, but would wait a little while and we would sit down and talk a few minutes longer; and he told us Satan was only his real name, and he was to be known by it to us alone, but he had chosen another one to be called by in the presence of others; just a common one, such as people have—Philip Traum.

It sounded so odd and mean for such a being! But it was his decision, and we said nothing; his decision was sufficient.

We had seen wonders this day; and my thoughts began to run on the pleasure it would be to tell them when I got home, but he noticed those thoughts, and said:

"No, all these matters are a secret among us four. I do not mind your trying to tell them, if you like, but I will protect your tongues and nothing of the secret will escape from them."

It was a disappointment, but it couldn't be helped, and it cost us a sigh or two. We talked pleasantly along, and he was always reading our thoughts and responding to them, and it seemed to me that this was the most wonderful of all the things he did, but he interrupted my musings, and said:

"No, it would be wonderful for you, but it is not wonderful for me. I am not limited like you. I am not subject to human conditions. I can measure and understand your human weaknesses, for I have studied them; but I have none of them. My flesh is not real, although it would seem firm to your touch; my clothes are not real; I am a spirit. Father Peter is coming." We looked around, but did not see any one. "He is not in sight yet, but you will see him presently."

"Do you know him, Satan?"

"No."

"Won't you talk with him when he comes? He is not ignorant and dull, like us, and he would so like to talk with you. Will you?"

"Another time, yes, but not now. I must go on my errand after a little. There he is now; you can see him. Sit still, and don't say anything."

We looked up and saw Father Peter approaching through the chestnuts. We three were sitting together in the grass, and Satan sat in front of us in the path. Father Peter came slowly along with his head down, thinking, and stopped within a couple of yards of us and took off his hat and got out his silk handkerchief, and stood there mopping his face and looking as if he were going to speak to us, but he didn't. Presently he muttered, "I can't think what brought me here; it seems as if I were in my study a minute ago—but I suppose I have been dreaming along for an hour and have come all this stretch without noticing; for I am not myself in these troubled days." Then he went mumbling along to himself and walked straight through Satan, just as if nothing were there. It made us catch our breath to see it. We had the impulse to cry out, the way you nearly always do when a startling thing happens, but something mysteriously restrained us and we remained quiet, only breathing fast. Then the trees hid Father Peter after a little, and Satan said:

"It is as I told you—I am only a spirit."

"Yes, one perceives it now," said Nikolaus, "but we are not spirits. It is plain he did not see you, but were we invisible, too? He looked at us, but he didn't seem to see us."

"No, none of us was visible to him, for I wished it so."

It seemed almost too good to be true, that we were actually seeing these romantic and wonderful things, and that it was not a dream. And there he sat, looking just like anybody—so natural and simple and charming, and chatting along again the same as ever, and—well, words cannot make you understand what we felt. It was an ecstasy; and an ecstasy is a thing that will not go into words; it feels like music, and one cannot tell about music so that another person can get the feeling of it. He was back in the old ages once more now, and making them live before us. He had seen so much, so much! It was just a wonder to look at him and try to think how it must seem to have such experience behind one.

But it made you seem sorrowfully trivial, and the creature of a day, and such a short and paltry day, too. And he didn't say anything to raise up your drooping pride—no, not a word. He always spoke of men in the same old indifferent way—just as one speaks of bricks and manure-piles and such things; you could see that they were of no consequence to him, one way or the other. He didn't mean to hurt us, you could see that; just as we don't mean to insult a brick when we disparage it; a brick's emotions are nothing to us; it never occurs to us to think whether it has any or not.

Once when he was bunching the most illustrious kings and conquerors and poets and prophets and pirates and beggars together—just a brick-pile—I was shamed into putting in a word for man, and asked him why he made so much difference between men and himself. He had to struggle with that a moment; he didn't seem to understand how I could ask such a strange question. Then he said:

"The difference between man and me? The difference between a mortal and an immortal? between a cloud and a spirit?" He picked up a wood-louse that was creeping along a piece of bark: "What is the difference between Caesar and this?"

I said, "One cannot compare things which by their nature and by the interval between them are not comparable."

"You have answered your own question," he said. "I will expand it. Man is made of dirt—I saw him made. I am not made of dirt. Man is a museum of diseases, a home of impurities; he comes to-day and is gone to-morrow; he begins as dirt and departs as stench; I am of the aristocracy of the Imperishables. And man has the *Moral Sense*. You understand? He has the *Moral Sense*. That would seem to be difference enough between us, all by itself."

He stopped there, as if that settled the matter. I was sorry, for at that time I had but a dim idea of what the Moral Sense was. I merely knew that we were proud of having it, and when he talked like that about it, it wounded me, and I felt as a girl feels who thinks her dearest finery is being admired and then overhears strangers making fun of it. For a while we were all silent, and I, for one, was depressed. Then Satan began to chat again, and soon he was sparkling along in such a cheerful and vivacious vein that my spirits rose once more. He told some very cunning things that put us in a gale of laughter; and when he was telling about the time that Samson tied the torches to the foxes' tails and set them loose in the Philistines' corn, and Samson sitting on the fence slapping his thighs and laughing, with the tears running down his cheeks, and lost his balance and fell off the fence, the memory of that picture got him to laughing, too, and we did have a most lovely and jolly time. By and by he said:

"I am going on my errand now."

"Don't!" we all said. "Don't go; stay with us. You won't come back."

"Yes, I will; I give you my word."

"When? To-night? Say when."

"It won't be long. You will see."

"We like you."

"And I you. And as a proof of it I will show you something fine to see. Usually when I go I merely vanish; but now I will dissolve myself and let you see me do it."

He stood up and it was quickly finished. He thinned away and thinned away until he was a soap-bubble, except that he kept his shape. You could see the bushes through him as clearly as you see things through a soap-bubble, and all over him played and flashed the delicate iridescent colors of the bubble, and along with them was that thing shaped like a window-sash which you always see on the globe of the bubble. You have seen a bubble strike the carpet and lightly bound along two or three times before it bursts. He did that. He sprang—touched the grass—bounded—floated along—touched again—and so on, and presently exploded—puff! and in his place was vacancy.

It was a strange and beautiful thing to see. We did not say anything, but sat wondering and dreaming and blinking; and finally Seppi roused up and said, mournfully sighing:

"I suppose none of it has happened."

Nikolaus sighed and said about the same.

I was miserable to hear them say it, for it was the same cold fear that was in my own mind. Then we saw poor old Father Peter wandering along back, with his head bent down, searching the ground. When he was pretty close to us he looked up and saw us, and said, "How long have you been here, boys?"

"A little while, Father."

"Then it is since I came by, and maybe you can help me. Did you come up by the path?"

"Yes, Father."

"That is good. I came the same way. I have lost my wallet. There wasn't much in it, but a very little is much to me, for it was all I had. I suppose you haven't seen anything of it?"

"No, Father, but we will help you hunt."

"It is what I was going to ask you. Why, here it is!"

We hadn't noticed it; yet there it lay, right where Satan stood when he began to melt—if he did melt and it wasn't a delusion. Father Peter picked it up and looked very much surprised.

"It is mine," he said, "but not the contents. This is fat; mine was flat; mine was light; this is heavy." He opened it; it was stuffed as full as it could hold with gold coins. He let us gaze our fill; and of course we did gaze, for we had never seen so much money at one time before. All our mouths came open to say "Satan did it!" but nothing came out. There it was, you see—we couldn't tell what Satan didn't want told; he had said so himself.

"Boys, did you do this?"

It made us laugh. And it made him laugh, too, as soon as he thought what a foolish question it was.

"Who has been here?"

Our mouths came open to answer, but stood so for a moment, because we couldn't say "Nobody," for it wouldn't be true, and the right word didn't seem to come; then I thought of the right one, and said it:

"Not a human being."

"That is so," said the others, and let their mouths go shut.

"It is not so," said Father Peter, and looked at us very severely. "I came by here a while ago, and there was no one here, but that is nothing; some one has been here since. I don't mean to say that the person didn't pass here before you came, and I don't mean to say that you saw him, but some one did pass, that I know. On your honor—you saw no one?"

"Not a human being."

"That is sufficient; I know you are telling me the truth."

He began to count the money on the path, we on our knees eagerly helping to stack it in little piles.

"It's eleven hundred ducats odd!" he said. "Oh dear, if it were only mine—and I need it so!" and his voice broke and his lips quivered.

"It is yours, sir!" we all cried out at once, "every heller!"

"No—it isn't mine. Only four ducats are mine; the rest . . . !" He fell to dreaming, poor old soul, and caressing some of the coins in his hands, and forgot where he was, sitting there on his heels with his old gray head bare; it was pitiful to see. "No," he said, waking up, "it isn't mine. I can't account for it. I think some enemy . . . it must be a trap."

Nikolaus said: "Father Peter, with the exception of the astrologer you haven't a real enemy in the village—nor Marget, either. And not even a half-enemy that's rich enough to chance eleven hundred ducats to do you a mean turn. I'll ask you if that's so or not?"

He couldn't get around that argument, and it cheered him up. "But it isn't mine, you see—it isn't mine, in any case."

He said it in a wistful way, like a person that wouldn't be sorry, but glad, if anybody would contradict him.

"It is yours, Father Peter, and we are witness to it. Aren't we, boys?"

"Yes, we are—and we'll stand by it, too."

"Bless your hearts, you do almost persuade me; you do, indeed. If I had only a hundred-odd ducats of it! The house is mortgaged for it, and we've no home for our heads if we don't pay to-morrow. And that four ducats is all we've got in the—"

"It's yours, every bit of it, and you've got to take it—we are bail that it's all right. Aren't we, Theodor? Aren't we, Seppi?"

We two said yes, and Nikolaus stuffed the money back into the shabby old wallet and made the owner take it. So he said he would use two hundred of it, for his house was good enough security for that, and would put the rest at interest till the rightful owner came for it; and on our side we must sign a paper showing how he got the money—a paper to show to the villagers as proof that he had not got out of his troubles dishonestly.

4

It made immense talk next day, when Father Peter paid Solomon Isaacs in gold and left the rest of the money with him at interest. Also, there was a pleasant change; many people called at the house to congratulate him, and a number of cool old friends became kind and friendly again; and to top all, Marget was invited to a party.

And there was no mystery; Father Peter told the whole circumstance just as it happened, and said he could not account for it, only it was the plain hand of Providence, so far as he could see.

One or two shook their heads and said privately it looked more like the hand of Satan; and really that seemed a surprisingly good guess for ignorant people like that. Some came slyly buzzing around and tried to coax us boys to come out and "tell the truth"; and promised they wouldn't ever tell but only wanted to know for their own satisfaction, because the whole thing was so curious. They even wanted to buy the secret, and pay money for it; and if we could have invented something that would answer—but we couldn't; we hadn't the ingenuity, so we had to let the chance go by, and it was a pity.

We carried that secret around without any trouble, but the other one, the big one, the splendid one, burned the very vitals of us, it was so hot to get out and we so hot to let it out and astonish people with it. But we had to keep it in; in fact, it kept itself in. Satan said it would, and it did. We went off every day and got to ourselves in the woods so that we could talk about Satan, and really that was the only subject we thought of or cared anything about; and day and night we watched for him and hoped he would come, and we got more and more impatient all the time. We hadn't any interest in the other boys any more, and wouldn't take part in their games and enterprises. They seemed so tame, after Satan; and their doings so trifling and commonplace after his adventures in antiquity and the constellations, and his miracles and meltings and explosions, and all that.

During the first day we were in a state of anxiety on account of one thing, and we kept going to Father Peter's house on one pretext or another to keep track of it. That was the gold coin; we were afraid it would crumble and turn to dust, like fairy money. If it did— But it didn't. At the end of the day no complaint had been made about it, so after that we were satisfied that it was real gold, and dropped the anxiety out of our minds.

There was a question which we wanted to ask Father Peter, and finally we went there the second evening, a little diffidently, after drawing straws, and I asked it as casually as I could, though it did not sound as casual as I wanted, because I didn't know how:

"What is the Moral Sense, sir?"

He looked down, surprised, over his great spectacles, and said, "Why, it is the faculty which enables us to distinguish good from evil."

It threw some light, but not a glare, and I was a little disappointed, also to some degree embarrassed. He was waiting for me to go on, so, in default of anything else to say, I asked, "Is it valuable?"

"Valuable? Heavens! lad, it is the one thing that lifts man above the beasts that perish and makes him heir to immortality!"

This did not remind me of anything further to say, so I got out, with the other boys, and we went away with that indefinite sense you have often had of being filled but not fatted. They wanted me to explain but I was tired.

We passed out through the parlor, and there was Marget at the spinet teaching Marie Lueger. So one of the deserting pupils was back; and an influential one too; the others would follow. Marget jumped up and ran and thanked us again with tears in her eyes—this was the third time—for saving her and her uncle from being turned into the street, and we told her again we hadn't done it; but that was her way, she never could be grateful enough for anything a person did for her; so we let her have her say. And as we passed through the garden, there was Wilhelm Meidling sitting there waiting, for it was getting toward the edge of the evening, and he would be asking Marget to take a walk along the river with him when she was done with the lesson. He was a young lawyer, and succeeding fairly well and working his way along, little by little. He was very fond of Marget, and she of him. He had not deserted along with the others, but had stood his ground all through. His faithfulness was not lost on Marget and her uncle. He hadn't so very much talent but he was handsome and good, and these are a kind of talent themselves and help along. He asked us how the lesson was getting along, and we told him it was about done. And maybe it was so; we didn't know anything about it, but we judged it would please him, and it did, and it didn't cost us anything.

5

On the fourth day comes the astrologer from his crumbling old tower up the valley, where he had heard the news, I reckon. He had a private talk with us, and we told him what we could, for we were mightily in dread of him. He sat there studying and studying awhile to himself; then he asked:

"How many ducats did you say?"

"Eleven hundred and seven, sir."

Then he said, as if he were talking to himself: "It is ver-y singular. Yes . . . very strange. A curious coincidence." Then he began to ask questions, and went over the whole ground from the beginning, we answering. By and by he said: "Eleven hundred and six ducats. It is a large sum."

"Seven," said Seppi, correcting him.

"Oh, seven, was it? Of course a ducat more or less isn't of consequence, but you said eleven hundred and six before."

It would not have been safe for us to say he was mistaken, but we knew he was. Nikolaus said, "We ask pardon for the mistake, but we meant to say seven."

"Oh, it is no matter, lad; it was merely that I noticed the discrepancy. It is several days, and you cannot be expected to remember precisely. One is apt to be inexact when there is no particular circumstance to impress the count upon the memory."

"But there was one, sir," said Seppi, eagerly.

"What was it, my son?" asked the astrologer, indifferently.

"First, we all counted the piles of coin, each in turn, and all made it the same—eleven hundred and six. But I had slipped one out, for fun, when the count began, and now I slipped it back and said, 'I think there is a mistake—there are eleven hundred and seven; let us count again.' We did, and of course I was right. They were astonished; then I told how it came about."

The astrologer asked us if this was so, and we said it was.

"That settles it," he said. "I know the thief now. Lads, the money was stolen."

Then he went away, leaving us very much troubled, and wondering what he could mean. In about an hour we found out; for by that time it was all over the village that Father Peter had been arrested for stealing a great sum of money from the astrologer. Everybody's tongue was loose and going. Many said it was not in Father Peter's character and must be a mistake; but the others shook their heads and said misery and want could drive a suffering man to almost anything. About one detail there were no differences; all agreed that Father Peter's account of how the money came into his hands was just about unbelievable—it had such an impossible look. They said it might have come into the astrologer's hands in some such way, but into Father Peter's, never! Our characters began to suffer now. We were Father Peter's only witnesses; how much did he probably pay us to back up his fantastic tale? People talked that kind of talk to us pretty freely and frankly, and were full of scoffings when we begged them to believe really we had told only the truth. Our parents were harder on us than any one else. Our fathers said we were disgracing our families, and they commanded us to purge ourselves of our lie, and there was no limit to their anger when we continued to say we had spoken true. Our mothers cried over us and begged us to give back our bribe and get back our honest names and save our families from shame, and come out and honorably confess. And at last we were so worried and harassed that we tried to tell the whole thing, Satan and all—but no, it wouldn't come out. We were hoping and longing all the time that Satan would come and help us out of our trouble, but there was no sign of him.

Within an hour after the astrologer's talk with us, Father Peter was in prison and the money sealed up and in the hands of the officers of the law. The money was in a bag, and Solomon Isaacs said he had not touched it since he had counted it; his oath was taken that it was the same money, and that the amount was eleven hundred and seven ducats. Father Peter claimed trial by the ecclesiastical court, but our other priest, Father Adolf, said an ecclesiastical court hadn't jurisdiction over a suspended priest. The bishop upheld him. That settled it; the case would go to trial in the civil court. The court would not sit for some time to come. Wilhelm Meidling would be Father Peter's lawyer and do the best he could, of course, but he told us privately that a weak case on his side and all the power and prejudice on the other made the outlook bad.

So Marget's new happiness died a quick death. No friends came to condole with her, and none were expected; an unsigned note withdrew her invitation to the party. There would be no scholars to take lessons. How could she support herself? She could remain in the house, for the mortgage was paid off, though the government and not poor Solomon Isaacs had the mortgage-money in its grip for the present. Old Ursula, who was cook, chambermaid, housekeeper, laundress, and everything else for Father Peter, and had been Marget's nurse in earlier years, said God would provide. But she said that from habit, for she was a good Christian. She meant to help in the providing, to make sure, if she could find a way.

We boys wanted to go and see Marget and show friendliness for her, but our parents were afraid of offending the community and wouldn't let us. The astrologer was going around inflaming everybody against Father Peter, and saying he was an abandoned thief and had stolen eleven hundred and seven gold ducats from him. He said he knew he was a thief from that fact, for it was exactly the sum he had lost and which Father Peter pretended he had "found."

In the afternoon of the fourth day after the catastrophe old Ursula appeared at our house and asked for some washing to do, and begged my mother to keep this secret, to save Marget's pride, who would stop this project if she found it out, yet Marget had not enough to eat and was growing weak. Ursula was growing weak herself, and showed it; and she ate of the food that was offered her like a starving person, but could not be persuaded to carry any home, for Marget would not eat charity food. She took some clothes down to the stream to wash them, but we saw from the window that handling the bat was too much for her strength; so she was called back and a trifle of money offered her, which she was afraid to take lest Marget should suspect; then she took it, saying she would explain that she found it in the road. To keep it from being a lie and damning her soul, she got me to drop it while she watched; then she went along by there and found it, and exclaimed with surprise and joy, and picked it up and went her way. Like the rest of the village, she could tell every-day lies fast enough and without taking any precautions against fire and brimstone on their account; but this was a new kind of lie, and it had a dangerous look because she hadn't had any practice in it. After a week's practice it wouldn't have given her any trouble. It is the way we are made.

I was in trouble, for how would Marget live? Ursula could not find a coin in the road every day—perhaps not even a second one. And I was ashamed, too, for not having been near Marget, and she so in need of friends; but that was my parents' fault, not mine, and I couldn't help it.

I was walking along the path, feeling very downhearted, when a most cheery and tingling freshening-up sensation went rippling through me, and I was too glad for any words, for I knew by that sign that Satan was by. I had noticed it before. Next moment he was alongside of me and I was telling him all my trouble and what had been happening to Marget and her uncle. While we were talking we turned a curve and saw old Ursula resting in the shade of a tree, and she had a lean stray kitten in her lap and was petting it. I asked her where she got it, and she said it came out of the woods and followed her; and she said it probably hadn't any mother or any friends and she was going to take it home and take care of it. Satan said:

"I understand you are very poor. Why do you want to add another mouth to feed? Why don't you give it to some rich person?"

Ursula bridled at this and said: "Perhaps you would like to have it. You must be rich, with your fine clothes and quality airs." Then she sniffed and said: "Give it to the rich—the idea! The rich don't care for anybody but themselves; it's only the poor that have feeling for the poor, and help them. The poor and God. God will provide for this kitten."

"What makes you think so?"

Ursula's eyes snapped with anger. "Because I know it!" she said. "Not a sparrow falls to the ground without His seeing it."

"But it falls, just the same. What good is seeing it fall?"

Old Ursula's jaws worked, but she could not get any word out for the moment, she was so horrified. When she got her tongue she stormed out, "Go about your business, you puppy, or I will take a stick to you!"

I could not speak, I was so scared. I knew that with his notions about the human race Satan would consider it a matter of no consequence to strike her dead, there being "plenty more"; but my tongue stood still, I could give her no warning. But nothing happened; Satan remained tranquil—tranquil and indifferent. I suppose he could not be insulted by Ursula any more than the king could be insulted by a tumble-bug. The old woman jumped to her feet when she made her remark, and did it as briskly as a young girl. It had been many years since she had done the like of that. That was Satan's influence; he was a fresh breeze to the weak and the sick, wherever he came. His presence affected even the lean kitten, and it skipped to the ground and began to chase a leaf. This surprised Ursula, and she stood looking at the creature and nodding her head wonderingly, her anger quite forgotten.

"What's come over it?" she said. "Awhile ago it could hardly walk."

"You have not seen a kitten of that breed before," said Satan.

Ursula was not proposing to be friendly with the mocking stranger, and she gave him an ungentle look and retorted: "Who asked you to come here and pester me, I'd like to know? And what do you know about what I've seen and what I haven't seen?"

"You haven't seen a kitten with the hair-spines on its tongue pointing to the front, have you?"

"No—nor you, either."

"Well, examine this one and see."

Ursula was become pretty spry, but the kitten was spryer, and she could not catch it, and had to give it up. Then Satan said:

"Give it a name, and maybe it will come."

Ursula tried several names, but the kitten was not interested.

"Call it Agnes. Try that."

The creature answered to the name and came. Ursula examined its tongue. "Upon my word, it's true!" she said. "I have not seen this kind of a cat before. Is it yours?"

"No."

"Then how did you know its name so pat?"

"Because all cats of that breed are named Agnes; they will not answer to any other."

Ursula was impressed. "It is the most wonderful thing!" Then a shadow of trouble came into her face, for her superstitions were aroused, and she reluctantly put the creature down, saying: "I suppose I must let it go; I am not afraid—no, not exactly that, though the priest—well, I've heard people—indeed, many people . . . And, besides, it is quite well now and can take care of itself." She sighed, and turned to go, murmuring: "It is such a pretty one, too, and would be such company—and the house is so sad and lonesome these troubled days . . . Miss Marget so mournful and just a shadow, and the old master shut up in jail."

"It seems a pity not to keep it," said Satan.

Ursula turned quickly—just as if she were hoping some one would encourage her.

"Why?" she asked, wistfully.

"Because this breed brings luck."

"Does it? Is it true? Young man, do you know it to be true? How does it bring luck?"

"Well, it brings money, anyway."

Ursula looked disappointed. "Money? A cat bring money? The idea! You could never sell it here; people do not buy cats here; one can't even give them away." She turned to go.

"I don't mean sell it. I mean have an income from it. This kind is called the Lucky Cat. Its owner finds four silver groschen in his pocket every morning."

I saw the indignation rising in the old woman's face. She was insulted. This boy was making fun of her. That was her thought. She thrust her hands into her pockets and straightened up to give him a piece of her mind. Her temper was all up, and hot. Her mouth came open and let out three words of a bitter sentence, . . . then it fell silent, and the anger in her face turned to surprise or wonder or fear, or something, and she slowly brought out her hands from her pockets and opened them and held them so. In one was my piece of money, in the other lay four silver groschen. She gazed a little while, perhaps to see if the groschen would vanish away; then she said, fervently:

"It's true—it's true—and I'm ashamed and beg forgiveness, O dear master and benefactor!" And she ran to Satan and kissed his hand, over and over again, according to the Austrian custom.

In her heart she probably believed it was a witch-cat and an agent of the Devil; but no matter, it was all the more certain to be able to keep its contract and furnish a daily good living for the family, for in matters of finance even the piousest of our peasants would have more confidence in an arrangement with the Devil than with an archangel. Ursula started homeward with Agnes in her arms, and I said I wished I had her privilege of seeing Marget.

Then I caught my breath, for we were there. There in the parlor, and Marget standing looking at us, astonished. She was feeble and pale, but I knew that those conditions would not last in Satan's atmosphere, and it turned out so. I introduced Satan—that is, Philip Traum—and we sat down and talked. There was no constraint. We were simple folk, in our village, and when a stranger was a pleasant person we were soon friends. Marget wondered how we got in without her hearing us. Traum said the door was open, and we walked in and waited until she should turn around and greet us. This was not true; no door was open; we entered through the walls or the roof or down the chimney, or somehow; but no matter, what Satan wished a person to believe, the person was sure to believe, and so Marget was quite satisfied with that explanation. And then the main part of her mind was on Traum, anyway; she couldn't keep her eyes off him, he was so beautiful. That gratified me, and made me proud. I hoped he would show off some, but he didn't. He seemed only interested in being friendly and telling lies. He said he was an orphan. That made Marget pity him. The water came into her eyes. He said he had never known his mamma; she passed away while he was a young thing; and said his papa was in shattered health, and had no property to speak of—in fact, none of any earthly value—but he had an uncle in business down in the tropics, and he was very well off and had a monopoly, and it was from his uncle that he drew his support. The very mention of a kind uncle was enough to remind Marget of her own, and her eyes filled again. She said she hoped their two uncles would meet, some day. It made me shudder. Philip said he hoped so, too; and that made me shudder again.

"Maybe they will," said Marget. "Does your uncle travel much?"

"Oh yes, he goes all about; he has business everywhere."

And so they went on chatting, and poor Marget forgot her sorrow for one little while, anyway. It was probably the only really bright and cheery hour she had known lately. I saw she liked Philip, and I knew she would. And when he told her he was studying for the ministry I could see that she liked him better than ever. And then, when he promised to get her admitted to the jail so that she could see her uncle, that was the capstone. He said he would give the guards a little present, and she must always go in the evening after dark, and say nothing "but just show this paper and pass in, and show it again when you come out"—and he scribbled some queer marks on the paper and gave it to her, and she was ever so thankful, and right away was in a fever for the sun to go down; for in that old, cruel time prisoners were not allowed to see their friends, and sometimes they spent years in the jails without ever seeing a friendly face. I judged that the marks on the paper were an enchantment, and that the guards would not know what they were doing, nor have any memory of it afterward; and that was indeed the way of it. Ursula put her head in at the door now and said:

"Supper's ready, miss." Then she saw us and looked frightened, and motioned me to come to her, which I did, and she asked if we had told about the cat. I said no, and she was relieved and said please don't, for if Miss Marget knew, she would think it was an unholy cat and would send for a priest and have its gifts all purified out of it, and then there wouldn't be any more dividends. So I said we wouldn't tell, and she was satisfied. Then I was beginning to say good-by to Marget, but Satan interrupted and said, ever so politely—well, I don't remember just the words, but anyway he as good as invited himself to supper, and me, too. Of course, Marget was miserably embarrassed, for she had no reason to suppose there would be half enough for a sick bird. Ursula heard him, and she came straight into the room, not a bit pleased. At first she was astonished to see Marget looking so fresh and rosy, and said so; then she spoke up in her native tongue, which was Bohemian, and said—as I learned afterward—"Send him away, Miss Marget; there's not victuals enough."

Before Marget could speak, Satan had the word, and was talking back to Ursula in her own language—which was a surprise to her, and for her mistress, too. He said. "Didn't I see you down the road awhile ago?"

"Yes, sir."

"Ah, that pleases me; I see you remember me." He stepped to her and whispered: "I told you it is a Lucky Cat. Don't be troubled; it will provide."

That sponged the slate of Ursula's feelings clean of its anxieties, and a deep, financial joy shone in her eyes. The cat's value was augmenting. It was getting full time for Marget to take some sort of notice of Satan's invitation, and she did it in the best way, the honest way that was natural to her. She said she had little to offer, but that we were welcome if he would share it with her.

We had supper in the kitchen, and Ursula waited at table. A small fish was in the frying-pan, crisp and brown and tempting, and one could see that Marget was not expecting such respectable food as this. Ursula brought it, and Marget divided it between Satan and me, declining to take any of it herself; and was beginning to say she did not care for fish to-day, but she did not finish the remark. It was because she noticed that another fish had appeared in the pan. She looked surprised, but did not say anything. She probably meant to inquire of Ursula about this later. There were other surprises: flesh and game and wines and fruits—things which had been strangers in that house lately; but Marget made no exclamations, and now even looked unsurprised, which was Satan's influence, of course. Satan talked right along, and was entertaining, and made the time pass pleasantly and cheerfully; and although he told a good many lies, it was no harm in him, for he was only an angel and did not know any better. They do not know right from wrong; I knew this, because I remembered what he had said about it. He got on the good side of Ursula. He praised her to Marget, confidentially, but speaking just loud enough for Ursula to hear. He said she was a fine woman, and he hoped some day to bring her and his uncle together. Very soon Ursula was mincing and simpering around in a ridiculous, girly way, and smoothing out her gown and prinking at herself like a foolish old hen, and all the time pretending she was not hearing what Satan was saying. I was ashamed, for it showed us to be what Satan considered us, a silly race and trivial. Satan said his uncle entertained a great deal, and to have a clever woman presiding over the festivities would double the attractions of the place.

"But your uncle is a gentleman, isn't he?" asked Marget.

"Yes," said Satan indifferently; "some even call him a Prince, out of compliment, but he is not bigoted; to him personal merit is everything, rank nothing."

My hand was hanging down by my chair; Agnes came along and licked it; by this act a secret was revealed. I started to say, "It is all a mistake; this is just a common, ordinary cat; the hair-needles on her tongue point inward, not outward." But the words did not come, because they couldn't. Satan smiled upon me, and I understood.

When it was dark Marget took food and wine and fruit, in a basket, and hurried away to the jail, and Satan and I walked toward my home. I was thinking to myself that I should like to see what the inside of the jail was like; Satan overheard the thought, and the next moment we were in the jail. We were in the torture-chamber, Satan said. The rack was there, and the other instruments, and there was a smoky lantern or two hanging on the walls and helping to make the place look dim and dreadful. There were people there—and executioners—but as they took no notice of us, it meant that we were invisible. A young man lay bound, and Satan said he was suspected of being a heretic, and the executioners were about to inquire into it. They asked the man to confess to the charge, and he said he could not, for it was not true. Then they drove splinter after splinter under his nails, and he shrieked with the pain. Satan was not disturbed, but I could not endure it, and had to be whisked out of there. I was faint and sick, but the fresh air revived me, and we walked toward my home. I said it was a brutal thing.

"No, it was a human thing. You should not insult the brutes by such a misuse of that word; they have not deserved it," and he went on talking like that. "It is like your paltry race—always lying, always claiming virtues which it hasn't got, always denying them to the higher animals, which alone possess them. No brute ever does a cruel thing—that is the monopoly of those with the Moral Sense. When a brute inflicts pain he does it innocently; it is not wrong; for him there is no such thing as wrong. And he does not inflict pain for the pleasure of inflicting it—only man does that. Inspired by that mongrel Moral Sense of his! A sense whose function is to distinguish between right and wrong, with liberty to choose which of them he will do. Now what advantage can he get out of that? He is always choosing, and in nine cases out of ten he prefers the wrong. There shouldn't be any wrong; and without the Moral Sense there couldn't be any. And yet he is such an unreasoning creature that he is not able to perceive that the Moral Sense degrades him to the bottom layer of animated beings and is a shameful possession. Are you feeling better? Let me show you something."

6

In a moment we were in a French village. We walked through a great factory of some sort, where men and women and little children were toiling in heat and dirt and a fog of dust; and they were clothed in rags, and drooped at their work, for they were worn and half starved, and weak and drowsy. Satan said:

"It is some more Moral Sense. The proprietors are rich, and very holy; but the wage they pay to these poor brothers and sisters of theirs is only enough to keep them from dropping dead with hunger. The work-hours are fourteen per day, winter and summer—from six in the morning till eight at night—little children and all. And they walk to and from the pigsties which they inhabit—four miles each way, through mud and slush, rain, snow, sleet, and storm, daily, year in and year out. They get four hours of sleep. They kennel together, three families in a room, in unimaginable filth and stench; and disease comes, and they die off like flies. Have they committed a crime, these mangy things? No. What have they done, that they are punished so? Nothing at all, except getting themselves born into your foolish race. You have seen how they treat a misdoer there in the jail; now you see how they treat the innocent and the worthy. Is your race logical? Are these ill-smelling innocents better off than that heretic? Indeed, no; his punishment is trivial compared with theirs. They broke him on the wheel and smashed him to rags and pulp after we left, and he is dead now, and free of your precious race; but these poor slaves here—why, they have been dying for years, and some of them will not escape from life for years to come. It is the Moral Sense which teaches the factory proprietors the difference between right and wrong—you perceive the result. They think themselves better than dogs. Ah, you are such an illogical, unreasoning race! And paltry—oh, unspeakably!"

Then he dropped all seriousness and just overstrained himself making fun of us, and deriding our pride in our warlike deeds, our great heroes, our imperishable fames, our mighty kings, our ancient aristocracies, our venerable history—and laughed and laughed till it was enough to make a person sick to hear him; and finally he sobered a little and said, "But, after all, it is not all ridiculous; there is a sort of pathos about it when one remembers how few are your days, how childish your pomps, and what shadows you are!"

Presently all things vanished suddenly from my sight, and I knew what it meant. The next moment we were walking along in our village; and down toward the river I saw the twinkling lights of the Golden Stag. Then in the dark I heard a joyful cry:

"He's come again!"

It was Seppi Wohlmeyer. He had felt his blood leap and his spirits rise in a way that could mean only one thing, and he knew Satan was near, although it was too dark to see him. He came to us, and we walked along together, and Seppi poured out his gladness like water. It was as if he were a lover and had found his sweetheart who had been lost. Seppi was a smart and animated boy, and had enthusiasm and expression, and was a contrast to Nikolaus and me. He was full of the last new mystery, now—the disappearance of Hans Oppert, the village loafer. People were beginning to be curious about it, he said. He did not say anxious—curious was the right word, and strong enough. No one had seen Hans for a couple of days.

"Not since he did that brutal thing, you know," he said.

"What brutal thing?" It was Satan that asked.

"Well, he is always clubbing his dog, which is a good dog and his only friend, and is faithful, and loves him, and does no one any harm; and two days ago he was at it again, just for nothing—just for pleasure—and the dog was howling and begging, and Theodor and I begged, too, but he threatened us, and struck the dog again with all his might and knocked one of his eyes out, and he said to us, 'There I hope you are satisfied now; that's what you have got for him by your damned meddling'—and he laughed, the heartless brute." Seppi's voice trembled with pity and anger. I guessed what Satan would say, and he said it.

"There is that misused word again—that shabby slander. Brutes do not act like that, but only men."

"Well, it was inhuman, anyway."

"No, it wasn't, Seppi; it was human—quite distinctly human. It is not pleasant to hear you libel the higher animals by attributing to them dispositions which they are free from, and which are found nowhere but in the human heart. None of the higher animals is tainted with the disease called the Moral Sense. Purify your language, Seppi; drop those lying phrases out of it."

He spoke pretty sternly—for him—and I was sorry I hadn't warned Seppi to be more particular about the word he used. I knew how he was feeling. He would not want to offend Satan; he would rather offend all his kin. There was an uncomfortable silence, but relief soon came, for that poor dog came along now, with his eye hanging down, and went straight to Satan, and began to moan and mutter brokenly, and Satan began to answer in the same way, and it was plain that they were talking together in the dog language. We all sat down in the grass, in the moonlight, for the clouds were breaking away now, and Satan took the dog's head in his lap and put the eye back in its place, and the dog was comfortable, and he wagged his tail and licked Satan's hand, and looked thankful and said the same; I knew he was saying it, though I did not understand the words. Then the two talked together a bit, and Satan said:

"He says his master was drunk."

"Yes, he was," said we.

"And an hour later he fell over the precipice there beyond the Cliff Pasture."

"We know the place; it is three miles from here."

"And the dog has been often to the village, begging people to go there, but he was only driven away and not listened to."

We remembered it, but hadn't understood what he wanted.

"He only wanted help for the man who had misused him, and he thought only of that, and has had no food nor sought any. He has watched by his master two nights. What do you think of your race? Is heaven reserved for it, and this dog ruled out, as your teachers tell you? Can your race add anything to this dog's stock of morals and magnanimities?" He spoke to the creature, who jumped up, eager and happy, and apparently ready for orders and impatient to execute them. "Get some men; go with the dog—he will show you that carrion; and take a priest along to arrange about insurance, for death is near."

With the last word he vanished, to our sorrow and disappointment. We got the men and Father Adolf, and we saw the man die. Nobody cared but the dog; he mourned and grieved, and licked the dead face, and could not be comforted. We buried him where he was, and without a coffin, for he had no money, and no friend but the dog. If we had been an hour earlier the priest would have been in time to send that poor creature to heaven, but now he was gone down into the awful fires, to burn forever. It seemed such a pity that in a world where so many people have difficulty to put in their time, one little hour could not have been spared for this poor creature who needed it so much, and to whom it would have made the difference between eternal joy and eternal pain. It gave an appalling idea of the value of an hour, and I thought I could never waste one again without remorse and terror. Seppi was depressed and grieved, and said it must be so much better to be a dog and not run such awful risks. We took this one home with us and kept him for our own. Seppi had a very good thought as we were walking along, and it cheered us up and made us feel much better. He said the dog had forgiven the man that had wronged him so, and maybe God would accept that absolution.

There was a very dull week, now, for Satan did not come, nothing much was going on, and we boys could not venture to go and see Marget, because the nights were moonlit and our parents might find us out if we tried. But we came across Ursula a couple of times taking a walk in the meadows beyond the river to air the cat, and we learned from her that things were going well. She had natty new clothes on and bore a prosperous look. The four groschen a day were arriving without a break, but were not being spent for food and wine and such things—the cat attended to all that.

Marget was enduring her forsakenness and isolation fairly well, all things considered, and was cheerful, by help of Wilhelm Meidling. She spent an hour or two every night in the jail with her uncle, and had fattened him up with the cat's contributions. But she was curious to know more about Philip Traum, and hoped I would bring him again. Ursula was curious about him herself, and asked a good many questions about his uncle. It made the boys laugh, for I had told them the nonsense Satan had been stuffing her with. She got no satisfaction out of us, our tongues being tied.

Ursula gave us a small item of information: money being plenty now, she had taken on a servant to help about the house and run errands. She tried to tell it in a commonplace, matter-of-course way, but she was so set up by it and so vain of it that her pride in it leaked out pretty plainly. It was beautiful to see her veiled delight in this grandeur, poor old thing, but when we heard the name of the servant we wondered if she had been altogether wise; for although we were young, and often thoughtless, we had fairly good perception on some matters. This boy was Gottfried Narr, a dull, good creature, with no harm in him and nothing against him personally; still, he was under a cloud, and properly so, for it had not been six months since a social blight had mildewed the family—his grandmother had been burned as a witch. When that kind of a malady is in the blood it does not always come out with just one burning. Just now was not a good time for Ursula and Marget to be having dealings with a member of such a family, for the witch-terror had risen higher during the past year than it had ever reached in the memory of the oldest villagers. The mere mention of a witch was almost enough to frighten us out of our wits. This was natural enough, because of late years there were more kinds of witches than there used to be; in old times it had been only old women, but of late years they were of all ages—even children of eight and nine; it was getting so that anybody might turn out to be a familiar of the Devil—age and sex hadn't anything to do with it. In our little region we had tried to extirpate the witches, but the more of them we burned the more of the breed rose up in their places.

Once, in a school for girls only ten miles away, the teachers found that the back of one of the girls was all red and inflamed, and they were greatly frightened, believing it to be the Devil's marks. The girl was scared, and begged them not to denounce her, and said it was only fleas; but of course it would not do to let the matter rest there. All the girls were examined, and eleven out of the fifty were badly marked, the rest less so. A commission was appointed, but the eleven only cried for their mothers and would not confess. Then they were shut up, each by herself, in the dark, and put on black bread and water for ten days and nights; and by that time they were haggard and wild, and their eyes were dry and they did not cry any more, but only sat and mumbled, and would not take the food. Then one of them confessed, and said they had often ridden through the air on broomsticks to the witches' Sabbath, and in a bleak place high up in the mountains had danced and drunk and caroused with several hundred other witches and the Evil One, and all had conducted themselves in a scandalous way and had reviled the priests and blasphemed God. That is what she said—not in narrative form, for she was not able to remember any of the details without having them called to her mind one after the other; but the commission did that, for they knew just what questions to ask, they being all written down for the use of witch-commissioners two centuries before. They asked, "Did you do so and so?" and she always said yes, and looked weary and tired, and took no interest in it. And so when the other ten heard that this one confessed, they confessed, too, and answered yes to the questions. Then they were burned at the stake all together, which was just and right; and everybody went from all the countryside to see it. I went, too; but when I saw that one of them was a bonny, sweet girl I used to play with, and looked so pitiful there chained to the stake, and her mother crying over her and devouring her with kisses and clinging around her neck, and saying, "Oh, my God! oh, my God!" it was too dreadful, and I went away.

It was bitter cold weather when Gottfried's grandmother was burned. It was charged that she had cured bad headaches by kneading the person's head and neck with her fingers—as she said—but really by the Devil's help, as everybody knew. They were going to examine her, but she stopped them, and confessed straight off that her power was from the Devil. So they appointed to burn her next morning, early, in our market-square. The officer who was to prepare the fire was there first, and prepared it. She was there next—brought by the constables, who left her and went to fetch another witch. Her family did not come with her. They might be reviled, maybe stoned, if the people were excited. I came, and gave her an apple. She was squatting at the fire, warming herself and waiting; and her old lips and hands were blue with the cold. A stranger came next. He was a traveler, passing through; and he spoke to her gently, and, seeing nobody but me there to hear, said he was sorry for her. And he asked if what she confessed was true, and she said no. He looked surprised and still more sorry then, and asked her:

"Then why did you confess?"

"I am old and very poor," she said, "and I work for my living. There was no way but to confess. If I hadn't they might have set me free. That would ruin me, for no one would forget that I had been suspected of being a witch, and so I would get no more work, and wherever I went they would set the dogs on me. In a little while I would starve. The fire is best; it is soon over. You have been good to me, you two, and I thank you."

She snuggled closer to the fire, and put out her hands to warm them, the snow-flakes descending soft and still on her old gray head and making it white and whiter. The crowd was gathering now, and an egg came flying and struck her in the eye, and broke and ran down her face. There was a laugh at that.

I told Satan all about the eleven girls and the old woman, once, but it did not affect him. He only said it was the human race, and what the human race did was of no consequence. And he said he had seen it made; and it was not made of clay; it was made of mud—part of it was, anyway. I knew what he meant by that—the Moral Sense. He saw the thought in my head, and it tickled him and made him laugh. Then he called a bullock out of a pasture and petted it and talked with it, and said:

"There—he wouldn't drive children mad with hunger and fright and loneliness, and then burn them for confessing to things invented for them which had never happened. And neither would he break the hearts of innocent, poor old women and make them afraid to trust themselves among their own race; and he would not insult them in their death-agony. For he is not besmirched with the Moral Sense, but is as the angels are, and knows no wrong, and never does it."

Lovely as he was, Satan could be cruelly offensive when he chose; and he always chose when the human race was brought to his attention. He always turned up his nose at it, and never had a kind word for it.

Well, as I was saying, we boys doubted if it was a good time for Ursula to be hiring a member of the Narr family. We were right. When the people found it out they were naturally indignant. And, moreover, since

Marget and Ursula hadn't enough to eat themselves, where was the money coming from to feed another mouth? That is what they wanted to know; and in order to find out they stopped avoiding Gottfried and began to seek his society and have sociable conversations with him. He was pleased—not thinking any harm and not seeing the trap—and so he talked innocently along, and was no discreeter than a cow.

"Money!" he said; "they've got plenty of it. They pay me two groschen a week, besides my keep. And they live on the fat of the land, I can tell you; the prince himself can't beat their table."

This astonishing statement was conveyed by the astrologer to Father Adolf on a Sunday morning when he was returning from mass. He was deeply moved, and said:

"This must be looked into."

He said there must be witchcraft at the bottom of it, and told the villagers to resume relations with Marget and Ursula in a private and unostentatious way, and keep both eyes open. They were told to keep their own counsel and not rouse the suspicions of the household. The villagers were at first a bit reluctant to enter such a dreadful place, but the priest said they would be under his protection while there, and no harm could come to them, particularly if they carried a trifle of holy water along and kept their beads and crosses handy. This satisfied them and made them willing to go; envy and malice made the baser sort even eager to go.

And so poor Marget began to have company again, and was as pleased as a cat. She was like 'most anybody else—just human, and happy in her prosperities and not averse from showing them off a little; and she was humanly grateful to have the warm shoulder turned to her and be smiled upon by her friends and the village again; for of all the hard things to bear, to be cut by your neighbors and left in contemptuous solitude is maybe the hardest.

The bars were down, and we could all go there now, and we did—our parents and all—day after day. The cat began to strain herself. She provided the top of everything for those companies, and in abundance—among them many a dish and many a wine which they had not tasted before and which they had not even heard of except at second-hand from the prince's servants. And the tableware was much above ordinary, too.

Marget was troubled at times, and pursued Ursula with questions to an uncomfortable degree; but Ursula stood her ground and stuck to it that it was Providence, and said no word about the cat. Marget knew that nothing was impossible to Providence, but she could not help having doubts that this effort was from there, though she was afraid to say so, lest disaster come of it. Witchcraft occurred to her, but she put the thought aside, for this was before Gottfried joined the household, and she knew Ursula was pious and a bitter hater of witches. By the time Gottfried arrived Providence was established, unshakably intrenched, and getting all the gratitude. The cat made no murmur, but went on composedly improving in style and prodigality by experience.

In any community, big or little, there is always a fair proportion of people who are not malicious or unkind by nature, and who never do unkind things except when they are overmastered by fear, or when their self-interest is greatly in danger, or some such matter as that. Eseldorf had its proportion of such people, and ordinarily their good and gentle influence was felt, but these were not ordinary times—on account of the witch-dread—and so we did not seem to have any gentle and compassionate hearts left, to speak of. Every person was frightened at the unaccountable state of things at Marget's house, not doubting that witchcraft was at the bottom of it, and fright frenzied their reason. Naturally there were some who pitied Marget and Ursula for the danger that was gathering about them, but naturally they did not say so; it would not have been safe. So the others had it all their own way, and there was none to advise the ignorant girl and the foolish woman and warn them to modify their doings. We boys wanted to warn them, but we backed down when it came to the pinch, being afraid. We found that we were not manly enough nor brave enough to do a generous action when there was a chance that it could get us into trouble. Neither of us confessed this poor spirit to the others, but did as other people would have done—dropped the subject and talked about something else. And I knew we all felt mean, eating and drinking Marget's fine things along with those companies of spies, and petting her and complimenting her with the rest, and seeing with self-reproach how foolishly happy she was, and never saying a word to put her on her guard. And, indeed, she was happy, and as proud as a princess, and so grateful to have friends again. And all the time these people were watching with all their eyes and reporting all they saw to Father Adolf.

But he couldn't make head or tail of the situation. There must be an enchanter somewhere on the premises, but who was it? Marget was not seen to do any jugglery, nor was Ursula, nor yet Gottfried; and still the wines and dainties never ran short, and a guest could not call for a thing and not get it. To produce these effects was usual enough with witches and enchanters—that part of it was not new; but to do it without any incantations, or even any rumblings or earthquakes or lightnings or apparitions—that was new, novel, wholly irregular. There was nothing in the books like this. Enchanted things were always unreal. Gold turned to dirt in an unenchanted atmosphere, food withered away and vanished. But this test failed in the present case. The spies brought samples: Father Adolph prayed over them, exorcised them, but it did no good; they remained sound and real, they yielded to natural decay only, and took the usual time to do it.

Father Adolf was not merely puzzled, he was also exasperated; for these evidences very nearly convinced him—privately—that there was no witchcraft in the matter. It did not wholly convince him, for this could be a new kind of witchcraft. There was a way to find out as to this: if this prodigal abundance of provender was not brought in from the outside, but produced on the premises, there was witchcraft, sure.

7

Marget announced a party and invited forty people; the date for it was seven days away. This was a fine opportunity. Marget's house stood by itself, and it could be easily watched. All the week it was watched night and day. Marget's household went out and in as usual, but they carried nothing in their hands, and neither they nor others brought anything to the house. This was ascertained. Evidently rations for forty people were not being fetched. If they were furnished any sustenance it would have to be made on the premises. It was true that Marget went out with a basket every evening, but the spies ascertained that she always brought it back empty.

The guests arrived at noon and filled the place. Father Adolf followed; also, after a little, the astrologer, without invitation. The spies had informed him that neither at the back nor the front had any parcels been brought in. He entered and found the eating and drinking going on finely, and everything progressing in a lively and festive way. He glanced around and perceived that many of the cooked delicacies and all of the native and foreign fruits were of a perishable character, and he also recognized that these were fresh and perfect. No apparitions, no incantations, no thunder. That settled it. This was witchcraft. And not only that, but of a new kind—a kind never dreamed of before. It was a prodigious power, an illustrious power; he resolved to discover its secret. The announcement of it would resound throughout the world, penetrate to the remotest lands, paralyze all the nations with amazement—and carry his name with it, and make him renowned forever. It was a wonderful piece of luck, a splendid piece of luck; the glory of it made him dizzy.

All the house made room for him; Marget politely seated him; Ursula ordered Gottfried to bring a special table for him. Then she decked it and furnished it, and asked for his orders.

"Bring me what you will," he said.

The two servants brought supplies from the pantry, together with white wine and red—a bottle of each. The astrologer, who very likely had never seen such delicacies before, poured out a beaker of red wine, drank it off, poured another, then began to eat with a grand appetite.

I was not expecting Satan, for it was more than a week since I had seen or heard of him but now he came in—I knew it by the feel, though people were in the way and I could not see him. I heard him apologizing for intruding; and he was going away, but Marget urged him to stay, and he thanked her and stayed. She brought him along, introducing him to the girls, and to Meidling, and to some of the elders; and there was quite a rustle of whispers: "It's the young stranger we hear so much about and can't get sight of, he is away so much." "Dear, dear, but he is beautiful—what is his name?" "Philip Traum." "Ah, it fits him!" (You see, "Traum" is German for "Dream.") "What does he do?" "Studying for the ministry, they say." "His face is his fortune—he'll be a cardinal some day." "Where is his home?" "Away down somewhere in the tropics, they say—has a rich uncle down there." And so on. He made his way at once; everybody was anxious to know him and talk with him. Everybody noticed how cool and fresh it was all of a sudden, and wondered at it, for they could see that the sun was beating down the same as before, outside, and the sky was clear of clouds, but no one guessed the reason, of course.

The astrologer had drunk his second beaker; he poured out a third. He set the bottle down, and by accident overturned it. He seized it before much was spilled, and held it up to the light, saying, "What a pity—it is royal wine." Then his face lighted with joy or triumph, or something, and he said, "Quick! Bring a bowl."

It was brought—a four-quart one. He took up that two-pint bottle and began to pour; went on pouring, the red liquor gurgling and gushing into the white bowl and rising higher and higher up its sides, everybody staring and holding their breath—and presently the bowl was full to the brim.

"Look at the bottle," he said, holding it up, "it is full yet!" I glanced at Satan, and in that moment he vanished. Then Father Adolf rose up, flushed and excited, crossed himself, and began to thunder in his great voice, "This house is bewitched and accursed!" People began to cry and shriek and crowd toward the door. "I summon this detected household to—"

His words were cut off short. His face became red, then purple, but he could not utter another sound. Then I saw Satan, a transparent film, melt into the astrologer's body; then the astrologer put up his hand, and apparently in his own voice said, "Wait—remain where you are." All stopped where they stood. "Bring a funnel!" Ursula brought it, trembling and scared, and he stuck it in the bottle and took up the great bowl and began to pour the wine back, the people gazing and dazed with astonishment, for they knew the bottle was already full before he began. He emptied the whole of the bowl into the bottle, then smiled out over the room, chuckled, and said, indifferently, "It is nothing—anybody can do it! With my powers I can even do much more."

A frightened cry burst out everywhere. "Oh, my God, he is possessed!"

and there was a tumultuous rush for the door which swiftly emptied the house of all who did not belong in it except us boys and Meidling. We boys knew the secret, and would have told it if we could, but we couldn't. We were very thankful to Satan for furnishing that good help at the needful time.

Marget was pale, and crying; Meidling looked kind of petrified; Ursula the same; but Gottfried was the worst—he couldn't stand, he was so weak and scared. For he was of a witch family, you know, and it would be bad for him to be suspected. Agnes came loafing in, looking pious and unaware, and wanted to rub up against Ursula and be petted, but Ursula was afraid of her and shrank away from her, but pretending she was not meaning any incivility, for she knew very well it wouldn't answer to have strained relations with that kind of a cat. But we boys took Agnes and petted her, for Satan would not have befriended her if he had not had a good opinion of her, and that was indorsement enough for us. He seemed to trust anything that hadn't the Moral Sense.

Outside, the guests, panic-stricken, scattered in every direction and fled in a pitiable state of terror; and such a tumult as they made with their running and sobbing and shrieking and shouting that soon all the village came flocking from their houses to see what had happened, and they thronged the street and shouldered and jostled one another in excitement and fright; and then Father Adolf appeared, and they fell apart in two walls like the cloven Red Sea, and presently down this lane the astrologer came striding and mumbling, and where he passed the lanes surged back in packed masses, and fell silent with awe, and their eyes stared and their breasts heaved, and several women fainted; and when he was gone by the crowd swarmed together and followed him at a distance, talking excitedly and asking questions and finding out the facts. Finding out the facts and passing them on to others, with improvements—improvements which soon enlarged the bowl of wine to a barrel, and made the one bottle hold it all and yet remain empty to the last.

When the astrologer reached the market-square he went straight to a juggler, fantastically dressed, who was keeping three brass balls in the air, and took them from him and faced around upon the approaching crowd and said: "This poor clown is ignorant of his art. Come forward and see an expert perform."

So saying, he tossed the balls up one after another and set them whirling in a slender bright oval in the air, and added another, then another and another, and soon—no one seeing whence he got them—adding, adding, adding, the oval lengthening all the time, his hands moving so swiftly that they were just a web or a blur and not distinguishable as hands; and such as counted said there were now a hundred balls in the air. The spinning great oval reached up twenty feet in the air and was a shining and glinting and wonderful sight. Then he folded his arms and told the balls to go on spinning without his help—and they did it. After a couple of minutes he said, "There, that will do," and the oval broke and came crashing down, and the balls scattered abroad and rolled every whither. And wherever one of them came the people fell back in dread, and no one would touch it. It made him laugh, and he scoffed at the people and called them cowards and old women. Then he turned and saw the tight-rope, and said foolish people were daily wasting their money to see a clumsy and ignorant varlet degrade that beautiful art; now they should see the work of a master. With that he made a spring into the air and lit firm on his feet on the rope. Then he hopped the whole length of it back and forth on one foot, with his hands clasped over his eyes; and next he began to throw somersaults, both backward and forward, and threw twenty-seven.

The people murmured, for the astrologer was old, and always before had been halting of movement and at times even lame, but he was nimble enough now and went on with his antics in the liveliest manner. Finally he sprang lightly down and walked away, and passed up the road and around the corner and disappeared. Then that great, pale, silent, solid crowd drew a deep breath and looked into one another's faces as if they said: "Was it real? Did you see it, or was it only I—and I was dreaming?" Then they broke into a low murmur of talking, and fell apart in couples, and moved toward their homes, still talking in that awed way, with faces close together and laying a hand on an arm and making other such gestures as people make when they have been deeply impressed by something.

We boys followed behind our fathers, and listened, catching all we could of what they said; and when they sat down in our house and continued their talk they still had us for company. They were in a sad mood, for it was certain, they said, that disaster for the village must follow this awful visitation of witches and devils. Then my father remembered that Father Adolf had been struck dumb at the moment of his denunciation.

"They have not ventured to lay their hands upon an anointed servant of God before," he said; "and how they could have dared it this time I cannot make out, for he wore his crucifix. Isn't it so?"

"Yes," said the others, "we saw it."

"It is serious, friends, it is very serious. Always before, we had a protection. It has failed."

The others shook, as with a sort of chill, and muttered those words over—"It has failed." "God has forsaken us."

"It is true," said Seppi Wohlmeyer's father; "there is nowhere to look for help."

"The people will realize this," said Nikolaus' father, the judge, "and despair will take away their courage and their energies. We have indeed fallen upon evil times."

He sighed, and Wohlmeyer said, in a troubled voice, "The report of it all will go about the country, and our village will be shunned as being under the displeasure of God. The Golden Stag will know hard times."

"True, neighbor," said my father, "all of us will suffer—all in repute, many in estate. And, good God!—"

"What is it?"

"That can come—to finish us!"

"Name it—um Gottes Willen!"

"The Interdict!"

It smote like a thunderclap, and they were like to swoon with the terror of it. Then the dread of this calamity roused their energies, and they stopped brooding and began to consider ways to avert it. They discussed this, that, and the other way, and talked till the afternoon was far spent, then confessed that at present they could arrive at no decision. So they parted sorrowfully, with oppressed hearts which were filled with bodings.

While they were saying their parting words I slipped out and set my course for Marget's house to see what was happening there. I met many people, but none of them greeted me. It ought to have been surprising, but it was not, for they were so distraught with fear and dread that they were not in their right minds, I think; they were white and haggard, and walked like persons in a dream, their eyes open but seeing nothing, their lips moving but uttering nothing, and worriedly clasping and unclasping their hands without knowing it.

At Marget's it was like a funeral. She and Wilhelm sat together on the sofa, but said nothing, and not even holding hands. Both were steeped in gloom, and Marget's eyes were red from the crying she had been doing. She said:

"I have been begging him to go, and come no more, and so save himself alive. I cannot bear to be his murderer. This house is bewitched, and no inmate will escape the fire. But he will not go, and he will be lost with the rest."

Wilhelm said he would not go; if there was danger for her, his place was by her, and there he would remain. Then she began to cry again, and it was all so mournful that I wished I had stayed away. There was a knock, now, and Satan came in, fresh and cheery and beautiful, and brought that winy atmosphere of his and changed the whole thing. He never said a word about what had been happening, nor about the awful fears which were freezing the blood in the hearts of the community, but began to talk and rattle on about all manner of gay and pleasant things: and next about music—an artful stroke which cleared away the remnant of Marget's depression and brought her spirits and her interests broad awake. She had not heard any one talk so well and so knowingly on that subject before, and she was so uplifted by it and so charmed that what she was feeling lit up her face and came out in her words; and Wilhelm noticed it and did not look as pleased as he ought to have done. And next Satan branched off into poetry, and recited some, and did it well, and Marget was charmed again; and again Wilhelm was not as pleased as he ought to have been, and this time Marget noticed it and was remorseful.

I fell asleep to pleasant music that night—the patter of rain upon the panes and the dull growling of distant thunder. Away in the night Satan came and roused me and said: "Come with me. Where shall we go?"

"Anywhere—so it is with you."

Then there was a fierce glare of sunlight, and he said, "This is China."

That was a grand surprise, and made me sort of drunk with vanity and gladness to think I had come so far—so much, much farther than anybody else in our village, including Bartel Sperling, who had such a great opinion of his travels. We buzzed around over that empire for more than half an hour, and saw the whole of it. It was wonderful, the spectacles we saw; and some were beautiful, others too horrible to think. For instance—However, I may go into that by and by, and also why Satan chose China for this excursion instead of another place; it would interrupt my tale to do it now. Finally we stopped flitting and lit.

We sat upon a mountain commanding a vast landscape of mountain-range and gorge and valley and plain and river, with cities and villages slumbering in the sunlight, and a glimpse of blue sea on the farther verge. It was a tranquil and dreamy picture, beautiful to the eye and restful to the spirit. If we could only make a change like that whenever we wanted to, the world would be easier to live in than it is, for change of scene shifts the mind's burdens to the other shoulder and banishes old, shop-worn weariness from mind and body both.

We talked together, and I had the idea of trying to reform Satan and persuade him to lead a better life. I told him about all those things he had been doing, and begged him to be more considerate and stop making people unhappy. I said I knew he did not mean any harm, but that he ought to stop and consider the possible consequences of a thing before launching it in that impulsive and random way of his; then he would not make so much trouble. He was not hurt by this plain speech; he only looked amused and surprised, and said:

"What? I do random things? Indeed, I never do. I stop and consider possible consequences? Where is the need? I know what the consequences are going to be—always."

"Oh, Satan, then how could you do these things?"

"Well, I will tell you, and you must understand if you can. You belong to a singular race. Every man is a suffering-machine and a happiness-machine combined. The two functions work together harmoniously, with a fine and delicate precision, on the give-and-take principle. For every happiness turned out in the one department the other stands ready to modify it with a sorrow or a pain—maybe a dozen. In most cases the man's life is about equally divided between happiness and unhappiness. When this is not the case the unhappiness predominates—always; never the other. Sometimes a man's make and disposition are such that his misery-machine is able to do nearly all the business. Such a man goes through life almost ignorant of what happiness is. Everything he touches, everything he does, brings a misfortune upon him. You have seen such people? To that kind of a person life is not an advantage, is it? It is only a disaster. Sometimes for an hour's happiness a man's machinery makes him pay years of misery. Don't you know that? It happens every now and then. I will give you a case or two presently. Now the people of your village are nothing to me—you know that, don't you?"

I did not like to speak out too flatly, so I said I had suspected it.

"Well, it is true that they are nothing to me. It is not possible that they should be. The difference between them and me is abysmal, immeasurable. They have no intellect."

"No intellect?"

"Nothing that resembles it. At a future time I will examine what man calls his mind and give you the details of that chaos, then you will see and understand. Men have nothing in common with me—there is no point of contact; they have foolish little feelings and foolish little vanities and impertinences and ambitions; their foolish little life is but a laugh, a sigh, and extinction; and they have no sense. Only the Moral Sense. I will show you what I mean. Here is a red spider, not so big as a pin's head. Can you imagine an elephant being interested in him—caring whether he is happy or isn't, or whether he is wealthy or poor, or whether his sweetheart returns his love or not, or whether his mother is sick or well, or whether he is looked up to in society or not, or whether his enemies will smite him or his friends desert him, or whether his hopes will suffer blight or his political ambitions fail, or whether he shall die in the bosom of his family or neglected and despised in a foreign land? These things can never be important to the elephant; they are nothing to him; he cannot shrink his sympathies to the microscopic size of them. Man is to me as the red spider is to the elephant. The elephant has nothing against the spider—he cannot get down to that remote level; I have nothing against man. The elephant is indifferent; I am indifferent. The elephant would not take the trouble to do the spider an ill turn; if he took the notion he might do him a good turn, if it came in his way and cost nothing. I have done men good service, but no ill turns.

"The elephant lives a century, the red spider a day; in power, intellect, and dignity the one creature is separated from the other by a distance which is simply astronomical. Yet in these, as in all qualities, man is immeasurably further below me than is the wee spider below the elephant.

"Man's mind clumsily and tediously and laboriously patches little trivialities together and gets a result—such as it is. My mind creates! Do you get the force of that? Creates anything it desires—and in a moment. Creates without material. Creates fluids, solids, colors—anything, everything—out of the airy nothing which is called Thought. A man imagines a silk thread, imagines a machine to make it, imagines a picture, then by weeks of labor embroiders it on canvas with the thread. I think the whole thing, and in a moment it is before you—created.

"I think a poem, music, the record of a game of chess—anything—and it is there. This is the immortal mind—nothing is beyond its reach. Nothing can obstruct my vision; the rocks are transparent to me, and darkness is daylight. I do not need to open a book; I take the whole of its contents into my mind at a single glance, through the cover; and in a million years I could not forget a single word of it, or its place in the volume. Nothing goes on in the skull of man, bird, fish, insect, or other creature which can be hidden from me. I pierce the learned man's brain with a single glance, and the treasures which cost him threescore years to accumulate are mine; he can forget and he does forget, but I retain.

"Now, then, I perceive by your thoughts that you are understanding me fairly well. Let us proceed. Circumstances might so fall out that the elephant could like the spider—supposing he can see it—but he could not love it. His love is for his own kind—for his equals. An angel's love is sublime, adorable, divine, beyond the imagination of man—infinitely beyond it! But it is limited to his own august order. If it fell upon one of your race for only an instant, it would consume its object to ashes. No, we cannot love men, but we can be harmlessly indifferent to them; we can also like them, sometimes. I like you and the boys, I like Father Peter, and for your sakes I am doing all these things for the villagers."

He saw that I was thinking a sarcasm and he explained his position.

"I have wrought well for the villagers, though it does not look like it on the surface. Your race never know good fortune from ill. They are always mistaking the one for the other. It is because they cannot see into the future. What I am doing for the villagers will bear good fruit some day; in some cases to themselves; in others, to unborn generations of men. No one will ever know that I was the cause, but it will be none the less true, for all that. Among you boys you have a game: you stand a row of bricks on end a few inches apart; you push a brick, it knocks its neighbor over, the neighbor knocks over the next brick—and so on till all the row is prostrate. That is human life. A child's first act knocks over the initial brick, and the rest will follow inexorably. If you could see into the future, as I can, you would see everything that was going to happen to that creature; for nothing can change the order of its life after the first event has determined it. That is, nothing will change it, because each act unfailingly begets an act, that act begets another, and so on to the end, and the seer can look forward down the line and see just when each act is to have birth, from cradle to grave."

"Does God order the career?"

"Foreordain it? No. The man's circumstances and environment order it. His first act determines the second and all that follow after. But suppose, for argument's sake, that the man should skip one of these acts; an apparently trifling one, for instance; suppose that it had been appointed that on a certain day, at a certain hour and minute and second and fraction of a second he should go to the well, and he didn't go. That man's career would change utterly, from that moment; thence to the grave it would be wholly different from the career which his first act as a child had arranged for him. Indeed, it might be that if he had gone to the well he would have ended his career on a throne, and that omitting to do it would set him upon a career that would lead to beggary and a pauper's grave. For instance: if at any time—say in boyhood—Columbus had skipped the triflingest little link in the chain of acts projected and made inevitable by his first childish act, it would have changed his whole subsequent life, and he would have become a priest and died obscure in an Italian village, and America would not have been discovered for two centuries afterward. I know this. To skip any one of the billion acts in Columbus's chain would have wholly changed his life. I have examined his billion of possible careers, and in only one of them occurs the discovery of America. You people do not suspect that all of your acts are of one size and importance, but it is true; to snatch at an appointed fly is as big with fate for you as is any other appointed act—"

"As the conquering of a continent, for instance?"

"Yes. Now, then, no man ever does drop a link—the thing has never happened! Even when he is trying to make up his mind as to whether he will do a thing or not, that itself is a link, an act, and has its proper place in his chain; and when he finally decides an act, that also was the thing which he was absolutely certain to do. You see, now, that a man will never drop a link in his chain. He cannot. If he made up his mind to try, that project would itself be an unavoidable link—a thought bound to occur to him at that precise moment, and made certain by the first act of his babyhood."

It seemed so dismal!

"He is a prisoner for life," I said sorrowfully, "and cannot get free."

"No, of himself he cannot get away from the consequences of his first childish act. But I can free him."

I looked up wistfully.

"I have changed the careers of a number of your villagers."

I tried to thank him but found it difficult, and let it drop.

"I shall make some other changes. You know that little Lisa Brandt?"

"Oh yes, everybody does. My mother says she is so sweet and so lovely that she is not like any other child. She says she will be the pride of the village when she grows up; and its idol, too, just as she is now."

"I shall change her future."

"Make it better?" I asked.

"Yes. And I will change the future of Nikolaus."

I was glad, this time, and said, "I don't need to ask about his case; you will be sure to do generously by him."

"It is my intention."

Straight off I was building that great future of Nicky's in my imagination, and had already made a renowned general of him and hofmeister at the court, when I noticed that Satan was waiting for me to get ready to listen again. I was ashamed of having exposed my cheap imaginings to him and was expecting some sarcasms, but it did not happen. He proceeded with his subject:

"Nicky's appointed life is sixty-two years."

"That's grand!" I said.

"Lisa's, thirty-six. But, as I told you, I shall change their lives and those ages. Two minutes and a quarter from now Nikolaus will wake out of his sleep and find the rain blowing in. It was appointed that he should turn over and go to sleep again. But I have appointed that he shall get up and close the window first. That trifle will change his career entirely. He will rise in the morning two minutes later than the chain of his life had appointed him to rise. By consequence, thenceforth nothing will ever happen to him in accordance with the details of the old chain." He took out his watch and sat looking at it a few moments, then said: "Nikolaus has risen to close the window. His life is changed, his new career has begun. There will be consequences."

It made me feel creepy; it was uncanny.

"But for this change certain things would happen twelve days from now. For instance, Nikolaus would save Lisa from drowning. He would arrive on the scene at exactly the right moment—four minutes past ten, the long-ago appointed instant of time—and the water would be shoal, the achievement easy and certain. But he will arrive some seconds too late, now; Lisa will have struggled into deeper water. He will do his best but both will drown."

"Oh, Satan! oh, dear Satan!" I cried, with the tears rising in my eyes, "save them! Don't let it happen. I can't bear to lose Nikolaus, he is my loving playmate and friend; and think of Lisa's poor mother!"

I clung to him and begged and pleaded, but he was not moved. He made me sit down again, and told me I must hear him out.

"I have changed Nikolaus's life, and this has changed Lisa's. If I had not done this, Nikolaus would save Lisa, then he would catch cold from his drenching; one of your race's fantastic and desolating scarlet fevers would follow, with pathetic after-effects; for forty-six years he would lie in his bed a paralytic log, deaf, dumb, blind, and praying night and day for the blessed relief of death. Shall I change his life back?"

"Oh no! Oh, not for the world! In charity and pity leave it as it is."

"It is best so. I could not have changed any other link in his life and done him so good a service. He had a billion possible careers, but not one of them was worth living; they were charged full with miseries and disasters. But for my intervention he would do his brave deed twelve days from now—a deed begun and ended in six minutes—and get for all reward those forty-six years of sorrow and suffering I told you of. It is one of the cases I was thinking of awhile ago when I said that sometimes an act which brings the actor an hour's happiness and self-satisfaction is paid for—or punished—by years of suffering."

I wondered what poor little Lisa's early death would save her from. He answered the thought:

"From ten years of pain and slow recovery from an accident, and then from nineteen years' pollution, shame, depravity, crime, ending with death at the hands of the executioner. Twelve days hence she will die; her mother would save her life if she could. Am I not kinder than her mother?"

"Yes—oh, indeed yes; and wiser."

"Father Peter's case is coming on presently. He will be acquitted, through unassailable proofs of his innocence."

"Why, Satan, how can that be? Do you really think it?"

"Indeed, I know it. His good name will be restored, and the rest of his life will be happy."

"I can believe it. To restore his good name will have that effect."

"His happiness will not proceed from that cause. I shall change his life that day, for his good. He will never know his good name has been restored."

In my mind—and modestly—I asked for particulars but Satan paid no attention to my thoughts. Next, my mind wandered to the astrologer, and I wondered where he might be.

"In the moon," said Satan, with a fleeting sound which I believed was a chuckle. "I've got him on the cold side of it, too. He doesn't know where he is, and is not having a pleasant time; still, it is good enough for him, a good place for his star studies. I shall need him presently; then I shall bring him back and possess him again. He has a long and cruel and odious life before him, but I will change that, for I have no feeling against him and am quite willing to do him a kindness. I think I shall get him burned."

He had such strange notions of kindness! But angels are made so, and do not know any better. Their ways are not like our ways; and, besides, human beings are nothing to them; they think they are only freaks. It seemed to me odd that he should put the astrologer so far away; he could have dumped him in Germany just as well, where he would be handy.

"Far away?" said Satan. "To me no place is far away; distance does not exist for me. The sun is less than a hundred million miles from here, and the light that is falling upon us has taken eight minutes to come; but I can make that flight, or any other, in a fraction of time so minute that it cannot be measured by a watch. I have but to think the journey, and it is accomplished."

I held out my hand and said, "The light lies upon it; think it into a glass of wine, Satan."

He did it. I drank the wine.

"Break the glass," he said.

I broke it.

"There—you see it is real. The villagers thought the brass balls were magic stuff and as perishable as smoke. They were afraid to touch them. You are a curious lot—your race. But come along; I have business. I will put you to bed." Said and done. Then he was gone; but his voice came back to me through the rain and darkness saying, "Yes, tell Seppi, but no other."

It was the answer to my thought.

8

Sleep would not come. It was not because I was proud of my travels and excited about having been around the big world to China, and feeling contemptuous of Bartel Sperling, "the traveler," as he called himself, and looked down upon us others because he had been to Vienna once and was the only Eseldorf boy who had made such a journey and seen the world's wonders. At another time that would have kept me awake, but it did not affect me now. No, my mind was filled with Nikolaus, my thoughts ran upon him only, and the good days we had seen together at romps and frolics in the woods and the fields and the river in the long summer days, and skating and sliding in the winter when our parents thought we were in school. And now he was going out of this young life, and the summers and winters would come and go, and we others would rove and play as before, but his place would be vacant; we should see him no more. To-morrow he would not suspect, but would be as he had always been, and it would shock me to hear him laugh, and see him do lightsome and frivolous things, for to me he would be a corpse, with waxen hands and dull eyes, and I should see the shroud around his face; and next day he would not suspect, nor the next, and all the time his handful of days would be wasting swiftly away and that awful thing coming nearer and nearer, his fate closing steadily around him and no one knowing it but Seppi and me. Twelve days—only twelve days. It was awful to think of. I noticed that in my thoughts I was not calling him by his familiar names, Nick and Nicky, but was speaking of him by his full name, and reverently, as one speaks of the dead. Also, as incident after incident of our comradeship came thronging into my mind out of the past, I noticed that they were mainly cases where I had wronged him or hurt him, and they rebuked me and reproached me, and my heart was wrung with remorse, just as it is when we remember our unkindnesses to friends who have passed beyond the veil, and we wish we could have them back again, if only for a moment, so that we could go on our knees to them and say, "Have pity and forgive."

Once when we were nine years old he went a long errand of nearly two miles for the fruiterer, who gave him a splendid big apple for reward, and he was flying home with it, almost beside himself with astonishment and delight, and I met him, and he let me look at the apple, not thinking of treachery, and I ran off with it, eating it as I ran, he following me and begging; and when he overtook me I offered him the core, which was all that was left; and I laughed. Then he turned away, crying, and said he had meant to give it to his little sister. That smote me, for she was slowly getting well of a sickness, and it would have been a proud moment for him, to see her joy and surprise and have her caresses. But I was ashamed to say I was ashamed, and only said something rude and mean, to pretend I did not care, and he made no reply in words, but there was a wounded look in his face as he turned away toward his home which rose before me many times in after years, in the night, and reproached me and made me ashamed again. It had grown dim in my mind, by and by, then it disappeared; but it was back now, and not dim.

Once at school, when we were eleven, I upset my ink and spoiled four copy-books, and was in danger of severe punishment; but I put it upon him, and he got the whipping.

And only last year I had cheated him in a trade, giving him a large fish-hook which was partly broken through for three small sound ones. The first fish he caught broke the hook, but he did not know I was blamable, and he refused to take back one of the small hooks which my conscience forced me to offer him, but said, "A trade is a trade; the hook was bad, but that was not your fault."

No, I could not sleep. These little, shabby wrongs upbraided me and tortured me, and with a pain much sharper than one feels when the wrongs have been done to the living. Nikolaus was living but no matter; he was to me as one already dead. The wind was still moaning about the eaves, the rain still pattering upon the panes.

In the morning I sought out Seppi and told him. It was down by the river. His lips moved, but he did not say anything, he only looked dazed and stunned, and his face turned very white. He stood like that a few moments, the tears welling into his eyes, then he turned away and I locked my arm in his and we walked along thinking, but not speaking. We crossed the bridge and wandered through the meadows and up among the hills and the woods, and at last the talk came and flowed freely, and it was all about Nikolaus and was a recalling of the life we had lived with him. And every now and then Seppi said, as if to himself:

"Twelve days!—less than twelve."

We said we must be with him all the time; we must have all of him we could; the days were precious now. Yet we did not go to seek him. It would be like meeting the dead, and we were afraid. We did not say it, but that was what we were feeling. And so it gave us a shock when we turned a curve and came upon Nikolaus face to face. He shouted, gaily:

"Hi-hi! What is the matter? Have you seen a ghost?"

We couldn't speak, but there was no occasion; he was willing to talk for us all, for he had just seen Satan and was in high spirits about it. Satan had told him about our trip to China, and he had begged Satan to take him on a journey, and Satan had promised. It was to be a far journey, and wonderful and beautiful; and Nikolaus had begged him to take us, too, but he said no, he would take us some day, maybe, but not now. Satan would come for him on the 13th, and Nikolaus was already counting the hours, he was so impatient.

That was the fatal day. We were already counting the hours, too.

We wandered many a mile, always following paths which had been our favorites from the days when we were little, and always we talked about the old times. All the blitheness was with Nikolaus; we others could not shake off our depression. Our tone toward Nikolaus was so strangely gentle and tender and yearning that he noticed it, and was pleased, and we were constantly doing him deferential little offices of courtesy, and saying, "Wait, let me do that for you," and that pleased him, too. I gave him seven fish-hooks—all I had—and made him take them, and Seppi gave him his new knife and a humming-top painted red and yellow—atonements for swindles practised upon him formerly, as I learned later, and probably no longer remembered by Nikolaus now. These things touched him, and he said he could not have believed that we loved him so; and his pride in it and gratefulness for it cut us to the heart, we were so undeserving of them. When we parted at last, he was radiant, and said he had never had such a happy day.

As we walked along homeward, Seppi said, "We always prized him but never so much as now, when we are going to lose him."

Next day and every day we spent all of our spare time with Nikolaus, and also added to it time which we (and he) stole from work and other duties, and this cost the three of us some sharp scoldings, and some threats of punishment. Every morning two of us woke with a start and a shudder, saying, as the days flew along, "Only ten days left"; "only nine days left"; "only eight"; "only seven." Always it was narrowing. Always Nikolaus was gay and happy, and always puzzled because we were not. He wore his invention to the bone trying to invent ways to cheer us up, but it was only a hollow success; he could see that our jollity had no heart in it, and that the laughs we broke into came up against some obstruction or other and suffered damage and decayed into a sigh. He tried to find out what the matter was, so that he could help us out of our trouble or make it lighter by sharing it with us; so we had to tell many lies to deceive him and appease him.

But the most distressing thing of all was that he was always making plans, and often they went beyond the 13th! Whenever that happened it made us groan in spirit. All his mind was fixed upon finding some way to conquer our depression and cheer us up; and at last, when he had but three days to live he fell upon the right idea and was jubilant over it—a boys-and-girls' frolic and dance in the woods, up there where we first met Satan, and this was to occur on the 14th. It was ghastly, for that was his funeral day. We couldn't venture to protest; it would only have brought a "Why?" which we could not answer. He wanted us to help him invite his guests, and we did it—one can refuse nothing to a dying friend. But it was dreadful, for really we were inviting them to his funeral.

It was an awful eleven days; and yet, with a lifetime stretching back between to-day and then, they are still a grateful memory to me, and beautiful. In effect they were days of companionship with one's sacred dead, and I have known no comradeship that was so close or so precious. We clung to the hours and the minutes, counting them as they wasted away, and parting with them with that pain and bereavement which a miser feels who sees his hoard filched from him coin by coin by robbers and is helpless to prevent it.

When the evening of the last day came we stayed out too long; Seppi and I were in fault for that; we could not bear to part with Nikolaus; so it was very late when we left him at his door. We lingered near awhile, listening; and that happened which we were fearing. His father gave him the promised punishment, and we heard his shrieks. But we listened only a moment, then hurried away, remorseful for this thing which we had caused. And sorry for the father, too; our thought being, "If he only knew—if he only knew!"

In the morning Nikolaus did not meet us at the appointed place, so we went to his home to see what the matter was. His mother said:

"His father is out of all patience with these goings-on, and will not have any more of it. Half the time when Nick is needed he is not to be found; then it turns out that he has been gadding around with you two. His father gave him a flogging last night. It always grieved me before, and many's the time I have begged him off and saved him, but this time he appealed to me in vain, for I was out of patience myself."

"I wish you had saved him just this one time," I said, my voice trembling a little; "it would ease a pain in your heart to remember it some day."

She was ironing at the time, and her back was partly toward me. She turned about with a startled or wondering look in her face and said, "What do you mean by that?"

I was not prepared, and didn't know anything to say; so it was awkward, for she kept looking at me; but Seppi was alert and spoke up:

"Why, of course it would be pleasant to remember, for the very reason we were out so late was that Nikolaus got to telling how good you are to him, and how he never got whipped when you were by to save him; and he was so full of it, and we were so full of the interest of it, that none of us noticed how late it was getting."

"Did he say that? Did he?" and she put her apron to her eyes.

"You can ask Theodor—he will tell you the same."

"It is a dear, good lad, my Nick," she said. "I am sorry I let him get whipped; I will never do it again. To think—all the time I was sitting here last night, fretting and angry at him, he was loving me and praising me! Dear, dear, if we could only know! Then we shouldn't ever go wrong; but we are only poor, dumb beasts groping around and making mistakes. I sha'n't ever think of last night without a pang."

She was like all the rest; it seemed as if nobody could open a mouth, in these wretched days, without saying something that made us shiver. They were "groping around," and did not know what true, sorrowfully true things they were saying by accident.

Seppi asked if Nikolaus might go out with us.

"I am sorry," she answered, "but he can't. To punish him further, his father doesn't allow him to go out of the house to-day."

We had a great hope! I saw it in Seppi's eyes. We thought, "If he cannot leave the house, he cannot be drowned." Seppi asked, to make sure:

"Must he stay in all day, or only the morning?"

"All day. It's such a pity, too; it's a beautiful day, and he is so unused to being shut up. But he is busy planning his party, and maybe that is company for him. I do hope he isn't too lonesome."

Seppi saw that in her eye which emboldened him to ask if we might go up and help him pass his time.

"And welcome!" she said, right heartily. "Now I call that real friendship, when you might be abroad in the fields and the woods, having a happy time. You are good boys, I'll allow that, though you don't always find satisfactory ways of proving it. Take these cakes—for yourselves—and give him this one, from his mother."

The first thing we noticed when we entered Nikolaus's room was the time—a quarter to 10. Could that be correct? Only such a few minutes to live! I felt a contraction at my heart. Nikolaus jumped up and gave us a glad welcome. He was in good spirits over his plannings for his party and had not been lonesome.

"Sit down," he said, "and look at what I've been doing. And I've finished a kite that you will say is a beauty. It's drying in the kitchen; I'll fetch it."

He had been spending his penny savings in fanciful trifles of various kinds, to go as prizes in the games, and they were marshaled with fine and showy effect upon the table. He said:

"Examine them at your leisure while I get mother to touch up the kite with her iron if it isn't dry enough yet."

Then he tripped out and went clattering down-stairs, whistling.

We did not look at the things; we couldn't take any interest in anything but the clock. We sat staring at it in silence, listening to the ticking, and every time the minute-hand jumped we nodded recognition—one minute fewer to cover in the race for life or for death. Finally Seppi drew a deep breath and said:

"Two minutes to ten. Seven minutes more and he will pass the death-point. Theodor, he is going to be saved! He's going to—"

"Hush! I'm on needles. Watch the clock and keep still."

Five minutes more. We were panting with the strain and the excitement. Another three minutes, and there was a footstep on the stair.

"Saved!" And we jumped up and faced the door.

The old mother entered, bringing the kite. "Isn't it a beauty?" she said. "And, dear me, how he has slaved over it—ever since daylight, I think, and only finished it awhile before you came." She stood it against the wall and stepped back to take a view of it. "He drew the pictures his own self, and I think they are very good. The church isn't so very good, I'll have to admit, but look at the bridge—any one can recognize the bridge in a minute. He asked me to bring it up. . . . Dear me! it's seven minutes past ten, and I—"

"But where is he?"

"He? Oh, he'll be here soon; he's gone out a minute."

"Gone out?"

"Yes. Just as he came down-stairs little Lisa's mother came in and said the child had wandered off somewhere, and as she was a little uneasy I told Nikolaus to never mind about his father's orders—go and look her up. . . . Why, how white you two do look! I do believe you are sick. Sit down; I'll fetch something. That cake has disagreed with you. It is a little heavy, but I thought—"

She disappeared without finishing her sentence, and we hurried at once to the back window and looked toward the river. There was a great crowd at the other end of the bridge, and people were flying toward that point from every direction.

"Oh, it is all over—poor Nikolaus! Why, oh, why did she let him get out of the house!"

"Come away," said Seppi, half sobbing, "come quick—we can't bear to meet her; in five minutes she will know."

But we were not to escape. She came upon us at the foot of the stairs, with her cordials in her hands, and made us come in and sit down and take the medicine. Then she watched the effect, and it did not satisfy her; so she made us wait longer, and kept upbraiding herself for giving us the unwholesome cake.

Presently the thing happened which we were dreading. There was a sound of tramping and scraping outside, and a crowd came solemnly in, with heads uncovered, and laid the two drowned bodies on the bed.

"Oh, my God!" that poor mother cried out, and fell on her knees, and put her arms about her dead boy and began to cover the wet face with kisses. "Oh, it was I that sent him, and I have been his death. If I had obeyed, and kept him in the house, this would not have happened. And I am rightly punished; I was cruel to him last night, and him begging me, his own mother, to be his friend."

And so she went on and on, and all the women cried and pitied her, and tried to comfort her, but she could not forgive herself and could not be comforted, and kept on saying if she had not sent him out he would be alive and well now, and she was the cause of his death.

It shows how foolish people are when they blame themselves for anything they have done. Satan knows, and he said nothing happens that your first act hasn't arranged to happen and made inevitable, and so, of your own motion you can't ever alter the scheme or do a thing that will break a link. Next we heard screams, and Frau Brandt came wildly plowing and plunging through the crowd with her dress in disorder and hair flying loose, and flung herself upon her dead child with moans and kisses and pleadings and endearments; and by and by she rose up almost exhausted with her outpourings of passionate emotion, and clenched her fist and lifted it toward the sky, and her tear-drenched face grew hard and resentful, and she said:

"For nearly two weeks I have had dreams and presentiments and warnings that death was going to strike what was most precious to me, and day and night and night and day I have groveled in the dirt before Him praying Him to have pity on my innocent child and save it from harm—and here is His answer!"

Why, He had saved it from harm—but she did not know.

She wiped the tears from her eyes and cheeks, and stood awhile gazing down at the child and caressing its face and its hair with her hand; then she spoke again in that bitter tone, "But in His hard heart is no compassion. I will never pray again."

She gathered her dead child to her bosom and strode away, the crowd falling back to let her pass, and smitten dumb by the awful words they had heard. Ah, that poor woman! It is as Satan said, we do not know good fortune from bad, and are always mistaking the one for the other. Many a time since I have heard people pray to God to spare the life of sick persons, but I have never done it.

Both funerals took place at the same time in our little church next day. Everybody was there, including the party guests. Satan was there, too; which was proper, for it was on account of his efforts that the funerals had happened. Nikolaus had departed this life without absolution, and a collection was taken up for masses, to get him out of purgatory. Only two-thirds of the required money was gathered, and the parents were going to try to borrow the rest, but Satan furnished it. He told us privately that there was no purgatory, but he had contributed in order that Nikolaus's parents and their friends might be saved from worry and distress. We thought it very good of him, but he said money did not cost him anything.

At the graveyard the body of little Lisa was seized for debt by a carpenter to whom the mother owed fifty groschen for work done the year before. She had never been able to pay this, and was not able now. The carpenter took the corpse home and kept it four days in his cellar, the mother weeping and imploring about his house all the time; then he buried it in his brother's cattle-yard, without religious ceremonies. It drove the mother wild with grief and shame, and she forsook her work and went daily about the town, cursing the carpenter and blaspheming the laws of the emperor and the church, and it was pitiful to see. Seppi asked Satan to interfere, but he said the carpenter and the rest were members of the human race and were acting quite neatly for that species of animal. He would interfere if he found a horse acting in such a way, and we must inform him when we came across that kind of horse doing that kind of a human thing, so that he could stop it. We believed this was sarcasm, for of course there wasn't any such horse.

But after a few days we found that we could not abide that poor woman's distress, so we begged Satan to examine her several possible careers, and see if he could not change her, to her profit, to a new one. He said the longest of her careers as they now stood gave her forty-two years to live and her shortest one twenty-nine, and that both were charged with grief and hunger and cold and pain. The only improvement he could make would be to enable her to skip a certain three minutes from now, and he asked us if he should do it. This was such a short time to decide in that we went to pieces with nervous excitement, and before we could pull ourselves together and ask for particulars he said the time would be up in a few more seconds; so then we gasped out, "Do it!"

"It is done," he said, "she was going around a corner; I have turned her back; it has changed her career."

"Then what will happen, Satan?"

"It is happening now. She is having words with Fischer, the weaver. In his anger Fischer will straightway do what he would not have done but for this accident. He was present when she stood over her child's body and uttered those blasphemies."

"What will he do?"

"He is doing it now—betraying her. In three days she will go to the stake."

We could not speak; we were frozen with horror, for if we had not meddled with her career she would have been spared this awful fate. Satan noticed these thoughts, and said:

"What you are thinking is strictly human-like—that is to say, foolish. The woman is advantaged. Die when she might, she would go to heaven. By this prompt death she gets twenty-nine years more of heaven than she is entitled to, and escapes twenty-nine years of misery here."

A moment before we were bitterly making up our minds that we would ask no more favors of Satan for friends of ours, for he did not seem to know any way to do a person a kindness but by killing him; but the whole aspect of the case was changed now, and we were glad of what we had done and full of happiness in the thought of it.

After a little I began to feel troubled about Fischer, and asked, timidly, "Does this episode change Fischer's life-scheme, Satan?"

"Change it? Why, certainly. And radically. If he had not met Frau Brandt awhile ago he would die next year, thirty-four years of age. Now he will live to be ninety, and have a pretty prosperous and comfortable life of it, as human lives go."

We felt a great joy and pride in what we had done for Fischer, and were expecting Satan to sympathize with this feeling; but he showed no sign and this made us uneasy. We waited for him to speak, but he didn't; so, to assuage our solicitude we had to ask him if there was any defect in Fischer's good luck. Satan considered the question a moment, then said, with some hesitation:

"Well, the fact is, it is a delicate point. Under his several former possible life-careers he was going to heaven."

We were aghast. "Oh, Satan! and under this one—"

"There, don't be so distressed. You were sincerely trying to do him a kindness; let that comfort you."

"Oh, dear, dear, that cannot comfort us. You ought to have told us what we were doing, then we wouldn't have acted so."

But it made no impression on him. He had never felt a pain or a sorrow, and did not know what they were, in any really informing way. He had no knowledge of them except theoretically—that is to say, intellectually. And of course that is no good. One can never get any but a loose and ignorant notion of such things except by experience. We tried our best to make him comprehend the awful thing that had been done and how we were compromised by it, but he couldn't seem to get hold of it. He said he did not think it important where Fischer went to; in heaven he would not be missed, there were "plenty there." We tried to make him see that he was missing the point entirely, that Fischer, and not other people, was the proper one to decide about the importance of it; but it all went for nothing; he said he did not care for Fischer—there were plenty more Fischers.

The next minute Fischer went by on the other side of the way and it made us sick and faint to see him, remembering the doom that was upon him, and we the cause of it. And how unconscious he was that anything had happened to him! You could see by his elastic step and his alert manner that he was well satisfied with himself for doing that hard turn for poor Frau Brandt. He kept glancing back over his shoulder expectantly. And, sure enough, pretty soon Frau Brandt followed after, in charge of the officers and wearing jingling chains. A mob was in her wake, jeering and shouting, "Blasphemer and heretic!" and some among them were neighbors and friends of her happier days. Some were trying to strike her, and the officers were not taking as much trouble as they might to keep them from it.

"Oh, stop them, Satan!" It was out before we remembered that he could not interrupt them for a moment without changing their whole after-lives. He puffed a little puff toward them with his lips and they began to reel and stagger and grab at the empty air; then they broke apart and fled in every direction, shrieking, as if in intolerable pain. He had crushed a rib of each of them with that little puff. We could not help asking if their life-chart was changed.

"Yes, entirely. Some have gained years, some have lost them. Some few will profit in various ways by the change, but only that few."

We did not ask if we had brought poor Fischer's luck to any of them. We did not wish to know. We fully believed in Satan's desire to do us kindnesses, but we were losing confidence in his judgment. It was at this time that our growing anxiety to have him look over our life-charts and suggest improvements began to fade out and give place to other interests.

For a day or two the whole village was a chattering turmoil over Frau Brandt's case and over the mysterious calamity that had overtaken the mob, and at her trial the place was crowded. She was easily convicted of her blasphemies, for she uttered those terrible words again and said she would not take them back. When warned that she was imperiling her life, she said they could take it in welcome, she did not want it, she would rather live with the professional devils in perdition than with these imitators in the village. They accused her of breaking all those ribs by witchcraft, and asked her if she was not a witch. She answered scornfully:

"No. If I had that power would any of you holy hypocrites be alive five minutes? No; I would strike you all dead. Pronounce your sentence and let me go; I am tired of your society."

So they found her guilty, and she was excommunicated and cut off from the joys of heaven and doomed to the fires of hell; then she was clothed in a coarse robe and delivered to the secular arm, and conducted to the market-place, the bell solemnly tolling the while. We saw her chained to the stake, and saw the first film of blue smoke rise on the still air. Then her hard face softened, and she looked upon the packed crowd in front of her and said, with gentleness:

"We played together once, in long-agone days when we were innocent little creatures. For the sake of that, I forgive you."

We went away then and did not see the fires consume her, but we heard the shrieks, although we put our fingers in our ears. When they ceased we knew she was in heaven, notwithstanding the excommunication, and we were glad of her death and not sorry that we had brought it about.

One day, a little while after this, Satan appeared again. We were always watching out for him, for life was never very stagnant when he was by. He came upon us at that place in the woods where we had first met him. Being boys, we wanted to be entertained; we asked him to do a show for us.

"Very well," he said, "would you like to see a history of the progress of the human race?—its development of that product which it calls civilization?"

We said we should.

So, with a thought, he turned the place into the Garden of Eden, and we saw Abel praying by his altar; then Cain came walking toward him with his club, and did not seem to see us, and would have stepped on my foot if I had not drawn it in. He spoke to his brother in a language which we did not understand; then he grew violent and threatening, and we knew what was going to happen and turned away our heads for the moment; but we heard the crash of the blows and heard the shrieks and the groans; then there was silence, and we saw Abel lying in his blood and gasping out his life, and Cain standing over him and looking down at him, vengeful and unrepentant.

Then the vision vanished, and was followed by a long series of unknown wars, murders, and massacres. Next we had the Flood, and the Ark tossing around in the stormy waters, with lofty mountains in the distance showing veiled and dim through the rain. Satan said:

"The progress of your race was not satisfactory. It is to have another chance now."

The scene changed, and we saw Noah overcome with wine.

Next, we had Sodom and Gomorrah, and "the attempt to discover two or three respectable persons there," as Satan described it. Next, Lot and his daughters in the cave.

Next came the Hebraic wars, and we saw the victors massacre the survivors and their cattle, and save the young girls alive and distribute them around.

Next we had Jael; and saw her slip into the tent and drive the nail into the temple of her sleeping guest; and we were so close that when the blood gushed out it trickled in a little, red stream to our feet, and we could have stained our hands in it if we had wanted to.

Next we had Egyptian wars, Greek wars, Roman wars, hideous drenchings of the earth with blood; and we saw the treacheries of the Romans toward the Carthaginians, and the sickening spectacle of the massacre of those brave people. Also we saw Caesar invade Britain—"not that those barbarians had done him any harm, but because he wanted their land, and desired to confer the blessings of civilization upon their widows and orphans," as Satan explained.

Next, Christianity was born. Then ages of Europe passed in review before us, and we saw Christianity and Civilization march hand in hand through those ages, "leaving famine and death and desolation in their wake, and other signs of the progress of the human race," as Satan observed.

And always we had wars, and more wars, and still other wars—all over Europe, all over the world. "Sometimes in the private interest of royal families," Satan said, "sometimes to crush a weak nation; but never a war started by the aggressor for any clean purpose—there is no such war in the history of the race."

"Now," said Satan, "you have seen your progress down to the present, and you must confess that it is wonderful—in its way. We must now exhibit the future."

He showed us slaughters more terrible in their destruction of life, more devastating in their engines of war, than any we had seen.

"You perceive," he said, "that you have made continual progress. Cain did his murder with a club; the Hebrews did their murders with javelins and swords; the Greeks and Romans added protective armor and the fine arts of military organization and generalship; the Christian has added guns and gunpowder; a few centuries from now he will have so greatly improved the deadly effectiveness of his weapons of slaughter that all men will confess that without Christian civilization war must have remained a poor and trifling thing to the end of time."

Then he began to laugh in the most unfeeling way, and make fun of the human race, although he knew that what he had been saying shamed us and wounded us. No one but an angel could have acted so; but suffering is nothing to them, they do not know what it is, except by hearsay.

More than once Seppi and I had tried in a humble and diffident way to convert him, and as he had remained silent we had taken his silence as a sort of encouragement; necessarily, then, this talk of his was a disappointment to us, for it showed that we had made no deep impression upon him. The thought made us sad, and we knew then how the missionary must feel when he has been cherishing a glad hope and has seen it blighted. We kept our grief to ourselves, knowing that this was not the time to continue our work.

Satan laughed his unkind laugh to a finish; then he said: "It is a remarkable progress. In five or six thousand years five or six high civilizations have risen, flourished, commanded the wonder of the world, then faded out and disappeared; and not one of them except the latest ever invented any sweeping and adequate way to kill people. They all did their best—to kill being the chiefest ambition of the human race and the earliest incident in its history—but only the Christian civilization has scored a triumph to be proud of. Two or three centuries from now it will be recognized that all the competent killers are Christians; then the pagan world will go to school to the Christian—not to acquire his religion, but his guns. The Turk and the Chinaman will buy those to kill missionaries and converts with."

By this time his theater was at work again, and before our eyes nation after nation drifted by, during two or three centuries, a mighty procession, an endless procession, raging, struggling, wallowing through seas of blood, smothered in battle-smoke through which the flags glinted and the red jets from the cannon darted; and always we heard the thunder of the guns and the cries of the dying.

"And what does it amount to?" said Satan, with his evil chuckle. "Nothing at all. You gain nothing; you always come out where you went in. For a million years the race has gone on monotonously propagating itself and monotonously reperforming this dull nonsense—to what end? No wisdom can guess! Who gets a profit out of it? Nobody but a parcel of usurping little monarchs and nobilities who despise you; would feel defiled if you touched them; would shut the door in your face if you proposed to call; whom you slave for, fight for, die for, and are not ashamed of it but proud; whose existence is a perpetual insult to you and you are afraid to resent it; who are mendicants supported by your alms, yet assume toward you the airs of benefactor toward beggar; who address you in the language of master to slave, and are answered in the language of slave to master; who are worshiped by you with your mouth, while in your heart—if you have one—you despise yourselves for it. The first man was a hypocrite and a coward, qualities which have not yet failed in his line; it is the foundation upon which all civilizations have been built. Drink to their perpetuation! Drink to their augmentation! Drink to—" Then he saw by our faces how much we were hurt, and he cut his sentence short and stopped chuckling, and his manner changed. He said, gently: "No, we will drink one another's health, and let civilization go. The wine which has flown to our hands out of space by desire is earthly, and good enough for that other toast; but throw away the glasses, we will drink this one in wine which has not visited this world before."

We obeyed, and reached up and received the new cups as they descended. They were shapely and beautiful goblets, but they were not made of any material that we were acquainted with. They seemed to be in motion, they seemed to be alive; and certainly the colors in them were in motion. They were very brilliant and sparkling, and of every tint, and they were never still, but flowed to and fro in rich tides which met and broke and flashed out dainty explosions of enchanting color. I think it was most like opals washing about in waves and flashing out their splendid fires. But there is nothing to compare the wine with. We drank it, and felt a strange and witching ecstasy as of heaven go stealing through us, and Seppi's eyes filled and he said worshipingly:

"We shall be there some day, and then—"

He glanced furtively at Satan, and I think he hoped Satan would say, "Yes, you will be there some day," but Satan seemed to be thinking about something else, and said nothing. This made me feel ghastly, for I knew he had heard; nothing, spoken or unspoken, ever escaped him.

Poor Seppi looked distressed, and did not finish his remark. The goblets rose and clove their way into the sky, a triplet of radiant sundogs, and disappeared. Why didn't they stay? It seemed a bad sign, and depressed me. Should I ever see mine again? Would Seppi ever see his?

9

It was wonderful, the mastery Satan had over time and distance. For him they did not exist. He called them human inventions and said they were artificialities. We often went to the most distant parts of the globe with him and stayed weeks and months, and yet were gone only a fraction of a second, as a rule. You could prove it by the clock. One day when our people were in such awful distress because the witch commission were afraid to proceed against the astrologer and Father Peter's household, or against any, indeed, but the poor and the friendless, they lost patience and took to witch-hunting on their own score, and began to chase a born lady who was known to have the habit of curing people by devilish arts, such as bathing them, washing them, and nourishing them instead of bleeding them and purging them through the ministrations of a barber-surgeon in the proper way. She came flying down, with the howling and cursing mob after her, and tried to take refuge in houses, but the doors were shut in her face. They chased her more than half an hour, we following to see it, and at last she was exhausted and fell, and they caught her. They dragged her to a tree and threw a rope over the limb, and began to make a noose in it, some holding her, meantime, and she was crying and begging and her young daughter looking on and weeping, but afraid to say or do anything.

They hanged the lady, and I threw a stone at her, although in my heart I was sorry for her; but all were throwing stones and each was watching his neighbor, and if I had not done as the others did it would have been noticed and spoken of. Satan burst out laughing.

All that were near by turned upon him, astonished and not pleased. It was an ill time to laugh, for his free and scoffing ways and his supernatural music had brought him under suspicion all over the town and turned many privately against him. The big blacksmith called attention to him now, raising his voice so that all should hear, and said:

"What are you laughing at? Answer! Moreover, please explain to the company why you threw no stone."

"Are you sure I did not throw a stone?"

"Yes. You needn't try to get out of it; I had my eye on you."

"And I—I noticed you!" shouted two others.

"Three witnesses," said Satan: "Mueller, the blacksmith; Klein, the butcher's man; Pfeiffer, the weaver's journeyman. Three very ordinary liars. Are there any more?"

"Never mind whether there are others or not, and never mind about what you consider us—three's enough to settle your matter for you. You'll prove that you threw a stone or it shall go hard with you."

"That's so!" shouted the crowd, and surged up as closely as they could to the center of interest.

"And first you will answer that other question," cried the blacksmith, pleased with himself for being mouthpiece to the public and hero of the occasion. "What are you laughing at?"

Satan smiled and answered, pleasantly: "To see three cowards stoning a dying lady when they were so near death themselves."

You could see the superstitious crowd shrink and catch their breath, under the sudden shock. The blacksmith, with a show of bravado, said:

"Pooh! What do you know about it?"

"I? Everything. By profession I am a fortune-teller and I read the hands of you three—and some others—when you lifted them to stone the woman. One of you will die to-morrow week; another of you will die to-night; the third has but five minutes to live—and yonder is the clock!"

It made a sensation. The faces of the crowd blanched, and turned mechanically toward the clock. The butcher and the weaver seemed smitten with an illness, but the blacksmith braced up and said, with spirit:

"It is not long to wait for prediction number one. If it fails, young master, you will not live a whole minute after, I promise you that."

No one said anything; all watched the clock in a deep stillness which was impressive. When four and a half minutes were gone the blacksmith gave a sudden gasp and clapped his hands upon his heart, saying, "Give me breath! Give me room!" and began to sink down. The crowd surged back, no one offering to support him, and he fell lumbering to the ground and was dead. The people stared at him, then at Satan, then at one another; and their lips moved but no words came. Then Satan said:

"Three saw that I threw no stone. Perhaps there are others; let them speak."

It struck a kind of panic into them, and, although no one answered him, many began to violently accuse one another, saying, "You said he didn't throw," and getting for reply, "It is a lie, and I will make you eat it!" And so in a moment they were in a raging and noisy turmoil, and beating and banging one another; and in the midst was the only indifferent one—the dead lady hanging from her rope, her troubles forgotten, her spirit at peace.

So we walked away, and I was not at ease, but was saying to myself, "He told them he was laughing at them, but it was a lie—he was laughing at me."

That made him laugh again, and he said, "Yes, I was laughing at you, because, in fear of what others might report about you, you stoned the woman when your heart revolted at the act—but I was laughing at the others, too."

"Why?"

"Because their case was yours."

"How is that?"

"Well, there were sixty-eight people there, and sixty-two of them had no more desire to throw a stone than you had."

"Satan!"

"Oh, it's true. I know your race. It is made up of sheep. It is governed by minorities, seldom or never by majorities. It suppresses its feelings and its beliefs and follows the handful that makes the most noise. Sometimes the noisy handful is right, sometimes wrong; but no matter, the crowd follows it. The vast majority of the race, whether savage or civilized, are secretly kind-hearted and shrink from inflicting pain, but in the presence of the aggressive and pitiless minority they don't dare to assert themselves. Think of it! One kind-hearted creature spies upon another, and sees to it that he loyally helps in iniquities which revolt both of them. Speaking as an expert, I know that ninety-nine out of a hundred of your race were strongly against the killing of witches when that foolishness was first agitated by a handful of pious lunatics in the long ago. And I know that even to-day, after ages of transmitted prejudice and silly teaching, only one person in twenty puts any real heart into the harrying of a witch. And yet apparently everybody hates witches and wants them killed. Some day a handful will rise up on the other side and make the most noise—perhaps even a single daring man with a big voice and a determined front will do it—and in a week all the sheep will wheel and follow him, and witch-hunting will come to a sudden end.

"Monarchies, aristocracies, and religions are all based upon that large defect in your race—the individual's distrust of his neighbor, and his desire, for safety's or comfort's sake, to stand well in his neighbor's eye. These institutions will always remain, and always flourish, and always oppress you, affront you, and degrade you, because you will always be and remain slaves of minorities. There was never a country where the majority of the people were in their secret hearts loyal to any of these institutions."

I did not like to hear our race called sheep, and said I did not think they were.

"Still, it is true, lamb," said Satan. "Look at you in war—what mutton you are, and how ridiculous!"

"In war? How?"

"There has never been a just one, never an honorable one—on the part of the instigator of the war. I can see a million years ahead, and this rule will never change in so many as half a dozen instances. The loud little handful—as usual—will shout for the war. The pulpit will—warily and cautiously—object—at first; the great, big, dull bulk of the nation will rub its sleepy eyes and try to make out why there should be a war, and will say, earnestly and indignantly, "It is unjust and dishonorable, and there is no necessity for it." Then the handful will shout louder. A few fair men on the other side will argue and reason against the war with speech and pen, and at first will have a hearing and be applauded; but it will not last long; those others will outshout them, and presently the anti-war audiences will thin out and lose popularity. Before long you will see this curious thing: the speakers stoned from the platform, and free speech strangled by hordes of furious men who in their secret hearts are still at one with those stoned speakers—as earlier—but do not dare to say so. And now the whole nation—pulpit and all—will take up the war-cry, and shout itself hoarse, and mob any honest man who ventures to open his mouth; and presently such mouths will cease to open. Next the statesmen will invent cheap lies, putting the blame upon the nation that is attacked, and every man will be glad of those conscience-soothing falsities, and will diligently study them, and refuse to examine any refutations of them; and thus he will by and by convince himself that the war is just, and will thank God for the better sleep he enjoys after this process of grotesque self-deception."

10

Days and days went by now, and no Satan. It was dull without him. But the astrologer, who had returned from his excursion to the moon, went about the village, braving public opinion, and getting a stone in the middle of his back now and then when some witch-hater got a safe chance to throw it and dodge out of sight. Meantime two influences had been working well for Marget. That Satan, who was quite indifferent to her, had stopped going to her house after a visit or two had hurt her pride, and she had set herself the task of banishing him from her heart. Reports of Wilhelm Meidling's dissipation brought to her from time to time by old Ursula had touched her with remorse, jealousy of Satan being the cause of it; and so now, these two matters working upon her together, she was getting a good profit out of the combination—her interest in Satan was steadily cooling, her interest in

Wilhelm as steadily warming. All that was needed to complete her conversion was that Wilhelm should brace up and do something that should cause favorable talk and incline the public toward him again.

The opportunity came now. Marget sent and asked him to defend her uncle in the approaching trial, and he was greatly pleased, and stopped drinking and began his preparations with diligence. With more diligence than hope, in fact, for it was not a promising case. He had many interviews in his office with Seppi and me, and threshed out our testimony pretty thoroughly, thinking to find some valuable grains among the chaff, but the harvest was poor, of course.

If Satan would only come! That was my constant thought. He could invent some way to win the case, for he had said it would be won, so he necessarily knew how it could be done. But the days dragged on, and still he did not come. Of course I did not doubt that it would win, and that Father Peter would be happy for the rest of his life, since Satan had said so; yet I knew I should be much more comfortable if he would come and tell us how to manage it. It was getting high time for Father Peter to have a saving change toward happiness, for by general report he was worn out with his imprisonment and the ignominy that was burdening him, and was like to die of his miseries unless he got relief soon.

At last the trial came on, and the people gathered from all around to witness it; among them many strangers from considerable distances. Yes, everybody was there except the accused. He was too feeble in body for the strain. But Marget was present, and keeping up her hope and her spirit the best she could. The money was present, too. It was emptied on the table, and was handled and caressed and examined by such as were privileged.

The astrologer was put in the witness-box. He had on his best hat and robe for the occasion.

Question. You claim that this money is yours?

Answer. I do.

Q. How did you come by it?

A. I found the bag in the road when I was returning from a journey.

Q. When?

A. More than two years ago.

Q. What did you do with it?

A. I brought it home and hid it in a secret place in my observatory, intending to find the owner if I could.

Q. You endeavored to find him?

A. I made diligent inquiry during several months, but nothing came of it.

Q. And then?

A. I thought it not worth while to look further, and was minded to use the money in finishing the wing of the foundling-asylum connected with the priory and nunnery. So I took it out of its hiding-place and counted it to see if any of it was missing. And then—

Q. Why do you stop? Proceed.

A. I am sorry to have to say this, but just as I had finished and was restoring the bag to its place, I looked up and there stood Father Peter behind me.

Several murmured, "That looks bad," but others answered, "Ah, but he is such a liar!"

Q. That made you uneasy?

A. No; I thought nothing of it at the time, for Father Peter often came to me unannounced to ask for a little help in his need.

Marget blushed crimson at hearing her uncle falsely and impudently charged with begging, especially from one he had always denounced as a fraud, and was going to speak, but remembered herself in time and held her peace.

Q. Proceed.

A. In the end I was afraid to contribute the money to the foundling-asylum, but elected to wait yet another year and continue my inquiries. When I heard of Father Peter's find I was glad, and no suspicion entered my mind; when I came home a day or two later and discovered that my own money was gone I still did not suspect until three circumstances connected with Father Peter's good fortune struck me as being singular coincidences.

Q. Pray name them.

A. Father Peter had found his money in a path—I had found mine in a road. Father Peter's find consisted exclusively of gold ducats—mine also. Father Peter found eleven hundred and seven ducats—I exactly the same.

This closed his evidence, and certainly it made a strong impression on the house; one could see that.

Wilhelm Meidling asked him some questions, then called us boys, and we told our tale. It made the people laugh, and we were ashamed. We were feeling pretty badly, anyhow, because Wilhelm was hopeless, and showed it. He was doing as well as he could, poor young fellow, but nothing was in his favor, and such sympathy as there was was now plainly not with his client. It might be difficult for court and people to believe the astrologer's story, considering his character, but it was almost impossible to believe Father Peter's. We were already feeling badly enough, but when the astrologer's lawyer said he believed he would not ask us any questions—for our story was a little delicate and it would be cruel for him to put any strain upon it—everybody tittered, and it was almost more than we could bear. Then he made a sarcastic little speech, and got so much fun out of our tale, and it seemed so ridiculous and childish and every way impossible and foolish, that it made everybody laugh till the tears came; and at last Marget could not keep up her courage any longer, but broke down and cried, and I was so sorry for her.

Now I noticed something that braced me up. It was Satan standing alongside of Wilhelm! And there was such a contrast!—Satan looked so confident, had such a spirit in his eyes and face, and Wilhelm looked so depressed and despondent. We two were comfortable now, and judged that he would testify and persuade the bench and the people that black was white and white black, or any other color he wanted it. We glanced around to see what the strangers in the house thought of him, for he was beautiful, you know—stunning, in fact—but no one was noticing him; so we knew by that that he was invisible.

The lawyer was saying his last words; and while he was saying them Satan began to melt into Wilhelm. He melted into him and disappeared; and then there was a change, when his spirit began to look out of Wilhelm's eyes.

That lawyer finished quite seriously, and with dignity. He pointed to the money and said:

"The love of it is the root of all evil. There it lies, the ancient tempter, newly red with the shame of its latest victory—the dishonor of a priest of God and his two poor juvenile helpers in crime. If it could but speak, let us hope that it would be constrained to confess that of all its conquests this was the basest and the most pathetic."

He sat down. Wilhelm rose and said:

"From the testimony of the accuser I gather that he found this money in a road more than two years ago. Correct me, sir, if I misunderstood you."

The astrologer said his understanding of it was correct.

"And the money so found was never out of his hands thenceforth up to a certain definite date—the last day of last year. Correct me, sir, if I am wrong."

The astrologer nodded his head. Wilhelm turned to the bench and said:

"If I prove that this money here was not that money, then it is not his?"

"Certainly not; but this is irregular. If you had such a witness it was your duty to give proper notice of it and have him here to—" He broke off and began to consult with the other judges. Meantime that other lawyer got up excited and began to protest against allowing new witnesses to be brought into the case at this late stage.

The judges decided that his contention was just and must be allowed.

"But this is not a new witness," said Wilhelm. "It has already been partly examined. I speak of the coin."

"The coin? What can the coin say?"

"It can say it is not the coin that the astrologer once possessed. It can say it was not in existence last December. By its date it can say this."

And it was so! There was the greatest excitement in the court while that lawyer and the judges were reaching for coins and examining them and exclaiming. And everybody was full of admiration of Wilhelm's brightness in happening to think of that neat idea. At last order was called and the court said:

"All of the coins but four are of the date of the present year. The court tenders its sincere sympathy to the accused, and its deep regret that he, an innocent man, through an unfortunate mistake, has suffered the undeserved humiliation of imprisonment and trial. The case is dismissed."

So the money could speak, after all, though that lawyer thought it couldn't. The court rose and almost everybody came forward to shake hands with Marget and congratulate her, and then to shake with Wilhelm and praise him; and Satan had stepped out of Wilhelm and was standing around looking on full of interest, and people walking through him every which way, not knowing he was there. And Wilhelm could not explain why he only thought of the date on the coins at the last moment, instead of earlier; he said it just occurred to him all of a sudden, like an inspiration, and he brought it right out without any hesitation, for, although he didn't examine the coins, he seemed, somehow, to know it was true. That was honest of him, and like him; another would have pretended he had thought of it earlier, and was keeping it back for a surprise.

He had dulled down a little now; not much, but still you could notice that he hadn't that luminous look in his eyes that he had while Satan was in him. He nearly got it back, though, for a moment when Marget came and praised him and thanked him and couldn't keep him from seeing how proud she was of him. The astrologer went off dissatisfied and cursing, and Solomon Isaacs gathered up the money and carried it away. It was Father Peter's for good and all, now.

Satan was gone. I judged that he had spirited himself away to the jail to tell the prisoner the news; and in this I was right. Marget and the rest of us hurried thither at our best speed, in a great state of rejoicing.

Well, what Satan had done was this: he had appeared before that poor prisoner, exclaiming, "The trial is over, and you stand forever disgraced as a thief—by verdict of the court!"

The shock unseated the old man's reason. When we arrived, ten minutes later, he was parading pompously up and down and delivering commands to this and that and the other constable or jailer, and calling them Grand Chamberlain, and Prince This and Prince That, and Admiral of the Fleet, Field Marshal in Command, and all such fustian, and was as happy as a bird. He thought he was Emperor!

Marget flung herself on his breast and cried, and indeed everybody was moved almost to heartbreak. He recognized Marget, but could not understand why she should cry. He patted her on the shoulder and said:

"Don't do it, dear; remember, there are witnesses, and it is not becoming in the Crown Princess. Tell me your trouble—it shall be mended; there is nothing the Emperor cannot do." Then he looked around and saw old Ursula with her apron to her eyes. He was puzzled at that, and said, "And what is the matter with you?"

Through her sobs she got out words explaining that she was distressed to see him—"so." He reflected over that a moment, then muttered, as if to himself, "A singular old thing, the Dowager Duchess—means well, but is always snuffling and never able to tell what it is about. It is because she doesn't know." His eyes fell on Wilhelm. "Prince of India," he said, "I divine that it is you that the Crown Princess is concerned about. Her tears shall be dried; I will no longer stand between you; she shall share your throne; and between you you shall inherit mine. There, little lady, have I done well? You can smile now—isn't it so?"

He petted Marget and kissed her, and was so contented with himself and with everybody that he could not do enough for us all, but began to give away kingdoms and such things right and left, and the least that any of us got was a principality. And so at last, being persuaded to go home, he marched in imposing state; and when the crowds along the way saw how it gratified him to be hurrahed at, they humored him to the top of his desire, and he responded with condescending bows and gracious smiles and often stretched out a hand and said, "Bless you, my people!"

As pitiful a sight as ever I saw. And Marget and old Ursula crying all the way.

On my road home I came upon Satan, and reproached him with deceiving me with that lie. He was not embarrassed, but said, quite simply and composedly:

"Ah, you mistake; it was the truth. I said he would be happy the rest of his days, and he will, for he will always think he is the Emperor, and his pride in it and his joy in it will endure to the end. He is now, and will remain, the one utterly happy person in this empire."

"But the method of it, Satan, the method! Couldn't you have done it without depriving him of his reason?"

It was difficult to irritate Satan, but that accomplished it.

"What an ass you are!" he said. "Are you so unobservant as not to have found out that sanity and happiness are an impossible combination? No sane man can be happy, for to him life is real, and he sees what a fearful thing it is. Only the mad can be happy, and not many of those. The few that imagine themselves kings or gods are happy, the rest are no happier than the sane. Of course, no man is entirely in his right mind at any time, but I have been referring to the extreme cases. I have taken from this man that trumpery thing which the race regards as a Mind; I have replaced his tin life with a silver-gilt fiction; you see the result—and you criticize! I said I would make him permanently happy, and I have done it. I have made him happy by the only means possible to his race—and you are not satisfied!" He heaved a discouraged sigh, and said, "It seems to me that this race is hard to please."

There it was, you see. He didn't seem to know any way to do a person a favor except by killing him or making a lunatic out of him. I apologized, as well as I could; but privately I did not think much of his processes—at that time.

Satan was accustomed to say that our race lived a life of continuous and uninterrupted self-deception. It duped itself from cradle to grave with shams and delusions which it mistook for realities, and this made its entire life a sham. Of the score of fine qualities which it imagined it had and was vain of, it really possessed hardly one. It regarded itself as gold, and was only brass. One day when he was in this vein he mentioned a detail—the sense of humor. I cheered up then, and took issue. I said we possessed it.

"There spoke the race!" he said, "always ready to claim what it hasn't got and mistake its ounce of brass filings for a ton of gold-dust. You have a mongrel perception of humor, nothing more; a multitude of you possess that. This multitude sees the comic side of a thousand low-grade and trivial things—broad incongruities, mainly; grotesqueries, absurdities, evokers of the horse-laugh. The ten thousand high-grade comicalities which exist in the world are sealed from their dull vision. Will a day come when the race will detect the funniness of these juvenilities and laugh at them—and by laughing at them destroy them? For your race, in its poverty, has unquestionably one really effective weapon—laughter. Power, money, persuasion, supplication, persecution—these can lift at a colossal humbug—push it a little—weaken it a little, century by century; but only laughter can blow it to rags and atoms at a blast. Against the assault of laughter nothing can stand. You are always fussing and fighting with your other weapons. Do you ever use that one? No, you leave it lying rusting. As a race, do you ever use it at all? No, you lack sense and the courage."

We were traveling at the time and stopped at a little city in India and looked on while a juggler did his tricks before a group of natives. They were wonderful, but I knew Satan could beat that game, and I begged him to show off a little, and he said he would. He changed himself into a native in turban and breech-cloth, and very considerately conferred on me a temporary knowledge of the language.

The juggler exhibited a seed, covered it with earth in a small flower-pot, then put a rag over the pot; after a minute the rag began to rise; in ten minutes it had risen a foot; then the rag was removed and a little tree was exposed, with leaves upon it and ripe fruit. We ate the fruit, and it was good. But Satan said:

"Why do you cover the pot? Can't you grow the tree in the sunlight?"

"No," said the juggler, "no one can do that."

"You are only an apprentice; you don't know your trade. Give me the seed. I will show you." He took the seed and said, "What shall I raise from it?"

"It is a cherry seed; of course you will raise a cherry."

"Oh no; that is a trifle; any novice can do that. Shall I raise an orange-tree from it?"

"Oh yes!" and the juggler laughed.

"And shall I make it bear other fruits as well as oranges?"

"If God wills!" and they all laughed.

Satan put the seed in the ground, put a handful of dust on it, and said, "Rise!"

A tiny stem shot up and began to grow, and grew so fast that in five minutes it was a great tree, and we were sitting in the shade of it. There was a murmur of wonder, then all looked up and saw a strange and pretty sight, for the branches were heavy with fruits of many kinds and colors—oranges, grapes, bananas, peaches, cherries, apricots, and so on. Baskets were brought and the unlading of the tree began; and the people crowded around Satan and kissed his hand, and praised him, calling him the prince of jugglers. The news went about the town, and everybody came running to see the wonder—and they remembered to bring baskets, too. But the tree was equal to the occasion; it put out new fruits as fast as any were removed; baskets were filled by the score and by the hundred, but always the supply remained undiminished. At last a foreigner in white linen and sun-helmet arrived and exclaimed, angrily:

"Away from here! Clear out, you dogs; the tree is on my lands and is my property."

The natives put down their baskets and made humble obeisance. Satan made humble obeisance, too, with his fingers to his forehead, in the native way, and said:

"Please let them have their pleasure for an hour, sir—only that, and no longer. Afterward you may forbid them, and you will still have more fruit than you and the state together can consume in a year."

This made the foreigner very angry, and he cried out, "Who are you, you vagabond, to tell your betters what they may do and what they mayn't!" and he struck Satan with his cane and followed this error with a kick.

The fruits rotted on the branches, and the leaves withered and fell. The foreigner gazed at the bare limbs with the look of one who is surprised, and not gratified. Satan said:

"Take good care of the tree, for its health and yours are bound together. It will never bear again, but if you tend it well it will live long. Water its roots once in each hour every night—and do it yourself; it must not be done by proxy, and to do it in daylight will not answer. If you fail only once in any night, the tree will die, and you likewise. Do not go home to your own country any more—you would not reach there; make no business or pleasure engagements which require you to go outside your gate at night—you cannot afford the risk; do not rent or sell this place—it would be injudicious."

The foreigner was proud and wouldn't beg but I thought he looked as if he would like to. While he stood gazing at Satan we vanished away and landed in Ceylon.

I was sorry for that man; sorry Satan hadn't been his customary self and killed him or made him a lunatic. It would have been a mercy. Satan overheard the thought, and said:

"I would have done it but for his wife, who has not offended me. She is coming to him presently from their native land, Portugal. She is well, but has not long to live and has been yearning to see him and persuade him to go back with her next year. She will die without knowing he can't leave that place."

"He won't tell her?"

"He? He will not trust that secret with any one; he will reflect that it could be revealed in sleep, in the hearing of some Portuguese guest's servant some time or other."

"Did none of those natives understand what you said to him?"

"None of them understood, but he will always be afraid that some of them did. That fear will be torture to him, for he has been a harsh master to them. In his dreams he will imagine them chopping his tree down. That will make his days uncomfortable—I have already arranged for his nights."

It grieved me, though not sharply, to see him take such a malicious satisfaction in his plans for this foreigner.

"Does he believe what you told him, Satan?"

"He thought he didn't, but our vanishing helped. The tree, where there had been no tree before—that helped. The insane and uncanny variety of fruits—the sudden withering—all these things are helps. Let him think as he may, reason as he may, one thing is certain, he will water the tree. But between this and night he will begin his changed career with a very natural precaution—for him."

"What is that?"

"He will fetch a priest to cast out the tree's devil. You are such a humorous race—and don't suspect it."

"Will he tell the priest?"

"No. He will say a juggler from Bombay created it, and that he wants the juggler's devil driven out of it, so that it will thrive and be fruitful again. The priest's incantations will fail; then the Portuguese will give up that scheme and get his watering-pot ready."

"But the priest will burn the tree. I know it; he will not allow it to remain."

"Yes, and anywhere in Europe he would burn the man, too. But in India the people are civilized, and these things will not happen. The man will drive the priest away and take care of the tree."

I reflected a little, then said, "Satan, you have given him a hard life, I think."

"Comparatively. It must not be mistaken for a holiday."

We flitted from place to place around the world as we had done before, Satan showing me a hundred wonders, most of them reflecting in some way the weakness and triviality of our race. He did this now every few days—not out of malice—I am sure of that—it only seemed to amuse and interest him, just as a naturalist might be amused and interested by a collection of ants.

11

For as much as a year Satan continued these visits, but at last he came less often, and then for a long time he did not come at all. This always made me lonely and melancholy. I felt that he was losing interest in our tiny world and might at any time abandon his visits entirely. When one day he finally came to me I was overjoyed, but only for a little while. He had come to say good-by, he told me, and for the last time. He had investigations and undertakings in other corners of the universe, he said, that would keep him busy for a longer period than I could wait for his return.

"And you are going away, and will not come back any more?"

"Yes," he said. "We have comraded long together, and it has been pleasant—pleasant for both; but I must go now, and we shall not see each other any more."

"In this life, Satan, but in another? We shall meet in another, surely?"

Then, all tranquilly and soberly, he made the strange answer, "*There is no other.*"

A subtle influence blew upon my spirit from his, bringing with it a vague, dim, but blessed and hopeful feeling that the incredible words might be true—even *must* be true.

"Have you never suspected this, Theodor?"

"No. How could I? But if it can only be true—"

"It is true."

A gust of thankfulness rose in my breast, but a doubt checked it before it could issue in words, and I said, "But—but—we have seen that future life—seen it in its actuality, and so—"

"It was a vision—it had no existence."

I could hardly breathe for the great hope that was struggling in me. "A vision?—a vi—"

"*Life itself is only a vision, a dream.*"

It was electrical. By God! I had had that very thought a thousand times in my musings!

"*Nothing* exists; all is a dream. God—man—the world—the sun, the moon, the wilderness of stars—a dream, all a dream; they have no existence. *Nothing exists save empty space—and you!*"

"I!"

"And you are not you—you have no body, no blood, no bones, you are but a *thought*. I myself have no existence; I am but a dream—your dream, creature of your imagination. In a moment you will have realized this, then you will banish me from your visions and I shall dissolve into the nothingness out of which you made me. . . .

"I am perishing already—I am failing—I am passing away. In a little while you will be alone in shoreless space, to wander its limitless solitudes without friend or comrade forever—for you will remain a *thought*, the only existent thought, and by your nature inextinguishable, indestructible. But I, your poor servant, have revealed you to yourself and set you free. Dream other dreams, and better!

"Strange! that you should not have suspected years ago—centuries, ages, eons, ago!—for you have existed, companionless, through all the eternities. Strange, indeed, that you should not have suspected that your universe and its contents were only dreams, visions, fiction! Strange, because they are so frankly and hysterically insane—like all dreams: a God who could make good children as easily as bad, yet preferred to make bad ones; who could have made every one of them happy, yet never made a single happy one; who made them prize their bitter life, yet stingily cut it short; who gave his angels eternal happiness unearned, yet required his other children to earn it; who gave his angels painless lives, yet cursed his other children with biting miseries and maladies of mind and body; who mouths justice and invented hell—mouths mercy and invented hell—mouths Golden Rules, and forgiveness multiplied by seventy times seven, and invented hell; who mouths morals to other people and has none himself; who frowns upon crimes, yet commits them all; who created man without invitation, then tries to shuffle the responsibility for man's acts upon man, instead of honorably placing it where it belongs, upon himself; and finally, with altogether divine obtuseness, invites this poor, abused slave to worship him! . . .

"You perceive, *now*, that these things are all impossible except in a dream. You perceive that they are pure and puerile insanities, the silly creations of an imagination that is not conscious of its freaks—in a word, that they are a dream, and you the maker of it. The dream-marks are all present; you should have recognized them earlier.

"It is true, that which I have revealed to you; there is no God, no universe, no human race, no earthly life, no heaven, no hell. It is all a dream—a grotesque and foolish dream. Nothing exists but you. And you are but a *thought*—a vagrant thought, a useless thought, a homeless thought, wandering forlorn among the empty eternities!"

He vanished and left me appalled, for I knew, and realized, that all he had said was true.

BIOGRAPHICAL NOTES

STEPHEN CRANE (1871–1900)

Born in Newark, New Jersey, the son of a Methodist minister, Stephen Crane emerged from conventional and pious beginnings to witness in twenty-nine intense years—and in many places—poverty and cruelty, fear and death. These experiences he recorded clearly and without flinching, both as newspaper reporter and as writer of fiction and poetry. His method was naturalistic and impressionistic; and as exemplified in his novel *Maggie: A Girl of the Streets* (1893) or in *The Red Badge of Courage* (1895), it is generally held to mark the beginning of "modern American literature."

From the beginning Crane showed more interest in observation and experience than in study. In his brief sojourns at Lafayette College and Syracuse University, books were slighted for boxing and baseball. Leaving Syracuse in 1891, he worked for a time as a reporter in New York. From his experiences in the Bowery and the East Side slums came *Maggie*. Later gun-running adventures off the Florida and Cuban coasts, including a shipwreck, were used in such stories as *The Open Boat* (1898). *The Red Badge of Courage,* however, was not the result of personal experience; it was written before Crane had seen war at first-hand, although its Civil War setting reflects an interest nurtured by reading and conversation since boyhood. Yet *The Red Badge* is not primarily about a particular war or battle, nor even perhaps concerned with a particular man, the protagonist Henry Fleming. The battle is the scene, and Fleming is its center, but the theme is man—or *a* man—and his thoughts and actions in one of the starkest encounters with fear and death which, as a man, he must face: the ordeal of combat. It is the truth and power with which this theme is expressed that has made the book notable since its first publication.

KAY BOYLE (1903–   )

A native of Ohio, where she was educated in music, painting, and architecture, Kay Boyle left America in 1922 to find her spiritual home in Europe; and everything she has written, since her first stories appeared in 1929, has been colored by her residence abroad. She will deny, however, that the essence of her novels would have differed had she lived in Cincinnati instead of Vienna, in the Adirondacks instead of the mountains of the Haute-Savoie. "The longer I live and the more I write," she declares, "the more completely am I convinced that my interest in people and in writing is of so un-national a character that, for me, the question of 'roots' in any particular soil or tradition is not of any moment." Many of her critics will disagree. Yet Miss Boyle might argue that her success lies not in the compelling details of the background of her novels (Europe during and between two wars) but in her concern with "the problem of man's responsibility to his time and the choices he must make." She is right: her people, their moral problems, and their destinies are always primary even if the European scene and the European character are her *métier.*

The Crazy Hunter (1940) is one of three short novels in her volume of the same name, and nowhere is her talent for fresh diction, rich symbolic texture, and sure control of language and metaphor better displayed. Her writings include *Thirty Stories* (1946), *The Smoking Mountain* (1951), *The Seagull on the Step* (1955), and *Generation without Farewell* (1959).

KATHERINE ANNE PORTER (1894–)

Although she has published relatively little since her first volume of short stories, *Flowering Judas* (1930), Miss Porter is known widely as one of the masters of her craft. One critic has called her stories "triumphs within their range of operation, works of perfection and intensity." A volume called *Hacienda* appeared in 1934, another called *The Leaning Tower and Other Stories* in 1944. During the decade between she also published three short novels: *Noon Wine* (1937), *Old Mortality* (1939), and *Pale Horse, Pale Rider* (1939). For many years she was at work on a full-length novel, *Ship of Fools,* which was published in 1962.

Miss Porter was born in Indian Creek, Texas, and has lived in Dallas, Denver, Mexico City, Bermuda, Paris, Berlin, Majorca, and California. She has worked variously as free-lance journalist, ghost writer, newspaper reporter, movie scenarist, critic, and teacher. As teacher, she gives this advice to young writers: "First, have faith in your theme; then get so well acquainted with your characters that they live and grow in your imagination exactly as if you saw them in the flesh; and, finally, tell their story with all the truth and tenderness and severity you are capable of;

and if you have any personality of your own, you will have a style of your own; it grows, as your ideas grow, and as your knowledge of your craft increases." It is advice she herself has liberally taken.

HENRY JAMES (1843–1916)

Henry James is one of America's major novelists, "a master of modern prose," as Philip Rahv calls him, "belonging to the company of Proust and Joyce." He has left an indelible mark on the art of the novel, both as critic and as craftsman. From the publication of his first volume, *A Passionate Pilgrim and Other Tales* (1875), through such triumphs as *The Portrait of a Lady* (1881), *The Wings of the Dove* (1902), and *The Ambassadors* (1903), James seldom faltered from his avowed purpose: to reproduce life as the intelligent observer sees it.

James' reputation was not always as high as it is today. The editor of the *Century Illustrated Monthly Magazine* called *The Bostonians* (1886) the most unpopular serial the magazine ever published. Arnold Bennett "simply could not read the novels" because they "did not seem to be *about* anything." H. G. Wells compared the James novel to a church, well-lighted but empty, on the altar of which one found, "very reverently placed intensely there, a dead kitten, an eggshell, a piece of string." Part of the reason for the delay in accepting James' kind of novel was a misunderstanding of what he meant by "life."

The fact that "life" for James meant generally upper-class, financially independent Americans at leisure in Europe is easy to understand when we recall that he left New York in 1875 to reside permanently in Europe, first in Paris, then in London, and finally in Rye, a small town in Sussex, England. The world in which James was at home is depicted by good conversation full of innuendo, irony, verbal refinements, and frustrating, elliptical indirections; and the subjects of this conversation are chiefly marriage, divorce, infidelities, moral degeneration, renunciation, codes of conduct, and ideals of attainment. His fiction is a record of the "inward life," what has been called the "subjective accompaniment" of a story rather than the story *per se*. One of his disciples, Ford Madox Ford, realized early that James was, above all, intent on revealing the pattern of life, not that "of birth, apogee, and death, but a woven symbolism of its own. 'The Figure in the Carpet,' James called it—and that he saw something of the sort was no doubt the secret of his magic."

Madame de Mauves was written before James was thirty. In the summer of 1873, he was "visited by the gentle Euphemia," the American heiress who, in his novels, was to ruin her life by marriage to a French baron. "She was what I might have called experimentally international,"

James recalls. "She muffled her charming head in the lightest, finest, vaguest tissue of romance." This is the germ of the story. If his better-known heroines Isabel Archer and Maggie Verver are exquisitely drawn, it is because he had women characters like Euphemia Cleve with which to experiment.

THOMAS MANN (1875–1955)

The circumstances of Thomas Mann's background, birth, and early life closely parallel those of Tonio Kröger. Born in the north German city of Lübeck, Mann was the son of a prosperous grain merchant and his partly Brazilian wife. Like Tonio's father, the elder Mann was of the patrician bourgeoisie: conservative, fastidious, highly respected, a senator of his town. Similarly, Mann's mother was the model for Tonio's: dark, musical, southern, "different from the other ladies in the town." Whatever traits he owed to his mother, Mann remained by heredity and environment predominantly bourgeois, and he had a keen awareness of the significance of his origin—an awareness which unquestionably intensified his natural inclination as an artist to inquire into the function of art and especially the relationship of the artist to the world about him. For Mann, as for Tonio, the dilemma was one of his dual nature—that of the *burger* turned artist—and the sense of isolation the artist feels in a bourgeois society. This theme of isolation is conspicuous in most of Mann's early works.

Among Mann's best works are the novels *Buddenbrooks* (1901), *The Magic Mountain* (1924), *Joseph and His Brothers* (4 vols., 1933–43), and the novellas *Death in Venice* (1913) and *Mario and the Magician* (1930). He was awarded the Nobel Prize for literature in 1929.

WILLIAM FAULKNER (1897–1962)

In 1950, William Faulkner won the Nobel Prize for literature. Not many years earlier he had been struggling for critical attention in America. "The way I look at it," he said, "this is an award for the last thirty years of my life. When I look back, it all seems a terrific job—not the physical labor of writing, but the sweat and anguish of the human spirit."

With the appearance of his novel *Sartoris* in 1929, Faulkner began the saga of Yoknapatawpha County, his mythical community in northern

Mississippi, his native state. Thirteen of his novels and numerous short stories are wholly concerned with the citizens of Yoknapatawpha. They have enlarged this legend to such proportions and with such complexity that it is sometimes necessary to remind ourselves that this world, though based on historical precedent and contemporary observation, is, in particular, the product of one man's genius and perseverance and fecund imagination. *The Sound and the Fury* (1929), *As I Lay Dying* (1930), *Light in August* (1932), and *Absalom, Absalom!* (1936) are the major Yoknapatawpha novels. Faulkner writes about other subjects: the Snopes clan, descendants of carpet-baggers (*The Hamlet, The Town, The Mansion*), a murder trial (*Intruder in the Dust*), the Civil War (*The Unvanquished*). But in all of his work he does more than recount a narrative; despite his protest that he is "just a man who lives to tell stories," his novels penetrate the problems of the human heart in conflict with itself. Only that subject, Faulkner believes, "can make good writing because only that is worth writing about, worth the agony and the sweat."

"The Bear," as it appeared in *Go Down, Moses* (1942), is a reworking and an expansion of two rather brief stories: "Lion" (*Harper's*, December 1935) and "The Bear" (*Saturday Evening Post*, May 9, 1942). In its final novella form it combines the story of a dog named Lion; the story of a young boy (Isaac McCaslin), his Negro-Indian guide (Sam Fathers), and their worship of the bear image; and finally the story of the McCaslin clan, of the sins of the Old Carothers McCaslin and the scars they leave on his progeny. For the readers of the whole Faulkner canon, "The Bear" serves nobly as beginning and end of the Yoknapatawpha legend.

JOSEPH CONRAD (1857–1924)

Although Conrad's fame rests largely on his tales of the sea and of the East, and on his treatment of the romantic and heroic, he is basically a tragic novelist. Morton Dauwen Zabel speaks of him as "essentially a moral and psychological realist whose profounder themes are concerned with problems of guilt and honor, with the tests of conscience and moral justice, and the secret recriminatory and retributive processes of the human personality." Born Józef Teodor Konrad Korzeniowski in Poland, Conrad was left an orphan when his father, an ardent Polish patriot who had been exiled by the Russian overlords, died in 1869. At seventeen he went to sea, and for twenty years (1874–1894) he was a professional sailor, rising after his apprenticeship in the French merchant service through the ranks to his own command. He traveled most of the seas of the world, and in 1890 (he was by then a British subject) made a harrowing journey up the Congo River which gave him the material for *Heart of Darkness* as well as the illness which plagued him intermittently for the rest of his life.

Written in 1898–99, *Heart of Darkness* was published in a volume called *Youth* (1902). It is a complex inquiry into a bizarre corner of human experience. Its action revolves in a style at once romantic and ironic about the greed, hypocrisy, and cruel stupidities all too characteristic of the early exploitation of the Congo. In a larger and deeper sense its theme concerns the effect of the savage, mysteriously enveloping jungle upon a man of extraordinary potentialities for good or evil. Conrad's characteristic style and themes may be found in this novella as in most of his fiction, especially the major novels, *The Nigger of the "Narcissus"* (1898), *Lord Jim* (1900), *Nostromo* (1904), and *Victory* (1915).

FRANZ KAFKA (1883–1924)

Franz Kafka's reputation is based on three posthumous novels: *The Trial* (1924), *The Castle* (1926), and *America* (1927). They earned for Kafka's name far greater national acclaim than the harassed young writer ever dreamed of achieving. Before his death from tuberculosis, at the age of forty-one, he had permitted the publication of a few volumes of short stories only because Max Brod, the German novelist, had practically wrenched them from him. Kafka ordered the manuscripts of the novels burned with all his other papers, but Brod chose to save everything. In 1935–37 Brod edited the *Collected Works* in six volumes, followed by a disjointed but informative biography of his friend, based on the rich and enlightening diaries, sketches, and unpublished letters in his possession. Several details of Kafka's life, as Brod tells it, are germane to an understanding of his remarkable novella, *Metamorphosis,* and especially to the causes of the guilt complex in which it had its beginning.

Kafka was born in Prague in 1883. His father Hermann was proud of his name, his thriving clothing business, and his Jewish heritage. Franz Kafka wanted none of the wealthy mercantile society in which his family moved. After a rigid German education, he entered the German University in Prague (where he met Max Brod) to study law. Once he had passed the examination for his doctorate in jurisprudence, he looked for a job that tolerated "indifference," by which he meant free hours in which to write. He thought he had found it first in an Italian insurance company and then in a workmen's compensation board, but they turned out to be joyless occupations that stifled his literary labors. His whole brief life was filled with the most intense frustrations, in parental relations, courtship, vocation, and physical health. He never married. He hated his work. He never finished his three long novels, even though writing was his escape. And he lived the last five years of his life in sanatoria.

There is of course a danger in reading Kafka's life-struggle into his work, yet Kafka invites that reading at every turn—for example, by naming the family in *Metamorphosis,* quite pointedly, Samsa. Does Kafka mean us to see in Gregor's transformation the symbol of moral disintegration which he himself experienced while living in a home where he felt isolated, by struggling all his life with a guilt complex out of his father's superiority, the world's cruelties, and his own sense of insufficiency? Does he emphasize his own degradation when he makes Gregor the model son, the support of the family, the very reverse of the Franz Kafka-Hermann Kafka equation? Or are we missing many of the symbolic overtones of the novella by reading it as thinly disguised autobiography?

MARK TWAIN (1835–1910)

The Mark Twain of *The Mysterious Stranger* (1916) is not the shrewd and salty American frontier humorist that most readers know from happy acquaintance with *Tom Sawyer* (1876) and *Huckleberry Finn* (1884). Begun in 1898 and not published until six years after Twain's death, *The Mysterious Stranger* is a profoundly personal story, the expression of a bitterness and a cosmic despair which, whatever their cause, reveal the pathetic paradox of an inner life of dissent and disillusion coexisting with the bright career of the American literary lion Twain had become. From the Missouri frontier village where he was born Samuel Langhorne Clemens, through his careers as journeyman printer, itinerant journalist, river boat pilot, prospector, and miner, he finally found his way into literature. By 1869, with the publication of *The Innocents Abroad,* Twain was famous, and for the next twenty years he wrote prodigiously and with unfailing gusto. He was successful beyond Tom Sawyer's wildest dreams. The fame was to endure, but not the prosperity. Business failures and family tragedy brought trouble and sorrow, complicated further perhaps by subconscious tensions and frustrations which are still the subject of critical speculation.

Despite its bitter hopelessness, its fatalistic determinism, *The Mysterious Stranger* has a certain sad beauty, even a compassion, which softens its essential nihilism. Without attempting to analyze Twain's metaphysics —and he was no trained philosopher—we can say that the story's chief impact is emotional rather than intellectual. It is a story of disturbing questions and ironies, with no certain answers. Their import, however, may suggest that it is Mark Twain himself who is the most pathetic figure of his story.